ALMOST
HISTORY

Also by Christopher Bram

HOLD TIGHT

SURPRISING MYSELF

IN MEMORY OF ANGEL CLARE

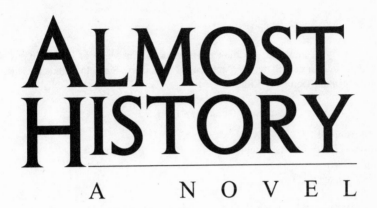

ALMOST HISTORY

A NOVEL

Christopher Bram

DONALD I. FINE, INC.

New York

Copyright © 1992 by Christopher Bram

All rights reserved, including the right of reproduction in whole or in part in any form. Published in the United States of America by Donald I. Fine, Inc. and in Canada by General Publishing Company Limited.

Library of Congress Cataloging-in-Publication Data

Bram, Christopher.
    Almost history / by Christopher Bram.
        p.   cm.
    ISBN 1-55611-231-9
    I. Title.
    PS3552.R2817A78   1992
    813'.54—dc20
    90-56068

                                    CIP

Manufactured in the United States of America

10 9 8 7 6 5 4 3 2 1

Designed by Irving Perkins Associates

To Mary Gentile

But history, real solemn history, I cannot be interested in . . . The quarrels of popes and kings, with wars or pestilences, in every page; the men all so good for nothing, and hardly any women at all.

—Northanger Abbey

Don't you think he's too close to the story?

—JOHN F. KENNEDY

ALL EMPIRES DECLINE AND FALL. The word itself suggests the ephemeral and doomed. It was a word I disliked during my twenty-plus years in the Foreign Service, thinking it can't when applied to American interests, a cynical way of dismissing our good work. But nothing is forever, nothing is pure.

I own a golf ball autographed by Richard Nixon.

(Yes, that's closer to the note I want to strike. I sound like a pompous ass when I attempt to do George Kennan or Dean Acheson. In describing a career that was small potatoes, I should stick to the potato's eye view.)

This golf ball is not something I cherish. I never admired or even respected Mr. Nixon during my years with the government. His golf ball holds no place of esteem in my little house in the Maryland suburbs. In fact, it wanders about the house of its own accord, appearing now in the drawer of the desk where I write this, now in the bowl of coconuts on my TV set and VCR, now in the dish on my refrigerator where I keep my car keys, unpaid bills and free condoms. I suppose I should either have the thing sealed in Lucite for posterity or toss it in my bag of practice balls where time, my persistent hook and a patch of weeds will rid me of it for good.

I once played nine holes with President Nixon, in 1969 at the Wack Wack Golf and Country Club in Manila. More accurately, I played with Chip Adkins, then chargé d'affaires to the Philippines, while Nixon played with Ferdinand Marcos. The two heads of state strutted down the fairway twenty yards ahead of us, each with a club in his hand, chatting and pretending to enjoy themselves. Marcos gave the more convincing performance. All around us strolled an army of press people, Secret Service men dressed like Mormons despite the heat and Marcos bodyguards. Nixon played a very anxious, distracted game, but then nobody could really concentrate on sport in those circumstances. It was all one could do not to bean a reporter or Marcos goon on the head.

Nixon was in Manila after flying out to the Pacific for the splashdown of the first men on the moon. He toured the Far East to prolong his vacation from the pressure in Washington over the Vietnam War. Even then I was struck that there was so much history—an American triumph in outer space, a bloody quagmire a few hundred miles away—looming over something as common-place as this quartet of middle-aged men in bilious knits and plaids knocking little white balls through the grass.

The Wack Wack was (and still is, I suspect) one of the most beautiful courses in Asia, a cunning series of vistas and hazards, Australian pines mixed with stands of bamboo along the fairways, palm trees towering over the greens like rubbery Roman columns. It was the same golf course where, one night three years later, Marcos staged an assassination attempt on a cabinet minister to give himself his final excuse to declare martial law. Machine-gun fire allegedly ripped through Juan Enrile's car as it drove past the thirteenth hole on the way back from the Malacanang Palace. It was later reported that Enrile and his men simply stopped the car on the back nine, got out and shot it up themselves.

Determined to win at everything he did, Marcos cheated at golf too. I once saw a goon surreptitiously scoot the boss's ball out of the rough for a better lie, and have heard tales from others involving duplicate balls and doctored scorecards. He did not cheat the day he played Nixon. He won honestly, but only by two strokes. Marcos was a bold man, not a stupid one.

We had time for just nine holes that morning before the rest of the day's scheduled events. We talked and laughed in the clubhouse locker room while we changed clothes, all regular guys. Marcos took his pants off himself, doing without his usual pair of valets. Nixon worked hard at appearing regular, going so far as to tell an off-color story, the punchline of which eluded everyone. I knew Nixon primarily as a face and voice on television. It was unnerving to undress so close to the jowls and square-tipped nose familiar to me from political cartoons, like undressing beside Mickey Mouse. Without meaning to suggest anything sexual, I admit I had a guilty desire to see the man naked. A peek would do. But no, Nixon slipped from his golf pants into his dress slacks as quickly as the shyest fat boy in gym class. I presume he waited until he got back to the Malacanang Palace to take a shower. He avoided looking at me and Adkins while we toweled off, although I do think I caught him checking out Marcos. (I can't believe I'm including all this.)

In suit and tie again, he called in one of his Secret Service men and sent him out for something. The man returned, utterly stone-faced in his sun-glasses, a dozen golf balls cupped in the bowl of his hands. "Mementos for the boys," Nixon explained. Sitting on a bench, he wrote his name on each ball and passed them to me, until I had my hands full of a slippery pile of white dimpled spheres. "Distribute them to the caddies," the Chief Executive

told me. "Something they can pass on to their grandchildren." He laughed as
he capped his pen, not nastily, but as if he suddenly appreciated the comedy of
the gesture, the absurdity of fame. Or maybe he realized from the looks on
Adkins's face and mine what a stupid act this really was. Marcos assured him
that it was for such thoughtfulness and generosity that the Philippine people
loved President Nixon.

Even with my big hands, I had difficulty carrying so many balls without
spilling them. I hurried through the heat and glare to the caddy pen, a clay
courtyard out behind the clubhouse with an open latrine and a porch roof of
green corrugated fiberglass. The "boys," the youngest of whom was over
twenty, sat in the green shadow of the porch, drinking San Miguel and listening to Nancy Sinatra on a transistor radio. "From the American president," I
announced as I approached. They jumped to their feet and came forward,
expecting a handsome tip. They saw only golf balls, and stopped. Then, baffled yet polite, they each took one, turning the balls around and around in their
fingers, as if there might be a trick involved. One of them laughed and said in
Tagalog, "What I want are Marcos's balls." Nobody else laughed; a Marcos
man stood among them, given away by his silk shirt and alligator shoes. I
wanted to laugh, but could not let America lose more face with these people
than we already had. Keeping all doubts and irony to myself, I still earnestly
played the game that summer.

When I was through, I had three or four balls left. Nobody asked for the
extras. I didn't know what else to do with them, so I loaded them into my
pants pockets, thanked the caddies again and rejoined the others. I did not
know how to return Nixon's unwanted balls to him. (The masculine analogy
in all this certainly gets tiresome, doesn't it?) I spent the rest of the day
tumorous with golf balls, unable to take them out until I put on my tux that
night for the lavish dinner given in the Nixons' honor. They flew on to Japan
the next day and we were able to get back to the quiet business of quarreling
among ourselves.

Over the following week, I gave away balls, I can't remember to whom. I
know I gave one to the Sullivan kids, who lived in Manila with their mother
while their father was attached to the embassy in Saigon. No dependents were
allowed in Vietnam and here was another family with whom I could play
Uncle Jim. I may have given one to Rosalita, my cook, although I can't
imagine what she'd want with it. In the end, I kept one for myself, assuming a
nephew or niece might get a kick out of having the president's scrawl to show
friends. It was three years before I got back to the States and saw my sister's
family again. In the meantime, the ball disappeared and I forgot all about it.
During that long sabbatical which I thought was permanant, I kept most of my
things in storage. Not until I retired for good and bought this house did I
unpack the many boxes of accumulated junk. I found the golf ball in a box full
of Balinese woodcarvings, amateur tennis trophies, an ornate brass lamp base

hammered out of the casing of an artillery shell and other debris one was reluctant to throw away.

Here it is, a Titlist 500, probably never used, with an illegible name circling it in blue ink, written as well as one can write anything on a small, lightly cratered globe. As with the world, so with a golf ball. It can't be worth any money; I don't know how an autograph dealer would go about authenticating the darn thing. But it still bounces. (There. I bounce it off my kitchen floor, which sits on cold concrete slab.) It hasn't gone dead yet, not as a golf ball anyway.

If there's a moral to all this, it eludes me. Except that I have no business writing a memoir. I may send these pages to you, the best of a bad lot, just to show you I *did* try. Your uncle is no writer. Reading what I've written, I fear my humor doesn't always come through and I alternate between the pompous and the smart-aleck. There are patches as cheerfully callous as the worst Watergate confessional. And I was never callous. Stupid or romantic, but never callous. Having been so blind about my life while I lived it, I can't bear the thought of being blind again on a second go-round.

The truth of the matter is I have no juicy anecdotes to tell, no state secrets to reveal, no story of my own. All I have is the tale of a career played out in the no-man's land between public events and private pathology. The latter might interest students of organizational behavior, but the habit of discretion forged by years in the State Department dies hard. There's much I'm reluctant to discuss, even with you. (Not the sexual. I certainly couldn't *write* about it, but you and I have no secrets in that department.) Let me leave history to the famous and you historians. I was there only on a brief visit, a tourist in the empire, a houseguest of history. That last phrase might look nice on my tombstone.

Good grief, Meg. Here I am at fifty-plus, already planning my own funeral. You see how attempting this has spoiled my equilibrium. I will forget the past, go out into the world and finish installing the new weatherproof gutters. Wisdom should express itself in silence.

JIM SET THE pencil down and sat back in his chair. Chair and desk were in the kitchen and it was cold there, despite his plaid flannel shirt and the sunny day outside. Framed in the window above the sink, the red leaves of a maple tree streamed in the wind like paper flames. The sky was a bright, pure blue. All around him, his empty house softly whistled and droned, as if with the sound of the Earth swerving through space.

Jim ran both hands over his scalp, wanting the thinning hair to assure him he really was old and therefore wise. He was not quite silent, though. He flipped through the pages in the yellow legal pad covered with tiny seismic zigzags, wondering what he had hoped to accomplish here, why the effort left him feeling so depressed. He hadn't actually wanted to write a memoir or meditation on history or whatever this was supposed to be. He couldn't remember where he had let this turn into a letter.

"Love, Jim," he wrote on the last sheet and gently tore the pages out. He folded them and wedged the bundle into a business envelope. Sending it on to his niece who taught history gave the exercise some kind of purpose, and got the evidence of failure out of the house. He addressed the envelope. He peeled off his reading glasses and set them on the desk, a pair of oval windows that watched him with their arms cooly crossed. He bounced the golf ball one last time against the floor before he dropped it in the drawer, then went out to the mailbox with the letter to his confidante, friend and accomplice.

1

WHEN HE ARRIVED IN 1953, Washington was still a city of trees and temporary buildings. The barrackslike offices erected around the Mall for the war remained in use, rows of khaki-colored shoeboxes under canopies of leaves. The tree-lined avenues and monumented traffic circles were full of bulbous new cars with chrome grills and little fins, like grinning pigs with wings. The newspapers were full of McCarthy.

Jim Goodall worked a minor Asian desk that spring, in the new State Department Building over toward the river. He spent fifty hours a week in his corner of the fifth floor, diligently preparing himself for his first assignment overseas. Twenty-five years old and fresh out of law school, Jim was tall and almost handsome, with cropped red hair and large athletic hands. Always farsighted, he wore reading glasses at his desk, hoping they made him look mature and serious. He tried to hide how excited he was, boyishly ecstatic he was where he had always wanted to be.

He had gone to law school only because it was the best route into the foreign service. Jim was seventeen when the war ended, so he grew up on war, missed taking part in it, then went to college surrounded by men who had been there. He wanted to serve; the foreign service appealed to his intelligence, ambition and virtue. Jim believed in his country with the same mix of passion and realism with which his grandfather, a Congregationalist minister outside Boston, had believed in God. There was room in their faiths for criticism, doubt and even jokes. "You're in the engine room of the world," Jim joked to himself. "Or at least the kitchen door."

Maps covered the new walls of the suite of offices where the minor Southeast Asian desks were thrown together. Across the hall was the breathless panting of a bank of teletype printers constantly rewriting nations. Long modern windows with long venetian blinds looked out across the treetops and river to Virginia. Jim sat in blue-edged fluorescent light and studied the Philippines.

They were sending him to Manila in July. Jim had wanted Europe, preferably along the Iron Curtain, but one had to start somewhere. And the more he
learned about his chain of islands—Spanish colony, then American, the Japanese occupation, independence, Colonel Lansdale and Ramon Magsaysay and
their campaign against the Huks—the more the post excited him. One could
do good work in such a place. One could start a career. He read every report,
memo and cable he could lay his hands on, memorized blocks of statistics,
wrote his own detailed report on the possible economic effects of the Philippines Trade Act of 1946 and, in his few hours alone in his studio apartment
near Dupont Circle, taught himself Tagalog, the chief language of the common people. Jim suddenly had more energy than he knew what to do with. He
began to play tennis again—he had been too busy with international law and
part-time jobs while he was at Boston University. He grew more physical and
restless, his desk no longer seeming big enough for his legs or elbows. He
caught himself smiling too much.

None of his peers appeared to experience anything similar. They were a
cool, sophisticated lot, most of them from better schools than Jim, their only
show of feeling a bit of self-consciousness in their smirks. The State Department was full of new people that spring. The new administration needed fresh
minds to fill the new building—and to replace all the old hands who had
resigned in frustration or fear. There was that going on, out in the unreal
world of newspapers and public opinion. *Reds in the State Department. More
Pansies in Pin-Striped Suits.* Jim was only annoyed by the noise in the distance. The jumbling together of Communists and homosexuals proved how
irrational it was, as if sex and politics had anything to do with each other. "A
hundred lavender lads," Senator Dirksen announced, "were fired from the
State Department last year." The word on the fifth floor was those men had
resigned of their own free will, worn down by the atmosphere of rumor and
too meek to fight back. Jim had no sympathy for them either. "If you can't
stand the heat, get out of the kitchen," he argued during discussions in the
cafeteria. The other junior officers agreed.

The political climate had little effect on the new men, except to make pin-
striped suits unfashionable. Jim's only firsthand experience of rumor and paranoia was with Bradford, a balding pink Anglophile in his late forties who
worked the Thailand desk around the corner from Jim. Bradford was said to
be on his way out. Nobody knew why. Nobody knew where the rumor origi-
nated, although for a man who'd been consul in Saigon to be stuck at a minor
desk stateside suggested somebody wanted to get rid of him. It was said Foster
Dulles himself wanted the man gone. Whatever the cause, a reputation of
doom hung over Bradford. Jim noticed people pretending not to see him when
they passed Bradford in the hall, or looking embarrassed when they had to
deal with him. Jim refused to give in to the rumors. He made a point of being
direct and friendly with the man, although Bradford made it difficult. He was
a strange man, cryptic and proud, as if taking perverse pride in his fate.

Bradford was sent with a pack of junior officers one evening to a reception at the Thai embassy, an opportunity for the new men to wear white dinner jackets and practice protocol on unimportant dignitaries. Bradford was supposed to show them the ropes, but he gave no advice, said nothing to put anyone at ease. Tiny Thai women in bright silk dresses, shy peacocks, stood around a room where everyone else was dressed in black and white, including the men on the embassy staff, as toylike and pretty as the women. Jim and the others stood above them, trying to remember not to bend down when they made conversation. A deputy-something spoke to Jim about the absence of nightlife in Washington—"Compared to Paris or even New York, your nation's capital is most definitely the sticks"—until Jim excused himself and went to the bar, where he found Bradford. He assumed Bradford had hurried off to take care of business or talk with Thai friends, but Bradford only stood at the bar and mournfully watched the room. Jim felt sorry for him. He tried to express his sympathy in a joke. "This can't be much fun for a man with your experience. Must feel like chaperoning a prom."

Bradford scornfully looked up, slowly remembering who Jim was. "Quite," he said, and demanded another martini from the bartender. "Prom night on the *Titanic*. Glub, glub. Which is Laotian for 'So long, sucker.' "

The man was drunk. Conversation was a bad idea. "I guess you've seen it all," Jim said respectfully.

"The foreign service used to mean something," Bradford muttered. "People from good families, names you knew. Now it's people with no names, no families, nothing but . . . superstitions." He looked straight at Jim.

Jim frowned and changed the subject. "Very handsome people, the Thai."

Bradford began to nod. "Oh yes. Quite. Beautiful, charming." He smiled. "And such fun to fuck."

Jim hated the way men like Bradford enjoyed being vulgar, always putting it in quotes, as if they thought their family trees kept them above dirt.

"Don't you know?" he continued when he saw Jim's reaction. "All wogs are. Except they take such pleasure in it you can never be certain if you're fucking them or they're fucking you."

"Excuse me." Jim set his unfinished beer on the bar and walked away. The man was drunk and unhappy. There was no point in getting angry with him. Jim wondered if Bradford were an alcoholic and that was why they were getting rid of him.

Back at the office Bradford remained his sober, jaded, doomed self, arrogantly sullen. Jim gave no thought to him. He was too contentedly busy that spring to give much thought to anything personal. He lost himself in his work and future. Jim intended to use one weekend before he left the country to fly up to Boston and visit his mother or at least drive down to Norfolk and see Ann, but there was always something to do. The spring grew greener and warmer. His report on the Trade Act was commended, passed around, then shelved.

He was reading Mindanao election returns into a Dictaphone one Friday when Dave Wheeler hurried past his desk, with frantic hair and his permanently rumpled gray suit. He had a sheaf of onionskin carbons in his hand, which he took around the corner to Bradford.

"Where did you get these casualty figures?"

"Those? A little bird. In point of fact, an old friend with the Red Cross."

"But they're *three* times what the French ministry tells us!"

"Vive la France," Bradford said drily.

Jim couldn't see them but he could hear every word. The office was all corners and no doors. Diffenbach, who sat at the Dutch East Indies desk across from Jim, looked up at the noise, glanced at Jim, shook his head and resumed reading a Dutch newspaper. People usually spoke in whispers here, but Wheeler was furious. Jim knew Wheeler only by sight. He'd been in Jim's orientation class, wearing the same unpressed suit, and was now with the Indochina desk, which had its own expanding offices down the hall, growing every month as the United States gave the French more arms and money.

"You think these figures are reliable?"

"It's very possible. My friend takes care of the inventory on medical supplies, which includes coffins. The French army doesn't provide their own, you know."

"Then why did you pass them on to us? These should've been sent upstairs!"

"Don't you know? I'm *persona non grata* up there."

"Yeah, but—" Nobody ever mentioned Bradford's doom to his face. "If these are true, they should be seen. These figures make it look like the Viet Minh are winning."

"Which was why I thought they might interest someone down your way. Has Foster seen them yet?"

"No. They came to me first. I screen all his material."

"Ah. Then it remains to be seen if they'll make it into *his* report."

Bradford remained perfectly blasé, already prepared to lose. Wheeler remained passionate.

"They have to at least consider this. They can't bury it."

"You'll see. Nobody loves Cassandra."

"I don't understand your attitude. You have something like this, and you just pass it along?"

Jim was impressed by Wheeler's anger. Everyone here was usually so polite and mandarin, himself included. Wheeler was beautifully passionate. Misled by his sloppy dress and boyish face, Jim had underestimated him.

"I'm making sure Foster sees these. You just better back me up."

"I will. Most definitely. *If* they get that far."

"They will, you'll see."

Wheeler came out from around the corner, still clutching his carbons, still breathing fire. He hurried past Jim and out the door.

Jim jumped up and followed him into the corridor. "Excuse me?"

Wheeler looked over his shoulder and stopped.

Jim forgot how deep and loud his voice could be. "Sorry. And sorry for eavesdropping. But I couldn't help overhearing what you told Bradford. Is that—?"

"The stupid bastard has *this* come to him." Wheeler shook the carbons at Jim. "And he's too lazy to do anything but pass them along."

"Or afraid," Jim offered. "He's a beaten man."

"Why did he even bother writing it up if he wasn't willing to go to bat—"

Wheeler stopped while a messenger pushed a trolley full of sorted envelopes past. He stopped long enough for them both to realize they couldn't talk about this out here. Other messengers and a few gray suits moved silently in the distance. The corridor was long and wide, its tiled floor checkered like a pale chessboard.

Jim didn't really want to defend Bradford or discuss casualty figures. He wasn't sure why he had run after Wheeler, except that he was impressed by the guy's passion.

Wheeler stood there, pushing one hand through his dark hair while he regained his temper. He looked half-Indian, with high cheekbones and faintly Oriental eyes. "You're the Philippines, right?"

"Temporarily. Until I go out to Manila in July."

"You're lucky. I wish I were getting out of this madhouse. Didn't come here to be a damn paper-pusher. And they don't even let you do that right. I'm going dead in this place."

Jim nodded, as if he knew the feeling. "You play tennis?"

"What? Not really." Wheeler was thrown by the new subject.

"You want to learn?"

Still confused, Wheeler shrugged and said, "Maybe."

"Saturday morning. You free? Rock Creek Park. You know where the courts are?" Jim raced through the arrangements, blurting them out just as he had blurted out the suggestion of tennis, without explaining to Wheeler or himself what he was doing. "I've got an extra racket. You have any tennis shoes?"

Wheeler agreed each step of the way, looking surprised and hesitant until the very end, when he burst out laughing.

"Something funny?" said Jim, laughing with him.

"You are, Goodall. But that's okay. I'm game. I'll see you tomorrow."

Back at his desk, Jim decided his behavior had been rather comic, a friendly bull in a china shop. Nevertheless, it had felt good to be impetuous, jumping into something without time for reflection. He did it so rarely anymore. And Jim really did want a chance to know Wheeler better.

Wheeler stood at the entrance to the courts the next morning, smoking a cigarette when Jim strode across the parking lot with two rackets under his arm. Wheeler looked different outdoors. His wild hair was less inappropriate;

his muscular legs suggested a maturity his face lacked. He was actually a good-looking fellow. His tennis shorts fit him a little too snugly, though.

With no more small talk than when they arranged this, they took a court and Jim began to lob balls to Wheeler. The burnt-orange clay was enclosed in fences similar to the open-air cages of the nearby zoo. A dozen games were already in progress, balls volleying like a dozen different heartbeats. Wheeler caught on very quickly. He was remarkably good-natured, patient yet exuberant, laughing at his own mistakes. Jim wasn't a great tennis player himself, making up in effort for what he lacked in grace, taking the game more seriously than it deserved. He tried not to take it too seriously today, but he enjoyed making Wheeler twist and stretch with tricky returns. Sinewy and slightly bow-legged, Wheeler's body was a rubber wishbone hopping around the court.

Afterwards, they sat in a pavilion with picnic tables, caught their breaths and talked. Jim had burned up enough energy that his words no longer outran his thoughts. They knew not to talk about work in public and said nothing about Bradford. They talked about sports, which Wheeler missed from college and the army. He was a year younger than Jim but had enlisted after high school, then went to college on the G.I. Bill. He'd been to a state university, so they could groan together over the self-importance and mannerisms of what Jim called the Whiffenpoofers. They recognized each other as two men of the people working their way up in the world. Jim secretly believed he was only regaining the position that would've been his if his mother had married more wisely, but he couldn't say that to Wheeler.

"Are you married?" Jim asked.

Wheeler threw his head back; his laugh was high and boyish. "You see how I dress. Do I look like somebody who's got a good woman looking after him?

Jim admitted Wheeler might do something about his appearance. He gave him the names of his barber and laundry.

"You're not married either," said Wheeler.

"No. For now. A wife and family can be a hindrance overseas, until you get yourself established." It was Jim's only thought on the subject.

"I've heard just the opposite. The right wife can smooth your way through the ranks. I'm seeing someone myself, but don't know if she's the one. Well, I spent twenty-four years being celibate. Another year or two won't kill me."

Which Jim thought a remarkably trusting thing for one man to confess to another; men their age usually spoke as if they were getting it regularly. He invited Wheeler back to his apartment, where they could shower and then grab lunch somewhere, but Wheeler said he had too much work waiting for him at home.

They saw a great deal of each other the following week. They ate together in the cafeteria every day, sometimes with others, sometimes alone. They were alone the day Wheeler reported his superior had killed Bradford's memo: the high casualty figures would not be going upstairs after all. Jim wasn't surprised. Wheeler was confused, his passion turned against itself by his respect for those in charge. They did their best to justify their superiors' behavior to each other.

"Foster says your friend's a certified frog-hater," Wheeler insisted. "He'll grab at anything that makes the French look bad."

"Bradford's got his hobbyhorses," Jim admitted. "Yes, I'm sure they know better than we do. Blind man and the elephant."

Jim looked forward to another game of tennis the following Saturday, so much that he was afraid to mention it to Wheeler for fear of letting his eagerness show. Not until Friday, when they were leaving the cafeteria after lunch, did Jim bring it up.

"Well. Tomorrow morning? Same time?" He slapped his hands together. "See you in court. Tennis court, that is."

Wheeler made a face. "I'd love to, Goodall. Only I'm taking Elaine out to Ocean City for the day. Thanks just the same."

"Ah? Oh." Jim was stunned, surprised they wouldn't be playing. And he was deeply hurt, he wasn't sure why. He jumped over his hurt and said, "You know, I've never been to Ocean City. Be nice to get out of town."

They stood at the bank of elevators. Wheeler looked blankly at Jim.

"We could take my car," Jim offered. "Yes, that could be lots of fun. And I'd really like to meet Elaine."

Wheeler turned away, embarrassed. "Uh, sorry. Maybe some other time, Goodall. Elaine thinks I've been neglecting her. You know. Women."

"What? Oh." Jim saw what a fool he just made of himself. He felt his face heat up, turning red.

"We'll play tennis next Saturday," Wheeler assured him. He gave Jim a smile weak with embarrassment and pity.

"Of course. If *I'm* free, that is," Jim said coldly. He did not want Wheeler to think he was so lonely and desperate he had to horn in on other people's social lives. "I hope you have a nice time," he added without conviction.

"Supposed to rain all weekend," Wheeler said, as if in apology.

Jim tried to lose himself in work that afternoon, going so far as to correct the mistakes in spelling and grammar of a field report from Luzon which would probably be going straight into a filing cabinet, never to be seen again. Jim could not understand how he could've done something as embarrassing as force himself on Wheeler, or why the mistake stuck in his thoughts. It was a social fumble, a minor *faux pas,* nothing more. Yet Jim could not forget it.

That night he ate in his usual restaurant near his apartment, sitting in a turquoise vinyl booth with the stack of foreign newspapers he read during dinner. The restaurant was full of bachelor bureaucrats who continued to shuffle papers while they ate. It was like dining in a library. Afterwards Jim took a long, rapid walk through the city, as calm and bosky as a country town after dark, even on a Friday night, a few curtained windows glowing among the leafy trees and dark shrubs, a solitary streetcar grinding down Wisconsin

Avenue. Jim felt there'd been something he looked forward to this weekend.
Then he remembered and was irritated with himself all over again.

He went home to the new apartment building with watery bricks of glass
around the entrance. The studio apartment upstairs was barely home. His only
furniture was a sofa which doubled as a bed, a card table and a folding chair.
Everything was temporary. Jim hadn't decided if he should keep this apartment when he went overseas, sublet it or what. He kept his diamond-patterned
copper necktie on when he sat at the card table to make notes for a report on
next year's pineapple crop. The sensation of constraint around his neck gave
Jim a feeling of focus and cool strength. He did not take the necktie off until
he stretched out on the sofa to study Tagalog for an hour before he went to
bed. Tonight he declined verbs.

"I love. You love. He loves."

The book had been published during the war by what was then the War
Department. The old blunt name was printed on the thick paper cover, a
beautiful plainness without pictures or decoration, only the name, title and
publication number.

"We love. You love. They love."

Jim set the book down. Damn, he told himself. He was suffering a return of
his old hero worship. And he had fixed that hero worship on Dave Wheeler.

He thought he'd outgrown that. All through college, hardly a semester
passed without Jim falling under the sway of one older fellow or another, a
veteran on the G.I. Bill who came to classes in khaki pants or army boots.
They were everywhere at U. Mass. after the war, smirking, joking old men in
their early twenties who'd seen it all. The guys who attracted Jim were the
loners, those who seemed faintly sad yet comfortable with their sadness,
which gave them a kind of masculine grace. One misunderstood Jim's infatuation, but the others accepted him as good company, an amusing little brother.
They drank too much and Jim drank with them, listening to war stories. The
real heroes downplayed any heroics involved and Jim worshiped them even
more.

What he felt for Wheeler was like a return of the old adolescent awe, Jim
decided. Wheeler had done nothing heroic—he'd been in the army in peace-
time, not even getting to Korea—but something in Jim felt Wheeler *would be*
a hero. He had the passionate nature and moral alertness Jim associated with
admirable acts. He wondered if Wheeler saw the same potential in him.

He knew he was being silly. These romantic notions were more appropriate
to prep school than to the State Department. But Jim decided he could be
amused by his infatuation now that he knew what it was: premature hero
worship. And it was nice to feel something besides the familiar self-love of
ambition and dry plotting of career, a moist private spot in his otherwise
practical life. Jim believed he could enjoy the emotion from a safe distance
until it passed. It always passed. He went into the kitchen and celebrated with
a cold glass of milk.

First thing Monday morning, Jim ran into Wheeler in the corridor. He was pleased to see Wheeler's rumpled suit and bow-legged walk coming toward him, pleased when Wheeler's cheekboned face went cockeyed in a sheepish grin.

"Have a good weekend?" he cheerfully asked.

"No," said Wheeler. "Was one helluva mess. I should've stayed in town and played tennis with you. God, I don't understand women."

"I'm sorry," said Jim, overjoyed. "A different kind of cold war?"

Wheeler laughed and shook his head. "The less said, the better. I should stick to the company of men. See you at lunch, Goodall."

The final draft of the pineapple report went quickly and easily that morning. Then, an hour before lunch, there was a telephone call from the assistant to the Assistant Secretary of State. Jim was wanted upstairs.

He stopped briefly in the men's room to comb his hair and adjust his tie. The call left him very excited and nervous. He had never been alone with the Assistant Secretary of State, had not even been up to the seventh floor since his orientation meeting three months ago. The assistant didn't say what this was about and Jim hoped they wanted to do something with his trade-agreement report after all.

The seventh floor corridor was identical to the one on the fifth floor, only quieter. Jim was received by a schoolmarmish woman who was secretary to the assistant of the Assistant Secretary. She ushered him through her office into a room next door, an oak-paneled library with a turkish carpet on the floor and bookcases that disappeared into shadows overhead. After the artificial brightness of the rest of the building, shadows seemed homey. In front of a window hung with green velvet drapes opened on gauze curtains was a mahogany conference table. Behind the table sat two men with slicked-back hair and boxy gray suits, neither of whom was the Assistant Secretary of State.

"Goodall? James?" said the man on the left, looking up from an open folder. "We won't take much of your time. Just a few questions."

"Federal Bureau of Investigation," the other man explained, his voice warmer and friendlier than his partner's. "Routine security check. Nothing important."

There was a flicker of nervousness, a twinge of self-consciousness. But Jim knew he had nothing to fear. In fact, he had enormous respect for the FBI. He was flattered they wanted to talk to him.

"My name's Hightower," said the friendlier man, leaning forward to shake Jim's hand. "This is Mr. Gardenia."

"Pleased to meet you," said Jim. Their handshakes were firm. Both men were Jim's age and they seemed like decent fellows. Being FBI, they too would've been through law school. Jim pulled out the leather chair on his side of the table and sat down. The chair was still warm.

"*Jim*. You have something to do with the Philippines," Hightower began. "What exactly do you do?"

Jim told him, careful not to make his work sound more important than it was. Hightower nodded while Jim spoke, as if this were an exam and Jim was answering correctly. Gardenia sat back and watched, the pencil in his hand idly tapping the steno pad in his lap.

"You work with Lyman Bradford," said Hightower.

"I work in the same office. Around the corner, in fact. But our countries have few relations with each other, so there's no need for us to work together. He's Thailand, you know."

"Where *are* they in relation to each other anyway?" Gardenia asked.

Jim told them, startled by their ignorance of geography.

"All those damn Chinese countries," Hightower said indifferently. "What do you know about Lyman Bradford's personal life?"

The question surprised Jim. "Very little. I don't know him socially."

"Is there anything you've seen or heard that's made you wonder about his character?" Hightower shrugged over the specifics. "Habits? Mannerisms? Vices?"

Jim remembered his thoughts on Bradford's drinking. Carried along by his respect for these men, he was ready to tell them, pausing to find the words that would make his uncertainty clear.

But before he could answer, Hightower said, "In particular, anything that leads you to believe Bradford's a homosexual."

"Homosexual?" Jim's mind went blank. He squinted at Hightower in disbelief.

"Sexual deviant," Hightower explained. "Pervert. Queer."

"*Bradford?*" Despite himself, Jim began to grin at the absurdity of the idea. "Bradford's married! He's got two daughters."

"Have you ever met his wife or daughters?"

"No. We don't socialize, as I said. But I can't believe—" Jim stopped, panicked for a second by his inability to refute the accusation. Then he laughed. "No, Bradford's not a homosexual. I'm perfectly confident of that. Oh, he *does* have those terribly English manners," Jim admitted. "But that's the Old Guard here. Their umbrellas and extended pinkies. They don't mean a thing."

"Considering what we know now about the English *and* the Old Guard," said Gardenia, "I'd say they mean plenty."

"You mean that nonsense in the newspapers?" Jim laughed. "Homosexuals selling us out to the Russians? You fellows don't believe that."

"You think it's nonsense," said Hightower drily, ambiguously.

Jim screwed up his face in another squint, as if trying to read Hightower without his reading glasses. His sympathy with these men, his trust of them, began to waver.

"Yes. It's ridiculous," he told them. "It has no logic. Communists think homosexuality's a disease of capitalism, bourgeois decadence. Why would a homosexual help his enemies? More importantly, where are all these homosexuals in the State Department? I haven't seen any."

Hightower and Gardenia sat there like stones, unpersuaded, unmoved.

Jim grew more heated. "Do you really believe . . . one of those people" —he was suddenly reluctant to use the word again—"has the discipline and emotional stability to pass all the tests and work here? No. Impossible. Even if they managed to get in, they'd go to pieces as quickly as a woman would in this place. Which proves to me it's nonsense. A sensationalistic fantasy cooked up to sell newspapers and politicians."

Hightower said nothing. Gardenia wrote something in his pad.

Their silence worried Jim. He responded with scorn. They were as foolish and gullible as anyone else in the outside world. Jim was indignant for Bradford's sake and relieved he hadn't tattled about the man's drinking. This wasn't national security, it was just gossip.

"Then you've never had any reason to suspect Lyman Bradford of sexual deviance?" said Hightower.

"None," said Jim. "Nor anyone else here."

A man less sure of himself might come away from this believing Bradford actually was a homosexual. It seemed like a subtle way of smearing the man. Jim suddenly realized that could be the real purpose of this interview. Who wanted to smear Bradford? Why?

Hightower took the folder from Gardenia and set it on a stack to one side. They were obviously interviewing others. "I think that'll be all," he told Jim. "We thank you for sharing your time with us."

Jim remained seated. He calmly locked eyes with Hightower. "Would this have anything to do with Bradford's memo on French casualties?"

Hightower blinked. "What memo might that be?"

He had to know, but Jim played along and told him. "A report on losses in Indochina based on the supply and demand of coffins. They were much higher than anything reported previously."

"Bradford discussed this memo with you?"

"No. I overheard him arguing with—someone from the Indochina desk." Jim didn't want to implicate Wheeler, although he didn't know what the implications were and assumed they'd be talking to Wheeler anyway. When trust died, you couldn't be sure of anything. "What I don't understand," Jim boldly continued, "is why, if these casualty figures are making someone unhappy, they don't simply prove them wrong with facts. Instead of smearing the source."

"Nobody's smearing anyone," Hightower said flatly. "This is only a routine security check. And we know nothing about this memo." He exchanged a glance with Gardenia.

"Of course you are aware," Gardenia told Jim, "you're not to discuss this interview with anyone. We're not in the business of spreading rumors."

"Of course," said Jim as he stood up, not believing that either.

As he turned to leave, Hightower said, "You're not married, are you?"

"No. I'm not."

Hightower leaned back in his chair, making himself comfortable. "You engaged or seeing anyone at present?"

Jim smiled to show he wasn't intimidated. "I believe that's personal."

"Just asking. It's been interesting talking to you. Thanks again."

"My pleasure," Jim said, nodded crisply and departed.

He strode through the secretary's office into the corridor, proud of himself for having held his own in there, for resisting the atmosphere of rumor. He was disappointed with what he glimpsed of this world, yet there was satisfaction in having seen through their game. Jim looked forward to comparing notes with Wheeler. Surely they'd be talking to Wheeler. Maybe together he and Jim could make some sense of the elaborate chess game being played with innuendos and reputations. Jim assumed it had been instigated by an outsider, someone high up yet not really part of the State Department. Heads came and went as regularly as hats here, affecting morale without changing the good nature of the body they perched on.

The fifth floor felt very real and sane after the visit upstairs. Jim confidently sat at his desk and read his pineapple report one last time before he sent it out to be typed. He heard the squeak and rattle of wheels from a chair around the corner: Bradford. The poor sot.

Jim took a looseleaf binder with him when he went down to the cafeteria, so people would think he was busy and let him sit alone. Wheeler would know otherwise. The bright high-ceilinged room was full of the clatter of cutlery and discreet murmur of shop talk. Negro stewards wandered about, refilling water glasses and coffee cups. Clouds of blue smoke began to drift up toward the cylindrical light fixtures, which hung from the ceiling like clockweights as men finished their meals and lit their pipes. Wheeler never appeared.

Not until Jim got up to leave did he see Wheeler, sitting by himself in a corner, his back to the room. Jim went over and happily pulled out a chair to sit down beside him.

"Didn't see you come in," Jim said. "I was sitting over there."

Wheeler glanced up, then went back to his food. "Right. I saw you. I was in a hurry. I didn't have time to chat."

Jim leaned in and lowered his voice. "They talk to you?"

"Who?" Wheeler didn't bother to look up.

"On the seventh floor."

"Why? Somebody talk to you?"

"Yes. Regarding Bradford."

"Hmmmm." Wheeler only took another bite of food.

And Jim realized his coolness was chosen, his avoidance of Jim deliberate. Wheeler looked different, his color gone, a clenched, closed-in quality about his jaw and eyes and even his nostrils.

"What did they say to you?"

"Nobody said anything," Wheeler irritably replied. "How could they, when nobody's talked to me?"

"They told me we weren't to discuss it," Jim admitted. "But I figured you and I—"

Wheeler turned and glared. "Then you damn well shouldn't discuss it, should you?" He glanced over his shoulder at the other tables, then lowered his head again.

Jim felt slapped, betrayed, heartbroken. It was a rejection of trust, a refusal of friendship. "Dave? What're you afraid of?"

"Nothing. Will you let me finish my lunch in peace?"

Hurt feelings turned into anger. He wanted to grab Wheeler's uncombed hair, yank his head back, look into his eyes and—Jim didn't know what he wanted to do.

"Suit yourself." Jim stood up to go, and glanced around the room to see if anyone *had* been watching them. All he saw were faces chugging on pipes and wagging in conversation. "See you later," he said coolly.

"Right," Wheeler muttered.

It took forever before an elevator arrived to take Jim away. He was furious with Wheeler for being afraid, disappointed with him for letting the men upstairs get to him. What was the guy afraid of? Being associated with Bradford? The shame of being questioned? Riding alone in the elevator with a young Negro attendant, Jim found his anger giving way to self-consciousness. "Is my tie on straight?" he asked the boy.

"Yessuh. Tie looks good. You got a fuzzy on your shoulder, though." He reached over to pluck it off.

Jim hurriedly brushed himself off before the boy could touch him.

Coming through the door to the suite of offices, he felt eyes look up at him. But when Jim looked, he saw only Diffenbach at his desk and Ayers at his, both back from lunch and drowsily going through papers.

Jim sat down at his desk. He opened and closed drawers before he realized he didn't know what he was looking for. Then he heard Bradford around the corner, opening and closing *his* drawers.

Diffenbach glanced up.

Jim froze. Did they think Jim and Bradford were signaling each other?

Jim set a folder full of clippings on his desk pad and pretended to study them. This was crazy. He felt on display here, scrutinized and wondered about. The very architecture of the room, all corners and no doors, seemed specially designed for self-consciousness. What was he afraid of? It was as though he'd caught Wheeler's fear, like a flu, without having a target for his anxiety. He tried to be angry with Wheeler for doing this to him, then found himself wondering if Wheeler were right to be afraid. Did he know something Jim didn't? Had Jim been wrong to brush off the interview so confidently?

Chair springs groaned around the corner as Bradford got up from his desk.

Keeping his head lowered, Jim watched through his eyebrows as Bradford strolled past, a harmless, pink-faced man in a baby blue seersucker suit. He ate his lunch at his desk, perhaps to avoid being avoided by people in the cafeteria, and was taking the wadded paper bag to the trash basket beneath the map of Southeast Asia on his way to the hall. He held his head high, proudly indifferent to the rumors and suspicions accompanying him like the loud creak of his leather shoes. Surely he knew. He went out the door, presumably to the men's room. No, there was something prissy about the man yet nothing unnatural. Jim remembered his crude remark about fornicating with Asians, but he'd only said that to shock Jim. Hadn't he? Jim couldn't imagine the man having sex with anyone, even a wife.

Then Jim saw Diffenbach watching him watch Bradford. Jim quickly turned to the next clipping, which included a grainy photo of half-naked bodies in a neat row on a dirt road, Huk rebels killed by the Philippine army.

What did Diffenbach know? He and Ayers and the others must've been upstairs today. Jim had been too busy with his report that morning to notice people's comings and goings, but surely everyone here had been upstairs. Everyone except Bradford. Or maybe Bradford too, so the man wouldn't get suspicious. With him they'd have to ask questions about someone else, of course, about Diffenbach or Wheeler. Or even Jim.

The smudged boys in white undershorts were corpses. The clipping was from the *Manila Chronicle*. Nothing so grisly could appear in an American newspaper. Jim suddenly felt he'd been looking at the picture for an unseemly length of time. What would anyone think who saw what he was looking at? Jim turned the clipping over, nervously, as though the investigation were not about Bradford but about him.

They thought Jim Goodall was the homosexual.

He looked up in a panic. The thought seemed so loud he feared other people could hear it. Diffenbach and Ayers continued with their work. Ayers yawned.

Jim closed his eyes, waiting for the idea to go away. The idea frightened him, frightened him most because it came to him as if it had been at the back of his mind all along, during the interview and his encounter with Wheeler and the woolgathering here at his desk, waiting only for the right train of thought to put him in touch with it. They believed Jim might be a homosexual.

He knew he had no reason to think that. Hightower and Gardenia showed no interest in his attack on the notion of homosexuals in the State Department, although they did ask if he had a girlfriend, didn't they? Dave Wheeler had seemed nervous over being seen with Jim, but he was only afraid of being overheard discussing the interview, wasn't he? The strongest argument against it was that Jim had angered no superiors, done nothing which would make anyone want to ruin his reputation, done nothing to lead anyone to suspect he was queer. Then why did he think it?

It was insane. He blamed the FBI for introducing the word *homosexual* into his thoughts, which made everyone suspect, even himself. Was that what Wheeler was feeling? With that vile word in his head, he misunderstood Jim's friendship. He looked for a way to assure Wheeler his intentions were strictly honorable, then wondered why he wanted to go to the trouble. A man who could think such a thing of you was not someone Jim wanted for a friend. If that's what Wheeler thought.

It was the not knowing that made this so maddening, the uncertainty that suddenly ran through everything. With a few questions, two know-nothing officials had destroyed the solidity of a world Jim had taken on faith. What began in skepticism ended in imagination run riot. It was being alone with these imaginings that frightened Jim. He'd been fine when he spoke to the accusers face-to-face. He felt he'd be fine if he could've spoken to Wheeler.

A clerk wheeled a cart full of cables, memos and mail into the room. Friendly without overstepping the boundaries, he handed Jim a bundle.

"Thanks, Bobby," said Jim. "Thank you very much." This was what he needed now: work. He went through the bundle, hoping to find something earth-shattering and important, waiting for his phantom fears to evaporate now that he'd chosen to ignore them. They merely subsided, but that was enough for the time being.

The end of the day found Jim standing in the cool marble of the front lobby, waiting for Wheeler. He had to talk to Wheeler and clear this up for good. It was Jim's only hope for any kind of peace of mind. But the lobby felt too public. Anyone seeing them here would think they were up to something, which would make Wheeler more guarded than ever. Jim stepped outside to the wide, shallow stone stairs out front, but that felt just as public. He went down the steps and a few feet up the sidewalk to watch for Wheeler from behind a wiry tangle of crepe myrtle.

Wearing hats and carrying briefcases, clusters of men came down the stairs and dispersed in all directions to bus stops and parking lots. Jim knew Wheeler did not rate his own parking space and had to park his car several blocks away. Jim intended to walk with him to his car, which seemed innocent enough. It was a pleasant May evening, still light outside, a sweet odor of mown grass coming through the harsh burn of car exhaust. Long shadows stretched across the grass and the angled shadows of bureaucrats undulated over the steps as people descended to the street. The hard geometry of the building's modern facade softened a little in the orange light.

Jim spotted Wheeler, bareheaded and alone, coming quickly down the stairs. His head was down, his body ramrod straight, his feet pedaling furiously beneath him. A battered briefcase jiggled in his hand. Jim was ready to call out, then thought better of it. He did not want to make Wheeler nervous.

Jim stood to the left of the stairs. Wheeler cut off to the right. Jim waited a moment, then followed him, up the street that curved around the building, then across the street to a little park and a run-down residential neighborhood. After another block, there were no other men with briefcases on the sidewalk.

Jim thought he should increase his pace and catch up with Wheeler. But not yet. He found it strangely exciting to follow Wheeler like this, as if they were in a movie and Jim was a detective or spy. Watched from fifty yards away, Wheeler's rubbery bow-legged walk was both comic and poignant. He swung his briefcase like a schoolboy swinging a bookbag.

Wheeler stopped at a crosswalk and waited for the light. Jim stopped too, still fifty yards behind him. When Wheeler glanced left and right, Jim resisted the urge to step behind a tree but stood where he was on the sidewalk. As if he wanted Wheeler to see him. And suddenly, Jim no longer felt like a spy or detective, but like a lovelorn adolescent pursuing his crush. Anyone watching them would think he was in love with the guy.

But when Wheeler stepped off the curb to cross the street, Jim stepped with him. He could not stop himself. And as he took more steps, as he translated the agitation in his head into something as simply physical as walking, Jim understood. He *was* in love with Dave Wheeler. There was no other name for his irrational behavior.

He knew he should stop, knew he shouldn't follow Wheeler a step further. He certainly couldn't speak to him now with this awful discovery fresh in his thoughts. But he followed Wheeler another block, and another, the front yards growing smaller and shabbier, the houses crowding closer to the street. As the sunlight faded in the trees, more birds began to sing, a cacophony of birdsong like an elaborate, unoiled machine overhead. Jim was horrified to find himself stepping deeper and deeper into his own stupidity, a perverse stupidity. At the end of a day crazy with accusations and fears of homosexuality, he was in love with a man.

Wheeler dug and rummaged in his pants pocket as he swaggered out into the street toward a car, a black DeSoto with a roof beetling over the windshield like a lowered brow. Jim stopped and watched from a distance as he unlocked the door, flung the briefcase into the back and climbed in. He had to use his choke twice before the engine turned over. Jim watched hypnotized—until he realized Wheeler would drive by him when he pulled out. Jim stepped into a narrow driveway flanked by overgrown boxwoods full of weeds. A moment later the black DeSoto rumbled past, muffler boiling and spitting underneath.

And then it was over. Jim felt it should be over. He came to himself again, a grown man in a gray suit and brown hat, standing in an unfamiliar neighborhood with a briefcase full of state documents hanging from one hand. The excitement that brought him here was gone, and all that remained was knowledge, confusion and quiet panic.

He resumed walking, trying to remember where he'd parked his own car, then remembered he'd walked to work this morning. He'd been so innocent and happy this morning, with nothing on his mind but the world market for pineapples. No, he was lying to himself again. He'd been worrying about Wheeler this morning, hoping no harm had been done by his attempt to invite himself along to Ocean City. What a fool he'd been to think this was only hero worship. Wheeler proved at lunch he was anything but heroic, yet Jim still worshiped him.

Finding a familiar avenue, he made his way toward home. He wanted to be logical and decisive about this. Full of divisions and departments, Jim seemed a bureaucracy of himself; it was time he brought his departments together. All right, he told himself. He *was* in love with Wheeler. Which was foolish and dangerous, dangerous in that it left him prey to paranoid imaginings. It had to be why he suddenly imagined this afternoon other people thought *he* was a homosexual. Was he?

Jim quickened his pace, threw more weight into his strides.

He couldn't be a homosexual. His feeling for Wheeler might be homosexual, but Jim wasn't. Point one: Homosexuals were womanly, artistic and sensitive, none of which Jim was. Point two: Homosexuality was about sex. And Jim didn't want sex with Wheeler. He didn't. All he wanted to do with him was play tennis. The thought of seeing Wheeler naked disgusted him as much as the thought of seeing him sitting on the toilet. Thoughts of sex of any kind left Jim cold, even sex with women. He'd dated a few in college but, finding himself uninterested and them confused, he'd not pursued it since. He knew his apathy to sex made him different from other men, but liked to believe his difference gave him an advantage, a place to stand outside a world fogged with daydreams of breasts and hair. Tonight he felt it left him with no place to stand, only this limbo where he was vulnerable to adolescent crushes and morbid fantasies.

It was dark when he entered his apartment. As soon as he closed the door and turned on a light, he felt painfully alone in the barren room, without even the noise and movement of city traffic to give the illusion of life. If only he had a friend in this city with whom he could forget himself. He'd hoped to find such a friend in Wheeler, but Wheeler was now part of the self Jim needed to forget. Self led to selfishness and sick thoughts. He collapsed on the sofa, feeling emotionally dead and empty. His deep depression seemed like delayed punishment for the selfish ambition and pride Jim had forgotten were sins.

He picked up the telephone and dialed the long-distance operator. He recited the number of his mother in Boston.

There was a moment of garbled chatter among miles of women sitting at switchboards, then the ringing of a phone in a townhouse apartment full of shabby gentility, bound sermons and English grammar books.

"Hello?" Even her voice wore a high collar and prim earrings. A concert of light classical music played on the radio in the background.

"Hello. Mother? How are you?"

"Jimmy! How are *you*?" Her teacherly voice turned worried and maternal.

"I'm fine," he assured her. "I'm calling just to say hello."

"One can say hello in letters, dear. Long distance is an extravagance except in emergencies.'' She was prudent, not miserly, a habit acquired from raising two children on a public-school teacher's salary after her father's death.

"Actually, I was calling about something in particular. I'm leaving next month for Manila, you know."

"You must be very excited. Is there something you need?"

"What I need, Mother, is to see you. I thought I might fly up this weekend for a quick visit." He'd been intending to see her sometime before he left. Hearing her firm matter-of-factness over the phone, he felt she might be what he needed right now to reconnect with reality.

"It's a lovely thought, dear, but airplane tickets are terribly expensive."

"I don't have enough time to come up by train."

"No," she said firmly. "I appreciate the thought. But what I'd appreciate more is if you would drive down and see your sister before you left."

"Why? What's the matter with Ann?"

"I don't know. Possibly nothing. I've heard from her only once since they moved back east. But you know your sister. Still waters run deep. I *hope* Rick's new job is working out. Especially with Ann due again."

"Again?" They had two children already.

"I won't criticize," she claimed. "It's her family. Nevertheless, I'd feel much better if I knew Rick were finally settled in a career."

"Hmph," went Jim, a wince made audible.

"Will you look in on them? Norfolk is only a few hours from you by car."

"Six hours," Jim told her. "But yes. I was planning to get down there anyway." Which was true, although he wondered if he actually would've gone without his mother obligating him to it. "I haven't seen them in, what? Two years? Not since they went out to California."

"Thank you, dear. I'll feel better when I hear what you think of the situation."

"In fact, I'll give her a call tonight and see what I can arrange."

"Wonderful. Very quickly, how're *you* doing?"

"Fine. Working hard. Tying up loose ends before I go overseas."

"Try not to work too hard. Have you been seeing anyone?"

"Uh, there's no point since I'll be leaving shortly."

"You're right. That's very practical and considerate of you, James. Do I detect a slight trace of southern accent in your voice?" She made it sound like cause for worry, a bad cold or fever.

"No, Mother. I've only been down here a few months. That's not enough time to give me a southern accent."

"Maybe. But I definitely hear something different in your vowels. Anyway, I don't want to run up your bill further. We'll talk again after your visit."

"Yes. Take care of yourself, Mother. Don't work too hard yourself. And don't let the little goops get to you." He packed in parting personal remarks before she hung up. "I love you."

"Love to you, James. G'bye." She said the last word so hurriedly it registered as just a click of tongue and pop of lips.

Jim hung up and sat there. He no longer felt alone. Now he felt tangled up in a snarled net of family.

He loved his mother. He loved his sister, too. But they were part of a childhood and adolescence full of mixed emotions. Respect for his grandfather the minister had been mingled with shame over their status as poor relations when they became part of his household. Admiration for his mother's independence after Boppa's death was bound up with embarrassment over their thinly disguised poverty and chagrin over having a mother who did something as public as teach school. He had hoped to outgrow these childish hurts and prides by outgrowing his family. Another sin.

He hunted through a pile of papers on the floor and found the postcard with his sister's telephone number. They'd moved from California to Norfolk in February for Rick's new job with a fertilizer company. What with Ann being pregnant again, Jim saw the obvious joke but avoided making it.

This time, he got a long-distance operator with a thick, noticeable southern accent. The electric ringing of the phone was different from the one in Boston.

Jim was suddenly connected with a screaming baby.

Then a young woman came on. "Frisch residence. Hello," she called over the crying.

"Ann? It's Jimmy. How're you doing?"

"Jimmy! Hi!" Her voice turned away. "Honey, here. Take Meg. It's my brother." She sounded impatient and short-tempered. The crying baby withdrew into the background. "Jimmy. Hello. Been meaning to write you. You're taking off to the Orient soon, aren't you? Japan, is it?"

"The Philippines. Which is why I'm calling. I thought I might—"

"No! Bad boy. Bad." Ann called out into the room. "Rick, honey, *don't* let Robbie do that!"

"Jiminy Christmas!" Rick hollered. "I only got two hands."

"Am I calling at a bad time?" Jim asked.

Ann laughed. "It only gets worse. What were you saying?"

Jim understood he had to speak quickly before the next interruption. "I wanted to see you before I left. I was thinking I might drive down this weekend. Would that be good for you?"

"Be wonderful. Rick? Jimmy's coming for a visit this weekend."

Rick's mumbled response could be either displeasure or preoccupation.

"Be fine, Jimmy. We'd love to see you. Did you want to stay here or did you want us to book a room in a motor lodge for you?"

"Let me see how my schedule looks. I might have time only to spend the day."

"Awww," went Ann. "Whatever. We'd love to see you, even just for a few hours. You haven't seen your nephew since he was born. And you've *never* seen your niece."

"I've seen Mom's home movies from her visit to San Diego."

"Not the same thing, believe me. It's been much too long, Jimmy. And I guess it'll be even longer before we see you again."

"I'll be coming back now and then," Jim said.

"You'll need directions. I'll turn you over to Rick. Honey? Here, I'll do that. Tell my brother how to get here. And be specific. He gets lost easily."

Rick came on. "Hello there, Jimbo." His voice was deep with exaggerated male camaraderie. "You catching this racket in the background? You still want to visit this zoo?" There was a hollow laugh before Rick switched to a brusque, businessy tone. "Got a pencil? All right. Take Route One down . . ." He gave dry, detailed directions without any friendly asides. He was only three years older than Jim but spoke as if Jim were a teenager and he were an adult. "Any questions? All righty. We'll be looking for you sometime Saturday morning. Give us a call if you get lost. Goodbye now." He hung up before Jim could ask for his sister again or offer closing pleasantries. They seemed to have no time for pleasantries.

Jim sat back and caught his breath. The things one grabs at when drowning in unhappiness, he thought. A condescending brother-in-law and an apartment full of babies. Well, it would take him out of himself, for a weekend at least. He wanted to see his sister and her children—he felt a duty to see them—but he also felt as if he were distracting himself from the pain in his head by slamming his hand with a hammer.

2

JIM WENT INTO WORK the next day without panic. Only his depression remained. The State Department seemed unreal to him. He felt he could see through everything if he looked hard enough, which made every smile, remark and memo translucent and questionable. But sharing a table and small talk with Diffenbach and others at lunch provided an anchor, assuring Jim nobody thought ill of *him*. At least nobody avoided him—nobody except

Wheeler. That hurt, even as Jim steered clear of Wheeler as the chief cause of his doubt and fear. Being in love with the man was indistinguishable from fear, a nervous anxiety focused on one person, a magnetic field where attraction was eerily mixed with the repulsion. Jim couldn't help stealing glances across the cafeteria at Wheeler, who continued to eat alone all week, apparently avoiding everyone.

They did not speak to each other until Thursday. Jim was washing his hands in the men's room. Wheeler entered, saw Jim, adjusted his jaw and continued in.

"Goodall," he said.

"Wheeler," Jim replied.

Their looks and nods were mediated by the mirror over the sink. Wheeler stepped into a stall and stood there, the unruly back of his head visible above the door.

Jim kept the faucet running so he wouldn't hear Wheeler urinate. "How're things at your end of the hall?"

"Business as usual," Wheeler said wearily. "The French are playing musical generals again."

If he'd seen Jim following him Monday, would he say this much? Jim pressed on. "Any repercussions from the fuss over Bradford's casualty report?"

"No. Thank God." He didn't deny there'd been a fuss. "One gets nervous when you find you've hitched your wagon to a falling star."

Was that the reason for Wheeler's odd behavior? He'd attached his name to a doomed man's project and blamed Jim for encouraging him. Homosexuality was a red herring that existed only in Jim's head?

The toilet flushed and Wheeler came out. Jim was still drying his hands on the coarse brown paper towels.

"Got any plans for the weekend?" Jim asked.

"Work. Just work." Wheeler's eyes timidly met Jim's in the mirror when he stood at the sink.

Jim hoped Wheeler would suggest another game of tennis, so Jim could tell him he'd made plans of his own. That appealed to Jim as a way of assuring Wheeler he was not in desperate pursuit of him, and at the same time slap Wheeler with the suggestion he'd ruined all chances for friendship. But Wheeler didn't mention tennis.

"Don't take any wooden nickels," said Jim as he hurried out the door.

HE WOKE UP early Saturday morning and left before the sun came up. He wanted to avoid the weekend traffic and get this over with as quickly as possible. Driving the bulky '49 Dodge through the sleeping city and across the river, however, Jim felt his depression lift. The traffic lights were with him all the way through Arlington, and south of Arlington there were almost no lights

at all. The only traffic out this early were a few trucks. It was good to be on
the road, rolling up and down the wooded washboard of northern Virginia,
fragrant night air pouring through the open windows of the enormous car, the
radio picking up hillbilly songs from a station in Cleveland. Jim wore his
necktie but his jacket was hung on a hook in the back. He drove with his
shirtsleeves rolled up and an elbow hanging out the window. He wished he
could drive like this forever.

Jim imagined he'd quit the foreign service and now worked as a traveling
salesman, driving from town to town, never staying in one place long enough
to care what people thought of him. He swapped jokes with customers and life
histories with hitchhikers—whenever one wanted company, there was always
a hitchhiking teenager or serviceman to pick up. Responsible to nobody, he
was freed from the tyranny of rumor, expectations, duty and ambition. But
Jim couldn't sustain the fantasy. He couldn't live like that, without a mission
in life. To live only for himself seemed the bleakest selfishness imaginable.
He'd be useless, nothing. He needed to be involved in the thick of things,
good works and the world. The pressure of secrets and worries in Foggy
Bottom might be what made him crazy, but Jim couldn't imagine leaving the
State Department. He'd be like one of those ugly, toad-looking fish from the
bottom of the ocean who, brought to the pressureless surface, expand like
balloons and burst.

The sun appeared, then disappeared in a low ceiling of clouds. The land
flattened out and there were fields and ramshackle farmhouses along the highway, threads of wood smoke rising from the kitchen chimneys. Jim slowed
down to pass a Negro leading a team of swaybacked mules who sashayed
along the shoulder. Coming south was like stepping back in time. Waiting in
the line of cars for the ferry to Norfolk, Jim watched a small steam locomotive
haul empty gondolas through a freightyard, a fireman actually shoveling coal
from the tender into the engine. He hadn't seen that around Boston since he
was a boy. The ferryboat arrived; the cars and trucks trooped on. Jim stood in
the bow as the ferry churned through the coal-dark water of Hampton Roads,
surrounded by tubby merchant ships and long low colliers, the misty air smelling of saltwater, burnt oil and coal dust. He saw a gray skyline across the
harbor and assumed it must be Norfolk. But it was the navy, battleships and
aircraft carriers stacked one behind the other like an image in a telescope,
their uniform shade of solid gray broken only by the great white numerals
painted on their bows, their superstructures towering over the piers and warehouses. After woodstoves and mules, this city of warships looked as surprising
as a Roman camp must have looked on the banks of the Rhine.

After the ferry, Rick's directions took Jim around the outskirts of old Norfolk, through flat miles of new houses under telephone poles and TV antennas,
down Military Highway past an abandoned airfield to a boulevard and acres of
green wooden housing like tourist cabins, until he came to the Ingleside
Apartments. His heart sank for his sister's sake. The apartments were a fleet

of two-story shoeboxes similar to the temporary buildings around the Mall, except these barracks were sided with shingles, like fish scales, and families lived in them.

Families with many children, apparently. Slowly driving around the treeless complex, Jim saw and heard children everywhere. Despite the threat of rain, they were out in number, packing a little fenced-in playground, squealing and racing about in the open areas between the buildings. One gang appeared to have ransacked somebody's living room, arranging tables, chairs and a floor lamp out in the patchy grass in an elaborate game of house. None of the children looked older than the war.

Growing up at a time when educated people had no more than two kids, Jim associated multitudes of children with poverty and Catholicism. Poor Ann, he thought. They may have grown up poor, but their mother at least knew how to keep up appearances. While Jim had climbed back up in the world, his sister had been dragged down.

Jim found her number and parked at the curb. He locked the car—there was no telling what these kids might try—before he remembered his coat still hung in the back. But this was family: he could arrive in shirtsleeves. He adjusted his necktie and starched white shirt in the sideview mirror, then went up the sidewalk. A small concrete slab with a metal awning served as the porch to Ann's apartment and the one beside it. There was a screen door. Jim peered inside and could see through a dark living room to the kitchen and back door, which was open too. A three-foot-high wooden gate was pulled across the doorway between the living room and kitchen. Mixed with the shouts of children coming from out back were voices that sounded like an adult conversation, until a music cue came on and proved it to be a soap opera on the radio.

Jim knocked on the screen door. The frame rattled in the jamb. The bottom screen was bellied out, stretched out of shape from the inside. Then Jim saw why. A small face appeared there, nose and mouth waffling themselves against the mesh.

It had to be his nephew. Jim was surprised by a flood of tenderness. He double-checked the apartment number, then crouched down to the boy's level. "Why, hello there. Hello." He softened his voice just as he did with cats and dogs. "You must be Robert."

The boy jerked back. "Mommy!" he cried. "Mommy!" He stomped and staggered into the shadowy apartment.

"Robbie, not now. I'm doing your sister." Ann's voice came from the kitchen. Her ears seemed tuned so she could hear her son through the different noises, but not the door.

Jim knocked again, harder this time, and called in. "Ann? It's me."

A face appeared in the kitchen, leaning back from something around the corner. "Jimmy!" Her grin and voice were stifled by a diaper pin clenched in her teeth. "Oh! Let me just—" She ducked forward again, out of view.

Jim pulled on the screen door, but it was hooked. He looked around inside, wondering where his nephew had gone.

"Here we are!" sang Ann, reappearing with a freshly diapered baby in her hands. She stepped gracelessly over the wooden gate into the living room and swung the baby into a playpen. "You're early!" she cried. "We weren't expecting you for another couple of hours." She hurried to the door and unhooked it.

Jim no longer saw his sister through a haze of screen. She closed the door and rehooked it before she looked at him again, her grin big and toothy, her eyes shining in the overcast light from outside. She wore pants and a man's shirt, the shirttail out and sleeves rolled up. Her hair was tied back in a paisley handkerchief.

He hugged her. They were not a hugs-and-kisses family, but an occasion like this required a hug. He was surprised by the solidity of her stomach against his and remembered she was pregnant again.

"Oh!" She caught herself and pulled away from him. "I didn't have time to pick up. Rick'll pitch a fit if he knows you saw the place like this." She began to grab up alphabet blocks, newspapers and rubber cars from the floor.

"Don't worry. Everything looks fine," said Jim. Actually, the living room was a wreck, toys scattered over the brown linoleum, dirty laundry heaped on one end of the sofa, the playpen crowding the small space with its own rickety squalor. A curly-haired, bandy-legged baby, naked except for its diaper, stood inside and gripped the bars. She watched Jim with enormous eyes.

"This the new one?" said Jim.

"That's right. You haven't seen her before." Ann stuffed toys and newspaper into a bushel basket and went to the playpen, expecting Jim to follow her. "This is Margaret. Your niece. Meg? This is your Uncle Jim."

Jim gazed down. She looked like a nice baby. "Where did Robert go?"

"Robbie?" Ann glanced around. "He's off hiding somewhere. He's shy around strangers. You have to let him get used to you. Here, sit. You've had a long drive. We can talk while I straighten up."

Jim sat on the edge of the blocky sofa with a plain brown slipcover, opposite the pile of shirts, bras and boxer shorts.

"Rick's up the road at Be-Lo, getting groceries. We don't have a thing in the house to offer you."

"No problem. I should've brought some groceries with me." Or something. Only now did Jim realize he should've bought a house present for Ann and Rick and toys for the kids, but he'd been too mired in self all week to think of that.

"Don't be silly, dear," said Ann, sounding like their mother. "We can feed a brother."

She hurried back and forth between the kitchen and living room, stepping over the gate each time, never bothering to open it. When she turned off the radio in the kitchen, Jim heard a television roaring in the next apartment.

People who couldn't afford to shoe their children spent money on TV sets, he thought contemptuously, before he noticed the dark-green oval screen in Ann's living room.

"Was going to do a load of wash," she explained, gathering up the laundry from the sofa. "But it looks like rain. Well, dump these in the washer and do them tomorrow. Out of sight, out of mind. You talked to Mother lately?"

"A few days ago. She seems to be doing well." He wouldn't mention he was here because of their mother's concern.

"We hope to get her down this summer, when school's out. Maybe find her an apartment here for a month or two, although Rick's not too keen on that."

"How is Rick? He like his new job?"

"As well as one can like any job. At least he isn't being run ragged by that —*uncle* of his. The s.o.b." Ann had to be very angry before she'd use even the initials for profanity. "Restaurant manager, my foot. He wanted us for cheap labor."

Jim humored her with a sympathetic nod. His brother-in-law had a degree in business, earned on the G.I. Bill, but he seemed incapable of working anywhere longer than a year. Rick had done sales work for a chemical firm in Buffalo, then office management for a company in Boston before he went out to California to manage a restaurant owned by his Swiss uncle. Richard Frisch was Swiss himself, his parents both immigrants with courtly Old World manners and sing-songy German accents. Jim had nothing against immigrants. The Swiss were an admirable people, good stock with a reputation for cleanliness and hard work. His brother-in-law had managed to grow up with no trace of a foreign accent and no evidence of Swiss practicality. To Jim, who'd known what he wanted to do with his life since freshman year in college, his brother-in-law's leapfrogging about the country from one job to another seemed the height of irresponsiblity, especially when he kept giving Ann babies.

"If you can't trust an uncle, who can you trust?" Ann was saying. "Not only did he have Rick washing dishes and waiting on tables, he docked the rent on our bungalow from Rick's salary, at twice what the place was worth. A real stinker."

Jim had to question his brother-in-law's judgment in getting into such a situation.

"There!" said Ann, collapsing into the brown chair that matched the sofa. A cigarette had appeared in her mouth on one of her trips to the kitchen. It looked as falsely tough there as it would in the face of a bobby soxer outside a malt shop. Ann, in fact, was wearing bobby socks. "What're you looking at, Love Bumps?" She addressed the baby, who still stood in the playpen, mouth wide open, big eyes watching her mother and uncle. "You've never seen this big, strange person, have you?"

"Ye-ye-ye-ye," went the baby, jigging herself on her little legs like a chimp, until she lost her grip on the bars and landed on her bottom with a thump. She looked startled and insulted.

Jim turned to share his grin with Ann, and found her solemnly watching him, mouth pulled taut across her teeth, the cigarette held off to one side.

"Something wrong?" he asked.

She smiled. "No," she said, her voice lowered by a little moisture in her throat. "Seeing you here makes me a bit homesick. That's all."

Jim smiled too. "For which home?"

Ann rolled her eyes. "Isn't *that* the truth." She laughed and stubbed out the cigarette in an ashtray with a beanbag base. "Let me see if I can coax Robbie out. We should try to get him used to you before his father gets home. Rick's not very patient with other people's shortcomings, even a two-year-old's." She got up and went off to where the bedrooms must be, calling, "Robbie? Oh Robbie."

Homesick, thought Jim, looking around the apartment and feeling nothing similar. He loved his sister and knew she loved him, but there'd always been a quiet distance between them, a friendly distance. She'd never understood any of his ideals or ambitions. He'd never understood her burning conventional desire for a husband and family, although he suspected it had something to do with the unconventional lives they had growing up. They didn't even have the bond of two siblings allied against a parent. During their years in their grandfather's household, their mother became an older sister to them, siding now with Jimmy, now with Ann, never asserting enough authority on her own to drive them together.

"Robbie," Ann said in the other room. "Come out from under that bed right this minute. You're not a baby anymore."

Jim's eyes fell on the playpen. He found his niece sitting there, staring dumbly at him. She closed her mouth when Jim stared back, drool shining on her chin. They looked at each other for the longest time, in mutual incomprehension.

Something banged at the door. "Wake up in there! I don't have eight hands!"

Jim jumped off the sofa and faced the door.

Rick stood outside the screen door, his arms wrapped around several bags of groceries while he knocked the door with his knee.

Jim stepped over to undo the latch.

"What in Sam Blazes—Jimmy!" He recognized Jim and swallowed his anger. "You're here already? Thanks. No, no. I got it all. Just lock the door behind me, will you?" Rick hurried through with the armload of bags and was stopped by the gate. He tried stepping over it, but the bags blocked his knees. "This—*damn* gate. Ann!" Profanity did not come easily to him either, but it came.

Jim stepped around and unlocked the gate. It folded back like an accordion and Rick went to the kitchen table, where he dumped the bags. "What a zoo, huh? We need that stupid gate to keep Robbie out of the kitchen. Back door won't lock. Well, I see you made it in one piece. Oh yeah," he added, remembering to hold out his hand. "How you doing, Jimmy?"

"Good to see you, Rick." Jim shook hands, an excessively hearty handshake meant to match his brother-in-law's gruff, overdone heartiness. Rick's real heart seemed elsewhere. He was not a naturally sociable fellow.

"Let me put this junk away," Rick said irritably. "Where's your sister?"

"Doing something with Robbie in the bedroom, I think."

"Ann, I'm home," Rick shouted.

"I hear you," Ann called back.

"How you doing out there, Meg-wump?" he asked his daughter around the corner.

"Nya-nya-nya," went the baby, back on her feet again now that her father was home, pressing her face between the bars to look at him.

Jim stood in the kitchen door, waiting for a conversation to begin.

Carrying cans to the cupboard, Rick looked uncomfortable seeing Jim still there. "Make yourself at home, Jimmy. Would you like a beer? I picked some up. I couldn't remember if you drank beer or not."

"I do. But it's too early, thank you."

"I don't drink it myself. Except when there's company. Which means almost never. But I thought you did, Jimmy."

Jim didn't like being called Jimmy. It was one thing coming from his sister, but coming from Rick it became a piece of his brother-in-law's condescension. Rick was older than Jim and, yes, he'd been in the army during the war. But Jim felt Rick hadn't established himself well enough to earn any right to look down on him. He didn't even look the part this morning. Wearing army khakis as work pants and a white T-shirt, his dark hair combed back in a glossy wave, he looked like a teenager who'd be more interested in tinkering with a jalopy than in making a career or raising a family. Their mother liked Rick and defended him sometimes, but Jim suspected she too had been taken in by the fellow's good looks, like his sister. Richard Frisch was handsome, in a dark, slightly lumpy, foreign kind of way. He looked Italian, not Swiss.

"Here we are," Ann sang out, leading a very small boy by the hand. The toddler walked with heavy feet, a little marionette, and stared straight ahead with enormous mournful eyes. "Here's Daddy," Ann sang, brushing a dustball from the boy's fair hair. "And here's your Uncle Jimmy."

Robbie broke away from his mother to scuttle past Jim into the kitchen. Throwing his arms around his father's leg, he looked back in terror at Jim.

"Robbie!" Rick snarled. "Jiminy Christmas, you're going to make me fall." He could not have looked more embarrassed than if the boy were a dog locked around his leg. He faked a laugh for Jim and pleaded, "Ann?"

"Robbie, c'mere," said Ann, taking the boy's arm and peeling him off Rick's leg. She sat in a chair and hoisted her son into her lap. "He's going through a difficult phase," she told Jim. "I think he's still a little J-E-A-L-O-U-S."

"He'd get over it more quickly if we stopped babying him," Rick grumbled, continuing to put things away.

Safely seated in his mother's lap, the boy coolly studied Jim. His seersucker shorts flared out and Jim could see the diaper underneath.

"He *is* a B-A-B-Y," Ann insisted. "If he seems old, it's only in comparison to his little sister." She laughed and bent over him. "Robert Gordon Frisch," she said tenderly. "You are such a goofus."

Even as a child, Ann had been the patient one, tolerant and flexible and slightly above it all, steeled by some kind of secret knowledge that she was right. She rarely became angry when she knew anger wouldn't accomplish anything, but quietly kept her grievances to herself. Still waters run deep, as their mother said. She made quite a contrast with her husband, who seemed more irritable now than he'd been before they went out to California. Failure had brought the man's natural impatience closer to the surface, Jim decided.

Ann picked a box off the table. "Oleo?"

"Sorry," said Rick. "I forgot. It all tastes the same anyway."

"Not to me it doesn't." Ann sighed, but she accepted that too. "We save real butter for special occasions," she told Jim. "You know me and my butter."

Jim smiled and nodded. One Christmas during the war, he bought a pound of butter, wrapped it up in fancy paper and bows and gave it to Ann as a joke. He'd never had a gift received more gratefully.

Ann fed Meg first. They had only one high chair and Meg sat there happily, pleased to have so many grown-ups about. Jim continued to stand off to the side, watching everyone as if they were a play.

Meg was put down for her nap, the high chair wiped off and Robbie set there to eat lunch with the adults: sandwiches and milk.

"Little bites, Robbie. Like this," Rick directed.

"How do you like your new job?" Jim asked. "Fertilizer, isn't it?"

"But chemicals," Ann quickly explained. "Rick's company doesn't do—manure."

Rick chuckled. "Firm used to market guano. Ship it up by the ton from South America. Now the only birdshit is in management."

"Richard," Ann groaned.

"What exactly is your job?" said Jim.

"Traffic management. Freight schedules and trains, things like that." He shrugged. "You know. Business."

"Does this look like a firm you'll want to stay with?"

Rick frowned. He glanced at his wife. He had to know that other people wondered about his constant changing of jobs. He took a swallow of milk and said, "Only time will tell. Life's different out here in the real world, Jimmy.

Nothing at all like Washington.'' He smirked. "All your bureaucrats and—pin-stripes.''

In that brief hesitation, Jim heard the absent words of the common phrase: *pansies in pin-striped suits.* Was that what his brother-in-law thought of him?

"And it's the Philippines you're going to next month?'' said Ann, not hearing the subtle exchange of blows between her brother and husband. "Weren't you there during the war, Rick?''

"No. Okinawa. *After* the fighting,'' he carefully added. "Then Japan during the Occupation. Mapmaking with the Signal Corps.''

"Tell Jimmy your story about the water buffalo.''

Rick made a face and tightly shook his head. "Jimmy won't want to hear that story. Robbie, no! *Drink* your milk.''

Jim had struck Rick in a raw spot, and Rick had struck back with an all-purpose insult. That's all that happened, Jim decided.

"I admit it,'' said Jim. "Washington's its own little world. Bureaucracy begetting more bureaucracy and paperwork about paperwork. But it's part and parcel of our new position in global affairs.''

"I suppose,'' said Rick. "Although, if you ask me, it's all one big racket. All our money going into army and navy, Marshall Plan and Grampa's Elbow. Those people won't appreciate what we're doing for them. This country has enough to do looking after itself. That's what I think anyway.''

Jim felt Rick was only baiting him, but he had to defend his government and job. "You don't believe the United States has an obligation to protect other countries from turning Communist?''

"You can't have a cookie, Robbie, until you finish everything, crusts too.'' Rick faced Jim with an embarrassed grin, uncomfortable the conversation was turning serious. "What do I know?'' he laughed. "I'm just a dumb business-man. But my gut feeling is if those people are stupid enough to want a way of life that has breadlines and no place for personal initiative, then let them. It's no skin off my nose.''

"What gets our goat,'' Ann automatically added, "is how the government spends *our* taxes on foreign countries. Isn't that right, dear?''

"We *are* paying Jimmy's salary,'' Rick admitted. "At least somebody we know is getting something out of it.''

Jim angrily chewed a mouthful of bread. He was infuriated to find this cynical attitude in his brother-in-law: apathy toward the world mixed with distrust of the government. It went beyond baiting or self-defense. Jim saw it as immigrant blindness, a second-generation refusal to see past the unskinned nose on your own face. And Jim's own sister parroted her husband. He wanted to tell them he was in the foreign service *for them,* that he was going overseas to protect his family at home. Which he was, in a manner of speaking, but Rick and Ann wouldn't understand such an abstract concept.

"There's more luncheon meat,'' Ann offered her brother. "I remember how you'd eat three and four sandwiches if we had the food in the house. Mother used to call him the human garbage pail."

"I'm fine. That was good," Jim muttered, wanting to let the argument drop.

It had grown darker outside and Ann leaned back to turn on the kitchen light. The mustard and mayonnaise jars on the painted table, the plastic plates and milk-filmed jelly glasses all looked very mean and sad in the harsh electric glare.

"I just had an idea," said Jim. "What if I take us out to dinner tonight?"

Ann's eyes opened wide. "Oh? Oh, it's been ages since we've eaten out."

Rick looked down. "You don't have to do that, Jimmy."

"But I want to. Someplace nice. You choose." Jim wasn't certain what he hoped to prove by this, but he liked the idea the more he considered it. "I didn't have time to pick up any presents. This'll be my present. Please. I've got plenty of money. I'm an overpaid bachelor."

"Yes, Rick? Please?" Ann pleaded. "I'd love to eat out tonight. Somebody else's restaurant. Good food. Real butter."

Rick looked peeved, having Jim know he couldn't provide his wife with something she wanted so badly. "I bought all those groceries," he complained. "And we'd have to find a sitter."

"I want to take everyone," Jim announced. "The whole family."

Ann's eagerness was slightly dampened. "Hmm. They've never been to a restaurant."

Rick snorted. "You'd be wasting your money, Jimmy. It's feeding time at the zoo with this gang."

"No. I'd like to take all of us," Jim insisted. "Something for them to remember me by when I'm overseas."

"They'll be fine," Ann assured her husband, and herself. "Just this once. It'd mean so much to Jimmy. And to me too."

Rick reluctantly gave in. "All right already. If it's so important to you people. And it's as good a chance as any for Robbie and Meg to begin to learn how to behave in a public place."

All at once, the shouting outside turned into shrieks and screams and something like birdshot peppered the back stoop. It had begun to rain and the mobs of children outdoors were running for cover.

While Rick went around the apartment checking the windows, Ann telephoned the Pine Tree Inn and made reservations for five o'clock. Jim felt stronger knowing he could provide something material for his sister's family even though they failed to appreciate what he provided abstractly.

IT RAINED ALL afternoon, trapping them indoors. Rick had intended to take Jim and Robbie down to the fertilizer plant, where they were unloading a potash ship from Germany today, but he said the rain would turn the docks and yards into a slippery mess of chemical mud. Jim watched a ball game with Rick on television. Ann rinsed out a diaper in the toilet and Rick shouted, "Can't you close the door when you do that!" Jim remained squeamishly conscious of a stink of ammonia and the rest coming from the big enameled diaper pail in there.

It was still raining when they left for the restaurant. They went in Jim's Dodge, which was bigger than Rick and Ann's Studebaker and had no toys piled in the back or fingerprints on the windows. Meg was zipped into a little pink suit with feet and a frilly bonnet. Robbie wore brown coveralls and a white shirt with a clip-on bowtie he kept tugging loose. Ann wore bright red lipstick and a touch of perfume and Rick appeared successful and adult in his gray business suit and striped necktie. They looked like a perfect family.

Dinner was a disaster.

The Pine Tree Inn was an enormous stuccoed house on the highway out toward Virginia Beach, everything in it arranged to suggest old plantation charm, which included elderly Negro waiters. The waiters terrified Robbie. He stretched his mouth open and howled each time one approached the table. Jim was embarrassed for the waiters' sake. Rick was humiliated by the looks the other diners gave them. Then Meg reached over from her high chair and spilled a bowl of Lynnhaven clam chowder into her mother's lap. She began to howl when she saw how upset Ann was. Ann rushed to the ladies' room to clean her dress off, and Rick had to deal with the two squalling children, his teeth clenched and his face red with anger. Jim attempted to calm Robbie— "Have an oyster cracker, Robbie. Hmmm, good crackers"—and the boy slid down from his chair to hide under the table, where he continued to sob. When Ann returned, Rick took Robbie out to the car to spank him. By the time they returned, Robbie sniveling and his face crusty with dried tears, the main course had been served and Rick's chicken livers were cold. He refused to let Ann send them back, but ate them in penance for agreeing to this. He refused to let Robbie have dessert, which meant nobody ordered dessert, and when the check came he argued with Jim over who should pay it, until Ann bluntly reminded him the rent was due on Monday.

They drove home in a knotted silence broken only when Ann said from the backseat, "Well, the lamb chops were good."

Back at the apartment, Jim sat out on the sofa while Rick and Ann put the children to bed. He felt stupid and useless, angry with Rick and angry with himself. What had he hoped to prove with his money tonight? What had he expected to accomplish by coming down here?

When the last sob and whine faded away in the children's bedroom, Ann came out, gently closing the door behind her. She collapsed on the sofa beside her brother and groaned.

"I think I'll drive back tonight," Jim told her.

She looked up, making a sour face. "Don't do that. Please. The worst of it's over, believe me. This'll be our only chance to visit."

"It's probably too late to get a motel room."

"You can sleep on the sofa. It's a comfortable sofa."

It looked too short for his long legs, but Ann sounded so plaintive he had to give in. "All right. If it's no problem for you. It *is* a long drive back."

Rick came out of their bedroom, dressed again in T-shirt and work pants. Not looking at either of them, he went to the television, turned it on and angrily sat in the armchair.

"Jimmy's spending the night," Ann told him.

"Of course," Rick grunted, eyes locked on the blue foxfire glow of the TV.

"C'mon, dear. It's not the end of the world," Ann timidly pointed out. "They're only kids. Now we know. Live and learn."

Rick lifted his hand to brush the subject away, a gesture of his fingers that looked faintly European. He still refused to look at his wife.

Ann sighed at Jim and tried to smile over the ridiculousness of children and her husband's temper and life in general. Then all the resilience and patience went out of Ann's face, and she looked tired and defeated. She leaned back to watch the television, crossing her legs and folding her hands tightly together in her lap.

Jackie Gleason stomped around a gray kitchen to the immense amusement of an invisible audience. Ann and Rick watched without laughing. The tin buzz of TV laughter played in air thin with anger and exhaustion.

Jim sensed something going on here that had nothing to do with tonight's failed dinner, that had been only tapped by the dinner. Family life, he told himself. Ann and Rick seemed like two kids playing house, only to find themselves overwhelmed by the game. Ann seemed so much younger than their mother had been, but then Jim had always known Ann as his little sister. Rick definitely lacked the maturity and patience to be a father. He was probably as impatient and short-tempered at work as he was with his family, and *that* was why he constantly changed jobs, Jim decided. His brother-in-law's ingrown anger silently dominated the room.

"You're due again in—five months?" Jim asked Ann during a commercial.

Rick glanced at them across the fist that propped his cheek.

Ann nodded, then bowed her head at Rick to signal they were disturbing him.

Despite her promise, she and Jim didn't get to "visit" that evening, but sat trapped and hypnotized by the television. Jim didn't own a TV and he saw how easy it was to be distracted and numbed by images constantly changing in one's own living room. When it was time for bed, Ann brought out sheets and blankets and made up the sofa.

"What a day, what a day," Rick grumbled as he stood up and stretched. "Goodnight, Jimmy."

Jim thought Ann might talk once Rick was gone, but she watched her husband leave as if he were something she had to finish. "Sleep well," she told Jim. "If you hear Meg in the middle of the night, just roll over and go back to sleep. We'll take care of her."

"I'm sorry it didn't go better tonight."

Ann shrugged philosophically. "It was a nice gesture, all the same. Good-night, brother." And she gave him a quick kiss on the forehead, humored him with a kiss the same way she probably kissed her children when her thoughts were elsewhere, then hurried into the bedroom to deal with Rick.

They were still talking in there, a quiet exchange of mumbles and coaxing behind the closed door, when Jim turned off the table lamp and climbed under the blanket. He resented Rick for demanding so much attention from his sister, for being a third child she had to obey as well as comfort. If *he* ever got married—But Jim couldn't imagine sharing his life with anyone under these circumstances. It was so crowded and messy. It made people irritable and narrow.

He struggled to make himself fit the sofa, resting his big feet up on the arm, then sticking them out to the side. Footsteps crossed the ceiling, people in the upstairs apartment. A carload of shouting teenagers roared past, a broken wing of light warping around the living room walls as the headlights swung by. A wasted trip, thought Jim, a lost weekend. He was sorry he hadn't stayed in Washington and played tennis, until he remembered there was nobody he could play with anymore.

DAVE WHEELER WAS angry with Jim and he had a knife. Jim had to calm him before Wheeler slashed Jim open. He wrapped his arms around Wheeler to pin the man's hands to his sides while he apologized to Wheeler for their misunderstanding and desperately looked for help on the deserted dirt road in the pineapple plantation. Jim was terrified holding Wheeler in his arms, frightened to have his mouth so close to Wheeler's warm face. But he couldn't let go because then Wheeler would kill him.

He woke up with a jolt. Something outside him had awakened Jim and he didn't know where he was. He heard a door open and close, and a baby crying. He was at his sister's. He rolled over on the sofa and caught his breath, trying to breathe away the strangeness of the dream. Jim never dreamed at home, or maybe he did but always forgot his dreams by the next morning, he wasn't sure. This dream seemed disturbingly familiar, as if he'd dreamed it many times before, and the violence of it excited him. It had been an awful dream, but eerily seductive. He heard a woman whispering comfort in the next room, a soothing tone that softly trailed away into deep, dark silence.

"INDUSTRY ON PARADE!" a baritone voice exclaimed. "Building today for a new and better America tomorrow!"

Jim looked into a pair of jet-black pupils, light brown irises whose filaments thickened as they opened the pupils wider, and a pulsing sky-blue plug with a wagging plastic handle. A baby furiously sucked on her pacifier and stared at him, holding herself up with two pink paws gripping the seam of the slip-cover.

"Morning, Jimbo. If you want to sleep, don't let the Meg-wump here bother you. C'mere, beautiful."

Rick leaned over to bring the baby back to him. He was sitting on the floor, a section of Sunday paper opened in front of him. He sat his daughter between his raised knees and continued to read the paper.

The sun shone outside and the front door was open, a cool, morning smell of rain-washed air coming through the screen door. The TV was on again, a program of industrial newsreels tootling cheerful music. Robbie sat in front of the television, apparently fascinated with shots of bottles speeding through an automated assembly line.

Meg began to swat the newspaper and make yipping sounds.

"Shush, darling. Shush," Rick whispered, brushing his unshaven chin in the baby's silky hair. "Mommy's sleeping."

This was not the family Jim remembered from last night. "Ann sleeps late?" he croaked.

"We let her sleep Sunday mornings. Least we can do, especially when she's had to get up the night before." Rick spoke of it calmly, kindly. "The Meg-wump wake you up with her crying last night?"

"Last night?" Jim remembered being awakened, and he remembered a dream. "No. Not at all. I didn't hear a thing." He drew his ugly feet beneath the blanket where nobody could see them.

"Truck," said Robbie, pointing at the television for his father's approval. "Truck, Daddy?"

"That's right," said Rick. "A dump truck. Robbie loves trucks and machines," he told Jim. "Ann thinks it means he'll be an inventor or engineer, but who knows?" Rick smiled and shrugged. "There's a pot of coffee in the kitchen when you're ready."

Jim nodded and rubbed his face, still adjusting to the strangeness of waking up in a roomful of people.

The bedroom door clicked open and springs creaked as a body climbed back into bed.

"Mommy!" Robbie declared over his shoulder.

"I hear her. Let's go say hi to Mommy," said Rick, standing up around his daughter, gripping her tiny hands and pulling her to her feet. "Upsa-daisy. Time to wake Mommy."

Robbie jumped up and raced into the bedroom. Rick followed with Meg wobbling in front of him, holding on to her father's thumbs. "Mommy!" Robbie cried in the next room. Knees banged against a bedframe, and bed-springs rattled as the entire family joined Ann in bed. Ann received them matter-of-factly, with mumbles and sighs.

Jim took advantage of their absence to get out of bed and pull his trousers on. He went straight to the bathroom, catching a glimpse of everybody piled in the big bed, Rick sitting at the foot of it, Robbie burrowing in the sheets, Meg crawling over her mother's knees, Ann herself invisible around the corner.

They were still in there when Jim came out and went to the kitchen to pour a cup of coffee. "Ann?" he called in. "You want some coffee?" He wanted an excuse to join them.

"No thanks, Jimmy. I'm asking for trouble if I try drinking anything in here." Her attention went back to her family. "Where you going, Love Bumps? Oh good. You already changed her. Is Robbie dry?"

Jim drank his coffee and listened to the sloppy domestic happiness in the next room. It sounded genuine. All Jim's thoughts from last night were turned around. He felt guilty for being so critical and full of pity for Ann, for failing to see what she and Rick had. Their life was dense and real while Jim lived in a world of abstraction where he was prey to every paranoid fear or morbid dream that came to him.

Rick cooked breakfast that morning, which seemed uncharacteristic until Jim remembered the restaurant in California. After breakfast, Ann loaded the washing machine in the kitchen. "I've got a couple of loads to catch up on to make up for yesterday," she explained.

"But it's Sunday," said Jim. "You're not going to church?"

Ann treated church as a matter of no importance; Rick was the one who looked sheepish. "We should. We will when we get the chance." He nodded at Robbie and Meg. "Right now, *they're* our church."

Jim showered and shaved, then put on a clean shirt and necktie for the drive back. He needed the necktie to remind himself he was an adult, a grown man whose life might be different from the lives here yet just as valid, just as healthy. But seeing his pampered, proper face in the cracked mirror of their medicine cabinet, his perfect cuffs and spit-shined shoes in this squalid bathroom with a diaper pail under the sink, Jim felt rich, guiltily rich. He was sinfully well off on his $6,000 a year plus overseas expenses, with nobody to spend it on but himself. His petty gift of dinner last night had been an irritable gesture made out of guilt. He needed to do more. Actions speak louder than words. Jim knew he was a better man in action than he was in reflection. He saw what he had to do.

When he returned to the kitchen, Ann was pulling a twist of wet sheets from the washing machine into a canvas hamper. "Should you be doing that? Here, let me help."

"I do this every day, Jimmy. No, no, you'll get your shirt wet."

"Where's Rick?" He thought he should approach Ann about this first.

"He's in the bedroom finishing some paperwork for tomorrow."

Rick was a good man, Jim told himself, a decent man whose only fault was an angry impatience brought on by the fear of failure, a fear of the future. Jim eagerly anticipated the future, but it must terrify a man with a family. Jim wanted to take some of the pressure off Rick and ease life for him and Ann.

"You going?" said Ann, dragging the hamper toward the door.

"Not immediately."

He followed her outside, where a series of diapers already hung on the line. The playpen had been moved outside and Meg sat there in the sun, happily banging blocks with a wooden mallet. In the bare ground beneath the gas and electric meters, Robbie pushed a toy truck around, his face hidden under a little black cowboy hat. Here and there in the treeless space behind the apartment buildings, clothes floated on distant lines: Ann wasn't the only pagan doing her wash on a Sunday.

"Rick's in a good mood this morning." Jim decided to approach the subject gradually.

"You mean after last night?" Ann played out a clammy sheet along the line, fastening it with clothespins as she went. "Well, Rick likes to make things difficult for himself. He doesn't take gas or Novocain when he goes to the dentist either. Don't ask me why."

Jim walked with her on the other side of the sheet. "I suspect living here doesn't help his temper."

"Pretty dismal," Ann admitted. "But it was the best we could do with the housing shortage down here. We've got our name on a couple of lists, but they're for houses that haven't even been built yet."

"You have the money for that?"

"We will."

Jim didn't believe her, but he could no more ask what Rick's salary was than he could ask Ann about their sex life.

"You know," he told her, "if you ever need financial help, I'm only too happy to give it."

Ann glanced at him, tightly smiled and hauled up the next sheet. "That's very sweet, Jimmy. A nice gesture. But we're fine."

"I don't mean it as just a gesture. I'm perfectly serious. You have two kids and a third on the way. I'm a bachelor. An overpaid government bachelor."

"Don't let Rick get your goat. I'm sure you're worth every penny they pay you."

"Even so, I'm paid more than I need. I'd like to help you and Rick."

Now that she saw he was dead serious, she stared at him over the clothesline. She lightly touched her tongue against her upper lip as the offer worked its way into her thoughts.

"A down payment on a house," said Jim. "I could help you there. I have two thousand dollars in the bank you could have right now. Within a year I'll have six thousand. There'll be even more further down the road." Putting it into hard facts and figures, he grew more excited with his proposition, overjoyed by it.

Ann began to look embarrassed, as if he *had* asked her about their sex life.

"Hospital costs for the new baby." Jim ducked under the clothesline to get closer to her. "College. What about college?"

She hid behind a nervous laugh. "It's too soon to worry about college, Jimmy."

"It's not too soon. How're you and Rick going to send *three* kids through college? What if I promised to pay for one of them?" Jim began to laugh at his impulsive rush of offers, tickled to hear himself talk like this. He had to stuff his big hands into his pockets to stop them from flying about in grandiloquent sweeps. "I'm ready to commit myself today. One college education. Or something, Ann. Please!" he pleaded. "I want to help."

She didn't laugh with him. She glanced at the back door and her children, then faced him again with an anxious mouth and a cool, practical look in her eyes.

Very gently, Jim said, "I remember how things were after Boppa died."

"Rick's in a much better position than Mother ever was. He *is*."

"I'm not saying anything against Rick."

"He's very proud," she continued. "Now more than ever. His pride's been hurt a few times. It'd be hard for him to take money from anyone, even a relative."

"But you do need the money," Jim observed.

"Oh yeah. We do," she said, sardonically matter-of-fact. "We have some debts. Nothing horrendous, but it galls me how we pay and pay and it only covers the interest. Banks are such a racket." She looked back at the apartment again, as if picturing Rick inside, yet she didn't appear guilty over having betrayed him for confessing this much to her brother, only challenged and practical.

"What if I *loaned* you the money to pay off the bank?"

"Maybe," she said, still looking away.

"I wouldn't charge interest. My interest is my interest in your family."

Ann didn't catch the pun. "Yes. A loan," she said. "We could begin to get our heads above water. You're in a position to loan us a thousand?"

"Yes."

Ann sighed, then nodded. She didn't embrace or even smile gratefully at Jim, but pulled a wet pillowcase out of the hamper and clipped it to the line. "Let *me* be the one to mention it to Rick. After you're gone, and not today either. Coming from you, Jimmy, he might take it as an attack on his abilities as a breadwinner."

Jim hadn't considered that possibility. He was doing this *for* Ann, not *to* Rick. "You couldn't take the money without telling him where it came from?"

"No. I pay the bills and it'd be easy to hide something like that, for a few months anyway. But no. I couldn't do that to Rick."

Jim nodded, respecting her wish and almost understanding it. "All right then. Talk to Rick in the next few days, let me know what he says and I'll wire the money to you. But I don't intend this as just a one-time commitment, Ann. For the future, anytime you need help and I'm in a position to give it, I will."

"Thanks, Jimmy. Heaven forbid we'll need it again, but it's good to know." Her smile turned guilty. "You don't think you should be saving your money for when you have your own family."

Jim laughed at her concern. "That won't happen anytime soon. If ever. You've said yourself you pity the girl who'd marry me."

"Did I say that? No. I couldn't have said that. Not seriously." She began to laugh with him. "When you meet the right girl, Jimmy—"

"I'm not the marrying kind. A confirmed old maid, that's me." He said it as a joke but suddenly understood, in a way he'd never understood before, how true it was.

"You're going to get lonely," Ann teasingly scolded.

"Which is why I want to help. You're my family. You and Rick and the kids." Even with his mocking tone and grin, Jim understood this was true too, and not just true but good and right and necessary.

Ann scoffed and shook her head. "Let me get a start on the next load," she said. "Give a holler if Robbie starts to wander off." She walked to the back door, the empty hamper swinging from one hand.

It was done. It wasn't as dramatic or conclusive as Jim had expected it to be, but he had made his offer and was confident something would come of it. He tried to bask in the glow of his good deed, but this felt more important than a simple act of charity. There was no rush of love or tenderness now that he had committed himself, only a ticklish awareness of future obligations, which might be what love really was, a nuisance of duties that held one in place like so many threads.

Jim approached the children, wanting to commemorate his new bond with them. "Hey there, Robbie. You want to play with your Uncle Jim?"

Robbie looked up, squinting in the sun. "No," he said and clutched his plastic truck, half as big as he was, expecting it to hold him to the ground if his uncle tried to pick him up.

"All right. Be that way." Jim was determined to show patience where his brother-in-law would lose his temper. "How about you, Meg-wump? You want a ride? A horsey ride from Uncle Jim?"

She cooed when he bent down into the playpen, then whooped when he lifted her to his shoulders. She felt less fragile than he'd imagined a baby to feel, loose and spongy. Holding her with both hands against the back of his head, her stubby legs on either side of his neck, Jim cantered around the wall of wet sheets and diapers, hoping Robbie would see how much fun this was and ask to be next.

Ann showed no surprise when she returned and saw her very proper brother galloping around in his necktie and white shirt with a giggling baby on his back. "She loves people," Ann declared. "Anybody. A total stranger could walk off with her and she'd be perfectly happy." Which undid some of Jim's satisfaction.

Nevertheless, driving back to Washington that afternoon, he felt very good about himself, better than he had felt in months. Committing himself to his sister's family made life seem simpler to Jim, easier. He wasn't sure why, but it did. Even before he received Ann's note a week later agreeing to the loan—there were final quibbles from Rick who wanted to pay Jim the two-and-a-half-percent interest he'd get if the money were in a savings account—Jim felt liberated, as if freed from another, trickier obligation. He was not alone. He had a personal life after all, a family and children, people he could think about when he needed to feel sentimental or loving.

Jim did not dream of violent embraces with Wheeler or any other man again, or could not remember such dreams the next morning, until six months later in a humid hotel room in northern Luzon, during an inspection tour, when he was awakened in the middle of the night by a small explosion in the police station down the street, set off by Communists or local gangsters.

3

A WATER BUFFALO walked on the sky, the flooded paddy full of white clouds and green shoots. A tiny boy on the animal's back grinned and made the A-OK sign of the astronauts.

In a marketplace full of black-haired men in white shirts, a grinning woman offered a small gold Buddha in one hand and an ashtray with President Kennedy's portrait in the other.

"Everything looks so dirty," said Mom. "This is the Philippines?"

"*Thailand,*" Dad impatiently told her again. "The Philippines was moons ago. Color in these is really something, Jim."

The Frisch family sat in the dark, Dad in his armchair, Mom in her rocker, Meg on the sofa between her two brothers. Uncle Jim sat cross-legged on the floor, his slide projector whooshing on the coffee table as it threw a window of world on the bedsheet draped over the door to the utility room.

Meg was enthralled. Just having a houseguest was an exciting change this summer in 1963. And this was Uncle Jim, who brought foreign countries with him. In the two long years since his last visit, Margaret Frisch had grown from a little kid interested in her uncle chiefly for the presents he brought, to an intelligent, thinking person who admired him as proof that life wasn't all Kempsville, Virginia. An adult who had no wife or children seemed both exotic and available to Meg. She was eleven years old.

Click-clack. A proud, pug-faced woman posed stiffly in a courtyard. Behind her was a red tiled roof and verandah with jalousie panels.

"Isn't she the Queen of Sheba," Mom observed. "Who is she, Jimmy?"

"Sirikit Kol. My housekeeper."

"That's *your* house?"

"Uh, housing's relatively cheap. Servants too."

"You sure had the life of Riley," Dad laughed.

Uncle Jim laughed with him, both of them laughing like grown men, a few deliberate ha-has. "It turns out to be more trouble than it's worth. I had fights with Sirikit because I like to get up early and fix my own breakfast."

The next slide showed jungle, a stand of leafy bamboo and, in the background, elaborate piles of gray-green stone like the dribble castles Meg made at the beach.

"Oh that's—! I'm sure Meg knows. What is that, Meg?" asked Mom.

"Angkor Wat," Meg said shyly, embarrassed yet pleased Uncle Jim would hear how smart she was.

"Miss Encyclopedia," Robbie snarled in one ear.

"Meggy-weg knows everything," sang Walter in the other. He'd recently begun imitating his big brother, but mocked her without Robbie's genuine malice. Meg jabbed him with her elbow.

More slides followed. The lost city looked nothing like what Meg had imagined from pictures in books, which promised enormous rooms that required only a few sweeps of the broom before she unrolled a sleeping bag and lived in them. These were ruins. With no roof overhead, twisted trees grew in the halls, great roots lifted stone slabs off the ground, thick vines like hairy snakes pulled down walls and choked eroded statues.

A man with mustache, sunglasses and gaudy Hawaiian shirt stood beside a naked pillar with a short-haired woman in khakis and a little girl in a pith helmet.

"Ceremonial stele," Uncle Jim explained. "Buddhist figures carved on one side, Hindu scenes on the other. The Khmers hedged their bets."

"These friends of yours?" asked Mom.

"Oh yeah. That's Dave Wheeler, who was my counterpart in Phnom Penh when I was deputy political officer in Bangkok. His wife Elaine and their daughter Jane. Jane must be about Walter's age."

"I'm nine," chirped Walter.

"Give you a Dewey button," Robbie muttered.

"I visited them for a week and we made the jaunt out to Angkor. This is all in Cambodia. Next door to Vietnam, but they've managed to keep the war from spilling over the border.''

"They look like a nice couple," said Mom.

"They are." Uncle Jim clicked to the next slide.

And there, standing beside the carved pillar, was Uncle Jim himself, hands on his hips, sunglasses hooked in his belt, his sunburned face screwed up in a squinty smile. Meg was startled to see him there. She knew he'd taken the pictures, of course, but this was like seeing on television someone she knew. He looked different, more vivid. The color slide made the hair on his arms orangey-red, like cayenne pepper, and gave his head a red-haired halo. Uncle Jim's forehead was even higher than Dad's, which went up just in the corners. His shirt and trousers were wet and stuck to his shoulders and knees. And handfuls of yellow scraps like flowers sprouted from the pattern of his shirt.

"You got butterflies!" cried Walter, pointing at the picture.

"I certainly did. Something in my sweat seemed to attract them. They were all over me whenever I stood still. When we got back to the hotel that night, I was powdered from head to toe with butterfly scales.''

"I'll be darned," said Dad.

Meg shivered with goosebumps, distressed and delighted by the idea.

A face appeared over the slide tray. "And that's the last one," he said. "The end." He turned off the projector and the vivid man went out like a light.

The table lamp snapped on. They were back in the family room, with the same tired green carpet and cardboard-colored paneling. But here was Uncle Jim on their floor, without butterflies, looking like an old college kid down there in his short-sleeved shirt and crewcut. His big freckled arms rested on his raised knees as he anxiously glanced around, turning a bashful smile to the niece and nephews behind him.

Meg felt that she alone understood how special this had been, how wonderful and exciting it was to have him here.

"That was really neat," she blurted out. "All those people and places, Uncle Jim."

Her words fell so short of what she felt that Meg cringed. She sounded like such a kid, which was why she usually kept strong feelings to herself.

"Right up your alley, wasn't it, dear?" said Mom, getting up to take the bedsheet down from the door. "Your niece loves books and ruins, Jimmy. She's a little like you were at that age.''

And Meg was full of love for her mother, who understood exactly what her daughter wanted right now.

Uncle Jim was looking at her, smiling at her, more curious than grateful for her interest.

Robbie leaned in front of Meg to snatch up the Balinese mask that lay face-up on the coffee table. It was a pig mask and he held it against his face. "Deba-deba-deba—That's all, folks!"

Uncle Jim burst out laughing, a real laugh, not like the ones he shared with Dad. "It does look like Porky Pig, doesn't it, Rob?"

"They didn't have Daffy Duck or Mickey Mouse?" he asked, nastily smiling at Meg to let her know he did this only to grab Uncle Jim away from her. He could be so queer.

"Their other masks represent Hindu deities," Uncle Jim explained, thinking Robbie was really interested. "I never saw another Porky Pig the whole time I was in Bali."

"The masks are lovely," said Mom. "And thanks again for the sarong. I don't know when I'll have an occasion to wear it, but it really is beautiful."

He had brought masks for the men and sarongs for the women. Meg had been disappointed with her gift, an envelope of dark blue silk embroidered with scaly thread. She wished Uncle Jim had brought her a book instead, or a canteen. A canteen would enable her to go off for weeks at a time into forests and jungles, alone.

"Sarong place, sarong time!" said Robbie, and Uncle Jim laughed harder than before. The littlest joke said by him earned their uncle's approval. Boys were supposed to get along better with men, and girls with women, but Meg knew she had more in common with Uncle Jim than her jerk brother did. There'd been a battle for his attention ever since he arrived.

Dad thanked Uncle Jim again for the slide show, said it was late and time for the kids to go to bed. Mom reminded Meg she'd be sleeping in the back room tonight, as if Meg could forget her uncle was sleeping in her room while he was here.

There was a short flight of steps to the kitchen and living room, then a regular flight of stairs to the floor with the boys' bedroom and Meg's. Meg waited until they were on their floor before she told Robbie, "You're such a creep."

"And you're a flirt," he sneered back.

"You're the flirt." She stood in the door to their room but didn't go in. "What makes you want him to like you anyway? You want his attention only because I want it."

"Guys can't flirt with guys, moron. Don't you know the facts of life?"

Walter collapsed on one of the twin beds, looking very sleepy and goofy, his last haircut so short his head looked like an enormous egg. "Meg and Uncle Jim sittin' in a tree," he mumbled. "K-I-S-S-I-N—"

"Oh shut up." Meg stomped into her room and slammed the door. "Peons," she muttered while she changed for bed, a new word she thought meant some kind of toilet. Walter used to be sweet, but he was turning into a creep like Robbie. And Robbie was getting meaner and queerer all the time. "Hormones," said Mom, which meant he was becoming a teenager and was one of the reasons he wouldn't wrestle with Meg anymore. The other reason was that he was so skinny and uncoordinated she could beat him. She knew about the facts of life from a book her mother had handed her. "If you have any questions, dear, be sure to ask me and not your father.'' But it was pretty much as Meg had figured out from dirty jokes at school, and not nearly as interesting as other things she read about in books.

The bookcase in her room, built by her father when they moved into this new house a year ago, was full of history and archaeology. She hoped Uncle Jim would notice all her books while he was here. Her library copy of Prescott's *Conquest of Mexico* sat on the built-in desk Dad also had made for her, along with Uncle Jim's magazines: *Time, Newsweek* and a fat gray one titled *Foreign Affairs*. His leathery blue flight bag sat on the floor next to a swollen briefcase with a combination lock of tiny gears and numbers. Meg wanted to see if she could figure out the combination, but she was afraid Uncle Jim would see the numbers had been changed.

In her long cotton nightgown, Meg slapped her bare feet down the wooden steps to the sweaty tiles of the family room.

"Meg, dear, you walk like a dockworker,'' Mom lightly scolded. "Ready for bed, Pumpkin? Did you want me to comb out your hair?''

She shook her head. She didn't want to be fussed over in front of her uncle, but wanted to appear independent and self-sufficient. "Goodnight, everybody.''

Uncle Jim looked at her curiously, expectantly. Maybe he expected a kiss, but they weren't a kissing family. Meg wouldn't feel comfortable kissing anyone right now.

"Leave the door to the utility room open,'' said Dad. "But shut your door so our talking won't keep you up.''

"Yes, sir.''

The gooseneck lamp in the little room was already turned on, the covers of the bed turned back. The room was used mainly to store stuff. Another of Dad's bookcases stood beside the bed, this one full of business textbooks from college and the ancient black *Encyclopedia Britannica* left to them when Gramma Goodall died. Meg would've liked to read about Angkor Wat before she went to sleep, but Dad would be able to see the light under her door. Besides, she wanted to listen to the adults. Adults were almost as good as books when there were no kids around to make them self-conscious.

"But Bissell wants to make Rick vice-president.''

"One of *four* vice-presidents. Oh, just another way of getting more work out of you. I bet Uncle Sam plays the same game. This last promotion give you more control, or just more responsibility?''

Uncle Jim spoke too softly for Meg to hear.

"Well, things are hopping at home too, as you'll find out if they keep you in Washington long enough. Dr. Martin Luther Coon.''

"Don't joke like that, Rick. Jimmy'll think you're a redneck.''

"Oh, your brother knows where I stand. I sympathize with what they want. I just think they're going about getting it the wrong way.''

"Considering the methods used in other countries," said Uncle Jim, "I think King and the others are handling themselves admirably."

"Maybe," said Dad. "Perhaps."

"I'm getting a Diet-Rite," said Mom. "Anyone want anything from the kitchen?"

Mom was bored with their newspaper talk. Meg was bored with it too, except Dad was speaking in a way she'd never heard from him before: carefully. He didn't scoff at or bait Uncle Jim the way he did other relatives. Dad didn't seem to like other people, and he might not like Uncle Jim, but he seemed to respect his opinions, which Meg found curious.

Mom's loafers clomped down the steps from the kitchen and stopped outside the utility room. "Good. I think she's asleep. She's had a very full day today."

"Where's Meg in school now?" Uncle Jim asked.

"Sixth grade, when they go back next month. I wish it were tomorrow. Blessed are the peacemakers. But Meg's a good kid. Middle children *are* supposed to be the best adjusted, you know."

Meg bit her lips together to keep from laughing at hearing herself praised.

"What grade will Robbie be in?"

And Meg was disappointed all over again, frustrated and annoyed. What was it about her jerk brother that fascinated Uncle Jim? Mom filled him in on the horrors of hormones and Uncle Jim sounded concerned.

"Psychology," Dad grumbled. "I don't believe in it. Anyway, I'm sure Jim doesn't want to hear a lot of nonsense about the kids."

"Rick doesn't like me fussing about them in public," Mom said good-humoredly. "But he fusses over them by building desks and things. Don't you, dear?"

"Well, I build things for the house. Doing is better than talking."

"How do you like the new house?" Uncle Jim asked.

"We like it," said Mom. "There's the golf course across the street and the kids can walk to the swimming pool there. It's still pretty rural out here and it was good getting out of Norfolk. We finally have some space. When I think of all of us packed in that little house—"

"Or the apartment you lived in before that," said Uncle Jim.

Dad laughed. "No point in digging up *that* horror."

The voices from the family room blurred with the chirring of cicadas coming through the window above her pillow. Meg dreamed that the braided pigtail pressed against her cheek was a ropy vine she climbed to escape the pygmies chasing her through the jungle.

MEG LOVED MORNINGS this summer. There was no school, Robbie slept late and Walter became human again. There was yellow sunlight in the backyard, dark green shadow in the front and the day felt cool and promising. This morning,

Uncle Jim's car was parked out by their mailbox, a strange old maroon Dodge whose hood narrowed like a snout between the paws of its fenders, the trunk and rear window curved like the rump of a sleeping cat.

He was still asleep when Meg crept into his room—*her* room—to get some clothes and her library book. Tangled up in the sheet, a huge bare foot with yellow calluses hanging beside the bedpost, he took up too much space in there. Meg decided she'd let him come to her today. She wasn't going to make a fool of herself fighting for his attention, "flirting" with him. If he couldn't see how terrific she was, that was his loss.

Uncle Jim continued to sleep, even after Robbie woke up and went downstairs to watch game shows in the family room.

"Time zones," Mom explained. "And there's that line in the ocean that makes them a day ahead or a day behind us. I heard him stumbling around at three o'clock last night. I guess his body hasn't caught up with him yet."

The idea that you and your body were not the same thing made no sense to Meg. Time zones, however, intrigued her and she imagined going backwards in time by flying around and around the world in the wrong direction.

Mom had words with Robbie over mowing the lawn. "I'll do it," he whined. "Later. The grass is too wet."

Meg took the hint and went out back with the hoe and bushel basket to weed Dad's tomatoes. They each had their chores, assigned by Dad and enforced by Mom, and Meg liked to get hers out of the way early, so she could read without guilt. She chopped and pulled for an hour, then brought the hammock out of the garage to hang it between the two sweet gum trees. She read how Cortez and his men, guests of Montezuma, were given a tour of the city they secretly planned to conquer. Meg especially enjoyed picturing the temples on top of the Aztec pyramids, "the heathens' diabolical obeisances proclaimed by hideous altars black with human gore."

When she went back in, Uncle Jim sat at their kitchen table.

"So what's the game plan around here? Anything special scheduled this afternoon?"

He spoke to Mom, who sat beside him swigging her first Diet-Rite of the day. He looked and sounded different, louder and larger than he had seemed last night, as though he'd been holding himself in when Dad was home. He sat in Dad's chair, one knee crossed over the other, the way girls were supposed to sit, his airborne foot wagging anxiously while he grinned and beamed.

"Morning, Meg-wump. What's that you're reading there?"

She showed him, ready to forgive his use of that old nickname.

"Prescott? I read him when I was about your age. Shamelessly romantic history. But fun. I didn't know kids still read Prescott."

As if Meg were just another kid and everyone read history.

Mom explained their day to Uncle Jim, how the kids went to the pool after lunch and gave her a few hours' peace and quiet. She encouraged him to go with them and have a nice swim. "You didn't bring any trunks? I think Rick's got a pair that'll fit you. They don't fit him anymore."

Walter came home for lunch and Robbie came upstairs and they piled onto the bench with Meg. She said nothing to Uncle Jim while Robbie was present, wanting to see if her brother courted their uncle for himself or just to compete with her. Robbie answered Uncle Jim's worked-up questions about hobbies with indifferent grunts while wolfing a peanut butter sandwich.

"A difficult age," whispered Mom when Robbie went upstairs to change. "I wouldn't mind his laziness if he weren't so apathetic about everything."

They were usually able to cheat on the hour Mom required between lunch and the pool, but today they had to wait for Uncle Jim. He finally reappeared, Dad's dark plaid trunks cinched around his waist and flaring like culottes above his knees. Meg thought almost everyone looked bad in bathing suits— Walter looked like a bean with legs, Robbie like a praying mantis, Meg herself a fool with a ruffled bandage around her chest—but Uncle Jim embarrassed her. He wore black leather shoes without socks; his legs were peeled tree trunks, their whiteness dirty with hair. Even Dad had more of a tan. Uncle Jim wore the same tattersall shirt he'd worn last night and Meg dreaded how he'd look when he took it off to swim. They gathered up towels and Meg took her book along, intending to hide in it at the pool.

"Everybody set? Well, off we go like a herd of turtles. See you later, Ann."

They went out through the garage, crossed the street and cut through the Lassiters' to the golf course, Meg worriedly glancing around to see if anybody saw them. Uncle Jim glanced too, proudly, like he wanted to be seen with his nephews and niece. The hot sun silenced the birds and kept the neighbors indoors.

They stopped at the edge of the fairway to wait while a pair of tiny figures snapped their balls toward the eighth hole. Walter automatically began to look around the shaggy grass for lost balls, which he sold to golfers. He had more cash that summer than his big brother or sister did.

"Uncle Jim, you play golf?" he asked, suddenly recognizing a possible customer.

"Oh, now and then."

"You gonna play with Dad, you think?"

Uncle Jim frowned. "I don't think so, Walter. I have to get back tomorrow and your father can't play on a weekday. One day, though." The indifferent frown abruptly dropped. "How about you, Rob? You like golf?"

"Buncha fat men hitting dinky balls with sticks," Robbie sneered.

Uncle Jim said nothing until they started across the fairway toward the grove of stunted pine and patchy grass.

"I don't understand you, Rob. If I were on summer vacation and lived in a place like this, I'd have no end of interests to keep me occupied." Uncle Jim smiled while he spoke, like a new teacher pretending to be your pal while chiding you about your potential. "Life is too short not to care about *something*."

"I care about stuff. I'm going swimming, ain't I?"

"You like to swim? That's good to hear. Swimming's an excellent activity."

Robbie rolled up his towel and snapped it at Walter, who happily bumbled along looking for golf balls again. Robbie pretended not to listen to their uncle, but Meg listened, cringing all the while. Uncle Jim sounded so fake.

"Yes, I wish I had more time to swim. A wholesome, healthy exercise. Good for coordination and the heart. And for diverting excess energy."

Where was the man Meg had imagined over the past year? The intelligent, worldly adult she expected to connect with as easily as she did with people in books? When Uncle Jim last visited them two years ago, he seemed just a big, awkward grown-up who didn't know how to talk to kids. Meg had thought that was only because she was young and dumb back then and couldn't see what he had to offer. Now she felt she hadn't been so dumb after all, that she was dumber now in fact, letting her imagination make up a wonderful uncle who'd share worlds with her.

The Kempsville Swimming Club was on the other side of the golf course, facing the highway and a cornfield. A squat pink cinderblock hut stood in the corner of a high wooden fence, the bright turquoise water visible through the fence's vertical slats. The hut housed a snack bar, damp smelly locker rooms and the pool's entrance. Lois, the assistant manager, knew Meg and her brothers by sight and clocked them through the turnstile. She paused and raised her painted eyebrows at Uncle Jim.

"This is our uncle," said Meg. "He has to pay the guest fee, doesn't he?"

"Why howdy-do," went Lois, tilting her perfumed beehive and batting her sticky lashes at him. *She* was a flirt. "We've never seen you here, Mr.—?"

"Goodall," Uncle Jim said, confused by her friendliness.

"You just passing through or will you be around for a spell, Mr. Goodall?"

"He's just here for the day. Give her a dollar," Meg told him, hurrying him inside before Lois found out he was a bachelor and they'd never get rid of her. Uncle Jim didn't seem to know how to deal with women.

Inside, the same sun burned brightly overhead, but the smell of chlorinated water and wet concrete suggested cool shade. Even the noise sounded cool, all kinds of splashing, loud thunks followed by raining water and the diving board's wobbly stutter, an AM radio station playing through the pool's public address system. "Wiiiipe out!" the recorded voice yodeled and another beach song came on. It was music for the teenagers who surfed at Virginia Beach, a half hour away, but all the kids pretended it was their music too. Robbie, who'd never been near a surfboard in his life, spent his allowance or cadged money from Walter to buy 45s of it. The music was just noise to Meg; Walter liked the records only because he could hook the big holes over his ears and become a Martian.

They went to their usual corner near the deep end, where there was grass
and flocks of aluminum lawn chairs. The mothers with small children congre-
gated at the other end, around the baby pool, shiny walruses in kerchiefs and
sunglasses. Meg noticed a few sunglasses being lifted while Uncle Jim pulled
up a chair next to Robbie's.

Mary Ellen Odell was already at the back of their corner, hanging out with
Tissy Price and the other seventh graders who read *Seventeen* and talked about
clothes and busts. They raised their sunglasses and began to whisper and
giggle.

It was Uncle Jim's legs, Meg thought. Also, he was the oldest man here—
the only grown man, in fact. The fathers were all at work and big brothers in
high school went to the beach. Uncle Jim stood out like a horse, even before
he took off his shirt. His chest was as pale as his legs and speckled with the
same red hair and a few freckles. Dad never took his shirt off in public
anymore, Mom kidding him about his tummy. Uncle Jim's tummy looked flat
and solid as he strolled over to the diving board. He stood on the board,
bending his knees and testing the spring of it, unaware of the women and girls
watching him. Then he stepped back, gracefully stepped forward, hit the end
of the board with both feet and flew, soaring out and down and into the blue-
green water, so neatly he left only a creamy fizz of bubbles.

Meg was surprised. She thought someone so clumsy with people would be
clumsy at everything else.

"A regular Tarzan," scoffed Robbie and he tiptoed over the hot concrete
toward the shallow end to enter the water slowly, one step at a time. Walter
had already jumped in and was splashing Harry Lassiter. Uncle Jim swam the
length of the pool, back and forth, cleanly arrowing around the skylarking
kids.

"Hello there, Meg Frisch. And how are you today?"

Mary Ellen Odell appeared beside her, smiling slyly between the curved
wings of hair she never got wet, speaking in that new gooey voice that gave
Meg the creeps.

"Hello yourself," said Meg. Last summer they'd been best friends. Now
Mary Ellen barely spoke to her unless she wanted something. Meg looked
over at Tissy Price and Mary Ellen's other new friends, whose identical white-
framed sunglasses were all aimed this way. "He's my uncle," said Meg.
"Since you're dying to know. And he's only here for a day, so don't waste
your time talking to him."

"Your uncle? Oh." Mary Ellen squirmed at Meg seeing through her friendliness so quickly. "Whoever do you mean? Oh, that man with you today. I
don't care about *him*," she lied, glancing back at the waiting sunglasses. "I
came over to show you my new swimsuit." She modeled the semi-bikini for
Meg, adjusting the top so it looked a little less wishful. "My mama bought it
at Rose Hall this morning. Don't you wish you had one too?"

"No."

"Why Meg Frisch," laughed Mary Ellen. "You can't be a tomboy your whole life."

Meg knew her body would reach puberty and betray her, but she saw no point in pretending puberty was already here. Mom had given her a training bra, which Meg tried to believe felt like the straps of a backpack she wore in the jungle; what it really felt like was a chihuahua harness.

"Better a tomboy than a Barbie doll," said Meg. "Go tell the other Barbie dolls my uncle's way too old for any of you."

Mary Ellen pouted. "You think you're hot snot, but you're just cold boogers, Meg Frisch. You are so stuck up."

She was stuck up? Meg responded with a lip-fart and, in her best dock-worker walk, she strode away from Mary Ellen and jumped feet first into the pool.

Cold silence. Then the percolation of bubbles escaping from her suit and ears. It was beautifully peaceful down there in the blue, Meg letting herself sink toward the curved basin and drain, her body wonderfully weightless and caressed all over. Then she felt two pigtails snaking around her head. She'd forgotten to put her bathing cap on and Mom would be mad as hops. It was too late to fix that now. Settling against the sloping floor, Meg heard a series of muffled percussions overhead, looked up and saw Uncle Jim's lean silhouette climb hand-over-hand across her sky.

Meg swam a little, jumped off the board a few times and experimented with holding her breath—holding your breath could come in handy in the jungle—until she felt she'd used the pool enough to justify coming here. She went back to her chair to towel off, read and sun her pigtails dry.

The Aztecs killed Montezuma, their own chief, which was a surprise. He kind of deserved to die, having been so stupid as to think Cortez was a great white god. Meg had felt sorry for the Aztecs for being so gullible, but now she felt sorry for the Spaniards who were besieged by thousands of angry Indians. One of the confusing things about history books was that Meg kept changing sides while she read, which was why she preferred archaeology and ruins.

"Come on, Rob. Don't be chicken. One more time."

Meg looked up and saw Uncle Jim standing beside the diving board with Robbie. He was teaching her brother how to dive. Reluctant and resentful, Robbie seemed to obey him. Meg wondered why.

"Don't give up, Rob. You almost had it that time. Anything worth doing is worth doing well." He shamed Robbie back on the board, showing him what to do from the side. "This time, don't just fall in, but push off with your feet and get your legs up."

"I can't do all that at once!"

"Sure you can. Come on. Nobody likes a quitter."

Meg resented the attention he gave her brother, but it was relentless atten-tion, bullying. Uncle Jim sounded like a different person yet again, forceful and confident. Robbie looked miserable, his skinny arms bundled around his hunched chest, his legs goosebumped and knock-kneed.

"When I say jump," said Uncle Jim, "jump. All right? *Jump!*"

Robbie jumped, weakly, his body flattening out and his outstretched hands spreading apart. He slammed the water with a loud smack, the splash parted neatly in the middle.

Uncle Jim stepped around to the ladder. "You okay, son? Here."

Robbie hauled himself up the ladder, his front teeth bared like an angry dog's, his chest raw and pink. He yanked his arm out of his uncle's grip.

"You were thinking too much. You have to do it without thinking. One more time while it's still fresh in your head."

"Uh uh." Robbie angrily shook his head.

"You almost had it, Rob. Now's not the time to stop." He lay a large hand on the boy's knobby shoulder.

Robbie twisted out from under the hand. "I'm cold. I'm tired. I let you teach me for ten minutes. Now lemme alone." He headed toward the grass and his towel on the lounge chair beside Meg's.

Uncle Jim followed. "Don't be a quitter, son. Nobody likes a quitter."

"I'm not your son!" Robbie's nose was clogged and he sounded like he was crying, his teeth-baring scowl screwing his eyes shut. "Just lemme alone. You're not my father. You're nobody."

Uncle Jim frowned and stood taller. "I'm your friend, Rob. I want to help you learn something. If you're going to be a crybaby and panty-waist—"

"I don't need your help! Why're you always trying to help us?" Once begun, angry words poured out in a rush. "We don't need your crummy help! We do fine without you. You think you can show up every couple of years and buy us with your money and junk. You can't! Dad does great without your help and Mom puts up with you only because you're her brother!"

Uncle Jim stared, his lips sealed, his jaw down. "Where did you hear I wanted—" He closed his jaw and tried to swallow his shock.

Robbie looked shocked too: he had told off an adult, and told so much.

Meg wondered where he'd gotten all that, if Robbie had made it up or heard it from Dad. She'd never heard any of it before, but her brother spent more time alone with Dad than she did. Uncle Jim stood above her, not giving Robbie the slap across the mouth she automatically expected.

Talk suddenly resumed around the pool. Everyone had heard her brother's outburst and now pretended to ignore it.

"I'm going home," said Robbie. "I'm sick of swimming." He grabbed up his towel and sneakers and hurried away, waiting until he was by the turnstile to put his sneakers on.

Uncle Jim watched him go, his trunks dripping coldly on Meg's left leg. Meg moved her leg and he saw her. "Your brother," he began calmly. "Your brother has a temper."

Meg felt she should say something. "He can be a real jerk."

He nodded, but said, "I guess I got carried away teaching him how to dive. Everybody has a breaking point."

"You can teach me, Uncle Jim."

He smiled at her, with only his mouth; his eyes were confused and sad. He sat on the lounge chair that had been Robbie's. "Some other time, Meg-wump. You've got your book to read and I'm all taught out for the day. But some other time."

Which was fine with Meg, who knew she'd only feel like a substitute for her brother. Uncle Jim sat there, elbows on his thighs, high forehead bent toward her while he thought and looked sad. Meg had never seen an adult have his feelings hurt by a kid. She wondered which of Robbie's words had done it. Uncle Jim brought them presents like any other relative, only his were exotic and strange. Meg didn't think he'd gone out of his way to *help* them, but if he had, what was wrong with that?

Walter approached, cautiously at first, then quickly when he saw nobody was angry anymore. He threw his towel around his shoulder and said, "What got Robbie mad?"

"Oh, stuff," said Meg. She and Walter watched their uncle together.

"Want a brand new Spalding golf ball?" Walter offered. "I got one back in my drawer I'll give you free, Uncle Jim." Walter could be surprisingly sweet and concerned when the spirit hit him; he hated to see people unhappy.

Uncle Jim laughed like a man and shook his head. "Thanks, Walt. But I've got tons of balls back in D.C. Uh, you kids about ready to hit the road?"

Meg and Walter nodded. Uncle Jim took his time putting his shirt and shoes back on, maybe to make sure they wouldn't catch up with Robbie on the golf course. He said nothing while they walked home. Silence made Walter uncomfortable, so he chattered away about Sambo, the Lassiters' Labrador puppy.

Robbie was out front mowing the grass when they came off the golf course. He'd just started and Mom stood in the driveway with her arms sternly crossed, keeping him at the task with a dirty look. Robbie pretended not to see them when they crossed the street.

"Have a good time?" said Mom, loud and chipper over the roar of the lawn mower. Robbie must not have said anything about what happened.

"Nice pool. I had a nice swim." Uncle Jim glanced at Meg, expecting her to understand he wasn't going to mention Robbie's outburst.

"Rick called from the office. He wants to have a cook-out tonight. So I got Robbie started on the lawn and Rick's picking up hamburger and buns."

"Great." He went through the garage into the house.

Mom stopped Meg and squeezed one of her pigtails. "Oh Meg," she groaned, as if wet braids were the worse tragedy she could imagine.

After Meg hung her chlorinated swimsuit on the clothesline with her brothers' suits and towels, she washed her hair under the bathtub spigot and sat at her mother's feet in the family room to let Mom brush and braid her hair.

Mom punished Meg secretly, vigorously tugging at the snarls and tangles while she spoke in the gentlest voice. The lawn mower droned in the backyard now and Uncle Jim had not come down from his room.

"Mom? Does Dad like Uncle Jim?"

"Hmmm. As much as your father likes anyone." The hairbrush stopped, then resumed its stroke. "Why? Did your uncle say something to make you think he didn't?"

But if Uncle Jim weren't going to mention what happened, then Meg couldn't either, even if it meant protecting her brother. "Naw. Just wondering."

"Little pitchers have big ears." When Meg didn't rise to the bait, Mom said, "Your father has his way of doing things and Jimmy has his. They don't always see eye to eye, but that doesn't mean they don't like each other. Or that we have to choose between them. Although your father *is* your father."

"Uh huh," said Meg and let the matter drop.

When Uncle Jim finally came downstairs, he was grinning and sounding the way he had last night, friendly yet restrained. Then the Rambler sighed out in the driveway and Dad came in, also grinning, not like himself but someone whose picture was being taken.

"Hello there, everybody. Hello, Jim. Have a pleasant day? Meg and Walter, bring in the groceries, will you. Leave the charcoal in the garage." When Mom leaned toward him, he said, "Yes?" as if he thought she were going to whisper something. "Oh," he went when she kissed him on the cheek instead.

Robbie finished the back stretch of lawn while Dad, in his home clothes, started the charcoal briquets and chatted with Uncle Jim about bermuda grass and the lack of topsoil here, all bulldozed away and sold to farmers by the developer. They were dull and adult with each other, not strange, and Meg began to feel it wasn't her business to wonder about her father and uncle, who were grown-ups and therefore above suspicion. She sat with Walter in the hammock, lightly pushing them back and forth with her longer legs. Walter contentedly leaning against her.

"You mow a terrific yard there, Rob," Uncle Jim called out when Robbie wheeled the heavy silenced mower back to the garage.

Robbie only nodded, confused and almost ashamed. He looked ashamed when they sat at the picnic table and ate the grilled hamburgers. He was careful not to make his bites too big, use too much mustard or do anything else that sometimes caused Dad to snap at him. Robbie seemed to be trying to make up for his disrespect to Uncle Jim by showing special respect to Dad tonight. He very politely excused himself to go inside and watch television.

As it grew dark, lightning bugs rose from the fresh-cut grass like bubbles in a tired glass of ginger ale, and Meg went around the yard with Walter catching them until they got into a fight over what to do with the jar of sparking insects. Walter wanted to let them go; Meg wanted to experiment with them, plucking their bulbs the instant they glowed and seeing how long they'd stay lit. She was in a coldhearted mood tonight, but irritably gave in to Walter's mushy concern for bug suffering. The adults remained at the picnic table, talking about taxes and septic tanks and Uncle Jim's old-model car.

Indoors again, everybody watched TV until it was time for bed. Dad stood and announced, "I've got an early day tomorrow myself, so I'll turn in too. Guess I won't be seeing you before you take off tomorrow, Jim." He spoke in a careful, friendly manner. "I hope we see you again before they ship you to your next station. You're always welcome down here."

Uncle Jim stood up, despite Dad gesturing that he remain seated. He shook Dad's hand. "Thanks, Rick. I've had a great time. You and Ann are very kind."

Dad gestured that away too and laughed. "Come on, kids. Bedtime. You'll see your uncle tomorrow." He herded them upstairs, his public cheerfulness giving way around the corner to his usual weary gruffness.

Uncle Jim and Mom were sitting on the sofa with the TV off, each of them holding a bottle of Diet-Rite, when Meg came back down in her nightgown.

"Goodnight, dear."

"Sleep tight, Meg-wump."

They both seemed eager to get her out of the way so they could talk and Meg wondered if Uncle Jim were going to tell on Robbie after all. But after she turned off the light and got into bed, leaving the door to the utility room cracked just an inch, all she heard was a silence so long and lazy Meg thought one of them had dozed off. Lightning bugs were easier to catch and study than adults.

"Something on your mind tonight, Jimmy?"

"What? Oh. Just readjusting, I guess. The way I always do when I come home after a long stretch overseas."

"I guess Washington changes every year."

"Actually, I meant here."

"Oh? Well, yes, this is your home too. But we change. The kids especially."

"And this house. It's nice."

"We've done very well for ourselves."

"The whole country's done well. Something I see more of each time I come back. Things aren't the way they were when you and I grew up, Ann."

"You think so? I can't really tell. I always feel it's a case of just *Rick* doing well. But I suppose you're right."

"Rick has done well. I don't deny that."

"Yes. He works very hard and he still doesn't know how to relax. But he's much happier with a little success under his belt. Not that he was ever a failure, but—you know."

Meg had never imagined her father could be a failure, or happy, for that matter. He'd always seemed to her the same timeless, irritable center of things.

"Rick's a good man. I like Rick."

"And he likes you, Jimmy. He does."

Uncle Jim didn't answer.

"Do you find yourself missing Mother this trip?" said Mom.

"I do. Or I miss knowing she's out there somewhere, thinking about us now and then. I was never as close to her as I should've been."

"You weren't. But I think that's natural for a male."

They were talking about Gramma Goodall, who'd died when Meg was eight. Uncle Jim had offered to fly everyone up to Boston for the funeral, but only Mom went. Dad stayed home with the kids and cooked pancakes for dinner, which was all Meg remembered of her first experience with death, that and Mom sitting in a dark bedroom on a rainy day, crying. She'd never seen her mother cry before and automatically began to cry too, not knowing why.

"Does it feel at all different," said Uncle Jim, "being my sister without Mother still around to make it so?"

Mom laughed. "What a strange thing to say, Jimmy. Were you my brother just to satisfy Mother? Why do you ask such a thing?" Mom grew disturbed and uncomfortable. "You're being silly. Was it to please Mother you offered to help us way back when?"

"No. You know I never told her, not even about the loan."

"Exactly. You did it because you're my brother, and you'll always be my brother, with or without Mother's seal of approval."

There was another patch of silence and Uncle Jim said, "In a perverse way, I'm a little sorry you and Rick never needed my help after that first time."

"Don't be sorry. You were a lifesaver. But it's not good for family to be beholden to each other. Financially. No, it was good to know the help was there if we ever needed it. And you've been important to us in other ways."

"Have I?" He sounded surprised, pleased.

"Certainly." But it took Mom a moment to come up with anything. "Your visits. Your news of foreign places. Your gifts for the kids. You mean a lot to the kids."

"Oh."

That must be the help Robbie had thrown in Uncle Jim's face that afternoon. Meg wasn't sure what it meant. Part of her was excited Uncle Jim wanted to give them money, as if all she had to do was ask and he'd hand her a hundred dollars. But she knew this was adult money, the large, abstract sums Mom handled with bills and checks the end of every month, money tied up with where they lived and who they were, better than the navy families who lived in the trailer park on the other side of Kempsville, money that had nothing to do with the money you used to buy books and candy. Uncle Jim spoke like his feelings had been hurt, like a kid who hadn't been picked by the team he wanted to play on.

"There's no special someone in your life right now, Jimmy?"

"My work, you know. One doesn't come into contact with many single women."

"I'm sure there'd be ways of meeting them. *If* you were interested."

THE SCREEN DOOR slammed and Meg woke up. She didn't remember falling asleep, but it felt very late, the house silent, the seams around her door black. She heard a slurp of feet whisking through the wet grass. Someone had gone outside. Meg jumped up and went out to the utility room and the back door, which was wide open, the screen door unhooked.

Every house out back was pitch-dark, as black and solid as the trees. The night air smelled like fog, yet the streetlight at the far end of the block shone clearly. Under the dampness was a fresh, clean aroma of mown grass, like watermelon rind. The night seemed so deep and still.

The rings of the hammock suddenly creaked against their hooks in the sweet gum trees. They'd forgotten to bring the hammock in and someone sat in it. Putting her face in the far corner of the screen, Meg could see a pale figure sitting out there under the trees, head lightly bobbing as he rocked himself back and forth.

Going outside at this hour seemed impossible, a mysterious taboo to Meg. But that was Uncle Jim in the hammock. She could follow him into this forbidden place. The screen door fluted loudly when Meg pushed it open. The cold wet grass sizzled as she walked through it, splashing her bare calves. She felt naked coming outdoors in her nightgown, but that was exciting too.

Uncle Jim stopped rocking when he heard the door and saw her coming. "Meg?" he whispered.

"Uncle Jim," she whispered back. Their voices sounded very strange and magical with so much silence and space around them.

"Shouldn't you be in bed?"

"Shouldn't you?" Meg was feeling bold, and whispering made her feel less like a kid, Uncle Jim less like an adult. She sat on the bench of the picnic table and faced him, a few feet away, her back to the table.

Uncle Jim resumed rocking, his back perfectly straight, his bare feet never leaving the ground. The belt of his trousers was unbuckled, as if he'd just pulled them on to come outside, and he wore a sleeveless T-shirt. "Nice out here, isn't it?"

"It is," said Meg. Looking over her shoulder at the house, she found it gazing down at them, the window of her brothers' bedroom and, at the other end, the window of her parents' room, solemn and blind beneath the barnlike roof.

"I couldn't sleep," Uncle Jim explained. "I just thought I'd come outside for a breath of air."

It was funny that an adult thought he needed to explain himself.

"Aren't you cold? Do you want to sit with me in the hammock?"

"Nyaah. I'm okay." If she sat with him, this would turn uncomfortable and mushy, when Meg wanted to keep it on a higher plane. "Why can't you sleep?"

"I don't know. Aren't there nights when you can't sleep? No, you're still too young for that."

The rings of the hammock clicked and creaked in their hooks. A lone automobile hummed past out on the highway beyond the soybean field.

"Where are you at in your book? Have you gotten to the Night of Tears?"

"The what?" said Meg.

"*La noche de lacrimas.* The night when Cortez and his men fought their way out of the city after the natives turned against them."

"No. They're still trapped in the city. The Aztecs just figured out Cortez wasn't a great white god."

"Well, no offense to Prescott, but I tend to doubt that great white god nonsense. There's too many other great white god stories for one to take them with anything but a grain of salt."

"Uh huh." Meg had no idea what he was talking about, but that seemed a small price to pay for being treated as an equal.

"Would you like to go to Yucatan one day? There's Mayan pyramids down there. The Aztec pyramids were all destroyed, as you know, but the Mayans were very similar."

Meg's heart suddenly lit up. Was he offering to take her? She carefully replied, "I guess."

"I'd like to see them myself. One day when you're older, maybe we could go down there together." His tone turned worried and uncertain. "Would that interest you at all?"

"Oh yeah! I mean, yes. When?" She was so excited she forgot to whisper.

"Shhhhh," went Uncle Jim, surprised by her reaction, then pleased by it, lowering his head and secretly smiling. Even in the dark she could see the smile. "When you're older, a teenager maybe. You'd get more out of it then, and I don't think your mother's ready to let you go out of the country anytime soon. But yes. That'd be something for both of us to look forward to."

A future so distant seemed more imaginary than real to Meg, which made the idea even more appealing. "I'd love that more than anything else in the world."

"Maybe Yucatan. Maybe Angkor Wat. We'll have to wait and see where I'm stationed when that time comes around. There's good ruins almost everywhere."

"Jungle," said Meg. "Anyplace so long as there's jungle."

Uncle Jim laughed. "The whole world's a jungle. But all right. I'll keep an eye open for ruins in a jungle, and you concentrate on getting a few years older." He'd regained his humor, his sadness was gone. He stood up and stretched and contentedly looked around the yard. "Well, I don't know about you, Meg-wump, but I'm going on in."

"I'm coming too," said Meg, getting up and walking beside him with her hands behind her back. "I'll be a teenager when I'm thirteen, you know."

"I was thinking more along the lines of sixteen or seventeen."

That seemed so far off as to be unreachable, yet it didn't spoil the joy Meg was feeling. "All right. I'll try not to die before I'm sixteen."

"It's a deal." He held the screen door open for her and hooked it behind them. With his hand lightly, then more firmly on her shoulder, as if realizing she wasn't made of glass, Uncle Jim steered her around the washing machine to her room. He stood in the door while she got into bed and whispered, "Thanks for keeping me company."

WHEN SHE WOKE up the next morning, she remembered last night and wondered if it had been a dream. But there was grass in her bed, green clippings that had stuck to her feet when she walked in the night.

Uncle Jim slept late again. He ate lunch with them before he left, making no mention to Mom of any conversation in the dark, although he smiled at Meg a lot while they ate. He hardly looked at Robbie, much less spoke to him. His vague promise of a trip, along with whatever it was that had happened yesterday at the pool, told Meg her brother had fallen out of favor and she had taken his place.

After he drove off, the house became very normal and dull again. Meg stayed home when Robbie and Walter went to the pool that afternoon, trying to read about the Night of Tears on the bed in the room that was hers again. The sheets and pillowcases hadn't been changed and there was a horsey, leathery smell of hair and aftershave on her pillow. She closed her book and clomped upstairs to her parents' room, where Mom was ironing.

"Hello, Skeezix. How you doing?"

"Oh, fine." Meg fell backwards on the enormous bed and lay there looking at the ceiling. She liked talking to Mom up here. The big room was full of sun in the afternoon, but the buzzing window fan kept the place from becoming too hot. The room seemed far away from the rest of the house, the TV and her brothers. "Uncle Jim says he'll take me to Yucatan one day." Meg wanted to try out the notion on her mother and hear how likely it was. "To see the Mayan pyramids. That's in Mexico, Mom."

"You're too young to go off gallivanting with your uncle, dear."

"I know. He said when I'm older. Fifteen." Shaving off a year wouldn't hurt.

Mom sprayed more starch on the collar of the shirt she ironed. Working up here alone seemed to relax Mom and make her easier to talk to. "Your uncle means well, Meg. His heart's in the right place. But you can't count on him doing everything he says."

Meg tugged hard at the reins of her pigtails. "You don't think he meant it?"

"I'm sure he meant it. It's just—fifteen's a long way off and, well, Jimmy's always been a little romantic and impractical."

"Romantic like mushy?"

"Impractical romantic. Idealistic." Mom resumed ironing, frowning as if she'd said too much. "All I'm saying is you shouldn't get your hopes up."

Meg relaxed. Her mother didn't really know; she was just lowering Meg's expectations, wanting to protect her. Meg didn't want to be protected. "Maybe when I'm fifteen I could go over and visit him in some embassy somewhere. What about that?"

"We'll have to wait and see. Although I don't think he'd want a young girl underfoot over there. Doing whatever it is he does."

Her squeamish tone suggested something new and awful to Meg. "You think Uncle Jim does bad things over there?" She suddenly pictured him killing Aztecs by the hundreds, but Cortez was Spanish and their family was American. Americans always helped people. They would've given the Aztecs CARE packages.

"I didn't say that," Mom quickly insisted. "I don't really know what he does over there. I'm not sure I want to know. His work or life or . . ." She concentrated very hard on ironing around a button. "It's one thing to read about those countries in books, Meg. But they're no place for girls or young women. Your place is at home, with a husband and family. Which is something you'll understand better when you get older."

Meg kept hoping her mother understood she wasn't like other girls, that she was going to do more with her life than wear pretty clothes or play housewife. Mom didn't understand her after all. Look at her over there, perfectly content pressing shirts and drinking Diet-Rite Cola, so smart about people in their house but blind to everything good and exciting in the bigger world outside.

Meg closed her eyes and pretended she was somewhere else, in a jungle with her uncle, where she looked for ancient ruins and he delivered boxes of canned soup and candy bars to villages of grateful natives.

4

TROPICAL BIRDS CACKLED in the little valley below, hidden under the hot canopy of treetops. The low ridge on the other side, treeless and dusty green with new scrub, suddenly gained a large bloom of orange smoke.

The sky banged shut and roared, as if an express train slammed through the air. The crump of the explosion itself crossed the valley a second later. Then more blooms appeared, a forest of explosions whose thudding caught up with the concussions of shells slamming overhead; the artillery barrage pounded the valley like a bass drum while the ridge disappeared in sunlit globes of brown and orange smoke. The smoke grew still and lost its shape as the last shock waves thundered in the cloudless sky.

Regaining their heartbeats and drawing deep breaths, people began to applaud. The First Lady lifted her face from Ambassador Earp's chest, laughed with him over her fright, then shared the laugh with her husband, President Marcos. While the Marcoses comforted and teased their twelve-year-old son, Bong-Bong, the ambassador checked his shirt for mascara smudges.

Jim sat three rows behind them in the reviewing stand. Roofed like the stands at a baseball stadium, the structure was full of Filipino politicians and their families this morning, wealthy men whose T-shirts were visible through the gauze of their cool, long-tailed barongs, comfortably fashionable women whose Spanish fans snapped open again and resumed fluttering. Jim and the other embassy men were expected to sweat stoically in white shirts and stubby neckties, the price of power.

"Fireworks at the palace would've been more convenient," grumbled Tom Lowenstein, the section assistant. "Or we could've zipped over to Saigon for the day."

"Think of it as batting practice at Fenwick Park," Jim muttered back.

They were at Crow Valley in a remote corner of Clark Air Force Base today in August, 1969, ostensibly so Marcos could show off his army and airpower to the new American ambassador. The base was American, of course, as was the hardware plowing up the ridge across the way. Jim hoped the gunners

aiming the artillery a mile behind them were American too, and no rounds
would fall short and blow everyone to kingdom come.

"Mr. President, Madame First Lady, Mr. Ambassador, esteemed ladies and
gentlemen," announced the professional voice over the loudspeakers. "Without further ado, we direct your attention to the far right. Let's give a warm
welcome to the *Huey Cobra helicopter gunship!*"

With a patter of blades indistinguishable from the applause, a tiny airborne
sports car flew into view. It buzzed across the valley toward the smoking
ridge.

"Hmmm. The Gold Dust Twins," said Lowenstein, nodding at two men
down below, Diokno and Aquino.

"Noted. Saw them when we arrived. Osmena's brother-in-law, too."

Most of today's guests appeared to be members of the "loyal opposition."
Marcos was up for reelection in three months and the real purpose of this
outing was to remind his opponents he had both the military and the American
government deep in his pocket, as well as to provide a little demonstration of
what that military could do to enemies. But Jim sensed no fear or discomfort
among the guests. Everyone seemed to enjoy the show and each other's company. Filipinos were the warmest, most genial people in the world, even toward those they were planning to murder. And the hosts and guests were cut
from the same cloth, all of them rich and most of them corrupt, their rivalries
as ideologically empty as the rivalries at a country club. There were a few
good thieves mixed among the bad thieves, but everyone assumed the worse
thief of all would be reelected. Marcos did not need to intimidate anyone
today.

The Huey Cobra circled the ridge like a bug, its invisible blades whipping
shreds of smoke into cones and question marks. It flew to a corner untouched
by the barrage and hung there, as motionless as a dragonfly. The machine
sparkled for a moment with a delayed burr like a chainsaw, the palm hut down
below evaporating in a dance of dust and splinters. There was little left for the
rockets that then shot from the helicopter like bursts from a roman candle.

More applause followed, and Marcos leaned over his wife to make a joke
with the ambassador. Earp threw his head back and laughed loud and hard.

A handsome man with a salt-and-pepper crewcut and a profile like Gary
Cooper's, Earp got along very well with the Thief of Thieves, far too well for
Jim's liking. Chip Adkins, who'd been acting ambassador during Jim's first
two months as political counselor, had been careful to keep some distance
between himself and Marcos. Not so Henry Earp, which seemed dangerous.
The embassy staff had had high hopes for the new ambassador, who was
supposed to be very independent and outspoken, a career officer whose career
had been on a siding because he didn't kiss ass in the State Department, until
he was sent here by President Nixon himself. He didn't kiss Marcos's ass
either, but seemed genuinely fond of the cunning little pig, enamored of him,
in love.

Jim had seen it again and again in his years with the foreign service: men sometimes fell in love with other men in power. There was no other name for these attachments that were so blinding and irrational. The men themselves were too busily heterosexual to recognize what was going on—the joke around the political section was that Earp and Marcos swapped anecdotes about their many mistresses—but Jim recognized and noted it, with the same calm matter-of-factness with which he noted the emotional streak in himself he sometimes interpreted as a spillover of celibacy, and at other times as proof of homosexuality. Jim could be as clear-eyed and detached in his observation of himself as he was in his observations of other countries. He had learned to acknowledge his homosexual streak without panic or any need to act on it. And knowing something like that about yourself gave you insights into others denied more normal men.

"Now for our grand finale," the proud announcer called over the loud-speakers. "An F–80 Shooting Star, flown by our own Commander Orestes Romualdez, will pass over the target. Let's see what happens."

"Romualdez?" said Jim. "Another of Imelda's nephews?"

"A second cousin. One of Eduardo's sons," Lowenstein explained. Government and military were a family affair and one needed a Philippine equivalent of Debrett's to keep track of the players. Lowenstein had family trees pinned over his desk.

The sky thundered again as a jet fighter roared over the reviewing stand. A silvery bullet, it shrieked over the valley and ridge toward the blue mountains in the distance, sun flashing on its wings as the plane banked to the left and came around to approach the ridge from the side. The jet flew close to the ground and in seconds finished its turn and raced across the crest. Specks like teardrops fell from the wings. The entire length of the ridge burst into a rolling cloud of red flame and black smoke, a fiery tidal wave that pursued the jet and almost caught it. A wall of heat hit the reviewing stand, as if the door to a furnace had been thrown open. People turned away in an effort to find air cool enough to breathe.

Then the heat passed, the long black cloud of smoke rolled up to heaven, its shadow passing through the valley and over the audience, and all that remained were a few fires burning on a long swath of black velvet.

"Whew!" went Lowenstein. "What's the encore gonna be? A hydrogen bomb?"

But Jim was too awed and shaken to laugh it off. He'd never seen anything like it at the many military shows he'd sat through, only in news footage on TV where you never felt the hot reality. It was horrifying yet beautiful, a disturbing, hypnotic temptation, as if Jim wanted something in his world to ignite like that and burn itself away. Then the confusing awe passed and he became himself again. "I better pay my respects to the Aquinos. You might say hello to Senator Diokno."

After the announcer thanked everyone for coming, a Sousa march began to play through the loudspeakers and people came down from the grandstand. The older women opened lace parasols when they stepped into the bright sun and daintily strolled in front of the view of the blackened slope and final flickers of burning napalm.

"We should've brought marshmallows," quipped Ninoy Aquino, a witty playboy who'd been a journalist during the Korean War and seen it all. "Or perhaps *we* were the marshmallows." That idea didn't seem to disturb him either. He was rich and had the invulnerable air of the rich. His dislike of Marcos caused him to attack the man in the Senate now and then, but nobody knew if that dislike stemmed from real political differences or if Aquino only wanted a bigger piece of the pie Marcos hogged. There was even a rumor that Aquino was still resentful of Marcos's conquest of the young woman they'd both courted many years ago, but Jim found that hard to believe. Imelda may have been Miss Manila of 1953, but Aquino had certainly made the better marriage in snagging the wealthy Corazon Cojuanco. Cory stood by with her arms folded in the butterfly sleeves of her yellow dress, impatiently waiting for her husband to finish his little chat with this minor American official. Filipina women showed more character in public than other Asian wives, especially when they had their own powerful families behind them.

"Goodall! Over here!" Ambassador Earp stood twenty yards away with President Marcos, under an enormous green golf umbrella held by one of Marcos's bodyguards.

"Excuse me, Senator. Mrs. Aquino. It's been nice to see you again." Jim nodded to each of them and went to see what the ambassador wanted.

They stood on the edge of the parking lot, where the guests were hurrying into air-conditioned limousines and the two modern buses Imelda used for her coterie of women friends—her Blue Ladies—and sip-sips—politely translated as "lapdogs." She was already inside a bus herself, which was a relief. Jim disliked being around her.

Earp had his arm around the short president's shoulders and softly spoke in one ear while Jim waited outside the green shadow of their umbrella. The baby-faced bodyguard in an aloha shirt gripped the handle in a beefy hand with scarred knuckles and coldly stared at Jim. Earp slapped the president on the back when he finished. "There you are, Goodall. You know my political officer, don't you, Mr. President?"

"Certainly. We've had the pleasure of several games of golf under your predecessor." With his plump cheeks and his widow's peak of black hair combed up to give him another inch of height, Marcos looked like a Chinese kewpie doll when he smiled, a doll with teeth. "A seven-handicap, if memory serves." He had a photographic memory and loved to show it off.

"Yet you always manage to beat me, Mr. President."

Marcos laughed and shrugged. "Competition brings out the tiger."

Earp laughed too. "Sorry to say my only game is poker." He slapped his hard stomach to announce he had other ways of keeping in shape. "Well,

Fred. I don't want to keep you from your luncheon. Give my regards to General Irons. And don't worry, I'll take care of our little *problema* pronto."

"Many thanks, Henry. I knew you'd understand. Talk to you tomorrow." Marcos strutted toward his waiting limo, his umbrella and bodyguard going with him. Out of nowhere, two more bodyguards appeared and walked on either side of him, the aloha shirt of one caught behind the revolver tucked into the small of his back.

Earp squinted in the bright glare at the departing object of his affection. His manner instantly turned brusque and clipped. "Called you over, Goodall, to see if you were staying for this air force lunch or going back to town. If the latter, I'd like some company on the ride in."

"My pleasure, sir. Let me give the car keys to Lowenstein and I'll meet you at your car." Jim strode through the saffron dust raised by the limos and buses racing off to the banquet at the officers' club. Lowenstein was waiting for him by their embassy Ford Fairlane. "I'm riding back with Earp," Jim said and tossed him the keys.

"Yeah? You think it'll be good news or bad news?"

"Damned if I know. Might be no news at all. Although I think he's promised Marcos another favor. More election fun and games, I bet. See you back at the office."

Clark Air Force Base went on for miles of savannah and hills before one drove past the hangars and runways. In the distance, gigantic B–52 bombers in camouflage shades of green and beige were parked in rows, although not nearly as many as there'd been before the bombing halt in 1968, a year ago. Most of the planes were based in Thailand now, continuing their bombing runs over South Vietnam and, some said, Laos and Cambodia, ready to bomb North Vietnam again at a moment's notice. Tom Lowenstein was right: it was absurd to play war here when there was the real thing on the other side of the South China Sea, an hour and a half away.

Jim sat in the backseat with Earp in the ambassador's air-conditioned Lincoln, Earp loosening his tie and making himself comfortable. "So, Mr. Ambassador." Jim used the title jocularly, still unsure what else to call their new boss. "What did *you* make of today's festivities?"

"Just Ferdy showing off his toys. Not like any of that was new to me, not after two years with Stilwell in Burma." Earp had been a captain during World War II, a fact he frequently dropped in the presence of subordinates to let them know he'd been around. Fifteen years ago, Jim would've found such a man above doubt or criticism. "What about you, sergeant?" Earp asked the stiff-backed Marine driving the car. "Guess it's old hat to you, too."

"Yes, sir. In 'Nam we saw that stuff from the inside," the man said woodenly, eyes locked on the road, both hands on the wheel.

"Yeah." Earp reached inside his trousers and vigorously scratched himself. "Heat rash," he muttered. "Looks like breaded veal down there with all that damn baby powder."

Jim smiled and lightly snorted, a respectful kind of laugh.

The highway outside the gates and sentry posts was lined with bars, burger stands, used car lots and strip joints, like the highway outside any military base in the United States. Beyond that the land reverted to the Philippines, diked acres of rice like green hairbrushes crowding the flat ground between the new highway and low, rocky hills on either side. Clusters of nipa palm huts hugged the roadside in cramped islands of banyan trees, naked children playing in the dirt of the highway's shoulder that was their front yards. Some jumped up and waved as the big car raced past. Jim disliked the way one could float along in leather upholstery and cool air that smelled like the inside of an expensive new shoe, look out through tinted glass and see so much poverty. In other countries, the roads were as poor as the people, the air-conditioning never worked and Jim rode with the windows down. The stink of things closed the distance between you and what you saw, a little.

"Jim. We got visitors from Washington next week," Earp announced.

"Again?" They were swamped with guests this summer, what with Nixon in July, the governor of California expected next month when Imelda opened her Cultural Center, scores of dignitaries and celebrities in between. The Marcoses seemed bent on entertaining the entire world.

"A Senate investigation team. The Subcommittee on Commitments Abroad or whatever it's called. Symington's hobbyhorse."

Jim's interest snapped to life. The Senate was studying the promises and deals made by the Johnson administration with their allies in Vietnam. Marcos had contributed an engineering brigade to the war, in exchange for large sums of U.S. aid, military and otherwise. It was high time somebody looked into that money. "And you want me to brief them on the situation? Tell them what we suspect?"

"I don't want you telling them anything." Earp settled back and faced forward, his handsome profile adamant and decided. "I'm letting them into the country under protest. Hardly in the saddle, the last thing I need now is a pack of congressional snoops imposing *their* values on our ally. Corruption is a way of life over here."

Jim was disappointed by Earp's decision, but not surprised. "We're not to cooperate in any way," he observed.

"Tell them nothing that hasn't already been included in reports to Congress. And be sure none of your staff gets the talking disease with these people. Ferdinand Marcos is the best thing to happen here since MacArthur. The country'd be anarchy without him. We're not going to do anything to help those numbnuts in Congress screw that up."

"Yes, sir." Marcos was part of the anarchy, but love is blind and Jim knew better than to attack Earp's loyalty head-on. Keeping his face and tone as bland as possible, Jim said, "I'm wondering though if we might tell them *something*. Otherwise, they're going to hunt around behind our backs. You know how those people are. They won't go away happy until they find something.''

"Hmmm. Good point. Throw them a bone?''

"Yes. Maybe the government's involvement in cigarette-smuggling. The skimming by Customs. The price-fixing in the sugar industry.''

Earp considered those and shook his head. "No. By American standards those sound like corruption.''

They *were* corruption by anybody's standards, but Jim offered them only as a prelude to the item he really wanted exposed. "Or maybe the unvouchered funds?''

"What funds are those?''

"The portion of military aid we pay directly to Marcos. The quarterly checks.'' Secret bonuses given as aid, yet accepted as bribes. Jim personally delivered one of the checks himself to the defense minister before he understood what they were. It left him feeling unclean, a bagman for gangsters.

"No, I think not. If that reached Congress it might come out in the papers. We can't have something like that becoming public over here, especially before the election. Might hurt Marcos with the voters.''

Which was the chief reason why Jim wanted to expose it. He should've guessed the ambassador would be smart enough to see the consequences.

"Anyway, we don't know for certain where that money goes, do we?'' Earp claimed. A new thought raised his eyebrows. "What if you told them about Imelda's brother?''

"Kokoy Romualdez?''

"Yes. His protection racket down in Leyte. The threats and extortion.'' Marcos himself must've fed that one to Earp. "We'll throw them the brother-in-law,'' Earp chuckled. "Everybody's got in-law troubles. They won't blame Marcos for Kokoy.''

Kokoy's racketeering was small potatoes compared to everything else, but Earp resolved that that was the bone they'd throw the investigation. Jim resigned himself to being able to talk only about Kokoy. At least he'd tried. He wasn't sure what he hoped to accomplish by exposing those payments anyway. Even something like that might not cost Marcos the election. Or if they did, there was no guarantee his successor would be an improvement.

Corruption *was* a way of life in Asia—tired old saw—and it was only the extent of Marcos's dealings that galled Jim. The man had a genius for greed, able to keep track of a dozen secret scams and at least two love affairs without losing his affable smile. It was kind of impressive. Jim had not noticed so much corruption during his first tour in Manila. He didn't know if it had become worse or if he only saw more now that he was higher up. There were times when Jim became depressed that his work required him to know so much and do so little about it. At other times he took perverse pride in the fact that he, a preacher's grandson, could live in this element and remain rational, becoming neither blindly righteous nor morally corrupt himself.

Earp gave final instructions on how the investigators should be handled. "They shouldn't be difficult, especially when they get the brother-in-law to chew on. Just a couple of numbnuts from Symington's office. And someone from INR traveling with them, but he should see things our way."

INR was the State Department's Intelligence and Research Bureau, foreign service people who went from embassy to embassy gathering data. Jim had been with them himself for two years. "Did they tell you who it was?"

"Yeah. Somebody Wheeler."

"*David* Wheeler?"

"That's right. You know him?"

The center of gravity shifted, the car accelerating to pass a crowded jeepney. A few grins and waving hands appeared in the mass of bodies packed under the converted jeep's roof, skirts and shirtsleeves flapping in the wind. Tropical landscapes were painted on the vehicle's chassis and hood, volcanoes and waterfalls.

"We've crossed paths a few times." Jim quickly suppressed his interest. "I had no idea he was with INR now. Haven't seen him in five or six years. With his wife in Phnom Penh."

"Then he's an Asia man. Good. He a team player?"

"Yes. I think so."

"He'll know better then to go opening doors to closets you tell him are empty."

"Yes, sir. He's a good man," Jim said drily. "He's married to a good woman."

Mountains of dark clouds were massing for the daily shower when they drove into the city. The subdued light brought out the gaudy colors of the tin and cardboard slums in Tondo, looking like a city dump in the distance. The sky opened up as they came down Roxas Boulevard, the bay on the right disappearing in a sweep of gray, the luxury hotels on the left turning on their floodlights. The blades of the tall palm trees lining the boulevard bounced in the heavy rain.

The American embassy stood on the Manila Bay side of Roxas Boulevard, a great white box with beveled corners and a lawn full of evergreens and Spanish bayonet. Going on to his residence in Forbes Park, Earp told the driver to drop Jim off at the front entrance.

"I'm leaving this in your hands, Jim. Don't let me down."

"No, sir. I'll take care of it."

A Marine had come out with an umbrella, expecting the ambassador himself to step from the car. Jim irritably let the solemn kid escort him through the few feet of lukewarm downpour to the bright, refrigerated lobby.

Everyone in the political section looked up when Jim entered the offices upstairs. Lowenstein was back and he must've told them their chief was riding in with the ambassador. Annoyed by their looks of curiosity and anticipation, Jim responded to the couple of hellos with no more than a curt nod as he strode back toward his office. He encouraged his staff to be informal and friendly with him, to avoid the respect that only got in the way when exchanging information and ideas, but this afternoon their forwardness rattled him.

"You have a good meeting with Mr. Earp?" asked Concepcion, his secretary, a university graduate who dressed dumb and feminine: mini-skirts and a bangy hairdo she said was inspired by Barbra Streisand.

"Tell Mr. Lowenstein that if he can shut his mouth for a few minutes"— Jim saw him out on the glassed-in porch with Blackwell, apparently filling him in on whatever he thought was happening—"I need everything we've got on the Romualdez family. And you're wearing too much perfume," he snapped. "I don't understand why an educated girl would want to do herself up like a concubine."

Concepcion looked stunned; Jim had never spoken to her like this before. "Sorry, Mr. Jim. I mean, Mr. Goodall. You want me to wash it off?" She jumped up. "The Romualdez family. I'll tell Tom and wash my face."

"I don't care. Smell the way you want." Jim stepped into his office and closed the door. He had no windows and he never closed his door when he was in there alone. He sat in his chair and propped his head with an elbow on the desk, the hand and thumb clamped across his mouth.

Dave Wheeler was coming. He'd be lying to Dave Wheeler.

So what? He told lies all the time, to outsiders and subordinates. "Men sent to lie abroad" was an old definition of diplomats. But Wheeler felt different. It wouldn't matter if he agreed with the reasons for lying or not, although Jim suspected he'd want to see Marcos exposed as badly as Jim did. Dave Wheeler had been terribly moral six years ago. They'd been terribly moral together in their nightly talks during the week Jim stayed with him and Elaine, talking to sustain the principles they had to keep on ice while they waited to reach positions where they could act on them. Now Jim was in such a position, except he'd been ordered to lie. Knowing he'd be lying to Wheeler made his justifications feel transparent and fake, lies to himself.

Jim knew he strained at a gnat after swallowing a camel—several camels, in fact. It was funny what the conscience snagged on. And it wasn't like Wheeler and Jim were close. Suddenly, six years ago, meeting in neighboring countries overseas, they were friends. Wheeler had initiated it in the course of official calls between embassies. "Come visit us. I want you to meet Elaine and Janey." And Jim had visited, a surprisingly enjoyable week with a day trip out to Angkor and passionate shop talk every evening, and no trace or mention of that time of confusion many years ago when Jim had been in love with the guy. There'd been other loves since then, nervous friendships with an edge of old-maid possessiveness: a couple of junior officers, a religious Marine lieutenant, a Finnish translator during Jim's year in Helsinki. Dave Wheeler wasn't unique and Jim had not been in love with him in Phnom Penh. No, he'd had a pleasant week of commonplace friendship with someone who'd once been the site of passion and turmoil, a comfortable friendship like the absurdly peaceful Cambodian village they found among the elaborate warlike ruins of Angkor.

There was a knock on the door and Lowenstein entered with a collapsed accordion of folders. Keeping all doubts and disagreement to himself while he told his assistant what Earp wanted, Jim felt he had swallowed his gnat.

"JIM!"

"Hello, Dave."

"Looked forward to seeing a familiar face."

"Likewise."

They shook hands in Jim's office, in front of Lowenstein and the two men from Symington's staff. Lowenstein had met the visitors at the airport and installed them in their hotel rooms at the Savoy. The Senate people looked soaked and wilted in their gray suits after the short walk across the boulevard to the embassy, their faces still dripping. Dave Wheeler looked damp but comfortable: a shortsleeved shirt, a loosely knotted tie. His old disheveled appearance had turned into something casual yet appropriate, and he'd grown a beard. Not a stuffy, pipe-smoking beard but a boy's beard, curly and untrimmed, that suggested a young college professor. He had an eager, wound-up quality that expressed itself in the rubbery tension of his bow-legged stance, the knot of his tight-lipped smile, the quick, sharp glance of his dark eyes. He still appeared young and Jim had to remind himself Dave must be forty now, just one year younger than Jim.

"How's Elaine?"

"Glad to be living stateside again."

"Janey?"

"Starts high school next month."

And that was the extent of personal words before Dave introduced Picard and Brown and disappeared into professional cool. Jim was disappointed in spite of himself. He gave his full attention to Picard and Brown, who were as anonymous and functional as the self-important ciphers he encountered from the FBI or CIA. They went into the screening room for the presentation Jim had put together with his staff, complete with slides of charts, graphs and photos of the players. People from Congress loved visuals.

"What about the rumors of government corruption?" Picard asked.

"I'm glad to hear you ask that," said Jim, turning away from the screen. "Tom, skip ahead to the Romualdez slides."

Jim went into detail on the corruption in Leyte and the involvement of the president's brother-in-law. Kokoy did not look particularly cunning or even bright in the photos they showed, more like a professional wrestler than a criminal mastermind. Jim included a couple of Imelda's scams, such as her Christmas charity drives for which Kokoy was her bagman. If that got back to Earp, Jim could claim there was no separating brother and sister. But Imelda was an amateur compared to her husband, a wife clumsily competing for her share of money and attention. A few junior staff members referred to the First Lady as "Lucy Ricardo," an allusion that had to be explained to Jim.

When the presentation was finished and the lights turned on, Picard and Brown expressed shock at Kokoy's crimes, amused contempt for Imelda's petty theft and satisfaction with the briefing. Dave said nothing. He sat with his arms folded and looked at Jim curiously, coldly. As the visitors left with Lowenstein to go over to Camp Aguinaldo for a briefing by the military attaché, Dave nodded at Jim and muttered, "Catch you later. Maybe."

There was no room for friendship here, Jim told himself when he was alone. And he and Wheeler weren't really friends. He had no reason to take Wheeler's disapproval personally. Jim fought his anger and guilt by becoming indifferent.

He worked late that day, as he always did when there wasn't a public function in the evening. After the last secretary and researcher went home, Jim took his newspapers and reports out to the glassed-in porch at the back of the section offices. He'd had the porch set up as a kind of den for his staff, with wicker furniture and sisal carpeting, a place where people could be themselves while they discussed news and policy. The plate-glass windows looked out on Manila Bay, now crossed with a glittering ladder of orange light as the sun sank toward the misty ridges of Bataan, the view framed by two white-barked coconut trees whose tattered fountain of leaves opened just above the third-floor porch. When Jim first noticed them, the nuts bunched tightly beneath the fronds had been lewdly suggestive. In time, they'd become just coconuts on a tree.

Sitting on the red cushions of the wicker couch, he read Blackwell's report on Muslim disaffection in Mindanao, read it with a pencil, correcting the grammar and phrasing as he went, an old habit that helped him concentrate. He believed clear thought required clear prose, even though he sometimes felt, handing the papers back for retyping, he had turned into his mother. He knew the staff treated the corrections as an idiosyncrasy, a joke. He knew they called him The Vicar behind his back, but that only amused Jim. His people seemed to trust and respect his abilities as their section chief, which was what mattered.

There were footsteps inside, a Marine guard making his rounds, or one of the cleaning people. Then the footsteps approached the porch. Jim turned and found Dave Wheeler standing there.

"Thought you'd still be here. Mind if I join you?"

Too surprised to speak, Jim gestured at the wicker chair opposite him.

Wheeler strolled in, hands in his pockets, wishbone legs bending as he looked around. "Nice view," he said and sat in the chair, his back to the window. He looked at Jim, his hands still in his pockets, the thin lips pinched in a smirk inside his new beard.

Jim watched him over the tops of his reading glasses; the tilt of his head made him feel stern and strong. He assumed Wheeler was here to talk about Jim's lies. "How was Camp Crame?"

Wheeler shrugged and made a face. Jim expected him to use the military briefing to talk about Jim's briefing. Instead he said, "You look like you've been taking good care of yourself."

"I do?"

"Yeah. No flab, no paunch." Wheeler grinned.

"I'm losing my hair," said Jim, his automatic response to all flattery.

"If you let it grow out, nobody'd know."

"I don't care about that. More scalp gets sunburned, that's all." They sounded like two middle-aged women, but what mattered was Wheeler's friendliness. Jim took off his glasses to make himself look friendlier. "You've kept *your* hair. And then some."

Chuckling, Dave kneaded his beard. "Yeah. A touch of the ape. Sets me apart in Foggy Bottom, but shows I'm in touch with the times."

"Then it's a political statement?"

"Political, personal, lazy. I hate shaving."

They nodded together, as if over the rigors of shaving. "Lowenstein taking good care of you?" said Jim.

"To be sure. What's the story on him anyway? Seems kind of dull. He has nothing to say, even when he's alone with me."

"Tom's a good man. He's just going through a cynical phase. We all go through it, but it seems worse for those with the highest ideals. Kennedy man." Which was true, although the real reason for his silence was that Jim had ordered him to be very careful about what he said. Lowenstein must be carrying out the order to its most cynical extreme.

"Wait until you see the next batch," said Dave. "No ideals, no passion, nothing. They seem to be choosing people for dullness. Like they're afraid anyone with intelligence or imagination has got to be a radical. It's the war. There's a siege mentality in Washington."

Jim shook his head in sympathy. "Anything is preferable to what life must be like back there. Even this paradise of snakes."

Dave let loose a laugh, the old boyish giggle which seemed out of proportion to Jim's crack. He looked straight at Jim and grinned. "Kokoy Romualdez, huh?"

Jim's guard went up again.

"They actually bought that, you know."

"Meaning you didn't?" Here it was, the real reason for Wheeler's chat.

"We both know there's far more rotten things going on here." He continued to hold his grin.

"Such as?"

Wheeler lifted himself up and drew his chair closer to Jim, too close. The proximity of beard disturbed Jim; he wanted to reach out and yank it.

"There's things you know, Jim, that you won't tell Symington's people."

"National security."

Wheeler shook his head. "Things that would show only what a stupid mistake we're making supporting Marcos. I read your last cables, Jim. You make it clear there's no Communist threat here, that the few remaining Huks became part of the criminal underworld years ago. They're an imaginary bogeyman. And we've hired a gangster to protect this country from them."

"Gangster," Jim scoffed. "You know the way of the world over here as well as I do. No, he's not Adlai Stevenson. Yes, we give them foreign and military aid. What else is new?"

"Two million dollars paid directly to Marcos himself. Without anyone in his own country knowing about it."

Jim flinched mentally, but Wheeler seemed to catch it in Jim's eye.

"Yes? You'd know more about those payments than I do, Jim. A bribe worked out under Johnson to insure Marcos would send token Philippine troops to Vietnam. And they're still going on. If word of that reached Congress, we'd not only stop those payments but could break Marcos over here."

"Do Symington's people know about these—*alleged* payments?"

"No. I was hoping you'd tell them."

"Since you know so much, or think you do, why can't you?"

"Because my source is classified. He can't testify in Congress."

"CIA?"

Wheeler nodded. "If I was subpoenaed, all I could give them is hearsay. We need to get solid information through another channel."

"Who exactly is *we*?"

"Nobody important," Wheeler admitted. "Some mid-level people in Southeast Asian Affairs. Everyone else is too busy with Vietnam to care what's happening elsewhere. Even Symington's people give the Philippines a very low priority."

"So there's a good chance your whistleblower will wreck his career."

"To be sure. What we hope for instead is that someone will leak information on the payments, the exact amounts and dates of the checks. If we have that, we can trace the payments through the Government Accounting Office, then show in Congress where the money went. We assume it'll be one of Marcos's bank accounts."

"Interesting," said Jim. "Very interesting"—pretending it was all hypothetical and Wheeler wasn't asking him to leak the information. "And what brave soul will present your findings to the subcommittee?"

"I will. If I get the goods." Wheeler tried to toss it off, cool and stoical, but he couldn't help himself: his mouth curved up in a guilty smile. "I like to live dangerously."

Jim was startled by Wheeler's foolishness, touched and tempted by it. His first impulse was to want to join him. His next was to stop Wheeler from ruining his own future. "But why Marcos? Why the Philippines? You've never spent much time here."

"When I heard about these payments I was outraged, disgusted. They're so blatantly wrong they're insulting. Don't you feel insulted?"

His indignation annoyed Jim; it seemed naive and inappropriate. "Have you ever leaked anything to the press, Dave?"

"No. I could've if the occasion arose, but no. Nothing important."

"I have," Jim whispered. "Twice. Nothing happened either time. The facts I passed on were either mangled or ignored by the time they appeared in print. There was a third time when my evidence was never used at all."

"This would go to Congress, not the press."

"Where it's as likely nothing will come of it, and more dangerous because it'll be so public." Jim drew a deep breath; there was no getting around the odds and he distrusted his desire to help Wheeler. It was too emotional, too personal. He resented Wheeler for using their friendship.

Jim sat back and crossed his legs. He laced his fingers together and parked the joined hands over his knee. "No, Dave. Sorry. I can't help you here."

Wheeler watched him, as if hoping another second of thought might change Jim's mind. Then he settled back in his chair and said, "Okay. I'm sorry too. But I understand."

There was no contempt or even disappointment in his voice. Jim had expected Wheeler to push and was ready to claim he knew nothing about these "alleged" payments. Perhaps Wheeler wanted to spare Jim the ignominy of more lies.

Wheeler twisted around to look again at the bay and low, dusty orange sun. "We'll be over here for a week. Up to Clark and Subic Bay tomorrow, then over to Bangkok and Phnom Penh. Picard and Brown go back, but I'll be in Saigon for a few days. The Caravelle Hotel from the twelfth through the seventeenth. Some business I have to take care of. You ever get to Saigon?"

"Not on this tour of duty." Jim felt Wheeler was telling him where he could be reached if Jim changed his mind.

"Crazy city. Wild. The war's turned it upside down. Tragic but exciting, like a burning house." He shook his head to himself, then smiled at Jim. "I sometimes think I could've stopped it. Pure hubris on my part. But I can't help wondering what would've happened if I'd fought to get those French casualty figures included in a report. You remember that? Around the time we first met."

"I remember some kind of stink about numbers." Jim was unnerved to hear that time in their lives acknowledged. "But I'm sure those figures were available through other channels. And I seriously doubt anyone would've been moved by the beating the French were taking. Look at Dien Bin Phu. No, it's crazy for you to think that."

"You're right. It is crazy. Still, one can't help feeling guilty for not having done more to stop it. And stupid. And cowardly." He looked over his shoulder again at the bay. "The thing was," he told the bay, "I was going through a crisis then. I was too afraid for myself to do what I believed was right. I behaved badly all around. Toward you too.''

''I remember you being—reserved,'' Jim insisted. ''That's all.''

''No, I shut you out completely. I wanted to have nothing to do with you. Or with Lyman Bradford's casualty figures. They were investigating Bradford for homosexuality. That panicked me. I had one bad case of homosexual panic.''

Jim heard the word before he heard what Wheeler was saying with it. ''You—?''

''I liked you and you obviously liked me. I became panicky about myself.'' He was facing Jim again, calmly, matter-of-factly.

Jim laughed, but all that came out was a cough from the back of his dry throat.

''Yes, silly wasn't it? But I was green and prudish. It was a prudish, naive time, unlike this decade. Not until I married Elaine did I become confident about myself and sex, sort out my feelings.'' He stopped and looked hard at Jim: studying his reaction? Remembering *he* wasn't married? What?

''Interesting,'' said Jim. He was too frightened and confused to know what else to say. ''Human psychology.''

Dave nodded. ''But what bothers me most about that crisis was how my panic prevented me from doing what I believed was right. I can't let that happen again.'' He looked yet again at the bay, checking it like a clock. He quickly stood up. ''I better be getting back to the hotel. I promised to have dinner with Picard and Brown. A night in Manila,'' he sighed. ''What do *you* do for fun these days?''

Jim was relieved by Dave falling back into chitchat. ''There's a racquetball court in the basement here,'' he said, standing up to say goodbye. ''You know me. If you're asking how to have a good time tonight, I'm the last person to tell you. I'm surprised one of Marcos's people hasn't tried to set you and your friends up with a little Philippine hospitality,'' he said with a successful laugh.

Dave laughed too. ''They did. Try, I mean. Brown was shocked, Picard tempted. What's the saying here? Three hundred years in a convent, fifty in a brothel?''

''Oh, they exaggerate.''

''Do you partake? In one form or another?'' He grinned harmlessly, but his eyes watched Jim, measuring his reaction.

''No. I don't.''

Dave shook his head, as if at Jim's purity, which was odd coming from a virtuous, happily married man. Then he grabbed Jim's arm just above the elbow. ''I'm glad we talked. Sorry I'm not spending more time in Manila.'' His thumb dug between the bone and bicep, his hand squeezing Jim's muscle. ''But I'll be in Saigon next week if you get over there.''

''I don't think my schedule allows it.''

The brown eyes in the chinks of smile fired a last look into Jim. He released the arm and backed away. "Whatever. I'll let you get on with your work. I know the way out. Take care."

He turned and walked through the office, now full of orange beams and long shadows rising level with the sun peering through the porch windows. His bow-legged swagger showed no trace of defeat or disappointment. Jim watched until Wheeler opened the door at the other end and, in the electric light of the corridor, turned to see if Jim were watching. He grinned goodbye and slowly closed the door.

Jim sat on the edge of the couch. What had happened here? How was one to read this?

Dave Wheeler wanted specifics on the unvouchered funds, that much was clear. He wanted them so badly he had confessed old mistakes and personal fears—grown men shouldn't talk like that. And he wanted Jim to meet him in Saigon, which was confusing and somehow threatening. Jim felt as if Wheeler were telling him to come to Saigon with the data, and he'd go to bed with Jim.

It was an absurd thing to imagine. Jim did not want to have sex with Wheeler. He did not want to have sex with anyone, which was why the feeling threatened him. Yet the feeling was there, planted by Wheeler's easy mention of homosexual panic and the way he had watched Jim and gripped Jim's arm. Maybe he meant to say he knew Jim was homosexual and could blackmail him with that if necessary. Maybe he meant nothing at all and was only being honest. People were sometimes themselves, without ulterior motives, even in the foreign service.

The sun had slipped behind Bataan and another lurid tropical sunset filled the sky, clouds flaring red and pink in the gold light, the vapor trail of a jet in the distance glowing like a strand of copper wire. The colored light poured a ghostly fire into the porch. Jim sat in the silent blaze and reconsidered his decision, wanting to sort out personal fears and imaginings from his desire to do what was right, challenged by his fear of Dave Wheeler. He often made decisions that were difficult to live with, but the most difficult were those he knew he'd made out of fear.

5

Jim took a Saturday afternoon flight from Manila to Saigon. Signing out of the country for the weekend, he claimed he was going to shop for antiques, not as preposterous as it sounded, what with objects from abandoned temples and archaeological sites all over Southeast Asia making their way to the shops and street markets there. Jim knew everyone thought he was going for sex. There were scores of bar girls and prostitutes in Manila, but The Vicar had a reputation to keep and he'd have to go to another country for his semi-annual woman. Such tawdry assumptions only amused Jim and made him feel safer with his secret. Tucked into the side pocket of his blue leather flight bag was a large envelope with the dates of checks paid to Marcos, a list of bank accounts and dummy corporations known to be the president's, and a Xerox of Jim's Eyes Only report on the Philippine government's billing of itself for that engineering battalion.

He carried a superfluity of secrets to make clear to Wheeler he did this not out of personal reasons of fear or friendship—he'd dismissed the sexual angle days ago as subjective nonsense—but because he wanted Marcos exposed. Jim felt good about his decision this afternoon. It was as though he needed to break with his routine of obedience and compromise every few years and *do* something, secret rebellions for the good of his soul. That's what happened when he leaked information to those journalists, twice in Indonesia, once in Thailand: nothing had been achieved, but he'd reestablished his moral credentials with himself. Marcos should be exposed and Wheeler was giving Jim the opportunity to do it. Jim flew over the South China Sea feeling very confident and full of purpose.

"You know what I fucking loved about R&R?" a soldier across the aisle was saying to his buddy. "You know what I fucking loved most about Manila? Toilets, man. Real fucking commodes. First day there, I sat on the pot all afternoon and flushed that sucker, just to feel the spray on my bony ass."

The Boeing 707 was full of G.I.'s returning to Vietnam after a week of Rest and Recreation in Manila, rangy men in gaudy civvies and cropped hair that made them all look like kids with big ears. There were a handful of obvious civilians, with redneck sideburns and guts, and a quartet of longhaired Filipino rock stars off to play the military circuit of clubs and mess halls, but the bulk of passengers were soldiers. They loudly yammered at each other about what a great time they'd had in Manila—modern plumbing and clean beds, but *fucking* was a verb as well as an adjective—and Jim couldn't help feeling sorry for them. He knew only half of them, maybe fewer, were going where there was combat, the rest returning to supply depots, garages and typing pools. But when the plane began its tight spiral downward, an identical, edgy silence fell over everyone.

The enormous jet circled down from the clouds to the airfield, without a long descent over countryside that would've exposed them to gunfire along the coast. There were no glimpses of Vietnam from the air. The country was first seen as one great air base, a criss-cross of runways, tarmac packed with rows of jet fighters, helicopters like gigantic enameled insects, more camouflage patterns of green and brown. All at once, the soldiers resumed their furious chatter as the plane taxied in.

The terminal was a concrete-floored warehouse, mobs of men and a few women crowding Customs, Immigration and the military check-ins. Everywhere were Americans in civvies, khakis and fatigues, outnumbering the Vietnamese travelers and officials four to one, making them look like foreigners in their own country. With his diplomatic visa and passport, Jim was able to hurry through the different stations and grab a cab out front, an old Fiat whose angry Chinese driver insisted on dollars, not piasters, and who refused to understand where Jim wanted to go until he repeated the order in French.

Jim crouched down under the low roof and looked out the open windows on the hot, violent ride to his hotel. Ten years ago, when he first visited here, Saigon still seemed French and civilized: broad avenues and squares lined with tamarind trees, sidewalk cafes, buildings like miniatures of originals in Paris. That city had begun to disappear the last time Jim visited, in 1966, when the American presence had jumped to the first of many peaks. Today the old city was completely buried under crowds of G.I.'s and hustling Vietnamese, ugly storefronts, the din of traffic and blaring radios. It was worse than Manila, which had never seemed civil. Diesel smoke coughed up by two-ton army trucks thickened air already soupy with blue-gray exhaust from frenzied motorcycles. Packs of South Vietnamese soldiers stood off to the sides, grumbling among themselves, short, paranoid and mean-looking. In '59 and even later, Jim had seen pairs of them walking hand in hand around Saigon, an old custom for friends that Jim found funny yet touching, young men holding hands even when they had rifles slung over their shoulders. Now they seemed to ape the macho toughness of their American guests.

The Poste, Telegraphe et Telefon Building opposite the cathedral had a hole punched high in its baroque facade, where the clockface had been, a ragged gap bandaged with cloudy plastic sheeting, damage left over from Tet last year.

The war was everywhere and nowhere. Saigon was part of the war without really being in it. But compared to the feverish energy of emergency here, the corruption of an ally in a nearby backwater seemed trivial. That was why Marcos could get away with so much. Nevertheless, Jim felt foolish, for a moment, as if he and Wheeler chased a loose dog in a village where a mad elephant smashed houses and trampled people. The thing was, they couldn't stop the elephant.

The lobby of the Caravelle Hotel was dark and cool, almost peaceful compared to the street. Three men argued in Swedish over how to load their movie camera. A fat Australian pleaded with a sulky Vietnamese girl in an *ao dai* and blue jeans. A colonel in baggy jungle fatigues demanded, then begged the elegantly dressed desk clerk for a room. Jim had wired ahead four days ago and the clerk said they were expecting him—after Jim slipped the fellow a twenty.

If Wheeler expected Jim to come, he would've checked with the desk to see if they had a reservation for J. Goodall. Sure enough, the desk clerk handed Jim a note along with his key: "Welcome to Dodge City. If you get in before 5, come knock on my door. Room 313. Dave."

The bellboy started up the air conditioner in Jim's stifling room after Jim tipped him five dollars. Jim took off his sopping shirt and stood by the half-cool wheeze of air for a minute, then washed his chest and armpits at the sink and put on a fresh knit shirt. He went downstairs to Room 313, the large envelope in his hand.

He had to knock twice before there was an answer.

"What? Huh? Hold on." The door opened a little and Wheeler's face appeared. He was red-eyed and lopsided, his wet beard crushed on one side. "No. No more photographers. Mr. Potato Head—I mean, Mr. Kissinger and I want to be alone."

"Dave, it's me. Jim Goodall."

"Jim? Oh." Wheeler shook his face and rubbed his eyes. "Jim! Hey!" He smiled, but only half his mouth responded. "Sorry. Was taking a nap and you know how those get in this climate. The craziest dreams. Here. Let me just—" He stepped behind the door and coins jingled as he pulled on some pants. He lightly jumped and snapped something shut. "Come in, come in," he said, his body now squeezed into a new pair of jeans. Denim looked peculiar on someone their age. "Let me get my breath," he apologized and closed the door behind them.

The room was cooler than the hallway, but not by much. The bed was stamped by the wet shadow of a body. Wheeler's chest was hairless and creased with red bedmarks. Jim had never seen him without a shirt.

Wheeler rubbed and slapped a little life into his face. "You made it. Great. Good to see you here, Jim. Uh, what brings you to this part of the world?"

"This." And Jim tossed the envelope on the desk.

That woke Wheeler up completely. He looked at Jim, then snatched up the envelope and sat on the bed. He tore the envelope open, pulled out the sheets and set them on his knees. He took long, unblinking looks at each page, blinked and moved to the next, as if photographing them with his eyes.

Jim folded his arms and leaned his back against the door.

"Damn. This is great," said Wheeler, going through the pages a second time. "This is perfect. If these don't nail him and his believers, there's no God. And we'll be very careful in how we use these, Jim. Nobody'll be able to trace anything back to you."

Jim nodded, feeling a twinge of shame that Wheeler was the one taking the risks. "I'll be curious to see what comes of it, if anything."

Wheeler hauled a suitcase out from under the bed, opened it and looked for a place to put Jim's pages. "I knew you'd come through on this. I knew you'd see it was worth doing, if I gave you some time to think about it. That's why I didn't pressure you or try to use our friendship while I was in Manila. I hope I didn't seem too cold."

"You didn't seem cold. I understood," Jim claimed. "Thanks for respecting my intelligence on this. We both know *something* needs to be done."

"Amen." Wheeler closed a compartment and left the suitcase open on his bed. "So!" He sat up, rubbing his palms against his thighs. "How long you here for?"

"I fly back tomorrow afternoon."

"Hmmm. There's somewhere I've got to be later tonight. But—" He gazed at Jim and hesitated. "We can have dinner together. We can spend some time tomorrow talking, if you don't have anything scheduled."

"Nothing," said Jim. "I was hoping we'd have time to talk."

"Great. Let me take a quick shower and we can go up to the roof for drinks. You ever been to the bar here?"

"Several times."

"Not what it used to be," Wheeler admitted. "But it's quieter than the terrace over at the Continental." He stepped around the corner into the bathroom and turned the shower on, a gurgle followed by an explosive squirt, then the steady spray.

The business of Marcos out of the way, Jim felt much better, unintimidated and in the right, pleased to be with Wheeler and looking forward to conversation. They could be friends again, equals.

Blue jeans hit the sill of the bathroom door, white jockey shorts spilling out. The hiss of water was broken by a body.

"Talked to Elaine this morning," Wheeler called over the shower. "Told her I might see you again. She said to say hi."

"That's nice," Jim said uncomfortably. "Tell her hi for me." In a minute the man would shut off the water and step into the room. The towels were stacked on the desk, the clean clothes in the suitcase on the bed. "Why don't I go on up and make sure we get a table?"

"You can," Wheeler called back. "Although it's too early to be crowded."

"No. I'm thirsty. I'll meet you up there."

Jim felt silly once he was out in the hall. He'd seen hundreds of naked men in locker rooms and showers around the world, without embarrassment or fear, only a friendly, academic interest in how their bodies compared with his. But he did not want to see Wheeler, not now when he was feeling so fond of him and comfortable.

It was good to be up on the roof and outside again, everything simplified to a hot afternoon and the cold ache of beer. The burnt breath of breeze was just enough to cool the coat of perspiration rising on Jim's neck and forehead. A canvas awning shaded the tables outside the bar, an airborne sidewalk café surrounded by a hazy vista of the river, other rooftops and distant hills. There was always a helicopter or string of them cruising over the smoky horizon. The only other people sitting outdoors were a pair of Japanese men, one of them reading Graham Greene, the other a Sergeant Rock comic book, and the fat Australian from the lobby, now accompanied by three Vietnamese girls. The girls chattered among themselves while the Australian glumly looked on. "Love Is Blue" played through the bar's loudspeaker, screening out the street and traffic noise below, reducing the constant sound of helicopters to a steady thumping, dogs wagging their tails against a floor.

"There. Feel wide awake now," said Wheeler, joining Jim at his table. His hair was wet and combed, his beard fizzed out and airy again, a pink sports shirt snugly hugging his chest. He wore mirrored sunglasses, which took some getting used to, and a big triumphant grin. "I'll have a vodka-tonic," he told the long-faced waiter. "And another beer for my pal. Looks like Los Angeles out there, doesn't it?" he told Jim. "You'd hardly know there was a war going on."

That started them talking about the war. They didn't argue but talked much as they had in Phnom Penh six years ago, trying out their opinions on each other, neither of them threatened when the other disagreed. Both worked from the unspoken assumption the United States should never have gotten involved in the first place. Jim believed there was nothing for them to do now but get out as gracefully as possible, what Nixon had proposed after his trip to the Far East when he announced the first troop withdrawals. Wheeler believed they should get out immediately, but only because it was too late to do what they should've done ten years ago: seize complete control of the government, overhaul the country from top to bottom—land reform, decent education, everything—and not give it back to the Vietnamese until they were ready for it, the way the British had with their colonies.

"You've become an Anglophile in your old age?" Jim charged with a smile.

Wheeler grimaced. "They made their mistakes, too. But I think their imperialism was more honest than ours, where we 'respect' our clients' autonomy. Which only means we support whatever shitheel happens to be in power.''

A moral rigor flavored all Wheeler's beliefs. Jim enjoyed hearing his point of view, which was fresh, unafraid of contradiction or foolishness. Wheeler not only sympathized with the war protests at home, he admired the protesters.

''I like their honesty, their clarity about things. Yes, they're naive, but we need a little naiveté again. Our generation is so bound up in complexity and irony we can't do a damn thing but go along with the machine. We become cogs in the system, ironic cogs maybe, but cogs nevertheless.''

''You talk like—what's the name of that book? *Greening of America.*''

Wheeler laughed. ''I read that. Silly book, but its heart is in the right place. No, I greened myself on my own. Through other channels.'' His grin was back, bent around a secret.

''Next you'll tell me you've dropped acid and seen God,'' Jim teased.

''No, not drugs. And definitely not God. But something new that's helped me cut through all the crap.''

Unable to see Wheeler's eyes, only his own skeptical glance doubled in the sunglasses, Jim couldn't tell if Wheeler were serious or mocking him back.

Wheeler grinned while he looked around—the tables nearest theirs were empty—then leaned forward on his elbows as if he were going to confess something dirty. Instead he said, ''You can tell me to go to hell, Goodall. But there's this question I have to ask you.''

''Yes?'' The two anamorphic Jims nervously squinted back at him.

''Are you gay?''

Jim had almost felt it coming. He was thrown, but not shocked, excited beneath his sudden coldness.

''Sorry. I forgot—'' Wheeler lifted the little mirrors up to his forehead. ''I forgot I was hiding behind these.'' The look in his eyes was gentle and interested, not at all accusing. ''Are you? Homosexual,'' he said softly.

Jim didn't know how they had gotten here. He was annoyed to be here, yet surprisingly relieved that someone—no, Wheeler in particular—at long last asked him that question. ''I think so,'' he said, and was frightened by his boldness. He quickly amended it to, ''I have that side emotionally. I think many men do.''

Wheeler smiled down at the table. ''Can I ask what *you* do for sex?''

''Nothing,'' said Jim. He felt taunted by the *you* and uncomfortable realizing a married man wouldn't understand this. ''There's that side to me. But I'm not that way. I don't believe in sodomy.''

''Do you have a heterosexual side?''

Jim pretended he had to think about it. ''I don't think so.''

''But you've never been to bed with a man?''

''Not really.''

Wheeler almost laughed. "What's that mean? Kind of? A little bit pregnant?"

"You know. Guys get drunk in college. Horseplay gets out of hand."

There'd been that veteran at U. Mass who misunderstood an undergraduate's friendliness, got drunk with the boy and wrestled with him, out of their clothes and into bed. Jim was astonished to remember it again, completely forgotten until he defensively tossed it at Wheeler. It was the heat and the beer, and things held back for so long had grown tangled together; Jim couldn't extract one piece without others following. He grew more embarrassed and annoyed.

"Kid stuff," he insisted. He covered his embarrassment with a laugh. "What made you bring this up anyway? If it has something to do with your— panic umpteen years ago, let me just say I never tried anything with you. I didn't. There was nothing I wanted to try."

Wheeler only smiled at his drink, looking quite pleased with himself.

There was a rumble in the distance, which could be thunder or might be an air strike in Cambodia, a hundred miles away. Jim used the look he gave the hills to check out the other tables and make sure there was still nobody close enough to hear what these two duffers discussed.

When he turned back to Wheeler, he found him still smiling sheepishly at his glass. The sunglasses on his forehead reflected two overlapping patches of sky. Another helicopter flew overhead, passing through one lens, then both, then the other, like a thought.

"I brought this up," said Wheeler, "because I have a side. That wants to be close to men."

"There," Jim instantly said. "Many men do and they don't express it in sex." But he knew that wasn't what Wheeler was saying.

He lifted his eyes to Jim. "I've found that's the best way to express it."

"You're bullshitting me. You're married."

"I am. And I love Elaine very much. But there's a side of me that needs to be with men. I've learned I function better if I swing a little."

Jim was excited, frightened, appalled. He felt very smart and very stupid simultaneously, having suspected all along something like this about Wheeler, yet refusing to believe it could be anything more than his own nervous imagination. He took refuge in the cold hard layer of disapproval that covered his emotions. "You cheat on your wife."

"I don't think of it as cheating. It's only sex. I rarely see anyone a second time and never a third. And I never do anything except when I'm overseas. Stateside, I'm the most faithful of husbands. You see, I love Elaine in the particular, and men in general. Doing both completes me."

"Does Elaine know how complete you are?"

Wheeler sighed. "No. I should tell her. I do feel bad about that. I think she's smart and tough enough to understand. But it's been good for our marriage. I always return from my trips abroad more affectionate and loving

than ever." He watched the changing shades of feeling on Jim's face, suddenly laughed and said, "C'mon, Jim. You've been around. I'm not the first
happily married FSO you've met with a secret life abroad. Or the first bisexual one either, I wager."

"No. You're not," said Jim. "But I can't say I respect the ones I've met.
The closet cases, I mean." He'd known several admirable men who cheated
on their wives with women, which confused Jim's system of values. But he
had no mixed feelings about the econ officer in Bangkok who visited the boy
bars regularly, or the deputy chief of mission in Jakarta who flew off for a
week in Ceylon with a homesick Peace Corps volunteer. "They always seem
to be yes-men, careful and conservative, unwilling to stick their necks out.
Either because they're afraid or because their secret gives them all the excitement they can handle."

"Do I seem like a yes-man?" said Wheeler.

"No. You don't," Jim admitted. "You're certainly sticking your neck out
on this other matter."

"I am. In part because of my sex life. Following my instincts there has
made me trust my instincts on more important things. And I've learned not to
sweat the small stuff. All right, maybe that means I'm immoral in my private
life. But it's helped me be more moral in public life."

"Small stuff?" said Jim. "Call me old-fashioned, but—" He shook his
head, more at himself than at Wheeler.

"Is your personal life really as squeaky-clean as you say, Jim?"

"Something make you think it isn't?"

"No. Except you seem to have become a bit careful and conservative."

Jim stiffened at having his own words thrown back at him. "You think I've
turned into a yes-man?"

"Not really, Jim. Not yet anyway." He gave Jim a long sympathetic look.
"A man can short-circuit in our line of work, all alone with his ideas, other
people's opinion of him and paranoia. You have an outside line—a ground, as
it were, that happens to lead to men. I think you're crazy not to use it."

"I use it. Without going to bed with anyone."

"You don't use it. It only gets in the way. That's what happened to me, not
only with that mess with Bradford, but again and again after that. Until I
found how easy the sex could be. And simple. And fun. You take all these
complicated desires and fears, roll them into a ball and—" He laughed as
giddily as a kid. He grabbed his drink, threw his head back to finish it and
came up grinning. He leaned forward again, covering Jim with his grin and
eyes.

Jim had to look into one black pupil, then the other, streaks of brown iris
tensing as they screwed tighter.

"I think you should express this side you have." An intimate, medicinal
gust of vodka. "You've helped me. I want to do something for you."

Go to bed with him? The idea had been there all along, waiting only for Jim to fall into it. There was panic, a rush of thoughts, the absurdness of doing something with Elaine's husband, Janey's father. What could they do? One of them would sodomize the other, the only act Jim could imagine between two men, either unclean or painful, the line he refused to cross. Ever since he resigned himself to homosexuality, Jim Goodall's final justification for celibacy had been his fear of sodomy. He was not being rhetorical when he told Wheeler he didn't believe in it.

"This thing I'm going to tonight," said Wheeler. "It's a party. I want you to go with me."

And the panic instantly stopped. Jim took a deep breath. "What kind of party?"

"Men like us. Like me anyway. I think it'd be good for you."

"Why?"

Wheeler laughed. "I don't know. Maybe I just want to have an old friend along. Maybe I want you to see you're not alone. I almost invited you downstairs, but I had to feel you out first and make sure. Well, knowing what I know now, I think it's a matter of grave importance I take you."

"A party of . . . pansies?"

"Wrong word for this bunch. Few fellows from the international community, some civilians, probably some servicemen. You seem to have the wrong idea of what kind of people share your inclinations."

Jim was so relieved this was all Wheeler wanted that he pretended to consider. "I don't know, Dave. I think I'd better pass."

"What else will you do tonight? Stay holed up in your room?"

"I'll think of something." But Jim realized he'd spend the night wondering what Wheeler was doing, imagining cruel and horrible mysteries in place of the obnoxious chitchat that was all that went on at any party.

"Nobody's going to bite," said Wheeler, almost reading Jim's mind. "And nobody's going to tattle on you either. They have their own asses to cover."

"It's not that. I just see no point in going somewhere I don't belong."

Wheeler leaned back and sighed, ready to give up on him. "What are you afraid of, Jim?"

"Nothing." He was hit in his most vulnerable spot. More important, he suddenly felt left out, excluded. It was a foolish thing to feel, but Jim did not want to let timidity and prudence exclude him from Wheeler's company tonight, no matter how much he disapproved of what the man was doing. Denied or spared the obligation of going to bed with him, Jim needed to glimpse Wheeler in this other life. "Oh, all right. I'll go."

"Yes?"

"If it's so damn important to you," Jim muttered. "Why not?"

"Good. Great. I knew you'd come around." Wheeler grinned yet again. "No. It'll be good for you. And fun. For both of us."

* * *

THEY LEFT DRESSED as they were, first to an American-style steakhouse on Tu Do Street around the corner from the hotel, eating home fries and broiled meat that may have been water buffalo, horse or even beef. Wheeler spoke critically of Prince Sihanouk for his policy of placating both Communists and Americans in Cambodia. Jim defended the man, but this time their disagreement took on an angry edge, a strained personal quality. Only now did Jim feel anything like anger with Wheeler, not for inflicting his new life on Jim, nor for what he'd done to Jim many years ago, but for his contemptuous views on Norodom Sihanouk.

The street at night was like the inside of a pinball machine, full of flashing lights, colliding pedestrians and pedocyclists ringing their bells. Wheeler commandeered a cab and they drove out of the nebula of carbon monoxide and neon toward the Cercle Sportif, the old French sporting grounds, and out past that to an old residential pocket of walled villas and poplar trees. Not until then did Jim ask, "Will you be, uh, going home with anyone tonight?"

"No. Not tonight."

The cab let them out at an iron gate in a stucco wall that would've been a back entrance in America. All wealth was turned inward here. They walked through a little courtyard to a polished oak door. Everything felt peaceful and civilized, quaintly European, with only the eternal Asian fragrance of sickly flowers and fermenting garbage to place them on a different continent.

Wheeler bounced a little on the balls of his feet after he rang the doorbell. "Relax," he told Jim. "You'll have a good time. I promise."

The door was opened by a Vietnamese boy with a white jacket and perfect triangle of chin and cheekbones. His smile was full of white, faintly concave teeth.

"*Nhut! Bon soir!*" Wheeler clasped the boy by the shoulder and introduced him to "*Mon ami,* Jim."

The boy shyly bowed and told them Georges and the others were in the back and all would be "beautified" by the arrival of Dave and his friend—Jim couldn't tell if it were the boy's French or his own that made it sound strange.

"Georges is our host," Wheeler explained as they followed the boy down a dim hallway, past a little Corot hung over a table with several household Buddhas. "Wife died five years ago. Son of a rubber baron. One of those French colonials time forgot, more French than the French."

But up ahead was the muffled sound of an electric guitar, jangly chords joined by the thudding of a drum, and a room full of electric green light. Watery light rippled in webs and washes over the ceiling and upper walls of a dark, empty living room, almost twitching in time to the music outside. Sliding glass doors looked out on an illuminated swimming pool, a rectangle of creamy green brightness. The boy gracefully gestured at the pool and glided to the right, leaving the Americans to stand and stare.

The pool was full of people. The sofas and chairs inside were covered with clothes: shirts and slacks and army khakis in discrete heaps, as if their wearers had suddenly disappeared, bodies popping like soap bubbles. The pool was just ten yards outside the glass and verandah but, confused by expectations and tan lines, Jim had to look again before he decided the men out there were naked.

"Damn," said Wheeler. "Impatient crowd tonight. Couldn't keep their pants on."

Jim angrily turned on him. "You *knew* this would happen? What kind of monstrosity did you bring me to? Is this an orgy?"

"Sometimes," Wheeler admitted and guiltily turned away. "Usually nothing happens until much later. I figured you'd be comfortable or gone by then."

Jim felt tricked, betrayed. "Why the hell didn't you tell me it might be like this?"

Wheeler began to lose his temper. "Because you're such a prig I knew you wouldn't come."

"Damn right I wouldn't! Why the hell did you need me here, Wheeler? You feel some perverse need to drag me down to your level of barnyard abominations?"

But instead of losing his temper, Wheeler only sighed and shook his head. "I don't get you, Goodall. You're really the Sunday-school teacher you pretend to be? All right. My mistake. I thought you'd drop your act once we were here. But if it's not an act, if you're really the sexless old lady you say you are, I'm not going to fight you." He sat on a silky striped sofa next to a pile of fatigues with sergeant's stripes and began to untie his sneakers. "You can get Nhut to call you a cab."

"You're joining them?"

"I always do. They look like a friendly group tonight."

Jim looked again, looking longer when he saw nothing sordid. Nobody appeared to be doing anything yet. It was the throbbing, shouting music that suggested wild abandon. A half dozen men stood waist-deep in water at one end with drinks in their hands, talking and laughing. A stocky fellow swam the length of the pool in a leisurely side stroke, his genitals a dark bud in the wrinkle of water. A long thin boy suddenly hoisted himself out of the bright pool, baring a white bottom before he climbed into the shadows. The servant who'd met them at the door was outside now, cut glass decanters in each hand, his clothes making everyone else look naked and obscene. He stood above the talkers, leaning over the water and light to refill the glasses they held up to him. Lit from below, he looked like a butler in hell.

One of the damned, a balding man with a mustache and silvery chest, turned away to lift his drink and wave at the living room.

"Somebody's seen us," said Jim.

"Georges. A very nice guy." Wheeler had his shirt off. He stood, hands wedged against his hips, pulling everything down until he twisted one foot and then the other out of the snarled legs. A bare ass in profile was only a continuation of thigh. There was a slight pad of stomach above his penis and baggy testicles.

Jim could not remember why the thought of seeing Wheeler like this had worried him that afternoon.

He faced Jim with hands on his hips, his weight on one leg, cool and unashamed. The beard intensified his nudity, an impatient grimace disowned it. "Are you going or staying?"

The fear was gone, but there was no desire either. All that remained was the aggravation of feeling challenged. "I'll stay. Go ahead. I'll join you."

"Fine." Wheeler received the change of mind without surprise or satisfaction. He pulled on the sliding glass door. The recorded music outside was unmuffled as the singer hollered, "No place for a street-fighting man!" before Wheeler hauled the door shut again. He moved toward the pool, breaking into a springy run for a few steps as he raised his hand hello. Every gesture seemed slightly exaggerated or in quotes when the person was naked. His buttocks lightly shimmied before one cheek flexed and squared itself as he dipped a foot in the water. He dropped in and waded toward the host.

What are you doing? Jim thought while he pried off his shoes. He had committed himself. He could not leave now without losing face, an appropriate attitude for an American in Vietnam, but beneath that was his feeling of being challenged, and an obligation to test himself with this experience. The taboos and boundaries that meant so much to him in the abstract seemed like timid excuses for doing nothing when the experience itself lay just beyond the glass. It would be a bad experience, a visit to hell, but he needed to submit to it for the sake of his pride and education, just as he submitted to the experience of corruption in other countries. He would not do anything that would hurt anyone, he promised himself. He could handle their hurting him.

He undressed quickly, angrily tossing his clothes on a chair. He noticed captain's bars on a fatigue shirt; there was an officer out there. Nothing in the civilian clothes suggested who those people might be, although a couple of skimpy panties like colored rubber bands said there were Europeans present. He was afraid he'd get a hard-on when he pulled off his shorts—his body frequently behaved with a mind of its own—but he remained soft and numb and had to give himself a tug before he faced the door. He rubbed his stomach to assure himself he was flatter than Wheeler. *In the destructive element immerse,* he thought, and opened the door.

The music was loud, the night air warm. He did not look at anyone as he crossed to the pool and jumped in feet first.

His feet instantly hit bottom. The pool was the same shallow depth from one end to the other. Jim recovered and felt himself clothed in mild water from the waist down. He glanced around and noticed figures noticing him. With knees bent so the water was up to his chest, he moonwalked toward the corner where Wheeler stood with their host and others. The water felt pleasant and familiar pressing around him, until the unfamiliar absence of anything binding his middle caught up with Jim and he realized he was all of one piece from head to toe. Even as a boy at the Y he'd always worn a suit.

"Ah. And here is our new friend, Jim?" The balding man with the mustache held out his hand from his position in the very corner, men standing against the pool walls on either side of him. "I'm Georges. A warm welcome to you."

Jim had to stand to shake hands with him. Seeing the others, he saw the water didn't hide anything, but displayed it like a great illuminated lens. All around him little anemones floated in beds of hair.

"It's a pleasure to be here, sir. Thank you."

"Not at all. The pleasure is all mine. I'm so glad you could come."

"You have a lovely house and grounds." Instead of hell, Jim found himself engaged in the old ceremony of courtesies, protocol without pants, like the bad dream of a foreign service freshman.

"You're too kind. One does what one can in this age. What're you drinking?"

"Beer?"

Wheeler laughed. "No, no. Give him scotch, a double scotch to loosen him up," he told the servant standing above them. Wheeler grinned at Jim, elbows parked on the white tiles painted with blue dragons, ankles crossed on the pale green floor.

"I must introduce you to my dear friends," Georges announced. "Phil. Vitold. Tony—I resist the temptation to call you Antoine like the saint. Soren. Luc. And Spike."

There were no handshakes, only nods, a couple of smiles and a few glances downward. With no last names, titles or jobs to give anyone an identity, they were only bodies, each split at the waist with heads and torsos shadows of what was bright and wavering underwater. Phil and Tony had army-short hair and redneck tans, just their faces and arms. The Europeans were tanned all over, except the graphic strips around their middles. Vitold must be Polish—he had a blond prizefighter face—and Jim wanted to ask if he were with the Communist bloc delegation from the U.N. He would've liked to talk about that, although the friendly bovine looks Vitold gave each speaker suggested he knew no English.

"Here you go," said Georges, passing Jim a large amber scotch. "Bottoms up."

Jim politely smiled, took a burning swallow and hurried to the wall beside Wheeler. That put him on the far end of the triangle and he felt safer standing by someone he knew. The alcohol unlocked his thoughts enough for him to worry how it would start and when.

There was sudden silence; then the music started up again.

"Fooking magic," said Spike. "I love the Dead."

The sideburned Brit—journalist? engineer?—referred to the new record now thumping and twanging through the speakers on the verandah. That started people talking about music, with Georges confessing he bought the most *au courant* in rock because his guests seemed to expect it. He preferred Edith Piaf and Streisand.

There were another six or seven men scattered around the pool—two sat side by side at the other end, sharing a cigarette that must be a joint—and Jim wondered if it would begin out there. Maybe these were the old men in this corner, although nobody looked as old as Jim felt, not even Georges, whose whiskers were tipped with white. Without trousers to give him a waist or paunch, George's middle-aged pursiness was indistinguishable from Tony's layer of baby fat. Tony must be army, but he had to be a clerk typist or something safe and sedentary. Phil too, or else he wouldn't be here, although Phil was short and sinewy, angrily biting the ice in his glass while the others chatted about music.

"Donovan is my fave," Tony announced, a shyly feminine turn to his voice and posture, his pretty face disguised by an anemic mustache.

"He might be fun to fuck," Phil grumbled. "So long as the wuss didn't sing to you afterwards." Phil's accent was half southern, half army.

Nhut kept reappearing overhead to refill glasses.

Out beyond the pool was a lawn, faintly lit by two smudge pots on poles whose scent of kerosene and incense seemed to keep the mosquitos away. Around the lawn was a coal-black wall of trees and ferny foliage, where Jim imagined a baffled Viet Cong sat watching this scene. It required an effort to remember there was a war out there. Closer to the pool stood a card table, with bottles of liquor and a silver tray full of jars and tubes. Out in the grass was the incongruous slab of a large bare American mattress.

Jim's hand underwater was lightly gripped by another hand, a smaller hand that gave Jim's palm a reassuring squeeze.

Dave Wheeler was smirking at Jim, as if to say, "See? This isn't so bad."

Dave had gripped Jim's hand many times, but in handshakes. Just the change of angle and the context gave touch an entirely different meaning. Jim nodded and gently withdrew his hand. He weighed the thought of doing something with Wheeler and found neither fear nor desire there, the emotional weight of the man dispersed by the presence of these other bodies. There was no desire in Wheeler's look and smirk either, just friendly concern. They were two boys standing with other boys on one side of a room at a dance, everyone working up enough nerve to approach the girls across the floor. Jim's chief feelings were an anxiety over making a fool of himself, and curiosity about what Dave would do. Maybe nobody would do anything. The longer they stood out here, the less sexual nakedness became.

There were yelps and thrashing out in the pool.

Everyone turned to look, erotic expectations and nerves springing out.

One man climbed another out there, wrapping his legs around a head. Then he rose against the flickering green ghost of the house, and Jim saw they were mounted for a chicken fight; another pair of men rose out of the water beside them. There were sighs and snickers here in the corner.

"Real nice," muttered Phil. "Like skinny-dip night at summer camp. I told you it was too damn early for a *debriefing*, Georges. Now everybody's too damn comfortable to start anything."

Georges shrugged. "One must be patient, Phil. And it is so pleasant to watch the boys and anticipate combinations. Later maybe I will turn out the light." He told the others in French that their bantam rooster was getting restless.

"Well, I can't just stand here twiddling my pubic hair," Phil said, setting his glass on the tiled curb. "I got to be back out at My Tho by oh-six hundred. Vitold, old buddy?" He put an arm around the shoulders of the tall man beside him, and his hand on the furry blond stomach. "I been looking at your Commie dick for the past half hour and it's getting old. Let's see if we can put a bone in it."

A drink still in his hand, Vitold passively looked down at the fingers combing and squeezing him a few inches underwater. Everyone looked at the penis and hand jumping back and forth in the shifting lenses of water. Jim felt himself thicken a little, as if the hand were touching him.

His stolid expression never changing, Vitold finished his drink and parked the glass behind him. He wrapped his arms around Phil, put a hand on Phil's ass and kissed him hard on the mouth.

It looked hideous, exciting and simple, all at once.

"Some enchanted evening!" a voice loudly sang out in the pool and there were the splashes of people coming in for a closer look.

Tony watched the kissing men, too fascinated to notice Georges gathering him up and kissing him from behind. More glasses clinked on the tiles and Spike swam out toward someone who'd caught his eye. Soren and Luc crowded in around Tony, helping Georges lay the smiling boy out on his back in the water, exploring him with their hands. And Dave Wheeler stepped away from the side, grinning mischievously over his shoulder at Jim before he faced Vitold and Phil, then the feeding frenzy around Tony, then all around the pool, looking for a party he wanted to join.

Frightened and excited, attention and nerves firing in all directions, Jim did the first thing that came to mind: he plunged behind Wheeler and threw both arms around him. He wanted to dunk the man or toss him or anything a kid automatically does when roughhousing in the water. But when he had Dave's back against his chest, and felt warm skin pressing his bare middle, Jim's body went blank.

"There. Glad now you changed your mind?" Dave whispered, leaning back into Jim's embrace. His arms were pinned against his sides at the elbow, but there was room for Dave to reach behind him with both hands and touch Jim's bottom, as casually as touching a shoulder or patting a back.

Jim was too excited to answer, an adrenaline excitement that was all in his nerves, not the skin or muscle, an excitement like fear that paralyzed and numbed him. His arms gripped Dave to hold himself up. He had never held anyone so still for so long, only formal embraces at state functions, brief hugs of female relatives, and angrily twisting wrestling matches in high school. His body knew only how to crush Dave's chest or get him in a headlock, muscles and bones suddenly angry with this man who'd been so righteous fifteen years ago and now cheated on his wife. Their nakedness seemed beside the point, until Jim looked over Dave's shoulder and saw a thick thimbled finger bobbing in front of him.

"There's a dental technician here who's absolutely gorgeous," said Dave, still glancing around.

Jim saw the Pole and the soldier squirming against each other while they kissed. He saw a head covering Tony's crotch while other heads covered the kid's face and chest, the boy wiggling and sighing as if being nibbled to death. Jim didn't want to do any of that, but knew he should do something, knew he and Wheeler looked like old fools just standing in the middle of an orgy. His mouth brushed a cartilaginous flower deep inside his focus, an ear, and Jim resisted an angry urge to bite it. His hand touched the pad of stomach that felt more muscular than it had looked indoors, then a loose thatch of buoyant hair and, when Dave didn't stop him, an erection. It felt like a stiff stick of warm rubber in his fist, with none of the disturbing pleasure he experienced inside his own skin whenever he clutched that shape. He didn't have that shape himself now, was too excited to feel anything of his own except adrenaline, fear and arrested anger.

Dave laughed. "Not a good idea, Jim. You can do better than me here. And we know each other too well." His hands playfully drummed Jim's ass. The left hand came forward and stuck itself between them. "See? You feel likewise. It'd be like necking with your brother."

The poke and crawl of fingers aggravated Jim's helplessness, a doctor's examination that made him feel his body was no longer private but this vulnerable, public thing. He released Dave and stepped back.

Dave turned around, grinning sheepishly. Jim was embarrassed to look him in the face after holding his dick. This was his colleague, Elaine's husband, Janey's father. Wheeler was right: they knew each other too well and there were too many emotions here.

"You need fresh blood," Dave cheerfully told him. "Who can I pair you with? You like them young? Closer to our age? Beefy, thin, what?"

"I can take care of myself, thank you." Jim fought against his anger. He didn't trust it, thought it might be a reflex of his body which knew only how to wrestle or play tennis and racquetball, activities that required a certain amount of fight.

"You'll be all right on your own?" said Dave, watching someone over Jim's shoulder.

"I'll be fine. Go screw a dentist. Have fun."

Dave laughed, patted Jim on the chest and eagerly waded past him.

Skin and nerves no longer touched, Jim waited for his body to become solid again, something more than this electrified net of panic and confusion. Lungs refilling with air as if he'd held his breath the whole time he held Wheeler, Jim stepped back to the side of the pool, intending to climb out. But he had no body to climb out with. The excitement in his nerves still disconnected him from his body.

When he could look again, he saw Wheeler on the other side of the pool, gazing up at a muscular square-jawed man who stood on the curb with his feet apart. He didn't look like a dentist; he looked like Sergeant Rock in the comic books and took swigs from a cut-glass decanter of liquor he held in one hand, the other hand stroking himself—male nudity was ugly with a length of hose sticking out of it. When Wheeler said something to him, the man set the decanter down and slipped into the water. He immediately took Wheeler in his arms, Wheeler wrapping his legs around the man's waist and the two of them rubbed face and beard together.

Jim did not feel disgusted or indignant—or jealous either. Abandoned by his own body here, he felt foolish, a wallflower, a failure. He did not want to do anything with Wheeler, but he felt shamed by him, beaten and outdone as if this were a game of tennis.

Bare feet slapped behind Jim; a new body leaped from the dark and splashed in the light. A slim arrow of black Asian hair and solid tan stood up a few feet away and Jim's first thought was that the Viet Cong he'd imagined watching from the bushes had become so excited he stripped and joined them. But it was the servant, Nhut, who'd shed his clothes and now coolly surveyed the guests, as if to see who needed to be waited on. When his friendly eyes fell on him, Jim instantly raised his hand to signal he was fine. Nhut nodded and glided over to Phil and Vitold, who promptly drew him into their embrace with strokes and kisses until, like a cell dividing, Phil and Nhut went one way —Jim wanted to be pleased a G.I. and a Vietnamese could get on so well together—while Vitold drifted over to Georges and the others as they tenderly carried Tony up the pool steps to the dark lawn and out to the American mattress. Jim's ability to judge and condemn was in suspension, like his body, as if he'd lost his right to judge Wheeler or anyone else because he couldn't get an erection.

A body burst from the water and Jim's heart jumped into his throat.

"Isn't this great! Isn't this fan-fucking-tastic!" demanded a wild-eyed boy with a brick-red face and white chest. His ears stuck out and he was lean, almost skeletal, catching his breath while he stared down at Jim in the water. His own erection wagged in front of him, an extra bone sticking out of his boniness. "What the hell. You got a minute?" he said, pushing Jim against the wall as if he had something to tell him.

Jim set the butts of his palms on the tiles behind him, ready to escape the pool.

"It's the principle of the thing," said the boy, grabbing Jim's hips. He took a deep breath and dropped down, squatting on the bottom with his hands on Jim's waist, his crewcut head awash like a flooded lawn. There was a soft tickle, then a warmer, harder wetness nibbled Jim's nerves.

His hands gripped the embossed tiles. The excruciating sensation continued for several seconds, a mush of tongue and nick of tooth pulling at him there. Finally the mouth let go and the boy leaped to his feet, water cascading down his closed eyes and lewd, blubbery smile.

"Thanks," said Jim, turning to the side in case the boy wanted to try again.

"Thought I could get you hard again but I guess you popped already and it's the principle of the thing, the principle, man! I'm putting my mouth around each and every cock here tonight!" the boy crowed. "Just for a taste. Make up for those miles of cock I never sucked in fucking high school or Danang. Cocksucking is the greatest. I don't care what the other fuckers say."

His jaw was askew and his pupils pulsing; the kid seemed to be high on something, but here he was, a naked body beside Jim with no emotional history or personal connection. He wasn't attractive either—big ears and a skinny body tanned in zones like a two-color map of Central America—but Jim had to see what he could do if he set his mind to it. He had to prove to himself he was not completely helpless.

The boy was glancing around in search of his next victim.

Jim placed his hands on the boy's shoulders—touching was less disturbing than being touched. He squeezed the back of a neck and stroked a birdcage chest.

The boy took a moment to understand what was happening. "Yeah? You don't look so bad either, big fella. Pitstop!" He fell against Jim and put his arms around him.

Jim fought the disturbance of being touched by touching harder. It was all hands and brain, Jim desperately groping a stranger to prove he could do something, straining to give pleasure when he couldn't take it. The boy opened and wrapped his legs around Jim's waist—the way Wheeler had his partner—and Jim could almost pretend they ineptly wrestled, until the boy tried to kiss him. Jim closed his teeth against the kiss and pushed his face past the mouth. They had slowly turned around and Jim could see the other side of the pool, where Sergeant Rock sat on the curb with the back of a man's head between his legs.

Dave Wheeler could do that? That was still Wheeler over there. Jim was shaken, intimidated, turning his back to the sight yet feeling he should do something for the rubbery hardness pressed against his stomach. One hand under a bony ass, Jim hoisted the boy out of the water to the side of the pool, feeling shamed into trying that. Level with his face and seen without reading glasses, genitals were unreal, hair and testicles hanging out as if the skin had been popped open by the erection sticking up like a broken mainspring. If Wheeler could do that, and this kid had too, then Jim felt he should.

"Yeah, my turn," said the boy.

Jim thought he could, pretending he bent down to suck the thumb of the fist that held yet another dick. This kid was nobody to Jim. All chlorinated skin and hair smelled identical. But when Jim had it in his mouth—a slender cylinder whose only distinction was a ding like a grain of sand against his tongue—nausea filled his throat and circled his eyes. He felt sick the way he had as a child when his grandfather forced him to eat steamed cabbage. It was a bizarre association, but Jim could almost smell cabbage steam, a sickly green odor of helpless disgust, his body revolting not against the warm tube in his mouth but against the memory of cabbage. He strained to get past that sensation, something in him expecting to enjoy this if only he could get around the memory. But his adrenaline nerves had resolved themselves into a body again, and the body was full of cabbage and nausea. Jim stretched his jaw open and emptied his mouth.

"Don't stop now, man," the boy gasped, grabbing Jim's head with both hands.

Jim angrily shook the hands off. "I don't do that. I can't. Sorry." He breathed deeply, trying to exhale the dead cabbage, unable to look at the boy's face.

"Shee-it." The boy began to laugh. "I don't get it with some of you people. Here we are, all queering away, but there's things too queer for some guys to do. Like eating cock. I say, if you're over the line, man, anything goes. *Anything*." He gave the whole business a philosophical sigh, then dropped back into the water. "No sweat. This was just to recharge my batteries. I'll get *beaucoup* blowjobs before tonight's over, and taste every dick in the house while I'm at it. Peace, old man." He actually gave Jim the peace sign, slapped him on the back and waded away.

Jim bent over, dipping his face in the water and rubbing it, trying to wash the nausea from his eyelids. He took a mouthful of metallic water and swirled it with his tongue before spitting it out. He turned his back to the pool and faced the darkness, elbows on the tiles, head in his hands, still breathing deeply. The mind was such a strange place: translucent green and yellow flakes of cooked cabbage. He was an adult and ate cabbage now, as well as eel, fish heads and iguana. He knew this was bound up in some way with his grandfather, an emblem or signal from the dead man who now sat in Jim's skin and entrails. Jim did not know what to do with that knowledge.

The music stopped. There was nobody left on the verandah to start the stereo up again. The lap of water and clatter of insects were clearer than the moans and whispers underneath. Somebody laughed.

Jim looked. There were still men in the pool, but not nearly as many as before, and the lapping water sounded like sex, but Jim saw only people watching other people. No, the boy who'd been with Jim now nuzzled the center of the Pole who lounged jadedly on the pool steps, a king on his throne. Two worm-pink bodies lay up on the side, forming not just a beast with two backs but one with a pair of legs at each end. There were figures out on the lawn. Dave Wheeler was nowhere in sight, unless he were part of the angular shape wrestling with itself like live Hindu sculpture on the mattress under the smudge pots. A string of loud, melodramatic groans was followed by mock applause and a taunting, "Take it like a man!"

Jim wanted to be disgusted. He wanted to take his self-disgust and turn it outward, use it as proof that this behavior was immoral and wrong. But he could convince himself only that it was wrong for him, especially when his body felt so weak and disconnected. He climbed out of the water into air and gravity.

He limped back to the verandah where he found a stack of towels and slowly dried himself off. He'd been celibate for too long, he told himself. He'd outlived sex, outgrown the opportunity and threat of it. That was for the best, he told himself. Homosexual attachments were difficult enough without the intimate messiness of sex involved. He wasn't a sexual person and had been a fool to let the situation and his fear of exclusion sweep him along tonight. Well, now he knew who he was and could confidently go on with his celibate life. At least he'd tried. Nobody could say he hadn't tried. His grandfather insisted little Jimmy did not have the right to reject steamed cabbage until he'd eaten an entire serving of it, no matter how sick it made him.

The air-conditioning inside was cold and Jim dressed quickly among the clothes of more sexual men. He still felt naked when he was dressed; clothes did not feel as important as they once were. There were those captain bars again. Jim had no idea whom that might've been and would have to ask Dave. He decided he'd wait for Dave, hoping that talking with him and expressing disapproval for what happened here tonight might help Jim recover his old moral strength. It was wrong what these men were doing. It *was*. Jim wanted to feel proud he had failed, but his strongest feeling was relief that he'd failed with a complete stranger and not with Dave Wheeler. That would've been too shaming.

His throat and mouth were dry and he needed something to drink. He couldn't go back outside now; there was nothing but alcohol out there anyway. He went through the door where Nhut had disappeared when they first arrived and followed a light on the other side of a darkened dining room into a large French-style kitchen. Copper pans hung on a beam over a heavy wooden table. He didn't see the woman until she jumped up from her pallet in the corner, frightened.

"Sorry," said Jim, as startled as she was. *"Pardonnez moi."*

A small, round-faced woman stood there blinking at him, apparently waking up. Why wasn't she at home and in bed at this hour? Surely she knew what kind of parties her employer gave—suggestive murmurs and lapping could be heard through the louvered shutters over the sink. Her blue tunic, cotton pants and plain sandals made her look very old-fashioned and traditional. Jim was indignant the Frenchman exposed such a woman to his debauchery. The mere presence of a woman in this house distressed Jim.

He apologized in French for disturbing her and explained he only wanted a Coke or soda. He looked for a refrigerator, but in this enormous kitchen there was only a small American model, like one you'd find in an office or luxury hotel room.

"No Coca-Cola, no Coca-Cola," she chanted, squaring her bulldog shoulders. *"Thé et vin, thé et vin."* When Jim said he'd fix the tea himself, she sternly shook her head and pointed at a straight-backed chair by the table. *"Moi chambre,"* she insisted in her pidgin French and grumbled to herself in Vietnamese until Jim obeyed her and sat down.

Watching her waddle between cupboard and stove on turned-out feet, Jim was reminded of Sirikit in Bangkok and his housekeeper in Jakarta and most of the housekeepers he'd had in Asia: tough little women who suffered their western employers with a tolerance that was sometimes purely formal, sometimes motherly. And not just their employers but all men, husbands, sons and brothers, as if steeled with a secret knowledge they knew men lacked. Jim thought briefly of his own mother and his sister Ann. Despite the occasional exception like Mrs. Marcos, women seemed to him more moral than men, or more practical at least. No woman would initiate anything so stupidly masculine as a war, an empire or an orgy.

She brought over a lovely teapot, cup and saucer on a tray, set them on the table and withdrew with a slight bow. Jim asked her to join him, gesturing at the chair opposite. She ignored the invitation and returned to her pallet, sitting down and closing her eyes again. Perpetua, his housekeeper in Manila, frequently joined Jim for coffee or tea, but Filipinas were more liberated, almost American compared to other Asian women.

Jim finished one cup of tea, then another, the astringent taste making him feel safer and more confident. Then the glass door out in the living room began to grind open and closed as the first people came back inside. They grumbled and laughed with each other like men coming into a locker room after a round of golf.

"Good booze, great grass. I drained the lizard so many times I can't believe I'm still standing."

"You see the prick on that Polack? Like a fucking mortar round. I think I'm in love."

"I ain't saying I didn't get off," said a third voice. "But I still wish there'd been some pussy here." He was answered by groans and catcalls.

A door to the right of the kitchen sink opened and Nhut entered, dressed in underwear and carrying his white jacket and black trousers. The woman jumped to her feet and berated him in Vietnamese.

Nhut saw Jim. "Some fun, yes?" he said, ignoring the woman.

Jim was disturbed the woman seemed to have a personal stake in the boy. Was she Nhut's sister? His mother? Jim couldn't tell how old she was and

Nhut treated her with the indifference with which most Asian men treat female relatives. The woman angrily directed Nhut to the table, then lit the stove
again and took down a covered bowl. She seemed furious with him for partici-
pating in the orgy, yet concerned he get something to eat before he went to
bed. Jim couldn't decide if this were the ultimate in love or culpability.

Nhut sat across from Jim, his elbows on the table, showing no guilt or
shame, looking contentedly exhausted. He shared a complicitous smirk with
Jim.

"Has anyone seen the guy I came with? The big fella losing his hair."
Dave Wheeler was out in the living room, apparently finished and getting
dressed. "Jim!" he called out. "You in hearing range?"

Jim was tempted to say nothing and let Wheeler leave without him. He
couldn't imagine looking Wheeler in the eye after all he'd seen. But he called
back, "Out here, Dave. In the kitchen."

"Just wanted to know where you were."

Dave swaggered through the door a minute later, hair and beard still wet,
completely dressed except for the sneakers he carried in one hand. He looked
as if he'd done nothing worse than had a nice long swim. "That's an idea,"
he said, seeing Jim's tea. *Thé, si vous plaît, Madame Drang,"* he told the
woman and sat beside Jim to put on his sneakers.

"Some fun, yes?" Nhut asked; it might be the only English he knew.

"Oh yeah. Good healthy discharge of libidinal tension. Good fun. I always
suffer a dose of postcoital depression afterwards," Dave cheerfully confessed
to Jim. "But just for a half hour or so. Protestant upbringing. No, I had a good
time. Guy I picked turned out to be a selfish pig, but I had a good time."

He didn't talk like someone who was depressed. The very notion annoyed
Jim, who'd had his depression *before* sex and found the idea of guilt afterwards to be dishonest and unfair. But it was difficult to connect this person
with the man Jim had seen naked and even embraced in the pool. It was
someone else whose dick Jim had held. In fact, in the dry glare of the kitchen,
it was difficult to identify Dave or Nhut or Jim himself with the naked men
outside.

"I can't get nooo-oh-oh satisfaction," someone sang in the next room. And
a naked man walked in.

It was Phil, the wiry little southerner who'd started it all, looking older in
overhead light, his redneck tan ugly, his nakedness inappropriate. A towel
hung around his neck. He ambled up behind Nhut, put both hands on the boy's
shoulders and spoke to him in Vietnamese.

Nhut laughed; the woman at the stove gave them an angry look, and turned
away.

"Can't you cover yourself up!" Jim snapped. "There's a lady present."

Phil glanced at the woman and faced Jim with a great sneer. "Who? You,
pal? This old mama-san's seen worse than my hairy butt. Oh all right. If it

makes *you* uncomfortable.'' He laughed and tousled Nhut's hair, then strolled out again.

"And you?'' Dave asked. "You enjoy yourself tonight?''

Maybe it was everyone's guiltlessness, maybe it was being called a lady by the little G.I., but suddenly Jim couldn't admit he'd done nothing.

"I saw you with that crazy kid,'' Dave laughed. "The one going from cock to cock like an urchin in a candy shop. Wasn't he a hoot?''

"Uh huh. No, it was interesting. I had a good time.'' Jim looked at the squat, long-suffering woman who stirred something in a pan at the stove. He admired women, but he did not want to be one. To confess he hadn't done anything out there and hated every minute of it would be like confessing he was moral and harmless, a woman. Jim had spent most of his life telling himself only men who were *like* women could have sex with each other, but tonight his system of symbols had been turned on its head.

"You probably feel a little down yourself right now,'' said Dave, catching the sorrow in Jim's face and voice. "Perfectly natural. But see? I knew you'd have a good time once you were here. Sex for fun is a great release. Burns the mind clean of morbid thoughts. Makes you forget everything else for an hour or so. And as somebody told me, fellatio is one of the nicest things one guy can do for another.''

Georges entered, wearing a short silk dressing gown, looking quite suave and pleased with himself. "I assumed this is where I find you,'' he announced. "You Americans always gravitate to the kitchen. You're eating? I am hungry myself.'' He gave the woman a new set of orders and sat down beside his servant. The household was divided by gender, not class or race. Delicately smoothing his mustache with one finger, his dressing gown exposing a chest covered with white hair, he looked quite distinguished, a younger brother of the top-hatted millionaire from the Monopoly game.

"It's over?'' asked Dave.

Georges shrugged. "Most of our soldiers had to go to report back to hospital. Tony too, alas. But our Polish friend is still at it. With Luc. Insatiable.''

There was a heavy clomp of boots and Phil returned. He wore canvas-sided jungle boots and army fatigues, the shirt unbuttoned but the bars on the collar clearly visible. *He* was the captain. "We're eating?'' he said, pulling out a chair. "Great. I should get some chow before I take off.''

Jim was shocked. He looked too young and sounded too coarse to be anything more than a sergeant, but this smirky, randy animal was a commissioned officer, with men under his command and important responsibilities. The name patch on his shirt read *Zacheray*. Captain Zacheray? Phil's personality changed shape and weight in Jim's eyes. He didn't know what to make of the man.

Captain Zacheray was looking at his watch. "Yeah, food. Wasn't going to have time to grab breakfast before I choppered out of My Tho this morning.''

"You're going out as soon as you get back?'' said Dave.

"Just an inspection tour. More intelligence bullshit. Fly around for a few hours, visit a few villages, make sure the Arvins have been doing their job." That was the ARVN, the South Vietnamese army which was taking over more tasks as the first American troops withdrew. "Just a look-see around the delta. I wasn't going to let a little thing like that make me miss Georges's monthly fuckfest."

"What about sleep?" Dave asked.

"Sleep? Sleep is a motherfucker," Phil laughed. "I got better things to do with my time. If I didn't have to be in My Tho, I'd grab Nhut here for another go."

Dave Wheeler had seemed like an impulsive, supercharged bundle of energy to Jim, but this Phil left Dave in the dust, made him look tame by comparison. Suffering nervous exhaustion, Jim could only sit there and listen while Dave asked Phil about his work and the war. He felt as superfluous as the woman who now cooked something French at the stove. For a moment Jim thought he smelled cabbage, but it was only baby onions.

"You spend a lot of time in the field," Dave was saying, "even though you're a staff officer." Apparently the two men knew each other from previous parties, but not all that well; Dave was clearly fascinated with the captain.

"Oh yeah. I'm no REMF. Rear echelon motherfucker. I'm no grunt either, although I did clock some time on the line. Got an ass cheek in both worlds. Right now I do mostly liaison between division and the Arvins. Which can get hairy. But I love the Vietnamese. Their officers are shit but the men are beautiful." And Phil gave Nhut another affectionate smirk.

"You Americans," sighed Georges, taking on that jaded look Europeans always assumed when criticizing Americans. "You expect everyone to love you."

Phil laughed. "I don't expect them to love me back. I just hope they do their job while I do mine and none of us gets killed."

Jim knew soldiers loved to lie, especially to civilians, making their lives sound more heroic and stoical than they really were. Jim fought his feeling of helplessness by poking at the man's capacity for lying. "I know it's none of my business," he told Phil. "But do you consider yourself homosexual? Bisexual? What?"

Phil glanced at Dave as if to ask, *Who is this jerk?* "You don't have to know what it's called to enjoy it," he sneered. "But no. I'd say I was queer. What of it?"

"That doesn't create problems for you as an officer?"

"I don't shit where I eat, if that's what you mean. Hell, I love the army and I love to fuck guys. Just got to use a little discretion. You live in a glass house yourself, pal. Although you got it easier in State than I do with Uncle Sugar."

"I know," Jim lied. "I was just curious how you handled it. Surrounded by men who hate homosexuals." What Jim really wanted to know was if this man were a liar, a lunatic or simply stupid. Then he'd no longer feel intimidated by him.

"There's queers all over the army," Phil told the entire table. "Tonight alone should've told you that. Some of us are more honest than others, that's all. For example, I've got these two tech sergeants on my staff, about my age, late twenties"—the guy was that young?—"who do *everything* together. They bunk together, eat together, shower together. I bet they even shit together. These guys are inseparable. They fuck together too, but not each other. One never goes to the skivvy house without his buddy and they take their whores side by side on separate beds. To hear them compare notes and make fun of each other afterwards, you know they spend the whole time watching each other fuck. The women are just accessories. Now don't tell me those guys aren't lovers. They just won't admit it."

"You've asked them?" said Jim.

"You kidding?" Phil howled. "They'd toss a grenade under my cot one night sooner than you can say 'faggot cocksucker.' Me, on the other hand, I knew what I wanted. Took me humping around in the jungle and almost getting my head shot off to realize life was too short not to do something about it. So I've been doing it. What can brass do to me if they find out? Ship me to 'Nam?"

The man was insane. The war had made him crazy. That was the best explanation Jim could come up with for Phil's ability to talk like this. When Jim turned to share his realization with Dave, he found Dave studying the man intently, curiously, more fascinated than ever.

"You've been in combat?" Dave asked.

"Sure. Why?"

"What's it like?"

Phil scornfully laughed at him. "What is it with you State Department bozos tonight? Gimme a break."

"I'm curious," Dave insisted. "I like to think I live dangerously. But I can't imagine what combat would be like. What I'd feel, how I'd act."

"Sometimes you don't feel a thing. And now and then it's the greatest high known to man. Either way you're scared shitless, but you often numb out while other times it's like this awful, beautiful rush."

That sounded to Jim like more G.I. bullshit, an insider bragging about what he knew and you didn't.

But Dave was impressed. "I've never even been shot at," he confessed. "I had rocks thrown through my window in Venezuela, but that's been it. I'll admit it. I've led a very safe life," he said guiltily.

The woman began to bring plates of food to the table, omelets for the Caucasians, a large bowl of dark noodles for Nhut. She stood respectfully behind Nhut until he ate a couple of bites and nodded his approval.

Phil hungrily dug into the food. "If you're really so hot to get shot at," he told Dave, "why don't you come with me to My Tho this morning?"

"You serious?" said Dave.

"Yeah. Why not?" He had a cruel, crazy grin. He had to be needling Dave, mocking both him and Jim for their safe, civilian lives. "I'll be honest with you—hmmm, tasty stuff, Georges—it's a milk run. Only a one in five chance we'd draw any ground fire. But it happens. So yeah. Come along with me."

Instead of laughing off the invitation as a joke, Dave sat back and rubbed his beard. "I'd like that. You're really serious? I promise I'd stay out of the way."

Jim couldn't believe what he was hearing. They were both insane. Or they were only showing off, playing games of machismo with each other, Phil trying to shame Dave into admitting he was just another REMF. Jim mentally criticized and dismissed this as adolescent braggadocio in order to fight his own stupid desire to join them.

Georges chuckled and shook his head. "You Americans," he said again. "Sexual orgasms aren't enough for you. You need new and different kicks. Silly boys."

"That's not it at all, Georges. I need this for my education," Dave argued. "Never been in the boondocks here. It'll give me a clearer perspective in Washington." The eager gleam in his eyes was anything but logical, a giddiness like his expression on the hotel roof that afternoon when he told Jim about his secret life. "Will you need to get any kind of clearance to take me with you?"

Phil shrugged. "What they don't know won't hurt them. Unless we get killed, but then we won't be around to suffer the consequences. No, I've got my own Huey assigned to me this morning and my word is God's word with the pilot."

They were serious. They were actually going to do it. And Jim would be left behind, safe and sane, as prudent as the woman who now sat on her pallet in the corner.

"It sounds very interesting," Jim told Phil. "I'd like to come too."

Dave turned and frowned. "You don't have to, Jim."

"I know I don't have to," Jim said sharply. "You have room for another passenger, Phil?" This was idiocy, insanity, but Jim had to go with them.

"There's room. Yeah, why not?" said Phil. "The more the merrier."

"What about your flight back to Manila?" Dave pointed out. "You have a plane to catch at three this afternoon." He wanted to protect Jim, which was annoying.

"We'll have him back in plenty of time. Hell, I should finish my rounds by ten and have one of my tech sergeants drive you back to town," said Phil.

"Good. Great." Jim was stunned yet pleased with himself. "Yes, I should get a glimpse of the war while I'm here."

"My pleasure," went Phil. "You're stationed in Manila, huh? You ever get to the boy bars in Ermita?"

"Uh, no. Too close to home," Jim lied. And he suddenly wondered how much sex had to do with this. If he couldn't have sex with men, did he think he could fix that by letting men shoot at him? No, he needed to be with Dave and Phil when they were shot at. If anyone actually shot at them. Now that he'd committed himself, Jim went back to his earlier suspicions that Phil Zacheray was a braggart, a liar, and nothing could possibly happen.

While Phil sang the praises of a male brothel in the Ermita district in Manila, Jim glanced at Dave, hoping to read something there that would steer his mind one way or the other. But Dave only smiled and shook his head when Jim's eye caught his, giving in to Jim's desire to come along.

Georges showed no surprise or concern. "Just be careful about your cocks," he told them. "You have very nice cocks and I'd hate to see harm come to them. But the good thing about this war is there are always cocks. If I lose one, your government sends others to replace it."

When Phil finished his food, he said they should be going. They thanked Georges for his hospitality. Phil said he hoped to be back next month, then gave Nhut a kiss on the cheek while he slipped some folded money into the waistband of the boy's shorts. The woman in the corner made a tight little smile.

Phil had parked his jeep out by the garage and the three men walked through the villa's backyard to get there. The electric lights in the swimming pool had been turned off and the whitening sky was mirrored in the perfectly still water. A goblet with an inch of brandy and a cigarette butt floated motionless on the surface. That was all that remained of the party, along with a crushed white tube on the curb, a few empty bottles in the grass and, lying face down out on the mattress, a naked body. It was Vitold, who might have been a corpse in the pale light except for the dry snores that could be heard beneath the early morning cackle and squeak of birds in the trees.

6

"YOU DRIVE LIKE YOU FUCK!" shouted Dave, clinging to the gunwale and seat of the speeding jeep.

"You should know!" Phil laughed and stepped on the gas to race around the next truck in front of them. They swerved in and out of an army convoy on a two-lane highway south of Saigon, their headlight beams glaring into canvas-covered caves filled with crated air conditioners.

Jim sat in the back and held on with both hands, keeping his body rigid while his nerves and heart raced with the belief they'd all be killed before they even got to My Tho. It was a weirdly liberating sensation, his fear and excitement driving out every other thought. After the furious self-consciousness of the past twelve hours, he was pleased to feel nothing but fear. He gladly left his life in the hands of an adolescent maniac who played chicken on the ground before taking them on an aerial joyride through a war.

Division headquarters at My Tho was a sprawling compound of vehicles, mammoth trailers and tents, an army slum surrounded by paddy fields that were greenish-gray in the predawn light. Captain Zacheray—it was difficult to think of him as "Phil" once they arrived and he hurried about, snapping orders and receiving salutes—commandeered helmets and flak jackets for Jim and Dave. They both looked like imposters with their knit sports shirts visible underneath, but the heavy helmet and weighted vest gave Jim a feeling of tough masculinity he needed right now. A previous owner had painted the words *Dumb Fuck* on Jim's helmet.

"Eat lead, Commie rat," joked Dave, continuing to grin despite the pained look in his eyes, like the beginnings of a hangover, as they followed Captain Zacheray toward the helicopter pad.

Fear subsided into nervous anticipation, until they were abruptly yanked into the sky.

The roaring Huey rocked forward as it lifted off. The lefthand panel door was slid back and Jim saw the earth drop out from under them. He'd flown in helicopters before, but never one this small or open. The Huey's interior was the size of a panel truck and Jim sat strapped to the sling bench beside Dave opposite the open door; the Huey banked hard to the left, as if to pour them out that door. It was like being hoisted skyward on an invisible cable, the helicopter swinging on the cable while the body responded with disbelief, expecting the cable to break any second now and drop them to the ground that fell further and further away. Then the machine straightened out, the landscape swung back and the body grew accustomed to its frightened disbelief, a bead of excitement like the bubble in a carpenter's level. As they gained altitude, the morning sun suddenly pierced the long curving slope of the ocean in the distance.

Captain Zacheray stepped back from the cockpit with a section of map folded under his clipboard. He didn't attempt to speak, only pointed at the map, then out the door. The roar of turbines and buzz of steel flooring made speech impossible. He gave them a brusque nod when he finished; the situation seemed to make him more serious and businesslike. Dave had lost his grin too, but he'd put on his sunglasses and Jim couldn't tell if he were exhilarated, frightened or bored.

The flat plain below was almost all rice paddies, rectangles and trapezoids fitted together like pale green slates in a stone floor, a few emerald clumps of trees and curving, silted creeks breaking the orderly terrain. The landscape gained color and shadows as the sun rose. Very quickly, they were far enough inland for the sun's reflection to race with them over land to the east, flashing in the criss-cross of canals, glittering over the width of a river, at one point flaring like a string of bright explosions through a chain of ponds. The plain was pitted with several of these chains of ponds, bowls of water at the center of large, geometrically perfect circles. Not until they flew directly over one did Jim realize the ponds were bomb craters, the perfect circles shallow depressions of exploded earth now green with grass. Each series of circles marked the bombing pattern of a single B–52 as it passed overhead years or maybe only months ago. It was strange to think one visit could do so much, or that the land could heal so quickly. Already the holes were part of the countryside, new dikes built around their circumference, cattle using one pond as a watering place. Stranger still, these geometrical scars were the only evidence of the war from up here, that and the orange network of ditches and bunkers surrounding a nearby emerald grove like the intricate tunnels of an ant farm. This high up, the world looked peaceful and safe.

Then the dozing soldier on the seat behind the cockpit roused himself and staggered to the open door. Jim had forgotten he was there, a sullen black man whose bare chest and shoulders bulged with muscles under his flak jacket. Whatever his duties were, the war gave him time to lift weights. Now he unlocked the heavy machine gun mounted by the door and swung it out on its swivel. But he only pointed it at the sky and inspected the chamber, opening and closing the gate around the ammunition belt.

The land was floating up toward them. Jim braced himself and listened for gunshots, although the noise inside the chopper was so loud there'd be no way of knowing they were being shot at unless they were hit. Jim watched the gunner at the door, an emerald canopy of trees swinging past as the Huey circled a grove. They hovered, yawed and dipped in, the grove revealing a village under its treetops, thatched roofs and walls and a natural pond like a puddle. Two women bathing small children looked up as the chopper nosed in, gathered up their babies and shielded them from the wind and dust pouring down from the blades. The machine bumped along the ground and the roar of rotors softened to a prolonged shriek as the Huey settled against its runners.

"First stop, gentlemen. Tan Thoi," said Captain Zacheray, stepping out the door without helmet or flak jacket, only his clipboard. "Let's see what's going down."

Jim quickly unhooked himself to follow Zacheray. With the blades still idling overhead, he automatically bent down when he got out and stayed down as he hurried over the bare ground after Zacheray. The air was already hot and thick, the sun painfully bright. After the pressure of noise on board, the continued warbling of the chopper sounded peaceful. Jim gradually straightened up as he walked.

The women withdrew quickly yet calmly with their babies toward the huts in the grove, passing an American soldier and Vietnamese civilian coming out to meet Zacheray. Jim caught up with him beside the pond, just as Zacheray finished saluting the soldier and shaking hands with the civilian. The men wore matching baseball caps and the civilian had black-framed glasses and the immobile frown of a fish. The soldier chewed gum and watched Jim while Zacheray spoke to the civilian.

The soldier lunged forward. "Lieutenant Curtis Carroll," he proudly announced, grabbing Jim's hand. "Fremont, Nebraska. Nebraska State. ROTC." He quickly recited himself as he stepped past Jim to shake hands with Dave, who'd come up behind them. "Pleased to be over here, doing my bit. For God and country."

"Put a lid on it," Zacheray groaned. "They're not journalists, lieutenant. Just happy campers from State."

The lieutenant sniffed, stepped back and resumed chewing, losing all interest.

Zacheray finished talking to the civilian and turned to Jim and Dave. "Nothing to see here, fellas. Just militia and a team of advisors. Hang out by the chopper and I'll get this over with as quickly as possible. Jackson!" he shouted to the gunner in the 'copter door. "Make sure my guests don't wander off, will ya?"

The gunner wearily lifted his hand to show he'd heard and Zacheray followed Carroll and the civilian into the grove. A few children had gathered shyly in the shade of a papaya tree and Zacheray petted one as he walked past. Most of the children followed the men, but a couple remained by the tree, looking out at the helicopter and the two Americans who stood idly in the sun.

"Damn," said Dave. "This is certainly the middle of nowhere."

Except for the grove and village in front of them, there was nothing but flat paddy fields all around, another grove in the distance, a line of water palms, and so much sky one might think they were near the ocean. The nearest paddy gave off a hot aroma of chaff and manure.

Jim began to smile. It was all absurd, but harmlessly so, he decided. Nothing would happen. He felt he'd misjudged Phil and the man wasn't crazy or dangerous after all. Jim should've known better than to judge him by what he was like off duty. His motor ran too fast when there was nothing to engage it, but he was clearly engaged now.

"Not such a bad place," Jim joked. "The garden spot of the Mekong Delta."

"Go ahead. Laugh. I must've been drunk or fucking nuts to agree to this."

The anger in Dave's voice took Jim by surprise. Armored in helmet and sunglasses, his face expressed nothing; Jim assumed Dave had been getting a kick out of this, was enjoying this ride as the heady goof Jim decided it to be. "Something the matter, Dave?"

"What do you think?" he snarled. "Here we are, in the fucking middle of nowhere. God only knows what can happen."

He wasn't kidding. "This was your idea," Jim told him.

"Yeah yeah yeah," Dave chanted, nervously looking around. "And I wasn't in my right head. I never am after something like last night. It's like I have to *prove* things." He grimaced at the ground, angry with himself for confessing so much, then aimed his mirrored sunglasses at Jim. "I wish like hell you'd done something to talk me out of this stupid stunt. Instead of being so hot to come along."

Jim kept his temper. "You're the man who said he liked to live dangerously, remember?"

"Yeah, well, it's one thing to fuck around with your sexual parameters. It's something else to fuck with life and limb. Especially when you have a wife and kid depending on you. You wouldn't know what that's like," he charged.

"No, I guess I wouldn't," Jim said coldly. The man cheated on his wife without compunction, but became the devoted husband again when he was scared. Jim kept the contemptuous thought to himself and said, "I doubt there's any real danger out here. If there were, this captain wouldn't have brought us along. He's just trying to spook a couple of nervous paper-pushers with his war talk." Dave disappointed Jim, but he didn't want to use his fear or fickle behavior against him. Forebearance made Jim feel superior, and superiority helped him contain his own anxieties.

"I hope to hell you're right. Let's get back to the chopper. It's standing out in the open that's making me paranoid. Plus the fact I've been awake for the past twenty-four hours."

They returned to the helicopter, where the pilot lounged in the plexiglass nose, leafing through *Sports Illustrated,* and the gunner crouched in the door, smoking a cigarette. Dave tried to occupy himself by striking up a conversation with the gunner, but Jackson had little to say except that he was from Milwaukee and had another ninety-three days in country before he went back to the States.

Captain Zacheray finally reappeared by the pond, accompanied now by just the Vietnamese civilian. They were followed at a distance by the same pack of curious yet skittish children, who crawled over each other like puppies while they giggled and pointed. Their innocence seemed quite touching, until Jim noticed one small boy whose arm ended at the elbow. The boy poked another boy with his stump, tickling him with it as matter-of-factly as another child might tickle someone with his hand, and Jim flashed on an image of his nephew, Walter, looking for golf balls in the weeds of a ditch. But that was in Virginia Beach, where there were no booby-trapped grenades hidden in the grass.

Zacheray slapped the civilian on the back and rotated a hand over his head to signal the pilot to start the engine.

"How many of these gook villages we hittin' today, Captain?" asked the gunner as Zacheray climbed in.

"Four, Jackson. And we don't call them gooks! These are our people and we call them Vietnamese. Save *gook, dink, slope* and the rest of that shit for the enemy." Zacheray shook his head and rolled his eyes at Jim and Dave as he ducked past them to the cockpit.

They lifted off again and wheeled around, the helicopter's defiance of gravity feeling more natural than the first time. After another landing, this trip would become perfectly routine. Nothing would happen, Jim told himself and knocked his knee against Dave's so he could smile at Elaine's husband and reassure him everything was fine. Dave sat very still, arms folded across his chest, mouth pinched tight in the beard beaded with sweat, fear expressing itself only in an irritable tapping of one shoe.

It was a short hop to the next village. They gained a little altitude and began to descend. This time, thatched and orange-tiled roofs were visible from overhead, only one end of the village covered by papaya and banana trees. The treeless end butted against a highway, a glistening strip of tar and oil on a wide dike that stretched across the scrambled checkerboard of paddies.

The Huey circled once, and then again. Three dark vehicles sat on the highway, squat boxes like coffins with antennas. Figures with the tiny green heads of insects wandered between the roofs of the houses. There were soldiers down there, ours. Jackson slowly swept one arm back and forth, letting the people know he saw them.

Zacheray rushed to the door to get a better look as they circled a third time. Something was wrong. He went back to the cockpit and jammed a chopper helmet on his head to use the radio mike. He angrily spoke to someone, either at headquarters or with the unit below. The Huey stopped circling and hovered beside the highway. Trying to look through the plexiglass window at his back,

Jim could see nothing. Dave remained motionless and watched Jackson, who coolly looked down on whatever was happening below.

The helicopter sank downward. Zacheray took off the chopper helmet and came back, shaking his head as if over some minor problem. A sideview of the village rose in the door as they settled in a dry paddy field. The noise level dropped when the engine no longer strained against air and gravity, but the pilot did not cut the power.

"Arvin!" Zacheray shouted. "A whole company!" He covered his head with a bulky combat helmet. "Not supposed to be here! It's a friendly village!" He jumped out the door and took off in long, exasperated strides across the cracked mud and hummocks of grass.

Jackson remained in the door, not touching the heavy machine gun that hung muzzle-down in its mount. Jim unbuckled his seatbelt and joined him.

"Gooks," Jackson grumbled, reaching under his helmet to take a cigarette from behind his ear. "Our gooks, so Vietna-fucking-mese." He lit the cigarette with a silver lighter. "Trust those little fuckers less than I trust Charlie. You know where you stand with Charlie."

The trees and haystack roofs of the village were fifty yards away, separated from the dry paddy field by a low hedgerow. To the left were acres of wet paddies divided by little knee-high dikes. To the right was the embankment with the highway. Zacheray scrambled up the grassy slope toward a handful of soldiers who stood self-importantly beside an armored personnel carrier. Below them, in the corner formed by the embankment and the hedgerow, men in undershirts and women dressed in black squatted on the ground. A few soldiers stood guard around the peasants, rifles hanging in their hands or laid across their shoulders like yokes. The oversized American helmets turned the soldiers into kids with buckets on their heads. More villagers straggled over the hedgerow and into the field, following the soldiers' pointed fingers to the corner. The running motor of the chopper blocked out the sounds accompanying the scene, but the action seemed to take place without panic or violence, only a weary air of inconvenience.

"What are they doing?" said Dave, who'd joined them in the door.

"Never know with Arvin," Jackson said. "Might be hunting VC. Might be here just to steal rice. Ain't that a pisser? Their army rips off its own people."

Up on the highway, Zacheray was waving both arms at a Vietnamese officer. The officer listened with one hand on his hip, his only movement an annoyed wag of the riding crop in his fist. When he flicked his free hand at Zacheray and turned away, Zacheray began to plead with the other men. They ignored him. He staggered down the embankment and walked toward the helicopter, more exasperated than ever.

"Assholes!" he shouted. "Left hand doesn't know what the right is doing in this godforsaken place." He did not climb aboard, but remained on the ground, glaring over his shoulder at the men on the highway. "Our people were yanked out last week. Another team of advisors. Nobody told us at division. Now this Saigon ass-kisser is claiming the village's VC and needs to be roughed up. Bastard's gonna undo in one morning the trust we took fucking months to pull together here. Hearts and minds?'' Zacheray spat. ''Hearts and assholes!''

''What'll you do?'' asked Jim.

''Not a fucking thing I *can* do. File a report on the bastard. Then have some dipshit desk jockey lecture me it's *their* country and we got to let the fucks run it whatever damn way they—''

There was a muffled pop from the direction of the village. Barely audible through the drumming of rotor blades, the sound might not have registered in Jim's head if Zacheray hadn't snapped around to look.

The soldiers in the paddy field spun around to face the village. The men on the highway froze for a second before one of them ran down the embankment, slipping and sliding. The peasants in the corner huddled closer together, throwing frightened looks at the soldiers who watched the houses and raised their rifles. A few children stood up and eagerly strained on tiptoe to see what was happening in their village.

A single shred of black smoke drifted above a thatched roof.

''Oh shit! Was that a grenade?'' Zacheray stepped away from the door, open palms held out at his sides. He walked toward the dissolving cloud of smoke; he suddenly broke into a run.

Jim and Dave stared at each other, excited and confused, then at Jackson. Jackson coldly watched the village, reaching back with one hand to grip the handle of the machine gun. His sweaty face gleamed like black glass.

We're going to be killed, thought Jim. But the thought didn't frighten him. He was excited yet detached, as if they were all characters in a movie he watched, a silent movie with the helicopter chattering like a projector. Any second now that movie could reach out and pull Jim into it; he was amazed at how calm he remained beneath his excitement.

Zacheray stood in a gap in the hedgerow, shouting and gesturing into the village. Pointing at the helicopter, he signaled someone to follow him. He came running back over the field, frantically jerking his hand at the men in the chopper door.

''Get out!'' he shouted as he raced up to them. ''Just get the fuck out!'' And he leaped at Dave, grabbed him by his flak jacket and pulled him to the ground. Jim jumped down and Zacheray rushed over to the cockpit, pounded on the plexiglass and shouted to the pilot. Jackson remained in the door, staring across the field.

Knots of Vietnamese soldiers stumbled toward them. Breathless and grimacing, they no longer looked like children. They carried bodies. The bodies were soldiers too, some limp, others twisting and kicking. Their green uniforms were stained black in patches that turned red on the hands of the men who carried them.

Jackson bent down and grabbed a body by its collar; he hauled the body across the floor. Other bodies were heaved up and loaded in. Jim automatically stepped over to help, but was shouldered aside by the next set of soldiers thrusting a man through the door. He stepped back with Dave to get out of the way. Dave watched with his mouth open and his hands on his hips. Jim's hand had touched wet clothing, but it was only a man's sweat, not his blood.

Blood streaked the steel flooring when Jackson dragged another body from the door. An upended boot quivered and kicked. A head rolled out and hit the ground—no, only a helmet.

"Fucking meat factory!" Zacheray hollered, pulling at soldiers to hurry them along. "Damn fools do everything in gangs! So six or seven caught it when the shit hit the fan! Booby trap!"

The soldiers stepped backwards after leaving their wounded in the door, some looking numb, others angry. An unwounded soldier clambered aboard, helped Jackson move a man, then squatted down and furiously ripped strips of white bandage from a kit to bind arms and legs.

Jim stood beside Dave, feeling no horror or fear, only an excitement that seemed obscene when he couldn't do anything to help.

When the last wounded man was on board, Zacheray looked around, motioned Jim and Dave away from the helicopter and signaled to the pilot. Jackson appeared in the door again and stood there, ashen and glassy-eyed, the floor behind him heaped with uniforms. He stared at Zacheray as the Huey rose like an elevator.

A dust storm roared over the paddy field, forcing the men below to shield their eyes with hands or forearms, rolling a discarded helmet bumpily over the ground. The roar softened to a buzz as the chopper swung over the armored vehicles on the highway and raced away through the hot sky.

It was suddenly quiet, strangely peaceful, and Jim realized they'd been left behind, stranded with a company of foreign soldiers in the middle of nowhere.

"He'll be back," said Zacheray. "Get those boys to a hospital, pronto." He spoke irritably, angrily, his mind on something else. He was looking at the officers up on the highway, then the soldiers who'd brought the wounded out, now scattered across the field, drifting toward the corner where the peasants sat watching and waiting.

Dave glanced at Jim, biting his lower lip. They walked with Zacheray toward the corner. Saucers of cracked mud softly broke under their feet.

"Little bastards," snarled Zacheray. "Soon as we turn our backs, the little bastards turn against us. They let Charlie into their village and let him leave a killer surprise for us. Fucking friendly, my ass. Arvin's gonna want to wipe this place off the map. Can't say I blame them."

No, it wasn't over, Jim told himself, looking all around as they strode across the field. Cold eyes were focused on the villagers. The massacre at My Lai had been over a year ago, but it had become public only this past spring. These soldiers were Vietnamese, not American, but there was clearly no love lost between the soldiery and populace here. And these men had seen their friends hurt. Vengeance was a very human emotion. Jim braced himself to witness something terrible.

"Stick close together and keep your eyes on me," said Zacheray. "There's no telling what might happen."

Jim was frightened by the thought of what they would see, but excited too, the excitement of a spectator who believes he's going to witness something awful yet real, valuable for his education. Not until he noticed the women and children again did his excitement disgust him. He seemed to have no trouble accepting the murder of grown men.

A dozen soldiers now circled the peasants. The peasants sat perfectly still, some with lowered heads, others stealing looks left and right. The soldiers angrily murmured among themselves and looked to their officers on the highway, waiting for a command or signal before they did anything. One very young soldier was crying, sobbing for a friend who'd been wounded. He gripped his rifle at waist-level and pointed the barrel at a man and wife who sat three yards away.

An ARVN lieutenant came down from the embankment, reaching the circle of soldiers and peasants just as the Americans did. He went up to Zacheray and spoke coldly to him in Vietnamese, pointing back at his superior.

The Vietnamese commander continued to stand like a statue beside the armored personnel carrier. Whatever happened, he appeared determined to remain aloof, refusing to dirty his hands.

Zacheray argued with the lieutenant. The lieutenant remained adamant. His sunglasses made him look lordly compared to his soldiers, machinelike compared to the peasants. He turned from Zacheray, unsnapped the holster at his hip and pulled out a square black pistol. *"Co ai o day là vee cee?"* he shouted at the peasants. *"Co ai vee cee?"* He cocked the pistol and stepped over to an old man in a frayed panama hat; he pointed the pistol at the man's face.

"Oh God," groaned Dave, gripping Jim's sleeve.

Jim frantically told himself: *This isn't your country. You're only a guest. You're not even supposed to be here.*

A baby began to cry. The mother swung the child into her lap and bent over it, trying to muffle its noise and hide the child from view.

"Co ai vee cee?" the lieutenant repeated. Who is VC? Which one of you is Viet Cong? That's what he must be asking. The old man closed his eyes and cinched his wrinkled mouth more tightly shut. Fear showed itself only in the spastic twitch of shoulders when he shrugged.

Zacheray had followed the lieutenant, standing close behind him. He suddenly stepped between the lieutenant and the old man. Very gently, Zacheray lifted the hand with the pistol and, before the lieutenant understood what was happening, snatched the pistol from his hand.

Jim let out the breath he'd been holding. The hand gripping his sleeve relaxed.

The lieutenant made a childish grab for the pistol Zacheray held at arm's length. Zacheray remained stonefaced while the man shouted and screamed at him, threatening Zacheray with the soldiers standing all around, then with his commander up on the highway. His tirade was sprinkled with *fock* and *asshool*. Zacheray snarled something at the man and nodded toward Jim and Dave.

The lieutenant looked at them, then hesitated. Guiltily glancing up at his commander, he slowly backed away from Zacheray.

Had Zacheray told him the two Americans were important men? Reporters or Congressmen? Whatever lie the lieutenant was told, he let Zacheray take charge. Jim was pleased his and Dave's presence might do some good after all, could even prevent a massacre.

But Zacheray did not dismiss the peasants and soldiers. He kept the pistol, pointing it in the air as he waded among the villagers. *"Co ai day vee cee?"* he called out, taking up the lieutenant's refrain. *"Co ai day vee cee?"* He watched people's faces, looking for something, someone. His lips were pressed tight against his bared teeth.

Jim and Dave stood just outside the circle, beside the soldier who'd been crying. The young man wiped his runny nose on his sleeve. His rifle pointed at the ground now that an American officer was in there. Rifles all around were lowered and the soldiers watched resentfully. Jim remained alert, relieved Zacheray was in control, trusting him to remain sane.

"Co ai vee cee?" Zacheray came to a young man in eyeglasses. The fellow sat on the ground, leaning over raised knees. He did not look up when Zacheray stood over him. *"Co ai?"* Zacheray repeated, and lightly tapped his head with the butt of the pistol.

The young man gripped his ankles and shook his head.

"Co ai." Zacheray placed the muzzle against the man's temple.

The man shook his head again, a tiny movement so as not to disturb the gun. The sinews of his neck stood out, drawing his mouth down in a grotesque frown. His eyes were closed.

Why him? Jim wondered if it were the glasses, which made him look like the village intellectual, the school egghead.

Zacheray lifted the pistol and stepped aside.

The man drew a deep breath, opened his eyes and took a quick glance to the left, before he saw Zacheray's boots and legs still in front of him.

Zacheray caught the glance and followed it, stepping through the people to another man, a younger man, a boy of sixteen or seventeen. He stood over the boy and looked back at the man with eyeglasses, who looked only at the ground. Zacheray gently laid his free hand on the boy's black-haired head and softly asked, *"Co ai vee cee?"*

The boy kept his eyes lowered, his mouth in a pout. He wore an American cowboy shirt with panels of paisley cloth at the shoulders. His bare legs were covered with scabs and overlapping scars of ringworm. He nervously rubbed one bare foot over the other and shook his head.

Zacheray's hand lightly stroked the boy's hair and Jim was reminded of his tenderness with Nhut last night at the villa. The distressed look on Zacheray's face made Jim think he might be tempted to kiss the boy.

Then Zacheray shouted, *"Co ai?"* He grabbed a handful of black hair and jerked the boy's head back. He glared down at the face, then angrily looked at the lowered faces around him, furious now, desperate for an answer.

The boy's eyes were wide open, terrified. His mouth opened and closed again without saying a word. A young woman sitting beside him kept her face buried in her shoulder.

Zacheray tossed the head forward when he let go of the hair. Looking utterly defeated, he took a deep, disappointed breath. He bent down, as if to whisper to the boy, placed the pistol against the boy's stomach and fired.

It happened so quickly it didn't seem to happen. There was a moist pop and Zacheray promptly stood up and called, *"Co ai vee cee?"* again, as though he'd done nothing extraordinary.

But the villagers drew back, scooting over the ground, mothers covering the eyes of their children. The young soldier with dried tears on his cheeks crowed at them, then laughed.

The boy lay curled up on his side. His arms and knees folded around a bright red stain on his cowboy shirt and he groaned on the air he breathed, a cry turned inside-out with pain. Zacheray stood over him, not even glancing down at the boy.

Dave Wheeler was gasping for breath—Jim felt Dave was about to scream and rush in to stop Zacheray. But it was Jim who wanted to scream. The muscles in his arms and chest vibrated with electricity: a horror that turned into rage, a blinding anger quicker than thought.

"You son of a bitch!" A hand grabbed his elbow to stop him, but Jim jerked the arm free and rushed in. "You cocksucking son of a bitch!" he shouted in Zacheray's face and dropped to the ground beside the boy.

The eyes were huge and open, the jaw stretched wide, the face turned to one side and rubbing against the chalky dirt. The arms around his stomach were covered with blood, but he was horribly alive.

"Idiot! Get the fuck out of here!" Zacheray shoved at Jim with his boot.

"Get this kid a medic, morphine, something! He's bleeding to death!"

"Damn straight he's bleeding to death. Why the hell you think I shot him? He'll be dead in five minutes and it'll make one of these fuckers talk!"

Jim felt furious and helpless. Before he knew what he was doing, he had jumped to his feet and grabbed the front of the captain's shirt. "You murdering cocksucker! You can kill a kid? What kind of man are you?" Finding how much bigger he was than Zacheray, he shook the man hard. Their helmets banged together.

Zacheray pushed back with one hand, then shoved the pistol between their faces, the barrel pointing straight up. He looked crazy enough to kill Jim. "Asshole! You're out of your fucking element here."

"Go ahead, shoot *me*. Show us what a man you are. A real man who can fuck boys and kill them too." Jim's anger grabbed at everything he knew about this man. "Coldblooded cocksucker."

Zacheray's wild look turned hard and steely. He grappled with one of the hands clutching his shirt. He took Jim's opened palm and forced the pistol against it. "You want to be the man? Here. Take it. Take it, you bleeding heart!" He squeezed Jim's fingers around the rectangular handle. "You think it's so damn cruel, you finish him off. Put the poor kid out of his misery."

Jim was shocked to find a gun in his hand. He did not know what to do with it except kill the boy's killer.

"Look at him, asshole! He's got another three or four minutes of that!"

At their feet, the boy thrashed like a landed fish, twisting around his stomach wound, pounding his head against the ground as if to knock himself out. The cracked mud around him was covered with a nervelike pattern of blood, yet the boy remained horribly conscious.

"You feel so fucking concerned, shoot him in the head. You got my permission. Do it! If you don't, nobody will. I'm the coldblooded faggot, remember?"

The bastard was right. Jim had to do something. He lifted the heavy pistol toward the face.

The boy saw the pistol. His head trembled, almost nodding, as if pleading with Jim to shoot. His face was inhuman with pain, mouth peeled back around gums and long teeth, an ugly cartoon with disturbingly human eyes. It was too awful, too intimate with those eyes looking out at Jim.

Jim knelt down. It had to be done. He took the boy's jaw in his left hand and turned the face to one side, gently. Jawbone and muscle quivered. Careful not to let metal touch flesh, Jim pointed the pistol to the left of the boy's ear, where a feathery, childish sideburn ended on beardless cheek. The curved jaw in one hand and flat pistol grip in the other jerked simultaneously.

A jolt went through the folded body, and Jim pulled the trigger again, terrified the first shot only added to the boy's pain, uncertain he even fired the first time. Something hard bounced back and stung his knuckles.

Suddenly, silence. The jaw he held was loose and heavy; Jim let go. The boy lay perfectly quiet, the pink mouth still open but his eyes calmly closed. There were two red holes like giant bites beside his ear. Jim heard black flies buzzing at the boy's stomach, then saw them floating over the halo of blood on the ground around his head.

Zacheray lifted Jim to his feet and pulled the pistol from his hand. "Get him away from here," he told Dave, who'd come into the circle. Without anger or remorse, Zacheray coolly turned away and resumed his mechanical chant: *"Co ai vee cee?"*

The soldiers looked merely puzzled as Dave led Jim past. Dave's body felt clammy and strange against Jim, his pale skin covered with cold sweat.

Glassy-eyed and breathless, Dave stood under Jim with one arm around Jim's waist, as if he thought Jim needed to be supported.

Irritated, almost embarrassed, Jim pulled free of Dave. "That was stupid. Very stupid," he said and took off in deliberate strides toward the grassy embankment ten yards away. He felt he should sit down after that.

"Are you all right?" Dave asked, keeping up with him. "How do you feel?"

"Fine." It was a bizarre thing to say, but then it was a bizarre thing to ask. Yet Jim did feel fine, or not fine but intact, as cool and solid as stone, intensely alert yet emotionless. When they reached the embankment, he did not sit down. He had too much nervous energy to sit and stood there, looking back at Zacheray and the peasants.

The corpse was barely noticeable in the crowd, even with the space the villagers had cleared around it. Zacheray continued to wade among lowered heads, waving the pistol and calmly addressing them.

"I can't believe I saw that," Dave muttered. He'd sat on the bank, elbows on his knees, head in his hands. One would think *he* had killed a man. "I don't want to believe I'm even here."

Something was happening in the circle. Zacheray had gone to an older man who sat behind the first man with eyeglasses. He rapped the older man on the head with his pistol. A woman sitting beside him screamed, embraced the man and began to chatter and point at the young man with glasses. Suddenly, the villagers were looking at each other, sharing disapproval over what this woman had done. They shared pity, not anger; the Saigon troops would soon be gone, but the VC would always be around to punish traitors. Without emotions to impede him, Jim understood everything he saw.

"What's happening?" said Dave. He had to lick his lips and swallow several times to get up enough saliva to speak.

"Phil's found his man."

"Oh shit. I can't watch that again." Dave lowered his head and shielded his sunglasses with both hands.

Zacheray went to the man and ordered him to stand up. But he did not use his pistol. Instead, he stuck the pistol in his belt and called two soldiers over. Obeying him, they tied the man's hands behind his back while Zacheray called the ARVN lieutenant over and spoke to him, apparently telling him what he was to tell his commander up on the highway embankment. Jim had forgotten all about the man up there. When Jim followed Zacheray's pointed finger, he saw the man talking on a telephone whose cord came from a hatch in the armored personnel carrier. He had one hand on his hip, as if proud of what had happened, as if it had all been his doing.

Then Zacheray clapped his hands and gestured at the village. The peasants stumbled to their feet, gathered up their children and began to hurry back toward their houses. The soldiers stood aside and watched them go. In half a minute, all that remained in the corner of the dry paddy field was a bundle of clothes with a pair of bare legs sticking out, a dead boy in a patch of spilled paint.

Jim stared at that, feeling nothing, knowing he should feel more. Instead of emotion, he found only hard rock beneath his thoughts. He was surprised he could kill a man and not go to pieces, almost proud of himself. No, he had only *finished* killing a man. He had to be careful not to make it worse than it was. Two soldiers went to the dead body, each grabbed a leg by the ankle and dragged the body over the ground and up the embankment toward their commander.

Zacheray came across the field with his prisoner, escorted by a single soldier. As they approached, Jim expected a look of hatred from the bound man, but the sullen eyes inside the glasses focused on nothing. All Americans and all soldiers must look alike to him. Zacheray pushed him to the ground a few feet from where Dave was sitting. When he shifted his feet against his ass to balance himself against the embankment, the soldier lifted his rifle to club him with the butt. Zacheray snapped at the soldier, who promptly stepped back. The soldier looked over his shoulder at the others, uncertain whose orders he should be following here.

"Happens every fucking time," Zacheray sighed, glaring at his prisoner. "The best and brightest young man in every two-bit hamlet is the one who's VC. Where the fuck's that chopper?" He scanned the sky and looked up at the embankment. "I want to get this prisoner out of here before Major Dipshit up there changes his mind."

"So it was this man and that boy who set the booby trap in there?" said Dave.

"Oh yeah. Probably. They had something to do with it at least, even if it was just to tell the local cadres our backs were turned long enough for them to rig their explosives. This fellow was definitely in on it."

"But maybe not the boy?" Dave asked timidly.

"No. I'm sure the boy was in on it too. I am." He barely glanced at Dave, but he refused to look at Jim.

"He was awfully young," Dave persisted.

"Yeah, well, they're recruiting them younger and younger as their veterans get killed off. The regulars from the north stick out like thumbs down here. But yeah, that kid was green as grass, too damn new to be any use to intelligence. And I needed to make an example of somebody. Arvin was hot for blood and they looked ready to exterminate the whole village."

Jim knew this was all for his benefit, an explanation, a defense. Jim had expected the captain to be furious with him for intervening, but anger was a luxury out here and the captain couldn't even look Jim in the eye, as if he were embarrassed over what had happened. Jim was embarrassed himself; it was the only clear feeling he found in his hard rock of emotion. Up on the highway they strapped the corpse to the personnel carrier as if it were a killed deer. Strange: a boy died and the two adults responsible were only embarrassed. Jim's natural impulse was to want to apologize for losing his temper, but that did not feel right either.

"Good thing then we came along when we did and they let you take charge," said Dave.

"I guess." Zacheray looked uncertain, getting more irritated with Dave's stream of questions. "But they didn't *let* me do anything. That shitheel major wouldn't even let me use his damn radio. I had to bluff my way through, pretend I knew what I was doing, and tell their shit-for-brains lieutenant my civilians were CIA. These people get real nervous around spooks." He broke off to study his prisoner again, then the empty white sky all around them. "We ain't out of the shit yet," he grumbled.

There was a motorized patter from the other side of the embankment. A moment later a helicopter appeared overhead, their helicopter. Zacheray stepped out and waved the chopper in, pumping one arm up and down to signal them to be quick about it. The Huey blew over the village with a gust of hot wind and settled in the field twenty yards away. The engine remained at full power, tail blades warbling, rotor blades panting. It was a comforting din and Jim was overjoyed to see Jackson standing in the door at his machine gun, as if the soldier were a dear old friend he hadn't seen in years.

Zacheray grabbed his prisoner under one arm and hustled him toward the chopper. He pushed him facedown on the floor and hoisted him through the door by the seat of his ragged black shorts. Jackson dragged him into a corner while Jim eagerly followed Dave out of the sun into the oily shade inside. Zacheray gave a final command to the Vietnamese soldier who tagged after them as he handed the fellow the automatic pistol, presumably telling him to return it to the ARVN lieutenant. They had come here unarmed. Zacheray jumped aboard and signaled the pilot to go.

It was a relief to see the world framed in an opened chopper door again, a joy to watch paddy field, highway and village drop away. Toy soldiers climbed the embankment to the armored personnel carriers. Tiny women went to a well between the haystack roofs to fetch water for their families.

Inside the Huey, Jackson strapped the prisoner to the floor, took off the man's glasses and tied white gauze around his eyes. Not knowing what else to do with the glasses, he stuck them back on over the blindfold. The man lay there, a stoical, nearsighted ghost. Zacheray had collapsed in the co-pilot's seat up front. Dave slumped on the sling bench beside Jim. Jim was suddenly exhausted too. He sank back, and his shoe stuck to the steel flooring. The metal was streaked with gummy rust: dried blood from the load of wounded soldiers. Jim noted that, yet was not disturbed by it. He was not disturbed by anything, which was strange. He was not the tenderhearted fellow he always feared himself to be.

They came to earth again twenty minutes later, and were instantly surrounded by an open-air warehouse full of the racket of trucks, fork-lifts and other choppers. The ground was sheathed with waffled steel mats. They walked across the helicopter pad to an air-conditioned house trailer, where typewriters chattered merrily. They seemed to walk out of war into a world of business. Enlisted men in clean fatigues looked up from their typewriters at the men in helmets and the barefoot, blindfolded prisoner who stood barbarically among the desks. While Zacheray turned the prisoner over to an interrogation officer, Jim took a long, cold drink from the Oasis water cooler beside the door.

Dave had removed his helmet, so Jim took off his, the flak jacket too, and felt lighter, almost naked in his knit shirt and summer slacks. He saw the words *Dumb Fuck* scrawled on the helmet.

"Just dump those on the table. I'll take care of them later," said Zacheray when he returned and saw the men fumbling with the borrowed gear. "What time's your flight?" he asked Jim. "Fifteen hundred, right? Three o'clock, I mean. Okay. I've called for a car and it'll get you back in plenty of time. It's not yet noon."

Jim was startled to hear it was still morning, amazed to realize his flight was today, not yesterday or the day before. Had he actually been in this country less than twenty-four hours? "Thanks, Phil. Appreciate that."

Zacheray nodded, frowning. "Let's step outside while we wait for your ride." He motioned them out the door into the heat and glare, glancing left and right as they went around the corner. Bareheaded again, he looked quite young, a sunburned, crewcut kid not much older than their prisoner, only a few years older than the boy who had died. When they reached the tarred roadway behind the trailer, he put one arm around Jim's shoulder, the other around Dave's, drawing them together as if to share a warm goodbye. He angrily whispered, "None of this happened."

Dave immediately replied, "Right. Nothing."

Jim hesitated, weighing exactly what Zacheray was asking of them. He assumed details would have to be suppressed, but was uncertain which ones.

"Jim. All right," Zacheray said firmly, putting a different meaning on Jim's silence. "We better clear this up before you go. We can't afford to have anybody mad about this morning. You must hate my guts right now. For what I did back there. And what I made you do. We were both very stupid. You lost your temper and I lost mine. You hit a nerve. I went a little crazy."

Jim was so certain he'd been completely in the wrong, it took him a moment to understand Zacheray was taking blame upon himself.

"I went a little crazy," he repeated. "I had no business dragging you into that, but you hit a nerve. I hated killing that kid. I did. Maybe there was a better way, but it seemed like the only way. The heat of the moment. I wanted to put you in my shoes in the worst way possible."

"I understand," said Jim, although he didn't, not completely. There were too many different motives to puzzle together. "I went a little nuts myself out there."

"I'm damn lucky you didn't blow my head off when I stuck that piece in your hand,'' Zacheray said, and made a dry little laugh. "But nobody can think straight in this place. I'm sorry, okay? No hard feelings?''

"None," said Jim.

"All right then. We don't mention this to anyone. It never happened.''

"Mum's the word," said Dave. "Just like Georges's parties.''

Zacheray glanced sideways, more uncomfortable over the mention of Georges than he'd been about the killing. But then a homosexual orgy would be a worse sin here than the killing of a Viet Cong suspect. "Okay. I'm glad we cleared that up. You're a good man, Jim.'' He slapped both men on their backs and stepped away. "Here's your ride.''

An army-green Mustang pulled up beside them, tires hissing in the half-melted tar. Zacheray opened the door for Jim and Dave and told the corporal at the wheel to take his very important guests to the Caravelle Hotel. "It's been real," he shouted, and slammed the door hard.

But it hadn't been real, Jim thought as the accelerating car threw him against the soft backseat. Dave peeled off his sunglasses and Jim saw his eyes for the first time in hours, ringed and bloodshot. Neither of them had slept for days, it seemed. No wonder the world seemed so thin and unreal. Dave glanced guiltily at Jim and said nothing. They couldn't speak about what had happened, especially in the presence of the driver up front.

Jim must have fallen asleep, because suddenly they were parked outside a hotel, city traffic honking and grinding around them, Dave opening the door. "Thank you, corporal," Jim automatically told the driver and followed Dave into the Caravelle Hotel. The same pack of Swedes sat in the lobby, still fussing over the movie camera they had fussed over yesterday when Jim arrived.

Dave went with him up to his room and watched while Jim stuffed clothes into his bag on the bed he'd never slept in. "You want company on your ride out to the airport?'' he asked.

"I'll be fine. You should clean up and get some sleep." Jim wanted to be alone as soon as possible, and on his way back to Manila where he could become himself again, the stuffy, well-meaning fellow his superiors and subordinates thought him to be. The presence of this witness blocked out that identity.

"Right," said Dave. "I do need sleep. Something to put more distance between me and this morning. How do you do it, Jim?''

"Do what?''

"Stay so calm.''

"Who said I was calm?'' But he was, wasn't he? Calm and detached. His strongest feelings right now were a fear of missing his plane, and an irritation with Dave for insisting he was so calm, somehow inhuman.

"I'm a wreck," said Dave, licking his parched lips to speak. "And I didn't do a damn thing. When I think how close we came to getting ourselves killed, how my stunt almost made a widow of Elaine and a—''

"Then stop thinking about it!" Jim snapped.

Dave looked at Jim and said, "You feel bad about that kid?"

"Of course," Jim said coldly. "I do." He zipped his bag shut.

"You shouldn't. I don't know what was going through your head back there, or Phil's head either. But you were right to do something. I just stood there."

"It was all very stupid and unnecessary. I don't know what I was thinking back there either. But it didn't change a damn thing, did it?"

"You saved that kid from two minutes of suffering. I know you must feel that's not much," Dave insisted. "But it's something. I admire you for that."

"Then you're a bigger idiot than I am." Jim hoisted his bag and went to the door, determined to end this conversation. He did not want his moment of insanity to be admirable or moral. He wanted it to mean nothing, to be as accidental and meaningless as a man tripping over a shoelace. He had gone a little crazy out there; he had lost his temper. That's all. "I've got a plane to catch."

Dave followed him out to the elevators. "Goodbye, Jim. And good luck. We'll be in touch."

"Yes?" Jim stared, baffled. He didn't want to be in touch. Without Dave's guilty glances to remind him he'd been there too, Jim could treat today as his own private nightmare.

"The papers on you-know-who," Dave reminded him. "The Senate hearing. I'll let you know the results."

"Oh yeah. That." The original deed that brought Jim here seemed like ancient history, small potatoes. "See what comes of it. If anything."

"I'll send you a note. Something discreet."

"Whatever." The elevator arrived and Jim stepped inside. "Good luck, Wheeler."

"You too. We'll need it."

The steel doors closed between them and Jim was alone again, free, as if none of it had ever happened.

He checked out at the desk. He grabbed a taxi out front, promising to pay the driver double if they got to the airport on time. With the man pumping his horn and lurching around traffic, Jim sat back, readjusted his legs in the confined space of the Fiat and thought about getting home, where he could have a hot shower, clean clothes and a good dinner fixed by Perpetua. A cool seafood salad might be nice tonight.

Then the bicep of his right arm began to twitch. The arm was awkwardly twisted around the flight bag on the seat and Jim shifted it into a more comfortable position. A new set of muscles began to tremble. When Jim lifted all weight off it, his entire forearm was quivering, spasms from elbow to wrist making his hand shake violently. He grabbed the wrist to stop the shaking. The outstretched fingers refused to close into a fist.

The cabbie swung his long black hair back and forth to the French pop song on the radio, oblivious to his passenger.

Jim flattened the shaking hand against his thigh, trying to keep it still until the spasms passed. His left hand held the quivering bones just as it had held a quivering jaw. And Jim saw a brown spot of blood on two knuckles of his right hand. Not his blood, but someone else's. He remembered a stinging sensation that accompanied the second gunshot. Like a splinter of bone, but it was only blood made hard by the velocity with which it splashed. Muscle and bone seemed to relive every detail, remembering more clearly than mind did. Mind was sickened, horrified. He had killed a man—a boy, in fact. He was a fool to think he could go on as if it had never happened.

The trembling stopped, first in his hand, then in his arm. The physical panic burned itself out, leaving Jim weak and queasy, sick with awareness. He had killed a man.

His legs were rubber when he climbed out at the air terminal; he had to lean against the cab while he paid the driver. But walking made him feel better, gave his body back to him a little. Inside the enormous, humid shed, he went straight to the men's room, splashed rusty water on his face and washed the spot of blood from his hand. It came off easily, without soap. The man in the mirror did not look like a murderer. He looked shabby and hungover, with a pink sunburned nose that hadn't been protected by the shade of the steel helmet, the rosy nose of a cartoon drunk.

He stepped out of the men's room just as they announced the boarding of his flight. Turning stern and pompous, he thrust ahead of the others, flashed his State Department I.D. and hurried through the check-in. Very quickly, he was walking down the carpeted aisle inside the familiar tube of little windows and futuristic high-backed seats. Isn't technology wonderful, he thought. You can be part of brutal war in the morning, then fly home in modern comfort that afternoon.

Young men entered the cabin in bunches, hooting and laughing as they took over whole sections of the plane. More G.I.'s on R&R, they wore civilian clothes that were stale and wrinkled from months at the bottoms of duffel bags. Surely they had witnessed terrible scenes, even participated as Jim had. They were killers, some of them, yet they seemed oddly innocent despite their swaggers and constant litany of shit and motherfucker, as noisy as schoolchildren starting a class trip. Their gift for forgetting was remarkable. They needed to forget, Jim told himself. Unlike Jim, they'd be returning in two short weeks.

There were a few women on board, unhappy wives and toughly smiling stewardesses, and more Filipino musicians this trip, two different bands apparently, one with hippie haircuts, the other looking country-western. The country-western group took seats around Jim, one fellow with anemic sideburns and a thin weedy mustache taking the window seat beside his. Jim noticed the fellow's cowboy shirt. The shoulder panels were madras, not paisley, but Jim had to turn away. Could he ever look another Asian in the eye without thinking of that boy? He found himself watching two soldiers across the aisle, one white, the other black, both of them about nineteen or twenty. As the plane pulled away from the gate, the white became more giddy, happily jabbing his buddy with an elbow. When the black groaned and swatted back, Jim expected their horseplay to end in an embrace and kiss, the two men to start necking.

They didn't, of course. Jim was startled he could imagine they would. But once the idea was introduced, he could not look at or think of the soldiers around him without picturing them in a swimming pool, naked and kissing. Georges's party had warped his mind, primed it with dirty pictures he could not control. Another pair of G.I.'s down the aisle, just crewcuts visible above their headrests, might be bareassed and touching each other. A stocky sergeant standing up to pull a magazine from the luggage rack could put his crotch in the face of the man beside him. Somewhere on board might be the very soldier whose cock Jim had tried and failed to take in his mouth.

Engines roaring, the plane raced faster, gathering speed before it jerked upward. Jim closed his eyes, hoping the sudden gravity would jerk him from this morbid fantasy. Instead, he imagined the slippery weight in his mouth now, with no trace of the nausea or helplessness he had suffered last night.

The jet rose steeply, and Jim felt his own weight lifting inside his fly. He crossed his legs to hide it, knocking the Filipino cowboy with his foot.

"Pardon me," Jim murmured, not looking at the man.

It was twisted, perverse, to think such thoughts after what happened this morning, to find his cock doing now what it rightly refused to do last night. Jim wanted to be proud he hadn't participated, needed to believe there was one area in his life where he behaved correctly.

Then the next thought struck him, and undid everything: *I cannot have sex with men. I can only kill them.*

Which was absurd. And frightening. And true. Jim had killed someone, which was the real perversity. The pornographic movies playing in his head no longer seemed so sordid or disturbing. They were sane and almost tender compared to the memory of a skull being blasted apart.

Pretending to look out the window, Jim studied the cowboy beside him, afraid of what he might see. But despite the shirt and black hair, the Filipino looked nothing like the Vietnamese boy. He was older, well into his twenties, with rounder eyes and thick lips, his facial hair so sparse his sideburns looked like they'd been done with a pencil. He appeared bored and restless.

"You fly this route often?" Jim asked.

The fellow turned and smiled; he was missing a tooth. "Oh yas. Meeny times this yar. Me and my brothers are country singers, you see. Tommy Memphis and His Lonesome Cowboys. You hear of us perhaps?" Very friendly and outgoing, the fellow was overjoyed to have someone to talk to. His lilting Filipino English was full of twanged syllables from Tennessee or

Texas, infected by the songs he imitated from records. His name was Cayetano, his friends called him Chick, and he and his brothers were returning home after a tour of NCO clubs in the Central Highlands. Sergeants and warrant officers were their biggest fans, he explained. Enlisted men preferred hard rock. He loved to sing but missed "the green green grass of home," a town in the Visayans where he had a wife and five children.

Jim listened and kept Chick going with new questions, although the fellow did fine on his own. He had no intention of trying anything with Chick. This was only a test, an experiment. Jim needed to see if he could speak with Asian men without being overwhelmed by the awful knowledge he'd killed one. Watching the little mustache twist and curl over the missing tooth, however, Jim suddenly imagined kissing Chick. He pictured himself taking that face in both hands and pressing his mouth to Chick's mouth. It was a sad, alarming urge, sad because Jim couldn't forget how easy it would be to put a gun to Chick's head and shoot him instead.

THE SENATE SUBCOMMITTEE on United States Security Agreements and Commitments Abroad began hearings in Washington on September 30, opening with the Philippines. Along with detailed testimony on the smuggling and corruption was an itemized schedule of payments obtained from the Government Accounting Office: the State Department had secretly paid $39 million to the Marcos government for the Philcag engineering battalion sent to Vietnam. A breakdown of bank accounts and corporate holdings produced by Senator Symington's staff suggested all the money had gone into Marcos's pocket. Exchanges between State Department officials and the subcommittee were made more heated by the fact this was a closed session and no TV cameras or reporters were present. The testimony would not become public until the subcommittee published its report.

"We threw our little party, private but satisfying," Dave Wheeler wrote on a picture postcard sent to Jim at the embassy—a personal letter might look suspicious. "We played pin the tail on the donkey. Photos should be out in a week. Elaine and Janey send love. Tarbaby don't say nothing. Dave."

But a week passed, then a month, and the report did not go out to the press. Kissinger's people sat on it for fear the facts might hurt Marcos's reelection. November arrived and Marcos won by a landslide. The report wasn't published until March, and even then it was heavily censored, facts expunged or presented as rumors. The amounts and recipients of the Philcag payments were deleted, so the charge seemed vague and unsubstantiated. Gone was any suggestion of Ferdinand Marcos himself selling soldiers for profit from his own private herd. Ambassador Earp saw the uncensored version and was furious with both Congress and whatever whistleblowing asshole helped them find their figures. Jim mollified suspicions Earp had about him by issuing a stern memo to his own staff reminding them where their loyalty lay. Earp was impressed by the memo, so much in fact that he sent copies to other sections in the embassy over his own signature.

It wasn't until after the gutted report appeared and good deeds were shown to be useless that Jim made his first visit to the Patpong.

Not to the Ermita, which was just a few blocks from the embassy in Manila, but to the Patpong in Bangkok. Manila was a small world where even the greenest boy could figure out where this American worked and ask for extra money, special favors, visas for himself and his family in exchange for his discretion. Jim had to wait until he could get away again, flying to Bangkok for the weekend.

The war had turned this city, like Saigon, into an American honky-tonk of bars and clubs and massage parlors. Jim had a few drinks in his hotel room, then disappeared into the neon rock-and-roll of the sex district, another middle-aged civilian in sunglasses. Sexuality was simply geography here. Jim found the street off Patpong Road that catered to men who wanted men or boys. The smoky gold light in a bar called Tulip was full of boys, although most Thai men looked adolescent to Jim until they became elderly. The boys employed by the bar wore white singlets and shiny silk gym shorts. Their very presence had a sexual gravity Jim never found in western strangers, or in any Asian men at all until the past few months, an erotic anonymity like the sex in dreams.

In the throng of white and Asian customers drinking along the bar, a boy crowded up against Jim, and smiled. His weight was as inexplicably friendly as the press of bodies in dreams where desire and memory conjure up a second person. He had a delicate mustache like a third eyebrow on his upper lip. His English was even more bare than Jim's Thai, which ten years ago had consisted of a few commands for household servants. Jim had to talk to him through the bartender: his name was It—a common Thai nickname—and he was new to the city. He'd never had an American and found Jim very distinguished and large.

The dream continued in a little "V.I.P." room upstairs. In reddish darkness by candlelight, without the bartender present to translate words, a smooth shadow prepared himself by sponging off at a basin. His smile seemed genuine; he had an erection. He kept the smile even when Jim stood naked beside him and It wrinkled his nose at the foreign smell of western sweat and diet. He happily sponged Jim down, like a man brushing a new horse.

There was a faint jolt of unease when Jim bent down to kiss, but then, inside the kiss, the flat map of the world suddenly became three-dimensional. He was amazed by the simplicity of it, the textures in his hands, the weightlessness of body and conscience when one was sexually excited. His grandfather was gone from his throat; Jim could do anything to this simple mystery who knew nothing about Jim except that he was large and distinguished and here.

When it was over, Jim felt guilty, although not soul-sick the way he'd expected to be, more foolish than sinful. Counting out It's "gift" of two hundred baht—prostitution was disguised as a friendly favor here—Jim felt like an ugly American, the power of money buying him sex just as it bought Philippine soldiers from Ferdinand Marcos. But It took the money with an easy smile and pressed his hands together for the slight bow that was a Buddhist thank-you. Jim envied him his lack of shame, his ability to mix business with pleasure. Back at the hotel, Jim told himself he'd never need to do this again now that he knew what the fuss was about, but he suspected his body would disagree.

He returned three months later, then four months after that, saving his visits for times of reward or need. If he could kill a man without reality coming apart, he could certainly have sex with one now and then. Sex remained in its own little room, just as the killing remained in another. In fact, the two secrets seemed to balance each other, like the deliberate flooding of a watertight compartment to counter the flooding opposite and save a damaged ship from capsizing.

With that other life below the waterline, Jim disappeared into his work at the embassy, playing the good subordinate with Earp, keeping all conscience and criticism to himself. He thought he could get through his tour in Manila with good marks and no conflicts. Then, on the night of September 22, 1972, President Marcos seized power by declaring martial law, and everything changed again.

7

THREE DAYS INTO 1973, on a cold, gray winter afternoon, Meg Frisch lay on her parents' four-poster bed and smoked a cigarette. Home was stultifying and she wished she were back at school, even with exams coming up. Her *Marx and Engels Reader* sprawled facedown on the nubbly white bedspread beside her.

"What time's Jim supposed to be here?"

"*Uncle* Jim," said Mom, "told us not to expect him before four."

The old black-and-white TV played at a low boil between mother and daughter, watched by neither of them. Mom sat sideways at the long sewing desk Dad had built for her, poking and tugging at the needlework kit Walter gave her for Christmas. She looked like an eccentric hermit over there, wearing one of Meg's William and Mary sweatshirts, Dad's woolly golf socks, her reading glasses perched on the bump of her nose with a length of red yarn tied to the earpieces and looped around her neck. Meg admired her mother's lack of vanity, but wished she had the independence of mind that went with it.

"I wonder what he knows about Henry Kissinger the rest of the world doesn't?" Meg asked the ceiling.

"I still don't understand why he couldn't have timed his visit better. I'm not ready for a houseful of guests."

Meg's exasperation returned. "You want me to call Doug and tell him not to come?"

Mom broke off a thread with her teeth. "What's done is done. Be rude to ask your friend to change his plans this late in the game. Not his fault Jimmy chose today to take some time off. Or that Robbie lost his apartment. Never rains but it pours."

They made everything so difficult here. Uncle Jim telephoned last night to say he finally had time for a visit, the first since his return from the Philippines. Doug Inge was driving down tomorrow from northern Virginia to spend two days with Meg before she rode back with him to Williamsburg. That was all, yet Mom treated it as a terrible imposition, a horrendous invasion of privacy. Meg didn't remember her parents being so neurotically private, but she hadn't spent this much time with them since last Christmas. The summer spent at summer school, without her annual fix of family, seemed to have changed Meg, making her more perceptive and irritable. Meg at twenty saw through everyone, and it was awful. She used to love chatting with her mother, but now all she could see were her mother's limitations.

"What gets me is why it had to be *now*," said Mom, hunting for a new spool. "He's been back for two weeks. If he wanted to see us so badly, he could've come *last* week, when the tree was still up."

"Maybe he had work to do. People to see in Washington. He had to explain why his last assignment is now a dictatorship."

But allusions to world events were lost on Mom. "Hmmm. Been so peaceful this past year. Just Walter and your father. Now all at once I've got you and Robbie and your uncle to contend with. And then this boyfriend to boot."

"Not a boyfriend, Mom, just a friend," Meg repeated with a groan. "Next time I come home I'll stay in a motel."

"No need for sarcasm, Miss Priss. You know what I mean. Your father's not wild about having so many people underfoot, and I'm the one stuck with keeping his feathers in place. Well, blessed are the peacemakers," she sighed.

There was a paragraph by Rebecca West, a recent discovery of Meg's, where West proposed that "idiocy"—derived from the Greek for "the refusal to go into public places"—was the female vice, an inability to see beyond private experience to the world-at-large. Meg had been wanting to quote it to her mother all week, but she couldn't. It was too insulting, too cruel, even if she included West's next statement that the male equivalent was "lunacy," a refusal to take seriously anything that wasn't public and as distant as the moon.

"Anyway, Doug's not coming until tomorrow, so Uncle Jim has us all to himself tonight," said Meg. "Lucky Jim."

Mom concentrated on rethreading her needle. "You might talk to him about law school while he's here. Maybe he can set you straight."

Meg gritted her teeth. This was their chief bone of contention, the real cause for Meg's frustration. "How?" she demanded.

"That it's hard work. Maybe too hard for someone likely to be dropping out in a few years to have a family."

Meg wanted her mother to be imaginative and intelligent, for other people if not for herself. She wasn't, which was both sad and surprising.

"What makes you think I *want* a family?"

"Don't sell yourself short, dear. Beneath your smarts, you're a passionate, caring person. You'd be much happier with a family than you give yourself credit for."

"Just because I went to law school wouldn't make me an old maid."

"I'm not saying it's impossible," Mom admitted, a change from the last time they discussed this. "I know there's women lawyers now. But I think you should look into it a little more before we mention it to your father."

Law school was a new idea. Meg had another year and a half of college left. She majored in history just because she had to major in something, and history was an old hobby. But Meg enjoyed a good argument and thought she'd make a good lawyer. She worried about becoming part of a corrupt institution, but trusted that being a woman insured she'd remain an outsider. All through Christmas break she'd been fighting her mother's assumption that women belonged nowhere near the game.

"But talk to your uncle," said Mom. "See what he thinks."

"Well, we know what Uncle Jim did with *his* law degree," Meg muttered. "Flitting about the world, making it safe for democracy."

The mocking tone caused Mom to glance up nervously. "Meg, dear? You will be nice to your uncle while he's here?"

"Why wouldn't I be nice to old Uncle Jim?"

The fake innocence did not amuse her. "You know exactly what I mean, Margaret Frisch. These books you're reading. Your friends at school. You've picked up a few too many ideas lately."

"You afraid I'll attack Uncle Jim for being a running-dog lackey of the imperialist warmongers?"

"I'm serious."

"So am I." Meg began to laugh.

"Things are going to be tough enough around here without you going after Jimmy with all guns blazing."

Meg gave up; it was like making faces at a blind man. "Oh Mom. I *like* Uncle Jim. I look forward to seeing him again. We haven't seen him in five years. But I want to talk to him about foreign policy," she confessed; she hoped to get into a good argument with an adult who'd argue back. "If we don't agree on everything, we can still be friendly," she claimed.

Mom frowned and settled into her needlework again, understanding that this was the most her daughter would promise. She stole another glance at Meg and quietly changed the subject. "I think we'll put Jimmy downstairs in the back room while he's here. And your friend on the family room sofa when he arrives tomorrow."

"I thought we were putting Jim in my room. And *I'd* sleep in the back room." With the family room just a door away.

Mom remained bent over her needle. "No. Not this visit. Not while this boy is here."

And Meg caught what she was discreetly saying. "*Mom.* Doug's just a good friend. That's all."

"Then it won't matter where you sleep, will it?"

"I thought if Doug and I wanted to talk late—and my bed's better for guests—oh forget it," she groaned. "Why should I care who's in what bed?" It was ridiculous, another piece of the idiocy of family life. Away at school, she'd been able to forget the humiliation of being treated as a household pet who needed to be protected from temptation. Meg rolled off the bed and gathered up her book and ashtray. "I've got to get back to my studying," she grumbled.

Mom watched her daughter leave. "This Doug," she said, on a softer, more sympathetic note. "He's not a boyfriend. But you'd like him to be one. Wouldn't you?"

Meg stopped in the door and rolled her eyes. "No, Mom. I wouldn't."

"Not just a little?"

"Nope. Doug is Doug. I like his intellectual curiosity. That's all. Men and women *can* be friends, you know. I should finish this chapter before Uncle Jim gets here," she declared and went down the short flight of steps to her own room.

Seeing through her mother's blind spots and limitations, Meg was alarmed to think Mom was still able to see straight through her. They *were* just friends, but friends who had sex now and then. Her mother wouldn't understand that, but then Meg didn't always understand it herself.

Sex was relatively new for Meg. She'd done it twice freshman year with a leering, narcissistic sophomore from her Violence in America seminar to commemorate the escape from home. Innocence out of the way, she could concentrate on the more interesting aspects of college life, the heady freedom of new ideas, book talk and beer—she disliked grass because being stoned ruined intelligent conversation. She met Doug last year in summer school. They were both drunk the first time it happened, but sober and deliberate on later occasions. "I feel awful because I don't love you," Doug guiltily confessed after the third time. "Nothing wrong with two good friends having sex," Meg assured him, improvising wisdom on the spot. She knew it was the woman's role to feel guilty about sex without love, but she didn't feel guilty. Doug was guilty enough for them both and, despite her assurances, it usually took him two or three weeks to overcome his scruples again. In the days in between, they continued their friendship, two intelligent people standing back to back and sharing comments about the world around them. The friendship was good, the sex fun, but there were mornings when Meg opened the baby-blue compact in her purse, saw the month spelled out in birth control pills and wondered if sex were worth the bother. It would be so much easier if Doug *were* in love with her, because then there wouldn't be this guilt that made his lust so erratic and unpredictable.

All right then, maybe her mother was right, but not for the reasons she imagined. Glancing through Marx in her bedroom, Meg fought free of motherly love by telling herself she could still slip downstairs and visit the family room sofa tomorrow night, when Uncle Jim was asleep.

An engine rattled and sighed out on the street.

Meg lifted the petticoat curtain above her bed and saw a car parked by their mailbox, a small red Pinto instead of the enormous Dodge she expected to see. But when the door opened and a man unfolded himself from behind the wheel, it was their uncle, fattened up by an unfashionable tweed overcoat, his bright pink forehead creeping into the ruffled nest of red hair. He pulled out a shopping bag full of packages and his old blue flight bag and walked slowly up the empty, oil-spotted driveway, worriedly looking around as if afraid he'd come to the wrong house. He seemed comic and sweetly awkward when seen from above. Wondering what he might mean to her now, Meg went downstairs to let him in.

She jerked the front door open and the suction of air banged the storm door like a gunshot. Out on the sidewalk, Uncle Jim looked up, startled. He lowered his eyebrows to stare at Meg as he approached, a blank stare that suddenly broke apart in the furious blinking of a man coming out of a daydream.

Meg pushed the storm door open. "Uncle Jim!" She exaggerated her greeting to make him feel welcome; he appeared so sad and lost out there.

"Meg?" He looked straight at her as he came up the porch steps, then remembered to smile. "Meg!"

"Who else?" she said and stepped aside to let him in, a cold cloud of air entering with him.

"My God, you've grown. I hardly recognized you." He dropped his bags and, before Meg could close the door behind them, threw both arms around her.

The icy leather gloves were a shock, and the embrace itself. They weren't a family for hugs and kisses, although Meg had found herself wanting to hug people when she arrived home this visit, Mom and Walter anyway. She'd assumed the impulse had something to do with her discovery of sex, but when Uncle Jim embraced her, she immediately wondered if touching were simply something in the zeitgeist, a symptom of changing times. Uncle Jim smelled strongly of aftershave and mothballs.

"Just look at you." A gloved hand gripped the shoulder of her sweatshirt while she turned away to shut the door. "I thought you were one of your brothers at first, until I saw your hair and thought you were your mother. When you first got married—when *she* was married, I mean."

Meg patiently smiled as she twisted her shoulder out of his grip. She had Mom's nose, but looked nothing like her mother, she hoped. "Mom!" she hollered up the stairs. "He's here!"

"I hear y'all! Down in a jiff! Let me get some shoes on!"

Uncle Jim looked around as he pulled off his gloves. "New wallpaper. Your father hang it himself? And there's furniture in the living room now. Looks good. You look good, too, Meg-wump. A real woman. It's great to see you again. Great to be back."

His physical presence felt as peculiar as his chatter. He had a middle-aged beefiness Meg didn't remember, male muscle and volume, but she'd never embraced her uncle so consciously before. He was a head taller than Meg, his face different shades of red and white, a combination of sunburn and cold. Peeled skin salted his metallic-pink eyebrows; his ears glowed in the heat of the house. Meg had forgotten her uncle was not just an idea but a body, with a body's cartoon idiosyncrasies.

"And everyone's home for the holidays. Your mother must be happy."

"Overjoyed," said Meg. "C'mon in, Uncle Jim. Why don't you take off your coat and stay awhile?"

"Right," he laughed. "Right," unbuttoning the long coat as he followed her into the shadowy kitchen. "I'm so excited to be here I still don't know if I'm coming or going." He laid the heavy, mothball-fumed tweed on the built-in bench behind the table, then sat down on the end of the bench, glancing around as if he'd never seen an American kitchen before. His grin hung on his face so long it looked unnatural. A striped dress shirt gaped at his throat without a necktie to hold him together.

"Would you like some coffee or tea? There's beer." The bottom shelf of the refrigerator was taken up with Robbie's six-packs.

"I'll have whatever you're having, Meg-wump."

She wished he'd stop calling her that. "Coffee then," and she filled a pot of water at the sink.

"So. You like college?"

A boring variation on the only question adults think to ask kids: You like school? Meg wanted her uncle to know her better than that. "I like it. It's difficult but exciting. How was Manila?"

"Ohhh, you know," he said. "Third World."

"Didn't the president there seize power in a coup last year?"

"Not a coup," he said, surprised she knew. "He exercised his legal powers to declare martial law, which amounts to much the same thing. You've been reading about that?"

"Off and on," Meg admitted. "Mostly in *Time*. The local papers never had much to say."

"Well, *Time*," he said and grimaced. His face came together in a way it hadn't when he grinned. "It's a fiasco. A tragedy. Only nobody seems to realize that. Nobody except a handful of stupid FSOs who think even a corrupt democracy is better than no democracy. Sorry." He held up his hand to stop himself. "It was on my mind on the drive down and I should spare you the boring details." He shook his head and chuckled, unable to look at Meg.

Before she could explain she wanted the details and would not find them boring, there was a clip-clop of shoes coming down the steps. Uncle Jim quickly stood up and turned around.

"Jimmy," Mom softly sang as she entered the kitchen. She wore her gray cardigan now and had retouched her lipstick. She looked as startled as Meg had been when he gave her a passionate hug too. "Hmmm, you've kept in shape," she said, lightly hugging back.

Frustrated the conversation was interrupted just when it became interesting —whose side was Uncle Jim on?—Meg watched the weird spectacle of old dogs trying out new tricks. It was as though the man hoped to make up in hugs for his failure with words.

"We're so glad you could make it down," Mom said when he released her, shooting Meg a look that dared her to say otherwise. "No, no. Sit, sit. Make yourself at home. Is that water for coffee, Meg? She's still a good kid, isn't she? You hungry, Jimmy? It's potluck tonight, but your niece can fix you a sandwich if you need something to hold you until dinner."

Uncle Jim insisted he was fine and Mom pulled out a chair to sit across from him. They smiled at each other with an affection that seemed sheepish yet genuine, even when neither knew what to say.

"There's late Christmas presents out in the hall. Nothing special. Just Tagalog barongs—Filipino shirts. I hope I have the sizes right."

"I'm sure they'll be fine. If we'd known you were coming, we would've kept the tree up. Rick takes it down the day after Christmas."

After Meg brought Uncle Jim his cup of instant coffee, she withdrew with her own cup to the corner, sitting up on the kitchen counter where she could watch them from a slightly elevated angle.

Mom filled him in on who was doing what in the family. She went on too long about the improvements Dad had made around the house and about the little cheerleader Walter was dating; Uncle Jim's nods and hums became mechanical, as though his attention had drifted back to the Philippines. She tread a thin line between honesty and deceit when she talked about Robbie losing his construction job after flunking out of college. "It's the economy, you know. Robbie's a very good carpenter. He takes after his father in that department."

"Takes after the wild boar in the behavior department," said Meg.

"He *can* be difficult," Mom admitted, sadly bowing her head. "There's times I almost wish he hadn't gotten such a high draft number. A couple of years in the service might've straightened him out."

Meg was embarrassed her mother could say such a thing, ashamed she said it in front of Uncle Jim. She might be narrow, but she wasn't stupid. "You don't really mean that, Mom. If Robbie'd been drafted, they would've sent him to Vietnam."

"I know *that*." She became flustered and spoke more quickly. "I don't wish that on anyone. But it's another terrible thing about this war. Otherwise, the army'd be the perfect place for a lot of young men to get their acts together."

Meg lost all patience. "Armies exist to fight in wars. Not to improve people."

"Don't contradict me, dear. I was only making a generalization."

Uncle Jim shared a look with Meg, but didn't smile, showed neither surprise nor pity.

"What about you, Jimmy?" Mom quickly changed the subject. "What's new in your life? I see you got a new car."

They talked about his new car for several minutes and Mom asked if he were going to stay in Washington for a while. He explained he didn't know yet, that he was between assignments. "Walking the corridors, as we say. But if I survived one term of the current administration, I can certainly survive another."

Meg asked if he were going to go to Nixon's reinauguration later that month.

"I'll be in town. But we in the State Department are outside of all that, Meg-wump. I might be stuck chaperoning Mrs. Marcos around, although I hope not. She's invited herself to town. This is the wife of the Filipino president," he explained to Mom.

Meg too needed to be reminded who she was. The Marcoses were not yet household names and Meg had been telling the truth when she said she'd followed events in the Philippines only off and on. Most of her attention went to books and classes; her interest in current events, which came in bursts, was generally focused on Vietnam and Cambodia.

"A friend and I are going," she said. "Not to the inauguration, but to a big rally at the Washington Monument. A kind of anti-inauguration. About the war and Christmas bombings."

"Your niece," said Mom, with an apologetic tone and soothing smile. "She has a mind of her own. She wants to go as much for the spectacle and being at a historical event as for anything else.''

Meg refused to let the lie stand. ''No. I'm going because I'm against the war.''

Uncle Jim looked at her, the skin around his eyes crimped with discomfort, the pink eyebrows lifted questioningly. But then he said, ''You will be careful, won't you?''

Meg had wanted him to take issue with her beliefs. She wasn't ready for his concern about her safety. ''There'll be a hundred thousand people there. People from Congress are speaking, Uncle Jim. Nothing bad can happen.''

''I've made Meg promise she's to get out of there at the first sign of trouble,'' Mom told him. ''But they've been having these demonstrations for years without any problems.''

Meg resisted the urge to correct her by mentioning Chicago and Kent State; there were advantages in having a mother with news amnesia.

Jim glanced from mother to daughter. ''I've been out of the country for five years. But, yes, we do things differently here. I don't imagine there'll be any problems. So long as Meg keeps her eyes open. Is your escort a man?''

''Yes.'' Meg wondered what difference that would make if the police started clubbing people.

''You'll be getting to meet him,'' said Mom. ''He's coming down tomorrow for a short visit before he takes Meg back to school.''

''Ah.'' The presence of an extra guest meant nothing to Uncle Jim. ''Well, so long as she's not alone, I think she'll be safe.''

The idea of Doug as any kind of protector was a laugh, but Meg let it pass.

''Don't mention anything about the rally in front of Rick,'' Mom asked. ''We don't want to get him going on that subject.''

Uncle Jim nodded, then looked again at Meg. He suddenly smiled at her, but it was a light, gentle smile, like a smile bestowed on a cat.

''Will you be at the rally, Uncle Jim?''

''Ohhh, I think not. Sounds like it's something for you young people. Not an old goat like myself.''

Meg remembered him being guarded and evasive in the past, but she'd assumed it was because he thought she was just a kid who wouldn't understand. Now she felt it was because she was an outsider, a civilian, a girl. She'd have to find a way to show him he was wrong.

''Look at the time,'' said Mom. ''I better get dinner started.''

She shooed Meg off the counter so she could get to the cupboards. She suggested Meg take her uncle downstairs to the family room, but Uncle Jim said he was fine where he was, that he enjoyed the chance to sit in a real kitchen and chat while his sister cooked. The overhead light was turned on and, with darkness outside the window and in the rest of the house, the Formica and vinyl formed a homey cubicle. Meg had no choice but to sit with her uncle. She knew she wouldn't be able to get him to talk about Marcos and democracy with Mom present, or find out where he stood on Vietnam, so she didn't even try. They talked about Dad finally getting the vice-presidency that had been held out to him as a carrot on a stick for the past ten years, and Meg's upcoming exams, sadistically scheduled between Christmas vacation and semester break.

Walter came home from basketball practice, entering through the back door and coming up the steps from the family room, feet like lead, his gym bag hanging from one simian arm. "Uncle Jim. Good to see you." He was too busy keeping his voice in a low, manly register for him to put much feeling in the greeting.

Meg watched to see if their uncle hugged men too, but no, he stood up and gave Walter a firm handshake. He looked uncomfortable with Walter, staring at his body then not quite looking at him at all, and Meg wondered if he'd confused him with Robbie, who was the one who'd never liked their uncle.

"Hey, hey. Uncle Jimbo!" Robbie crowed when he came in. "How's it hanging, man? You been losing your hair. How about a brew, bro'? After a long day on the road, the only thing better than a hot babe is a cold beer."

Robbie usually wasn't this bad. It was a show for the sake of their guest. Uncle Jim did not look offended. He stared at Robbie, confused and amazed, as if his nephew were a new animal, a mixture of breeds he couldn't figure out. Robbie had shoulder-length hair and long sideburns that ran along his jaw, but the peace sign plastered on the back of his denim jacket was captioned: "Footprint of the American Chicken."

"You were right next door to 'Nam, Jimbo. You get any gook ears over there? That's what my wheels need right now. A chopped-off ear like a piece of dried fruit, hanging from my rearview mirror."

Uncle Jim bit his lip and glared at Robbie, his throat tightening in disgust.

"Ignore him," said Meg. "He's turned into a real loser."

"Yeah? Better that than a libber egghead."

"Kids," said Mom. "Will you *please* cool it. Go downstairs and watch TV, Robbie."

"Whatever you say, Big Mama. You're the boss." He went down the steps with a can of beer in each hand and turned on the television.

Mom wrinkled her forehead and smirked at Uncle Jim: Blessed are the peacemakers.

Dad came in through the garage and they heard him and Robbie greet each other with their usual strained tolerance. Then Dad came up the steps, wearing his business smile and one of his eternal gray suits and white shirts. Only his neckties changed with the times, growing wider and slightly colorful.

"Jim. Good to see you. Have a good drive down?"

"The house looks good, Rick. Congratulations on the promotion."

Dad winced and smiled and brushed aside the compliments with a courtly wave of his fingers. Meg had thought only Uncle Jim had aged, but he made their father look older too: the thin threads of hair in his widow's peak, shirt bellied at his belt when he threw his shoulders back. Dad stepped over to peck Mom on the cheek and whisper with her at the stove.

Dinner was eaten in the dining room that night; Robbie and Walter were too large now for everyone to fit at the kitchen table with Uncle Jim here. Conversation was limited but peaceful. Uncle Jim said little about Manila except to mention the shock of coming from a tropical climate to a cold one. Dad was amiable and almost relaxed at first. As dinner progressed, however, he became more conscious of Robbie's noisy, sloppy eating, the elbows on the table, the face so close to the plate his hair got in his food. It was as though Uncle Jim's presence made him realize again what a pig his son had become. Finally, with a nervous smile and a look of personal hurt in his eyes, Dad said, "Robbie. You eat like you were raised by wolves."

Robbie's only response was to grin maliciously at their father and stuff a whole boiled potato into his mouth.

After dinner, they adjourned to the family room and Uncle Jim gave them their shirts, white gauze with white flowers embroidered up and down the fronts.

"*Men* wear these over there?" said Robbie. "Juicy-fruit city."

"They're lovely, Jimmy. They really are," said Mom. "Although you can see right through them, can't you?"

Walter went up to Mom's room to phone his girlfriend. Robbie left to meet some friends down at the beach. They might've been able to talk then, except Dad turned on the television. Even Uncle Jim seemed hypnotized by the bright colors and insistent laugh track.

"I'm so glad you could make it down," Mom told him during the first commercial. "Nice to be with family again, isn't it?"

Meg rocked in the rocking chair, growing more agitated and sullen. "I need fresh air," she announced. "I think I'll take a walk."

"You do that, dear. Walk off some of that nervous energy."

Uncle Jim came out of his trance and turned to Meg. "Mind if I join you? Or did you need to be alone?"

"Not at all. I'll get our coats." This was exactly what Meg wanted and she was pleased her uncle proposed it himself, without prompting. He too wanted a real conversation.

Mom distractedly watched them get ready. "Don't go *too* far, Meg," she pointedly called after her when they went out through the garage.

After the stale warmth inside, the air felt alive with cold, carbonated with it. There was no wind, no sound except the crunch of frozen grass under their shoes when they walked around the side of the house. Moonlight lined the tall, magnified nerves of the bare sweet gum tree out front.

"So what exactly happened in the Philippines?" Meg asked before they reached the end of the driveway.

Uncle Jim chuckled, broken clouds spurting from his mouth and nostrils. "We don't need to talk about that, Meg-wump."

"I don't mind. I'm curious."

"Actually, I'm trying to forget about it while I'm down here. Which way do we walk?"

Meg started them off to the right, where the street led away from the golf course. She was annoyed to find herself up against the old adult reticence about discussing work. Even Dad became so evasive and private when asked about the fertilizer trade that one would think he worked for the Mafia. In a way, Uncle Jim did, didn't he?

"So peaceful out here," he half-whispered as they walked. "I can't get over how still everything is."

There were no sidewalks, but no traffic either; they walked in the middle of the street. All the Christmas lights were down. Every house was folded in upon itself for the night, low moonlit hulls with an occasional set of curtains or blinds leaking yellow through the shrubs. The solitary streetlight at the corner illuminated a swatch of colorless lawn.

"Your parents seem to be doing well."

"Oh yeah." Meg had burned to get away from her family to talk about real issues, but all her uncle wanted to discuss was family.

"Walter, too. Robbie, on the other hand—" Another gust of cloud shot from the corner of his mouth. "I don't quite know what to make of Robbie."

"He's an ass," said Meg, deciding to leave off the second half of the word. "They keep expecting him to outgrow whatever bad phase he's going through, and he just grows into something worse."

"I'm surprised at the way he's turned out. Your father always seemed to be such a—uh—strict father."

"He's that, all right. And it all got aimed at Robbie. But it didn't take." Meg had a hundred different theories about her family—that it was Dad's high expectations that drove Robbie into manual labor, and Mom into the idiocy of private life; that Dad would've been happier as a cabinetmaker than as a corporate executive; that he had a middle-class income but working-class values—and she was tempted to share some of that with Uncle Jim, except she didn't want to talk about family. "I don't know what Robbie's problem is," she said. "He's overcompensating for something. Maybe he's a latent homosexual."

But Uncle Jim didn't laugh at her joke. He wasn't shocked either, but turned his head and asked very earnestly, "What makes you think that, Meg?"

"I don't, Uncle Jim. Not really. I was just saying that to be funny." She had to laugh to make her humor clear.

"Ah," said Jim, and he laughed with her.

"Robbie doesn't have the originality to be latent anything. It's just one of those things you can say about anyone to explain weird behavior." She hesitated; she'd said it herself about Uncle Jim, back at school when he was an idea and not a real person walking beside her.

He faced forward again, chuckling and shaking his head. "One of the clichés of our psychological age," he said cheerfully.

His ease with the notion surprised her. She and Doug had been speculating about the sex lives of parents and relatives, and when Doug took her little hypothesis about a bachelor uncle too seriously, she had to explain that even if it were true, Uncle Jim was too prudish and uptight to recognize such a thing in himself, much less act on it.

"And Freud says everyone's bisexual," she added. "So if it's true for everyone, it doesn't really explain anything, does it?" Even when she hadn't had her uncle's personal presence to defuse the idea, Meg hadn't taken it very seriously. It had felt like a private joke, sacrilegiously drawing a mustache and tits on a favorite family photograph.

"It doesn't," said Uncle Jim. "How about you? How are you doing?"

At first she thought he was asking if she were bisexual; she was tempted to tease him with her ideas about that. But then he asked specifically about William and Mary and her classes there, and Meg jumped at the chance to talk about herself. She told Uncle Jim about her paper on nineteenth-century programs to annex Cuba, written for her favorite teacher—the department's token leftist, who was trying to direct Meg into feminist studies.

The street ended in a larger street with Meg's old elementary school on the other side. She led them across the street into the playing fields to the left of the low slab of brick and windows. Behind the school was a farmer's field, acres of blue-gray stubble stretching to a distant horizon stitched with a line of bare trees. The sky was an ocean of blueness around a full moon, all stars hidden by the bright frozen bubble of light.

"You consider yourself a feminist?" Again there was no shock, only earnest curiosity.

"Naturally. But if I wanted to do history, I'd want real history, not piddly little monographs about antebellum child care. *If* I wanted to do history. Actually, right now I'm thinking about law school." And she began to tell him about that.

He seemed interested at first, then listened with his head bowed as they stepped over the patchy ground, hands burrowing deeper in his coat pockets. He abruptly said, "*I* went to law school, you know."

"Yes, I knew that." She waited for him to lecture her on how difficult it was or ask if law schools accepted women nowadays; there was a note of warning in his voice and posture.

Instead he said, "I hope you're not intending to enter the foreign service."

"No." She didn't want him to think for a minute she was emulating him. "If I went to law school I'd want to practice law."

"Good. I'm relieved to hear that. Very good."

He sounded sincere, not at all disappointed she had other plans. Meg wondered why. "You don't want me following in your footsteps?"

"I don't recommend it, no," he said drily. "Only the mediocre thrive in the foreign service. If you have any ambitions about doing good in the world, forget the foreign service."

Meg was flattered he understood she wanted to do good, then surprised that he understood. Not until she had those thoughts did she realize he was confessing something about himself. "But that can't be true, Uncle Jim. You've been in the foreign service your whole life."

"I rest my case."

He had to be teasing her. Without any streetlights nearby, the moonlight seemed bright as day, until one tried to read the expression on another person's face.

"Get out of here," she scoffed. "You're not mediocre." She took his competence on trust, just as she believed in her father's business acumen.

"I am. In my secret way. It's the secret of my success. It's why I'm being considered for an ambassadorship or even an assistant secretary of somebody else's affairs."

"But that's good. *Isn't* it?"

"I would've thought so in younger days. But it's also their way of buying you off. They ignore the message but reward the messenger, which somehow makes it all right." He tried to sound dry and humorous, yet he sounded only dry.

"Was your message from the Philippines?"

He responded with another laugh, another cough of cloud as substantial as his head in this light, only paler. "You won't let go of that, will you? I'm sorry, Meg. I shouldn't use you as an ear. I'm usually able to keep these things to myself. I don't know why I'm boring you with them tonight."

"I'm not bored," Meg insisted.

"You should be." He shook his head at himself and hoisted the coat around him with his pocketed hands, the collar riding up like a monk's cowl. "I don't know what kind of illusions you have about Uncle Jim overseas. He's just a bureaucrat, a sociable paper-pusher. He shakes people's hands, then writes reports on whether their palms were sweaty or not. He collates and synthesizes other people's reports categorizing handshakes and sends his findings to Washington." The wittier his words, the more bitter the voice became. "The desk officer for your country reads the report, sifts the dross from the gold and sends the gold to his superiors, usually. Say what you may about Foggy Bottom, the people there actually know a hawk from a handsaw. No, the problem comes at the top. Nobody knows what to do with this gold, this wealth of knowledge. We're top-heavy with gold turning into lead. Knowledge without power is just paper. And power without knowledge is a blindfolded German in a china shop, pleased as punch he's picked up one vase nicely enough, not hearing the other vases crashing around him."

Meg had never heard her uncle talk like this before. The chaos of metaphors sounded crazy, only he didn't speak in a rush but repeatedly paused to choose new images, grinning sardonically at what he came up with. The obfuscation seemed deliberate, a way of talking about something he couldn't address otherwise. Here it was, the moment she'd been waiting for all day, and Meg couldn't follow half of what he was saying.

"You've shaken Marcos's hand?" she asked, attempting to play his game.

"Oh yes. More times than I care to admit. A bastard, pardon my French. But one can no more blame him than one can blame those animals who eat their young. No, my grouse is with our people. For three months now I've been sending my gold to Washington. Not just me, but a handful of us in Manila, going behind the ambassador's back. For the past week I've been taking my gold door to door, hoping someone would buy if they could see I wasn't a troublemaking malcontent but a good company man, like themselves."

Meg couldn't tell if he were being obscure to be secretive or if he simply assumed she knew more than she did. "Can I ask—what exactly is your gold?"

"That there is no Communist threat in the Philippines. That this state of emergency is a complete fraud. That the United States has no business giving Ferdinand Marcos its blessing."

Meg finally had the key to what her uncle had been saying. Good, he was on the right side.

"But many in the department knew that already. For those who didn't, these were inconvenient facts they didn't want to hear. But the overall consensus seems to be: what a pity the showplace of democracy in Asia is now a dictatorship, but at least they're *our* dictatorship."

"The American empire at work," Meg sadly declared.

Uncle Jim turned his head to look at her, keeping his smile. "Perhaps," he said. "That's one way to see it. Where do you stand on foreign policy, Meg? You're smart, you're in college. I presume you're in the opposition." He wasn't threatened in the slightest.

"When what we do is wrong," she said, a half-lie with enough truth she didn't feel like a liar.

"I don't know what your professors tell you, or what you and your friends tell each other. But we're not the omnipotent bad guys some would have us believe." His dry tone took on a faint uncertainty. "There are no good guys. There's bad guys and worse guys. The best one can hope for is to defend the bad against the worse."

They had reached the baseball backstop in the far corner of the school grounds, the farmer's field of rag and stubble on the other side of a deep ditch. They passed behind the chain-link cage and went back the way they'd come, the moon behind them now, a pair of long, faintly haloed shadows pushing through the salt sparkle of frost in front of them.

"I don't want you thinking your uncle is any kind of idealist. No righteous moralist with a flaming sword. You lose both ideals and ideology early on in my line of work." The uncertainty deepened, becoming weary or sad.

"Rather, you don't get to use them. But you hope, you assume, that when the day comes when you can change something for the better, you'll be able to use those beliefs. Well, my day came and went and I couldn't change a damn thing. It's not the first time, but—" A new thought caused him to lift his head, then sadly shake it.

Meg was amazed, embarrassed and grateful. He had cracked the shell of fake omniscience that frustrated her about most men, and shown the uncertainty inside. She was excited by the gift yet did not know what to do with it.

"Do you think about leaving the State Department?"

He looked up again, surprised by the question. "No. I don't. Not really"— as if he'd never considered it before. He quickly glanced at Meg, then faced forward again. "No. I'd be a fool to pack it in, especially now with an ambassadorship in the offing. Maybe they'll give me a nice, safe country where nothing happens. Yes, I'd like that right now. A nice, safe, *warm* country," he chuckled, adjusting his coat as if he were readjusting his shell. "Cold out here. I must be talking to keep my teeth from chattering."

"There's nothing else you'd like to do besides work in the foreign service?" She wanted to keep the confidences coming. "Aren't there other things you can do with your law degree?"

"Practice law? Now there's an idea," he said humorously, without sarcasm. "Hang out my shingle in a small town in the middle of nowhere. When you finish law school, Meg, we could hang up our shingles together. 'Frisch and Goodall.' Sounds like a clean, reputable firm."

The moment for confidences had passed. He humored and teased now, asking Meg if she played golf and jocularly lecturing her on the advantages of a good golf game for any ambitious lawyer. Meg gave in and let Uncle Jim chat about the need for healthy exercise by anyone who worked with their brains.

But as they came back up the street and turned the corner near the house, he suddenly said, "Interesting to talk about work with someone outside it all, reducing everything to basics. It gives one a different handle on things. Thanks for hearing me out, Meg."

"My pleasure." She waited for him to explain what he understood now he hadn't understood before.

Instead he said, "You're sharp, Meg. Dangerously sharp." He laughed and threw an arm around her, pulling her up against him. The air was too cold for her to smell mothballs this time, their coats too bulky for Meg to feel anything except a clumsy weight knocking against her. But she was pleased to be appreciated, even pleased he didn't tell her more. It was a compliment to her intelligence he hadn't told her everything, the way people tell their troubles to a pet they assume won't understand a word.

"Have a nice walk, kiddos?" Mom asked when they came inside.

"Lovely," said Uncle Jim, and Mom looked relieved.

Not until she went to bed and lay in the dark reconstructing their conversation did Meg wonder why she'd been so polite and careful with her uncle. He'd offered her a peek at the inner life of a public man—ideals and compromise and contradictions—only to snatch it from view while pretending he'd shown her everything. He seemed to think they'd had a wonderful conversation, when all along Meg had felt they were only on the verge of one. She suffered similar frustrations in more personal talks with Doug, although Doug was more forthcoming than her uncle, and Jim's experience was far richer, complex and mysterious than that of any college kid.

She should have pressed him harder about his work in the world, his resignation to failure, his personal life. His hypothetical homosexuality was back in her thoughts: it had to be latent and unconscious—the one real homosexual Meg knew at school was an exaggeration of everything she disliked about women, too much vanity and flashy emotion. But she couldn't dream of asking Uncle Jim if he'd gone to bed with anyone, male or female. It seemed too cruel, too much like picking apart lightning bugs the way she had as a kid to see how they lit up.

There was a ruthlessness in Meg's curiosity that frightened her, a hint of violence she could let out only when reading books or watching movies, never with living people. She wished she'd been more ruthless in asking about her uncle's work, pushing past his reticence to achieve real intimacy with him. She was sorry Doug arrived tomorrow and she wouldn't get another chance this visit to make real the bond tonight's walk merely suggested.

8

JIM WOKE UP THE NEXT MORNING in what looked like a family storeroom: they put him with the Christmas lights and their rolled American flag. He wasn't in Manila or even Washington, but home. It actually did feel like home this morning. Shaving in the tiny downstairs bathroom, Jim experienced none of the morning despondency that often came over him when he watched his bleak face in a mirror. He was not alone here, not after his remarkable talk last night with Meg.

He had come expecting less than usual, just the ritual visit to Ann and her family that marked his return to the States, only to discover his niece. Her assumption of intimacy astonished him. He'd never understood Meg's fascination with him when she was a bookish tomboy or chubby teenager; it was an interest Jim had done nothing to earn or deserve. But now she was a slender, swaggering, sloppy college student who could talk and listen like an adult, and Jim was amazed by how much they could say to each other. It was as though Meg had been fascinated with him all along because she somehow knew this time would come.

Jim worried he had told her too much last night, but her intelligence threw him off guard. It was a student's intelligence, brash and innocent, and he wasn't sure what she knew and what she only pretended to know. She didn't know enough to avoid certain topics, not yet understanding there were real horrors outside her haven of home and school. But he liked the innocence in her politics, her belief in right and wrong that was neither righteous nor self-congratulatory. Jim knew not to believe everything he read in newsmagazines, but when he arrived and saw Meg was in college now, he braced himself for the disdain that college students were said to have for anyone belonging to "the Establishment." But no, either the media exaggerated or, more likely, his niece was smart enough to understand that nothing was as simple as it seemed, that even a diplomatic lackey had his reasons.

Jim was drinking coffee at the kitchen table with Ann when Meg came down to refill her own cup; she was studying for exams this morning. He gave her a conspiratorial smile that Meg answered with a smirk before going back upstairs to her room.

"She's a good kid," Ann said once again, not fully understanding how fine her daughter really was. But Jim felt affectionate toward Ann too this morning. Her obsessive concern with house and home that sometimes annoyed Jim, even when he blamed it on the ad hoc households of their childhood and their mother's straitened circumstances, did not seem so narrow and wrong to him this visit. Yes, there is this way too, he thought, and it looked like a wisdom of sorts compared to the worthless mess of his own life.

"Is this a boyfriend who's coming today?" Jim asked.

"I don't think so," Ann whispered. "Meg's interested in him, but I gather he's not interested in her. You know how fickle men can be."

"I'm sure Meg can take care of herself. She has her head screwed on straight." Jim automatically disliked the young man. He pictured an arrogantly masculine frat boy, or one of those smug campus radicals he read about in *Time*. What he really feared was that the new guest would bring out a different side to Meg and spoil Jim's intimacy with her.

Meg's friend did not arrive until that afternoon. Jim, Ann and Meg all sat at the kitchen table and watched him eat a ham sandwich.

"Great sandwich, Mrs. Frisch. Especially delicious after the long drive down. Thank you for fixing it."

"You're welcome, Doug. No bother at all."

The boy looked utterly harmless. He was definitely a boy, pale and blond with faint stars of acne on his hairless chin. He was short—Meg's height, in fact—and his hair was long, not like Robbie's but like Meg's, parted in the middle and sloped over his ears, both of their heads looking like thatched roofs. Meg had slouched back in her chair, watching Doug with a contented smirk, looking more like a big sister than a woman in love.

"I hope I'm not inconveniencing anyone by coming down. I didn't know Meg's uncle would be here."

"No bother in the slightest," said Ann. "We just stick another plate on the table. I hope you don't mind sleeping on the sofa."

"The more the merrier," said Jim, giving his sister a wry smile to let her know he knew otherwise.

"To tell you the truth, Mr. Goodall, I'm glad our visits worked out like this. Meg's told me lots about her uncle in the foreign service."

"Don't believe a word of it," Jim laughed and glanced at Meg, expecting to share another complicitous smile. Meg was grinning at Doug.

"Watch out," she said. "Doug likes to study people."

Doug giggled without a trace of embarrassment. "I like people. Their infinite variety."

"You're a voyeur," Meg growled, delighting in the word.

"No. I just think other people's lives are more interesting than mine." Even that was said in a flippant manner, with a smile for Jim. He had the strangest smile. Doug's mouth was absurdly wide, the lips very thin, the rest of his face so pale and featureless the sealed smile stood out as though drawn there in crayon. Even at rest, the mouth formed a smile. A haircut might improve Doug's looks, but there was nothing one could do with that insipid smile.

"Well, kiddos," said Ann, "what're your plans for the afternoon?"—implying she wanted them out of the house.

Doug said he'd never been to Virginia Beach and would like to see the ocean. Meg jumped on the idea, saying she'd love to show him the Atlantic. "Want to come with us, Uncle Jim?"

Her invitation surprised him. Boyfriend or not, he assumed they'd prefer to be alone. "You don't need an old duffer tagging along."

But Meg insisted and Doug joined in—"I'd like to hear about Manila, Mr. Goodall"—and even Ann encouraged him to go. Jim gave in, hoping to see what his niece was like with a peer, secretly pleased to be included.

While they went to get their coats and Jim was still sliding out from behind the table, Ann whispered, "Well?"

"This boy?" Jim whispered back. "He seems pleasant enough. Very well spoken. Very polite."

"Too polite, if you ask me. I wish he didn't remind me of Eddie Haskell."

The reference escaped Jim, but he thought he knew what she meant. "With me there, you can rest assured they won't be checking into a motel while they're out," he joked.

Ann didn't laugh. "Kids these days don't need motels," she said. "When Meg's at home, I expect her to behave herself. What she does while she's off at school is none of my business. I'd rather not know, to tell you the truth."

Jim was shocked to hear his sister talk like that. It was depraved coming from a mother, and a preposterous thing to say about Meg. Kids were rumored to be as casual as rabbits nowadays, even girls, but Jim knew Meg was different. It sounded as though she spent most of her time in the library anyway, and this boy seemed no more capable of sexual conquest than a pimply adolescent in a church choir.

Shaking his head over the very idea, Jim followed the kids out to the yellow Volkswagen bug parked behind Jim's Pinto. Doug kept his hands to himself, in the bottom pockets of a baggy army field jacket. Jim felt the boy did not have the right to wear that jacket. Army surplus had meant something back when Jim was in college, and only veterans wore it, not whey-faced youngsters. Jim knew this was a silly thing to feel about a jacket, but he felt it.

He insisted on riding in the back so that Meg and Doug could sit together up front. The doors thunked shut like thumps on a tin drum, the engine puttered like a lawn mower and Doug talked about an upcoming exam. Jim glanced down at the books scattered on the floor of the backseat: Yeats and Marx and Sartre, and something called *Our Bodies, Ourselves,* which appeared to be for women. He was about to ask Meg if it were hers, when he flipped to a detailed diagram like an overhead view of a battleship. Then he read the names of the various parts. He snapped the book shut and returned it to the floor. Eggheads, he thought, dismissing his embarrassment. The world to them was nothing but books and idle ideas.

VAST AND OPEN, almost deserted on a winter afternoon, the beach was a beautiful surprise. A pale sun hung above the hotels and motor lodges, but the sky over the water was a smooth expanse of dusty blue, the one faint puff of cloud out there actually the full moon again, a transparent ghost of itself in daylight. Ocean boiled and broke along a shelf of sand packed solid like sandpaper, sheets of water sliding up the beach before they slid back into the breakers that pedaled furiously without getting anywhere.

"The mighty Atlantic," Meg declared.

"Feels good," said Doug, taking a deep breath of cold and salt.

They walked along the boardwalk, Meg in the middle, Jim on her seaward side, upwind from her wildly blowing hair. Other bundles of coats and scarves strolled past them, and a few stick figures wandered along the strand in the distance.

Jim felt he must have been here one winter years ago, before the bigger hotels were built, except the position of the sun seemed wrong and he realized he'd confused a summer visit here with memories of a Baltic resort in Finland. His sense of place was full of scrambled geography.

"What? No feeling of oceanic transcendence?" Doug mockingly asked Meg.

"I'm not going to get sentimental about the beach. All it means to me is sunburn and headaches and sand in your shoes. And the shame of being hosed down naked in the backyard by our father before he'd let us in the house."

"Until you were how old?" asked Doug.

"Eighteen," Meg replied, remaining deadpan until Doug laughed.

The presence of Doug did bring out a different side to her, not a bad side but someone more spirited and willing to be silly than the serious young woman who'd walked with Jim last night. There was also a mocking quality that had only been hinted at before, friendly bites all directed at Doug. When Doug finally noticed the moon and observed, "Look, a diaphanous slice of moon," then admitted to Jim that, yes, he'd like to be a poet, Meg tauntingly added, "Or a philosopher or elementary school teacher or a Zen monk. Doug's a basketcase of ambitions."

The boy pleaded guilty with a laugh. "I like to keep my options open."

"It's what I love about Doug. He makes *me* feel decisive."

"I'm very decisive. I've decided to let my life choose me, instead of the other way around."

"An existential Buddhist," Meg tenderly scoffed. "But don't let him fool you, Jim. His gentle soul business is mostly an act."

That too drew only a guilty smile and laugh. "What about you, Mr. Goodall? Did you choose the foreign service or did it choose you? It was something you just stumbled into, right?"

"No. It was something I chose for myself. God knows," he confessed, caught off guard by the question.

"Really? You wanted to see the world?" asked Doug. "Or did you have dreams of power?"

It was said half-jokingly, so Jim felt free to answer with a joke. "I think I wanted to play the lead in *Lawrence of Arabia.* I ended up with a bit part in *The Godfather.*"

Not until he saw the look on Meg's face did he realize he'd said more with the joke than he'd intended. As with Meg last night, there was something about talking to kids that caused him to say aloud things he never said even to himself.

"Remember *Lawrence of Arabia,* Meg?" He instantly covered his tracks. "We saw it together during one of my visits the year I was in D.C. between Thailand and INS, which was ten years ago."

Meg remembered. She rolled her eyes and told Doug about her mother's reluctance in letting Uncle Jim take a little girl to a "war movie." Violence was strictly for boys.

"Wasn't T.E. Lawrence a homosexual?" asked Doug.

Jim grimaced slightly. "Oh, there's been speculation. People speculate about anyone after they're dead."

"All I remember about the movie is camels and desert and getting thirsty," said Meg, smiling fondly at Jim, almost protectively.

The sky behind the hotels now glowed bright orange, casting long blue shadows across the boardwalk into the blue of the beach and ocean. The moon became denser as it rose, more substantial.

"Getting late," said Jim. "Shouldn't we be heading back?"

"I guess," sighed Meg. "Been nice getting out of the house. Hard to be ourselves at home."

Jim knew he could be himself only when he was alone, but this was definitely preferable to the tense courtesy he expected at the house when Rick got home. He respected his brother-in-law, yet never felt comfortable around him. Robbie added a whole new tension of his own, a malice Jim couldn't help believing was what Rick hid under his politeness. "What're you saying, Meg? Did you want to go someplace else?"

"Eat out, you mean?" They seemed to be reading each other's minds, attributing to the other what they wanted themselves.

"Just an idea. Would your mother be upset if we phoned and said we were grabbing a bite down here?"

"I don't know. It was going to get awfully crowded at the table tonight," she pointed out. "Doug?"

"Whatever you two decide," he said, smiling his passive smile.

Jim wanted to be decisive. They came to a phone booth in the arcade of a boarded-up snack bar and he volunteered to call Ann. Not until he heard the first ring did he realize how rude this was, visiting his sister and then going off with Meg and her friend.

Ann was surprised, but did not protest. "This isn't something the kids talked you into, is it? No, I don't mind. I wasn't sure what Rick might make of this Doug anyway. Have a nice time and don't let Meg talk your ear off."

"Now I feel guilty," Jim said humorously after he hung up. "I've jilted the mother to be with the daughter."

"She can live with it," said Meg. "Let's go eat and get warm."

Most of the hotels and their restaurants were closed for the season along Atlantic Avenue. Meg knew a diner called the Puritan Inn near where they'd parked the car. They went there. It had been years since Jim had eaten in a diner and he nostalgically took a seat in a red vinyl booth beneath half-open venetian blinds. Meg sat opposite him while Doug went off to find the men's room.

"Well?" she said just as her mother had, only Meg gave the word a hopeful ring.

"He's pleasant. A little young, maybe. But no. I like him." What else was there to say about Doug?

"Good. He likes you too. I can tell," said Meg, as if Jim might care one way or the other.

The warmth of the restaurant brought back feeling in Jim's ears and produced a prickling in his legs. When Doug returned, Jim noticed the cold had put color in the boy's cheeks and nose, giving his vague face character. Meg's face was already full of character, her mother's sharp nose and chin emerging under the curious brown eyes she'd had when she was a teenager, a little girl, even a baby, her expressive, lipstickless mouth poking or pinching with every new thought that came to her, a witty mouth. She lit a cigarette, her third or fourth since Jim's arrival, but he did not think it his place to scold. Jim felt she deserved better than Doug, someone harder, more solid, but he could not tell her that either.

"I have this thing about eating out," Meg happily confessed while she read the menu. "Probably because Dad refused to take us to restaurants when we were kids. Ever."

"I once took the whole family out to dinner," said Jim. "Years ago, when you were a baby. An absolute disaster."

"Then it's your fault I'm this way," Meg teased.

Doug asked what Meg was like as a baby, and Jim had a difficult time remembering anything worth telling. Then Doug asked about his early years in the State Department, during McCarthy, and Jim explained that had never affected him firsthand, he knew about it chiefly through the newspapers, like everyone else.

"I warned you," said Meg. "Doug likes to study people."

"Only people who interest me," Doug said boldly, and asked Jim what his most interesting post overseas had been.

"Bangkok?" Meg suggested. "When you went to Angkor Wat?"

Jim gave in to their curiosity and humored them with tidbits, trivial anecdotes about life overseas. He remembered things he'd stopped noticing years ago, such as the fact that a single American company had the furniture contract with the State Department, so you found the same furniture in every embassy and government-leased apartment around the world. "Whether you're in Jakarta or Helsinki or Timbuktu, there it is, the same dreary plaid sofa with a matching armchair."

"You were in Finland?" said Doug.

"Two years. Before my last tour in the Philippines. They've begun shifting personnel to different regions, ostensibly to keep us from 'going native.' What it actually does is keep us incompetent on a global scale."

"But you were in Manila when the Marcoses seized power?"

Meg lowered an eyebrow and tucked a corner of her mouth at Jim, signaling she'd said nothing to Doug about Jim and martial law.

"I was," said Jim and shrugged the matter aside. "Business per usual in the Third World," he sighed.

But Doug was not put off. "You've met the Marcoses? What're they like?

Are they really as evil as they look? Is Imelda the brains behind Ferdinand or is she just a dumb housewife?''

Doug knew a great deal about the Marcoses, far more than Meg. The placid smile and constant questions no longer felt innocent. Answering Doug with evasive nothings, Jim suddenly wondered if the boy might be some kind of agent, a college student recruited specifically to meet Jim Goodall's niece, court her and insinuate himself into her family to learn what Goodall really thought of Ferdinand Marcos.

It was too preposterous a scenario to entertain for longer than a second. To imagine anyone going to such lengths was the height of paranoia and hubris. Everyone knew what Goodall thought and that he didn't matter.

"You've made a study of the Marcoses too?" Jim laughed.

"I just read some articles in the *Washington Post*," Doug replied.

"Doug's from northern Virginia," said Meg. "Inside the Beltway. Where they follow that stuff." She sounded resentful, annoyed Doug knew more than she did. Jim was reminded of the way she used to compete with her brothers for Uncle Jim's attention.

"Is your father with the government, Doug?"

"No, sir. He teaches high school. Retired air force, though."

"Ah." That might explain the boy's respectful behavior, which seemed at odds with his bohemian appearance: a conditioned respect for adults in positions of authority. Jim relaxed again, feeling amused by his comic paranoia—this wasn't Manila. Nevertheless, once the idea that Doug was not what he seemed entered Jim's thoughts, it would not go away. The boy seemed to be hiding something behind his peaceful smile and cheerful questions, an ulterior motive, a secret interest. Or maybe it was only the gentle self-effacement that didn't seem quite genuine, as though the boy smugly believed he would never be invisible in Jim's eyes.

"Power fascinates me," said Doug. "Corruption too."

Jim laughed again. "Well, I was in a position of no power at all over there. Which Meg got to hear about in all its glorious boring detail last night." He winked at her, wanting Meg to know he did not intend to share with Doug what he'd shared with her.

Meg smiled at Jim and sat back, relieved.

"I didn't mean you, Mr. Goodall," Doug quickly apologized. "I meant the Marcoses. They seem like the absolute in corrupt evil, from what little I've read."

"What you've got to understand," Jim said automatically, "is corruption is a way of life over there. But here's our food."

The waitress arrived with several plates balanced up and down her arm, a homey woman with a homely face and soft Tidewater accent.

"Meat loaf," Jim told her. "I can't tell you how long it's been since I've had plain old-fashioned meat loaf." He chatted with her for a full minute about the joys of meat loaf, savoring the pleasure of sounding like a typical American.

Another suspicion accompanied Jim's ticklish consciousness of the boy, but Jim took it even less seriously than the possibility Doug might be a spy. The boy was Meg's beau, and he was not Jim's type anyway.

IT WAS AFTER ten when they returned to the house. Robbie was out, Walter on the phone again in the kitchen, Ann and Rick upstairs watching TV in their bedroom. Ann came down to make sure the doors were locked and to see that there were blankets and sheets for Doug on the sofa. She sat and visited with them for a few minutes, asking how the ocean was. "Try not to stay up too late," she said when she finally stood up to go. "And try to keep it low."

"I think I'll retire shortly myself," Jim told her.

"You hear that, Meg? Don't keep your uncle up with your yakking. You and Doug save your all-night bull sessions for school, okay?"

"Yes, ma'am."

Ann wished them all goodnight and went up the stairs, the vent under the steps to the kitchen squeaking like a bird, the wood of the main flight groaning inside the family room closet.

The three of them quietly sat there, Meg and Doug on the sofa, Jim in the rocker, waiting for someone to speak. Ann's suspicions, her fears for her daughter, were what gave the silence a sexual edge. Meg and Doug had barely touched at the beach, had not even held hands. Jim decided it was safe to leave them alone.

"Don't mind me," he said. "I'll probably sit up and read, but your chatting won't disturb me. I promise not to listen," he joked.

"Good night, Mr. Goodall."

"Good night, Uncle Jim." Meg addressed him as uncle again, after experimenting all day with plain Jim. She did not get up to kiss him goodnight but remained on the sofa with Doug.

Jim pulled the door to the utility room shut, then the door to the guest room too, but could hear them whispering and giggling while he changed into his pajamas. When he came back from the little bathroom on the other side of the washer and dryer, he left the door to the guest room opened just a foot, so he might catch some of what they said out there.

As soon as he climbed under the covers and put on his reading glasses, however, there was a knock on the closed door. "Goodnight, Uncle Jim," Meg called through the door.

" 'Night, Meg-wump," he called out, although he'd decided to stop using that nickname; he'd noticed the wince behind Meg's eyes each time he called her that. Hearing the metallic twitter of the vent when she went up the steps, Jim resumed his search of the bookcase. His sister was as foolishly fearful about Meg as Jim had been about Filipino agents.

The books were all paperback novels, thick, foliated cubes of yellowed print, the words *epic* or *sprawling* on the cover of each. The jackets promised the joys and sorrows of several generations in a single family, fortunes and children through several decades, history from a woman's point of view, all getting and begetting. A couple had family trees opposite the title pages, and most had collages of people on their covers, happy old people and miserable young ones, a wise-looking middle-aged woman usually somewhere in the middle. Jim assumed the books were Ann's, an expression of nostalgia for something that never quite existed.

The door to the family room snapped open. A pair of naked legs whisked past and the bathroom door clicked shut. Jim listened to the different sounds of water in the bathroom, wondering if Doug was actually naked. Two minutes passed before the bathroom door opened again. Bare legs flashed through the light from Jim's door. "Goodnight," Doug whispered as he went by, smiling face bent sideways to glance through the door.

"Doug?"

"Sir?" The face reappeared in the partially opened door. His legs were definitely naked, but he wore a brown sweater above them, white briefs peeking below.

"Sorry," said Jim. "I thought for a moment you were wearing a mini-skirt."

Doug laughed and pulled the sweater down so it actually did look like a short dress. "Cold. Needed something else to sleep in beside my skivvies." His bare feet danced on the cold tiles, yet he lingered in the doorway, accidentally pushing it further open when he leaned against it. "You're going back to Washington tomorrow?"

"Oh yes. Have tons of paperwork to finish. And I'm still not settled in my old apartment. The last sub-tenant left quite a mess."

The boy's calves were fizzy with blond hair, his thighs long and hairless. Sitting up in bed in pajamas and reading glasses, Jim felt like the wolf chatting with Little Red Riding Hood.

"Where in D.C. do you live, Mr. Goodall?"

"Near Dupont Circle."

"You ever go to—? There's a bar near there. I can't remember the name." He idly reached overhead with both hands to grab the doorframe and hang there. The sweater climbed up; hips wrapped in a white band of underpants fell out.

"I'm the wrong person to ask about night life. I've been away five years, and never went out much when I was there."

The boy was neatly tucked in up front. Blond down blurred the eye of his belly button and the elastic waistband was crimped like the edge of a pie crust. Detached and bemused, logical and interested, Jim experienced no excitement or panic. He could not quite connect this blond shadow of American boy with the dark, opaque bodies he'd held in Bangkok or even the soldiers he'd watched in a swimming pool. Did the boy realize he was flirting with Jim?

"I sometimes get into Washington when I'm home, you know. Drinking age is only eighteen there." He blandly smiled between his raised arms.

"You play any sports, Doug?" Jim thought he should explain his interest in the boy's middle.

"Uh-uh. Shows, doesn't it?" he laughed, looking down and letting go of the frame to lift up his sweater. "Babyfat. No love handles though." He took a small handful of flesh. "No big ones anyway." He stepped into the room, still displaying his stomach. "Do you mind?" he asked, pulled the sweater down and sat on the foot of the bed. "The floor's freezing."

Jim quickly shifted his feet under the blankets, giving Doug as much room as possible.

The boy folded pink feet into white thighs, his pretzel of legs half-turned toward Jim, the corner of bed sagging under his weight. "You play sports though. Weren't you some kind of jock in college?"

The boy *was* flirting with Jim, teasing him at least. He knew. And Jim felt the only way he could know was because he was that way himself. The pieces instantly snapped together—the cool curiosity that seemed like spying, the self-effacement that didn't efface, the unromantic friendship with Meg—and the boy made perfect sense. He sat on Jim's bed and waited for Jim to do something.

"Just tennis in college. Golf and squash came later. Maybe we should close the door?" said Jim. "If we're going to sit up talking."

Doug glanced at the door, and faced Jim with a crooked, knowing smile. "Nyaah. I'll be going back out to the sofa in a minute."

"Fine." And it was fine. Jim had mentioned the door simply to explore what the boy might want from him. This was an intellectual problem, not a sexual one. Even if Doug were his type, this was Virginia Beach, Virginia, and Jim's sister and her family were scattered overhead.

"No team sports?" said Doug. "No horsing around in the showers with the guys after the big game?"

It was an impressively subtle approach, yet they were talking around the same thing, weren't they? "No, I was one of those sensitive lone wolves who showered and got out of there as quickly as possible."

"That's good. I don't like those loud, chuff-chuff-chuff jocks. My father's like that, you know. All that overdone, macho masculinity."

"You don't see yourself as masculine, Doug?" Was that why the boy seemed so vague and sexless? He wasn't effeminate, but there were no hard male edges to him either.

"Not really. But I'm not going to fake what I'm not, the way most guys do." He drew his hair out of his face and behind his ears with both hands. "Masculinity is a lot about fakery. Women are more authentic than men, don't you think?"

"I can't say I've stopped to think about it." Maybe they weren't talking around the same thing after all. Gender and sex were two unrelated subjects for Jim.

"They are. Women can be physically affectionate with each other and even sleep together without the world falling apart. Men can't."

The placid, lightly sealed smile widened, becoming pinched at the corners; the transparently blue eyes looked straight at Jim beneath the long colorless lashes.

"Did you ever see or read *Women in Love*?" Doug asked.

Something cracked in the darkness outside the door. Doug turned toward it. Jim heard the creaking of steps, one by one, as somebody very slowly came down the stairs. Doug glanced back at Jim, still smiling, still sitting cross-legged on the bed, making no move to jump off. He calmly faced the door again when the vent in the steps to the kitchen began to tweet.

"Meg?" Doug softly called out.

The tweeting stopped. It resumed and Meg appeared outside the two sets of half-open doors, cautiously looking in.

"Meg?" Jim said automatically. "I'm sorry. I thought we were keeping our voices down."

Her large brown eyes stared at them. Her mouth was open and her arms hung at her sides, shoulders stooped as she hunched down to peer inside. "Oh," she said and stepped into the light, rubbing one eye. "I thought I heard voices. I couldn't remember who was down here." But her face wasn't heavy with sleep, her hair not at all tangled. She looked vulnerable and confused with doughy white legs and a rumpled longtailed man's shirt, but her eyes were wide awake, darting between Jim and the boy on Jim's bed.

"We've been talking about sports and masculinity," Doug told her, showing no trace of embarrassment or fear.

Jim decided he looked innocent enough, reading glasses sitting on his nose.

Meg's confusion gave way to a wan smirk for her uncle and a look of irritation at Doug. She stood in the door and put her hands on her hips. "C'mon out of there," she told Doug. "Let my uncle get some sleep."

"In a minute, Frisch. Come on in. Get off that cold floor." Doug made room for her on the bed, lifting his rump over Jim's legs.

"Yes, the more the merrier," Jim said drily, shifting his legs to the middle away from the warm weight of thighs. "For a few minutes anyway."

Meg gave in with a sigh and padded over, mouth twisting ironically. "Regular pajama party here, isn't it?" she said, sitting on the bed with her feet on the floor. She crossed one leg over the other and there was a glimpse of flowered panties in the split of shirttail.

"Except I'm the only one who appears to wear pajamas nowadays," Jim observed.

Meg gave the joke the polite smile it deserved, then continued the smile over her shoulder to Doug. "You can't stay put, can you?"

"You're one to talk." Doug remained terribly pleased with himself.

"You're just full of surprises."

"Is it my fault I like to talk to interesting people?"

Jim's legs were pinned down with Meg's weight on one side, Doug's on the other. He seemed to be trapped at a lover's quarrel. Meg had come downstairs to be alone with Doug, only to find Doug in bed with Uncle Jim, figuratively speaking.

"You're awfully tense tonight," said Doug. "Here." He put his hands on either side of her neck and began to squeeze her shoulders.

Meg cut her eyes at Jim, amused Doug did this in Jim's presence. "Throw us out the second you get bored with us," she said.

Jim assumed she'd come downstairs only to kiss and neck with Doug—it was, after all, the family room sofa and Meg had to be even more innocent than Doug. But Jim was humiliated for Meg that she had to go to the man instead of the man coming to her. Ann was right: Meg loved a boy who didn't love back. It must hurt her: the looks of resentment at dinner that Jim had mistaken for sibling rivalry, the glare of irritation when she found Doug sitting on Jim's bed. He wanted Meg to understand it wasn't her fault, that she was a remarkable, attractive woman, only this boy did not love women. If Doug didn't have the courage or self-understanding to explain himself to Meg, Jim certainly did.

"You realize, of course," Jim told her, "I'm leaving tomorrow morning."

"Uh huh." Her head was tilted back while Doug massaged her shoulders. "It's been good seeing you, Uncle Jim. It really has."

"So when will I get to see you again?" he affectionately asked.

Meg wiggled her shoulders to make Doug let go. "You coming down again anytime soon? I'll be on break again right after exams."

"Maybe you could visit me," he suggested. "You said you're coming to D.C. for the inauguration?"

"Yeah. My last exam's that Friday morning. I'm getting a ride up that afternoon."

"How about then? You're more than welcome to stay at my place."

"I'd love to, but—" She looked back at Doug. "I'm staying with Doug's family in Annandale. We're driving in the next morning with some friends to that rally."

"Come with us to the rally, Mr. Goodall," Doug said cheerfully. "Or do they let you go to things like that?"

"No, I could go. If I were so inclined." He wouldn't be able to have the kind of talk he wanted with Doug present, or the hordes of chanting college students he pictured being there. "Here's another option," he began. "What if you came into town Friday night? There's a round of inaugural eve parties, all Democrat, a sort of wake for Nixon's new term. I have to make an appearance at several and you could come with me, Meg. Nothing glamorous, but it'd give you an opportunity to see some of your uncle's world firsthand."

Meg's eyebrows were raised, her interest piqued, but she was frowning. "I'd like to, only I'd be a fish out of water at something like that." She looked to Doug for advice or encouragement.

"No worse than your uncle is," Jim assured her. "I might also add that Mrs. Marcos is scheduled to be in town. She's certain to be at one of these parties. I could even introduce you."

"Imelda Marcos herself!" Doug said excitedly. "You gotta go, Frisch. You'd be a fool not to. A dictator in the flesh!"

"The wife of one," Jim pointed out.

But Meg only sighed and weaved her head back and forth, smiling at her inability to make up her mind. Jim knew this kind of social timidity from Ann, and was surprised to discover it in Meg.

"You gotta, Frisch. Don't be chicken. Then you can give me the inside scoop."

Meg grimaced and gritted her teeth.

Without thinking, Jim automatically said, "If you're afraid your uncle won't be company enough, bring your friend along."

Doug snapped an eager, breathless grin at Jim.

Meg stared at him.

It was like a move you make when you're playing tennis, your body thinking for you and the mind taking a split second to catch up: the wrong move. Jim feared Meg attributed an ulterior motive to the invitation that wasn't there. It was Meg he wanted to see, not Doug.

"Yes, yes!" cried Doug. "You have to now, Frisch. Say yes. Come on." Doug leaned forward, knees pressing against Jim's legs, and he embraced Meg from behind, arms bundling her shirt against her breasts while he whispered in her ear. A hand briefly stroked one breast.

Meg automatically leaned backward into the embrace. She began to giggle, then pushed Doug away with a jab of her elbow. "Oh all right. You guys," she laughed. "Okay. It'll be very educational for me, won't it, Uncle Jim?"

"One would hope," he told her. The embrace threw him, then the fact that including Doug spoiled the whole purpose of the invitation. But when it didn't backfire and make Meg suspicious, he realized he was pleased Doug would be there. He told himself this would provide another opportunity to study the boy more closely before he gave Meg his conclusions. And Doug seemed like the kind of boy who'd be adept at mingling at parties. At one gathering or another, Jim could be alone with his niece and warn her.

"This'll be nifty," said Doug. "Thank you, Mr. Goodall. Oh boy. I can just see the look on Larry's face when we tell him we're meeting *Imelda Marcos!*"

Doug did not seem to suspect anything either. As they discussed the where and when, Meg grew as excited as Doug. "So long as I don't have to dress like I'm going to the prom," she said. They would drive into the city that night, meet Jim at his apartment and he'd take them on a tour of parties inside the very government they'd be protesting the next day. The duplicity seemed part of the appeal for Meg.

"Now that it's settled," said Jim, "I really think it's time we all went to sleep." Being alone might give him a better grip on what was going on here.

Meg thanked him again and leaned in to give Jim a goodnight kiss on the forehead. His eyes darted to the loose collar of her shirt, but did not want to notice her breasts, which was like acknowledging his niece might have a sex life. When she drew back, her brown eyes narrowed at him for an instant, a look that could be either a conspiratorial wink or a worried wince.

Doug climbed off the bed, giving Jim's right knee a quick squeeze through the covers as he crawled over. "This'll be great. I can't thank you enough, Mr. Goodall."

Meg herded Doug from the room, smiled gratefully at her uncle and pulled the door completely shut. He heard the door to the family room click shut too.

But even when Jim took off his glasses and turned out the reading lamp, he did not feel alone. He listened to them out in the family room, wondering what they were doing and what it would mean. There were a few hisses of whispers, giggles, then a groan. And there was a whisper of touch around Jim's right knee, the shadow of a hand gripping him where Doug had squeezed it good-bye. It might have been nothing more than a grab to keep his balance when he climbed over. Jim tried to reconstruct the grip in his memory, the position of thumb and fingers, and the nervous shadow disappeared.

You think too much, he told himself, knowing he should think about what he had gotten himself into by inviting Meg and Doug on his inaugural eve rounds. Instead, he listened and waited for something. When he heard the sharp tweet in the steps as Meg went up to her room, he thought that's what he was listening for: he'd been a fool to worry there'd be any kind of monkey business with Meg. But then he continued to wait and listen, lying on his back in the shapeless dark. There was no shush of blankets when someone got up from a sofa, no snap of a slightly warped door being opened. Nothing.

JIM WOKE UP in an inexplicably good mood, like the mood of anticipation after a wonderful dream, high hopes that linger even when you remember it was just a dream. Jim rarely remembered his dreams anyway; he accepted the mood as a gift horse and didn't inspect its teeth.

His happiness continued while he showered, shaved and packed, then joined Ann and the kids in the kitchen. They seemed a typical pair of sulky, sleepy-eyed kids this morning, with no potential for malice or mystery. Ann's sunny presence brought everything back to earth. She treated the news he was taking them on a tour of Washington parties as a sweet gesture, as though he'd offered to take them to the zoo, which in effect he was.

"Don't be a stranger," Ann said when it was time for him to go. She expressed sorrow he couldn't stay longer and hoped they'd see more of him now that he was back in Washington. Jim knew his sister well enough to understand she was sincere, about what she felt at this particular minute anyway. He shook Doug's hand and paid no attention to the boy's premature thank yous over meeting Imelda. He hugged Meg, and was uncomfortably conscious of breasts flattening against him; hugging was still new to Jim and he couldn't dissociate it from sexual situations. He held her by the shoulders, looked deep into her eyes a moment—he half-expected a frightened, pleading look, which wasn't there and shouldn't be—but could think of nothing to say except a very solemn, "Thank you, Meg."

Meg laughed at his solemnity. "You'll be seeing me in two weeks, Uncle Jim," she said, treating his grave goodbye with the lack of seriousness it deserved.

Jim was on the road by ten o'clock.

The sun was out and the brightness of land and sky were evenly matched, unlike the tropics. Jim enjoyed driving the new car. The Pinto rode close to the earth and fit him more snugly than the old Dodge had. The highway to Washington was interstate all the way, smooth and seamless. A long bridge with a tiled tunnel now crossed over and under the wide, steel-blue harbor instead of the pokey ferryboat. What shipping was out there today was all cargo-container vessels; the colliers, coal dust and smoky tugboats were things of the past. The sky was a clear, cold shade of blue so fine Jim wanted another word to describe it to himself: cobalt or cornflower or baby-eyed blue.

Jim turned on the radio and fiddled with stations, hunting for news. The war could've ended or a new one started while he was at Ann's without his hearing a word. All he found were police sirens of rock music. He settled on a station where the announcer spoke softly and the songs were less electrical, a channel that should have a good news program. The Pinto seemed to race with a fast song, then float for a slow one, music breaking up the somnambulistic drone of highway and heater.

He didn't know much about history; he knew nothing of trigonometry—a song had caught Jim's attention, its melody so sweet and gentle he could actually follow the words. It was a schoolboy's wistful plaint that he was ignorant and dumb, but he knew he was in love and the world would be wonderful if the other person loved him back.

Jim began to smile at the song, a silly smile that began in his chest and went straight to his head. The happiness he'd experienced all morning slowly connected with that smile and song, connected in the glands beneath his eyes. There were no tears, only a pleasantly ticklish softening there; a feeling of lightness ballooned in his chest. Jim knew it wasn't just the song that moved him. He wasn't musical. He waited until it ended before he used the lyrics to identify why he was so pleased with himself today: he was in love with that boy.

Or infatuated or smitten or something. It was preposterous to call his happiness love. There was nothing lovable about the kid except the possibility he might be homosexual and might like Jim. There was nothing sharp or solid in his personality to justify Jim's interest, or that could block his interest either. But what a pleasant surprise it was to stumble upon love again.

Jim had not been in love—or infatuated or whatever one called his periodic fixation with this or that junior officer, embassy guard or European male—in over three years, not since his discovery that he could have sex in Bangkok. Or no, before then: not since just before his visit to Saigon.

More songs played on the radio, all of them love songs. It was as bad as the Philippines, where they sang about nothing but love. Those songs meant little to Jim; they were background noise at receptions and garden parties, tales of woe about people dying for love, either through suicide or being murdered by a jealous swain. A passionate people, the Filipinos. Today's songs were sweeter, tender and regretful.

Excitement, affection and fear gravitated around the image of a pale face with blue eyes and an improbable crayon smile. What did one do with such feelings? Four years ago Jim would've used them to invite Doug to play tennis or racquetball. Most people were reported to have sex with the person they loved, only Jim never had. He fell in love with Caucasians and had sex with Asians, a division of labor that enabled him to keep everything under control. Divide and conquer, he reminded himself. And yet, what if one were able to combine the two? Despite his blond hair and command of English, Doug seemed as smooth and gentle as the rent boys in the Patpong, a friendly smile and willing body, a place where Jim could work off his semi-annual need for physical affection.

He had not been to Bangkok since July. After martial law was declared, there was too much happening for him to slip away for a weekend, first the arrests, then the American businessmen who wanted assurances, then the detailed reports Jim put together on his own to show Washington what he thought they should know, before he understood they didn't want to know. He wondered if his excitement this morning was only backlogged lust. Where could he go for relief now that he was home again? But his tentative euphoria did not migrate to his groin the way thoughts of bare asses did when he knew it was time for another trip to Thailand. He did not picture Doug's ass; he did not picture his body at all. And Jim did not want to dismiss his nervous joy as a simple case of unappropriated testosterone. It was more interesting than that, more mysterious.

Fresh green signs overhead announced the exit for Williamsburg and the College of William and Mary. Jim had forgotten he'd be passing near the boy's college. His niece's college too.

Poor Meg. She loved a boy who didn't love her back, who was more likely to be in love with her middle-aged uncle. No, Jim could not claim that much for himself. But something was missing between Meg and Doug, something she wouldn't understand. Meg did not know men the way her Uncle Jim did. He wanted to save her, protect his niece from heartbreak over the insincere love of a confused homosexual. The obvious solution, of course, was for Jim to seduce Doug, killing two birds with one stone, because Jim would also be helping the boy understand where his true interest lay. What a good deed that would be. What a nice man Jim was. Was it his fault there would be something in it for him?

No, the scenario was much too neat to be plausible, as absurdly self-serving as the bits of wishful thinking concocted by the National Security Council, fantasies of rationalization where the good of a small foreign country happened to coincide with American interests. *Realpolitik* transformed a Filipino mobster and his wife into the Kennedys of Asia. Jim's celibate imagination transformed an animal itch into selfless love that could benefit everyone concerned. Jim knew it was ridiculous to expend on that itch energies once used to unravel the hidden agendas of Ferdinand Marcos. But nobody cared what Jim believed about Marcos, so why not use that energy to amuse himself with fantasies of love?

Nothing could happen. Meg and her friend were coming with him to a few cocktail parties, that's all. But when his euphoria began to disperse in doubt and scruples, Jim wanted to bring it back. Slipping outside the range of the radio station that endlessly played love songs, Jim twisted the dial back and forth through the airwaves, hoping to find another frequency that would tell him what he wanted to hear.

"STUFFY UNCLE JIM is a big old queen," said Doug.

Meg cut her eyes at him. They were alone, in Doug's car on the way to the mall to look at people and get some air. There was no nastiness in Doug's tone of voice, but Meg found herself on the edge of losing her temper. "Don't call him that. He's my uncle. And he's not stuffy, just . . . old-fashioned."

"But he is gay," said Doug. "I'm sure of it." His mouth stretched across his face in a know-it-all smile. "You should've seen the way he was checking me out last night before you arrived."

"What, you were testing him? Is *that* why you were with him? And why you sat on his bed?" The detail made her angry with a quickness that startled her.

His shoulders shifted embarrassedly, but he did not lose his smile. "It wasn't premeditated. But yeah. I guess I was curious how he'd respond."

Meg had avoided thinking about last night. She'd told Doug she might be down later, when Uncle Jim was asleep. Not only was Jim still awake, Doug was keeping him up. But the sudden knot in the pit of her stomach when she saw them together went beyond mere annoyance with Doug for spoiling her plans. She didn't know what she was afraid of, but there had been a wave of panic before she regained herself with irritation, then amusement. She'd been too shy to mention any of this to Doug today. But he brought it up.

"Did he *ask* you to sit on the bed?"

"No. But you should've seen his face when I plopped myself down."

"You're cracked. He just wanted you to leave him alone."

"He suggested we close the door. But I didn't want to go *that* far. Anyway, I knew you were coming so nothing could happen."

"You were teasing him?"

"I guess," he said hesitantly.

"But that's cruel, Doug. Don't you see how cruel that was? You're not like that," she insisted. "Cruel."

"I told you. It wasn't premeditated. But I was curious. You're the one who said he might be gay but was too uptight to know it."

"It's insulting to come on to somebody like that, even if they don't know they're being insulted." It suggested a malicious streak in Doug she'd never seen before. Or no, she suspected something in him, a great blind spot, a mysterious absence he disguised with consideration and consciousness of other people, a coldness like the coldness Meg feared she contained at her own center. But nothing so deliberate as cruelty. "I bet he didn't realize you were flirting with him. It probably went right past him."

"No. He knew. And he knows what he is."

"What makes you so damn sure?"

"The way he checked me out. And some of the things he said."

"Like what?"

They came to a traffic light and Doug concentrated on the clutch and gear shift. He bent over the wheel and smiled up at the light. "He stared at my stomach and asked if I played sports. I told him I thought women were more authentic than men and he said he never thought about women."

"Hmmph." Meg distrusted Doug's admiration of women, his claim he envied them; Doug knew so few women. "What else?"

"I'm trying to remember. It was mostly the way he looked at me." He glanced sideways at Meg, beginning to understand she might not be overjoyed to hear this about her uncle.

The light changed and the Volkswagen lurched forward.

"He probably thought you were weird," Meg called over the snare drum of changing gears. "Probably thinks we're both weird."

"Not so weird to stop him from inviting us up to meet Imelda," said Doug, his smile triumphant and self-assured again.

Now Meg had new reasons to regret accepting the invitation. Not only did she have to worry about clothes and makeup and making a fool of herself in the company of overdressed strangers, there was her uncle's opinion of Doug to consider, the faint possibility Jim might think Doug was interested in him and would spend the evening studying Doug, scrutinizing him, giving Doug his full attention.

She felt a sudden urge to slap Doug across the face. She had to squeeze her hands under her armpits to stop herself from hitting him. "Why should it matter to you anyway? He's *my* uncle, not yours."

"I want to meet Imelda too."

"Screw Imelda. I mean if my uncle's queer or not."

"I'm sorry." His voice went soft and squishy, his usual overdone note of apology when he understood he was in the wrong. "I thought you'd be interested in what I thought. I didn't know you'd get upset."

"I'm not upset. Not with my uncle. I'm upset with you for treating him the way you did."

"You're right, Meg. I apologize. Scientific curiosity got the better of me. And it is none of my business," he admitted, a little too quickly, but his desire to repair any damage done seemed sincere.

Meg closed the subject by pointing out Krispy Kreme Donuts as they drove past and told Doug how her idea of intellectual bliss in high school had been to go there late at night with "the guys"—a couple of egghead rebels from Superior English—drink hot chocolate and argue about *2001: A Space Odyssey*.

She pushed her uneasiness to the bottom of her thoughts. When it briefly returned at the mall—Doug pointed out an angel-faced little boy sitting by a tubbed tree and said, "Future newscaster or male prostitute"—Meg realized she wasn't as disturbed by the idea that Uncle Jim might be consciously queer as she was by Doug wanting to believe he was.

But on the way home Doug said, "I guess I'll be in the guest room tonight? Downstairs? Alone?" She knew what he was saying. They were both too shy to propose sex in advance, Doug out of guilt, Meg out of pride, their timidity in talking about that an odd exception to their willingness to explore everything else under the sun. Even last night Meg had said simply, "Maybe I'll come down to see if you're all right." She did not want to admit to herself how frustrated she'd been when Uncle Jim stopped them from doing anything.

Doug got along disturbingly well with everyone at dinner that night, talking to Dad about the fertilizer industry, Robbie about cars, Walter about girls. He was such a chameleon. Mom only smiled and offered him seconds. He and Meg watched television alone for an hour after the others went to bed, never mentioning later, then Meg said goodnight and went up to her room. She studied for another hour, until she felt everyone upstairs was fast asleep. She considered masturbating and going to sleep herself, as a kind of punishment of Doug, but tonight was the last chance for a victory in her secret war of independence against home and family.

A light was on. Again, both doors were open, but Doug sat in bed alone, reading Sartre. He smiled when she closed the door and sat down beside him. He closed his book and kissed her. They barely spoke; they were not the same people they'd been before.

She loved being undressed by him, enjoyed his voyeuristic thrill in the theatricality of sex. They left the light on and nudity in this room had the flush of childhood embarrassment, those moments of shame as intense as sex before Meg knew what sex was. Doug was very free with his hands and mouth, very naked with his penis standing in its little Nazi helmet. He preferred touching to being touched, and liked to make love with his mouth, which had been a surprise. He drew her out into the sweetly nerved textures in her breasts, then down to the lilylike fold of flesh. Pale blue eyes watched from between her legs while he smiled into her, until genitals and loins began to inhale for sneezes that were all in the nerves, blowing away every other sensation. Meg strained to keep her joy in the back of her throat: her brothers slept in the room directly overhead.

Doug always finished quickly during intercourse, so he saved that for last. She wrapped her arms and legs around him, and gently gripped him with a third hand. She would love to stay like this forever, all uneasiness and distrust of Doug gone, washed from her nerves in breathlessness. His face took on that stressful, stoic, comic look, and she lightly placed a hand over his mouth. He showed less interest in his own orgasm than he did in hers, just as he often preferred to let the other person talk, but lately his gasps and moans had been getting louder, as if trying to match Meg's, and she was afraid he might forget where they were.

He went into his usual funk afterwards, thinly disguised with timid pecks and caresses. He immediately pulled his underpants back on, as if ashamed his penis was now such a wet, raw thing. Male biology puzzled Meg. Her own nakedness was a wonderful relief after sex. If Doug were capable of conversation now, she would've climbed into bed with him to chat and touch, but his guilty coldness after sex made her feel she should be guilty too. If Doug ever loved her, she could be in love with him, but it was good to know he couldn't love her uncle either. Meg put on her shirt and panties, kissed Doug goodnight and crept back upstairs, feeling slightly rakish and very pleased with herself.

9

Washington was familiarly unreal despite the changes. Streets were cut open and boarded over where they were finally excavating a subway system beneath government offices and row houses. The trees planted years ago to replace the doomed elms along the main thoroughfares remained slight and stunted, the city more barren than ever in winter. There were more glass and concrete office buildings, more underground garages. The sixties had come to D.C. while Jim was away, leaving brightly patched hippies scattered around Dupont Circle and a stale stink of marijuana or hash in Jim's studio apartment. He'd sublet it to a young Iranian financial analyst with the World Bank, but all kinds of people were trying out new experiences nowadays. The capital of the free world still shut down at six o'clock when everyone went home to Virginia or Maryland, the wide sodium-lit, bone-colored avenues looking deader than Manila after Marcos declared his midnight curfew. The American flag flew at half-mast during the first weeks of the new year; Truman had died.

Foggy Bottom felt painfully different because of its sameness: the spirit of the place was thin and sour. The chessboard corridors and drably painted walls now suggested an old hospital; the urgent chitter of teletype printers had been replaced by a more insidious electronic hum. There were few familiar faces about. Diffenbach was up on the seventh floor, one of those quiet fellows who live their careers in anonymity, then suddenly reappear several rungs up the ladder. O'Brian was gone, off with a New York law firm. Lyman Bradford had quietly retired years ago, of course; Jim read a brief yet fulsome obituary in the *Foreign Service Journal* while he was in Manila. And Dave Wheeler was down in Caracas with his wife, out of INR and back on a career track, a deputy chief of mission. Jim hadn't heard a word from him since the cryptic postcard three years ago. Wheeler's colleagues in Intelligence and Research spoke highly of his independence and boldness, assuming he'd left the bureau only because too long a stint there hurt one's future: INR was very unpopular on the seventh floor. Jim wondered if Dave had jumped ship for more private reasons, frightened into grabbing the safer, more conventional life, one where he could take his wife along to keep him from temptation and harm.

After he returned from Virginia Beach, Jim resumed "walking the corridors." Not literally—they gave him a small office outside the Southeast Asian secretarial pool while he awaited word on his next assignment—but he had too much time on his hands, no role or task in which he could lose himself. He could not continue his one-man campaign against martial law, knowing now what an exercise in futility that was.

The week after Christmas had been a sorry round of meetings and briefings, hearty handshakes across various desks followed by mechanical nodding and condescending sighs from listeners who began to frown at their gold-plated wristwatches and glance through their calfskin appointment books. Even the Philippines desk officer, a stuffy child with a crewcut and the soul of a telephone book—surely Jim's generation had not been as dull as the new junior officers were—gently treated Jim as a foolish old fogey. Only Abramowitz and Reuter in INR paid attention to what Jim had to say, just as they'd been the only people to respond to his first reports from Manila, cabling him for additional data, Reuter meeting privately with Jim when he came to Manila in November. But there was only so much INR could do. Policy decisions were made on the seventh floor, and maybe not even there. It took Jim several days to understand there might be a different reason for the State Department's lack of concern. It wasn't that they had bigger fish to fry or even that anyone sincerely believed Marcos was the benevolent reformer they said he was. No, the real reason the State Department supported martial law was because they were completely powerless. Every decision that mattered was now made by Kissinger and the National Security Council. The best way to hide your superfluity, from both yourself and others, was to fervently support whatever was happening, even pretend it was your own doing. Jim's suspicions seemed justified when Abramowitz took him to lunch with an NSC staffer, a former college professor who said more crudely what Jim had been hearing all week: "Marcos is the best thing that could happen to that fucked-up backwater. We've been jerking ourselves off over there with all this democracy shit. Orientals don't want democracy. They want to spread their legs for a tough, take-charge kind of guy. Yeah, this Communist-threat talk is bullshit, a gimmick to sell the man to the peons. But the man's a war hero, he's promised land reform, an end to corruption *and* our continued use of the bases at Clark and Subic Bay."

They weren't stupid, they were brutally practical, which was almost impossible to combat. Stupidity can be corrected with facts; cynicism in the name of *realpolitik* could be fought only with values or ideals, airy things you began to doubt yourself when they made no impression on your opponent. Even speculation about the longterm effects of martial law meant nothing to the former professor, who could conceive of the future as little more than that time when his superior would be remembered as the wizard who restored balance to the world with Vietnam and China, the American Metternich. Well, Jim too once had thought of history in such confident, self-adulating terms. He was surprised when the former professor telephoned the next day to say Dr. Metternich himself would like to meet with Jim; he had fifteen minutes free on Tuesday afternoon. Jim was disappointed but not surprised when, telephoning Tuesday morning to find out which entrance of the White House went to the National Security offices, he was told both Kissinger and the former professor had canceled all appointments for the day. Jim learned from the *Washington Post* that they'd flown to Paris for the resumed peace talks with North Vietnam.

It was hopeless, useless, dead, a corpse that should be buried and forgotten. No newspaper or journalist showed the slightest interest in what had happened over there. The righteous indignation in Congress and the press that had been Ambassador Earp's chief worry when his golfing buddy seized power never materialized. Jim had done everything he could. And yet, when he returned from his sister's, he did not feel finished with Marcos. He looked through the cables and reports he'd sent from Manila over the past three months, hoping to find a new argument, something that could convince even Kissinger that American support of Marcos was a mistake. *Easily construed as an action for personal gain. Financial discrepencies of the gravest order. The suspension of habeus and custody of persons appears directed as much at political opponents in legally recognized parties as at possibly subversive elements.* It was all so careful, cool and loyal. Turns of phrase Jim had intended to be scathingly ironic seemed as dry as dust. The habit of loyalty was burned too deep in him, the discipline of formalities, the trust in means and ends that enabled one to play the game by their rules. Jim wished he'd written, *This is criminal. This is vile. It is a sickening piece of hypocrisy for the United States to support this action.* But righteous passion without an audience who could be moved by anger was indulgent and personal. His continued obsession with Marcos began to feel almost neurotic to Jim.

You spend your life waiting to do good, able to live with yourself in the meantime because you sincerely believe you will do good when the opportunity finally presents itself. Your opportunity's here, Jim thought, and you can't do a damn thing. No, there'd been other opportunities, some ignored, others acted upon, but no good had come of them either. Jim didn't know why this time should feel so different, why he couldn't lie to himself again and smooth away his failure with the belief there'd be other, more important opportunities for good deeds in the future. Something in Jim had changed, died away or come to life.

Thinking this through one night in his old restaurant with turquoise booths and knotty pine paneling—only its prices had changed in twenty years—Jim remembered he'd said something similar to Meg, had begun to formulate these ideas while talking with his niece during their late-night walk in the suburbs. He wished he'd told her more. She was smart and sane and authentic. With Dave Wheeler gone, there was nobody here with whom he could speak his mind the way he had that night with Meg.

He looked forward to seeing her again at the end of the month. He wished she were coming alone. The presence of her friend turned what could be a wonderful evening shared with a bright young relative into a social obligation, a messy chore, the boy a distracting reminder of how foolish an adult imagination could get.

Jim's fantasies about Doug stopped almost as soon as he drove back across the Potomac. There was something about Washington that smothered thoughts of love and sex, bringing Jim back to reality. He couldn't even remember what Doug looked like. He kept seeing sky-blue eyes in a Thai or Vietnamese face. It was actually a relief to realize the boy was only travel porn, a fantasy to take out during a long drive by car, peruse and discard, a pleasant distraction from martial law. As for the possibility that Meg was in love with a homosexual, he should talk to her about that before jumping to conclusions. Maybe she wasn't in love. Maybe Doug wasn't that way. Sharing his suspicion about Doug, of course, would mean filling Meg with suspicions about her uncle.

He thought about telling Meg. He wanted to tell Meg everything, one day. Jim seemed to have spent his entire life talking mostly to himself, but it was nice recognizing there was somebody out there who would listen when the time came.

THE MONTH PASSED slowly. Jim initiated a report written with Reuter proposing the State Department pressure Marcos to release Senators Aquino and Diokno, for the sake of world opinion if nothing else. Once out, it was hoped the two men would work to free other, less famous prisoners. Doing that much enabled Jim to feel more himself again. One of Imelda's Blue Ladies telephoned repeatedly, pleading with Jim to do everything possible to get her daughter and son-in-law invitations to the Inaugural Ball. He politely informed her the Marcoses must have more powerful friends in the administration than a former political officer. The truth of the matter was the White House wished Imelda and her friends would stay home. It was one thing to praise a family of gangsters as the saviors of Asia; it was something else when they invited themselves to your wedding.

Jim picked up his tux at the cleaners on Thursday. The mechanized racks were jammed with plastic-sheathed dinner jackets, chiffon gowns, beaded satin dresses, a couple of saris and a single African ceremonial robe, the whole city apparently getting laundered for the weekend of receptions and balls.

In his apartment Friday evening, Jim sat on a footstool in his undershorts, a sheet of newspaper on the parquet floor, and diligently spit-polished his black dress shoes. He preferred the simple, private life of his studio apartment to the complicated households he had to keep in Asia—Finland had been modern enough that one could live simply—but there were times like tonight when he missed having a servant to handle the details. He shaved, showered, then slipped into the different layers of the elegant monkey suit. He inspected himself in the mirror hanging on the inside of his closet door, fussing with the springy black tie, checking the neat swoop of jacket over his rump—he'd had the tux made in Hong Kong four years ago. Jim hoped Meg wouldn't be put off seeing him in this imperialist costume. He liked to think the outfit suggested James Bond, despite his thinning ginger hair, the exposed dome of forehead, the pink skin that never tanned, only burned and peeled and burned again.

The doorman buzzed. "Mr. Inge."

Jim remembered that was Doug's last name. "Send them up, Zack." He gave one last pat to the hair crisp with Brylcreem over his scalp, closed the closet door and put on an avuncular face for Meg.

The doorbell rang.

Jim strode to the door and opened it.

And there was the boy, hands in his coat pockets, shoulders thrown back, blue eyes underlined with his enormous, close-mouthed smile—how had Jim forgotten that insipid smile? The carpeted hallway behind him was empty. "Hello, Mr. Goodall."

Jim noticed a wide striped necktie and blue blazer and jeans—the boy wore *jeans* tonight?—under the wool overcoat; he looked around the boy's head into the hall again. "Where's Meg?"

"Ah. Yes. Well. Meg." The hands in his pockets casually flapped the coat open and shut. "Meg's running late. You see, sir, the people she's riding up with live on Old South time. They were supposed to leave at noon, but she called an hour ago to say they wouldn't be leaving until about now. She's furious, as you can imagine, but what can she do? She asked me to call you, explain and apologize about Mandrake being so unreliable—that's the friend who's driving. Or if I wanted, she said, I should come in without her."

Jim stared while Doug blithely rattled away, Jim's irritation turning into anger.

"So here I am. I hope you don't mind it's just me tonight. But I didn't want to blow my chance to meet Imelda Marcos."

"Meg's not coming *at all*?" Jim was angry the boy came without Meg, galled by his presumption Jim could share tonight with a mere acquaintance. He seemed to think Jim should be pleased to see him.

"No, sir. And she's real upset. But she asked me to arrange it so we can meet tomorrow, either at the rally or parade, whichever makes you more comfortable. She's spending tonight at my place, so I'll see her when I get home. We're coming in tomorrow with two other friends from school, more reliable than Mandrake." The pocketed hands perched on his hips, drawing the overcoat back and displaying the jeans with a starburst of creases at the middle. "Will that be good for you, Mr. Goodall?"

"Damn it to hell, are those the only pants you own!"

The smile was slapped from Doug's face. His shoulders collapsed as he took his hands from his pockets and nervously watched Jim. "I'm sorry," he said, in a very soft, vulnerable voice. "I wasn't thinking." He seemed to understand for the first time Jim might not want to see him without Meg.

Jim felt foolish for losing his temper, for being angry the boy was here. Without his usual confidence or ease, Doug looked like a harmless child.

"Would you rather I not come along tonight?" he timidly asked.

"Don't be ridiculous," said Jim, wanting to undo his anger. "I don't care what you wear. I'm just upset Meg didn't take the trouble to call me herself. Let me get my coat and we'll be off." No, he could not be so cruel as to send his niece's friend back home, chastised and rejected.

"She would've called," said Doug. "Except it's pay phones in the dorm and she was out of quarters, so I told her I'd take care of it."

"That's no excuse. She could've called collect." Buttoning up his tweed coat, Jim stepped out into the hall with Doug and locked the door. "Never mind. What's done is done. We'll be making the rounds by foot and cab. It's going to be hell finding a parking place tonight. Did you have any trouble parking?"

Jim decided to be friendly. It wasn't Doug's fault the night had been fouled up, or that Jim had imagined certain things. He was just a kid, a thoughtless, irresponsible kid who assumed the world revolved around his whims. Riding down in the elevator, Jim noticed the glitches of razor nicks along Doug's cheek, and a little vapor of blond hair missed when shaving. Jim's suspicions and fantasies of a couple of weeks ago seemed to have been about somebody else entirely. If he was uncomfortable, it was just because he wasn't sure what to say to Doug. Meg was their only bond.

They walked to the first party. The night air was very cold yet damp, and lace doilies of old snow still lay on the ground from the snowfall earlier in the week. Jim's shoes clicked martially over the wet sidewalk. Doug regained his smile, but it was less placid and self-assured now; he too seemed a little lost without Meg there to provide continuity. His tone changed wildly from one sentence to the next. He answered Jim's idle question about how exams went with a cocky, "You don't really want to hear about that." Then, as they went up the steps of the slightly shabby music-box villa that housed the Cosmos Club, he said in a small, guilty bleat, "I'll try not to embarrass you." When they'd checked their coats and stood in the entrance to a large room with yellow walls and green wainscoting, Doug surveyed the black tuxedos and rainbow prism of gowns and contemptuously declared, "The powers that be. Swilling champagne from plastic goblets."

Actually, this party was the powers that were, or almost were: old Washington, retired FSOs, a few administrators of liberal foundations, rich people interested in science or travel and a handful of politicians old-fashioned enough to be loyal to politically useless friends. Many of the men looked rather dowdy, but the women dressed fashionably no matter what their age was. Jim liked these people, their manners, their lack of ulterior motives, their harmlessness.

"James Goodall! It's been eons and eons." An older woman stepped forward to take Jim's hand, Mrs. Sebastian Weed, wife of the ambassador when Jim was in Thailand ten years ago. A lean, handsome woman in an elegant blue dress, only the crepe skin of her neck and unnatural perfection of her dentures belied her age. Mrs. Weed had been a perfect foreign service memsahib, with a photographic memory for names and faces and a genius for small talk. "My, you're looking quite dashing these days, James. And who's your young friend?" she asked, bestowing her genteel smile on the boy who stood much too close behind Jim.

Only then did Jim realize what people might assume about Doug. Everybody knew Goodall was a bachelor, which suggested nothing when he was alone. He almost introduced Doug as his nephew, until he remembered *nephew* was even more suspect. "Douglas Inge, a friend of my niece in college. Who unfortunately couldn't join us tonight." Jim watched Doug gingerly take Mrs. Weed's hand and greet her with a fawning smile. "Mrs. Weed," Jim told him. "An old, dear friend of mine. You should help yourself at the bar, Doug. Or, if you're hungry, there's a buffet table in the corner."

Happily, Doug took the hint. He asked Jim and Mrs. Weed if they needed anything, then sauntered off, glancing all around at the people he passed, apparently looking for famous faces.

"I'm terribly sorry," said Jim, "but I can't remember what Mr. Weed's doing now."

Mrs. Weed laughed off Jim's apology—she was not one of those wives who were insulted that other people didn't follow their spouses' careers—and proceeded to tell him about Mr. Weed's work with UNESCO, the lovely trips they'd taken and their daughter's new job at a museum in Milwaukee. Jim had chaperoned the daughter to a few parties when she visited her parents in Bangkok, a college girl as nervous with Jim as Jim had been with her. "Give Linda my regards the next time you speak to her," he said.

While they chatted, Jim repeatedly looked around to see where Doug was. The boy parked himself at the bar, standing there with a plastic goblet in his hand and gazing around the room, happily taking in champagne and people. Jim relaxed a little when he noticed other young people scattered through the party, some dressed as elegant miniatures of their parents, others as shaggily collegiate as Doug. There was even another boy wearing jeans, with a malcontent's ponytail and beard. Doug did not stand out. So long as he didn't tag after Jim like a lost puppy, things would be fine. Jim had no important business to discuss with anyone tonight; all he had to do was appear at a few parties and remind various people he existed.

"If you're looking for grand panjandrums," said Mrs. Weed when Jim stole another look at Doug, "there's only Georgie Kennan down from Prince-ton. He's holding court over by the window. So smart. So serious. I couldn't get through twenty pages of his memoirs. But now everybody wants to write memoirs, even Sebastian. When you write yours, James, try to limit yourself to one volume. We must be kind to the trees."

"I have no memories to memoir," said Jim with a laugh.

"You've just returned from—Rangoon?"

"Manila."

"Ah," went Mrs. Weed, and Jim thought she might ask about martial law or maybe something she'd heard about Jim's stand against it. But an amused, mischievous shine came into her eyes and she cocked her head to say, "Then you've dealt with Mrs. Marcos. She certainly sounds like quite a character. Is there any truth to the rumors about her use of feminine charms with men from the embassy? Meeting with them alone, virtually sitting in their laps while she tries to talk them to her point of view? On a love seat?"

Jim chuckled. "She can be a very forward woman."

"Then she's even tried it with you? You poor man."

"No comment," said Jim, using their timeless phrase as a joke.

"You're no fun. Still the scrupulous, silent one. No, I can't quite picture Mrs. Marcos chasing *you* around the room," she teased. "Oh there's Katzenberg. He was with us in Nairobi. No, Auckland. I better say hello to him. If you're still around when the weather turns warm, James, we'll have to have you over for tennis. In the meantime, good luck. It's been so nice to see you."

"It's been delightful seeing you again, Mrs. Weed."

Jim decided he felt comfortable enough now to get a drink. Doug still stood with his back to the bar, yet another fresh goblet of champagne in his hand, his mouth still creased in his tireless crayon *V.*

"Enjoying yourself?" Jim asked while the black bartender—the only black in the room except for an ambassador—fixed him a scotch and soda.

"It's fascinating," said Doug. "Like a scene in *War and Peace.*"

"With plastic cups," Jim reminded him, but the crack amused him now and he repeated it with a smile. "You should wander about and eavesdrop. It could be very educational. That's George Kennan over yonder."

"Yeah? We read one of his books in Russian History," said Doug, looking through the bodies toward Kennan. "You don't mind?"

"I'm not your mother, Doug. All I ask is that you show discretion and not go around comparing Nixon to Hitler. It's always best at these things to keep your ears open and your mouth shut."

"Right," said Doug and he finished the champagne in his hand, picked up another and headed off in the direction of George Kennan.

Jim worked his way through the party, talking about the Christmas bombing of North Vietnam with a retired air force officer, UNESCO with Mr. Weed himself—who was far more solemn about his duties than his wife had been—and the pros and cons of various books on golf with a senator who'd played eighteen holes with Jim in Manila two years ago. Nobody talked about Marcos and martial law.

When he felt he'd stayed long enough, he looked for Doug but the boy wasn't with the men bunched around Kennan. Jim found him by the door with one of the miniature adults, a boy younger than Doug who haughtily lectured him.

"Time to go," Jim said brusquely. "We have a full night ahead of us." He wanted to make clear by his tone he did not want to be introduced or explained.

"Yes, sir. Happy salvation to you," Doug told the other boy and followed Jim out to the marble entrance hall.

"Who was that?" Jim asked while they waited for their coats.

"Just some kid who was telling me how he was a heroin addict when his father was ambassador to Greece, but now he's hooked on Jesus and everything's peachy."

Jim fought the temptation to ask more so he could figure out who the ambassador was. "George Kennan have anything interesting to say?"

"Nyaah. Somebody tried to get him to talk about Kissinger, but all he wanted to talk about was sailing the fjords of Norway."

The street outside was filled with taxi cabs and limos. Jim flagged a taxi and they swung down Embassy Row toward the Naval Observatory. "The next party should be much, much flashier," Jim told Doug. "A reception at the Iranian embassy and they're notorious for putting on the dog. It'll be more international too, with a heavy dose of the jet set. Parasites with too much money, but that's something we have to keep to ourselves."

"Then why're you going?" A boozy cheerfulness washed away any note of disapproval in the question.

"Because there should be a few congressmen present, State poohbahs and National Security people. When you're hunting elephants, you don't turn up your nose at a particular water hole because jackals go there too."

"Will Imelda be there?"

Jim smiled; everyone seemed obsessed with Imelda Marcos tonight. "Maybe," he said.

The front of the Iranian embassy was a blazing white billboard of light behind a screen of bare poplars. A column of limousines and taxis was backed along the curb and around the semi-circular drive to the entrance, where doormen opened car doors and ushered people in and out. Jim told the cabbie to let them off in front of the South African embassy across the street. The grand reception didn't justify the wait, and Jim preferred to slip in unobtrusively.

Under the baleful gaze of the shah himself—a large oil painting of the man in his brocade uniform hung opposite the entrance—the reception hall was a

Noah's ark of furs, every woman and even a few men arriving silky with mink, leopard, ermine and other mammals. Two peasant-faced Iranians in white uniforms with gold braid and pearl-handled pistols in their holsters flanked the servants checking coats. The fashions underneath were elegant and daring. Women wore suede dresses and a few men had ruffled shirts with their tuxes. Jim even saw a man whose shirt was apricot instead of white. Doug pointed out a woman in a sleek black dress and a chrome tube around her throat that went from her collarbone all the way up too her chin.

"Curious," Jim admitted.

"Is it supposed to be jewelry or a neck brace?" said Doug.

Jim had to laugh. The boy could be very fresh and funny. His jeans stuck out here far more than they had at the Cosmos Club, but Jim was pleased to have him along now, could even enjoy his company.

The lights in the ballroom were turned up full to show off the clothes and their owners, diamond-white light flashing from the crystals of the chandeliers on the necklaces, earrings and sequins flaring down below. Tuxedos stood out like black holes in the dazzle. Enormous silver bowls full of ice lined the buffet table, little Petri dishes of pearl-black caviar set in the center of each. At the middle of the table, surrounded by flowers, was an ice sculpture of the head of Richard Nixon. The glassy block was watched over by another white-gloved guard whose chief duty seemed to be to wipe the pointy nose with a handkerchief now and then before it dripped.

Going to the bar together, Jim asked for another scotch, Doug more champagne; the champagne here was French and served in crystal flutes. Blue eyes watching people while he pursed his mouth to sip from the narrow glass, Doug had the contented concentration of a boy blowing across the top of a soda bottle. He nibbled his lips around the taste. With a sudden smirk he said, "I can almost understand how this way of life could corrupt people."

"It gets very old very fast. For those of us without a sensuous streak, there's no difficulty in maintaining an ironic distance."

"You don't have a sensuous streak, Mr. Goodall?" The tone was mocking, the eyes perfectly amiable.

"Not really," Jim told him. "Oh, athletics, I suppose. A few other indulgences now and then." He lifted the scotch to claim this was one. In fact, Jim drank so infrequently he wondered if his second scotch were what made him enjoy chatting with Doug. There was a telltale numbness in the tip of his nose.

The small orchestra at the other end of the room shifted from Glenn Miller to "The Fool on the Hill." Jim could see couples gliding by the bandstand.

"Do you dance, Doug?"

Doug giggled. "Thanks, but I better pass."

Jim's face went warm and he covered his embarrassment with his own laugh. "I ask only as a point of information. My own dancing has been compared to a wooden Indian."

Doug laughed and said, "I'm not much of a dancer either."

"No? I'd assumed somebody your age, loose-limbed and unself-conscious as you seem, would enjoy dancing."

"Uh-uh. Not me." He was staring at something, and Jim followed his gaze to a stately African dignitary murmuring in French with a demure blonde. The man's blue-black face was scored with geometrical scars from an old tribal initiation rite; the gold-framed black square of a digital watch peeked from the cuff of his dinner jacket. Doug turned back to Jim and said, "Do you think the West violates indigenous Third World cultures?"

The jargon made Jim smile. He motioned Doug to the side, away from the African diplomat and Iranian bartender. "*Violate* is too strong a word. The old colonialism was often rape. The new colonialism—westernization, Coca-colonization as one wag calls it—certainly has its ugly side." Jim kept his voice low and frequently glanced around to insure he offended nobody. "But those indigenous cultures aren't exactly pretty either. There's nothing pretty about poverty, disease or feudal restrictions. In Asia, for example, people in villages *want* a door into the wider world. They know it's out there. They want western freedom, money and goods."

"So it's more seduction than rape?"

Jim disliked the sexual metaphors that always accompanied this topic, and Doug's smile seemed awfully knowing. "No. It's more mutual than seduction. Although the results certainly aren't mutual. I admit it. I prefer the relative innocence of Philippine rural life back in the early fifties, when I was first there, to the mishmash it's become. But that's not what *they* wanted. They might miss it now that they've lost it. But there's no way we could've prevented them from getting what they wanted. Burma is ruled by a Buddhist theocracy, but all their restrictions against the taint of the West only make western goods more valuable there."

Doug's knowing smile was unshaken by Jim's argument. Meg would've listened more closely, asked for details, tactfully argued with questions. Jim suddenly felt guilty for discussing such things with this boy instead of with Meg.

"And so on and so forth," said Jim, making mock of his own long-windedness and surveying the room, looking for someone important he should be chatting with instead of Doug.

"Whoever's fault it is, it's really great to see this rot from the inside," Doug said. "Glittering rot, like exotic fruit bejeweled with green flies." He giggled at his flamboyant phrasing and Jim realized the boy was not knowing and judgmental, he was drunk.

"Good. I'm glad you're getting something out of this," Jim coldly declared. "I still wish Meg could've joined us though. I miss having her along tonight."

"I'm kind of glad she's not here," said Doug. "Meg's great and all that, but she wouldn't have gotten into this. No. She would've hated it. There's times Meg can be a real drag."

All Jim's irritation and distrust of Doug instantly returned. He lowered his eyelids a fraction and said, "That's a peculiar way for a man to talk about his girlfriend."

Doug guiltily laughed, then shrugged his shoulders. "We're not really a couple, you know."

"No? What are you then?"

"I like Meg. She's smart and well-read and full of stories and ideas. I enjoy being with her. I'm just not in love with her."

"Why not?"

Doug snorted at the question—it *was* a ridiculous thing to ask anyone. "I dunno. Maybe I'm not a very passionate person."

Which was the excuse Jim had made to himself all those years before he understood his indifference to women. At least he'd had the good sense not to get too close to anyone who might misunderstand his friendliness and be hurt.

"Does Meg know this?"

"Oh sure. I've always been honest with Meg. But that doesn't stop her from feeling differently about me than I do about her. You know how women get sometimes."

"Hmm," went Jim, indignant for his niece, annoyed with Doug, and furious at himself for thinking about the boy sexually again. "Excuse me, Doug. I see somebody I should speak to. Don't wander off. I'll be back in a minute and we'll go. You might watch it on the champagne. Try some caviar."

Forget it, Jim told himself as he stepped around a huddle of Taiwanese executives. You don't really want to protect Meg. You only want to go to bed with that boy. Looking back at Doug from ten yards away, Jim was struck by how physical the boy had become, with a body as well as that ideogram of a smile, a confusing presence of cocked hips and slumped shoulders and a head he tossed to flip the hair out of his face before he took another swig from the flute. His presence could not have been stronger among the overdressed adults if he'd been naked, except none of the people nearby so much as glanced at him. He was apparently something only Jim could see.

When Jim ran into someone he knew, an English economist who'd advised oil companies when Jim was in Indonesia, he put all thoughts about Doug in a back compartment of his brain and gave his full attention to a conversation about life in Tehran, where the economist now lived with his family. "Everything's higglety-pigglety over there. The English language has become a status symbol. Even the merchants are getting in on it, only they don't always say what they think they're saying. My favorite mangling is a package of condoms which reads, 'For sanity of penis.' Isn't that lovely?"

On his way back to Doug, Jim passed the bearded professor from the National Security Council who'd lectured him about Marcos. Jim tried to signal him with a nod, then a raised hand, but the man didn't see him, or pretended not to.

Doug stood at the buffet table, blinking while he explored his mouth with his tongue. "So this is caviar," he said.

"One more stop and we'll call it a night," Jim announced. The wisest course of action was to finish the evening as quickly as possible and send Doug back to Annandale. For sanity of penis.

They retrieved their coats and joined the furs and polyglot chatter of people queued up just inside the door to wait their turn for a cab.

"Hey, Jim," said Doug much too loudly. "You promised me Imelda Marcos." Champagne made the boy insolently intimate.

"If she wasn't here, she might be at the next party," Jim said wearily.

"She better. I don't want to think you got me here on false pretenses." Doug giggled to show he was teasing.

Jim cut his eyes at the boy and hoped nobody heard.

The last party was in a posh residential enclave off Wisconsin Avenue and above Georgetown. The taxi glided down tree-lined streets winding around deep, snow-spotted lawns. A sudden pack of expensive cars parked along the curb showed where the party was: an enormous Tudor house with boxwood hedges and a flagstone walk. The presence of four matching white limos announced that Imelda and her court were somewhere inside.

Jim immediately saw her from the front hall while he took a ticket for his coat. She sat in a wing-backed chair that had been moved to the center of the cozy living room full of fumed oak and brass fixtures. Her face hidden from view by people standing in attendance, an olive-skinned hand with gold bracelets gracefully twisted and turned like a charmed snake while she spoke. Everyone laughed in unison at something she said. The little feet crossed at the ankles and tucked beneath the chair wore red high heels tonight; she had to wear flats when she appeared with her husband.

"We going to talk to her?" asked Doug, eagerly shifting from side to side to see her face through her audience.

"In a minute. I'd like a drink first." Jim stepped into the room, looking for a bar or butler. He didn't understand why Imelda made him so edgy and irritated tonight. He had nothing to win or lose from her now, but he no longer had the armor of an official role to play either, which left him feeling very vulnerable. He motioned Doug toward the leaded window with hexagonal panes behind the grand piano. A sleepy pianist played leisurely jazz variations on the Philippine national anthem. It was a quiet, civilized gathering, the fire crackling in the stone hearth, the conversation going at a low boil, nobody speaking louder than the guest of honor. Most of her entourage mingled with the other guests.

"Is that her lover standing behind her?" Doug whispered. "The silver-haired guy holding her drink?"

"*No*. Just Jack Valenti. He does something in Hollywood. A friend of the family."

A pair of current favorites among her Blue Ladies sat on a sofa, softly chittering like parakeets into both ears of the elderly corporate lawyer who sat between them, in pig heaven. An army officer in a tux—he had the Napoleonic stance of most Filipino colonels—conspired in the corner with the lobbyist who was their host while keeping an eye on his First Lady. And one of her sip-sips, a hairdresser or decorator, sulkily draped himself by the fireplace in a shirt so thick with ruffles his front seemed to have exploded in white flowers. His bored gaze fell briefly on Jim and Doug, then slipped off, never dreaming he had something in common with them—which he didn't, not really. Jim despised the frivolousness and effeminacy of Imelda's coterie of lapdogs.

"Scotch and soda," he gruffly told the black butler.

"You got champagne? Wait, I change my mind. Make mine scotch and soda too." Doug smiled at Jim, then resumed his study of Imelda. He leaned in very close and whispered, "The banality of evil."

Jim frowned and tightly shook his head to silence the boy. Imelda might be banal but she wasn't quite evil. Vain, self-important and greedy, her sins were trivial compared to her husband's. She was a bad joke and Jim sometimes suspected Ferdinand encouraged his wife to indulge herself in order to distract people from his own more serious crimes. Yet tonight her presence unnerved and angered him. The official role that once kept Imelda out had also enabled Jim to keep his personal feelings in. She sat here like a mannequin in rust-red Ultrasuede, a mascot of Jim's failure, an emblem of his ineffectuality.

"But she will talk to you?" said Doug. "Even though you're her enemy?"

Jim grabbed the boy's shoulder to shut him up. "Not enemy," he whispered sharply. "Critic. Foreign service is in no position to be anyone's enemy." The hand felt muscle and bone beneath the jacket.

Eyes still watching Imelda, Doug leaned against Jim to hear his whispers better.

Jim smelled hair and warm skin and his hand automatically gave the shoulder an affectionate squeeze. "Besides, she can't imagine they have any enemies," he continued. "Only misunderstandings, which she assumes she can charm away." Even Mrs. Weed had heard about the private summit talks on the love seat. Imelda had tried it once with Jim. His colleagues came away from the First Lady's cooing and pawing nervous wrecks, but Jim had remained perfectly calm and courteous, his only difficulty the peppery sensation of her perfume burning in his nose. You can't sexually intimidate someone whose compass points elsewhere. His thumb lightly dug along the groove between collarbone and muscle while he gazed disdainfully at Imelda.

The butler came with their drinks and Jim promptly let go. "Thank you," he told the man. "Cheers," he told Doug and took a deep swallow, hoping alcohol would separate his two different trains of thought. While he consciously judged and condemned Imelda, the rest of him seemed to think about going to bed with Doug.

"Quality stuff," said Doug, rattling the ice in his glass. He took on a more stoical, masculine pose with the scotch than he'd had with the champagne. Was it some kind of signal that he now drank what Jim was drinking?

"Well, drink up. We should make our hellos to Mrs. Marcos and get the hell out of here."

Jim thought that would make the boy linger over his drink. Instead Doug gulped it down and faced Jim with a grin.

"All right then. She's the wife of a head of state. Treat her with the same respect and care you would the mother of a rich girl you hope to marry"— which was what they'd been told in protocol class twenty years ago. "Let's get this over with." He wheeled around and stepped briskly toward Imelda Marcos. "Madame First Lady?"

"*Jeem.* What a pleasant surprise."

She looked up at him with her perfectly stenciled smile and eyebrows, still Miss Manila of 1953 and incapable of leaking a single sincere emotion. Her face and hair were much too tight for that.

"We were *so* sorry when they took you from us," she said poutily, offering him a handful of bright red fingernails. "Your president must have needed you so badly." There was no trace of sarcasm. A genial winner, Imelda could be quite sweet to losers.

Her lack of rancor and the faint tickle like enameled beetles in his palm brought back Jim's feelings of failure and helplessness. He remained dry and cordial. "I have someone here who wants to meet you, Madame President. Douglas Inge, a friend of my niece."

"*Imelda Marcos!* I mean—Madame President. What an honor!" Doug bowed when he took her hand and Jim feared he might actually kiss it. The boy overdid it terribly, but he didn't seem to be mocking her.

Imelda responded with her little munchkin titter. "Douglas? That is our favorite American name in my country. 'I shall return?' Shall you return, Jim?" She didn't wait for an answer. "I didn't know you had a niece. That's good. Family is important to us too. Is she here tonight?" Her soulful eyes theatrically searched the room.

"Unfortunately she couldn't make it tonight." Just having this woman refer to Meg made Jim's skin crawl. If Imelda was corruption then Meg was purity and Jim felt relieved she wasn't being exposed to this.

"Too bad. I could tell her what a fine and upright man her uncle is. He had such a moral reputation in Manila," she told her audience. "People used to call him the Vicar."

Everyone laughed and Jim had to make a polite smile. If his staff nickname had made its way to the Malacanang Palace, it was safe to assume his position on martial law was known there as well.

"You are in school, Douglas? What subject do you study?"

When he told her English, she went into a little speech about the University of the Philippines having the finest literature program outside the United

States and how Doug must keep them in mind when he applied to graduate school.

Jim stood by with his hands clasped behind his back, patiently waiting for Imelda to finish so he could decide what to do about Doug. He already seemed to have decided.

"We shouldn't take up any more of your time, Madame First Lady," Jim said when she paused to catch her breath. "I hope you'll have a pleasant stay in Washington. My regards to President Marcos."

"Thank you, Jim. I am sure Ferdinand remembers you fondly. One hopes the winds of time will bring you back to Manila. And it was so nice meeting you, young man." She bared her Chiclet teeth at Doug.

"The pleasure was all mine and I can't tell you how much—"

Jim laid a firm hand on Doug's shoulder, gave Imelda an apologetic nod and steered the boy toward the door. The hand remained there until they were out in the front hall.

"Imelda Marcos in the flesh," Doug gloated while he pulled on his coat. "I can't believe I met her. And she knows *you* by your first name."

The way she knows her servants and sip-sips, thought Jim. He was disturbed by the genuine pleasure Doug had taken in meeting the woman. How could Meg be attracted to such a boy?

A taxi cab outside was dropping off a junior naval officer and pretty young woman. Jim signaled the cab from the door. He waited until he and Doug were sitting in the back and on their way home before he said, "You seemed quite taken with the banality of evil tonight."

"Yeah, well. Strange people fascinate me. Was I laying it on too thick?" he asked nervously.

"One could say that. Although she brings it out in the best of us."

"She's a trip. What a weird, seductive woman."

"Only with those who want to be seduced." No, Jim could not pretend he wanted to seduce Doug out of a selfless desire to protect Meg. But that result, that additional benefit, should cancel out the fact that this was his niece's boyfriend. He should stop splitting hairs about this and act. He could not be as ineffectual with his own needs as he'd been with the needs of a foreign country. Jim turned to Doug and sternly said, "You've had an awful lot to drink tonight. Are you sober enough to drive home?"

"Am I drunk?" Giggling, he touched his own cheeks and forehead as if that could tell him. "I'm so excited right now I don't know what I am."

"I'll fix some coffee when we get back to my place," Jim said with weary exasperation. "I don't want to have to worry about you having an accident. If worse comes to worse, I suppose you *could* spend the night."

"Oh?" Doug was silent a moment. "Let me see how I feel when we get back," he said and went off again on the subject of Imelda, asking if it were true she once sang "Hello, Dolly" at the White House for Lyndon Johnson.

When they arrived at Jim's building, Doug stumbled when he climbed out. "Damn. Maybe I am drunk."

"I thought as much. Well, come on up. I'll make some coffee while we decide what the game plan should be."

"Right," said Doug. He followed Jim inside, grinning drunkenly at his feet. Riding up in the elevator, he asked, "Can I call home and see if Meg's there yet?"

"Of course."

Jim unlocked his door and turned on the light. He took Doug's coat and hung it with his own in the foyer closet. "There's the phone next to the armchair."

The apartment felt very stark with Doug glancing around at the salmon plaid sofa against one wall, the leather armchair and long maple dresser opposite, the half-empty bookcase between the two windows with closed venetian blinds. Jim could not remember the last time he had someone in here besides his cleaning lady. It was like seeing the place for the first time and he was surprised by the bareness of his life. The parquet floor looked dry and chipped. There were nail holes in the wall where his Iranian tenant had hung a few pictures; Jim had no pictures of his own.

"Momma! Hello dere. It's me. Your son, the ne'er-do-well."

Doug sprawled in the armchair and prattled away on the telephone. Jim stepped past him to the narrow kitchen to put the kettle on for coffee, then went back to the foyer and his clothes closet to remove his tux. Behind the open door with the mirror on the back, he tried to decide what his next move should be. He had never seduced anyone in his life. Even in diplomatic arrangements Jim simply presented the facts and stepped aside, making no attempt to charm or bully his way through. In the Patpong in Bangkok he simply presented himself in the right bar, an anonymous American in a sports shirt and sunglasses. He didn't have to say to anyone, "Let's have sex" or "I'm a homosexual." Being there said it all, along with a friendly smile at the right boy who smiled back and the assumption there'd be a "gift" of saffron and bronze baht notes afterwards. Jim wondered if slipping a twenty-dollar bill into Doug's coat pocket without telling Doug might undo his inhibitions about making the first move.

"Uh-huh. Uh-huh. Yeah, yeah, yeah. I'll talk to her in a minute. You're not excited I met somebody famous? No, she's Argentina. Imelda's the Philippines. It's like shaking hands with Mrs. Adolf Hitler!" Doug looked up when Jim came out to remove his studs and cuff links at the dresser; he disparagingly rolled his eyes over his mother. "I am. I told you I was. Champagne and scotch. You won't believe the way people scarfed up the booze at the Iranian embassy."

The studs and cuff links lightly clinked when Jim dropped each one in the copper dish on the dresser, a sinister sound like bullets being removed by a surgeon.

"All right already. Let me ask him." Doug covered the mouthpiece of the phone. "My mother *insists* I spend the night. She thinks I'm too drunk to drive."

"Fine," Jim said drily, amused the boy's mother was helping him.

"Mom? Mr. Goodall says no problem. But we still have to work out what to do about tomorrow. Maybe I should talk to Meg."

Jim returned to the clothes closet to remove his shirt. He took off his shoes and tucked them into their pocket in the leather shoe bag hanging beneath the mirror. He decided it was too soon to remove his trousers. The sleeveless undershirt fit snugly around his flat stomach and showed off his square, freckled shoulders. Only from the neck up did he look like what he was, somebody's pompous, middle-aged uncle.

When he came out from behind the door, Doug's tone on the telephone had become huffy and defensive. "It's not my fault Mandrake screwed up! Be pissed at *him,* Frisch, not me. No, I wasn't taking advantage of anyone. You told me yourself—what was I supposed to do, sit home and watch the clock grow whiskers? I don't see why you're so bent out of shape. Yeah, of course he's here. Sure." He covered the mouthpiece again and his tone snapped back to amused disparagement. "Meg wants to talk to you. She's furious at everyone. I think she feels left out." He thrust the receiver at Jim and jumped up to shut himself in the bathroom.

Jim settled his face in the horns of the phone. "Meg?"

"I'm really sorry, Uncle Jim. I'm so angry I could kill somebody for the way everything got screwed, but I'm really sorry you got stuck with Doug. I told him he *might* go in without me. I didn't think he really would."

The disembodied voice threw him. He had never heard Meg angry and he could not quite connect this voice with the young woman he'd been thinking about off and on all evening. He hid his confusion by continuing the stern, masculine tone he'd been using with Doug. "I proposed this evening in the first place for *your* sake, Meg."

"I know. I wanted to be there. I really did."

"You could have arranged things better."

"I know, Jim. And I'm sorry. I never dreamed Mandrake could be *six hours late.* Or that Doug would actually go in without me. You're *my* uncle, not *his.*"

Meg didn't want them to get together without her? Jim wondered if she knew more about both of them than he thought she did.

"How are you two getting on?" she asked worriedly. "Is he being oh-so charming or just a pest? He can get really obnoxious when he's drunk. How drunk is he?" She was locked into a note of apology, but there were flickers of anger underneath.

"Very drunk. Dull drunk. Nothing to do but put him to bed and let him sleep it off. I could've killed him myself for the way he carried on with Mrs. Marcos. You certainly know how to pick them, Meg." He heard himself growing more dishonest and tried to cancel it with a chuckle. "Well, I've handled visiting congressmen and businesspeople away from their wives. I can deal with a college kid who can't hold his liquor."

"Okay. Good," said Meg, her mind put at ease about something. "Will I get to see you tomorrow? After a mess like this, I really hope we get to see each other."

"Definitely. What have you and our inebriated friend worked out?"

While Meg explained that she'd be riding in with Larry and Trish in the morning to meet Doug at the rally—it had been decided Doug wouldn't have time to drive home to Annandale before Larry and Trish came by to pick them up—Doug came out of the bathroom. He sauntered past without looking at Jim, going straight to his bookcase. He stood there inspecting titles, loosening his tie, then shaking off his blazer and draping it over the back of the wooden chair. He gave Jim a smirk over his shoulder.

"All right then. Eleven o'clock, the Washington Monument. I'll do my best to be there, Meg-wump. We can finish this tomorrow. We all need our shut-eye for the big day."

"Again, Uncle Jim, I'm sorry about what happened."

"I don't blame you. Goodnight, Meg. I love you."

"Goodbye, Uncle Jim."

He hung up, took a deep breath and wiped the hand against his black trousers. It was only a guilty imagination that made him think she knew what might happen. And he would tell her afterwards. Jim pushed aside all sympathies and doubts in order to act.

"You won't be needing coffee after all," he announced and stepped into the kitchen to turn off the boiling water. "Would you like a nightcap?" he called out.

"Uh, sure."

Jim never drank at home, so his cabinet was full of various bottles given as gifts over the years. He filled two tumblers with Dutch herb-flavored gin, which should be enough to keep Doug loose and kill the taste of copper in Jim's mouth.

Doug closed the copy of *Seven Pillars of Wisdom* and returned it to the shelf when Jim brought the tumblers out.

"Here's a new experience for you. Cheers."

Jim downed his in a single tilt. Doug sipped at his.

"Different," he said and nodded appreciatively. He seemed less drunk now than he'd been in the cab or on the phone. "Poor Meg. She takes everything so personally." He swallowed without having taken another sip. "Are these the only books you have?"

"The only ones I keep. I throw away a lot on my travels." There was a coldness in Jim's tone he couldn't shake, a stern authority that came with the suppression of doubt. He was standing very close to Doug but the boy refused to look at him.

Jim stepped away, set his glass on the night table and began to stack the sofa cushions. "Let's go to bed." Leaning the cushions against the wall, he looked over at Doug to see how he responded. "You realize, don't you, we'll be sharing a sofa bed?"

Doug's eyes darted from one wall to the other. "Oh. There's no bedroom. Ah. This is all you can afford?"

"It's all I need when I'm in the States." Jim took the handles and lifted the folded mattress and springs from the depths of the sofa, then unfolded the fact of the bed across the room. "Come on. Lights out in five minutes. We have a long day tomorrow."

Doug looked away from the bed, embarrassed by it, then sat in the wooden chair beside the bookcase and began to untie his shoes, very slowly, like a man undressing for a doctor's examination.

Jim turned on the lamp on the night table and turned off the overhead light on his way into the bathroom. If not romantic, it was less clinical. He brushed his teeth, used the toilet—his penis looked skeptical—and took off his trousers, which he hung by the cuffs on their special hanger. He removed his socks and garters and rubbed his calves to erase the pink bands left by the elastic. A man in boxer shorts and garter tracks looked too absurd to seduce anyone. He hadn't seduced him yet, had he? Should he wait until they were in bed or did he make his intentions clear before then?

When Jim came out, Doug was already in bed. The blanket was pulled up to his bare shoulder, a wing of blond hair covering half his face; he lay on one side with his back to the rest of the bed. His eyes were still open but he didn't turn to look when Jim stepped around to his side of the mattress. Doug's necktie, shirt and jeans were draped on the chair.

"All set?"

"Uh huh," Doug answered indifferently.

Jim knew he should say more, knew now was the time to make clear what he wanted and discover if Doug wanted it too. But he didn't know what to say even after he turned off the light and they became invisible. He lifted the blanket and climbed into the creaking warmth. Doug did not roll over to receive him, but remained on his side, breathing steadily. His warm legs radiated beneath the covers.

A siren began to wail in the distance, a police motorcycle escorting a limo full of dignitaries back to their embassy or hotel. The motorcade's route seemed to circle the bed in the blotchy, imperfect darkness before fading into silence.

Worse than doing the wrong thing was doing nothing at all. Jim took a deep breath and said, "I should warn you, Doug. I'm a bit drunk myself tonight. And I like you very much." He had laid his hand on a hip sheathed in soft cotton.

Doug lay perfectly still. "I don't know, Jim."

"What? If I'm drunk or if I like you?" His thumb flicked the dry waistband.

"Feel my chest," said Doug.

Jim reached around to spread his hand over the cage of bones; a heart furiously kicked inside. The ribs expanded to take a breath.

"You're gay, aren't you?" said Doug. "Homosexual"—as if Jim might not know the slang word. "I've never done this before."

Not *that,* but *this:* they were halfway there. "Would you like to?" Jim's hand caressed hairless skin and a goosebump of nipple. This hairlessness had a smoother grain than the silk of Asian skin.

"I thought I did." His voice was very small and panicky. "I thought I could let it happen. But my body says no. It's all nerves right now and I feel sick to my stomach."

And Jim was divided again, between sympathy for Doug's distress and a determination to make love to him. He moved his hand down to rub Doug's stomach and make him feel better.

"All right then. We don't have to do anything," Jim whispered. "Let me just hold you for a minute, and we can go to sleep."

Jim slipped his other arm beneath Doug and shifted them closer together, front to back. Organs continued to twitch and percolate under the skin. Forcing himself on Doug, Jim wondered if he really were drunk.

"I'm sorry," Doug said sadly.

"We don't have to do anything," Jim repeated, brushing his chin against Doug's shoulder. He could taste the smell of his whole body, baby shampoo and gin and butter—butter was the only association Jim had for the aroma he had never smelled on Thai skin. His hand continued to stroke the down on Doug's stomach, until he slipped his fingertips beneath the waistband.

When Doug pulled an arm free, Jim thought he'd gone too far. But instead of stopping Jim, the hand groped backward and gripped Jim's shorts.

"You wanted to fuck me?" he said accusingly.

"No. I didn't. It hurts if you haven't done it before."

The hand relaxed, then groped more intimately, weighing and thumbing Jim through the safety of cloth. "Never touched another guy's dick before," he said, awed with himself.

Jim's excitement was indistinguishable from fear, the feeling joy was too fragile to last another second. This had nothing in common with sex in the Patpong, where there was no suspense and Jim went to bed with ideas of men, whole races of men. This was a particular man, someone with whom Jim had imagined love. In the weeks since they met, through the hours of challenge, annoyance and doubt tonight, Jim had forgotten he was in love with Doug, and that there was a chance the boy might love him back.

Jim slid his own hand into the pocket of hip and elastic and found Doug: just crinkly hair and pigeon-egg testicles, but here, arched over his knuckles, was the bent spring of an erection.

"Let's get rid of these," he said, using the hand inside the briefs to pull them off.

Doug rolled over as he lifted up and extracted each knee. He faced Jim—he had a face, an open mouth and frightened eyes deep inside Jim's farsighted focus. The eyes closed when Jim held the back of his head in one hand and caressed his face with the other.

Jim held Doug's jaw in his palm when he kissed him. Lips squashed open and a birdlike tongue darted into Jim's mouth, but the sad, inward curve of jawbone enabled Jim to taste another man's tongue and teeth, deepening his need to go inside a living mouth. It was how Jim began every kiss.

Doug abruptly pulled back, as if frightened. But he was grinning, looking sweetly depraved as he caught his breath. "You too," he said and pulled at Jim's shorts, pulling them down while Jim whipped his undershirt off over his head. They had knocked the blankets back and were completely exposed to each other, doubly exposed with extended cocks and eyes adjusted to the dark.

"You're something else," Jim laughed. "I love"—but he couldn't say it yet—"being with you like this."

Doug laughed too, and rubbed his hand and face against Jim's chest, fascinated by the texture of hair and muscle. Amazed he could touch or kiss another American anywhere, Jim stroked Doug's bottom and licked the rim of his ear. They had crossed the border from suspense into sex and the clearly marked map of separate bodies and various taboos was obliterated. It was all so simple and shameless, body no longer divided against consciousness, but the two meeting in Jim's love for the man in his bed. Pressing the warm, mildly bitter, sculptural weight of him between his tongue and palate, Jim felt he could slip all of Doug into his mouth, and keep him there. It was beautiful when Doug determinedly did it to Jim, not just the sensation but the hope there might be love here if Doug could do that.

"Did you want to fuck?" Doug asked, now excited by the idea.

"Not our first time." Jim wanted him to know there'd be other times.

"So how do you have an orgasm? I might shoot any second, but I want to see you first."

Jim had to do it himself. Maybe it would be different with Doug, but he didn't want their joy in each other to grind down in effort and anxiety. He lay back with Doug in one arm, kissing his mouth and breathing his hair while he gathered his excitement in his free hand. Doug did it for him briefly—"Like touching myself except you're thicker"—but it seemed to work better when Jim did it. The shame of Doug watching fed his excitement, spun the strands tighter. He stopped kissing Doug to shut his eyes and picture a naked man, any naked man seen across a room. He pictured Doug: a trigger was pulled and the gate snapped open. Jim made a fist with his ass and clenched his teeth as all thought and sensation flew from him in incontinent jolts.

His body reappeared in a thin film of evaporating sweat. Jim came back to life with a deep breath, as though he'd been underwater. And here was Doug in his arm, the very person Jim had imagined in order to finish.

"Ah," said Doug, dabbing Jim's stomach. "You did." He stroked his chest and kissed Jim on the cheek.

Jim was painfully naked after a climax, stripped not only of clothes but of dignity and desire. And Doug wasn't someone who'd take Jim's baht notes, thank him politely and never see Jim again. He spoke the same language, knew Jim in the real world; he was friends with Jim's niece.

Jim was not yet ready to see the world outside this bed.

He hoisted Doug up to cover his nakedness. Cradling warm skin and weight on top of him, Jim was surprised by how tender he felt toward Doug, a mournful need unlike his usual coldness after sex.

"Oh yeah," sighed Doug, squirming against Jim's stomach. "I'm ready." His legs straddled Jim's legs to slide in the spill.

He was beautiful up close and Jim wished he could put on his reading glasses to see him better. He held his back and bottom. He tensed his stomach muscles to help him along.

In just a few strokes, Doug was grinning and making faces. His breathing deepened into moans and he lifted his head to get more air in his lungs. He arched his back and rocked harder against Jim, the moans quickening, building, becoming higher. Until his mouth stretched wide open for a strangled cry, a string of cries from the back of his throat and base of his spine. Then, with a final thrust of hips and a moan full of disappointment it was over, he collapsed against Jim.

Jim was amazed. No wonder Doug hadn't been sure if Jim had finished. Awed by the privilege of seeing such ecstatic abandon, pleased by his own role in it, Jim held on to Doug. The breathing weight in his arms seemed to go very deep into Jim, not stopped by skin or lust or whatever prevented human touch from getting too far inside. He wanted them inside each other, Doug in him and Jim in Doug, rolled up in a ball like a pair of socks.

Doug slid off and flipped over on his back, his ribcage still heaving.

"So," said Jim. "Was it as awful as you thought it'd be?" Despite everything he felt, Jim heard himself teasing like an elder.

Doug opened his eyes and blinked a few times. He lifted his head to look at himself. "Messy when it's both guys," he said unhappily.

Jim's front was thickly splashed too, most of it Doug, but that had more to do with age than emotion. Jim sat up, found his boxer shorts and reached over to wipe Doug off. He did not want to leave him, not even to get a towel.

"No, I'll do it," Doug said testily, snatching the shorts and rolling away from Jim.

Jim mopped himself in plain view. "We should sleep well tonight," he said. He was not yet ready to admit aloud how important this had been to him. "What're you looking for?"

Doug leaned over the side of the bed, bony haunches in the air while he fished for something. "My skivvies."

"What do you need those for? Come on, Doug." He was gentle but firm, pulling the boy down beside him, then bringing the blankets up over them. "It's friendlier like this."

Doug squirmed, turning on his side with his back to Jim again. "I should warn you," he said. "I feel very weird right now."

"After sex all animals are sad," Jim said automatically. He felt the boy was exaggerating his mood, which made Jim wonder if he'd been exaggerating his pleasure too. Jim could still feel him bouncing against his stomach. "I must say, though. You did seem to enjoy it."

"Oh yeah. Was great." He sighed, then turned his head so Jim could see his face. "Really. I always get like this."

Jim was touched to hear a man confess so much. Sex itself was an intimate confession, but conversation was even more personal. The only other time Jim had lingered afterwards was with an ambitious young man who worked to improve his English by asking Jim endless questions about American cars, appliances and farm animals.

"I thought you said this was your first time."

"With a guy."

"You've slept with women," said Jim.

"Oh yeah." Doug tried to cover his forlorn tone with a little arrogance. "Well. Two," he admitted.

"And how did this compare?"

The shoulder blades scissored up in a shrug. "Was different. Interesting." He thought a moment. "Women last longer. Which is great, but it's kind of intimidating too. They have the greatest orgasms."

All Jim wanted to hear was which experience Doug preferred.

Doug rolled over on his stomach, able to steal a look at Jim after he protected himself with his sexual credentials. "But this was nice," he insisted. "Different. Exciting." He frowned. "I don't know why I was so scared at first. I don't think I was scared of you. My own body scared me. I've been wanting to do this for a long, long time."

"With a man," said Jim, not wanting to claim too much too soon.

Doug pinched his mouth shut and nodded. "I like women. I like having sex with them. Sometimes. But I can't stop thinking about men. Even though they scare me and I don't like them as people. Not the way I like women."

If he said the right thing, Jim could prevent another Dave Wheeler from happening, or for that matter another Jim Goodall. "I like women, but I only fall in love with men. I stick to men. That way nobody gets confused or hurt."

"You've never had sex with a woman?"

"No."

"Then you really are gay." He looked at Jim with a faintly smug smile. "Aren't you afraid of other people knowing?"

"You have to learn not to worry about that."

"See, I worry about it nonstop. I don't know why. You read enough Sartre and modern philosophy and you see how slippery everything is. Other people aren't any more real than you are, so it shouldn't matter what they think." He buried his face in the pillow and made a little moan. "You must think I'm a real flake rattling away like this."

"Not at all. You're more honest and intelligent than I was at your age." Doug's openness made him seem worthy of love, and capable of loving back.

"I'm not. I got to be the most dishonest, insincere person I know. Even my fascination with other people is fake. Friends think I study them because I want to be a poet or philosopher or something. But I think the real reason is to keep them from studying me. Because as soon as they do they'll see what I am."

"Homosexual?" said Jim. Not *horny* or *bisexual* or any of the other excuses, but the thing itself. No wonder Doug had been frightened.

Doug nodded. "God, I am such a cliché," he groaned.

Jim smiled. "Not to me."

Doug smiled back, propping himself on his elbow. "When did you first figure me out?"

Jim laughed. "I still haven't figured you out. But I guess I first began to suspect something that night at my sister's when you came into my room. You seemed to be flirting with me."

There was an embarrassed whine that ended in giggles. "I was flirting, wasn't I? Oh God. You see, even then I was being dishonest. I didn't know what I was doing. I thought I was testing you. I mean, you're old enough to be my father. I never dreamed I could think of somebody like you this way. But when I felt you were interested in me, I began to think about what might happen if we were ever alone together."

They were like two golfers replaying their game in the clubhouse. "You were testing me?"

"That's what I thought anyway, flashing you, then sitting on your bed. I had to check out Meg's theory her Establishment bachelor uncle was really a homosexual. I was so obnoxious."

All thought and feeling suddenly stopped. "Meg knows?"

"Half knows. She thinks you might be gay but that you're so moral and repressed you don't recognize it about yourself." He broke into a grin. "We sure proved her wrong on that one."

Jim had forgotten Meg's involvement. His first impulse was to dismiss her as a minor character here, a bit player. But that felt terribly disloyal. And part of Jim was thrilled she called him correctly, a knowledge that both frightened and pleased.

"Strange," said Doug. "I feel more comfortable lying here talking than I ever have before after sex."

"What does Meg know about you?"

"I'm not sure. I've never told her. She must know something. She's very smart, you know."

"Isn't she a little bit in love with you?"

"I don't think so. She might've wanted us to be lovers in the beginning, but now we're just best friends. Yes. That's all."

The uncertainty at the end of that statement worried Jim. He didn't want to know, but he owed it to Meg to know. "Is she one of the women you've slept with?"

Doug looked straight at him, as if he hadn't quite heard the question, then grinned despite himself. "Isn't this weird? I keep expecting you to act like a very conventional grown-up, disapproving of this and that, even after what we just did. But—no. She's not."

Jim wanted that to close the door on Meg, keep her out of this, but it didn't. He wasn't even certain what it would change if she had slept with Doug.

"I've thought about it," Doug admitted. "We both have. But we are best friends and I'd feel too guilty."

"Yes," said Jim. "Are you thirsty? I am. Right back." He climbed out of bed and stepped toward the kitchen, hoping verticality would clear his thoughts about Meg. There was a world outside the bed, wasn't there? Jim winced at the light when he pulled the refrigerator door open.

"You're in good shape for someone my father's age," Doug called from the darkness.

Jim looked down at his body, in livid color again, copper hairs glued against his boxy front, testicles hanging so low his penis looked incidental. He took out a bottle of Gatorade and closed the door over the light.

"Thanks," said Doug, taking the bottle and swigging from it while Jim climbed in beside him. "How does the State Department deal with you being gay?"

Jim took a swig from the bottle. "What're you suggesting? You won't tell on me if I don't tell on you?" He said it as a joke, but it wasn't a joke, was it?

Doug thought a moment. "I assumed we weren't going to tell anyone."

"I think we should tell Meg." Did that make Jim feel better?

"I guess." Doug sighed and scuttled up against Jim, laying an arm across his stomach. "Sometime."

Jim was sitting against the sofa part of the bed. He set the Gatorade on the floor to wrap one arm around Doug against his chest. It was the first time they'd really touched since finishing and Jim was reconnected with his happiness. His frets about Meg were only something on the outside of that happiness. "How do you think she'll react?"

"Dunno. She'll probably be jealous."

"Jealous?"

"Yeah. She'll feel left out. Feel we were off being guys together." Doug spoke sleepily, contentedly, his warm breath tickling. He draped a leg over

Jim's leg. "Meg wishes she were a guy. She's kind of a feminist. About
herself. She doesn't particularly like other girls."

No, Doug didn't understand. It would be more basic and primal than trivial
feelings of exclusion. Meg would be shocked, appalled, disgusted her uncle
was a real homosexual, not an abstract one, and that he had betrayed her by
sleeping with her best friend. If he had slept with one of her girlfriends from
school it would be bad, and this was worse. She did not know how terrible the
world could be or that there were far more horrible things one man could do to
another than put his sex in your mouth.

"I'll be the one to tell her," said Jim. "Eventually. Maybe a letter would be
best."

"Hmmm." Doug snuggled closer. "This is great. Being with someone else
and feeling you can doze off any second."

"You're right. We should get to sleep. Be a long day tomorrow." Jim
shifted down and adjusted his side against Doug's front. "Are you comfortable?"

There was no answer. Doug was already asleep.

Jim expected to lie there for a long time, Doug in his arm and Meg across
the river, unable to doze off while he sketched a mental draft of a letter that
explained everything. But he had gotten no further than *Dear Meg* when the
warm contentment under the blankets rolled into his thoughts and he was fast
asleep.

10

THERE WAS A CURIOUS GAME OF PRETEND the next morning,
a pleasant air of playing house. Jim put on a bathrobe and made coffee while
Doug stayed in bed. He brought the *Washington Post* in from the hall and they
read the news while they drank their coffee, Jim in his robe in a chair beside
the bed, Doug sitting up in bed. Doug took two aspirin with his coffee, but
then seemed fine. He looked nice in daylight, colors in his paleness, his

shaggy blond hair comfortably disheveled, the wide mouth still comic yet beautiful too. When Jim commented on the time and suggested they take a shower, Doug got up and stretched without embarrassment. His nudity looked perfectly at home in the apartment, more domestic than erotic. They showered together, enjoying the game of being unashamed in each other's presence.

Jim waited until they were fully dressed and the bed neatly folded back into the sofa before he asked, "When will I get to see you again?"

"I'm not sure. Meg's staying until Sunday, you know. But I'll be home all next week on semester break." Doug began to smile to himself. "Maybe I can come into the city sometime during the week?"

"Good enough." Jim took out a sheet of department stationery and wrote on it. "Here's my home number and the address here. And my work number too. Call me as soon as you know."

"Great." Doug folded the paper and slipped it into a pocket. "Maybe we could see a movie or something."

"Or something," said Jim with a friendly smirk.

Doug smirked with him. They pretended this wasn't what it was, but both of them clearly knew, which made it a friendly game and not a guilty denial. If last night could be repeated next week, then maybe this had a future, whatever it was.

Not until they were downstairs and passing the doorman did Jim wish he'd given Doug a final kiss or feel before they went out in public.

"Morning, Mr. Goodall. Y'all off to see the parade?"

"Eventually, Leon. But I think we'll check out this antiwar rally. I've never seen one and it's certain to be the last."

The doorman made a face. "Have a nice day. Watch it you don't get your pockets picked."

Out on the street Doug asked, "You really believe this'll be the last demonstration?"

"I'm very bad at prophecy, but the war is just about over. In the words of Dr. Kissinger, 'Peace *is* at hand.' "

He felt wonderful this morning, full of good spirits despite the gray sky overhead, despite the peculiarly southern cold that chills the skin without numbing it, cold seeping into bones and joints. He didn't feel the cold after walking a block. They walked the mile to the rally. The wide avenues were almost deserted this morning, shoppers knowing better than to come to town today, many of the streets closed off by the parade route. Pennsylvania Avenue above the White House was packed with families, men with crewcuts, women in scarves, children in ear-flapped hats that made Jim think of the fifties. The parade would not start for another hour and the reviewing stands down by the White House appeared empty. A peddler pushed a grocery cart out in the street, full of American flags, Redskin pennants and yellow stuffed animals.

"Nixon lovers," Doug jeered as he and Jim made their way further west, looking for a place where the police would let them cross. "Dick Nixon before he dicks you."

"Oh, they're just here to see a celebrity," Jim said in their defense, feeling kindly toward all humanity this morning. This crowd seemed neither political nor passionate.

They crossed a few blocks up Pennsylvania Avenue and passed between Victorian government buildings to Constitution. They joined a scattered stream of people moving east in the direction of the Washington Monument, most of them Doug's age but many adults too. On the right, the park that had been filled with temporary buildings when Jim first came to D.C. was an open park again. Black treetrunks stood over hard shells of snow scattered around the brown grass; the Reflecting Pool was visible in the distance, a long strip of frozen, cracking mica, and beyond that the stony box of the Lincoln Memorial. On the left, buses from a dozen different companies were parked along the White House side of Constitution Avenue. Jim assumed they'd brought some people to the rally and others to the parade, until he noticed how they were parked tightly front to back, without enough space for even a child to squeeze between them. A solid wall of buses stretched up the avenue toward the metallic echo of a single voice becoming three or four different voices in a set of loudspeakers, buses hired by the police for the sole purpose of separating the rally from the parade.

A gap at the next cross street was sealed off with blue sawhorses. Behind the barricade stood a troop of D.C. police, the visors of their riot helmets up while they muttered among themselves and watched the crowd straggle past. A few swatted gloved hands with nightsticks in an effort to keep warm.

A half-dozen mounted police, also wearing riot helmets, moved in a solemn single file alongside the buses, sitting high on their arrogant, muscular brown horses.

The ghostly faces of a couple of soldiers peered out through the tinted glass of one of the buses.

Jim suddenly remembered Meg, and was frightened for her. This was Washington, not Manila or Jakarta, and Jim kept seeing men and women his age and older among the college students walking in the street, people not very different from the crowd waiting for the parade, not at first glance. But a young woman would be in great danger if anything happened, if the police and soldiers were to rush in. His old habits of prudence and alarm had snapped on, keener than ever because his niece was somewhere nearby. Jim nervously watched for armored riot cars, tear-gas launchers and automatic weapons.

A helicopter hung in the open sky off to the right, not a Huey or even a police chopper, but a glass bubble with the letters of a local television station on its tail. Down below, the long slope beneath the Washington Monument was solid with people, a massed carpet of so many colors it appeared black with color.

"What a show!" Doug exclaimed, delighted with everything. "What an orgasm of history! It's like being inside the six o'clock news."

No, nothing terrible could happen here today. There were too many adults present, too many TV cameras around the platform in the foreground, and the announcer was introducing Bella Abzug, a member of Congress. As he and Doug followed the others into the milling edge of the rally, Jim paid less attention to the threat of police and soldiers at his back, but his feeling of anxiety remained.

"The criminal hypocrisy of a president who bombs a people back to the peace table!" the loudspeakers proclaimed in the harsh accent of a woman from New York.

As Jim and Doug made their way uphill toward the white monument behind the crowd, Jim noticed that only people around the platform responded to what Abzug was saying. Further back, they just listened quietly, many young people sitting on ponchos, older people in lawn chairs they'd brought. There was an unease that may have been only the cold weather, but many people appeared uncertain why they were here. They seemed to know the war would end soon no matter what they did today, yet nobody took any pride or satisfaction in the passionless way it concluded.

Most of the flags around the base of the Washington Monument still flew at half-mast for Harry Truman. Others flew upside down at the tops of their poles and one flagpole was bare. A small fire burned on the ground, a pack of longhaired teenagers warming their hands over it, kids tossing in slats they untwisted from the dune fence they had knocked down. There was no park ranger present, no police at all up here to stop kids from destroying government property or flying the flag however they pleased. The smoke carried a nauseating stink of burnt nylon and Jim realized the missing flag had been thrown into the fire. A vague sense of dread continued to hang over him. Jim suddenly glanced up and saw the great square mass of granite towering overhead, more than the stone blockhouse he saw at eye level but something that continued upward in the overcast sky, making no sense at all when seen this close.

"Jim!"

He looked.

She stood ten yards away, holding one hand over her head like a student wanting to be called on. She muttered something to someone standing nearby. A green knit cap was pulled down over her ears. She was grinning, but her eyebrows were pinched together—against the cold?

"Meg! Good!" Jim called out and started toward her, stealing a quick glance at Doug. The crayon smile gave nothing away. But when he looked back at Meg, her grin wavered while her eyes darted from Jim to Doug and back again.

"You came," she said brightly as Jim stepped up to her. "I was worried you wouldn't."

"I felt I owed it to you after last night." He hugged her hello, his arms fitting themselves naturally around the body inside the bulky coat. When he released her, she was looking at him as though he'd whispered something in her ear. He leaned back slightly, afraid she might smell Doug on his skin. "Was worried we wouldn't be able to find you in this crowd. Quite a turnout, isn't it?"

"Yeah. It's great. Really great," she said, her mother's sharp nose pointed up at Jim, her father's brown eyes taking him in.

"Hey, Frisch. You made it in. Great." Doug set his hand on her shoulder, and gave her a kiss on the cheek.

Meg frowned. "What was that for?"

"Huh?" Doug's cheeks were red, but that was only the cold. "I'm happy to see you. And sorry last night got so screwed up."

"I'll live with it," she muttered, drew a deep breath and shook her head. "Oh Jim, this is Trish and Larry." She introduced two kids Jim hadn't noticed standing beside her. "This is Jim Goodall. My uncle in the State Department."

They could muffle all suspicions in the presence of other people.

"Pleased to meet you, Mr. Goodall." Larry was a short, stocky boy with waffled cheeks and a dustball of beard on his chin. He shook Jim's hand firmly, determined to be his equal. "This must be a new experience for you. Seeing things from the other side of the barricade."

Trish, with long straight hair hanging down the front of her navy peacoat, shyly smiled and nodded when Jim took her hand.

"Yes, it is new," Jim told everyone. "Interesting. A more mature, well-behaved crowd than I'd imagined. Noticing all the police on our way over, I half-expected to see a mob with pitchforks and torches preparing to storm the castle. At least burning the monster in effigy."

"You missed them burning a flag," said Meg.

"Those punks over there." Larry nodded at the teenagers around the fire. "They thought it'd be funny to torch a flag and a whole mess of us rushed over and told them their ass was grass if they tried burning another. Just because we're antiwar doesn't mean we're anti-American, y'know?"

"Jesus," Trish groaned. "Just a symbol. I don't see why everyone got so bent out of shape."

"Hey. Call me old-fashioned, but I don't like seeing my country's flag wasted. Especially by a bunch of kids who think it's a joke. I remember the April twenty-third demo back in 1971." Larry told how one group of protesters defended a flagpole outside the Treasury building against another group, one defender swinging on the rope and kicking the attackers back while the police looked on in confusion. Larry had been coming to antiwar demonstrations in D.C. since high school and spoke with the cool self-importance of an old pro.

Meg stood there listening to Larry, although she must have heard his stories

before. Her hands were stuffed in her coat pockets and she appeared at ease, a
little bored maybe.

"But Inge got to go inside the belly of the beast last night," she suddenly
said. "Didn't you, Inge?"

Doug grinned at her gratefully, taking that as his cue to match Larry's
experience with his own. "Oh yeah. Got to see the Establishment at play." He
began with the Cosmos Club and George Kennan, then all the conspicuous
consumption at the Iranian embassy, slowly building toward the promised
meeting with Imelda Marcos.

Jim listened closely, afraid the boy might give away the secret undercur-
rents of the evening. He could feel Meg watching him. Each time he threw a
friendly glance in her direction, however, she was watching Doug or, once,
looking off in the distance toward the banners and placards down front.

"Sounds to me like you really got into it," Meg grumbled.

"Maybe," Doug said proudly. "Nothing human is alien to me." He
grinned again, not at Meg but at Jim, a giddy, cocky grin.

Meg snapped her head around to stare at Jim, then turned away, embarrassed by what she saw.

Larry asked Doug who else was in Imelda's entourage besides Jack Valenti.
Trish wanted to know what jewelry Imelda was wearing.

Jim bent down, turning his back to the others and softly told Meg, "You
didn't miss anything last night. Just boring chitchat and people in fancy dress.
But I *am* sorry you weren't with us."

"Uh huh." She looked up at him, twisting her lower lip under her front
teeth. "You and Doug hit it off okay?" she said, a sarcastic curl in her mouth
and voice.

"Uh, yes. Doug's okay. When you get to know him."

What did she know? How did she know? Jim wondered if his happiness
shone through his discomfort. He took on the bland, stupid look he used with
journalists, especially European journalists who assumed American diplomats
had little intelligence and no imagination.

"Meg? Are you angry about something?"

"No. Just feeling weird. Weird and creepy and paranoid." She looked past
Jim toward Doug and the others, who went on about Imelda, paying no attention to Meg's exchange with her uncle.

"Are you paranoid about anything in particular?" He didn't want to know,
but he'd be even more suspect if he didn't ask.

"Forget it." Meg looked at the different groups of people milling around
them. "This feels really creepy right now. For us to be yakking, like this was a
tea party, while everyone else is so concerned about cities being bombed and
people getting killed."

A shiver went through her body. Her teeth began to chatter and she angrily
folded her arms in front of her chest.

"You're cold, Meg. Here." Jim put his arm around her and reached up with his other hand to chafe her warm.

She ducked beneath his arm and stepped away. "I'm fine. I can take care of myself."

"Didn't you bring any gloves? Here. Wear mine." He pulled at one of his gloves.

"I'm not a baby." She stepped around him and walked up to Doug, who stopped his story to look at her. "Guys," she said. "We gonna be here a while?"

"I thought we'd hang out until Jerry Rubin speaks," said Larry. "Then see what's going down over at the parade."

"Okay. I'll be back. I got to walk around a little. My feet are numb and I just got to—walk around. Okay?"

"You want company, Frisch?" Doug spoke idly, pretending nothing was wrong, making clear he didn't really want to go with her.

"I'll walk with you," Jim told her.

"No." She vehemently shook her head and backed away from everyone. "I want to be by myself for a few minutes. Okay? No big deal, damn it." She turned and started down the slope, arms still folded across her chest, head bent forward, the gentle gradient making her short steps very quick and heavy.

When Jim looked straight at Doug, the boy only sighed, lifted his eyebrows and smiled sheepishly, as if to say: *Poor Meg.*

"I remember my first demo," Larry declared. "It stirs up all kinds of heavy stuff."

Trish said nothing, only glanced curiously at Jim, then off at Meg.

The rally was to the right of the straight line formed by the monument, Reflecting Pool and Lincoln Memorial. Meg was headed toward the left, where a few solitary specks of people wandered on the brown and white grounds between the frozen pool and rime-encircled Tidal Basin.

"I need a walk myself. We'll be back shortly," Jim announced.

"Good luck." Doug said it with a blitheness that annoyed Jim. Surely he understood what was happening, yet he showed neither fear nor concern.

Jim walked briskly, without breaking into a run. He would catch up with her soon enough. She already knew. She had read it in the air. He'd been a fool to think for a minute it was the police who'd made him so uneasy when he arrived here. The best he could do now was to explain the extenuating circumstances or let Meg know precisely what it was she knew or—no, he didn't know what he could tell her, only that he needed to tell her something.

Off to the right, a voice continued to echo against the federal buildings, a male voice now that emphasized a few key phrases. "Our Christmas present to the people of North Vietnam . . . the blood on American hands . . . a peace *without* honor."

Jarred by her heavy-footed walk, Meg's bent head bounced between her shoulders. She had to hear the shoes breaking through a patch of snow behind her, but she didn't look back or slow down. She didn't quicken her gait either.

Jim fell in step beside her. "Meg. I'm sorry. I know you wanted to be alone. I just wanted to ask why."

She kept her head down so all Jim saw was the bulky weave of green yarn in the cap Ann must have knitted for her.

"Because I hate feeling stupid. I hate feeling other people know something they're not telling me. It makes me think I'm very stupid and paranoid."

The sound of Meg punching herself with words strengthened Jim's resolve to tell her. "You're not stupid, Meg. In point of fact, you have good cause to be paranoid."

She looked up at him, her eyes wide open, not frightened but amazed, impressed that she'd been right. "You and Doug? Yes?"

Jim nodded. "Last night."

She faced forward again, her mouth parted open; a few strands of hair were blown across her face as though she'd walked through a spider web. *"Why?"*

They were on level ground now, the open space stretching in front of them with nobody in sight except two kids sliding out on the ice of the frozen pool.

"Because I'm homosexual," Jim calmly told her. "I don't know what you suspect about your uncle, Meg, or what you know about men like me. But I am homosexual. It's a fact about myself I've told very few people. But it's something I've wanted to tell you, Meg. Before now. I realize this might shock or even disgust you," he admitted. "But it's what your uncle is, the way he was born."

"And *that's* why you did it?" she demanded. "Homosexuals can't stop themselves with another guy? You *had* to fuck him?"

Her anger stunned him, the quickness of it cutting through all respect and fear and love of him. She did not pause at confusion or disgust, but went straight through to anger.

"It didn't matter he was *my* friend. You thought I'd be too stupid to figure out what was going on. You should've seen the two of you back there," she said scornfully. "Doug looking so damned pleased with himself. You looking *so* guilty."

"I am guilty, Meg. I've handled this very badly." Jim had braced himself for tears, expecting Meg to be hurt and helpless. He had never had a woman angry at him like this. His natural impulse was to defend himself with anger of his own, but he had no right to be angry and she did.

"Now it makes sense. What an ass I was. What a dumb stupid twat." Her anger turned against herself and that hurt him. "I knew something was up. When we talked on the phone last night? Before then too, but I thought that was just me. Being neurotic and paranoid, feeling put out because I didn't get to meet *Imelda Marcos*." She bit at the name with special contempt. "How long you been planning this, Jim? Did you plot it with Doug back in Virginia

Beach? Is *that* why you invited us up? You were hoping I wouldn't get here in time and you'd have Doug all to yourself?''

"No. It was you I wanted to see, Meg. What happened last night was not premeditated.''

"Yeah? You were both drunk, and when a man's drunk and horny he just can't help himself, can he? 'I want to suck your cock, Doug.' 'Oh sure, Mr. Goodall. Sir.' ''

Jim turned away, appalled she knew such words, but Meg remained alongside him, glaring into his face.

"Or no, you probably didn't even talk about it. *Women* talk. *Men* do. So what did you do? Tell me. Did you fuck him?'' She twisted the question like a knife in both herself and Jim.

"Meg! It's not important what we did.''

"Oh? Another holy masculine secret *I* wouldn't understand! All right then. Can you tell me who started it? You or Doug? Who made the first move?''

"I initiated it,'' Jim admitted.

"Uh huh. And did he put up much of a fight? Did you have to work real hard seducing him, *reasoning* him into it?''

"He was already interested, Meg. Your friend is homosexual.'' Jim could justify himself with that fact.

"You think so? You don't think he was just being polite? Or curious? Nothing-human-is-alien-to-me Inge?''

"He's homosexual. I suspected he might be, or I wouldn't have instigated anything. I had to find out, Meg. For your sake as well as mine.''

She screwed her jaw to one side when she heard his last statement.

"And for Doug's sake too,'' Jim added. "I've been in his shoes. It's a difficult thing for a man to admit to himself. He only confuses the people around him until he comes to terms with it.''

"Doug's queer?'' she said. "He's queer.'' She looked away, trying out a mocking scowl her mouth couldn't sustain.

"You didn't suspect it of him?''

"Shit,'' she muttered, her anger momentarily suspended. It returned the instant she looked at Jim again. "And *that's* why you did it? To save me from the big, bad homosexual? Uncle Jim to the rescue. My hero. My protector.''

"I don't claim I did it solely out of—''

"He didn't go into a killer depression when he was through?''

"Uh, no.''

"But he finished like that.'' Meg snapped her fingers. "Didn't he?''

Jim stopped walking and just stood there.

"Yes?'' Meg turned and faced him, dark eyes flaring after each blink. "We fuck too. You didn't know that?''

All the strength and confidence Jim had built up against her disappeared. "He said you didn't.''

"He was lying. And you believed him? He's a shitty liar, when he knows he's lying. But *you* believed him," she said contemptuously.

Jim suddenly hated Doug. He felt exposed and humiliated, and he wanted to blame Doug.

"I'm sorry, Meg. This changes everything."

"Does it? How?" She seemed to know it did, yet insisted Jim be the one to put it in words.

But all that came to mind were biblical prohibitions against looking on a parent's nakedness, although Meg wasn't his daughter, and the passage about Adam and Eve hiding their nakedness from God and each other. Their coats covered them to their knees, but Jim could not bear to look at Meg.

"When did you and Doug last . . . do anything?"

"A couple of weeks ago. In Virginia Beach, in fact. The night after your visit."

"Are you in love with him, Meg?"

He said it very gently, wanting only to find a conventional reason for his feeling of shame and trespass, but Meg shivered and turned away, as though he'd said something cruel.

"You think a girl won't sleep with a guy unless she's in love with him? Ha! What century you living in, Jim?"

"You're not?"

She felt the outside of her coat pockets, then reached in and brought out a cigarette. "I dunno. Didn't think I was." She frowned at the cigarette in the petite hand that peeked from the baggy sleeve of her coat, seeming to want the sight of it to remind her how tough she was. "Shit. I feel so hurt right now it's like I must feel—" She closed her eyes and didn't open them again until she lit the cigarette. "Why? Are you in love with him?"

Jim did not know what answer might make it easier for her, so he told the truth. "I honestly don't know."

"You going to see him again?"

"I thought I wanted to. Before I knew the extent of your involvement." Doug no longer seemed lovable, was not the promising future whose existence had enabled Jim to submit himself to Meg's anger; the door to the future was shut.

"Why should that change anything? See him. Don't think you're doing me any favors. I'm not going to feel better knowing you're making another big sacrifice for me. I should warn you though. Doug's got the libido of a snail. A month can go by before he wants sex again. Or maybe that's just with me." She spoke hurriedly, as if in an effort to outrun her pain. "Did you ask him about me before or *after* you did anything?"

"Afterwards," Jim admitted.

She gave that a scornful snort, before the pain caught up with her again. "Ugh. It makes my skin crawl. The idea of you two lying in bed, talking about me. Laughing at me for being such a dumb twat."

"Nobody was laughing at you, Meg. We talked with respect and consideration."

Meg grimaced and closed her eyes again. "I bet. Big shit. Damn." She had to open her mouth to draw a deep breath. "Why the fuck should it matter to me?" she hissed at herself. "I feel like such a *girl*." She snarled the word as the ultimate tag of contempt for anyone who could feel so much pain and confusion. She bit her lip at Jim, furious he'd heard her say that, then stood very straight and looked around, sweeping the spider web from her eyes.

"I'm sorry, Meg. I was very stupid and thoughtless."

She ignored him. "We should be getting back," she announced.

They stood halfway to the Lincoln Memorial. At this distance, the amplified speech playing over the hivelike hum of people massed beneath the monument was not much louder than the cannonade of bass drums coming from Pennsylvania Avenue. The barricade of buses and police was invisible from the low ground along the frozen pool.

"You can face Doug now?" said Jim.

"I don't have any choice. I'm spending the night at his house, then catching a bus home tomorrow."

"You can stay with me tonight. If you like."

She narrowed her eyes at Jim. "No. It's easier for me to be with Doug. I always expected less from Doug."

That stung, which Jim thought was only right. "Did you want me to go back with you to the rally? Or would you rather I went home?"

"I don't care. Don't you want to be with your *buddy*?"

He didn't, but he told Meg, "What matters now is what'd make *you* most comfortable."

"Nothing's going to make me feel better, okay? So do what you want and don't pretend you're doing it for me."

"All right then. I'll go home."

"Fine." She looked toward the monument again, frowning over the idea of returning.

"You're going back to Williamsburg or Virginia Beach tomorrow?" He wanted them to part, but at the same time he needed to know he'd be seeing Meg again.

"Ginia Beach. Semester doesn't start for another week," she mumbled.

"Maybe I'll come down and visit you at school next month. When some of the smoke has cleared?"

Her head jerked around to look at him, not pleased but confused and hurt. With blue eyes one looked straight through to sky and nothingness, but with brown eyes one seemed to see the soul itself sitting just inside cheekbones and brow.

"I don't care," said Meg. "Any message you want me to give Doug?"

"No. None." Jim hoped that might convince her she was more important to him than any boy could be.

"No skin off my nose. Okay then. Goodbye." She spun around and walked away, her head held high, one hand in her pocket, the other with its cigarette hanging at her side.

Jim stood there, watching, waiting for her to turn and wave or at least look over her shoulder. He wondered if she wanted him to run after her again. He let her go, watching her grow smaller as she marched down the monstrous fairway toward the slope crawling with people. Without her ferociously hurt face in front of him, he didn't need to protect himself with lies. He seemed to have known all along that what he'd done last night would hurt Meg. What he hadn't guessed was that his hurting her would mean so much to him.

When she became a speck among a hundred other specks, Jim walked across creaking, discolored ice and up the slight incline to Constitution. He walked back the way he'd come this morning with Doug, when he'd been so blind as to believe one's own happiness could justify anything. It was dangerous to be happy. You forgot other people and betrayed them.

At Pennsylvania Avenue, he had to stop and wait with the others while a mammoth high school band joyously pounded and trumpeted "Land of a Thousand Dances."

JIM TURNED ON his television when he got home and poured himself a shot of the herb-flavored gin. Live coverage of the parade was interrupted with occasional reports from the rally and recorded highlights from the inaugural address at noon. "Because of America's bold initiatives," intoned the jowly basset hound whom Jim had seen clumsily scribble his name on a dozen golf balls, "nineteen seventy-two will be remembered as the year of the greatest progress since the end of World War Two toward a lasting peace in the world." Watching his parade from inside the cantilevered swoops and wings of the inaugural pavilion, the man repeatedly stretched both arms over his head and twitched peace signs at the floats and marching bands reflected in the bulletproof glass. There were no reports of violence or confrontation from the demonstrators—Jim wondered what Meg and Doug might be saying to each other. Film rushed to the studio from the TV chopper provided a God's-eye view of the rally. Watching television in Washington was a new experience for Jim, familiar places and even events he'd seen for himself repeated and made strange by the camera angles and framing, personal reality refracted in a house of mirrors. Everything looked sluggish from high above, the rally a mud puddle of people, the few lone figures scattered along the narrow white pool nearly invisible. He thought he saw one figure hurrying away from another, but it was like imagining one could see the dance of molecules in the air and there was no knowing when this footage was shot.

He spent the evening in, hoping somebody might call, although he didn't know what he could say now to either Meg or Doug. He numbed himself with television and occasional doses of gin. He wondered what Meg would say to her mother when she got home tomorrow. It served Jim right that the rest of his family would learn who and what he was.

Nobody called that night or the next morning either. Jim walked over to the State Department to pick through some papers and get away from his phone. The entire city felt hungover after yesterday. There was almost nobody downstairs in the department gym. He played a couple of listless games of racquetball with a paunchy desk officer, recently divorced and at a loss as to what to do with his Sundays. Walking back home, Jim noticed a couple of red-eyed teenagers shivering in short jackets on the lip of the dry fountain in Dupont Circle. He'd heard tales about hustlers hanging out here and assumed that's what these boys were. Jim felt no interest in them today, only regret he hadn't come here for sexual relief instead of letting lust discharge itself disguised as an infatuation for his niece's boyfriend. Life had been simpler when he kept his elements apart, each in its separate sphere. He had destroyed everything by mixing them together.

There were no telephone calls Monday morning at work. That afternoon, however, Jim received a call from the seventh floor: he was to report immediately to the Assistant Secretary in charge of African affairs, someone Jim had never worked with. The man received Jim alone in his office. He curtly announced they had a new post for Jim. The Seychelles: Jim was to be the ambassador. The curtness was only a man-to-man pose; the assistant secretary assumed Jim would be overjoyed. An isolated handful of islands in the Indian Ocean, the Seychelles was a place where nothing ever happened, the staff was minuscule and the post was known as just a stop for career officers on their way up or down the ladder. But Jim would be an ambassador, one more rung up in the service, and during the two or three years he was out there people would forget any bad feelings that had developed over his opposition to Marcos. The assistant secretary mentioned none of this; he didn't have to. As a matter of form, he gave Jim a week to consider—the post did not become open until the end of March—but clearly assumed Jim would accept. Jim assumed so himself, but when their fifteen minutes were over and he was on his way back downstairs, Jim was startled to realize he could go on with his life once more as if nothing had changed. The ease of it disturbed him.

It was late that afternoon when Doug called. "Jim. Hey there. Guess who. Just calling to see if you might be, uh, free this evening."

"How's Meg?"

Doug cheerfully explained he'd put her on a bus Sunday morning and she should be safe and sound in Virginia Beach by now. "I was thinking I might come into town tonight. Can I drop by your place?"

"Yes. We need to talk, Doug. Come by the apartment after six."

"Sixish? Okey-doke. See you then." He hung up before Jim could finish making clear he was displeased with what they'd done and wanted to see him tonight only to hear about Meg.

Doug ran late. Jim wondered if he knew what was coming and had changed his mind. But then the doorman called up and the bell rang and here was Doug again, pink-cheeked and eager, wearing the army field jacket Jim didn't think he had the right to wear.

"Did you hear the big news?" he excitedly asked. "Johnson died. LBJ himself. I heard it on the radio coming in. He died this afternoon. It's ironic, almost poetic. What with everything else happening."

The aroma of skin and hair, as unique as a fingerprint now that Jim's nose was tuned to it, distracted him. "No. I hadn't heard. That's too bad. Have a seat, Doug." Jim motioned him toward the armchair.

Doug tossed his jacket over the back of the chair, plopped down and stretched out, his legs spread in front of him. "It's good to see you again, Jim." The bland smile looked lewd and complicitous tonight. A wily twitch of his forehead jerked his eyebrows up and down.

Jim went straight to the point. "I was very disappointed to learn you didn't tell me the whole truth about yourself and my niece."

"Yeah. Well." Doug showed neither surprise nor fear. "I knew it'd make you feel funny. So I had to fib about that. Is there anything to drink?"

"Let me finish this first," said Jim. He put his hands on his hips, needing a posture of authority to undo the fact that he'd kissed and fellated this boy. "I don't like liars. And I don't like sleeping with someone who's slept with my niece. There are too many taboos involved. Too many other people who're getting hurt."

"We straightened out all that."

"How?"

Doug sighed and shook his head. "Meg never wants to see me again. Period. I can't blame her. It's her right. She was a good friend and I'm going to miss all our conversations. But you can't make an omelet without breaking a few eggs, right?"

"That's all you feel?" Jim was shocked at the absence of remorse or guilt, the shallowness of his regret. How could he ever have imagined he was in love with such a person?

"I feel bad," Doug claimed. "I felt really bad Saturday night when we got my car and were alone for the drive home. I thought her silence was the worst, until she started chewing me out. Said I'd been using her as a disguise, that I was a coward for having sex with her, then that I'd used her only to get to you. But after a while, you can take only so much of that before you go, 'Okay, I am shit. Take it or leave it.' And she left it."

There was nobody at home in this body, no one Jim could hate or admire. There was nothing you could do with this body except have sex with it. Listening to Doug skate over the pain they'd inflicted on Meg, Jim could find no feeling for him except lust.

"Has she come to any new conclusion about me?"

"You?" He had to think a moment. "She's pissed at both of us. 'You bastards. You assholes.' But all I remember is what she said about me in particular. Don't worry. I didn't blame it all on you, make it sound like you raped me or something.''

"I'm much obliged," said Jim. The boy was too self-involved to be of use even in letting him know where he stood with Meg. Jim turned away and lifted a cushion from the sofa. "You know where the booze is, Doug. Help yourself if you'd like a drink first."

The bland smile became an excited grin. "Okay. Great. I promised my mother I'd be home at a decent hour tonight. Oh, I brought you a present." He reached back to take something from his coat pocket, a paper bag with the receipt still stapled to the top, and a plump white tube inside. "I been thinking all day today about things we didn't try the other night."

This time there was nothing timid or sentimental about sex. Jim thought he wanted it simply to get rid of it, confused and ashamed he could still want sex with this boy. But if his heart wasn't in it, his body was, mouth and fingers going everywhere, as though the absence of feeling were a vacuum that could be filled with skin. Doug treated the roughness as an exciting game, until Jim ignored his sudden change of mind and continued in, Doug wincing and gasping before he relaxed into the pleasure behind the pain. Curled around each other, Jim did not picture a homey pair of rolled-up socks this time, but two snakes swallowing each other by the tail, a circle tightening into a knot that would finally tremble, flash and disappear.

HE WOKE UP to find the lights still on and the covers kicked back, the room cold and smelling like fish and oil. A body lay facedown beside him. Jim wasn't frightened, only surprised the body had followed him halfway around the world to reappear in his bed. He sat up and leaned over to look more closely. No, of course. This was somebody else. It was Doug, shoulder blades rising and falling as he dozed, his face turned to the other side. They'd both dozed off after finishing. Jim lay back down, wondering why he should imagine such a thing, what it meant for him to confuse a boy he'd killed with one he had fucked. Doug looked perfectly happy, enviably blissful while he dozed in a world that went no further than the undamaged envelope of his flesh. His body was very warm.

Jim felt a sudden tenderness that had nothing to do with who Doug was, only who he wasn't. He wanted them to continue, despite the harm they had done, despite Jim's guilt, despite the intense coldness at the center of his need.

11

UNCLE JIM. Dear old Uncle Jim, who spoke like a butler and sometimes a used-car salesman. Who gave imperialism a human face, complicating everything Meg believed about American power because he was so scrupulous and ineffectual. If he were a homosexual, he'd be a nice, ineffectual one. Now she knew otherwise. The American empire had come home, petted Meg on the head and fucked her boyfriend.

It was like being kicked in the stomach, then slapped in the face, pain followed by insult and humiliation. She'd been betrayed by Uncle Jim, by Doug and her own stupidity. All of it hurt, but she kept coming back to her stupidity. Meg prided herself on intelligence and an ability to confront anything, yet she hadn't seen Doug was queer or imagined her uncle could want him. She must have suspected something or else she wouldn't have become nervous the night she found them together, then furious when she arrived at Doug's house and heard he'd gone in without her. But she'd refused to believe her emotions until they brazenly walked up to her at the rally, all guilt and satisfaction, the flip sides of carnal knowledge. They might just as well have been holding hands, the selfish assholes, the smarmy fags.

Meg hated the words that came from her anger. She despised being the injured party; there was no dignity in it.

She called Sunday afternoon from the Greyhound station in Norfolk. They weren't expecting her until that evening, but Walter was home and Mom said he'd drive in to pick her up. "You get to see your uncle?"

"Only for a half hour. I'll tell you about it when I get home."

A bus station on a grim winter's afternoon was the perfect setting for Meg's squalid state of mind. Her hair and clothes stank from the half pack of cigarettes she'd smoked during the long trip home. Diesel exhaust blew in from the loading dock each time someone opened a door. The men were all sailors in civilian clothes, swaggering about or sprawled in the coin-operated TV chairs; the women were mostly black, many stranded with armloads of restless toddlers and crying babies.

Walter entered and saw her. Watching his gracefully graceless, slouching walk as he came over, an unhurried giraffelike lope, Meg thought: *he'd* never have sex with a guy. Robbie might, just to be perverse, but not Walter. It was disturbing to have to consider such a thing about your own brothers.

"Hey there, Meg. You ready?"

"Hi, Walter. I can get that," she grumbled when he tried to take her bag.

He strolled her out to the car with both hands nesting in the front pouch of his sweatshirt. "Washington okay?"

"Yeah."

"See Uncle Jim?"

"A little."

A new idea was worrying her. Meg needed to ask Walter, but did not know how. She waited until they were in the car and on the road to the interstate before she said, "Did Uncle Jim ever act queer around you?"

Walter thought a moment. "Naw. Kind of duddy sometimes. But nothing looney. You mean strange queer, right?"

"Right. Strange." She couldn't name it to Walter, could not share what she knew and he clearly didn't.

"Nope. Always seemed fine to me. Little lonely maybe. Nothing nuts."

"Just asking," said Meg. "No particular reason." To pursue the subject with Walter felt wrong, a violation of *his* ease and innocence. Despite her anger, she could not sincerely believe Uncle Jim had ever tried anything with Walter or Robbie. It takes two, and neither of them were Doug. But the idea of it, even as a possibility, made her uneasy, made the whole family seem terribly vulnerable and in need of protection.

Dad was out in the garage when they got home, contentedly working at his lathe. He looked up from a spinning, warbling blur of table leg to give Meg an embarrassedly preoccupied smile when she and Walter passed through, then readjusted his stance and resumed in a spray of wood chips. Robbie was stretched out on the sofa, his mouth wide open while he slept through a cowboy movie, a couple of cans of beer on the floor. Mom came down to the kitchen and insisted on fixing Meg a cup of instant coffee, chiefly as an excuse to sit with her at the table and hear about exams, the trip to D.C. and Uncle Jim.

Meg told her everything, up to a point.

"You wouldn't have had much fun at those parties anyway, dear." Mom picked that as the cause for her daughter's foul mood. "All those phonies putting on the dog. You would've hated every minute of it. I'm sorry you got to see Jim only for a few minutes"—Meg said he needed to rush back to the office after bringing Doug to the rally—"but I can't say that surprises me either. Men who live for their work put a very low importance on human contact. He's my brother and I love him dearly. But Jim's never been very good with people outside a job situation. Women especially."

Meg hesitated, tempted to explore exactly what her mother knew about their uncle. But she couldn't know. Meg decided to keep the truth to herself, not to protect Uncle Jim but to protect her mother. It would be awful enough telling Mom her brother was a homosexual, without the ugly fact that he'd gone to bed with a boy whom Mom had met, someone Jim had first encountered under this very roof. It was all too close to home. Protecting her mother gave back some of the pride Meg had lost over her own stupidity.

Mom asked about the rally, then Doug's family. "Are they nice?"

"Nice enough. His mother spoils him rotten. That's probably why he's so selfish and irresponsible."

Mom lifted her eyebrows at that, then studied Meg a moment before she gave the matter a philosophical shrug. "Yes. You don't really know a person until you see their home life. Well, you said yourself he was just a good friend."

"Yeah." Meg decided not to fight her mother's understanding that something had changed. "Maybe I thought there were other possibilities, but there're not and I'm not going to lose sleep over it."

"There's plenty of other fish in the sea."

"Uh huh. I better go unpack my stuff," she said. Meg carried the heavy bag up to her room before her mother's tactfulness gave way to tacky sympathy.

She was not in love with Doug. She'd decided on the long bus ride she'd never been in love with him; her pain wasn't jealousy. If Doug had slept with another man—Larry, say, or Mandrake—she wouldn't feel nearly as hurt as she did now. Her anger with Doug was mostly anger with herself for not understanding sooner who he was, for letting things go on the way they had for so long. When she finally lit into him Saturday night—her brooding silence had not bothered him—he seemed to think it meant acceptance; she was infuriated by his repeated bleats of "I'm sorry," but only as evidence of what an insincere coward Doug had always been.

Her anger with Jim was different. It felt moral and justified. She wanted to be proud of everything she told him at the rally. She was still stunned with how much she'd instantly understood in that flash of anger: his masculine arrogance, paternalism and self-deception—he really was the empire personified. But the anger itself frightened Meg, the violence of it, the way it cut into her as well as Jim, cutting deeper than intellectual pride. She wanted to believe it was revulsion over learning he was a real homosexual, not just a hypothetical one, but her disgust with body parts and sex acts felt forced, a cover for something else. It was almost as if she felt judged that Jim chose Doug over her, which was stupid. She knew now Doug was nobody, and she did not want to sleep with her uncle. She didn't, she told herself. Sex wasn't a shortcut to intimacy but a detour, a dead end. And yet Jim chose that over loyalty to Meg. It didn't matter now if he continued to see Doug or never saw him again. The truth had been revealed. Meg waited for her anger to cool so she could be as contemptuously indifferent toward Jim as she was about Doug.

* * *

HOME WAS A place where Meg did not have to think or feel too much. She lay low during her week there, watching television, reading, going to the movies one afternoon with Walter when his girlfriend said she had no desire to see a new western about Robert Redford killing Indians. Meg considered giving Carter Mason a call, the only guy from her Superior English/Krispy Kreme set who wasn't off at school or in the navy. But she hadn't seen Carter in over a year and wondered what it might mean if he too turned out to be gay. All smart, unconventional men were now suspect. The day after Kissinger announced an agreement ending the war, Meg purchased the paperback of *Fire in the Lake* at the mall. The righteous indignation she experienced reading about past crimes and errors in Southeast Asia was cleaner and more satisfying than the raw emotions about people close to her.

She returned to school the following week. William and Mary had a homey, bookish gloom in winter. Rain spattered the worn brick walks outside, radiators sizzled and snorted in the overheated rooms. It was never cold enough to snow here, only rain, but Meg associated rain with the privilege of being able to stay indoors and read. A good harsh smell of wet wool disguised the scents of soap and perfume in the dorm her first afternoon back.

Trish dropped by and sat on the windowsill while Meg put her clean clothes away. "I am so depressed to be back," she moaned. "This place is the pits. What're we doing here, Frisch?"

Seeing Trish's dark horsetail of hair and familiar long jaw made Meg nervous. Trish and Larry were Doug's friends as well as hers. She'd have to say something about the change.

"It's nothing dramatic," Meg calmly announced, "but I've decided not to see Inge this semester. Socially or otherwise."

"I *knew* it!" Trish crowed. "I could feel it in the air last Saturday. The shit hit the fan, right? Right? So what happened?"

"I wised up to what a jerk he is, that's all."

Trish's face became soft and pitying. "Do you want to talk about it?" She could be as knowing and condescending about feelings as Larry was about political protests. "Did it have anything to do with that cousin or uncle who was there?"

"No." But Trish and Larry had seen how pissed she was the morning they picked her up at Doug's house. "Not really. Inge taking advantage of my uncle's invitation was just part of it. I've been giving more than I got and decided the only solution was to end it." There was no temptation to tell Trish the truth. Doug was too unimportant now for Meg to want to betray his secret, and the truth was too humiliating.

"I saw it coming," Trish congratulated herself. "Larry didn't, but I sure did."

"Don't think you have to choose between me and Doug. I just want you to know that if I suddenly get up from a table or don't join you guys at the Dirty Delly, it's not you I'm avoiding. And tell Larry not to go playing peacemaker, okay?''

''Gotcha. Doug's more Larry's friend than mine anyway. I always kind of wondered what you saw in him, Frisch. He's smart and charming, but there's something not-there about him, something weaselly. Good company when there's other people around but—Larry thought he only needed to get laid. Guys think that's the solution to everything.''

Meg shuddered, knowing how much Trish knew, wishing Trish would just shut up. They weren't close friends. In fact, they'd be no more than acquaintances without the connection of Doug and Larry.

''You sure you don't need to talk about it? You sound awfully cold and logical for somebody giving a guy the kiss-off.''

''Can we just drop this, Bickle? It's starting to get real boring.''

''All right already. Whatever you say.'' Trish surrendered with both hands held up. ''I just want you to know I understand. And I'm here if you ever need to talk about it.''

Talking to Trish about the movies they'd seen, Meg decided it was time she found a new set of friends, people who didn't know Doug or her relationship with him. Anti-intellectual men might make a nice change, or very intellectual women, women with enough passionate interest in a specialized field they could talk for hours without mentioning lust or boyfriends or anything personal.

She was afraid Doug might come by her room their first night back, but he didn't. She registered for classes the next day at Blow Gym—the tired puns had a new kick this morning—but she did not run into Doug among the students milling from table to table on the springy wooden floor of the basketball courts. She signed up for the second semester of American Foreign Policy. Doug had taken the first semester with her, but Braun was one of Meg's favorite teachers and she would not sacrifice a course with him to avoid Doug.

He wasn't in Foreign Policy the first day of classes. Meg did not see him in the Caf either, although Larry said he was back. She wanted to be pleased she scared him enough he was avoiding her. That afternoon she went to Asian History, a new subject for her. Shortly after the elderly, turtle-faced professor arrived, Doug sauntered in, looked around for an empty desk, and saw Meg.

She hadn't imagined his bland, noseless face in its gable of blond hair would be so bare and characterless. He looked as surprised to find Meg here as she was to find him. Except for occasional references to Buddhism, all from one book, Doug had never expressed any interest in Asia. Meg was here because of *Fire in the Lake*. She feared Doug was here because of somebody's influence.

He gave her a mechanically sheepish smile and sat on the other side of the room.

When the interminable class was over—the professor announced there'd be little discussion and much memorization, then proceeded to recite dates and dynasties—Meg gathered her books, gritted her teeth and walked over to Doug.

"Fancy seeing you in here," she said.

"Yeah. Well." Doug remained seated. "I've become curious about Asia. And I knew you'd want to stick with Braun, so I figured I'd take something else. Give you some space."

"How considerate. Have you seen my uncle since the rally?"

His tongue poked inside his cheek, as if poking memory. "Yeah."

"More than once?"

"Uh huh."

Her stomach began to bind up. "Just asking. He gave me the impression he might not see you again. But I guess not. No surprise. That's all I wanted to know." She swiveled on her heel and walked away, out into the hall and down the stairs.

It didn't change anything one way or the other. Jim had deceived her there too—and himself.

Not until Meg was outside and striding through the cold wind toward Swem Library did she wonder what they were going to do now that Doug was back in school. Would Doug go home every weekend? Would Jim come here? "Maybe I'll visit you at school when the smoke clears," Jim had told her. But the smoke hadn't cleared; a fire still burned. Maybe the jerks were even in love, although when Meg asked each of them last Saturday they both said the same thing: *I don't know.* She'd been elbowed aside by two men who had no idea what the hell they wanted.

The next day Meg went to the department offices and switched from Asian History to American Social Trends after 1875. It wasn't just because of Doug. The Asian History class looked dry as chalk.

Once the semester was under way, she lost herself in work. Ethics went from the truisms of Epicurus and Bentham into endless, irresolvable arguments about draft evasion and Nazis. Disappointed by the course, Meg sneered, "If Hitler didn't exist, the philosophy department would have to invent him." Doug was the only person she knew who might've appreciated the quip. The new semester in Foreign Policy began with the Spanish-American War, which led directly to a brutal war in the Philippines.

Meg had known there were troubles in the former colony's past, but had no idea how extensive and bloody they had been. The United States helped the Filipinos liberate themselves from the Spanish, then McKinley changed his mind and decided to make the islands an American possession. "Benevolent assimilation," he called it, arguing that the Filipinos were not yet ready to govern themselves. The Filipinos disagreed. They fought a guerrilla war that didn't end until over two hundred thousand "natives" died. Braun compared it to Vietnam and the parallels were considerable, right down to an antiwar movement at home. There was a striking antiwar cartoon from the period, a scratchy steel engraving of American soldiers in peaked-brim hats aiming their rifles at four barefoot, blindfolded children. The caption read, "Kill Every One Over Ten."

The picture took hold of Meg's imagination. She wanted to know the details behind it, how much truth or exaggeration it contained. A paper wasn't due until the end of the course, but Meg immediately began to research the Samar massacres. In 1901, in reprisal for a bloody ambush of American soldiers on the island of Samar, General Jacob Smith commanded that every inhabitant of the enormous island capable of bearing arms be killed. When Major Littleton Waller, the officer charged with carrying out the order, asked him to be more precise, Smith said anyone over the age of ten. There was no recent book in the library that told the full story. Meg turned to old books, old newspapers on microfilm, then the U.S. Senate hearings after the war, which included testimony from soldiers who had participated in the campaign. Some of the men were appalled by what they had done, most treated the killings and the destruction of villages as just what the "goo-goos" deserved. One man cheerfully remembered a military band standing on a beach and playing "There'll Be a Hot Time in the Old Town Tonight" while a village of nipa palm huts burned brightly and soldiers danced with each other or the sobbing village women. Major Waller was more moral than his commander. "We are not making war on women and children," he told his troops. They killed only grown men.

"You can't go to the library on a Friday night!" Trish groaned when Meg got up after dinner at the Caf. "Come with us to the movies."

Larry said, "You've let this Doug thing turn you into a real grind."

"Fuck you. It's got nothing to do with him. I'm getting a good start on a couple of papers before the semester gets crazy. See you later."

She didn't tell them what she was researching. They'd find it peculiar, even morbid. And it was morbid, this fascination with old bloodshed, although it wasn't the violence that held her so much as the attitudes and contradictions in the men who could do such things. Major Waller's ability to draw a humane line through his inhumanity intrigued her; butchery should know no bounds. Stranger still was his loyalty to General Smith after the nation became outraged over reports of slaughter from all over the Philippines, and Waller was offered up as a scapegoat. During his trial in Manila, Waller said nothing about Smith's orders until Smith himself testified and put full blame for the killings on his subordinate officer. Only then did Waller present the original instructions, written out in Smith's impeccable copperplate script. Waller was exonerated, Smith tried, convicted and discharged. What kind of blindness was at work in Waller's distinctions and loyalties? What kind of masculine psychology?

Meg knew early on that Uncle Jim was buried somewhere in her fascination with this story, if only in the coincidence of the Philippines. Yet the deeper she went, the cooler her anger with him became. It was still there, dispersed in the facts of what happened seventy years ago, but if dead facts diluted the anger, the anger also brought those facts back to life. Meg was pleased by the way history took her out of herself without denying or breaking with that self.

This went on for two weeks, then three and four, Meg filling an entire notebook with facts and quotes and observations. She read Mark Twain and Finley Peter Dunne to get the anti-imperialist point of view. She read the memoirs of army officers for whom the Philippines had been a single episode in careers that went back to the Civil War and campaigns against the Indians, or forward to World War I. The dry, self-important maunderings or purple passages of adventure prose offered occasional glimpses into a strange ethos of military duty, discipline, sacrifice. And people said *women* were masochistic. Meg gathered so much material she became worried she'd never be able to pull a coherent paper from this. Go deep enough into any subject and it opens out into everything else. Still, she could not let go.

She saw Doug only from a distance that month, brief sightings of him skulking across campus or sitting at the other end of the cafeteria. Without anyone saying anything, they'd worked it out so Meg had their friends at dinner, and Doug had them at the nightly bull sessions in the local beer-and-sandwich shop. That was fine with Meg. She stayed at the library until it closed at eleven, then read or studied in her room until two.

One night Meg was sitting in the lobby of the library, smoking a cigarette before she returned to the bound periodicals on the second floor. The library was one of the newer buildings, its lobby a tall box of marble veneer and plate glass, the furniture modern and already shabby. Meg sat in a tilted wire saucer covered with frayed padding, flicking her cigarette in an ashtray like a long-stemmed steel mushroom. People around her chatted about classes and sorority parties, TV shows and boredom. Her chair faced the floor-to-ceiling glass that separated the lobby from the reference room in the back, so she saw Doug coming from the magazine racks a good thirty seconds before he saw her.

He walked with his usual smug lope, pretending to be taller than he was, his head tilted back to keep his hair out of his face. The glass door made a grinding ring when he pushed it open and saw Meg.

She was surprised by her coolness of emotion, then her feeling of strength when Doug nervously looked away. She lifted her hand and gave Doug a nod to see if he'd come over. He did, his gait slowing, his hair falling in front of his ears as he lowered his head. He worked his mouth into a thin smile.

"How's Asian History?" she asked.

He looked puzzled. "I was going to ask you. I transferred out."

"So did I," Meg said and laughed through her nose. "That's funny. Well, I don't think either of us missed anything there." Stretched out in the chair, Meg looked up at Doug uncomfortably looking down at her. They might have been gazing at each other from either end of a telescope, with Meg at the wrong end so Doug appeared very small and distant. "How're things?"

"Fine."

"Uncle Jim?"

He turned his little nose to one side, trying to look around the question to the anger he assumed lurked behind it. "Different," he said.

"Really? In what way?"

"This and that. You won't want to hear."

"Tell me. I'm curious." Meg spoke coldly, but she suddenly wanted to hear what had been happening these past weeks, amazed she hadn't wanted to know before now. She'd been intrigued by the doings of men who died before she was born; she should want to know what went on between her uncle and Doug. "Then you've been seeing him since school started?"

Doug readjusted his stance and looked her in the eye. "Uh huh. I've been going up there every other weekend."

"He hasn't come down here?"

"No. I've asked, but he won't. I think he's afraid of running into you."

Meg wanted to leave herself out of this. "So how's he different?"

Doug drew a deep breath and looked around. "I can't talk about this with you. There's too many people around here anyway."

"All right. We'll go someplace private." Meg tilted forward and the dish of chair tipped her to her feet. "Let's go out to the staircase. Come on. I'm not going to bite your head off. I want to hear what's happening in the wonderful world of men."

He reluctantly followed her into the stairwell beside the elevator, then down the stairs to the lower level. Overhead, shoes loudly tick-tocked as students came down from the stacks, but nobody came down here. The audio-visual department was closed for the night and the emergency exit was wired with an alarm. Meg crossed her arms and settled her back against a white plaster wall. Doug positioned himself beside the steel railing opposite, holding on with one hand to pull himself up for a speedy getaway.

"You said he's changing," Meg persisted.

"Yes." Doug looked up the narrowing rectangle of the stairwell. "He's demanding. He gets more and more demanding."

"Good for him. I should've been more demanding. If I had, I would've found out the truth about you a lot sooner."

Doug hung his head and delivered the routine bleat. "I'm still sorry about this, Meg. I know you don't believe me, but I am."

"I believe you. I just don't think it changes anything." She was pleased by how mature and objective she sounded. "You were dishonest and cowardly, but I can't hold you fully responsible for that. I realize now that guys like you and my uncle are like dogs. Dogs can be perfectly well behaved when they're alone with people. But put another dog in the room and they just can't help themselves."

Doug frowned. "Okay. It was selfish. But it wasn't cowardly. Or all right, maybe I was a coward with you but I'm proud I was finally selfish enough to do what I needed to do. I'm just sorry it was with your uncle."

"A man's gotta do what a man's gotta do," Meg scoffed. "Even a man who's not a real man, huh?"

He gave her an exasperated sigh. "Go ahead. You have a right to be angry. But you're not going to make me ashamed of being gay."

"Well. Love has certainly shown you the light. Lucky you." It was his smugness that irritated her, not the idea he'd found love. "So why don't you see him *every* weekend? Why haven't you dropped out of school to move in with him?"

Doug hesitated, drumming his fingers on the steel railing. "We're not in love. I don't know what we are. But whatever it is, it's almost over."

"Yes? It sounds to me like *he's* in love with you, if he's so demanding." She felt mildly indignant for the sake of her uncle.

"No. He's erratic-demanding. Like he doesn't know what he wants, but he wants it very badly."

"Sex," said Meg, sarcastically pointing out the obvious.

"Oh yeah. He gets very intense there." Doug lowered his head, blushing, then smiled slyly over his embarrassment. "It gets scary sometimes. But I kind of like that."

"He hurts you?"

Doug laughed. "It's not whips-and-chains scary. It's more like—he thinks it's wrong, but that's a turn-on for him. It makes him ferociously passionate, out of control."

Meg was startled by how easily she accepted the idea her stuffy, wooden uncle could be sexually wild. He was in such different, disconnected pieces in her mind, and sex was only one more country, another island in the archipelago. "But he's not in love with you?"

"No. Because outside of bed—" Doug shrugged. "We talk. But we run out of things to talk about. You know me. I like to listen. But so does he. We went to a movie once and all he could say afterwards was that he liked it." He gave her a smirk, acknowledging that *they'd* never had that problem.

"He doesn't talk about his life? The countries he's seen? His work? Old love affairs?"

"Not really. He'll tell a story now and then, but it's very rehearsed and self-conscious. Like when my father comes out with a story. That's something else weird. He's beginning to remind me of my father."

"Beginning?" Meg laughed scornfully. "Isn't that what's been going on all along? I know how hung up you are on your father."

Doug looked horrified. He grimaced and shook his head. "Another good reason for me to be glad it's ending."

"Have you talked about this with Jim? Or do you just *wish* it were ending?"

"We haven't talked about it," Doug admitted. "But it'll be ending soon enough. One way or the other."

"What does that mean?"

"He's going overseas again. They've assigned him a new country," said Doug, surprised she didn't know.

"Really? When? Where?"

"End of the month. Some island in the Indian Ocean. He's going to be an ambassador."

Meg suffered a stab of pain. All her feelings of strength and superiority came apart and she felt excluded that she'd had to learn this through Doug.

"He didn't tell you?"

"I haven't heard a word from the asshole."

"He says he keeps meaning to write you. He hasn't?"

Meg shook her head. Why should it matter to her that he hadn't told her himself? "You going with him to this island paradise?" she sneered.

"I couldn't. Even if he asked me. And he hasn't."

So this was the way it ended, she thought. Her uncle ripped through their lives, upending everything in his path, then blew out to sea again, guiltless and unchanged.

"You see how I can say he's not in love with me either," Doug explained. "It's been a learning experience for all of us. But it wasn't in the cards. There was just too much against it from the start. Including the fact that we both feel guilty over what we did to you."

Meg stared at him in disbelief, not knowing whether to laugh or punch him. "You didn't do anything to me. You've been doing it to each other," she said sternly. "Do what you want to do next. But don't pretend for a minute you're doing it for me."

"Meg, I just wanted you to know—"

"I'm tired of being used as everybody's excuse or symbol here. I'm sick of being apologized to. It's bad enough I have to be the captive audience for your 'learning experience.' "

"You asked me what was happening," Doug said defensively.

"I did. Yes. And now I know. It's over. Too bad. I thought you deserved each other." She kept biting off phrases so he wouldn't mistake her disdain for anger. She didn't understand why she sounded so angry. She should be pleased Doug and Jim would go their separate way, that Uncle Jim was disappearing into the world again. She looked up at the white echoey stairwell. "I should be getting back to Manila, 1901," she said.

"I know it sounds perverse," Doug began. "But I've enjoyed talking to you like this again."

Meg made a face at him, although she wasn't surprised he could say such a thing. She started up the steps.

Doug stepped with her. "When this is over, do you think there's a chance we'll be friends again?"

"Oh God, Inge. You are such a—how should I know? How in hell should I know?"

"Just asking. Goodnight, Frisch."

They reached the lobby floor and Doug went out. Meg continued upstairs to the second floor and her one-person table against the painted cinderblock wall. She sat there over the notebook filled with Major Littleton Waller, breathed the spice-cabinet smells of old paper and various bindings from the rows of steel bookcases, and wondered why she hadn't been able to tell Doug they'd never be friends again. She should want it to be finished, just as she should want Doug and Jim finished, concluded episodes of history she alone might understand. The participants themselves seemed to understand nothing. Uncle Jim was off to yet another station in the empire where he'd disappear up his own ass again, which wasn't much different from disappearing up Doug's. It wasn't as though Meg *enjoyed* the idea that they thought about her each time they got together, using her as a human cat-o'-nine-tails if Doug were to be believed. It wasn't as though she felt a proprietary interest in this affair, the sacrificial goat as maid of honor. No, it was just that Meg believed more should come of this emotional turbulence than a "learning experience" for Doug, new objectivity for herself and a piece of ass for Uncle Jim.

The crowded notebook backed by the volumes and bound periodicals piled on her table gave Meg no pleasure or pride tonight. Understanding now seemed like a consolation prize awarded to the outsider. Her interest in Littleton Waller bore too close a resemblance to her idle curiosity about two men fucking themselves silly. Meg no more wanted to be a gay man than she wanted to be an army officer killing Filipinos, but she resented the way both experiences rubbed her face in the fact that the world would always be *out there,* sealed off by stupidity and maleness.

IN THE DAYS that followed, Meg gave no thought to Uncle Jim except when she went to the post office. There was no letter from him behind the little window of her box, which was fine with her. Uncle Jim was dead and all Meg wanted now was something to make it official, like a funeral.

She returned from the library one evening to find Trish lounging in the TV room of their dorm with a couple of girls who wore curlers and bathrobes. "Why aren't you off with the gang?"

"I'm bored," Trish groaned. "With the Dirty Delly and Larry and the same old jokes night after night. I decided to stay in and hang out at the boob tube just for a change of pace."

Meg wondered if she'd had a fight with Larry. "You want to go get a beer? Just us. Not the Dirty Delly but someplace different."

"Sure." Trish seemed only mildly pleased by the idea, but Meg felt it was right and necessary they go off together and talk, although she wasn't sure what they'd talk about.

They went to the Cave, a tavern in the basement of a restaurant down the street from their dorm. The walls were plastered in lumps and folds to simulate the subterranean, the place full of shadows broken by pools of red and yellow light. Trish took a booth by the jukebox and Meg went to the bar to get a small pitcher of beer. An older crowd came here, fewer students and more townies than one saw at the Dirty Delly and elsewhere. Meg saw Dr. Braun over in the corner, sitting at a table with other history teachers and their grad students, all male, the aftermath of some kind of seminar or departmental gathering. Meg waved hello across the room and Braun gave her a smile and a friendly flash of his steel-rimmed glasses. One of the grad students turned to look, then returned to the discussion when he saw it was nobody important.

Meg sat in the booth and filled their glasses. "How's Larry?" she asked, deciding to get that over with as quickly as possible.

"Fine. God, is he fine. I'm bored shitless with everything being so fine." Trish sat hunched over her elbows, long hair hanging down like the wings of a sulky vulture. "Talk and fuck, talk and fuck, that's all anyone ever does around here. I want to be a nun or a junkie or something different, just for a new experience."

Meg had no sympathy for boredom tonight. People who complained about being bored usually presented it as proof of what deep, hungry souls they had, with the implication you were shallow if you found life interesting.

"Tell me I'm crazy. Tell me how lucky I am to be white and middle class and safe from harm in the dullest little school in America. Tell me to change the subject. *Anything,* Frisch. I feel you're judging me when you sit there saying nothing."

The demand caught Meg off guard. "Sorry. I don't know what to say. I'm not even sure what you're talking about, Bickle."

Trish frowned, then sank back with a long, blubbery lip fart. "I don't know either. Except that I've got everything I want, and I'm still not happy. I want to want something else, but I don't know what."

"You want to suffer?"

Meg said it as a joke, but Trish seriously considered it. "No. I don't think so. Unless it was real dramatic and there was no physical pain involved."

"What if Larry started seeing somebody else and didn't tell you?" It was as close as Meg could get to explaining why *she* wasn't bored.

"That wouldn't be much fun. On the other hand, if *I* started sleeping with somebody else—" Trish rolled her head back and laughed. "What about you?"

"Me?"

"Aren't you bored? Or is there something you want that you don't have yet?"

"Power," said Meg, perfectly deadpan.

Trish laughed, then grinned at Meg, intrigued. "What kind of power?"

"Oh, I don't know. Political."

"You want to save the world?"

"Sure. Why not? Or have the power to destroy it, then not destroy it. That'd be nice too."

Trish bobbed her head up and down, pretending to take this seriously. "Not me. I like being powerless. No responsibility there. One advantage to being a woman."

"Maybe that's why you're bored," said Meg. "If you thought there was any chance you could get power, then you could get interested in something outside yourself." Under the cover of her joking banter, Meg heard herself turn serious. "I can't resign myself to being female."

Trish studied her, lifting her heavy chin and looking down at Meg, a skeptical horse. "Why're you so contemptuous of other women, Frisch?"

Meg experienced a mild jolt. How had they gotten here? "What're you talking about? I'm not contemptuous of women."

"No? Indifferent, then. Cool. Or no, it really *is* like contempt."

Meg shifted uncomfortably under the accusation, looking for a way to disprove it. "Bickle," she began, "you go on and on about how bored you are. And now, when I don't share your holy boredom, you say it's because I'm contemptuous you're a woman. Gimme a break."

"It has nothing to do with that. And it's not just with me. Name one woman you respect and admire."

"You're being ridiculous. What're you accusing me of anyway? All right then. Emma Goldman."

"No. Somebody alive. Someone you know personally."

Meg's mind went blank, so she mockingly declared, "My mother."

Trish laughed and shook her head. "Uh-uh. I know you well enough to know you love your mother, but you don't respect her. That's okay. I've got mixed feelings about my mother too."

"I have mixed feelings about everyone," Meg insisted. "Regardless of gender."

"Maybe. But you have stronger mixed feelings about men."

It was true. Meg was disturbed that it was true, guilty to find even her usual disdain for Trish turned into the stuff of sexual politics. She stole a glance over at the history table, wishing she were with the men discussing weighty, impersonal issues that did not reflect on her. "What women do *you* admire?" Meg said accusingly.

Trish emptied the rest of the pitcher into their glasses. "*Admire* isn't the right word. But there's times I respect *you*. Which might be why I get angry when you don't take me seriously."

The compliment was even more troubling than the accusations. Meg shrugged it aside and laughed. "Don't respect me. I'm a mess."

"You're very self-contained and on top of things. Like with Doug."

Meg frowned. "I do take you seriously, Bickle. As seriously as I take anyone."

Unconvinced, Trish only sighed and looked away. She slowly surveyed the room and said, "Do you realize we're the only unattached women in here tonight?"

Meg looked and saw it was true. Two girls sat with two men in a booth beyond the bright, smoke-filled light over the bar, but the rest of the clientele was male.

"Why is that?" said Trish. "Or when you do see women drinking in public, they're always in little packs, never one-on-one, the way you see guys?"

"Sisterhood is powerful," said Meg.

Trish winced. "See how mocking you get? What I'm saying is maybe it's not just you. It's something we're all taught. I know when *I* see two women alone, I just assume they couldn't get a date that night. Or that they're dykes, which is disgusting of me, isn't it? When I see two guys together, I don't automatically assume they're fags."

"I do," said Meg. "I consider the possibility anyway."

Trish looked away in frustration, as though Meg had killed all serious conversation by saying the most absurd thing imaginable.

"Have you ever considered that?" Meg asked.

"Considered what?"

"Sex with a woman."

Trish lowered her eyebrows and stared.

"I haven't," Meg quickly added. "I wonder what that says about me?"

"It says you're normal," Trish instantly told her.

"Maybe. Although—" She was wondering aloud, meaning nothing by it. This was new, her recognition that she had never had sexual feelings about women, not really, only abstract thoughts similar to the way she once thought about her uncle's latent homosexuality. It seemed a constriction of imagination, a failure of nerve.

"Quit it, Frisch. You're making me nervous."

"I can feel sensuous about stiff new paperback books and even some men I know are twits. Why not women? What difference does a penis make?"

"Look," said Trish. "When I said I wanted you to take me seriously, this isn't what I had in mind."

"I know." Meg was surprised by how upset Trish sounded. "This has nothing to do with you. It's something I've never considered before. I'm wondering what it means. Maybe you're right. Maybe I am contemptuous of women."

Trish remained nervous and uncomfortable, turning around to glance at the Budweiser clock over the bar. "You spook me, Frisch. Whatever happened with Doug sure brought out a cold, perverse streak in you."

"This has nothing to do with Doug," Meg calmly declared, then suffered an uneasy fear that she imitated her uncle in believing she *should* think sexually about women. He pinched her life no matter which way she turned. "Forget it. Let's talk about something else. Should we get another pitcher?"

"Not for me. I should be heading back."

Opening the subject of lesbianism, Meg seemed to have closed the door on whatever intimacy Trish wanted. Did Trish have sexual feelings or fears about Meg? Meg hoped not. She couldn't reciprocate, not even the fears. Meg decided to pretend nothing had happened. "Okay. I think I'll say hi to Braun before I go."

"All righty." Trish finished her beer and pulled on her coat. "I'll go on back. I'm zonked. See you later, Frisch," and she fled.

Meg hadn't intended to spook Trish, yet it now felt as though she'd done it in deliberate retaliation for Trish's accusation that she was indifferent to women. Meg didn't dislike women. She didn't know what to feel toward them, and lust was no solution. She suddenly worried that she'd been colonized by male attitudes and could think of her own kind only as men did, with either lust or indifference, and Meg did not feel lust. She gathered her coat under one arm and approached the history table, hoping their indifference—or lust —would give her a feeling of solidarity with women.

But Dr. Braun greeted her with friendly respect. An overweight leftist with a bearish beard and flannel shirt, he was the teacher who'd attempted to steer Meg into feminist studies. "Margaret Frisch, one of my best students," he told the others. Except for Braun, all the men seemed slightly drunk, the looks and smiles they gave her amiably fogged with beer. They paused in their heated discussion of a dissertation on Huey Long when Braun mentioned Meg's paper on the Samar massacres.

"Where they killed everyone over ten," announced a grad student with a long neck and enormous adam's apple, showing off to his teachers. "There's a famous newspaper illustration. You should look it up."

"I already have," Meg told him, showing off as well. "It's a political cartoon and it exaggerates. Despite the order, we didn't kill any women or children."

"You're defending what they did?" the grad student said scornfully.

"I'm not defending anyone. Those are the facts."

Dr. Hinckle, a babyfaced professor with a goatee and boozy southern accent like a mouthful of marbles, insisted Meg join them, then almost drove her away by adding, "Nothing civilizes a table of rowdy men like the company of a smart and pretty young woman."

But Meg pulled out a chair and sat down, intending to stay just long enough to see what history teachers were like off-duty, to study them. Very quickly, they forgot she was even here and argued the pros and cons of Huey Long, the politics of paternalism and the class struggle in the New South, topics Meg knew nothing about. Her invisibility, however, felt more like a privilege than a punishment here, an opportunity to play the fly on the wall. The men were passionate yet good-humored in their disagreements, their egos shored up by facts. They *were* drunk—Dr. Hinckle became slightly maudlin when comparisons were made to Lyndon Johnson and he fervently defended the man—but Meg was impressed that they were so full of their vocation the alcohol uncovered nothing but history in each man, all the way down.

Ralph, the graduate student with the adam's apple, arrogantly leaned back in his chair and said little, smugly watching his teachers make fools of themselves. Meg thought he looked like a fool.

When Dr. Braun got up to go, he asked Meg if she needed a ride anywhere, his tactful, nonpatriarchal method of suggesting he felt responsible for her. He didn't press when Meg said her dorm was down the street and she'd be fine.

The others slipped away while Dr. Hinckle continued a long, rambling monologue about northern contempt of the southern mind, punctuated with courtly smiles and looks of adoration at Meg. In the end, all that remained were Dr. Hinckle, Ralph and Meg.

"Here's an idea," Dr. Hinckle announced. "Why don't we all go back to my place for a nightcap and some Tammy Wynette? You too, Ralph. Ralph rents the apartment in my basement," he explained.

Meg was tempted but prepared to say no, when Dr. Hinckle stood up and stumbled sideways. Ralph leaped up and caught him.

"I'm fine. Just let me adjust my verticality." But he continued to lurch about, as boneless as a rag doll.

"Give me a hand," Ralph said irritably.

"Yes, another crutch!" cried Dr. Hinckle, reaching for Meg with his free arm. "Man needs the support of a strong woman!"

Meg wedged herself under his arm.

"We're right around the corner," Ralph told her, neither apologetic nor pleading. "It'll take only a few minutes."

"I don't mind." Meg began to laugh at the situation. She was short and Ralph was tall and Dr. Hinckle hung between them at a slant.

"Cockeyed Jesus," the teacher giggled as they hauled him up the steps outside. "This is so embarrassing, Margaret Frisch. You'll never want to have a class with me after tonight."

Drunk as he was, Dr. Hinckle remained a gentleman, doing nothing to take advantage of the situation except steal an occasional whiff of Meg's hair. She wondered if he and Ralph were lovers.

"You're a senior?" Ralph indifferently asked as they stumbled along the sidewalk.

"Junior."

"Hmmm," he hummed, without looking at her.

"LBJ!" sang Dr. Hinckle. "Nobody takes him seriously! But he was a great man. He was for all of us. He was for that little old black lady in Selma, Alabama!"

"What're you doing your dissertation on?" Meg asked Ralph.

"It's over your head."

"Try me."

"The Marshall Plan. With anti-Communism as a cynical disguise for the global expansion of American capitalism after World War Two. American money is the cancer of the postwar world."

"America bad, everybody else good?" Meg said mockingly, although if Ralph had taken the opposite stand she might just as easily have argued this herself.

"When you've read as much as I have, you'll come to the same conclusion," Ralph haughtily declared.

"Yankees," snarled Dr. Hinckle. "What they did to the South, they're doing to the whole damn world!"

Dr. Hinckle's house stood behind a larger house at the bottom of the hill in back of the Cave. The porch light was on and his front door was unlocked. Dr. Hinckle regained the use of his legs when they got him through the door.

"Music! We got to get back to our roots," he insisted. "I got Tammy Wynette. I got Willie Nelson." He stumbled toward his stereo, then suddenly stopped and hung there, glassy-eyed and open-mouthed, his blond beard covering his throat. He made an abrupt pirouette and collapsed on his back on the sofa. "How did I get so shitfaced?"

"We're going now," said Ralph, motioning Meg to the door. "Goodnight," and he pulled the door shut.

"Will he be all right?"

"He'll be fine. He gets like this a lot," Ralph grumbled. "Ever since his divorce. What I don't understand is how an educated man like that would want to play the redneck cracker."

Meg automatically disagreed with anything Ralph said. "I think it makes him more human."

He smiled condescendingly, then looked her up and down in the light of the porch. He was dark and spindly and not conventionally attractive, with heavy circles under his eyes and that bare rock of an adam's apple. Being alone with him felt eerily sexual.

"Let me show you my place," he said.

It might have been different if Meg liked his intelligence and wanted to know him better. His combination of grad-school arrogance and older-man cool—he was twenty-four or -five—left her feeling she knew all there was to know about Ralph, and would not want to see him again after tonight. "Sure," she said. "Why not?"

She followed him around the back of the house to a single-room apartment that had once been a tool shed or storeroom. A sink, stove and refrigerator stood against one wall; a mattress covered with books and loose papers lay on the floor.

"Don't do much entertaining," Meg quipped as she took off her coat.

"The life of the mind," Ralph self-importantly sighed. "I suppose I could fix some tea or coffee. Or there's gin."

"You didn't invite me here to fuck?"

He stared at her, as though she were a chess piece that had just moved itself.

"Yes or no?" Meg demanded. "If it's no, I should go back. I've got a ten o'clock class tomorrow."

"And I thought you might be a straight-A goody two-shoes. Well." He congratulated himself with a smirk. "Let me clear off the bed."

Meg was not sure what she expected to prove to herself. It was more than horniness. She wasn't even aware she was horny until Ralph was kissing her on the mattress and undoing buttons. She imagined it would be like having sex with his dissertation, the only thing about him she found interesting and not an unappealing notion in her current frame of mind. But it was mindless, excitingly brainless, kissing and groping this man whose opinion meant nothing to her, a furiously physical escape from convention, uncertainty and pride.

Ralph seemed to think he did it to her, so she let him know this was her doing, pulling off her bra before he could, pulling down his pants when he tried to undress gracefully. He was long and loose in the dark, a bamboo-jointed praying mantis. Meg felt very neat and compact in comparison. He had no imagination and kept laying her down to nuzzle her breasts, holding her wrists to stop her from touching behind his privates. He would not kiss below her navel. Covering her with his warm, knotted length, he placed a knot against her fold, lightly pressing until she unfolded inward and the power of her own sex climbed into her breasts and throat. She breathlessly reminded him again to be careful. "I have perfect control," he murmured, stirred around, and she had no choice but to embrace and trust him. It was frustrating to remember she was not invulnerable after all. She had angrily flushed her pills down the toilet when she returned from Washington, which was stupid, very stupid, as if she had imagined she could not have sex again for a long, long time.

THERE WAS SOME unease when Meg woke up the next morning in a strange bed with a hard pillow, musky sheets and a hairy, baggy-faced man. She liked the fact she was naked but hated seeing the messy room in daylight and Ralph's gloomy, unshaven face. She rolled off the mattress to wash up and get dressed.

Ralph remained in bed, nervously watching her. He relaxed and clasped his hands behind his head when he understood she was leaving. "I suppose we'll see each other around the department or at the library?"

"Probably." She screwed her feet into her loafers, then found her coat. "But if we don't, last night was fun."

He hesitated, afraid that agreeing would commit him to something. "We were both a little drunk," he claimed.

"You might have been. But I wasn't. I was horny and you were handy. Thank you."

"Uh, you're welcome." He looked confused, an actor hearing someone else speak his lines.

"Go back to sleep," she told him. "Goodbye, guy. I know my way out."

"It was nice meeting you," Ralph called after her.

All feelings of guilt or strangeness lifted as soon as Meg stepped outside and started up the hill toward campus. The sun was out and the morning carried a muddy scent of spring thaw; birds tittered and squeaked. She had plenty of time before her first class and decided to walk around before she returned to the dorm to shower and get her books. Walking toward the town post office, she felt very good about herself, freed from something.

It may have been nothing more than sexual relief, but Meg wanted to think it went deeper than that. She enjoyed discovering she could have sex without feeling she'd placed her heart in someone's hand. She could have sex the way men had sex, which might make her as bad as a man except she would not go about it with their thoughtless egotism and presumption. Her egotism would be thoughtful and deliberate. A woman who behaved like a man would have to be stronger and more aware than any man was. She felt she had the strength to do that, refusing to play either good girl scholar or clinging bimbo, the only roles men seemed to offer.

The post office was nearly deserted at this hour, an undisturbed shaft of dusty sunlight angled through the Colonial-style windows to the pigeonholed wall of bronze and glass boxes. Meg unlocked her box and found a lone letter inside, a business envelope with her address written in a hand so small and neat it looked typed. The return address was in D.C.

She calmly dug her thumbnail under the flap and pulled out a folded sheaf of yellow legal paper. The paper was covered with the same inhumanly neat blue handwriting, more like printing than writing, the letters in each word not always connecting.

March 15, 1973

Dearest Meg,

I hope school is going well and you enjoy your classes. I apologize for not writing sooner.

I have intended to write for some time now, but wanted to wait until various pieces finished falling. They are still falling and I admit this was only an excuse for silence. The best I can do is inform you of recent thoughts, and give you news of a major change in my life. Forgive the bureaucratese that enters my phrasing, but I am unaccustomed to writing in the first-person singular. Know that any coldness in what follows is inadvertant and I am full of tender regard for you.

I feel you should be the first to know of the step I've taken. I probably won't tell your mother until sometime next week by phone, without of course giving her the full explanation. Doug was here this weekend—it was not a good visit—and I could not tell him before I had told you. My news is this: last Thursday I handed the Assistant Secretary of State my letter of resignation. I am leaving the Foreign Service.

The events of these past six weeks have made me understand what a monster I've become. Love, cut off from the rest of my life, has become a blind bull in the bureaucracy of myself. I hurt those close to me. I cannot forgive myself for hurting you. I am a bull in the proverbial china shop, as thoughtlessly selfish in love and sex as our friend Doug, without his excuse of youth.

I am not leaving to be with Doug. We finished with each other long ago and have only been going through the motions. Not only are we mutton and lamb, the affair was a matter of crossed wires from the start. I was in love with the possibility of love. Doug was in love with the novelty of sex with a man, as I should have been at his age. The sacrifice of personal life I made for the State Department left me underdeveloped, a middle-aged adolescent who can't tell the difference between love and sex, who felt obligated to turn the latter into the former by sheer force of will. It's only made matters worse.

Query letters have been sent to various corporations with overseas business in Asia. On paper, at least, my experience looks valuable and I should have no difficulty finding a position in the private sector. I am writing to firms in New York, Los Angeles, San Francisco and Boston. I will not stay in Washington. I cannot be myself here. I don't know who I am, but there are too many people here who think they do, so I have to leave if I hope to find out.

You showed me the way, Meg. On that first night in Virginia Beach, before Doug's arrival muddied the waters, you heard my complaints and wisely told me I should resign. It was an idea that had not occurred to me since my first days in the Foreign Service. As Doug may have told you, they offered me an ambassadorship in the Seychelles, a bone thrown to me for my stand on Marcos. I accepted the post until I understood it would solve nothing, and remembered your advice.

I will not lie to you or myself. If the sacrifice of personal happiness—or the pursuit thereof—had produced anything in the way of good deeds done, I would not turn my back on public life. But as I made clear to you that first night, I couldn't save anyone, could not save a country. It's time I at least try to save myself.

I sit here at home on a Sunday night, writing my thoughts as they occur to me, sipping scotch to loosen my inhibitions. I had intended this to be a rough draft, but will send it to you uncensored.

My decision may be as foolish as what went before. You be the judge, Meg. I sometimes feel you know me better than I know myself. I have been a poor uncle to you, and a very bad friend. It'll be some time before I'll ever be able to face you again. But your stern judgment is appreciated. I feel less alone knowing you are out there, judging me.

Much love,
Jim

Meg looked up from the letter, and found herself walking in a bare corridor of elm trees, like the warped ribs of a ship's skeleton, birds singing in the limbs. She'd automatically walked while she read, without looking where she went, and it took her a moment to realize she was back on campus, in the tree-lined promenade behind the Wren Building.

She flipped through the letter again, wondering what to make of it, feeling too many things to know how she felt. She *didn't* know Jim, and resented his claim that she did. Her suggestion that he quit had been a knee-jerk response to his complaints and she'd forgotten she said it. She felt disappointed, *cheated* he was leaving the State Department, where her critical judgment could look through him into larger issues, a window on politics and power. She did not want to be judge to a private citizen.

And yet, beneath her irritable, clearer thoughts, Meg twanged and vibrated, excited by the letter. Something terribly dramatic had happened, and her uncle insisted she be the sole witness. Despite herself, she was pleased, flattered and grateful.

Years later, when she understood that every passionate choice could also be an unconscious escape, Margaret Frisch wondered what she'd been fleeing when she chose a career writing and teaching history. There was the narrowness of her family, of course, and the limbo of being female. But there was also the example of her uncle, something she'd pursued as well as fled. They'd been like two people passing each other in a revolving door, Meg going out, Jim coming in, each inadvertently pushing the other through the spinning chase of doors.

12

THINGS HAPPENED QUICKLY when Jim left the foreign service. Freedom was a shock, a rush of events like the rush of images after a blow to the head. Offered several positions, Jim accepted one with RCA, sold his apartment and moved to Los Angeles.

He'd spent much of his life in smoky new cities of glass and sun that were constantly compared to L.A., yet Jim knew the place itself as chiefly an airport and acronym: LAX. Three weeks after he arrived, Jim was in love again—with Los Angeles. He knew he shouldn't be. Serious people were expected to hate it, loathe the uniform round of gorgeous days, the lack of a center, the feeling everyone and everything were brand-new and could not last. The white and pastel sugar cubes crowding the hillsides and valleys seemed as changeable as the swirl of traffic bowling through the freeways. Palm trees grew like weeds, not trees, barely scratching the edges of too much bright sky. A little more sun and the city would completely disappear, an overexposed photograph. Jim loved its sunny impermanence, which must mean he wasn't serious anymore. He didn't know what he was. He felt like a man who hadn't known he'd spent his life in prison until he stood outside the gate, blinking. He did not look back, not yet.

He grew a beard, then shaved it off when he found he looked academic, not bohemian. He became Southern Californian, washing his car as frequently as he'd once shined his shoes. He wore colored shirts and wide neckties in the highrise office whose floor-to-ceiling windows were tinted like sunglasses. He worked in strategic planning at RCA, on a longterm study of electronics firms in South Korea, Taiwan and Singapore. Asia was hot and Jim had been in greater demand than he'd imagined. RCA planned to compete with Japan in the market everyone expected to open in China, not directly but by investing heavily in foreign companies, pitching Asian against Asian. If these new firms entered the American market too, RCA would be in a good position to buy them up and make their profit that way. It was all a game of profits and numbers, one Jim enjoyed playing; no governments would be toppled, no dissidents imprisoned or tortured. He happily played the game for a few hours every day, then put away his toys and went home.

Jim took an apartment in Marina del Rey temporarily while he got a feel for the city, then found he liked it there and stayed. His semi-furnished one-bedroom faced a courtyard with a swimming pool and Jacuzzi, like the court-yard of a big motel, a few pine trees towering over tubby, pineapple-trunked palms. He sat on his second-floor balcony with newspaper and coffee on Sunday mornings, listening to neighbors laugh, scold their children and make love behind drawn curtains and open sliding glass doors. Jim enjoyed their invisible company. After the nervous, determined privacy of public life, he was gently surprised by the careless openness of private lives here. He was as alone as he'd been in Washington, yet solitude felt less confining now, less lonely.

He went out jogging every evening after work, trotting down the street to Venice Beach, fifteen minutes away. He pumped along in the bicycle lane of the Promenade on the way out, past the carnival midway of gift shops, snack bars, old people and hippies, then returned along the beach, clutching his hips while he gasped for air and his run slowed to a walk on the shelf of wet sand. The sun would be going down in the chalky blue air above the ocean, the blue-gray sweep of coastline to the left dissolving in white mists coming off the mountains. The sudden coolness after the heat of day was so keen you could drink it. The deep desert of beach glowed for a few minutes in the soft candlelight of sky. Jim's mind emptied itself completely when he ran, a beautiful absence of thought that sharpened his senses and left him seamless. In that state of mind, just looking at one of the muscular rhinoceroses who thudded down from the weightlifting yard for a swim, or two husky-voiced teenagers sharing a joint under the pier, or a young man in baggy shorts and shirt innocently asleep on the rumpled sand with the *I Ching* over his face was as intensely erotic as kissing each of them.

Jim began with the bars, just looking at first, then meeting men his own age. They wanted youth, of course, but Jim only wanted information and they were happy to oblige. They told him about Griffith Park, the baths and, yes, the boys who hung out at the bus stops along Santa Monica Boulevard *were* for sale. Jim picked up a very tanned, slightly stoned long-haired blond one evening on his way home from work as easily as he might have picked up a quart of milk. The boy swaggered about Jim's apartment, expressing disdain for the furniture and disbelief that Jim had no drugs to share. He simply lay there, showing neither the friendly professionalism of Thai prostitutes nor Doug's amateur eagerness, and Jim had to think about Doug to keep himself excited. He did not want to think about Doug. All love had ground itself out in sex, a wildly desperate sex powered by Jim's resentment that it was only sex, not love. There wasn't even that with the hustler. Jim finished, returned the boy to Santa Monica Boulevard and decided he had to start fresh. Doug had spoiled him, with hope if not with love, and Jim couldn't go back to Bangkok.

"You got to find boys who're looking for daddies," explained Rory, an advertising executive from Oklahoma who wore cowboy boots and leisure suits and drove a Mercedes. Between "sons" at the moment, Rory sat at the front of Stardust in West Hollywood every Friday night, joking with cronies while they checked out the young men coming and going. Jim enjoyed their company, the easy camaraderie of men out duck-hunting together. He did not think he wanted to be a daddy, though.

It was at Stardust that Jim met Tony, a small black-haired boy who nervously cruised Jim from across the room. He looked startled when Jim smiled and came over—Jim startled himself with how easily he went to the boy. Tony was older than he appeared; he taught kindergarten, although his petite frame and childlike complexion suggested he'd only recently finished kindergarten himself. He was slightly effeminate too, which Jim accepted as a challenge to his laws of attraction. Tony couldn't believe his luck when Jim invited him home; Jim couldn't believe anyone would want him so badly. Tony followed Jim in his own car back to Marina del Rey, and didn't leave until Sunday evening.

They saw each other every weekend for a month while Jim waited to fall in love. Tony loved Jim from the start, carefully, discreetly, keeping his adoration under control with gentle teasing about Jim's "butch arms" and "hot buns." Jim had assumed he'd automatically love anyone who loved him, but he did not love Tony. He was not sure why, except there was no mystery to Tony, no shadows. He was sweet and clear, all there, without masculine snags or armor. Jim kept coming back to Tony's effeminacy as an explanation, although he didn't know why that should bother him. Despite his slightly wiggly walk and hoarse, androgynous voice, Tony was quite tough. When Jim lied to him over dinner and said he'd met someone else—it seemed easier that way—Tony was silent a moment, then smiled and said he knew it couldn't last. "I like to dance, you like to run. Well, it was fun rolling around in that kinky patch of chest hair." Jim was surprised at how little guilt he felt afterwards. Failure to love back was not the terrible crime he'd imagined it to be. He simply wasn't ready yet. Jim decided he owed it to himself to stay loose while he explored his possibilities, keeping love dissolved in a solution of sexuality.

He tried a leather bar, thinking butch might be more his line. He owned no leather and they had Jim check his shirt at the door of a smoky, shadowy place surrounded by warehouses. Jim strolled among the beards and motorcycle jackets, leather vests and chaps. In the pauses between songs from the juke-box, the room creaked like an old sailing ship. The sullen maleness of the place was too overdone to seem sincere, as foreign to Jim as the platform shoes and eye glitter of the handful of David Bowie clones at Stardust. A short man with a close-cropped beard and motorcycle cap walked up to Jim, sneered at him and tweaked Jim's left nipple. Jim went home with him to a little cottage in Echo Park. The man would not let Jim kiss him, which was excitingly frustrating, then handcuffed himself to his bed and dared Jim to fuck him. Jim might have enjoyed the game of resistance if the man hadn't continued to snap commands, first that Jim slap him across the face, then that Jim bite his nipples hard. Knowing the real injury one man could do to another, Jim found this playacting disturbing. "Yeah, I was right," the man said afterwards. "You're a pussy. Now get out of here."

Gay life was a new country, or a lot of new countries, a United Nations of eros. "Don't tell me you're a rice queen," snarled Rory one night at Stardust when he caught Jim eyeing an Indonesian-looking fellow who stood at the pinball machine. Rory explained the term and told Jim there were actually bars for men who had the hots for Orientals. "You should check one out, Jimbo. While you're playing kid-in-the-candy-store."

Which Jim did, visiting the Lady from Shanghai, a bar near Little Tokyo whose narrowness was disguised with darkness and mirrors. The Asians were mostly young, the Caucasians middle-aged and overweight—stocky, compla-cent men like former drill sergeants, the sort of American one saw frequently in Asia, contractors, engineers and mechanics who worked in the Orient be-cause they enjoyed the easy access to booze and sex, whatever their tastes. It was odd stumbling upon a pocket of that in downtown L.A., and Jim nearly turned and walked out again, for fear of being mistaken for one of them. But he stayed, bought a beer and wandered the room. The middle-aged men lounged like lords along the bar. The younger men stood out by the dark mirrors that doubled their number. Jim found he attracted the kind of attention here only a young hunk might get at Stardust. Well, age *was* venerated in Asia. He chatted with a coquettish boy whose flirty eyelashes made Jim nervous. He struck up a conversation with an older, more self-contained young man named Robert, who said he played the cello. His speech was full of the odd, oblong vowels of Southern California and, when the subject came up, said his grandparents had emigrated from mainland China in the 1920s. "But I hate rice queens, y'know? I want to be liked for me, not the angle of my eyelids." He then admitted *he* had a fetish for redheads, smiling sheepishly at Jim.

They saw each other for two months, through the screen of each other's fetish, the redhead and the Asian. Jim needed to discover if he had a secret obsession with Asian men, if that had been the mystery missing in Tony and others since Doug. No, or it didn't translate to Robert anyway. Robert was very courteous, cheerful and horny, so courteous Jim took two weeks to understand they had nothing in common except lust. The mystery of race was trivial compared to the mystery of Robert's being a musician. Classical music was a closed book to Jim. He went to a concert with Robert, and even bought a few records in an attempt to open that book, but the book remained sealed shut. When Robert confessed over dinner that he'd fallen in love with another musician, a red-haired clarinetist, Jim understood perfectly.

He went to the Lady from Shanghai one more time. He was trying to catch the eye of a beefy Filipino in the corner when a short Caucasian strutted into the bar, impatiently glanced about and hoisted himself on to a barstool. The man looked vaguely familiar. Jim couldn't figure out why until the fellow leaned forward to whisper to the bartender, and was lit from below by a light behind the counter, just as he'd once been illuminated in a swimming pool. It was Phil Zacheray, Captain Zacheray. He was stouter and had sideburns now, and he seemed to be a regular at this bar. Because of what happened five years ago? But he did not appear haunted, only older. Jim was deliberating over whether he should go up and say hello, when Zacheray waved to a boy in the shadows and called him over. No, this was not a good time. It would not be right for Jim to inflict the past on Zacheray, or on himself either, not now when they both enjoyed the present so much.

It was 1974 and journalists liked to claim America had been "traumatized," first by Vietnam, then by Watergate. The very notion amused Jim. "As if the two minutes the average American devotes to world events each day while reading the newspaper or watching Walter Cronkite could have any psychological effect," he wrote in a letter to Meg.

I was in a bar the night Nixon delivered his resignation last month over national television. Everyone stopped to listen. We were quite respectful, knowing this was an historical moment we'd want to share with our grandchildren, or rather, our nephews and nieces. But all I could think about was the young man with curly hair and a mustache who sat beside me. (Afterwards, when I told him I once played golf with Tricky Dick, he thought I was conning him and moved to the other end of the bar.) No, our withdrawal from Vietnam was an enormous relief, and Watergate little more than a soap opera that confirmed most people's assumption that their government is all —pardon my French—horseshit. Maybe I'm simply reading my own feelings in the population at large, but I believe my reading is closer to the truth than that of pundits who claim the population is in a state of shock.

Jim sent letters to Meg every now and then, usually when he felt the need to write down his thoughts and share them. "At one extreme is the world," he wrote on another occasion,

> an abstraction of numbers and names. At the other extreme is the narrow life of the village. After living so many years in the world, I've now come home to the village. The gay ghetto is as isolated as any village in the jungles of Sumatra or tiny island in the Visayans, but it is as real as they are too, as solid, immediate and necessary.

Meg wrote back infrequently, one letter for every three or four of Jim's, brief, polite notes usually about her classes and plans. She never referred to the recent past. She didn't respond to Jim's news of the present either, except for the occasional slogan, "Hope you're still enjoying yourself," which had a sarcastic ring in Jim's head. He felt she merely tolerated his letters, yet wrote back to keep them coming, superstitiously reluctant to break the chain. He knew their correspondance meant far more to him than it did to Meg.

She finished William and Mary in 1974 and was accepted by several graduate schools in history. Jim thought that was a step down from her original ambition of going to law school, but he congratulated her and added, "Writing history is healthier than attempting to make it." Meg went to the University of Wisconsin where she reported the winter was so cold her nose hairs froze with each breath she took, and the enormous lake beside the city and campus became a desert of ice, with secret fish living underneath. Her letters grew more newsy, friendly in their comments on place and people. When Jim found a fat envelope in his mailbox one evening, his first thought was that Meg had finally opened up, letting loose all the anger, confusion, intelligence and love she'd been holding back, making her peace. Inside was yet another short note, and the Xerox of a ten-page proposal for a master's thesis: "The Invention of Masculinity."

Jim fixed himself a scotch and soda before he put on his glasses and went out to the balcony to read it. But the proposed thesis had nothing to do with him, not really. It began with the claim that masculinity as we know it was a recent development. "The male ideals of silence, strength, stoicism and solitude would be quite alien to men of the generation of 1860." There was a paragraph from a letter written by a Major Thomas Curry to his wife during the Civil War, a passionate, heartfelt passage about death, fear and love. The next quotation came from a letter written in 1901 by an American officer in the Philippines named Littleton Waller, florid yet dead rhetoric about honor and duty that Jim found himself skimming. Finally there was the closing paragraph of *A Farewell to Arms* where the narrator can say nothing about the death of the woman he loved except that he sat with the corpse, then walked back to his hotel in the rain.

These samples represent an emotional shift in masculine style to a pseudo-stoicism unlike the genuine stoicism of an earlier age where strong emotion was always acknowledged before the individual came to terms with it. The New Masculinity attempted to deny emotion altogether. In its crudest terms, sometime after 1900 men could no longer cry in public, although this is only one facet of a many-faceted evolution of identity. Under the guise of dis-passionate selflessness, men were freed to become self-pitying and self-absorbed, without becoming self-critical. What drove them to this refuge?

Meg then cited some of the causes and effects she hoped to explore: the urbanization of American life accompanied by the growing popularity of the cowboy myth in dime novels; the threat of women represented by the suffrag-ette movement; the identification and demonizing of male homosexuality after the turn of the century; America's new role as a world power, which meant men could not afford to expend their energy examining anything so ephemeral as emotions.

In conclusion, this will not be a speculative polemic or feminist critique, but an objective, well-illustrated uncovering of the roots and historical nature of "man."

Jim's initial reaction was to dismiss it as airy cleverness from the ivory tower. How much did anybody know about what people thought and felt a hundred years ago? Were men really that different back then? How much could a twenty-three-year-old girl know about men even in the present? Nev-ertheless, the more holes Jim poked, the more intrigued he became with the notion that what he'd wrestled with his whole life was merely historical, a passing fashion like the hats men were once expected to wear. He assumed that's what this was about: heterosexuality. Jim could not remember the last time he'd cried, but he had escaped this trap of masculinity by becoming gay. Hadn't he? He read the handwritten note enclosed with the Xerox:

Thought you'd like to see the thesis I'm *not* writing. Not yet anyway. My advisor has steered me away from it, which is actually a relief. It's insanely ambitious, far too ambitious for a master's or even a doctoral dissertation.

But one day, when I've mastered the sources needed to support it. My advisor feared it would be too belle-lettery. But along with his valid arguments—my advisor *is* a he—I got the distinct feeling he was thoroughly uncomfortable with the project itself. He kept crossing and uncrossing his legs at our meeting before he said he couldn't understand why a woman wanted to pursue this subject. But who else except a woman could understand there was a subject here? Adam named the animals, but he doesn't like it when the animals turn around and name him.

Feel free to respond with suggestions or critiques. Hope you're still enjoying yourself.

As always,
Meg

Jim wrote back that night, commending her theory for its ingenuity, wondering how she'd go about proving it, regretting she couldn't write about it yet. "I doubt Adam's naming of homosexuality as something wrong is as recent as you say, until I remember the various ways it's treated in Asia," Jim wrote in pencil.

One can get dizzy thinking about the elasticity of human nature, the possibilities offered not only by different cultures but different periods of history. In my own case, much I assumed was written in stone has been erased and rewritten in a few short years. Imagine what a century could do. We need to distinguish between our true skin and our old clothes, shuck the clothes and walk naked in the wide, open spaces.

Jim knew he went off on his own tangent, but his letters were always like that, monologues delivered past Meg to the world at large.

SOMEBODY LAUGHED, AND Jim woke up naked in a dimly lit cell. He lay on a narrow bed looking up at four walls that didn't go all the way to the ceiling, a grid of chicken wire stretched across the top. There was the hiss of showers outside, a man laughing again, somebody loudly snoring. Humid smells of sweat and soap and the whiff of disinfectant helped Jim to pretend he was in an army barracks, or jail, but he knew he was back in ManLand. He had no idea how long he'd slept; his wristwatch was with his clothes downstairs in a locker. He had nothing with him except the towel on its hook and a key on the string around his neck. There had been a fat, bearded, hippielike fellow who made up in tongue for what he lacked in muscle, but he was gone too. Jim did not feel naked; he did not feel anything except sour and foolish, feelings he knew would pass with a hot shower.

He did not start going to the baths until his second year in L.A. Originally he believed sex should be very private and personal, with at least the possibility of future meetings and better acquaintance. But after a few one-night stands that had been thoroughly enjoyable, sudden intimacy with a friendly, nameless body no longer seemed decadent. Jim required they at least be friendly. There were anonymously beautiful young men who expected their breastplate chests and little two-fisted bottoms to express what needed to be said, haughtily looking off when anyone paid attention, even the other beautiful men they eventually took into a cubicle. They only *seemed* to be the majority at ManLand. Jim treated them as scenery and concentrated on the people with open faces and lived-in bodies, not unattractive but different, various. Here he sometimes had sex with men his own age, which was interesting. He went to the baths when he wasn't seeing anyone, and only when he was in a particular mood: bored and restless for no clear reason, mentally listless yet physically anxious in a way not even a run along the beach could smoothe away. A trip to the baths snapped him back to life. If he felt slightly glum and stupid afterwards, Jim accepted that as purely physiological, and it was simpler and more tangible than his earlier state of mind.

He jumped up, knotted the towel around his waist and went to take his shower. The pale fluorescent lighting stopped time at three o'clock in the morning, but it felt much later. The slap of Jim's feet on the sweating floor sounded very loud; there was nobody else about, none of the men who roamed the hall at all hours, only differently tuned snores from the cubicles. Jim imagined a blazing noon outside. It was a weeknight and he couldn't remember if he had any meetings scheduled for the morning. There was no clock on this floor. Instead of going down the stairs to the showers, Jim went up toward the roof garden to take a quick look at the sun.

He pushed on the door and there was no bright flash. It was still dark outside, still night, a deep hush like a long sigh. The passing of cars down in the street was part of that sigh. Jim let the door gently shut behind him and stepped over the cool patio tiles, toward the railing silhouetted against the amber halo of a streetlight just below the roof. A tall redwood fence closed the roof on three sides, but to the west, where the land sloped down and no buildings stood high enough for anyone to see what went on up here, there was a railing and a view. Jim gripped the top rail with both hands and looked out on the city: dusty orange, sodium-lit boulevards curving past the white light of billboards and the dark ranges of houses and scrub. It wasn't much of a view, but a surprise after the cramped spaces below, the distance slightly dizzying after so much closeness. His bare skin contracted in the dry cool. Only the genitals under his towel retained a loose feeling of nakedness, as if body were just a shadow of clothing and he didn't exist without anything to swaddle or bind him. He had stepped out of the world and even Los Angeles had more weight than Jim Goodall. He looked up at the sallow blue-grayness of night sky and followed it overhead and down again. It shaded into a bright blueness above the fence to the east, where the sun would be coming up. The roof garden was pitch-black against that aura, the dark bulbs of two tubbed fruit trees standing above the sawtoothed line of fence.

A tiny red spark at the base of one of the trees began to glow, a soft pink face blossoming behind it in the darkness. The face suddenly disappeared and the spark weaved back and forth. "Here," a choked voice called out.

Nobody answered and Jim understood the voice meant him. "No thank you," he said, but stepped toward the spark, curious. The pink face had appeared so low in the darkness there hadn't seemed room for a body, as if a severed head sat on the tiles. Jim stood directly above him before he understood the man was stretched out on one of the wrestling mats sunbathers used during the day. He had a joint in his hand and seemed to be naked, with his towel rolled up under his head.

"Was getting a moonburn," he said. "But the moon went down. Have a seat." Skin squeaked when he scooted to one side.

Jim lowered himself to the leathery mat, sitting up with one knee raised so the man would understand this was a social visit. "I came up to watch the sunrise," he explained.

"Yeah? Getting to be that time, I guess." He took another toke on the joint, offered it again to Jim, then licked a thumb and finger and winked the spark out. "So this is L.A.," he sighed. "Not the friendliest town."

"You're visiting?" Jim could not guess his age; the weary voice suggested someone too mature to be getting stoned by moonlight.

"Yup. Business trip. Stay here and save on the hotel. Meet a few natives. You a native?" He laid his hand on Jim's thigh and petted it.

"I've been here two years now."

"Maybe that's why you're still friendly. Nobody talks here. It's all eat and run. If you know what I mean." He gave the leg a squeeze and let go.

"I'm Jim," said Jim, holding out his hand.

The man laughed and shook it. "I'm Joe." He did not let go when they finished the grip, but lightly held on, rubbing his thumb over the knuckles.

"What line of business are you in, Joe?"

"Cookies. Wholesale baked goods. I come down from Seattle four or five times a year to see how our product's getting displayed in the chains."

His hand continued to hold Jim's, fingering and exploring it, idly scratching a dog while chatting with its owner. Jim's hand automatically touched back, without interest, until he found a smooth metallic band around the base of one finger.

"We handle sales through the main office, so there's no commission on these jaunts. But I've found little bonuses of my own."

Jim held the ring, lightly turning it round, chivvying it up to the knuckle, the rest of his hand enclosing the delicate finger.

The man laughed, understanding Jim's interest. "Yup. Afraid so. But knuckles get fat and I can't slip the damn thing off when I play hooky."

"You have kids?"

"Three. *You* married?"

Jim shook his head. "Boys? Girls?"

Again the man laughed. "We shouldn't talk about them here."

"No." Jim lifted the hand and brushed his lower lip over the knuckles, wiry hairs and loop of metal. He disapproved of the man for being married, for cheating on his family and himself.

A hand stroked Jim's back. "I don't know if I can get hard again. But we can try. Do you kiss?"

Still holding the hand, Jim bent down and kissed a bristly mustache that opened into a mouth. His body opened out on the cool mat and his towel came undone. He did not know why the man excited him. He knew the man only as a mustache and wedding ring, then a furry front and fat bottom. Jim groped again for the hand with the ring. The deceit fascinated Jim, the network of secrets and lies that surrounded this, binding Jim into something large and complicated. They were not alone. Jim imagined the man's family watching, standing out there like the highrise offices he knew were scattered beyond the redwood fence. Not that Jim wanted to hurt his wife and children. They could never know about this. But Jim knew, and that was enough to tie him into their life, giving sex weight and meaning. The crime of it excited Jim, his complicity, although he found the man so tender he thought Joe might be a good father, even a good husband when he was at home. He liked to hug and kiss and they ended up half-sitting, half-sprawled in a tangle of legs, pulling on each other like two kids in a cellar. The man closed his eyes and grinned when he came. When Jim followed—spasms straining deep inside for something to shoot—it was as though his entire body were pulled through an opening the size of a wedding ring.

They lay on their backs, catching their breaths. The sky was now light enough for them to see who they were. Joe was somewhere in his late thirties, with dark hair and a heavy build, a Jerry Colonna mustache and teeth, too comic to look like a father. "I couldn't tell what you were when we started," he told Jim with a smile. "An old man with a young body, or a young man losing his hair. But there you are." He jostled him with his foot.

"A pig in a poke," said Jim. He propped himself on his elbows to look around. The sun hadn't come up and the roof garden was still all shadows, paler now. And Jim saw two men in towels sitting on a bench in the far corner, sullenly facing him and Joe out here on the wrestling mat; one of them quietly smoked a cigarette. Jim reached for his towel, wondering how long they'd been there, fearing he and Joe must look like a heap of peeled potatoes in this light. He remembered his fantasy of being watched by Joe's family, and was embarrassed by how perverse it was.

Joe slapped him on the stomach. "Want to hit the showers?"

In the white tiled room that a few hours ago had been the scene of hypnotic stares and bold groping, a handful of men quickly showered before they went home or straight to their jobs. One young fellow stood very still, shaving himself without a mirror, his genitals still plumped out by a cock ring. Jim followed Joe down to the lockers and saw more of who he was: bright red briefs, a yellow shirt, slacks with flared legs and a necktie as wide as a lobster bib. He was a salesman and quaintly lower middle class.

No, decided Jim. He wouldn't hold himself responsible for his thoughts during sex, but to continue them in the light of day was folly. And Jim had been here before. It was a step backwards when he needed to move forward, only it seemed he couldn't step in any direction without revisiting an old error.

"When do you go back to Seattle?" he asked.

"Start the long drive home tonight. But that's why I had to make the most of this morning." He grinned at Jim, his mustache displaying his big teeth. "It should keep me going until my next trip down."

Jim took out his wallet. "Here's my card. Next time you're in L.A. and want to see a friendly face, or need a place to stay, give me a call."

Joe looked at the card, uncertain what to make of the offer. "Gee. What a nice gesture, Jim. But—it won't be another three or four months before my next trip down."

"Whatever," said Jim, understanding nothing would come of this. He shook hands with Joe and wished him a safe trip home.

"You too. Happy trails," Joe laughed, hoisted his suitcase and went out the door.

JIM ASSUMED HE'D never hear from Joe, which was just as well. But three months later there was a call at work from a Mr. DeVichiello. He reminded Jim who he was—"The cookie salesman from Seattle"—and asked if the offer of a place to stay were still good. It was, tentatively. Joe stayed with Jim for three nights while he toured supermarkets in Greater Los Angeles. A few months later, he was back again. His visits became a regular feature in Jim's life. Jim waited to grow bored with the arrangement, or for one of them to fall in love, with each other or somebody else. But it became and remained a friendship, casual and good-humored, with sex where other friends might play golf or go bowling.

Jim enjoyed the sex, but what he liked best was the conversation afterwards: Joe wanted to talk about his family. It was odd at first having a man in your bed with his head in your lap, the light from the living room showing you both were still naked, complaining about his wife's most trivial tics or fearing he wasn't strict enough with his kids. Joe spoke about them so matter-of-factly he didn't seem to be using the subject of family to deny what he'd just done, not consciously anyway. Jim tried telling him a little about his life in the foreign service, but travel and politics were too abstract to interest Joe, who listened politely, then turned the subject back to his kids. He liked to talk about his kids, especially his daughters, although Teresa was not the pal she'd once been now that she was in junior high. His son, John, however, worried and frightened him.

"Six years old and he can be such a baby, bursting into tears if you look at him cross-eyed. Still wanting to be held and kissed. Kissing is for girls, immigrants and babies, I tell him."

"But *you* like to be kissed," Jim said.

Joe frowned. "No. He's got to learn to be tough. That's all."

Jim cautiously suggested, "You're not afraid of hurting him by being too cold?"

"I don't want him to turn out like me."

He was not quite the happy hypocrite he pretended to be. He believed homosexuality was a weakness, like alcohol, that had to be kept under control or it became a vice. He had made a private contract with himself never to get into bed with his wife within twenty-four hours of having sex with somebody else. He loved his wife and was utterly faithful to her—in Seattle. He waited until he was out of town before he visited the baths, propositioned hitchhikers or read Gordon Merrick novels. This sexual friendship was as new to him as it was to Jim.

"I am his one-man Bangkok," Jim wrote to Meg after the first year.

It probably shocks you. A few years ago a friendly affair with a married man would have shocked me, but it seems perfectly natural once you're inside it. I wouldn't mind meeting a second or third Joe to take up the slack between visits, but all I've managed are more short-term affairs with other honest, thoroughly gay men like myself. Well, I spent the first half of my life falling in love with men. I'm spending the second half sleeping with them. In the end I will have lived a complete life.

Mao died and the China market still didn't open up. Overseas planning and investment were shifting to the manufacture of products for the American market, with high hopes for video cassette recorders. Carter was elected president. Jim wasn't registered to vote in California, but he liked Carter, especially after the man confessed in an interview that he'd "known lust in his heart." Jim understood why people snorted and smirked at that, yet he enjoyed hearing a public figure be as scrupulously innocent as he'd once thought himself to be.

On Christmas Day, Joe called Jim at home to say Merry Christmas, and confess he'd been promoted; he would not be coming to L.A. anymore. Jim offered his congratulations, said it had been fun while it lasted and that friendships go on whether you see the other person or not. Joe was very quiet and Jim could hear children bickering in the distance.

He went into a mild funk that January, a kind of emotional winter that made up for the absence of winter in Los Angeles. He wondered if maybe he'd been in love with Joe after all. Watching Carter's inauguration on the evening news

—seeing the winter coats, the bare trees in the background, hearing the familiar bump of wind in the microphones—Jim realized it had been almost four
years since he started his new life, a whole term of wild oats and exploration.
His funk wasn't Joe, it was boredom. He needed to find a lover, or buy a
house, or try a new city, something different. He went to a new bar in West
Hollywood that night and fell in love with a young blond bull who let Jim buy
him drinks but refused to go home with him. No, it wasn't love but it was
different, this fixation with the unobtainable. Jim returned to the bar week
after week, hoping to break the bull's resistance and charm him into bed.
When the bull finally gave in, sensing Jim was getting bored with the game, it
was the dullest lay Jim had ever had, like rubbing against a lukewarm side of
beef.

Another year passed and Jim was at his desk, simplifying the English of a
report from South Korea, when his secretary buzzed and said he had a call
from Washington. He assumed she meant Washington State, which would be
Seattle. He promptly picked up the phone. "Hello."

"Hello, Jim? Jim Goodall?"

"Speaking." The voice at the other end was not Joe's.

"*Jim!* Hey. It's Dave Wheeler. How you doing?"

"Dave?"

"Yes!" He laughed. "From your old days in the State Department. You
haven't blocked that out completely, have you?"

"Dave. What a surprise." Dave, Joe: Jim felt as though time had short-
circuited; he stalled while he got his bearings. "Well, well. How's Elaine?"

Elaine was fine; she and Dave had a house in Georgetown now. Janey was
fine, working on the Hill for a Congressman from Massachusetts.

"A real Washington family," said Jim. "I assume you're still in the Department."

"Afraid so. Which brings me straight to the reason I'm calling. You had
your fill yet of getting rich and fat in the private sector?"

Jim relaxed a little; the call was not personal. "I've gotten neither, but no. I
like it here, Dave. You should try it sometime."

"You never get the itch to come back?"

"I can't say that I have. Not really." Jim was curious only about why they
might want him, and why Wheeler was the one calling.

"There's some important people here who'd like to talk to you about coming back, Jim."

"Such as?"

"Patricia Derian."

"Who she?" There were very few women in the State Department, and
none in important positions.

"The new director of Human Rights. Carter brought her in. He's a big
believer and the bureau's been expanded. We're up on the seventh floor, Jim.
I'm Derian's deputy."

"Congratulations. The seventh floor." Jim had been away long enough to hear how ludicrous that sounded. "Seriously. You deserve to be up there at the top." He did not want Dave to think he was envious.

"The important thing is I'm now in a position to do good work. And single out a few good people to help me. Even bring back a few from the dead."

"I'm quite alive, thank you. I was dead back there, but now I'm alive. Not interested."

Dave only chuckled. "That was much too quick to be sincere, Jim."

It was, and Jim disliked being seen through. He swung his chair around and faced his tinted view of the city, the harsh contrasts of light filtered out by the polarized glass. "I've got a very nice position here. Why should I swap it for a badly paid desk back in the depths of Foggy Bottom?"

"We wouldn't waste you here, Jim. You'd be sent overseas as a human rights commissioner or monitor, whatever we end up calling them. It's good work. Necessary and valuable work."

"Where?"

"Too soon to say. We're considering different people for different posts. But I've recommended you for Manila."

"Huh." He intended to laugh, but all that came out was a single, stranded syllable. His mind went blank at the thought of Manila.

"Things are different, Jim. They've changed. You'd have a direct channel to us and wouldn't have to answer to the whims of an ambassador or desk officer. What happened over Marcos under Kissinger can't happen again."

A gleam of light sailed across the darkened sky, the filtered flash of sun on the body of a jet far out over the ocean. Jim watched it, feeling disdainful, amused, challenged and resentful.

"Can you at least consider coming east to talk? We'll fly you here, put you up, wine and dine you. Be a chance for you to see how much things have changed."

"Will I get laid?"

Dave missed a beat, then chuckled again. "That's a service you'll have to procure on your own. All we can promise is the hotel room."

Jim had said it just to let Dave know how much *he* had changed. "I don't know, Dave. I think I'd be only wasting your time."

"You wouldn't. We'd at least get a chance to pick your brain about the Marcoses."

"Slim pickings," Jim muttered, and yet he couldn't deliver a flat no. "Let me sleep on it, Dave. Okay, I can at least consider coming in to hear your sales pitch. Let me look at my schedule and we can talk tomorrow."

"Good enough. That's all I ask for now. Meet with us. I know Pat would really like to meet you. Other people too. You've developed something of an underground reputation here for your stand on Marcos, Jim. You have a small but devoted following."

Jim disliked being stroked with false flattery; Wheeler had once been more subtle in his methods. "I *said* I'd sleep on it, Dave. Talk to you tomorrow. My best to Elaine."

"I look forward to seeing you again, Jim. We have a lot of catching up to do. Take care."

Jim hung up and sat there, tightly swiveling in his chair while he tried to think. Manila and Washington. Marcos and Wheeler. Catching up with Dave Wheeler again—so who was out in front? He tried thinking about Dave sexually, as someone to compete against or fuck, but sex didn't enter into his feeling of aggravation. What disturbed him was that Dave was still out there, playing that idiot game, while Jim was in here, playing this harmless and sane one. Glancing around at his chrome furniture and tinted view, Jim felt very successful, wise and cowardly.

HE WAS MET at the gate at National by a junior officer as dry and prematurely middle-aged as the generations of young men who'd preceded him. He had sideburns down to the tips of his earlobes, but then so did Vice-President Mondale. He took Jim to his hotel, then straight to the State Department building. Outside, Washington in April had its usual clouds of blossoms and first new leaves like colored smoke. Inside, it was like revisiting an old school, the corridors narrower and more commonplace than Jim remembered, yet full of emotions that seemed too large for them. Jim came as a tourist, leaving his jacket at the hotel to show how uninterested he was. He almost came without a necktie, but decided that would look too contemptuous.

Dave was on the phone when the junior officer brought him in. He grinned enormously at Jim, dismissed the junior officer with a nod and signaled Jim with a raised finger he'd be finished in a minute. "No, we'll have to pull an end run around EAP on that. Holbrooke's being a turd again."

His hair was shaggy and full of gray, as if to compensate for the youth he'd kept in his face. Jim looked through the fortyish face to a face he remembered from twenty years ago, the cheekbones and long squint he had thought made Dave look like an American Indian. He had shaved off his beard and put on weight. Jim continued to study him, looking for one of the various Dave Wheelers he'd known over the years.

"Keep up the good work." Dave flipped the phone into its cradle and jumped up. "Jim!" he said, coming around his desk. "Goodall! How are you?" He seized Jim's hand and slapped him on the shoulder. "You look good. California agrees with somebody. Have a seat. Would you like some coffee? Soda? I told Pat I'd bring you in when you got here, but we got time to visit. Sit down, sit down."

Jim lowered himself into a swaybacked chair while Dave sat against the front of the desk. "You look good," Jim lied.

"Oh no. My appetite's finally gotten ahead of my metabolism." He pinched a thick fold of stomach through his shirt with both hands. "I don't get the exercise I used to get."

"No late-night swims with the guys?"

He smiled. "Ohhh—I don't do that anymore."

"Not at all?"

Dave glanced at the closed door to his office. "Right to the point, huh, Jim? How's my sex life?"

"A perfectly natural question, considering the last time we saw each other." Jim kept his voice and face bland. He needed to bring up the subject, not just with Dave but in this building, to prove to himself he'd outgrown both.

Dave folded his arms and maintained his smile. "No. My feasting-with-panthers days ended years ago. Just a phase I was going through. I got too old, I guess. And too busy." He twisted around to hunt among the loose papers piled on his desk.

But something horrible had also happened the last time they saw each other. It seemed to have disappeared without a trace behind Dave's breezy manner and professional smile, but maybe not.

"You might want to look at this when you have a minute." He passed Jim a thick booklet bound with staples. "But not before you eat."

Report on the Philippines, Amnesty International, 1975. Jim turned back the cover page, then closed it. "I'm probably the last person on earth you'd want to send to Manila. I'm not very popular with our ally. Marcos knows exactly where I stand on him."

"By sending you, we'd let him know exactly where *we* stand."

"Ah. Then you want me chiefly as a symbol."

"No. We want your integrity and experience too."

"And my homosexuality?"

Dave shrugged. "No sweat. We assume you'll show discretion."

"We?"

Dave shook his head and chuckled again. *"I,"* he confessed. "I've gotten into the *we* habit of speech, being part of this. But no, the others know only that you're a perennial bachelor, which covers a lot of sexual territory."

"I don't know how discreet I can be, Dave. I'm used to getting laid regularly. It's what's important to me, far more important than collating reports at RCA. I can't go back to my old life."

"You know, Jim? You sound like someone who's spent a lot of time trying to argue himself out of something he wants to do."

Jim gave him an exasperated sigh. "I'm simply pointing out the obvious facts of the matter."

"Uh-uh. You want to come back on board, or else you wouldn't be here. You're hesitant because you were burned the last time. I understand. But I believe a man with the rectitude and capacity for indignation to resign in protest over a moral wrong would jump at the chance to help right that wrong.

I'm hoping I can prove to you how much we've changed since your last go-round." He checked his watch. "Would you like to meet Pat?"

Jim was amazed at Dave's belief he'd quit over Marcos. He didn't immediately correct Dave, as if he wanted to enjoy being misunderstood in such flattering terms. He followed Dave down the hall toward the director's office.

The door between the reception area and the office of fumed oak was wide open. Dave stuck his head in without knocking. "Pat? I've got Jim Goodall here. The Marcos Goodall."

Jim had forgotten the director was a woman. She stood when they came in and held out her hand. Jim wasn't sure if he should shake hands with her as if she were a lady or a man; their handshake was a clumsy compromise. She was Jim's age, maybe a year or two younger, with a long, slightly leathery face that suggested a lady cattle rancher despite her full lips and fluffy bangs. She wore no jewelry and only a trace of lipstick. A cigarette was burning in her ashtray and a can of Coke sat on her desk. "Jean? Hold all calls for the next five minutes," she called through the door to her secretary. "Make yourselves at home, gentlemen. So you're Goodall," she said, leaning forward on folded arms, speaking with a slight southern accent. "I've heard a lot of fine things about you. I read your cables and reports as well. Time certainly proved you right on that happy couple. Too bad you weren't high enough up the ladder for your resignation to get the attention it deserved. No matter. You did what you had to do."

There it was again, the admiring misapprehension. It felt so good Jim had to remind himself it *was* a misapprehension.

"Here's what you're up against, Goodall." She spoke as if it were a foregone conclusion Jim would be joining them, but then superiors always spoke like that. Listening to a female take that tone was a new experience. But her command of the facts was so strong and quick he became more interested in them than in Pat Derian.

The administration was tying foreign aid to human rights. Governments that imprisoned people without trial, tortured political prisoners and even murdered them would be ineligible for American funds, whether they were on the left or right, dictatorship or democracy. It was that simple. The Human Rights Bureau investigated reports of abuses, then made their recommendation on whether aid should be continued. They could use their powers of friendly persuasion and talk of world opinion to cajole governments into good behavior, but their only real power was the power of the purse. In most countries, middle and sometimes junior officers represented the bureau, visiting prisons and speaking to local journalists along with their other duties. There were several places, however, where experienced, full-time personnel were needed: South Korea, Iran, Chile and the Philippines.

The new policy had its enemies. Congress was behind it, and the White House of course, but much of the State Department itself thought it a big mistake to mess up *realpolitik* by snooping into other countries' private affairs. Several ambassadors obstructed the work and one had complained so sharply to Washington that his man had been recalled. It was worst in the East Asia and Pacific region, whose director worked actively to sabotage the program. The acting ambassador in Manila who supported the policy had just been replaced by a man chosen chiefly for his opposition to it.

"So anyone you send there can count on being hated inside the embassy as well as outside," Jim observed.

"Hated by everyone except those we hope to help," Derian quietly declared. "There's some six thousand political prisoners still in the jails. I see you have the Amnesty report." She nodded at the booklet rolled up in Jim's hand. "Even the embassy people who think we're a pack of nosy parkers admit the report is basically accurate, give or take a thousand prisoners. And such fine detail as whether one labor organizer was repeatedly kicked in the gut or in the face. The report concentrates on the main island and barely touches on the others."

"Things are usually worse the further you get from Manila," Jim muttered, rolling the booklet a little tighter. "Do these monitors have any authority with anyone?"

"Not really. Your title will be special assistant to the ambassador, and he has to give you an office but any other cooperation you get will be up to you."

"Just like you were CIA," said Dave. He'd been sitting there watching Jim's face, measuring his interest.

"He can ask to have you recalled, but we promise to stand behind you to the best of our abilities. There's no telling where the balance of power will be six months or a year from now. Oh, and I should add you'd come back in as an FS–3. Which is probably half the salary you're making now."

Jim laughed. "You certainly know how to sell a guy."

Derian nodded. "Just putting all the cards on the table. We respect you too much to deceive you, Goodall. I'd rather play to your better instincts. And Dave's feeling you'd like to finish what you couldn't start four years ago. You pulled a few punches in your reports, but I picked up a nice righteous indignation between the lines. You kept your outrage under control, which is what we need now."

Jim remembered planting little twists and barbs of phrase and was pleased someone had finally noticed them.

"All right, Goodall. That's the whole ball of wax." She stood up to signal the meeting was over. "Any further questions, just ask Dave. If you decide against it, nobody will think less of you. But it's been good meeting you. I've learned the Department isn't all old boys and tap dancers. There are people like you and Dave who've somehow managed to keep their principles intact, in hibernation until the circumstances came along when they could use them."

"See you later, Pat," said Dave, escorting Jim to the door. "Thanks."

"Interesting lady," said Jim in the corridor. "Where did she come from?"

"Remarkable woman. The spoils system, believe it or not. She campaigned hard for Carter and, when it came time to reward her, she asked for Human Rights. The old hands assumed a woman would be easy to handle and the bureau would remain toothless. But no, she's a fighter. In another day and age, we'd say the lady had balls."

"What do you say now?"

Dave laughed. "That she's got testosterone."

They returned to Dave's office and Jim braced himself for another volley of arguments on why he should return. Instead Dave said, "I've got a couple of final calls to make, but do you have plans for tonight? Elaine and I would like to have you over for dinner."

"Elaine? God, I haven't seen her since—" Jim was frightened by the thought of seeing her, then excited, before he realized he was thinking about someone else, as if all women were the same person. Even Derian had made him think of Meg, both in her quickness with facts and her smoking. "Sure. That'd be nice. I'd like to see where you live."

It was after five and Jim sat in the empty outer office while Dave made his calls behind a closed door. Jim still had the Amnesty report rolled in his hand, but did not open and read it. If he knew the details of what was happening over there, it would be more difficult to walk away. He felt less free than he'd been when he arrived, a false pride like a face in a mirror telling him he owed it to the world to take this post. Such noble posing was only the product of everybody thinking he had resigned in protest over his government's acceptance of Marcos. Their misunderstanding was farcical, almost as funny as the fact that something in Jim wished it were true.

Dave finished and said they could go. They went out to a parking lot squeezed between two annexes in the back, where Dave's Volkswagen Rabbit was parked beside a Cadillac. Jim waited until they were out in traffic before he finally said it.

"You and your boss are operating under a gross misconception."

"In regards to policy?"

"In regards to me. I didn't quit over Marcos. I quit for personal reasons. I wanted a life. I wanted to find myself." The phrase embarrassed him and he added, "I wanted to get laid."

Dave smiled and cut his eyes at Jim. "It may have worked out that way. But the real reason was your disgust with the system. Your frustration over being able to change nothing."

"Dave! I quit so I could fuck guys."

"No. You might tell yourself that. But I know you better."

"Do you now?" Jim began to laugh; this was too ridiculous.

"All right then. I don't know everything. But I do know I once saw you go apeshit when an army officer shot a kid in the stomach."

Jim hadn't thought either of them could bring that up, but here it was, with office workers in neckties or lipstick looking dully ahead in the cars all around them.

"I just stood there, afraid of doing anything. But you weren't afraid. You jumped in and ended the boy's suffering."

"That wasn't me. That was anger. Temporary insanity. I'm not proud of what I did."

"Good. You'd be a bastard if you were. But it *was* you, Jim. You knew one man's suffering was inexcusable, even when it was intended to save a whole village. The sacrifice of one for the benefit of many, and all that pragmatic horseshit. You couldn't accept that and had to do something, even if it meant becoming a murderer yourself."

Jim turned away, grimacing.

"What happened that day has been with me ever since," Dave continued. "I thought I could hide from it by concentrating completely on my career, becoming a 'tap dancer' as Pat says, anonymous and successful. A good family man too. But no, I couldn't get out of my head what you did and I couldn't do in that paddy field. When I heard this loose cannon of a woman was being made director of Human Rights, I started maneuvering to come in with her, thinking here was an opportunity where I could make good. Maybe this time a kid wouldn't have to die."

Jim was silent a moment. "You're a cagey fellow, Dave."

"What makes you say that?"

"This isn't the first time you've tried to seduce me. In one form or another."

"No, it's not," he admitted. "But it's always been with the truth, Jim. And always for a good cause."

His honesty left Jim without a response. They were already in Georgetown, toy houses and tree-lined streets visible behind the shops and restaurants along Wisconsin Avenue.

"You telling the truth when you say you don't have sex with men?"

"I am. I can still find men attractive, but I don't want to sleep with them."

Jim could muster no erotic feeling for Dave. It wasn't the man's middle-aged appearance that blocked out sex, but a feeling that a line into the past had been snapped and sex no longer had anything to do with who they were to each other.

"What happened over there scared you straight?" Jim said.

Dave frowned. "Maybe. My occasional adventures with men were only a sideshow. It scared me into understanding how much I loved Elaine. I told her everything. We had a couple of rocky months, but it left us very close. My itch for adventures stopped."

Brick townhouses hugged the narrow street and each other, a net of branches overhead catching the pale clouds of new leaves and blossoms. Dave swung the car into a little driveway that ended fifteen feet from the street against a closed garage door. He jerked on the parking brake and turned off the engine.

"The experience scared *me* gay," said Jim.

"Yes. Well. That's because you're a real homosexual, Jim." Dave was smiling. "The experience shook us down to our priorities."

A pale face appeared in the wavy glass window of an antique brick house beside the garage, watched them a moment, then disappeared.

"Does Elaine know about me?"

"Yes."

"The killing too?"

Dave nodded. "She's far tougher than I once gave her credit for. Hell, she's chatted with scar-faced generalissimos over brussels sprouts, she'll have no trouble being comfortable with you. Let's go in."

Jim wished she knew nothing about him, but if she must know one half, at least she knew the other too: a murderer *and* a homosexual.

"Jim Goodall. Lord, lord. How many years has it been? Why the last time we saw each other, you were being eaten alive by butterflies at Angkor Wat."

She had changed, of course. He didn't remember her southern accent sounding so strong, or her neck being so short. In Cambodia she'd been a weary young woman with a bouffant hairdo and a morbid fear of fruit and water. Now she was a veteran embassy wife, a professional whose noisy friendliness betrayed nothing personal, although Jim suspected the extra squeeze she gave his hand signaled something.

"You'll have to excuse me. I just got home from work myself. Oh didn't Dave tell you? I'm over at H.E.W. Dear? Show Jim the house, fix him a drink and then I can use your expertise in the kitchen."

Ten minutes later, Jim sat in a lawn chair outside their kitchen, a tumbler of scotch in one hand, the Amnesty booklet still rolled in the other—he kept meaning to set it down somewhere. The little backyard was a cool, green open-air room with flowerbeds heaped along the walls and a spray of apple blossoms fountained over the patio. At his back, Jim heard Elaine and Dave quietly chat about household matters while they washed vegetables and chopped meat, as if Jim weren't here.

They all knew too much about each other, yet it didn't seem to bother Elaine, or Dave either. The only person it disturbed was Jim, which made him feel overly sensitive, shamefully vulnerable. He wanted to reach a final decision about turning down the job, but other things kept breaking into his thoughts—nervousness in the presence of a woman whose husband he no longer loved, memories of a boy's death, echoes of a niece, the strangeness of being misunderstood as a hero, even the bosky cool of a spring evening—as if Jim were trying to think and feel everything at once. He remembered being able to think or feel only one thing at a time, following it through to its conclusion without being dispersed in memories and emotions. He was no longer capable of that, no longer qualified for decisive action. A turtle popped from its shell, Jim had made himself completely unfit to handle the work they wanted him to do, which would require emotional narrowness and linear thinking. There was no way he could consider accepting this job.

With that in mind, Jim unrolled the Amnesty report, peeled back the cover page and began to read.

"So. *Accounts Rendered or Deferred: A Boston Merchant in the Age of Jefferson.* What did you think? Anyone?"

Thirty-six anonymously young faces settled back and stared, sitting out there in an autumn jumble of sweatshirts and sweaters. As terrified of bombing as any stand-up comic, Meg still began every class on a wave of stage fright, even this semester with the prospect of success suddenly before her. Her good news was less than a month old.

"All right then. I admit Rufus Flagg isn't my idea of a fun guy either. What fascinates me about this book is how the author uses logbooks and ledgers to construct Flagg's private life, a detective story about a common man."

Hearing they were free to dislike Flagg, students began to respond to the man. He was a greedy bore, a New England Scrooge whose only concern during the birth of the nation was how it might affect business, a bad man. It continued to amaze Meg that even now, in 1978 after Vietnam and Watergate, freshmen still believed the world divided into saints and sinners, good and evil. She'd thought her chief obstacle would be the cynical belief it was all bullshit, but only her brighter sophomores thought that. Pointing out Flagg's human qualities, she could begin to disabuse students of moral certainty by putting them in Flagg's shoes.

History 201—American History to 1865—was a basic survey course required by all majors. Grad students and junior faculty treated it as a menial chore, but Meg enjoyed teaching "civilians." She liked the challenge of keeping their attention, involving them in discussion, making them understand this story might also be about them. She liked to perform. Her good news at the start of the semester was that she could continue to perform. She had finished her dissertation over the summer—"Reading, Writing and Empire: The Thomasites in the Philippines, 1901–1913," the American schoolteachers who came over after conquest, named for the *U.S.S. Thomas* which brought the first shipload—and her advisor said it was good. Then, with her doctorate a near certainty, Meg was offered a new contract that put her on tenure track. She was close to achieving everything she'd worked toward for the past four years, achieving it far more quickly than most. Success was exciting and strange, confusing on the top yet an enormous relief down below. Meg might be what she thought she was, a historian.

"I'm sorry, but I still don't get why we're wasting our time with this man," said Glick, a conventionally bright student who already had law school and a career in politics written all over him. "It's not history. It's just one man complaining about business and family."

"History is only the big public events, Mr. Glick?" Meg tried not to spar sarcastically with her students, but this exchange might lead somewhere.

"Well, yeah. The ones that affect us. *History* history. The stuff in our outside reading never has anything to do with what's in the textbook." The textbook was a standard narrative. The supplemental readings chosen by Meg were all bits of social history.

"Anybody else?" she asked. "Agree or disagree? Mr. Glick's made a good point. Why read about Rufus Flagg? Why waste our time with social history?"

Somebody offered a commonplace about getting the flavor of the past. When another student observed that Rufus Flagg made the past more real for her, "like it is in novels," Glick came back with the argument that novels were trivia and stories like Rufus Flagg's were just distractions from the real story, interruptions. "What does this guy's worrying about marrying off his daughter have to do with the debates on the Constitution?"

"It's the kitchen and the moon," Meg declared.

Everyone looked baffled.

"Social history and what Mr. Glick called *history* history. How *do* they connect?" She began to laugh at herself; the class was going well enough that she could afford to goof. "I'm sorry. The kitchen and the moon is my private language for this, the two opposite poles of human experience. At one end you have the kitchen: personal life, domestic life, absolutely indifferent to the world outside. And then there's the moon, distant and abstract, the spectacle of public life. It's not a female moon, but a lunatic moon, an abstract moon." She almost described it as a male moon, but calling the images male and female would take her from the point she wanted to make. "This is derived from Rebecca West, but you don't need to know who I'm stealing from. Years ago, the study of history was all moon. Now we're trying to work the kitchen in, and they do seem like different realities. It's difficult to understand how to connect the two, just as it's hard to connect them in real life."

Alice, the calf-eyed, short-haired freshman, raised her hand. "How do *you* connect them?"

"Well, as a historian I look for episodes where the two interact, the public and private, so I can see how they affect each other."

"No, what I meant was—how do you connect them in real life?"

Meg feared that that was what Alice wanted to know. Alice regularly came up after class to ask for further reading suggestions. When males courted her like that, Meg knew they were simply brown-nosing; it felt different from women, Alice's need for attention coming off her like a schoolgirl crush.

"Luckily I don't have to worry about that," Meg claimed with a flustered laugh. "My only concern as a historian is connecting the two in my work. But the absence of any strong connection between Rufus Flagg and what we think of as *the* major event of his time suggests . . .''

Pushing on to her point—the sheer inertia of private life is as much a part of history as the momentous changes—Meg was sorry she'd brushed Alice off. It was a good question, but not one for class, and not one she knew how to answer. Meg was in neither the kitchen nor the moon these days, but floating somewhere in between, a privileged post that enabled her to study both.

Finding a connection in the lack of connection, Meg went on to explore how the undeclared war and embargo did affect Flagg, the role they played in business failures he blamed on himself, working out from Flagg to the American responses to the Napoleonic wars that seemed dry and vague in the textbook, then back to Flagg again and the remnants of Puritan ethos in his self-criticism. Students began to defend him uncomfortably, as if seeing their fathers in Flagg—if not themselves. It turned out to be a good class after all.

When it was over and everyone straggled out the door, Meg expected Alice to approach and ask more questions. She didn't, and Meg feared she'd hurt the girl's feelings by snubbing her. She should have deflected the question more gently. Meg blamed the excitement of performing, which sometimes caused her to ride roughshod over students. One thing she feared about success was that her new confidence might make her callous, insensitive. She had to be more careful.

Meg went upstairs to her new office, collapsed in the chair and unwound with a cigarette. There was a strumming of nerves after every class, especially a good one. She had her own office this semester, a windowless room not much bigger than a library carrel, but it felt very snug and homey with her name on the door. On the walls were Meg's 1905 map of the Philippines, like a diced snake, a photo of women in shirtwaists and men in straw boaters having a picnic in the jungle, and the Toulouse-Lautrec print that was a gift from Ron Pulaski: a happy couple lay buried up to their eyes in a featherbed and quilt. Meg relaxed and wondered again how many years it would take to expand "Reading, Writing and Empire" into a real book that other teachers could use the way she'd used Rufus Flagg.

Knuckles rapped on the open door and there was Ron Pulaski himself, apologetically tall and bearded, a tweed jacket over his hospital whites. He had a bundle of mail in his hand.

"Saw you hadn't checked your box yet, so I knew you were in." He passed Meg her mail. "Had a couple of hours free while waiting for a tissue sample, so I bicycled over to see if you were in."

"I'm glad you caught me," said Meg, understanding what this meant. She flipped through the university memos and an unpaid bill for library copying costs. "You can't have dinner tonight?"

"Sorry." He made a long face—he had a long face anyway and his droopy eyes made sorrow look sweet on Ron. "I have to run these tests tonight during the operation. Schedule change. I hope you don't mind."

"No, I understand." There was a letter from her uncle, with Philippine stamps and a Manila postmark. She wondered if he were there on business or pleasure; she hadn't heard from Jim all summer.

"Would you like to go get coffee?"

"Sure." She looked up from the letter. "Or how about a walk? I'd enjoy a walk right now."

"Even better."

Pulling on a baggy, coatlike cardigan, Meg slipped Jim's letter into a pocket, intending to read it later. "Oh, I almost forgot," she said, and went up on tiptoe to kiss her lover hello.

They'd been seeing each other since May, sleeping together since June. Ron was thirty-three, a pathologist from Chicago who worked at the university hospital as a gastrointestinal specialist. Their romance had run through its romantic phase, the giddy, mutual surprise of two people discovering someone they really like, and had not yet found its next identity. He clearly loved her, and Meg thought she probably loved Ron, but with so much else happening this past month it was difficult for her to distinguish one excitement from another. Unlike unrequited love, which announces itself by running into a brick wall, requited love seemed to flow into everything else. It was a new experience for Meg.

She had had a couple of departmental romances with other grad students her first year in Madison, brief pairings made edgy by the competitiveness that continued even in infatuation. And intradisciplinary lust spoiled what Meg enjoyed most about sex, which was the way it took her out of her head and into her body for an hour or two. She had a couple of flings outside the department, and a complicated two-month affair with an English instructor named Catherine. Meg felt challenged by Catherine's interest in her, and curious, but her heart wasn't in it and Catherine was right when she accused Meg of using her to experiment with herself. Meg had hoped to keep that guilty truth a secret, but Catherine's emotional awareness was exhausting. After the Thomasites took over her life, Meg had no room for love or sex. She met Ron during final revisions, when she badly needed to come up for air.

It was windy outdoors, the blue of the lake glowing and fading as clouds raced over the sun. Ron and Meg walked toward the water under the bright red maples and flame-yellow aspens that spit leaves against the prairie sky.

"You look Virginia Woolfish in that sweater," said Ron.

"Woolf in cheap clothing."

Ron grinned. "How was your three o'clock?"

"Good. Quite good, in fact. Although I may have hurt a girl's feelings when she asked a personal question. I've got to find the middle ground between authority figure and pal."

She explained what happened and Ron didn't scoff at her concern. "Nice thing about my work is I deal with people's sections, not their emotions. But the kitchen and the moon?" His grin expanded in delight. "I like that."

"It was just a goof, something to get their attention and show them I'm not always the pompous academic. Don't you have any private jokes about serious matters? Private imagery?"

"I was just asking myself that. Yes, I see my world defined by the liver and the history professor."

Meg laughed. "No, you don't. If your world was that narrow, I wouldn't be wasting my time with you."

Ron had claimed she was lucky to be dating a pathologist: he had more normal hours than most doctors because the dead can keep until morning. It didn't always work out that way, but Meg didn't mind. He had his calling just as she had hers and they respected each other's vocation. Meg once joked that they both worked with the dead, but that Ron's findings had more immediate, practical uses. Ron enjoyed hearing about Meg's research and teaching, and he envied her ability to confront packs of living strangers; he saw himself as neurotically shy. But Ron wasn't the absentminded scientist he pretended to be in social situations, or the gloomy, self-involved geek his casual dress and shambling posture suggested. He looked quite beautiful in bed and could be very warm and defenselessly human after sex. He loved to talk after sex, discussing her work and life as well as his own while they loitered in a nest of bare arms and legs beneath the covers—the Toulouse-Lautrec print was not an idly chosen gift. Sex with Ron took Meg out of her head and into the body and back to the head again, but with tenderness and comfort accumulated along the way. She felt thoroughly comfortable with Ron, possibly too comfortable.

"My chief fear about success is that it'll make me thoughtless and callous with my students," Meg continued.

"I thought your chief fear is that it'll make you complacent about being the perennial observer."

Meg laughed. "That was last week. This week I'm afraid it'll make me a *complete* egotist." Her excited confusion over succeeding kept tossing up new reasons for why she should be dissatisfied over the achievement, without really injuring her satisfaction.

"I think you deserve to enjoy your success. For a little while at least."

"Oh I do," said Meg. "I most certainly do."

They came to the strip of beach outside the cafe in the Student Center. A few months ago they'd watched summer school students in cut-offs and swimsuits skylark or launch sailboats here while they met on the terrace for lunch. Two months from now the lake would be a desert of ice.

"You made any Christmas plans?" Ron asked, as if he too had been picturing the lake frozen.

"Oh, go home and see my folks, I guess. Why?" She thought he might suggest they take a trip together to somewhere warm.

"I'm taking a week off. Was wondering if you'd like some company when you went to Virginia."

"And meet my family?" Meg frowned.

Watching her reaction, Ron idly shrugged. "Just an idea. I wouldn't dream of inflicting my family on you, but yours sounds quite sane."

"They are, in their own quiet way," Meg admitted. Having escaped from her parents, Meg could appreciate them now. They weren't the reason for her sudden unease, her feeling of constraint. "I don't know, Ron. It wouldn't be much fun. And if my mother met you, I'd never hear the end of it. 'He's so nice, so sweet, *and* he's a doctor.' "

"And that'd be bad?"

Meg laughed and moaned. "I'm not ready to share you yet," she claimed. "Maybe it's just neurotic, but I'm afraid my mother's seal of approval might turn me against you." She apologetically took his hand in hers.

Ron seemed to accept her lie. He had enough neuroses of his own to indulge Meg in hers, even an invented one.

Her real reason for resisting was that such a trip might make their relationship too solid, too definite. Ron had never mentioned marriage, or even the possibility of Meg moving in with him, but she sensed those questions in the fond, timid looks that occasionally punctuated his silence this past month. The fact he hadn't mentioned their living together proved to Meg he really did love her. Love made him alert enough to understand she'd say no.

She gave his large, soft hand a gentle squeeze, sorry to be so difficult. "It was probably going to be a hit-and-run visit anyway. I should be getting back here to prepare the defense for my dissertation." Her review panel was in January.

"Sounds pretty impregnable already, from what I read and your advisor told you."

"It might be. But I'm not."

Did she love Ron? She thought she did. Then why was she reluctant to take the next step? Meg wasn't sure. She'd tried telling herself she could do better than Ron, but that wasn't it. Meg had felt differently over the summer, when Ron was new and everything else in her life had not yet begun to fall into place. Now, committing herself to Ron felt too much like declaring her life was complete, finished at the premature age of twenty-six. It wouldn't finish her, of course, but that's how it felt, suggesting to Meg she had deeper fears about academic success than were expressed in her little sparks of doubt. Success was a trap and she needed to keep one door open, not yet ready to house herself for good in the metaphorical kitchen.

Hand in hand, they walked along the lake, Ron explaining the tests he'd perform on liver tissue tonight, Meg guiltily flicking an envelope her free hand found in her sweater pocket.

13

A DARK GREEN, RATTLING OCEAN OF SUGAR CANE covered the plateau. Clouds of black smoke boiled along the horizon, looking like war from this far away, but they were only burning off the fields in preparation for tomorrow's cutting. Fire consumed the leaves and tops of the stalks, driving snakes and rats into neighboring fields or out into the clusters of peasant huts, the haciendas where the owners lived, even the streets of the nearest town. That morning Jim had seen a rat with singed fur limping down the alley behind the police station.

"I am not CIA," he repeated once again, first in English, then in Tagalog. He knew no Ilongo, the language they used in this part of Negros. "Tell them that, Father."

Father Dulag told the cane worker and his wife something. It was Sunday and the couple were still dressed in the casual, freshly laundered clothes they'd worn to church. They sat outside the man's thatch-and-clapboard house, at a bamboo table under a peaked roof of shaggy brown nipa palm. The house and yard were wedged in a rocky hollow surrounded by cogon grass and the tattered vertical banners of banana leaves. The endless cane fields began on the other side of the dirt road where Jim had parked the Mustang he rented three days ago in Bacolod City. The man's children played around the car, sitting on the hood, dancing barefoot on the hot roof.

"I am not looking for Communists," Jim insisted. "What I want are reports of violence on the part of the police or plantation owners. His name will not be used. The fact he was beaten by police won't be used as evidence he's NPA. All I want are a few details so I can give my superiors a clearer picture of how bad things are down here."

It was what he'd been telling people all day through Dulag, and the priest should know it by heart. With his black-framed glasses and white shirt with ink stains around the pocket, Dulag looked more like a shipping clerk than a priest. He and an Australian missionary, Father Gore, had been quietly working to organize and protect the cane workers from the owners and their thugs, and the local police who were indistinguishable from the thugs. Despite a letter from Jim's contact with Amnesty International, they did not completely trust this visitor from the American embassy. Dulag was willing to give Jim a chance, but insisted he use no names and refused to pressure or prompt anyone into talking. That decision must be left to them. Dulag lifted his eyebrows at the cane worker when he finished translating, two thick quotation marks around everything he'd said.

Exchanging glances with his wife, the man said he had no problems with the police, that he'd heard of terrible injustices suffered by others who messed in politics, but he was not a political man. "Life is difficult enough now that my wife and I must work in other people's fields after losing our own." That, at least, was how Dulag translated.

There was a long glossy scar on the man's left arm, but that would be from a slip of his own machete. There were probably even more scars like that on the legs inside his neatly creased jeans; Jim saw one on the wife's ankle. Everyday life here was brutal enough, yet Jim needed evidence of special brutality. He had come to Negros as a tourist of brutality. He knew he looked like a tourist in his drenched knit shirt and narrow-brimmed fishing cap, a new Polaroid camera hanging from his neck. He carried a steno pad, but that was only a prop; nobody told him so much he needed to write it down.

Jim gave up on the man. He took the cigarette pack from his damp pocket and offered another to the man, his wife and Dulag too, asking through Dulag how many children they had. Jim carried several cartons in the trunk of his car, to be used as bribes to officials and for the small courtesy of sharing cigarettes with strangers. He even smoked one now and then himself, to earn their trust.

Relieved the interview was over, the man luxuriated in the cigarette and became very chatty and hospitable. He made a drinking motion with his hand, then cheerfully sent his wife into their little house. Jim hoped it would be water and not more tuba, their palm wine.

The man was proudly counting off his children on the fingers of one hand, Dulag wearily translating half of everything he said about them, the two voices going simultaneously, when the man abruptly stopped. He listened to something in the distance. Jim heard it too: the chainsaw buzz of a motorcycle out on the road. They all knew who it was. Jim had met Sergeant Presquito that morning when he visited the police station to announce his presence in the neighborhood and claim he'd been sent by the American embassy merely to look into the living standards of the peasantry. Since then, Presquito had passed Jim and Dulag out on the road several times, ostensibly making his rounds but clearly checking up on them. This would be the first time he would see where they had stopped and who spoke to the visiting American.

The man gritted his teeth and stared at the short stretch of road visible from the table, framed by his house on one side, the parked car and wall of banana leaves on the other.

Then the buzz shifted down, wobbled and changed direction, becoming fainter. When Jim saw a cloud of white dust jetting across the ocean of cane in the distance, the tall stalks hiding both the motorcyclist and the road he took, he shared a sigh of relief with Dulag.

But the cane worker didn't look relieved. He knotted his face in shame and disgust, then angrily rubbed his face with one hand. He suddenly snarled at the priest and gestured at Jim. Dulag answered uncertainly. The man insisted.

Dulag turned to Jim and said, "He wants to show you something. I told him it was his decision."

The man stood up and Jim stood too, intending to follow. The man only stepped to the corner post of the pitched roof, looking over to make sure he was just out of view of his children playing around the car. He turned his back to Jim and lifted his shirt.

Jim knew what was coming. The bare back was covered with stripes, puckered ribbons of raised skin in the meat on either side of the spine. Jim had to resist his impulse to touch them. The shiny scars were real, skin broken open by repeated blows with a thin cane or car antenna. Jim had become an expert on scars.

"Who did this to you?"

The man jerked his head toward the cane fields where the motorcycle had disappeared. He kept his shirt up, insisting Jim get a long, hard look, spitting angry words over his shoulder.

Jim explained through Dulag what he wanted while he snapped the camera open. "I won't show your face. I won't write down your name."

The man glared at Dulag, then pulled up his shirt so it completely covered his head.

Jim stepped closer until the viewfinder was filled with a map of scars. He released the shutter, the camera whirred and a square of white cardboard popped out in front.

There was a sharp cry from the house. The woman stood in the door, three wet cups in one hand, a straw-plaited jug in the other. She shouted at her husband as she hurried toward him. He yanked his shirt down and shouted back.

Jim watched the white square take on colors and lines, trying to ignore the fear and anger he had caused, the woman pointing at their house and children, the man pounding his chest with a fist. It was terrible enough that a man had been beaten like this, that a woman could not make love to her husband or even embrace him without feeling the humiliation carved across his back. But for a foreigner to come to your house and take a picture—

The exposure was good; Jim would not need to ask for another.

The wife continued to shout. The husband lifted his hand and threatened to slap her. Dulag stepped in to stop the husband and calm the wife.

"Nobody will know this is you." Jim held the photo so the man could get a quick look, then lowered it, ashamed of what he showed him. "I'll be very careful with this. I promise."

Dulag was too busy with the wife to translate. The husband only stared at Jim.

"I'm sorry," said Jim. "I don't know what else I can do." He bowed his head and walked away.

The children scattered when he approached the car. One small boy had climbed inside to sit behind the wheel; he left the door open when he leaped out and ran giggling after the others into the brush. Jim sat on the scalding upholstery, leaned over and unlocked the glove compartment to stick the fresh photo in the envelope with the other photos he'd taken over the past three days. He turned on the engine and waited for Dulag.

The priest got in and slammed the door hard. "The wife does not want to be a widow."

"I guessed that on my own, thank you." He put the car into gear. "Where to now?"

"I think you should see José Olempos."

"Will *he* talk to me?"

"He won't. But his grave might." Dulag refused to look at Jim. "He was murdered last year. By Presquito or someone working for Presquito."

Jim ignored the blatant message there. "All right. I suppose I should get a picture of his grave. Is it marked? A rumor substantiated by a gravestone is better than nothing."

"If it's Polaroids of corpses you want, you should go riding with Presquito."

Jim kept his temper. It was the heat that made them angry with each other, the ugliness of what they had witnessed and could do nothing to stop. What could he hope to accomplish in his brief visit? His mere presence at people's doorsteps put them in danger.

"I don't like this anymore than you do, Father. It's idiotic. It's obscene. The reports you and Father Gore have been sending should be enough to convince anyone. But my people insist on hearing it from one of their own."

Dulag nodded at the glove compartment. "How many of those photos have you taken?"

"On Negros, six. Maybe seven."

"You will show them around Manila?"

"I'm not sure what I'll do with them," Jim admitted. "Show them to the American ambassador, in hopes they'll wake him up to the conditions down here. Send them to Washington with my report."

The priest remained skeptical, chilly.

"I assure you, Father, I'm not keeping a personal scrapbook of wounds I peruse at my leisure," Jim said bitterly. But it was pornographic, this collecting of photographs, this invasion of privacy. The bodies had been invaded once before by the police, but that first invasion didn't fully justify this second one.

"Your government," began Dulag with a sigh. "They will say this is a local matter and has nothing to do with Marcos or them."

"Maybe. Probably. But I have to keep trying, until I find the incident or crime that kicks somebody's conscience open."

They drove past the rear entrance of a large hacienda, where a guard in unmarked fatigues stood in the shade of a gatehouse with a shotgun under his arm. Behind him was a garden and the back of a villa, like a glimpse of California circa 1925. A few hundred yards further down the road, behind a high chain-link fence, were the wooden barracks where most of the migrant cane workers lived. Jim wished there were a way he could get in there and talk to those people. He had to make do with the handful of families who still owned an acre here and there along the foothills, where the ground was too rocky for cane and not worth stealing. Life had always been bad on Negros, but under Marcos a few rich men and their banks were able to buy out the small farmers through mortgages and intimidation, reduce the population to peonage, then keep them in line with the police and military. Not even the Church could protect the people. The violence was directed against attempted unions and strikes, and against the Communists. There were Communists now, real ones, scattered throughout the Philippines. The Huks had been replaced by the NPA—the New People's Army—which included embittered union organizers, university students, even priests. After years of crying wolf, Marcos had created a situation that made wolves inevitable and often admirable. Jim wouldn't have been surprised if Father Dulag himself were NPA.

Dulag had lit one of his own cigarettes from the lighter in the dashboard. "I disagree with Father Gore," he said. "I don't believe there's the slightest chance you might be CIA."

"Is that what Gore thinks?" Jim almost laughed. They were obsessed with the CIA over here, believing it to be omnipotent and omnipresent, the explanation for everything from the rise of Marcos to the lateness of the monsoon season. "But you believe otherwise."

"You're not cunning enough. You're too self-conscious. Too impatient. You're like a priest fighting a crisis of faith."

"Maybe I'm a CIA operative fighting a crisis of faith."

Dulag shook his head. "No. You are here for your own personal, private reasons. And that is why *I* don't trust you."

Jim knew exactly what he meant. What *am* I doing here? It was a question he asked himself almost daily.

Up ahead on the straight dirt road, a white cloud appeared with a motorcycle and rider in front of it, Sergeant Presquito again, racing toward them. He rode without a helmet, his long hair blowing behind him, his Hawaiian shirt pressed flat against his oil-drum chest. The only detail that announced he was more than a biker out on a Sunday joyride was the plump black holster at his side, with the wooden butt of a revolver sticking out. He grinned and waved at Jim before pulling his red neckerchief over his beard as he roared past and plunged into the cone of dust spinning behind the Mustang.

He too probably thought Jim was CIA, but then the Filipinos, as everybody said, were the most naturally friendly people on earth.

WHAT AM I doing here?

Pale green tiles and yellow cinderblock walls echoed every whisper and bootstep under the fluorescent lights, more like the entrance to a gym or indoor pool than the reception area of a jail. This jail was at Camp Crame in Manila and Jim stood at the front counter, waiting for the officer of the day to return from the toilet and take him to his monthly interview with Ninoy Aquino.

Seven years after his arrest, Aquino was still in custody, still awaiting trial. So much else had changed in the world, but not that. One of Jim's few specific duties was to visit Aquino once a month and see he was being properly looked after. Manila was full of political prisoners, but Aquino was the only one famous enough for Washington to follow regularly. Unable to persuade Marcos to release the man or at least bring him to trial—Aquino was too articulate for anything as public as that—the Human Rights Bureau could only make sure he was given enough attention that an accidental fall from a window or lonely suicide in his cell would be immediately suspect, although Jim felt that wasn't what stopped Marcos. No, Marcos kept his former rival alive for purely personal reasons, because of old social ties—they were fraternity brothers—or as a favor to his wife—Imelda had dated Ninoy before she met Ferdinand—or maybe just for the game of sparing an enemy's life. If cruelty was often arbitrary, why not kindness too?

Jim usually enjoyed seeing Aquino. The man knew the Americans could do little for him and used these visits as a chance to talk. He was as garrulous and witty as ever, and was one of the few people in Manila who could speak his mind without fear. Aquino had sustained himself in prison with a regimen of sit-ups and push-ups, and by reading every book he could lay his hands on, including a complete set of the *Encyclopedia Britannica*. Today Jim brought him biographies of Thomas Jefferson, Thomas Paine and Karl Marx. A round-faced corporal flipped through the books, looking for hacksaw blades between the pages and paying no attention to the titles. Jim stood on the other side of the counter and watched.

There was a faint moan in the distance.

It sounded at first like a man making love—the damp air and echoey silence suggested the baths in Los Angeles for a second—but this was a military jail in Manila and Jim's mouth went dry. He listened more closely and heard another moan from the hallway around the corner, then sobs and more moans.

The corporal heard nothing until he glanced up and saw the look on Jim's face. "Someone getting sick," he said. "Prisoners always getting bellyaches and moaning in their cells."

But the heavy door to the cellblock was pulled shut and there were none of the usual jailhouse noises of radios playing and men singing. The moans came from the offices around the corner and had a regular, official rhythm.

The corporal picked up the phone and dialed. "We have a man from the American embassy out here," he said in Tagalog. "Thank you." He hung up and told Jim, "I remind the captain you are waiting," then flipped through one of the books again.

The moans suddenly stopped. Perhaps they were waiting for Jim to leave before they resumed the interrogation; perhaps they'd simply placed a strip of tape over the suspect's mouth.

Jim took on a jaded, cynical look while he swallowed the dryness in his throat. If he could find out who it was, he might be able to make enough inquiries to keep the person from disappearing. "Who do you have in there? NPA terrorist? Another damn university student, I bet. Those spoiled rich kids are nothing but trouble."

The corporal was a poor boy from the provinces and his resentment of urban money caused him to open up a little. But he had no idea who they were interrogating. That was the Presidential Security Unit back there and they had their own private entrance. The PSU was Marcos's personal secret police, paying close attention to special matters that might be missed by the Philippine police's CSU or the Army's MSU or the NISA, the National Intelligence and Security Agency—a dictatorship acquired more departments and acronyms than any welfare state. The corporal said he disliked the PSU. "They are so *bastos,* so high and mighty. And they sometimes have women back there. *Dios ko.* One should never treat girls that way. Pretty girls most of all."

Jim was never able to find out whose moans he had heard. It wasn't the first time he knew someone was in danger yet could do absolutely nothing to help them. He kept expecting to burn out or go numb, but hadn't, yet.

WHAT AM I doing *here*?

He was in the Folk Arts Theater of Imelda Marcos's new Cultural Center, sitting in the presidential box behind the First Lady herself. Between the finny peaked shoulders of her brocade dress, the fat of her neck crinkled each time she turned to flirt with Ambassador Gough. As always, she had him eating from the palm of her hand. Very tall and handsome, Gough kept bending his courtly smile toward Imelda. Ferdinand sat to her left, glum and preoccupied, letting his wife have full charge of the evening. This was a little theater party she'd arranged for the American ambassador and select members of the embassy staff; no wives were invited. It was the opening night of a new production of *South Pacific,* with a minor American TV star specially flown over to sing the female lead.

Wexler, the yes-man deputy chief of mission, was here, and Chase, the economics officer, and Holmes, who was only the assistant administrative officer, but he was one of the few blacks in the foreign service and that was enough for Imelda, who now fancied herself an unofficial leader of all Third World peoples. Jim wasn't sure why he'd been included. By now the Marcoses had to know everything about him—everything. Nevertheless, Imelda remained friendly, mockingly intimate, as though she confidently believed she could bring Jim around if the need ever arose. Ferdinand treated him as a harmless nuisance, an attitude shared by Colonel Enéro, who sat behind Marcos and beside Jim tonight, a bald, pug-faced man in a full dress uniform stiff with ribbons and medals. Rumored to be Marcos's illegitimate half-brother, Ishmael Enéro was head of both the PSU and NISA. On the other side of Enéro was Captain Aguilar, his executive officer, wearing a dinner jacket instead of a uniform here, presumably so he could hide a shoulder holster underneath. Aguilar discreetly watched the tiers and boxes on either side. At the back of the box stood two of Imelda's favorite sip-sips, Dominick and Gus-Gus. Dominick was her dress designer, Gus her hairdresser.

While Marcos and his officers barely noticed the show and the Americans pretended to have a good time, Imelda thoroughly enjoyed herself. She lifted her doll-like hand for each song and gently conducted the singers, until finally, when Bloody Mary sang "Bali Ha'i," Imelda could contain herself no longer. She sang too, softly at first, then full-voiced, turning to serenade Ambassador Gough with one hand pressed over her heart.

Nobody laughed. Jim heard Holmes tightly whine as he held it in, but Holmes was new and dissociation was not yet second nature to him. Gough smiled, honored by the First Lady's singing. In the boxes on either side, people leaned forward to see if it were actually Imelda who accompanied the singer down below. Marcos continued to stare at the stage, too lost in whatever he was thinking to hear his wife.

Only Imelda seemed to get any fun out of absolute power. Seven years of martial law had exaggerated the couple's differences, turning her into a kind of court jester, hardening him into a stony Buddha. There were rumors Marcos was ill and that's why he'd become so sullen and stern, but absolute power had to be exhausting, endless vigilance and the constant work of punishing enemies and rewarding friends, without rewarding them with too much power of their own—Jim noticed that Juan Enrile, the defense minister, was absent tonight. Seven years ago, Marcos had been capable of enormous charm, not nearly as witty as Aquino but almost as talkative. Now there were few people in the world he needed to charm. He silently sat there like a dog guarding its bone, a man keeping an entire country locked inside his head.

Intermission arrived and everyone adjourned to the red velvet reception room behind the box. Marcos took Colonel Enéro out into the corridor to discuss privately whatever new scheme or counterplot he had worked out during the first act. Gough brought Imelda a glass of champagne and stood beside her tall, Spanish-style chair while she held forth on her belief that music could bring harmony and peace to the world. "I'd like to teach the world to sing," she said, hummed a few bars of the Coca-Cola jingle that included the phrase and laughed at herself. Gough watched for the return of Marcos, with whom he needed to discuss the renewal of leases on the American bases.

Jim had hoped to use the interval to confront Enéro but decided Captain Aguilar would do. All Jim expected to accomplish was to remind them someone was watching. He approached the man with a mild smile. "Good evening, Captain."

"Mr. Goodall," Aguilar responded with a friendly nod. He was tall for a Filipino, with a boyishly handsome face, aviator glasses like Marcos's, heavy eyelids and a Spanish grandparent somewhere in his bloodline. His manner was smooth and educated. "Are you a fan of the Broadway musical?"

"Can't say that I am." Jim readjusted his smile. "I heard some distressing news while I was out at Camp Crame last week. That the PSU has a special room out there, in addition to their offices at the Palace. This room is sometimes used for beatings and torture."

Aguilar closed his eyes and nodded. "We interrogate prisoners out there. It's an exaggeration to call it torture. No worse than the 'grilling' your police give suspects in the United States. And you should know by now how we Filipinos love to embroider for dramatic effect."

"I heard this man screaming while I was out there. It was not a routine interrogation."

Aguilar accepted that too. "It's possible. Our men sometimes get carried away in their fervor. But all is fair in love and war." He gave the business a bored sigh. "And there is a war going on."

There was giggling. Jim looked past Aguilar and saw Christian and Gus-Gus watching them from the corner, Christian whispering and Gus smirking while the pair sipped their champagne.

Aguilar lowered his lids and looked Jim squarely in the eye. "If you'll excuse me for saying so, I find your government's concern for human rights admirable but naive. And hypocritical. What happens in Communist countries, Cambodia for example, is far worse than anything that happens here."

"They're the enemy. We expect better from our friends. And besides, we don't give foreign aid to Communist countries."

The captain seemed to be studying Jim, measuring him in a way that had little connection with their routine remarks about policy. "Still, your President Carter has been very slow about putting his money where his mouth is. This program is little more than a p.r. campaign. Window dressing. That is the phrase?"

Jim nodded. It had proved to be just that, despite Dave Wheeler's promises, despite Pat Derian's battles with Holbrooke and East Asian and Pacific Affairs. The recent overthrow of the shah had made Carter skittish. Here in the

Philippines, the renewal of leases on the bases at Subic Bay and Clark was far more important to the ambassador than a few nasty stories about tortured dissidents. The Philippine government knew that, which was why Imelda remained friendly with Jim, and why Aguilar could amiably continue this discussion.

"I mentioned Camp Crame only for your own good," Jim claimed. "The PSU in particular needs to be careful about their methods, since anything they do wrong might be blamed on President Marcos. That could hurt American support of him if it made the news back home."

"Then perhaps I *should* look into it," said Aguilar. "Did you get the name of the man whose screams you heard?"

He was trying to learn exactly how much Jim knew, and Jim didn't want to admit he knew nothing. "Only his last name. I have it written down, but can't remember it offhand."

"Was it Lollio? Tommy Lollio." His expression remained playful, yet he lowered his voice to say the name. "Last week you said. Tuesday?"

"Yes, it was Tuesday." Torture wasn't so commonplace there'd be many candidates in a given week, but what startled Jim was that Aguilar gave him a name. The captain wasn't stupid. Either he intended to trick Jim or he was deliberately giving him a useful piece of information.

"Then it must have been Lollio. University student." Aguilar solemnly nodded to himself.

"I'll have to check my records." If Tommy Lollio actually were the name of the man he'd heard tortured—Jim would visit the university the next day and ask around—did Aguilar hope Jim might be able to protect this fellow?

Aguilar's dark eyes gave away nothing. "Yes. I will look into that. Although I doubt there's anything either of us can do about it. What's done is done. Colonel Enéro will be embarrassed that our people got carried away, and that you overheard."

"Maybe we can keep this student from disappearing."

Aguilar made a scornful snort. "Mr. Goodall. This is not Cambodia. Or even Argentina or Chile." He looked away toward the door into the corridor, where the bell signaling the end of the interval was ringing, and Marcos and Enéro would be returning.

"I understand you went to law school, Captain?"

"Yes. As did President Marcos. As I understand you did yourself, Mr. Goodall. But there were not many career opportunities for lawyers when I got my degree. I saw the future and it was police work."

"You didn't happen to be out at Camp Crame last Tuesday?"

The hooded eyes coolly stared at Jim. The captain said, "Thank you for your time. If you'll excuse me, I have duties to perform." He went out into the box to survey the theater before the president and First Lady took their seats.

Jim saw Ambassador Gough frowning at him from across the room. Dominick and Gus-Gus sauntered past, and Gus cut his eyes at Jim. When Jim

glanced back at Gough and Imelda, Imelda was smirking at Jim, almost winking. Jim struggled to block out these distractions while he tried to understand
what Aguilar intended.

They all returned to the box but remained standing until Marcos and Enéro
came back. The rest of *South Pacific* passed quickly. Lieutenant Cable was
saved from love for an Asian girl by getting killed. Nellie Forbush accepted
love with her French planter, despite his own touch of the tarbrush in two
Eurasian children by a previous marriage. The performance was warmly received. When Imelda stood to applaud, a standing ovation spread through the
tiers and across the orchestra seats like the overflow of a bathtub.

The Marcoses and their guests left together, riding down in an elevator
hung with blue velvet to a special side entrance, where floodlights and TV
crews were waiting. Ambassador Gough made a brief statement about this
classic of the Broadway stage being an appropriate tribute to the love affair
between the Philippine and American people, publicly thanked Mrs. Marcos
for a lovely evening, waved to the cameras and joined his staff in the embassy
limo.

"Whew," he said, sinking back in the black leather upholstery. "The
woman is certainly a charmer, but it can be draining having to match her smile
for smile." A lanky midwesterner with sandy hair, a basketball player in
college, Gough was in his mid-forties but had kept his look of corn-fed youth.
Jim was the old man in this crowd, having just turned fifty.

They had a motorcycle escort up Roxas Boulevard to the embassy, a mile to
the north along the bay. The bright lights of traffic and hotel entrances were
made a firefly shade of green by the tinted windows of the limousine.

"Shall we start the post-mortems now?" asked Wexler. "Or did you want
to stop off and do them at the embassy?"

Every social function, no matter how trivial, was followed by an informal
debriefing, the participants sharing impressions, overheard remarks, fresh gossip. Gough said they could quickly do that on the ride back to the embassy.
"I'd like to get home at a decent hour or my wife'll think I've eloped with
Imelda. I doubt there's much to discuss anyway. We were too busy smiling to
get into any interesting conversations."

Jim calmly announced, "I think I picked up something interesting from
Enéro's executive officer."

Gough impatiently groaned and looked away.

"If it's more torture-related scuttlebutt, Goodall, we don't need to hear it,"
said Wexler, automatically speaking for the ambassador.

"This was more than just scuttlebutt." Jim continued to address Gough.
"The captain let slip the name of the man I think I heard being interrogated
when I visited Aquino last week. A university student."

"You *think* you heard," snapped Wexler. "Rumors of rumors, cobwebs and
dishwater. You're making enemies for us peddling your secondhand gossip."

Jim kept his temper. "Those pictures I brought back from Negros were more substantial than gossip."

"That's the boondocks. We can't hold Manila responsible for that, no more than one can blame Washington for what some redneck sheriff down in Alabama might do," said Wexler, watching his chief.

"The screams I heard were hardly gossip either. Now I have a name and can find out where he is. If he's still alive." Jim glanced at Chase and Holmes, not expecting them to take his side, only wondering where they stood privately. Chase remained dry and aloof; Holmes looked faintly embarrassed.

Gough had continued to gaze straight ahead, letting Wexler be angry for him. He finally turned to Jim and said, very sternly, like an adult speaking to a child, "I don't like having to remind you that we're in the midst of some very important negotiations, Goodall. We can't afford to make the man think we're out to get him. You can stick your nose anywhere you like, so long as you don't stick it too close to Marcos. Not until the base renewals are signed."

"Sir, those renewals have been in negotiation for the past two years now," Jim pointed out.

"That's our priority. I can't afford to have you rocking the boat by running down a few excesses of the constabulary. Understand?"

"I'm sorry, Ambassador, but running down excesses is my job. If I didn't pursue this case, I'd be neglecting my duties."

"Damn it to hell, Goodall!" There, Jim had finally succeeded in breaking Gough's smooth confidence. "If you continue to pursue this, I'll have no recourse but to demand you be recalled."

"Very well, Ambassador. That's your prerogative. But my duty is to find out everything I can, no matter whose toes I step on." It was an easy stand for Jim to take. If Gough did succeed and Jim were recalled, he'd be freed from the futility of this impossible mission.

They drove past the guardhouse outside the embassy and pulled up at the entrance so Chase, Holmes and Jim could get out. Wexler would ride out to Forbes Park with Gough, where he had his own wife and family, and the pair could use the ride to discuss this further.

"Think about it," said Gough as Jim stepped out. "We don't need more enemies here. And the Human Rights Bureau doesn't need more enemies in Washington." He pulled the door shut and the limo purred away.

Chase wished them a quick goodnight and hurried off to his car. Jim asked Holmes if he needed a lift to the embassy housing compound, which was a few blocks back down Roxas Boulevard.

"Thank you, no. There're some requisition forms I need to look over before I go home. Up in my office," he unnecessarily added. "Goodnight." He went inside and Jim saw him show his identification to the Marine officer on night duty.

Jim understood Chase and Holmes perfectly. He was a dangerous man to be seen with. Chase was a dried-up character anyway, a pocket calculator of a fellow who restricted all comments to the economic situation, which was an absolute disaster under martial law. While South Korea had gotten development and prosperity in exchange for its loss of personal liberty under President Park, the Philippines stagnated with unemployment and poverty. As for Holmes, he couldn't afford to get anywhere near Jim. Not only was he junior officer—Manila was Holmes's first overseas post—he was black, which Jim assumed made him as careful about his standing at the embassy as a woman or homosexual might be.

Jim did not think they knew about him, not yet anyway, or else they'd try using it to pressure or discredit him. He was prepared for that.

Jim drove through the noisy, flashing party district behind Roxas Boulevard to an elevated highway that swung away from the bay toward the glassy black towers of Makati, the new commerce center. He had a house in Urdenata Village, one of the housing developments that surrounded Makati like fortified parks, islands of suburbia protected from outsiders by walls, electrified fences and security guards. Jim needed privacy this tour, and a house in a wealthy enclave was the only alternative to an apartment in the embassy annex. A security guard waved Jim through the gate and he entered a palm tree colonnaded street of ranch-style houses that was indistinguishable from middle-class streets in Phoenix, San Diego or, of course, Los Angeles.

His housekeeper, Tammy Lacaba, had gone home and Jim walked from room to room, turning on a few lights. There was little evidence of the Philippines anywhere inside the house. The furniture was Early American, purchased in suites by the owner, a trade lawyer who had moved with his wife to Hong Kong to protect his new wealth. What with campaign contributions to Marcos and solicitations for Imelda's "charities," success could be very expensive in Manila. He rented his house to Jim at a surprisingly cheap price, trusting the presence of someone from the American embassy would safeguard his belongings as well as give him a useful contact for future favors.

Jim left his shoes in the living room, draped his jacket over the leather recliner and went into the kitchen, which was utterly American too, except for the garish chromo of the Virgin Mary that Tammy had taped to the refrigerator. The figure, half-Spanish, half-Malay, held out her heart in one hand as though offering a piece of fruit. Jim poured himself a glass of iced tea from the pitcher inside, then sat at the kitchen table with legal pad and pencil to write out his encounter with Aguilar while it was still fresh.

He'd been at it for a half hour when the doorbell rang.

Jim didn't know any of his neighbors. There should have been a call from the gate if it were someone from the outside. He went to the door, stepping very quietly and keeping away from the windows, and peered through the peephole.

The porch light was off and all Jim could see was a lone silhouette against the softly lit street. The visitor was alone and humming a tune from *South Pacific*.

Jim opened the chained door and the column of light fell on Gus-Gus. He still wore his buff-colored tux with the elaborately ruffled shirt and was grinning from ear to ear; he had perfectly bonded porcelain tablets of teeth.

"Hello, Jim Goodall."

"What're you doing here?"

"House call. Aren't you going to ask me in?" He had a lilting tone that made everything he said sound gently mocking.

Jim closed the door to unchain it, then quickly opened and closed it behind Gus before more mosquitos and moths flew in.

Gus stood in the hall, bouncing on his heels, glancing into the living room. He had a roundish face that suggested he was fat, although he wasn't fat, only short and slightly stocky. "Are you alone tonight, Jim Goodall?"

"As always. You here on a special mission from Imelda?"

Gus laughed, a two-note "Hu-haaaaa!" like the high end of a trumpet. He shook his head, gazed up at Jim and began to sing:

I was cornholed in Kansas in August,
Rolled in the hay on the Fourth of July.
And if you can note
The great lump in my throat,
It's the cum of a wonderful guy.

"Dominick taught me that tonight," he explained. "I never hear it before. He learned it from the queens when he lived in San Francisco many years ago. You ever hear it before, Jim Goodall?"

"Can't say that I have." Jim had his hands on his hips, hesitating. "Oh okay," he finally said. "But I have an early day tomorrow."

Gus grinned. "Do you have any beer? I'll be getting ready." And he waltzed down the hall toward Jim's bedroom, singing his song again.

Every week or so, for the past two months, Jim had been visited by Agusto Luna, known in Imelda's circle as Gus-Gus, the First Lady's hairdresser.

Imelda had tried throwing women at Jim, beautiful, seductive girls who were intended as both a bribe and a means of tapping the new special assistant's private thoughts. Nobody was certain what the division of labor was between Marcos and his wife—she had her own people who sometimes seemed to be in competition with his people—but the girls appeared to be Imelda's doing. When they didn't work, she sent him her hairdresser. There was no other explanation for why the fellow showed up at Jim's house one evening with a blow-dryer and scissors and the claim he'd been dying to do something with Jim's scant hair. "The hell with it," thought Jim and sat the fellow in his lap. Understanding his powerlessness here, he felt he had nothing to lose. Afterwards, he understood he might have something to gain. If Imelda used Gus to spy on Jim, Jim could use him to tell the Marcoses what he wanted them to hear.

When Jim returned from the kitchen with a beer for Gus, Imelda's spy was still undressing and neatly hanging up his clothes. He had draped a blue silk handkerchief over Jim's desk lamp for a romantic, underwater effect. "Thank you," he said when Jim gave him the beer. "I want to wet my whistle."

Jim stepped over to his dresser to take off his own clothes. "So what does Imelda want to know tonight? What I thought of the show? Who I talked to and what they said about her?"

Again Gus laughed. "You are a very funny fellow, Jim Goodall."

Jim had let Gus know from the beginning he understood his real reasons for coming here. Gus always treated it as a peculiar little American joke. If it weren't true, however, Gus would be deeply insulted.

"I liked the show," Gus said. "Dominick put it down as bad, compared to the production he saw in the States fifteen years ago. But all I know is the Mitzi Gaynor movie."

Gus was twenty-seven, a protegé of Dominick's. It was through the older man he'd gained access to Imelda's circle. A hairdresser was low in the pecking order of her court, and a sure sign of how unimportant Jim was. The Marcoses hadn't used this yet, apparently hadn't even passed it on to their dear friend, the ambassador. They were saving it for the future, if Jim ever became a threat, not knowing that a man who didn't care would be invulnerable.

"Did you tell your wife you wouldn't be coming home tonight, or just that you'd be late?"

"Late only. I too have an early day tomorrow."

Gus sometimes spent the night. And he was married, with two sons, which hadn't surprised Jim. Most of Imelda's sip-sips were married, not so much to hide as to have children and continue their family lines. Being tight with the Marcoses was a boon that benefited their immediate families, their in-laws, their cousins, everyone. According to Gus, his wife didn't mind his sleeping with men so long as he stayed in Imelda's good graces.

"No no no," he scolded when Jim began to take off his shorts. "We save those." He had kept on his own skimpy, slightly frayed nylon briefs—a touch of poverty under his gaudy tux. His well-fed body was sheathed with a layer of babyfat, the hairless skin hiding his smooth muscles; his round shoulders were as narrow as his hips.

Jim sometimes wondered if he could've done better by holding out, if Imelda would've sent a muscular bodyguard or lean, ambitious army officer. But Gus was attractive enough, his slight effeminacy barely noticeable, and he was very easy to be with.

He smiled and came around the bed to Jim. "Hmm, *guwápo*," he said, running a hand through the graying hair on Jim's chest, stroking the stomach that no number of sit-ups could make perfectly flat again. He slipped both hands under the waistband in back and slowly drew the shorts down. "Boing," he whispered.

Because, despite everything Jim knew and felt, his body was excited.

Gus knelt while Jim stepped out of the shorts, then stood up so Jim could do the same for him. "Boing," he whispered again, more softly than before.

Jim brushed his chin in the mossy black hair, then ran his cheek up smooth skin to the nipples—Gus had the most sensitive nipples—before gathering him in his arms and kissing him very hard and deep.

All knowledge and distrust of Gus lifted during sex. They didn't disappear but lifted, hovering just above sex, intensifying and anchoring it. Jim was excited to expose himself with a spy, to be with a man who did this not only for mere sex but for reasons of state. Gus did it for sex too. He overdid his murmurs and gasps, his "Oh God" and "You are so *guwápo,* so beautiful," but those weren't lies, simply exaggerations to heighten his pleasure. He liked older men, older Americans in particular, which was perhaps another reason why he was chosen for the job. And he liked the fact that this American didn't play straight to his gay, but could do to him whatever he did to Jim. Neither of them wanted to be fucked: Gus claimed Filipinos didn't do that, then that it would mean a loss of face for him as a father—Jim couldn't untangle the cultural from the merely personal in Philippine sexuality—while Jim had finally accepted that something in him refused to relax there. But Gus and Jim did everything else to each other: tongues and fingers, cocks and balls. Gus knew how to enjoy the moment at hand, even when he knew the next moment would be spent asking questions and storing up casual remarks. They did their best to prolong the moment at hand.

They ended up top-to-bottom on the bed, Jim making love to a face that had legs for arms while another mouth and hand finished Jim down below. Jim's stoppered moans produced new moans in Gus, as if Gus were his megaphone. Gus breathlessly shifted around to straddle Jim's face right-side-up on all fours. Jim still enjoyed having him in his mouth, the little piston thrusting and catching against his tongue. But when the moans outside began to quicken, tighten, Jim had enough detachment to remember a different moaning. He suffered a rush of tenderness for Gus, and fear for him, before the piston tensed and Jim's mouth was suddenly very full, as if with his own saliva.

Gus lifted up and rolled off Jim's face with a satisfied whimper.

Jim discreetly emptied his mouth in a handful of bedsheet.

Gus lay grinning at the ceiling while he caught his breath, his smooth, unscarred body marked only by three neat patches of black moss, his nipples and mauve genitals. He had far more identity than Jim's old dreams of sex in the Patpong. There were times when Jim could imagine being in love with Gus if the circumstances were different. But tonight he was relieved that Gus was with the enemy, and safe from harm.

His spy twisted around to face Jim, half-curled on one side like a cat. "You are so hot, Jim Goodall," he said, fingering one ear, brushing some hair over Jim's scalp. "Oh. What do you know about the new man in the box tonight? The black man."

Whenever Jim wondered if his assumptions about Gus might be only a habit of paranoia, Gus said something to give the game away.

"I'm curious," he claimed. "Aren't black people in the U.S. angry and rebellious? Is this man happy to work at the embassy or is he disaffected?"

Jim couldn't help smiling. This wasn't a word in Gus's everyday vocabulary; he was too artless to make an efficient spy. If Imelda hoped to get her claws into Holmes, her understanding of American life was even flimsier than Jim had presumed. "No, Holmes is probably quite happy. He's out of the ghetto and on his way up in the world—if he was ever in the ghetto. He's more loyal and gung-ho than I am."

"I see. Just curious." Gus nodded to himself while he committed this to memory.

Jim could feel annoyed with Gus, but never angry. He leaned forward, kissed him on the hip, then slapped his bottom. "You'll want to take your shower now."

Gus usually jumped in as soon as they finished, saving all postcoital chat for then. Jim followed him into the bathroom. The high-tech blue-tiled stall was big enough for a small orgy, with a little steel bench built in along one side. Hot water and good plumbing were a luxury here and Gus took advantage of Jim's facilities every chance he got, sometimes showering before sex as well as afterwards, and even in the middle of it. He closed his eyes and smiled under the shock of black hair plastered down his face.

Jim felt hairy and old standing in there with him. He took a bath mitt and began to soap and scrub Gus's back.

"Hmmm. I feel much better, Jim Goodall. Earlier I was very tense."

Jim couldn't tell if Gus liked to use his full name for the sheer joke of it or to keep a little distance between them. "What were you tense about? Troubles at the palace?"

"With my family. My wife's brother is moving to Manila and I have to find a place for them to live. Nnnnnh."

"Mrs. Marcos can't help you?"

"Ha." Gus turned petulant. "Everyone thinks I am sucking on the golden tit just because I do the lady's hair. No, one does her favors just to stay in good with her. She never does you favors back."

Jim held him across the chest while he gently scrubbed his bottom. Having sex with a spy was not nearly as peculiar as giving him a friendly wash afterwards. "What kind of favors do you do for her?"

"Hair favors. Here." He took the mitt from Jim, turned him around and began to do him. "Your family," he said, changing the subject. "They never ask you for favors. Everyone in America is too well-off to go to family for money and jobs and places to live. You are lucky."

"I suppose," said Jim. "I've offered to pay my niece's airfare, trying to get her to come over for a visit. But that's different. You're right. We don't depend on each other financially. Only emotionally. Sometimes." He wanted to say "philosophically," but that would be too difficult to explain—his back to Gus, Jim's thoughts had wandered elsewhere. "What do you know about Captain Aguilar's family? Whose brother or cousin is he?"

"Aguilar? He's a nobody from the sticks. Another toad of the Scrotum"— the sip-sips' nickname for Colonel Enéro. "You should have heard the way the Scrotum talked to Dominick tonight, called him a flit to his face. 'Get out of my sight, you flit.' I think he's an old queen himself."

"Does Mrs. Marcos like Captain Aguilar?"

"She doesn't know he exists."

"What about the president?"

Gus stopped scrubbing. "What makes you so interested in Aguilar? He's nobody. And he loves women. Nothing but women. Don't even waste your time thinking about him."

Jim wanted to laugh. "Too bad. He's sort of attractive."

But Gus didn't hear it as a joke. "He's cunt-crazy. He has three and four girlfriends, *and* a wife. He doesn't like men."

"I didn't think he did," Jim assured him. "I was just curious about who his friends are."

Gus curled his upper lip at Jim. "I saw you flirting with him tonight. I thought, 'Haha, is he barking up the wrong tree.' "

This was getting silly. "I was asking him about an arrested student."

"Uh huh. I bet."

"A student I suspect was tortured by the police."

Gus frowned, pinching his mouth and nose together. He stepped into the spray to wash off his front. "I don't care if you have the hots for Aguilar or not," he insisted. "I just wanted you to know he likes women." He thrust his face under the water to end the subject.

Gus hated it whenever Jim mentioned anything specific about his work. He pretended not to believe the few details Jim told him or, in some cases, that it was only what those people, terrorists and murderers, deserved. When Jim returned from Negros and told Gus everything he'd seen and heard, *wanting* him to pass it on to Imelda, Gus was moved to tears and Jim thought he could win the man to his side. But then Gus said, "That is so sad. I don't even want to think about it. Life is full of pain and we should concentrate on what's good and beautiful. There's too much negativity in the world."

Jim could not feel contempt for such tenderhearted indifference, only frustration and pity. How else could Gus live with himself in this paradise of snakes?

By the time they finished and were toweling each other off, Gus was back to his cheerful, bantering self. Jim could not feel contempt for that either. He too contradicted himself wildly from moment to moment, mixing business with pleasure, brutality with farce, righteous indignation with callous aloofness. He wasn't sure who he was anymore, and there was nobody here who could tell him.

* * *

THE GUARD IN a blazing white shirt and gold epaulets stood with his back to the high chain-link fence, one mahogany arm parked comfortably on the submachine gun that hung from his shoulder. Jim stood over the shouting men and women inside the fence.

Out on the glassy black lake of light, the huge airliner rippled and shimmered like a silk flag as it taxied in. It grew more solid, lost its wiggle and halted. A stairway into air was wheeled across the tarmac to the door.

The crowd cheered when the first passengers came out. Names were cried and children lifted overhead while family and friends tumbled down the ramp, people returning from months of work in the States as nurses, gardeners, maids and chefs. They wrestled with cardboard suitcases, straw bags and boxed TV sets as they streamed over the pavement, happily shouting to the people screaming and waving behind the fence.

Jim hadn't seen Meg in six years and was afraid he might not recognize her. But then he saw her.

She lurched backward when she stepped out the door, into the furnace. She lowered her head and charged down the steps, fighting the heat, then trying to ignore it while she strode toward the gate and glanced all around, wanting to take in everything. She did not appear professorial. She was slimmer than Jim remembered and had long straight hair that hung behind her back. A shoulder bag heaved against one hip and a suitcase dragged her down as the heat caught up and melted her stride.

"Meg!" Jim shouted. "Meg Frisch! Wisconsin! Goodall! Frisch!"

He had to shout different names before one finally caught her ear in the babble of voices along the fence. She looked, and seemed to see him, although she continued walking toward the gate, her eyes screwed tight, her mouth hanging open.

For a split instant, Jim experienced a flicker of panic, a fear that he'd been wrong to insist on this visit.

But the limp mouth suddenly closed in a smile. She grinned and turned, going up on her toes to break into a run—only to sink in the ooze of heat. She drunkenly staggered toward the fence, grinning and gasping for breath.

"Welcome to Manila," he said with a laugh.

"Uncle Jim! Hello." Even that left her winded.

People around them kissed each other on the mouth—mouths were small enough to get through the diamond-shaped mesh. Jim's hand was too big for him to get more than three fingers out to Meg, but he stuck them through.

She grasped them with her thumb and index finger to shake him hello, and began to laugh, at the heat, her exhaustion and the absurdity of this fence. "How do I get out? Or in—or just through? God, this heat's given me brain damage."

"Don't worry. You'll get used to it. Salt tablets and water," he told her.

"Go around to the gate to Customs—I'll meet you there, flash my papers and facilitate procedure. I was planning to meet you inside, but couldn't wait to see you, Meg, even if it was just to watch you getting off the plane. It's really good to have you here. We're going to have a great visit."

"Over this way?" said Meg, lifting her suitcase and nodding.

"Yes," said Jim, regaining control of himself. "Meet you inside."

Meg trudged toward the gate and Jim crossed the gravel yard of the visitors pen into the dark terminal. He'd been chattering away like a schoolboy at her, rushing to say everything at once. He was amused with himself, surprised to be so excited. He had downplayed the importance of this visit, treating it as simply a three-week break from his customary solitude and the routine futility of his work, but Jim was genuinely excited to see Meg again. After all these years. There was none of the shame he'd always felt in Los Angeles whenever he thought about facing her again in person. It was as though his return to Manila had given him back his right to see her again, which he knew was a foolish notion. What it really gave him was something to show Meg in addition to his egotistical stick of self.

Hurrying down the long, half-cooled corridors of Manila International toward Customs, Jim was very excited and pleased and only slightly anxious to think Meg had come halfway around the world to see her uncle again.

14

MEG CAME TO MANILA FOR RESEARCH. That was the practical purpose for her trip. Expanding her dissertation on the Thomasites into a publishable book, she needed to investigate the archives, even though the best collections for her period were all in the United States. The National Library in Manila had been destroyed in 1945 when MacArthur recaptured the city from the Japanese, but Meg assumed she'd find something here, if only a keener sense of place. She owed it to herself to visit the country she'd studied off and on since her days as an undergraduate. Uncle Jim's offer of a round-trip ticket and a roof over her head were too good to ignore.

And yes, it'd be interesting to see Jim again, useful and informative.

Meg knew there were other, more personal emotions masked by her intellectual curiosity—her surprise over Jim's return to the foreign service, for one—but her chief excitement when she boarded her flight in Chicago was anticipation over visiting a country, not seeing an old relation. She prepared herself for a working vacation in the tropics, glimpses of poverty, hours in libraries and a friendly, low-keyed visit with an uncle she'd once worshiped, then hated, then finally accepted as merely human. She had no fantasies about getting an inside look at American foreign policy or the Human Rights program. All of that took place behind closed doors. Meg was prepared to see little during her three-week visit except what scraps her uncle chose to share.

She was not prepared, however, for the biological confusion of traveling by air against the Earth's spin. Thirty-six hours compressed into twenty, spokes of daylight pierced the airborne, all-night party when Meg's body insisted it was still dark outside. She hoped the swing through time wouldn't prematurely trigger her period. Meg was even less prepared when they landed, and she stepped from air-conditioned shadow into the blaze of noon. Despite the constant complaints she'd read in letters and memoirs, she had no idea the heat was like this, a thick fire that drained her body and went straight to her head. Drugged and breathless, she felt her way to the ground, wondering how her subjects had managed in long skirts, furbelows and corsets. When she caught sight of Uncle Jim in her stupor, he looked like a hallucination. Meg assumed she'd be met by a driver holding her name on a piece of cardboard, but there was Uncle Jim, standing very tall and pink and calm in a mob of furiously happy Filipinos, a white canvas tennis cap perched on his head. When he spoke, he sounded as loud and manic as the people around them.

Everything continued to come at her in pieces even when she got out of the sun: Jim's damp embrace when he met her inside, the cheerful efficiency with which he handled officials and took her past the long lines, the compact, toylike machine guns the policemen carried in the terminal proper, the steady bombardment of questions about her flight and family and plans as Uncle Jim hurried her toward the front entrance, carrying her bags as if they were weightless.

When Meg saw he was about to rush her back outside again, she had to stop. "Can we wait a minute? I have to catch my breath. I don't mean to be such a baby, but the sun here—"

"I'm sorry. I forget what it's like before you get acclimated. Here." He set her suitcase down to give her a place to sit. "Right back," he said, and Meg sat there catching her breath and feeling like a fool until he appeared in front of her again with a cup full of ice and a bottle of Perrier. "I should've met you in Customs with this in hand," he said as he poured. "I forget what a shock the tropics can be for the neophyte. And when you factor in jet lag to boot."

Meg sipped and waited for her fog to clear. She looked around at the international anonymity of an air terminal, its only identity the prominent number of brown faces and tropical clothes. A rainbow-colored centipede of laughing Japanese men in sports outfits trooped past.

"Sex tour," said Jim. "Japan uses the country as a giant bordello. Other countries do too, but the Japanese are much better organized," he amicably explained. "Wait in here and I'll go get the car. See if I can get the air conditioner going and things cooled off before you get in." And he was gone again, taking her shoulder bag with him.

Meg sat and sipped, already feeling better. Just being still for a few minutes helped. She felt good enough to be annoyed that her uncle had seen her like this, helpless and out of it, a kid again.

A Toyota pulled up out front and the horn beeped. Uncle Jim got out and looked around, clearly afraid to leave the car unattended. Meg had enough strength to pick up her suitcase and meet him at the door. He took the suitcase from her. "Sorry. There're magicians here who can snatch the contact lenses off your eyes if you're not paying attention. You okay now?"

It wasn't nearly as bad outdoors as it had seemed before. The seat inside the car burned through her cotton slacks, but a blast of cool air from the dashboard blew on her wet face and sopping blouse.

"I knew it'd be hot. But I thought it'd be like the South in August. I've been living in Wisconsin too long."

"You'll get used to it," Jim assured her. "And you've arrived at the hottest time of the day. I forget my first tour here, which was back in the fifties before air conditioning became commonplace. I was weak as a kitten for days. But then everyone's energy level was low."

"People probably made less trouble before the invention of the air conditioner," Meg said.

Jim laughed. "Americans in particular. That's a jeepney up ahead." He pointed out a small, gaudily painted truck with a roof and seats in back, picking up brightly dressed passengers at a bus stop.

Except for the jeepney, the landscape around the airport looked dissonantly American: American cars and the concrete honeycomb of an American hotel under construction. They drove out toward a large highway with what looked like a junkyard on the other side, hidden from new arrivals by a high fence covered with billboards advertising Shakey's Pizza, Love Bus Tours, the Bataan Golf and Beach Resort ("Come back to Bataan") and Chicken-in-a-Bikini. They stopped at a traffic light facing the signs, and young boys in T-shirts and shorts swarmed between the cars, waving at the drivers and puckering their lips at them in kisses. A giant bordello, thought Meg.

"Cigarette boys," said Jim. "They sell them individually. You need one?"

"I brought a couple of cartons," said Meg, relieved things weren't so bad that children were selling themselves at each traffic light.

The light changed and the boys stepped nonchalantly through the ferocious traffic to the roadside. Meg read more billboards as they drove down the highway—Girl World, Seagram's, an American horror movie called *Halloween*—until they passed the last one and she looked back to see the junkyard behind them. Children prowled the lanes between heaps of junk that were actually shacks, homes, the junkyard a muddy slum of cardboard, tin and green corrugated plastic under a forest of TV antennas.

"You'll get used to that too," sighed Jim. "Or used to seeing it at least."

"My only surprise is they did such a half-assed job of hiding it." Meg wanted him to know she was quite tough-minded.

"The Marcos way," said Jim. "Feeling better?"

"Much." Her head was clear enough for Meg to notice her uncle. "It's nice to see you again. You're looking good."

"Oh, all right for an old man," he snorted.

He looked much as Meg remembered him, only pinker. His tennis cap was off. He hadn't lost any more hair and it lay combed back from his forehead, pale copper covering his pink scalp. Tiny red capillaries had broken out in his cheeks.

"How long's it been?" she asked. "Five years?"

"Six. Inauguration Day, nineteen seventy-three." He glanced at her, and smiled, as if to say: *I remember.* "Here's what I've got planned," he announced. "Let me know if it meets with your approval."

It was too soon to jump into the past and Meg too wanted to get a better idea of what her visit would be like. They would take it easy today and tonight, Jim said, while Meg's body caught up with her. Then tomorrow he would show her a little of the city. After that, she'd be on her own until the weekend, when they'd drive up to Baguio, the summer capital in the mountains. The following weekend, he'd go with Meg on her six-day trip to Samar. She wanted to visit one of the other islands while she was here, and Samar was the scene of an important chapter in her book, contrasting the bloody reprisals of Major Littleton Waller with the experiences of two women teachers who arrived one month later.

Meg had hoped to go down to Samar alone. "Can you afford to take off that much time from your work?"

"Oh yeah. My work." He laughed. "That's turned out to be a very bad joke. They'll be glad I'm out of their hair for a few days, if they even notice. But you'll get an earful about *that* before your visit's through."

Meg nodded. She was curious, although not at all excited or eager to hear. She believed the whole Human Rights program was a scam, a public relations ploy, and dubious her uncle had only recently understood that. She wondered how much he'd tell her.

They were approaching a set of highrise office buildings identical to the ones stuck like stakes in the center of any medium-sized American city. Jim explained it wasn't Manila but Makati, a new satellite of the city. An unfinished apartment building stood beside the road, an empty bookcase of concrete floors with vines circling the pillars and knotting over the ground. A sign out front said *Love at Work,* with a faded picture of Imelda Marcos, identified as *Your Minister of Human Settlements.*

They drove along a stretch of brick wall, palm fronds and vines dripping over the top, and the car turned into the gate of what looked like an army post. Jim mockingly saluted the Filipino guard in the booth, and they were suddenly in a miniature Beverly Hills.

"Yes, it's weird," said Jim. "Very weird. And disgusting, but what can you do? It's a country with no middle, only wild extremes."

There were many evergreen trees, a few carefully plucked palms of various shapes and sizes, and short lawns so neat they looked painted on. A dwarf in a cowboy hat swaggered around an oval bonfire of flowers, his body twisted like bonsai, wetting the blossoms with a hose. The car swung into the driveway beside him.

"Mabuháy, Tommy," Jim told the man when he got out, spoke to him in Tagalog and introduced his niece. "This is Tommy Suka, my gardener."

The man lifted his hat and bowed his head, then began to bicker at Jim. Maybe Tagalog only sounded like bickering to Meg, because Jim never lost his smile while he listened, thoughtfully scratched his neck and gave his consent. He took Meg's bags from the trunk and led her up a short slate walk flanked by extraterrestrial shrubs whose cactuslike leaves were wounded with crimson flowers. "Tommy refuses to speak English on the grounds it corrupts his soul. He may be right."

The interior of the house was as American as its new-old brick facade, and air-conditioned. A pretty Filipina in a crisp white dress appeared in the living room while Jim set the bags down in the hall, keeping respectfully at a distance until Jim introduced her. "Tammy Lacaba, my housekeeper."

"You'll have a lovely visit," she announced, beaming as she stepped forward and seized both Meg's hands. "Tell me what your favorite foods are. Give me your laundry. We'll have much fun, you and I."

"Yes. Thank you," said Meg, glancing at Jim and wondering what to make of the girl's impulsive welcome. She looked younger than Meg.

"Would you like refreshments, Jim? I have made iced tea."

While Tammy returned to the kitchen to get things ready, Jim took Meg and her bags down the hall to the guest room, pointing out his study and his bedroom along the way. "A country of extremes," he repeated. "Feast or famine. It's far more house than I need, and a beautiful garden is wasted on me. Tammy and Tommy I inherited from the landlord. When in Rome—" He showed her the guest-room bath and suggested she might like a nice long shower before joining him for tea. "Take your time. It's really good to have you here, Meg. Really." He smiled at her knees, and ducked down the hall.

Meg was glad to be left alone for a few minutes. His eagerness felt more like fear than joy, and he seemed to think she was judging him, which had to be why he kept criticizing this life before she could. Meg wished he wouldn't. The fact of the matter was she felt too overwhelmed right now to judge or criticize anything. She wanted to enjoy the intense strangeness, the vertigo of this dream where the familiar was surrealistically scrambled with the new, the irresponsible freedom of observing things she couldn't change. Maybe she'd judge her uncle later—maybe not—but she disliked having the role forced on her the way he'd gently forced other roles in the past.

SHE FELT VERY good after a shower, exhausted yet solid, her fatigue all in the sweet meat of her body now. She put on clean clothes and sat with her uncle on a long, comfortable sofa. He seemed more relaxed, less frantic and fragmented, more accustomed to having a guest; he probably had very few visitors.

"I thought we'd have an early dinner, then you could go straight to bed if you like. I need to swing by the office for an hour or two, but Tammy's here until seven if you need anything."

There was already an ashtray on the table; Meg didn't need to ask. Jim said he'd offer her a drink but was afraid alcohol might knock her out in her current condition. They drank iced tea and talked like adults while Tammy set the table in the dining room. There was a heady aroma of garlic from the kitchen.

Naturally, he wanted to hear about the family, which he knew only from Mom's newsy Christmas cards. Meg had not been back to Virginia since the birth of her nephew eight months ago, but she thought Walter would be a good father and she liked his wife, Bard, who was very tough and funny. An executive something at a wholesaler—Meg couldn't remember what they sold —Walter put his wife through law school and Bard was working in a small firm outside Richmond.

"So there's a lawyer in the family after all," said Jim.

"I wouldn't have been very good at law."

"Too cutthroat?"

Meg laughed. "Life in the ivory tower has its own share of slashed gizzards and stabbed backs." She continued with family, describing Robbie's marriage, which Mom believed had finally made him a member of the human race. Meg's theory was that Gladys Fay merely gave Robbie someone to lord over and protect, but his paternalism had made him more responsible, even considerate. They lived in Raleigh.

"How's your mother coping with an empty nest?"

"She loves it. She's delighted, much to my surprise." Meg explained how Mom had become less a mother and more a wife, she and Dad closer to each other than they'd ever been when Meg was growing up. Jim seemed surprised by that, having assumed all along they were a perfectly happy couple—he must not know many married couples. Meg didn't tell him how she occasionally regretted the change, how after years of fighting her mother's cautious concern she was sometimes disappointed that most of Mom's attention was now directed elsewhere.

"And what about you?" he asked. "Seeing anybody? Living with anyone?" He treated it as a perfectly innocent question but the blandness of his tone was overdone.

"I've been seeing someone. For the past year, in fact."

"A whole year? That's great. Then it's something serious?"

Meg laughed and took a deep breath, not knowing how to explain Ron. "I'm not sure how serious it is. I like him. He's a good man. And he loves me. But I don't know where the relationship is going."

"You don't love him?"

"I love his self-possession. I love how he gives me plenty of space. I love" —they *were* adults—"to be in bed with him. But I don't love the idea of marrying him, which is what he'd like. I'm not leading him on. He knows where I stand. He's very patient and understanding, which—" Only made it worse, but Meg didn't know how to explain that to Jim. She didn't really want to talk about Ron. "It's your typical, modern academic courtship," she claimed. "Maybe I'm just not ready to settle down yet."

Jim nodded away his look of mild confusion. "I saw an intriguing T-shirt in L.A. just before I left. On the front it said: 'A woman without a man is like a fish without a bicycle.' "

Meg cocked her head at him, not over the familiar slogan but at his assumption this was a matter of sexual politics. "How about you?" she asked, and lowered her voice. "Or can you do that over here?"

Jim looked hesitant and Meg remembered Tammy could probably hear them from the kitchen. But then he smiled and said, without whispering, "There's a fellow I see now and then. Nothing remotely serious. I neither love nor particularly like him."

"A friendship with sex?" All the affairs he described in his Los Angeles letters had sounded like friendships with sex, if that much.

"No. Just sex," he cheerfully confessed. "Made interesting by extenuating circumstances."

"How so? It's somebody at the embassy?" She glanced toward the kitchen, afraid she'd been too loud.

Jim laughed. "No. Outside. And don't worry about Tammy. She's cool." He shook his head and chuckled at himself. "It's too tricky and complex to get into just yet. Maybe I'll be able to explain it later, when you have a better idea what it's like here at Kafka-in-Paradise."

"Fine." His aloofly smiling tone put her off, like the breezy note of the sex talk in his letters, an embarrassing mix of sheepishness and gloat. There had been something perversely satisfying about those letters, the spectacle of her uncle revealing himself as just another liberated gay man rattling away about once-forbidden trivialities, although Meg had also been disappointed to see Jim so shallow. Apparently he had returned to his old line of work with that sexual smugness still intact.

Tammy announced dinner and they moved to the chrome-and-glass dining-room table, Jim insisting Meg sit facing the sliding glass doors so she could look out at his tropical backyard. He explained the dishes as Tammy brought them out: *gambas al ajillo*—enormous peeled shrimp marinated in garlic; *lapu lapu inihaw*—grilled fish with more garlic; and garlicky stewed meat called *adobo*.

"Stewed dog," said Jim after Meg took a bite.

"Tastes like chicken," Meg observed.

Tammy screamed with laughter. "It *is* chicken! Your uncle is a joker. Dog is *aso* and only country bumpkins like Tommy eat it. No fear, no dog!" She returned to the kitchen, slapping both cheeks to stop herself from laughing.

"I see I can't shock you," said Jim.

"Probably not." Meg took a swallow of water to cool her mouth. "You said your work has turned out to be another bad joke?"

"Oh yes. To be sure. I've been orphaned in the crossfire of office politics back home, EAP versus Human Rights. EAP won," he indifferently said, cutting away the eyes and spiky antennae of a large brown shrimp.

"EAP is—?"

"East Asian and Pacific Affairs, Richard Holbrooke, director. Smart man, with Vance and Clark Clifford on his side. Thinks of himself as a hardnosed realist and of Human Rights as a pack of bleeding hearts who only muddy the waters. The overthrow of the shah and the mess in Iran threw things his way. Washington's afraid of losing more of their so-called friends. So we're a toothless dog, free to bark all we please but everybody knows we can't bite." He did not sound bitter or indignant, only resigned, with some of the same smiling smugness he used when talking about sex.

"Are the abuses very bad here?"

He finished chewing what was in his mouth. "There's worse places. You can say that about anywhere, but the abuses here *are* relatively light. It's generally people held in prison without trial. I spend a lot of my time visiting prisons and jails. It's dreary, depressing work."

"Do you come across any incidents of torture?" Meg heard herself taking on his glib, slightly bored tone.

"A few. Although it's difficult to distinguish between a standard police interrogation and what can accurately be called torture. It's not like Argentina or Iran. Extreme measures are neither widespread nor methodical. They don't have to be. The government broke the opposition years ago. There was a resurgence of student protest last year before I arrived, which accounts for most of the people I seek out in jails. And there're a few pockets of NPA up in the mountains, which accounts for most of the arrests outside Manila. But it's a benign if erratic tyranny. The worst excesses were during the first years of martial law. You won't see any massacres or concentration camps while you're visiting.''

He wasn't telling her everything, but Meg couldn't decide if he were protecting her or only himself. She was surprised he told her this much so soon. ''Are you sorry you came back?''

''Yes and no,'' he said after a pause. ''Try the shrimp. I know they look like gigantic bugs, but they're quite tasty.''

''What makes you *not* sorry? The lifestyle? Getting away again? Anything in the work itself?''

''Getting away?''

''I thought maybe you felt more comfortable in foreign countries.''

''California was foreign enough to satisfy me there. No.'' He paused for dramatic effect. ''I returned thinking I could do right what I did wrong before. I've learned there's nothing I could've done, which justifies my having quit in the first place. When my contract is up, I can go back to private life for good, without regrets.''

''You weren't happy in private life?''

''Oh, I don't know.'' He smiled and shook his head. ''I felt like I'd rushed things, jumped ahead to dessert without finishing my vegetables. So here I am. I say it's spinach and I say the hell with it,'' he laughed.

If he could be only humorously half-honest at the personal end of the subject, maybe she could get to him through the larger issues. ''Very few people had much faith in the Human Rights program from the start, you know. At best, it was just a show. At worse, moralistic imperialism.''

''It *is* moralistic imperialism,'' Jim conceded. ''A missionary imperialism. But since we're already committed to the economic and military varieties, why not go ahead and include a few do-gooder principles? No harm done, and it might even help.''

''But does it help? Or does it only disguise the blows?''

He glanced up, understanding this was what she believed. ''Maybe,'' he admitted, neither surprised nor offended. ''But one can't help wanting to soften the blows people get with bare fists, even if it's just to disguise them.''

''Wouldn't it be better if people saw these punches for what they were? Then they might fight back.''

''I think these people know they've been hit.'' He said it gently, without righteousness or certainty.

''Of course. What I meant was—'' What did she mean? An argument that made perfect sense in classrooms and coffee shops in Madison sounded naively brutal after seeing the slums outside the airport. How much harder did she want this country beaten?

''You might be right,'' Jim abruptly admitted. ''There's times I feel my job would be easier if things were worse than they are. I could at least make the people back home see what's going on here. But I'm no good anymore on the longterm scheme of things.''

"No," Meg conceded. "Of course it's right to help a few individuals. What disturbs me is how the program is used by the government to flatter itself with the idea it's good and moral, while it continues to engage in business as usual." There—that's what she really wanted to say.

"They have no cause for self-congratulation," Jim declared and sliced his fish. "Do you ever hear from our friend Doug?"

"No." The change of subject threw her, although she sensed some kind of connection hidden underneath. "Not directly. Have you?"

"No. Not since I moved to L.A." Two blue-gray eyes watched her through the wiry copper eyebrows while he put a forkful of fish in his mouth.

"I get reports from mutual acquaintances," she told him. "Last I heard, he was living in New York, doing odd jobs, still calling himself a poet. He's published a few, in a gay magazine."

"One of those beefcake publications?"

"I don't think so. I'm told this one has literary pretentions. And he has a boyfriend, someone he's lived with for the past three years."

"Good for him," said Jim, giving the news a polite nod. "Good for him." He treated Doug as only mildly interesting; Meg wondered if Jim'd mentioned him only to stop them from talking about his work.

"You haven't been in touch with him at all?"

He shook his head. "I spoke to his mother once. When I was in Washington interviewing for this post, I gave his house a call. I assumed he didn't live there anymore but was curious about where he was. His mother said he'd moved to New York." A sad look was gathering in his eyes—sentimental regret over lost love? Then the look focused, and fell solidly on her. "I still feel bad about what I put you through."

"Yes?" The sorrowful look alarmed her.

"I betrayed your trust. It was terribly selfish and irresponsible of me. I'm still not sure how I could do such a thing."

"You were horny and at loose ends. Doug was curious and available." After all these years, it felt very strange to talk about that again, especially after discussing foreign intervention and torture. "Feelings were hurt. There was a lot of messy emotion. But you opened a few eyes, yours and Doug's as well as mine. An education for everyone concerned."

He looked surprised she could discuss it so calmly. "What did *you* get from it?"

"Oh, the obvious. That gay men don't have horns and a tail. They can be your boyfriend or your oh-so-butch uncle. And it reinforced things I already half-knew. That good people can behave badly. That as a woman I was always going to be on the outside, with or without sex, so I damned well better get used to it."

He frowned, although she'd made the last comment without anger or resentment. "Do you ever suspect," he cautiously began, "that what I did has anything to do with your attitude toward men? Your distrust of them."

Meg stared at him. He looked so guilty and sincere. She laughed, a single burst like a bark. "No! I like men. I feel comfortable around them. I know where I stand with men. Yes, I'm skeptical, but that's a natural, intelligent attitude to take. And remember, I grew up with two brothers." He seemed determined to make the incident the most important event in her life. "I picked up far more skepticism from that than I did from our little episode. No, I can't blame you for any of the mess in my life, thank you."

"What mess?"

"Oh, this and that." She hadn't intended to bring conversation around to herself, but here she was. "The usual is-this-what-I-really-want-to-do doubts about any goal once you attain it. I like teaching. I like the challenge of being a woman in history—we're still freaks, you know. But now that I've got my shoulder through the door, I worry about what I've become. An academic? Those who can't, teach? The eternal know-it-all spectator?" She gave herself a mordant sigh.

"Yes, well. That's something all of us go through now and again," he said automatically. "But I'm relieved to hear you don't feel you have a grievance. With me, I mean. I didn't *think* I scarred you. But one never knows which actions will stick and which ones won't." He lowered his eyes while his mouth took on a slow, half-embarrassed smile. "Good, then. I feel much better now that we've finally talked about that."

Was he serious? Yes, he actually wanted to think they were finished with the subject, which should have pleased Meg. She too wanted to get it behind them and move on to more important issues. She expected him to ask about her teaching or book or dissatisfaction. Instead, he looked at his black-faced watch and said he should be going shortly.

"Make yourself at home while you're here. Don't feel shy about asking Tammy for anything you want. Oh, if you need to use the phone for any reason, I should warn you that there's the slight possibility it could be tapped."

"Yeah?" He had to be either showing off or teasing her.

"I'm not absolutely certain. But dictatorships can be terribly inefficient. There's a chance some minor functionary in the bowels of this or that bureau has decided to waste his time monitoring my calls." He treated the matter as an absurd joke.

"There's nobody I know in Manila except you."

"No? For future reference then, in case you meet someone. You and I are protected as American citizens, but we have to be careful not to get nationals into hot water. Let me think. I feel there was something else I wanted to tell you."

"I'm probably going straight to bed," she reminded him.

"Yes, you must be exhausted. And I have a full day planned for tomorrow.

If you have any peculiar dreams, they're called hypnogogic visions and are perfectly natural for anyone who's just arrived in the tropics. Something to do with the body's response to the heat and loss of fluids. Nothing to worry about.''

"I could use a few visions," Meg muttered.

He grinned. "It really is good to have you here," he told her yet again. "We'll have time for plenty of conversations like this while you're visiting." He stood up, stepped to the kitchen to give final instructions to Tammy, then crossed the living room toward the front hall. "Catch you later," he called back, went out the door and was gone.

Suddenly she was exhausted. The fatigue in her limbs swept into her head and her energy collapsed. She looked over the remains of fish bones and juices from a meal that now sat heavily in her jet-lagged stomach, a couple of imaginary shrimp antennae swishing about inside. She smiled at her exhaustion, and at herself for forgetting her low expectations while talking to her uncle. How else did she expect him to behave? She should just let everything wash over her—country, Jim, talk—without attempting to decipher or judge. She'd been trying to read their conversation as though it meant something, like guessing at the pattern of a piece of embroidery from the stitches and snarls of colored thread on the flip-side—Meg had recently begun experimenting with more feminine metaphors.

She went to the kitchen, thanked Tammy for a wonderful meal and said she was going to take a nap.

"I can cook American too," Tammy announced. "But your uncle wanted your first meal to be real Philippines. Sleep tight. Don't let the bedbugs bite."

Meg would have liked to sit with Tammy and learn something about her life, but there would be time for that. She drew the curtains in her bedroom and began to undress. The air conditioner bothered her, not the noise of it or the cool, but the fact she needed its protection. She hoped her body would adjust and she wouldn't have to spend her entire stay in the Philippines sealed up in bubbles of air-conditioning, looking out through windows. One can resent a window even while appreciating the privilege of a view.

The sheets and pillowcase were pleasantly cool at first. When she closed her eyes, she saw a rich green tapestry of embroidered leaves that opened like a curtain to the gray skeleton of a building under construction. Cartoon vines slithered like snakes around the concrete supports and under the flooring, lifting the slabs and holding them aloft in a new configuration of broken cakes and enormous fluted beanstalks. *Love at work,* thought Meg, conscious enough to remember the sign outside the abandoned project.

15

He let her sleep when he came home, then gently knocked on her door early the next morning. After a shower and two cups of coffee, Meg was intensely awake and eager to get out, her long hair neatly folded out of the way in a simple leather disk and dowel. Jim found her a pair of sunglasses and a white tennis cap identical to his own and they climbed into the car.

Jim knew they'd only begun to settle personal matters the previous afternoon. Attempting to address their past head-on had made him realize you couldn't talk away an old grievance in a few sentences. He assumed Meg already understood that, or else she wouldn't have brushed aside the subject so quickly. He took her dismissal as a sign that they should wait, and that she could be perfectly at ease with him while they became more accustomed to each other. Jim assumed she was emotionally smarter and more conscious than he was. He had to keep his own feelings as dull as possible for his work here, but he was excited by the prospect of being with someone who could afford to follow every shade and detail of emotion. It would be good to be personal again, he told himself. It would be interesting to see Manila through the eyes of a brainy woman.

First they drove to the embassy, where Jim could leave the car while they toured by jeepney and foot. Meg wanted to see where he worked, which pleased him. He took her through the imposing foyer into the dim corridors and cluttered offices, back to his own small office in one of the many annexes added over the years. "Largest plant and staff of any embassy in Asia," he said, showing her the view from his window of yet another annex, the processing center for visas to travel—and work illegally—in the U.S. On their way out, they ran into Wexler. "A niece, huh?" Gough's toad said with a leer. Jim was embarrassed for Meg, but she seemed quite amused and tough behind her sunglasses. "So they *don't* know about you," she commented when they were outside again.

A salty lukewarm breeze off the bay rustled the palm fronds above Roxas

Boulevard and kept the city's bouquet of burnt fuel and rotting fruit in back of the long facade of waterfront hotels. They rode up the boulevard in a crowded jeepney covered with murals of the Virgin Mary, like a Mexican chapel with chrome ornaments and tires. Jim had to stoop to sit under the low roof, but Meg could sit up straight, damply gummed to Jim and a friendly older woman who asked where Meg and her husband were from.

They began in the Intramuros, the old walled city north of the embassy, so Meg could get a feel for the Manila she was writing about. "Most of this is a reconstruction of what was demolished during the war," he explained as they entered a Spanish gate, but Meg already knew that. There was the machine-gun fire of jackhammers in the distance and one of the churches wore a rickety skeleton of bamboo scaffolding. Inside the church, Jim pointed out a grotesque wooden figure of a dying Christ, not crucified but garroted, strangled to death in the Spanish style with an iron band around his neck; the cracked whites of his eyes bulged painfully.

"If you'd come around Easter, we could've witnessed a real crucifixion. It's an annual event in a small town to the north. Men volunteer to be nailed to a cross for a few hours, in penance for their sins."

When Meg made a face and said she had no desire to see anything that masochistic, Jim confessed he'd managed to miss the Good Friday processions and carnage, despite all his years in the Philippines. "I've never understood self-inflicted pain. The other pain is awful enough."

They wandered in and out of dark, clammy churches and along hot, dusty streets. Jim kept the packs of would-be guides and begging mothers at bay by dismissing them in Tagalog—he trusted Meg could see there were far too many for them to give anyone money. They left the walled city and crossed the street to the Manila Hotel, stepping inside the slightly stained white wedding cake for a look at the high-ceilinged lobby full of murky shadows and ghosts of the American raj, banished today by a tour of overweight veterans and their wives waiting at the front desk. Out in the sun again, the broad sandy promenades of Rizal Park were relatively deserted on a weekday morning, the strips of lawn a yellowy green in these final weeks before the rainy season. The deciduous trees looked sparse and Mediterranean against the flickering light of the bay. A pack of girls and boys in jeans, students or hustlers or both, lounged in the shade of a stunted live oak and eyed the American couple without interest.

"I recognize this park," Meg announced. "From a photograph of the execution of José Rizal." She described a bizarre picture from 1896, in the days before the Americans came. Here in a public park, a line of soldiers in white held back a Spanish and mestizo crowd sporting opera hats and parasols. In the foreground, Rizal the revolutionary stood with his back to an assembling firing squad, a little man as bourgeois as his spectators, dressed in a dark suit and bowler hat. "It's quite surreal," said Meg. "Like something from a Bunuel movie."

"Interesting," said Jim. "No, Americans don't have a monopoly on cruel absurdity here." He pointed out the ugly concrete box on one side of the park that housed the National Archives and Library, where Meg would begin her research. He asked how she was holding up.

"Hot. A little spacey. But pleasantly so."

He took her to the park cafe, where they collapsed in two chairs under a mammoth flamingo umbrella. He wrote out their orders on a little pad the elderly deaf-mute waiter handed him. All the waiters at the cafe were deaf, he explained to Meg. "Whatever happened to 'The Invention of Masculinity'?"

She had removed her sunglasses and hooked them in the front of her shirt. She nakedly blinked at him a moment before saying, "Oh. You mean my idea for a thesis."

"Yes. It sounded quite intriguing. Why're you writing about teachers in the Philippines instead?"

"I dunno," she began, looking surprised he remembered, skeptical he wanted to hear. "It was insanely ambitious. The Thomasites seemed much more do-able." She was prepared to leave it at that, but when Jim persisted— and the waiter brought a tall glass of ice and cloudy papaya juice she held against her neck before taking a deep swallow—she began to talk about her field, carefully at first, then more eagerly when Jim maintained his interest.

Meg still believed her theory that masculinity was a recent invention. She hoped to write about it one day, when she'd mastered the sources and found a story she could hang it on. Her master's thesis on representations of women in dime fiction had been a dreary, tiresome task with only themes to explore and no real people. She found she needed people she could like or dislike to keep herself excited during the long haul of a project. Ideas and larger social themes worked best for her when they came in the course of telling a story. Understanding that, Meg had hunted around for an incident or life as a topic for her dissertation. She almost went back to a story she'd written about as an undergraduate, the trial of a Marine major after the Samar massacres in the Philippine-American War. "But the man didn't interest me anymore. I was burned out on atrocities, men as killers, bloodshed and violence. But reinvestigating Littleton Waller, I stumbled upon the letters of a woman who came to Samar while he was still there. A teacher from Massachusetts named Emily Chalmers. She met him on a picnic in the jungle and mentioned him in a letter home: 'a charming marionette with a head stuffed with old orders.' Her collected papers were at Sarah Lawrence and I read through them, thinking she might give me a new angle on the massacres. Instead, I became fascinated with *her* work, the teaching and bureaucratic battles and the Thomasites in general. Maybe what they accomplished isn't so wonderful either—literacy as intellectual colonization—but their intentions were good, and good intentions are more complicated and interesting than blind brutality." She closed with an apologetic laugh. "Sorry to tell such a shaggy dog story. But you asked how I got to the Thomasites."

"No, I'm intrigued," said Jim. "I had no idea historical research could be so autobiographical."

"It's not," she said. "Not really. But there needs to be a personal element, for me anyway. To keep myself involved."

"I was thinking in particular of you being a teacher yourself."

"Yeap. A colonizer of young minds," Meg mockingly confessed.

Jim suspected he was somehow involved too, in the setting of the Philippines if nowhere else, but he couldn't mention that without making himself sound hopelessly narcissistic.

"And there's the hook that this story has women as well as men," Meg continued. "The commissioner was male, but there were as many women as men out on their own in towns and villages. I get tired of writing about men without women, and sick of the accusation I'm male-identified."

"Male—?"

"Identified. It's the feminist version of the old line, 'She won't be happy until she grows a pair between her legs' "—Meg growled the phrase in a gruff bass. "Which is ridiculous. I want to write about people doing things in the world, which until recently meant men. But with the Thomasites I've been able to study women's mistakes as well as men's, their whole different balance of sympathy, racism, stiffness and accomodation, the same elements but put together differently." She began to laugh. "All right. Maybe my book *is* autobiographical. Maybe I express myself best only when I'm writing about dead people."

"You express yourself in your work," Jim told her.

"Yes. Yes, I do." She sounded surprised he said that, amused and satisfied.

Jim had said only what seemed obvious to him, but he pursued it, asking to read her dissertation. Meg hadn't brought a copy but she promised to send the manuscript of the book when she finished. Rewriting it for publication, she was putting in all the anecdotes and personal asides she'd had to leave out to satisfy the professional requirement that dissertations be unreadable.

And that seemed to be the end of the matter. But when they moved on to other topics—their scheduled trip to Samar, the itinerary for this evening—something had changed between them. Jim couldn't identify exactly what, but Meg seemed more relaxed and open, with fewer darting glances and hesitancies in her conversation. There'd been a carefulness to her that Jim didn't notice until it was gone. Perhaps it was nothing more than a show of interest in her work that put Meg at ease, but their detour through the Thomasites seemed to settle something, if only a fear all conversation would be at the extremes of personal grievance or touristy chitchat.

THEY RETURNED TO the house that afternoon for naps and showers before they went out again for a tour of Manila at night. Jim put on a fancily embroidered barong, more for Meg's amusement than his own comfort—even with a T-shirt underneath, Jim was painfully conscious of the body hairs pricking through the gauze. Meg wore her long hair loose again, with a silk blouse and flowing trousers that made her appear quite feminine without lipstick or mascara.

Once again Jim left the car at the embassy. They took a cab to the southern end of the bay strip for dinner in the restaurant on the roof of the new Philippine Plaza Hotel. A feathery blaze of crimson, pink and gold filled the sky and bay, the black shapes of Bataan and Corregidor floating unharmed in the fire. Down below in the Ermita, bars and clubs leaked red neon on the streams of people crowding the narrow streets. Jim pointed out the Pasig River far to the north, following the shiny band inland with his finger until he found for Meg the bend where the ivory box of the Malacanang Palace stood.

After dinner, they descended in a glass elevator through the atrium with its artificial jungle and waterfall to the disco beneath the hotel. "I thought we'd start the expedition with something familiar," Jim explained, to which Meg replied the only disco she knew was the one in *Saturday Night Fever*.

It was early yet and the booths on the terraces around the dance floor were filled with an older, more western crowd than Jim expected. A few Japanese men savagely frugged with graceful, smiling Filipinas under the flashing lights and spinning police car cherries. Jim gave a barechested young man in harem pants a fifty-peso note—three dollars—and requested a table as far as possible from the incessant shriek and crump of music. "World War Two with a beat," said Meg.

They were seated in a dark corner beside a six-foot centerpiece of calla lilies and bird-of-paradise plants. The disco was called Oasis, which explained the palm tree silhouettes painted on the lavender walls, and the harem pants. Ordering drinks, Jim felt shy about noticing their waiter's smooth chest and protuberant navel, or the fact the fellow wasn't wearing any underpants. Then, deciding he had nothing to hide from Meg, Jim watched for its jiggle when the waiter turned to walk away.

"No worse than some of my undergrads in cut-offs," Meg observed. "The boys can be as bad now as people used to say girls were."

"This is rather modest compared to what you see in some clubs in the Ermita. There the waiters compete with the floor shows. Sometimes they *are* the floor show. Which can be quite peculiar when they come back afterwards and ask if there'll be anything else."

"Sex shows," said Meg, very matter-of-factly.

"Yes. Well, my experience is limited to boy shows, of course. And only one. A friend insisted on giving me a tour of gay Manila. Rather innocent," he claimed. "Two boys—young men, in fact, although that does go on, sad to say. But two young men stood in a shallow plastic tub and gave each other a friendly bath."

"Rubba-dub-dub," said Meg.

"And beyond. They have a thing about cleanliness here, so I suppose it has special erotic meaning." He was amused by the ease with which he described this to Meg. Gus had also taken him that night to a bar whose floor show was for sale—a dozen young men sat naked in a row of chairs on stage, listlessly pulling on themselves while they waited to be noticed by the customers drinking at the tables—but Meg didn't need to hear about that. Jim had found the spectacle of sex reduced to a police lineup sad and depressing.

"This bathtub show is one of the places we'll be seeing tonight?"

"Uh, I hadn't intended to take you. No."

"Women aren't allowed?"

"There were women the time I went," Jim admitted. "With their husbands or boyfriends, which was odd."

"Maybe they go for bath tips," said Meg. "I'd like to see this place."

Jim laughed, pretending Meg was joking, although he knew she wasn't. "No. I think not."

"How come? You have me curious. I've never watched two men having sex. It could be very educational." Her persistance was playful, with nothing malicious in her smile.

"I don't know, Meg. I'd feel strange seeing that with my niece."

"But why? You've made me a witness to so much else in your life. Why draw the line there?"

"Witness?"

"It's what you said in one of your letters. I'm your witness and judge. I don't want to judge, but I would like to witness. This bathtub show at least."

He had said that, hadn't he? He still believed it too, but the idea had an ugly sound when expressed aloud, even as a joke.

"I think of you more as a confidante. A friend," he explained.

"I can be that too. Don't look so nervous!" she said with a laugh. "You should see the expression on your face. I mentioned it only because I can't understand why you're so shy about taking me to this club."

"Let me think about it. I'm not as modern as I'd like to be, you know."

The waiter returned with their drinks and Jim put himself at ease again with a sip of scotch. Meg lit another cigarette and sat there, taking in the people on the dance floor and booths.

"Did you want to dance?" asked Jim.

"Maybe later. I'm not much on dancing." She was watching someone behind Jim. Her eyebrows came together. "What's happening down there?"

Jim twisted around to look. Off to the center of the terrace below theirs, two policemen in white helmets went from table to table, escorting a man in a white dinner jacket. The man spoke briefly to the customers, who promptly stood up, took their drinks and moved elsewhere. More boys in harem pants rushed over to shift the abandoned tables together. The policemen withdrew and the man in the white dinner jacket surveyed the disco with his hands on his hips: Captain Aguilar from the PSU.

"You might get to witness something after all," said Jim. "They appear to be setting up for a V.I.P. and his guests. Or *her* guests, as the case may be."

Yes. A moment later, when Aguilar finished securing the area, a herd of smiles descended the stairs, in gold chains and silky clothes, surrounding a giddy, bubbling Imelda Marcos. She bubbled for the sake of a very tanned, tall American whose perfect smile looked more effortless than any politician's smile. When Filipinos around the room dutifully applauded—tardily joined by a few foreigners—Imelda pretended with a flurry of hand gestures the applause was for her guest.

Jim patted his palms together; Meg only stared.

"It's really her," she muttered.

"In the flesh. She likes to get out and mingle with the *hoi polloi*. I have no idea who that is with her."

"He's a movie star," said Meg. "A celebrity, only—I can't quite remember his name."

Imelda graciously sat in the chair the movie star held for her, then the rest of the entourage swept in around the table. Jim spotted Dominick, with an arm around the waist of a bashful waiter, which meant Gus was probably somewhere in that gaggle. Once everyone was seated, it was impossible to distinguish faces against the flicker and flash of the dance floor. Imelda herself was reduced to a solid hairdo and extravagantly articulate left hand. One could feel people throughout the room struggling to forget she was here, but it was like trying to ignore the presence of a television camera crew. Not even the thudding music could muffle her: the couples on the dance floor lurched and spun self-consciously.

"We could quietly slip out," said Jim. "Or I could take you down and introduce you."

Meg smirked. "Let me think about it. Finish my cigarette. Maybe have another drink." She wasn't joking.

"She won't bite your head off," Jim assured her. "She can be quite charming, in fact."

"I don't want to be charmed. No, I'm afraid of what I might say to her. Or of hating myself for what I don't say." Frowning, she studied Imelda again.

"She's relatively innocent, compared to her husband anyway. So far as I know she hasn't had anyone thrown into prison."

"But she's part of it," Meg declared. "I don't believe in innocent wives. Ignorance is no excuse and willed ignorance is just as culpable as consent." Meg faced Jim again, smiling at herself as she shook her head. "Call me neurotic, but I'd rather *not* meet Imelda Marcos."

"No problem," said Jim, surprised by her attitude. Most people would jump at the chance to meet someone so notorious. "Uh oh. We've been spotted."

Standing by the aisle like a maitre d', Captain Aguilar was gazing up at their corner, his face tactfully angled away from Goodall and a young lady friend. Not until Jim lifted his hand did Aguilar smile and acknowledge they'd seen each other. He jauntily trotted up the steps to their level.

"Mr. Goodall." He smoothly shook Jim's hand. "One doesn't expect to see you 'on the town.' "

"Captain Aguilar, my niece. Dr. Margaret Frisch." Jim included her title to weaken the obvious assumptions, although Aguilar should know through Gus what Jim's tastes were. "A history professor at the University of Wisconsin."

"Not a professor yet. Not even full faculty," muttered Meg, studying Aguilar with her face half-turned toward Jim's.

Aguilar delicately adjusted the frame of his aviator glasses, the better to examine Meg with his heavy-lidded eyes. His smile was congenial, authoritative.

"The captain is with the Presidential Security Unit. He's the right hand man of Colonel Enéro, who's right-hand man to Marcos himself."

Aguilar laughed. "You exaggerate my importance, Mr. Goodall. I am more the left hand of a left hand, which is why I'm playing chaperon to the First Lady and her friends tonight." He glanced back to see where they were.

"I'd invite you to join us, Captain, but I know you're busy."

"Not at all. Now that everyone's settled in, I can spare a minute. May I?" He pulled a chair and turned it toward Imelda. "You're visiting your uncle? You have an excellent guide. He knows Manila quite well. How long will you be here?"

Meg looked at Jim, understanding the question might be more than just idle chat.

"Three weeks," Jim answered for her. "She's finishing a book on the Thomasites."

"The Thomasites? You don't say." Aguilar leaned to one side, resting his elbow on the back of his chair. "My grandfather tells stories of being taught by Thomasites."

"Really." Meg was polite but skeptical.

"Oh yes. An American lady came to his village in 1910, 1915? He said she looked like a beautiful ghost. She taught them how to spell *apple*." He chuckled. "Even though they'd never seen an apple before."

"Where was this?" asked Meg.

Ilco norte—northern Luzon, the Marcos family's home province—but Aguilar didn't know the teacher's name; his grandfather called her simply the Pale Lady. He told other bits and pieces as he remembered them, periodically looking down at Mrs. Marcos's party or sharing a smile with Jim. There was an ulterior motive to this visit, but Jim couldn't tell if he were the object or Meg herself. If Aguilar hoped to get an inside line on Jim, he'd do much better picking Gus's brain than Meg's. But he was said to be a womanizer, and Meg—even under the name Dr. Frisch—was an attractive woman tonight. Jim trusted her to recognize and know how to handle that possibility.

"Good evening, Jim Goodall."

Think of the devil: It was Gus. He stood behind Jim, bouncing on the balls of his feet to the music, jiggling the gold charms hanging low in his open shirt. He grinned slyly.

"I could not believe my eyes when I look and see *who* the captain is chatting up. And then I see this pretty woman with the ravishing hair—well!" His effeminacy was turned up full, either because he'd been performing for Imelda's guests or deliberately to annoy Jim. He gave Meg a sarcastically appreciative look, swinging his hips as he gazed. His black hair was lightly puffed up and frozen in place with hairspray.

"Gus, this is my niece, Meg Frisch. Meg, Mr. Agusto Luna."

"A niece, huh? A niece." He leaned over the table to examine Meg's face; he was drenched in cologne. "I am looking for the family resemblance. No. All I see are the large noses. But all Americans have big noses. You have very lovely hair though. I do hair, you see. Mrs. Marcos's hair and the hair of her very best friends."

Aguilar remained aloof and amused. "You'll have to excuse our friend, Dr. Frisch. Gus is what we call a sip-sip."

"A sip-sip? You call *me* a sip-sip?" The insult made Gus even more outrageous, one hand indignantly slapping the air over Aguilar's head. "Jim Goodall, you are going to just sit there and let this man call me a sip-sip?"

Jim had never seen him so indiscreet and obnoxious. He might have found it funny if Meg weren't present. "Gus, stop being such a nuisance. Please."

"Macho man," said Gus. "Macho, macho man. I want to be a macho man," he sang, with the song now playing in the speakers over the dance floor. "Do you want to dance, Jim Goodall?"

Jim laughed, dismissing the invitation as a joke, sharing the joke with Meg. She looked attentive yet unthreatened, calmly taking it all in.

"How about you, Captain? Dance with the silly sip-sip."

But Aguilar was watching Mrs. Marcos again. She'd stood up, patches of her dress shimmering like fish scales. She took the hand of the American movie star and led him down the steps toward the dance floor.

"You'll have to excuse me. Duty calls," Aguilar told Meg. "This has been fascinating. I hope we'll be able to continue while you're here." He gave Jim an officious smile and nod. "Mr. Goodall."

Aguilar made his way down to the flashing dance floor, then idly wandered along its perimeter. The First Lady and the American star pumped their arms at each other to the beat of "Macho Man," the star smiling off into the distance, Imelda unable to take her eyes off the star. She loved occasions that created rumors.

"Look at that dress," sniffed Gus. "Dominick could dress her in the latest, smartest best, but all she wants is sequins, more and more sequins. She can be such a disappointment."

"You do her hair?" asked Meg.

"Yes. You like it? It looks good?"

"Lovely."

"Thank you. I could do much more for her, but that is how she wants it. Tight and shiny. Like some hearts I know." Gus was looking at Jim, his mouth in a critical pout. The departure of Aguilar had made him slightly less frantic. "And you are Jim Goodall's niece?" he drily asked.

"Yes. He's my mother's brother."

"I've told you about Meg," said Jim, deciding there was no hiding the fact that Gus was more than a casual acquaintance. "This is the niece I've been inviting to visit. She'll be staying with me for three weeks."

"Hmmmph." The pout opened into a sly curl on one side. "I need to see you tonight, Jim Goodall."

"Tonight's no good," said Jim, smiling at Meg, clearing his throat for Gus. "We'll be out late, as I'm sure you will be too. Mrs. Marcos is something of an insomniac," he explained to Meg. "Whether she's out on the town or entertaining at home, she rarely turns in before dawn."

"I can slip away," said Gus. "What time will you get home?"

"No, Gus. Not while I have company."

"Don't worry about me," said Meg. "If you two need to, uh, discuss something, I can make myself scarce."

"It's nothing that can't wait until later," Jim declared.

Gus accepted with a heavy, melodramatic sigh. He suddenly smiled at Meg and fingered the air much too close to Jim's face. "Did you ever notice the teeny little blood vessels on your uncle's cheeks? They look just like the red threads in American dollar bills. Beautiful, very beautiful." There was a cunning look of triumph in his smile, as though he thought he'd just ruined Jim completely in his niece's eyes.

Meg cocked her head to look, her mouth pinched tight to keep herself from grinning.

"Old age and sun," said Jim.

Another boy in harem pants appeared beside Gus. "Mr. Luna? Your party is asking for you. They have an emergency."

Gus waved the boy away, but looked and saw Dominick beckoning with both hands. "Ugh. Mrs. Cocojuanca must want to dance. I am her date for tonight but she dances like a caribao. Stay right here. I *will* be back," he bossily announced, turned and hurried down the steps, shaking his arms to get into character for dancing with one of Imelda's more important Blue Ladies.

"Let's get out of here," said Jim.

"Can we? Won't your friends be upset?"

"They know where to find me. Unless you *want* to stay."

Meg rolled her eyes. "Not me. I'm suffering a cognitive overload here." But she didn't seem panicked or stressed, only amused by all the new impressions furrowing her mind. She kept her amusement to herself while Jim set a handful of peso notes on the table and escorted her along the rear wall to the exit. Out in the lobby, as they stepped past the cool swish of water swirling among banana plants at the foot of the waterfall, Meg let out a loud snort. She clamped her hand over her mouth to stop a guffaw, but it was too late. Her body bent over, shook and stumbled. "Her hairdresser?" she squeaked. "Imelda Marcos's hairdresser?"

Jim chuckled with her as he took Meg's arm to whisper, "Try not to say her name too loudly. Call her 'she' while we're in public."

"Right. Sorry. It's just—" She inhaled sharply, but catching her breath only gave Meg more giggles. "I'm sorry, Jim. But it *is* funny. He's the one, right? The man you're seeing."

Jim nodded. It was funny, wasn't it? He didn't need to feel ashamed Meg knew. "It has its comic side," he confessed aloud.

"For a minute I thought that captain was the one. Although I couldn't understand why he seemed to come on to me," she whispered as they continued toward the doors. "But then *he* came up, and I saw he was jealous of me. I knew right away."

"Jealous? Of you?" Filipinos were notorious for their hair-trigger jealousies, but one needed to be in love to be jealous. "No, Gus was only being difficult."

"Whatever. He was looking daggers at me, even after he knew I was your niece. But a hairdresser, Jim?" A new wave of giggles shook the arm Jim held. "How far the mighty have fallen."

He let go of her when they entered the revolving door. Outside the night was hot and humid and noisy. Doormen blew their whistles, cabs blew their horns, and the guides who'd bribed the security guards for the right to work the hotel entrance shouted out promises of "The real Manila! Sensuous Manila! Manila after dark!" The broad sidewalk under the illuminated hotel fronts curving up the bay was full of red-faced families and well-dressed couples, and the policemen whose chief duty was to keep hustlers and beggars confined to the side streets. There was a slight press of air from the land toward the water now, so each side street exhaled its own bad breath of gasoline and garbage, sour bodies and fried fish.

Meg's steps fell in alongside Jim's and she walked very close to him. "I'm sorry, but I have to ask," she said, seriously, nervously. "Isn't it kind of dangerous? *Her* hairdresser. What if she and her husband find out? Won't they try to use it against you?"

"Gus was her idea in the first place. The Marcoses are renowned for their hospitality." But Meg deserved an honest answer, and it was safer talking on the street than in the lobby of the Philippine Plaza. "He's their spy. A very friendly, personable spy, as you saw. And knowing he's their spy, I can use him myself. My private hotline to the Malacanang Palace. Messy, but not dangerous."

"I see." She did not sound convinced. "I guess you know what you're doing."

"I don't." Jim laughed at the quickness with which he admitted that. "Not really. But I've learned not to give a damn. I don't sweat the small stuff anyway. One learns to go with the flow in this madhouse. Let's try this street.''

He didn't intend to end the conversation, but there was so little space on the crowded sidewalk after they turned that they could no longer walk beside each other. Nor had he intended to prove his case by plunging Meg into the Ermita's monstrous extremes of poverty and pleasure, but here they were. Above the traffic and crowds, extravagant electronic signs glowed gaily on stucco walls with leprous patches of peeled paint and cramped rows of closed wooden shutters. A tender ballad coming from a bar gave a dreamy, slow-dance quality to its stretch of street, the Filipina teenager and middle-aged American ahead of Jim clutching each other more tightly as they walked. Up a narrow alley between McGirls and Shakey's, a baby was crying among the squashed bundles of trash. Even Jim had to look twice to assure himself the bundles were people, whole homeless families who slept now so they could search the garbage cans for fresh scraps at three in the morning. He looked back at Meg, giving her weak, philosophical smiles over his shoulder. Seeing this with her was like seeing it new, despite all his years in Asia. No, it didn't justify Gus, but yes, he had hoped to prove something by rubbing her nose in it. Meg looked neither alarmed nor appalled, but she walked with her arms folded across her breasts.

When they were able to talk again, it was in a bar inside a small, dimly lit shopping mall off Adriatico Boulevard, chosen by Jim when Meg pointed out the marquee proclaiming, ''The Filipino Beatles!'' At the far end of a long room whose walls were covered with red carpeting, a band sang perfect imitations of Beatles hits to a handful of men outnumbered by hostesses. Meg had little to say about the quiet despair of the place, or the loud, desperate insanity of the streets outside. Instead, she wanted to know more about *her* circle, and Captain Aguilar in particular.

''He seemed kind of—human? But he's with the secret police?'' she whispered.

''Yes. But quite human. He might even be a decent fellow, or would be under different circumstances. I still don't have a fix on him. But quite human, quite intelligent. And quite the ladies' man too.''

''I felt that. Although I couldn't tell if he were interested in me as a woman, or me as Jim Goodall's niece.''

He was impressed by how quickly she caught on. ''Probably a combination of both, with more the former than the latter. He should know by now how unimportant I am.''

''So what do I do in situations like that? I mean, how careful should I be about what I say?''

''About what?''

''About everything. But you in particular.''

It was a good, practical question and Jim should have raised it himself. He thought a moment and said, ''Just use tact and judgment. My hours and where I go each day are things they already know. My opinions they can figure out on their own. So don't worry about inadvertantly giving away any secret plots or schemes. You're not the houseguest of James Bond. You're only staying with the local welcome wagon for political prisoners.'' He didn't want to give the impression his work was more significant than it actually was, and he did not want to alarm Meg over dangers that would probably never appear.

They never did find the boy bath show that night. Jim led Meg up and down a few streets, then said he'd have to get the address from Gus.

16

IT WAS A COMEDY, Meg told herself, a frivolous farce. Out in the streets was frivolous tragedy, glitz and poverty, Las Vegas piled on Calcutta, a feverish spectacle that amazed and exhilarated until something in the soul gave way and grew sick of the wild extremes. But in the private theater of her uncle's life, it was all privileged comedy: movie stars, dashing secret police officers, the madcap wife of an offstage dictator, occasional trysts with the woman's snippy hairdresser. For someone who was just visiting, the sane response was laughter. Laughter was not inappropriate. Was it?

Those were the thoughts that remained the next day, while Meg worked in the fluorescent flutter and mildew of the Rare Books Room at the National Archives. It felt odd returning to history after last night, although the past was as chaotic as everything else here. The collection was a wreck, files were missing and many old books were tied up in string, their glue and bindings eaten away by insects or mice. Meg found the shriveled mummies of three mice at the bottom of a box of unsorted letters from the 1930s, poisoned by something in the ink. There was a soft, pencillike scratch of panic behind the shelves each time Meg ventured into the stacks. The librarian, an elderly flirt with rimless, half-moon glasses on a face like a wizened apple, loaned Meg a flashlight for the aisles where the lights were burned out. He blamed the

Americans for this state of neglect. Filipinos were more interested in the history of the United States than that of their own country, and the only people he ever saw down here were the same handful of eccentric historians, visiting American scholars and married women who used the deserted room for meetings with their lovers. "We are a romantic people," he told Meg fondly. "Except about our past."

She met Jim at the embassy when the day was over to ride back to the house. Meg felt quite comfortable with him after yesterday, even after last night. It didn't hurt to discover a streak of comic error in Jim's life, and he continued to ask about her work, a pleasant change from friends whose attention wandered when the topic of history went on too long. As for his own work, Meg didn't know if she should believe him or not when he dismissed it so quickly. In her experience, men who spoke about their importance were invariably lying, while those who lightly ridiculed themselves often told the truth, although not always.

They spent the evening in, where Jim introduced her to Philippine television: torrid soap operas on stagey sets, a beauty contest with a young American announcer, an ancient episode of "Bonanza." The news broadcast gave special attention to the Communist threat against Somoza in Nicaragua— "I'm surprised they dare mention it, what with the parallels," said Jim—and spent ten minutes on a local crime of passion where a man shot his wife's lover, and the wife now pleaded for the court to forgive him as she had. Imelda Marcos used a gold shovel to inaugurate construction of a hospital. "Nothing is expensive when it helps the people," she nobly told the camera, and Meg was appalled with her all over again. Meg knew she should get over it, but something about the woman affected her viscerally. She was everywhere, giving the regime a human face, and it was a vile joke that the face she gave it was female.

"How much power does Imelda actually have?"

"Good question," said Jim. "Not as much as she pretends, that's for certain. Ferdinand's given her a few fiefs as playthings, such as her governorship of Metro Manila. But beyond that nobody knows for sure how much say she has. My theory is none at all. You've seen her. She's much too flighty and sincere to be the cynical manipulator other people think she is."

Oddly enough, Meg found herself wanting to believe in a cunning Imelda, a supersubtle woman who only played the fool to throw her enemies off guard. In a world where everything was equal, women should be as evil as men. It was a line of argument that put Meg at odds with most of her feminist colleagues.

MEG WOKE UP early the next morning, showered and dressed and went out to the kitchen for a badly needed cup of coffee. Imelda Marcos's hairdresser sat at the kitchen table.

"Good morning, Dr. Frisch," he said and stood up.

For a moment she thought he was a dream, a delayed hypnogogic vision. But it was definitely the gay Filipino from the other night, his singles bar swinger's outfit replaced with jeans and a tight knit tangerine shirt, his catty manner replaced by old-fashioned chivalry.

"Does my uncle know you're here?" She'd heard his shower running when she came from her room. She heard Tammy in the back with the washing machine.

"He should. I spent the night. Cream or sugar?" He poured Meg a cup of coffee and joined her at the table. "I came by very late, after you went to bed. I'm relieved we didn't wake you. I struggled to enjoy myself silently, but one can lose control."

It was much too early to picture her uncle having wild sex with this fellow.

"I see you smoke too, Dr. Frisch. Please. Take one of mine." He lit the cigarette for her.

Smoke and coffee enabled Meg to think more clearly. "Gus, right? Call me Meg. Not even my students call me Dr. Frisch."

"Whatever you say, *Meg*. I'm sorry if I was a bitch the other night. But now I know for certain you're your uncle's niece." He grinned with a mouthful of beautiful white teeth; she couldn't tell if they were Asian teeth or dentures. He had a soft brown babyface and faintly Chinese eyes.

"You thought I was a girlfriend? You don't know my uncle very well."

Gus happily shrugged. "He likes men but maybe he likes women too. I like men but—" He held up his left hand to show her a ring. "Six years, two sons," he declared. "I'm no sad *tita*, no sorry queen. I am a family man."

"Does your wife know?"

"*Que ba!*" he laughed. "She knows. She eggs me on." Common idioms became strange again in his overly precise accent; nobody's English quite belonged to them here, whether they were Filipino or bureaucrat. "She's happy I'm friends with someone as nice and important as your uncle. Now she knows not to worry on nights I don't come home."

"Lucky her."

"Hu-heeee!" A boy's laugh. "You Americans. Everything must be this or that. But we are too full of life to limit ourselves. We are a very sensuous people. A romantic people."

"So I've heard." What was this thing Filipinos had about explaining themselves to Americans? Meg wondered if they actually believed it or only made it up as they went along.

"And we are a family people too. Family is enormously important to us. Just because a man likes to love men doesn't mean he cannot be a father. I'm a wonderful father, and a good husband too."

Meg didn't know how to get at that, so she asked about his wife—Eleanor, who was three years older than Gus and the second cousin of a second cousin —and his sons—Nonoy, five, and Matthew, four. They had a nice apartment in the new complex Imelda had built along the waterfront outside Tondo, the old slum district where Gus still had a few relatives. "I pulled myself up by my bootstraps," he declared. "It's right I must help them too. But there are so damn many," he moaned.

He was so innocently cheerful it was difficult to condemn either him or his situation, although it'd be interesting to hear his wife's side of the story.

Jim came into the kitchen and went straight for the coffee pot with an elaborate show of unconcern. "Oh good. I hoped you two would have a chance to get better acquainted."

"Gus was just telling me about his family."

"Ah," said Jim, treating the fact Gus had a family as a matter of no importance. "He has two beautiful sons."

"You've met them?"

Gus laughed. "One day. Eleanor wants very much to meet your uncle," he claimed to Meg. "But the right occasion hasn't yet arisen."

Jim gave her a very solemn, blank look when he sat at the table.

No, it wasn't the friendly sexual free-for-all Gus pretended it to be, although it was difficult to imagine this sunny courtesan was the spy Jim had described either. The two men didn't touch or look at each other like people who'd made love the night before; there was neither tenderness nor guilt, only a mild sheepishness Jim disguised by asking everyone what they wanted for breakfast.

When Tammy came in from the laundry room, she treated Gus's presence as perfectly commonplace, showing annoyance only when Jim and Gus went through the refrigerator together, looking for leftovers Gus could take home to his family.

In the driveway was an old-model sports car whose top was up and patched with electrician's tape. Gus hugged Meg goodbye; his body was more solid than it looked. "I'm so happy we can be friends, Meg. I will tell everyone I know what a swell and pretty *niece* your uncle has. *Ciao,* Meg. *Ciao,* Jim Goodall." Gus climbed into his car with the bag of shrimp and cake, waved at them through his windshield as he backed out, then roared off down the street.

Not until they were on the road themselves did Jim address Gus's visit. "I hope that wasn't too awkward for you. But it was much easier letting him spend the night than trying to send him away."

"No problem. I enjoyed talking to him. I don't expect you to change your routine while I'm here."

"Yes, well. Actually, I think he came last night because of you."

"He thought I was your girlfriend," Meg said with a snort.

Jim frowned, then scoffed. "Only because it'd mean he'd lose his foot-up with Imelda while you were here. No, his chief reason for visiting was that Mrs. Marcos insists on knowing what everyone is up to, even me. She wanted Gus to find out who you were."

"He asked nothing about me. He talked only about himself," Meg pointed out, wondering if this spy routine were something Jim imagined in an attempt to justify a very peculiar affair.

"That's Gus for you. Not the world's most efficient spy. It's one of the things I like about him."

"And his being married? Do you like that too?"

"Hmmm?"

"I just wondered if you had a thing about married men? Men who're involved with women anyway. That cookie salesman you wrote me about. That guy from your first days at the State Department. And Doug, of course."

He was not alarmed by the idea, not even by the inclusion of Doug. "You know," he said, "I've asked myself that."

"Really?" She was surprised. "So what's the appeal? Is it the illusion of straightness? Normalcy? The deceit?"

Jim laughed, a motorized chortle behind closed teeth. "I don't know. You're right, though. There's something. Although what's going on between Gus and me is completely different."

"You think so?"

"Gus is a matter of the moment, reasons of state and sexual availability. I don't mean to say he can't be pleasant company, or that I wish him harm. But we're just two whores using each other," he happily confessed.

He danced away from one dangerous truth to dance around another, never really addressing either. If it had been another man talking, Meg might have believed the masculine posturing.

"You ask some difficult but interesting questions," said Jim, and Meg felt she was in the tiresome role of playing his conscience again.

"White woman's burden," she laughed.

MEG SPENT THE day at the archives reading through a series of first-person articles about the "good old days" that ran in the *Manila Times* shortly after the war. The librarian had remembered them and he ordered a set of enormous, dusty ledgers brought out on a hand truck. The newspapers were not yet transferred to microfiche and, opened up, each volume of crumbly, orange paper completely covered Meg's table. Her arms and T-shirt and even her face became smudged with dirt, but there, among photos of executed Huks and advertisements for 1951 American cars, Meg found anecdotes about shirtwaisted teachers in nipa palm classrooms, the Thomasites from the students' point of view. Much of it was nostalgic nonsense, yet there were details she could use, including a Samar man's humorous memories of Miss Emily Chalmers, the very woman whose letters Meg had read. The discovery of a reversed perspective made this dustbin exciting. The man mentioned the massacres once, as simply the "misfortune."

Meg had been at it all afternoon, filling her notebook with scrawl she hoped she could decipher later, when she began to feel someone watching her. She wondered what the librarian wanted from her—they were the only ones here today—but refused to look up until she finished copying out this paragraph.

"Dr. Frisch?"

He stood on the other side of her table, not the librarian but someone wearing a loose, Technicolor shirt.

"Just a sec," she muttered and quickly finished.

A man with an apologetic smile and tinted aviator glasses gazed down at her, someone she'd never seen before, in a blue Hawaiian shirt.

"Pardon the interruption. I thought it might be you, but your hair was different. Now I see. You wear it up. Very becoming."

Meg recognized his gracious manner before she remembered the suggestive, crepe-lidded eyes. "Captain Aguilar," she said.

His lean, military stance was draped with the flowered shirt, his high cheekbones softened by the skewed teardrop lenses. Something scented held his glossy, brushed-back hair in place.

"What a coincidence to run into you," he said. "Or maybe not." He glanced around to see if they disturbed anyone: there was only the librarian leafing through a magazine and watching them over his glasses. "Our chat about my grandfather made me want to look up details about his village. I hoped to be more helpful when we ran into each other again. I should've guessed you might be here yourself."

No, Aguilar came looking specifically for her. Why? Meg was skeptical, curious, nervous. The man had an immediate sexual gravity and her first thought was that he wanted to seduce her. It was a ridiculous thing to think. More likely was the possibility he hoped to learn something about her uncle.

"You shouldn't have bothered. I doubt you'd find anything in this rat's nest anyway. But thank you just the same."

He bowed his head and leaned forward, one slim brown hand covering Meg's notebook. "Do you have a minute?" he whispered. "Can we talk?" He had a half-smile that reminded Meg of the romantic leers from last night's soap operas; he had seemed much smoother at the disco in his dinner jacket.

"Sure," said Meg, gesturing at a chair. He didn't need to resort to romance to find out she knew nothing about her uncle.

Aguilar kept his smile, but shook his head. "Back there perhaps?" He pointed at the darker aisles between the shelves in the corner.

Meg's curiosity was stronger than her fear. She felt challenged by the idea of talking with a man from the secret police, the chance to glimpse that life up close, but knew she should do it out in the open. "We could go across the street to that cafe with deaf waiters. It's almost closing time and I could go for something cold to drink."

Aguilar looked scornful. "Please," he said. "I have only a few minutes." His smile returned. "This will be more private."

Meg hesitated. What could happen? She forcefully scraped her chair when she stood up, to get the librarian's attention.

The old man watched Meg follow Aguilar toward the stacks, disappointed, almost heartbroken. He looked too frail to be of much help if Meg needed to call out to him. Aguilar gave the man a brief, insincere smile over his shoulder as he stepped behind a bookcase stuffed to the ceiling with rolled documents.

And Meg followed him. A new panic fluttered in her stomach and below. She felt stupid for not listening to her panic, but guilty for being afraid, even when she told herself she wasn't afraid of Aguilar because he was Asian, but because he was with the secret police. Following him down the aisle toward the windowless back wall, she saw he was her height, no taller. She tried to use that to excuse her passivity. The worst that could happen would be an attempted grope or forced kiss. What was she afraid of? She was the niece of a man with the American embassy.

Their soft-soled footsteps were silent and the only noise back here was a frantic scratch of pencils.

Aguilar turned left and stopped in a blind alley between the last bookcase and the cinderblock wall. He faced Meg and signaled her to come closer. A light in the next aisle illuminated him in sections. His face was in shadow. His whispering made his words simultaneously sinister and corny. "I know this isn't the best circumstance for a *tête à tête*. But I wanted very much to see you alone after the other night."

Meg positioned herself three feet away, an escape route at her back, her arms folded across her chest. "I'm listening."

"I don't know where to begin." He lay an arm over an outcrop of books, getting his hand uncomfortably close to her shoulder. "Would you describe your uncle as a man of principle?"

"In most areas, yes." She was too startled hearing Jim mentioned to say anything except the truth.

"Not his sex life. I don't care about that." His tone became clipped and hurried. "But his professional life, his official duties. Does he believe what he professes? Human rights and all that shit."

The reference to his homosexuality jarred her, then the realization that this wasn't about her at all. Of course. Her first suspicions had been absolutely right. "Yes. He does," she said, automatically indignant for her uncle's sake.

"You don't think there's a chance he can be bought? By the PSU or the president or the president's friends?"

Meg was amazed at how calm and clear her thoughts were now that she understood what he wanted. "I don't think I should be talking about this with you."

"Please. I have to know." The face in shadow was stern, aloof.

"Then talk to him, not me. Although I seriously doubt you'll get very far with my uncle."

"You know that for a fact?"

"No. I don't. I've only been here four days. Talk to him, not me."

"You're a blood relative. You know him better than anyone else in Manila.

Please. In your opinion, that's all I ask, is there any chance his loyalty could be bought? For love or money, if somebody named the right price?''

"In my opinion?"

"That's all I want to know."

In her opinion, Jim could inadvertantly betray someone in the gray area of personal relations, but could never betray anything so large and clear as a principle. Or if he could, and this was his chance for a handsome bribe, Meg was right to protect him from temptation.

"In my opinion. No. Definitely not."

Aguilar frowned and looked away, irritably nodding to himself.

Meg wondered what he hoped to gain, and what Jim had to sell.

"All right then." He reached back and lifted his shirt to tug at something wedged under his belt. "That was my impression too. Here. I'm putting my life in your hands."

He held out a square brown envelope whose underside was dark with sweat. He shook it at Meg.

"Take it. Please."

She took it. There was something hard and flat inside, a disk the size of a lady's compact.

"I don't know what to do with it, but maybe your uncle will."

"What is it?"

He shook his head. "The less you know, the better. All I ask is that you tell nobody except your uncle who gave it to you. Can you promise me that?"

She held the envelope between them, sorry she had accepted it, hoping he'd take it back. "Why should you believe any promise I gave you?"

"You seem very honest, innocent and proud."

"I'll say I'm innocent. I have absolutely no idea what this is about."

"Just give that to your uncle. He'll understand. He can explain why nobody can know where it came from, no one with my government or his either. Unless things change completely." He lifted his chin and swallowed. "In which case, I might need one of you to testify on my behalf."

She stared at him, demanding he explain.

He answered her look by saying, "Even the most pragmatic of men need to indulge their conscience, and all that shit."

"But until what changes?" asked Meg. "The government here? With this?" Her fingers squeezed the shape inside the envelope.

"I don't know. It depends on what use your uncle has for it. I only needed to indulge my conscience," he sneered, fiercely contemptuous of what he was doing. "He should understand *that* too. Just promise me you'll give it to him, and that you'll mention it to no one else."

"All right. Yes. But I can't make any promises for him." She should turn this over to Jim and let him decide what was real and what was only the echo of too many bad movies. Aguilar's agitation seemed real, but the melodrama around this envelope felt like a put-on, a joke.

"Okay. My life is in your hands," he declared. He drew his shoulders back and regained his dinner jacket smoothness. "I suspect our paths will cross again during your visit, Dr. Frisch. You'll understand, of course, when my small talk is even smaller than it was the other night. Oh, could you wait a minute after I leave before you return to your table?"

"Yes?" This was already over?

"The librarian's never seen me before, but I assume he knows who you are. He has a nephew with the NPA, but that doesn't preclude his cooperation if the police ask about any Filipino visitors. Better that he think I'm a would-be masher."

Nothing was what it seemed; everyone suspected each other. She wanted to ask why he put any faith in *her* opinion of Jim.

"Thank you for your time. Enjoy your stay in Manila, Dr. Frisch." And he left, briskly stepping past Meg and around the corner, setting off another scribble of mice. She heard him loudly clear his throat as he passed the librarian's desk.

Meg stood there in the dusty, mildewed stacks with a dozen unanswered questions, feeling foolish and skeptical and excited by the damp brown envelope in her hand.

"You opened it?" said Jim.

"I told you I did."

"And that's all that was inside? No note, no clipping, just that?"

"Just that."

The envelope lay between them on the front seat of the Toyota, its contents set neatly on top: a small white Super–8 reel snapped into a blue plastic lid. Jim glanced at it one more time, then didn't look at it again while he drove.

"What do you think it is?" Meg asked.

"A movie of something. Or nothing. Who knows?"

"Political prisoners?"

"Maybe. Although I can't imagine Aguilar going from jail to jail with a movie camera. I won't know until I look at it."

"When will you watch it?"

"Oh, sometime. I think I saw a projector back at the house."

His lack of excitement puzzled Meg. After meeting him in the entrance hall of the embassy as scheduled, she had waited until they were out in the car before she told Jim about Aguilar's visit and gave him the envelope. He quickly pulled out the reel and popped it open to see that there was actually film wound inside, then started up the car with a look of cool indifference. Meg assumed the look was for the sake of anyone who could see them in the parking lot and for the Marines who saluted at the gate as they drove out. But Jim remained calm and detached even when they were on the highway, even when he asked her to repeat in full detail everything Aguilar had said.

"These people have the damndest idea of a practical joke," Jim suddenly announced. "I don't mind him pulling my leg. What galls me is he went out of his way to upset you."

"I'm not upset. Just curious. He seemed awfully angry with himself for someone pulling a practical joke."

"Yes, well, these people are terrific actors. You can never tell where they're coming from."

But Jim himself was a very poor actor. Nobody in his right mind could dismiss this so easily. He had the preoccupied, inwardly engaged look of someone listening to a speech on headphones, even when he smiled at Meg. This was a Jim she had never seen before, coldly serious, secretly solemn. She wanted to see him at work, and she was determined to see what was in this spool of film.

When they got back to the house, Tammy had already left for the day. Without stopping to take off his tie, Jim looked through the closet in his study. "The owners left a projector behind with the other junk they don't use any-more. I guess it's all video cameras nowadays for people with money," he told Meg, who stood watching from the door. "Here it is." He pulled a black plastic suitcase out and set it on his desk. "Now to figure out how to work the damn thing."

Meg came in to help set it up. She was surprised he hadn't tried to send her away. They pointed the projector at a patch of ivory wall six feet away and Meg was able to thread the leader to the large take-up reel. Aguilar's little reel hung at the front of the machine like a hypocephalic head.

Jim waited until he was closing the curtains before he said, "Maybe I should watch this by myself first."

"I thought you said it's probably nothing."

"More likely than not. But there's an outside chance it isn't."

"If I'm going to be used as a go-between, I think I deserve to see what I've been involved in. Even if it isn't a joke."

Jim stood by the window, frowning.

"Good God," she said. "I've been reading and writing about atrocities for years. You're not going to protect me from anything I don't already know goes on. If it *is* something like that."

"Yes? All right. We can watch this together. Whatever it is."

He sat in a chair beside the desk and faced the wall. Meg sat behind him, beside the projector, able to see only the back of his head.

"All right, let's see what we have," he sighed.

Meg turned the switch. The curtains leaked daylight around the edges, but the projector was close enough to the far wall for the image to be as sharp and bright as the screen of a color television:

A horsey Filipina in a sunsuit turned an embarrassed smile toward them. She bent down to put her arms around two small children, a naked little boy and a gap-toothed girl in pink underpants. They stood on cracked pavement by an inflatable wading pool, a covered patio and small concrete house to the left.

"*This* is his moment of conscience?" said Meg.

"Wait," said Jim, watching very closely.

There was a blip of light and the children again, this time with a stocky man who had a pale, jagged scar on the left side of his face, running from his temple to his chin. The children laughed when their father lifted one and then the other up on each shoulder. He laughed when his son gripped his short hair like reins.

The camera swung into shadow. The automatic exposure caught up under the covered patio, where the naked toddler sat kicking his feet in a rattan chair next to a refrigerator that stood outside the house. The screen door opened and the little girl stumbled out, her head completely swallowed by a wobbly white army helmet. She had to tilt her head back to see where she was going.

"Policeman and his family," said Jim. "That's PSU headgear."

The mother sat her children at the patio table to feed them pineapple cut in slices like watermelon. Their faces were nibbled around the edges by the bright light behind them.

Another blip of light and the movie was indoors, with the seasick yellows and greens of fluorescent lighting. It looked like a kitchen, but one much too large for the house outside. Three men in black T-shirts and fatigue pants stood by the cabinets drinking beer. The counter was covered with bottles. There was a gap in the cabinets where a stove should have been. One soldier scowled at the camera and indifferently flapped his hand at it. The camera dipped, glimpsing a bed in the middle of the kitchen floor, a mattress with brown stains.

"Where are we?" asked Meg, but Jim didn't seem to hear.

Suddenly a girl stood with the soldiers. The camera was further back now, ignored by the men who surrounded and teased the girl. Faces did not read clearly in the murky, septic light. The girl looked sleepy or stoned, her head hanging down, her long hair hiding half her face. She wore a filthy T-shirt, jeans and eyeglasses. The soldiers abruptly looked off to the left, as though someone outside the frame had spoken. A younger, mild-faced soldier with a little mustache like a shadow on his lip chucked the girl under the chin and touched her eyes. He spoke to her as he set her glasses on the counter. The girl began to undress.

"Meg, you don't have to watch this."

The quick, cold tone of Jim's voice made Meg understand that what looked like could happen actually *would* happen.

"I do. I have to see this," she hissed, surprised by her own anger, the tension of the muscles squeezing her legs together, her hands and genitals closing into fists.

The girl had stumbled to the bed, smudged sexless dough without clothes. Two soldiers pushed her down on her back. The third, the mild man with the undergraduate's mustache, wheeled a little dolly to the bed, a collapsible luggage cart with black boxes strapped to it. He took a pair of handgrips, tongs like the clamps of jumper cables, only smaller, more delicate, and tapped them together a few times. He applied one to the finger of a weakly clenched hand a soldier held out to him—the other two soldiers were kneeling on either side of the bed, holding the girl's arms and blocking her face from view. She lay nervously still, like a woman on a doctor's examining table. She twitched when the man brushed the second pair of tongs against her breast. Her body stretched and arched when the man gripped her breast and held it with the tongs.

It seemed too leisurely to be real. Meg wanted to think the scene was staged, faked, but if anyone wanted to fake this they'd know what to empha-size. The lack of emphasis, the distance and silence made it more real, forcing the mind to fill in the gaps: the black boxes on the cart were car batteries, the clamps burned the finger and nipple when the electrical circuit was closed. Meg's body understood before her mind did. She could feel it in her own breasts, not the fierce shot of pain, but the nauseating ache that would follow such pain. She suddenly understood that each time the men made faces, the woman was screaming.

The amplified, accelerated clockwork of the projector trapped Meg with the girl.

Meg closed her eyes only to open them again, needing to see that this was not happening in her head, but on the wall, in the past, in the recent past. That this was something that actually happened made her less culpable for watch-ing. Unlike fictional movies, this was about more than the fact that people watched it.

The mustached man went about his task with no expression. One of the soldiers restraining the girl shut his eyes—and kissed the air above her head, pretending this was sex.

The camera swung away, not in disgust but distracted by something new. To the far left of the kitchen cabinets stood a thick figure in olive drab, watching the men and girl across the room. But that wasn't what caught the camera's attention. It darted back to the right a little, and a door being opened from the outside.

"Oh my God. Was that Enéro? Colonel Enéro watched this?"

Jim sounded thrilled to recognize someone he knew. Meg had forgotten he watched this with her. She was appalled they could watch this together, sick-ened to think Jim knew the people involved, and angry that he could be excited by anything in the film.

"It looked like Enéro. Maybe they'll show him again. Ah, and here's *your* friend."

The new arrival standing in the open door in jungle fatigues was Captain Aguilar himself. He stared at the camera, then in the direction of the girl and bed. He showed no surprise or shock at what was happening, but looked straight into the camera again, more concerned that he was being filmed than that a girl was being tortured.

His head snapped to the left. The camera followed to the thick-set man in olive drab again. He was covering his face with one hand now, angrily gesturing at Aguilar with the other. The camera swung away, flashing past Aguilar who marched toward it. The camera bobbed, found the three soldiers and the naked body, and the image flashed white.

Film continued to unwind from the spool, but the square on the wall remained white. What they saw had lasted less than two minutes.

"So the captain took the man's toy away, and kept his film," Jim muttered. "Damn. I wanted a better look at Enéro."

"Do I turn it off?" Meg's voice was hoarse, her mouth dry.

"Yes, yes. But leave it threaded. I'll need to run that back and forth a few times to see the details." Jim swung around in his swivel chair and saw Meg sitting behind him. He hadn't been smiling, but there was an excited, eager look on his face that froze when he saw the expression on hers.

She felt sick with anger. Anger was the only way she could hold off the nausea in her throat and crotch, an anger so strong she could not limit it to just the men in the movie, but found it including Jim for watching so intently, and herself for ever feeling that it was safe to laugh.

Jim lowered his head and took a deep breath. "I'm sorry, Meg. I would never have let you watch if I had any idea it was going to be a woman."

"What difference does that make?" But it did make a difference. Awful as it would've been to watch a man tortured by men, the scene would have felt more alien, less connected to her own experience, less sexual. "I asked to see it. I had no idea it would be anything so—" Just stopping to think of a word caused her stomach to knot and her arms to freeze. "No, that's not something you did to *me*."

Jim frowned at the projector. "I had no idea myself it would be half that explicit. Terrible," he said. "Absolutely disgusting." But he couldn't disguise his satisfaction in having the horror recorded on film. "I need a drink. You must need a cigarette. Let's get away from this thing."

There was a rubberiness in her legs when Meg stood to follow him into the hall. It seemed worse with the projector off and the experience completely inside her head and body. Sitting at the kitchen table, she had to make a fist a few times before she could light a cigarette. The muscles were watery, as if after a mild electric shock. Jim stood at the counter, clinking ice cubes into glasses, and Meg remembered it had been a kitchen in the movie. Not even dreary, commonplace kitchens seemed safe anymore. The ludicrous picture on the refrigerator of the Virgin Mary offering her heart—"Is that a piece of raw liver?" Meg had joked—was no longer comical.

Jim gave her a glass of scotch and ice, then stepped back and stood at the counter, as if afraid she wouldn't want him near her.

"Why were they drinking?" she asked. "At first I thought they were having a party."

"They have to get a little loaded to do what they do. Even in the Presidential Security Unit, there's not enough real sadists who'd be able to do that sober."

"But that's your job over here? Following things like that, recording and reporting them?"

Jim nodded and took another swallow. "You knew that. You're well-informed about what goes on in the world."

"Yes, but—" Had he misled her or had she been fooling herself? "You said all you did was visit prisons. And not much of *that* went on here. I never dreamed you'd actually see it."

"I don't. This was the first time. What we just saw together is the clearest, most damning piece of evidence I've encountered in my year here." Another swallow, to give him time to think. "I feel bad you had to see it with me."

But Meg refused to let this be about her. "Who is she?"

"I don't know. That's something I'll have to find out."

"What did they want from her?"

"She looked like a university student. Maybe the girlfriend or sister of an NPA suspect. They wanted to know what she knows. She might even be NPA herself."

Meg wanted specifics that could make the naked body real, get it out of her own body and head, out into the world where the girl could be helped. She couldn't remember her face once the glasses had been removed, only the faces of the men watching her. "Do you think— she's still alive?"

"Yes," said Jim. "Probably. She'll be hidden away in their jails somewhere, or she might even have been released from custody. In which case it'll be more difficult to find her." Seeing the skeptical look Meg gave him, he added, "They're peculiarly legalistic when it comes to political prisoners here. This isn't Cambodia or Argentina, as people are quick to tell you. In Manila anyway, it's very rare they resort to illegal murder."

"That was legal?"

"If the case ever got to court, that would appear as a routine police interrogation."

"But they weren't even asking any questions," Meg said angrily.

"The questions come later. This was to soften her up. Although one got the distinct impression this wasn't her first session." He looked into his ice, ashamed he knew so much.

"This was like a show being put on for that colonel."

Jim nodded. "That's what it looked like. And that's what makes this piece of film so valuable. Proof of extreme measures, watched by Marcos's own chief of security." The eager look he'd hidden since the end of the movie poured into his eyes, a cold blueness in his face. "Our friend wasn't exaggerating when he said he'd put his life in our hands."

"You can do something with it?"

"Definitely. A picture's worth a thousand words."

"You'll send it to Human Rights in Washington?"

"Maybe." The copper eyebrows were pinched together, the high forehead creased with a single, unfinished furrow. "I've sent them other items they weren't able to do a damn thing with, but one would assume something like this . . ." He left the statement unfinished when he caught himself thinking aloud. "I don't know yet. I have to consider this. Very carefully."

She had hoped he would send it away and other hands would finish this, but it had been an automatic, cowardly hope. "What do you want me to do?"

"Keep your mouth shut." He smiled, afraid that sounded too harsh. "But you already know that. No, we can't mention a word of this to anyone. Not to Tammy, Gus, people at the embassy."

"I don't know any embassy people."

"They'll come sniffing around sooner or later. Sooner, if they get the feeling something's up. They have their cozy relationship with Marcos to protect. We have to be even more careful around them than we do with any nationals. So play dumb. Or play the absentminded professor with them."

Meg cringed, feeling that's what she'd been playing all along. "I can keep my mouth shut. I'll be extremely careful about anything I say. Only what do I say if I—?"

"What?"

"If I see Captain Aguilar again?"

"You won't."

"He won't want to hear what's happened to his movie? What your reaction was and what you're going to do?"

"He'll be curious. But he'll be more prudent than ever now that it's out of his control. A man who was afraid to meet with me alone, who had to wait until I had a houseguest he could contact on the sly, is going to be extremely paranoid about who he's seen with for the next few months. If this film sees the light of day, he *is* a prime suspect."

She pictured Aguilar in that room, so cool and blasé in the presence of obscenity, as though he'd seen it a hundred times before, then the suave, unruffled man at the disco. "Why is he doing this? If he's one of them. He is, isn't he?"

"I don't know. I'd pegged Aguilar as your basically good man who'd sold his name for a mess of pottage. He's smarter than the others, but that only makes the lies you tell yourself more clever. And success in your field is a great opiate. But like the man told you, even pragmatists need to indulge their conscience now and then. This movie fell in his lap and he had no choice. It's easy to do nothing, so long as you don't see a damn thing you can do."

"He seemed to think you'd understand why he did it," said Meg.

"Hmmm." Jim ignored her suggestion of similarities between Aguilar and himself. "What I'd like to know is how long he's been sitting on this. And who else has seen it. Surely whoever developed it."

"Labs are all automated now," Meg told him. "They never know what movies they're processing."

"Really?" He looked pleased to hear that. "Then Aguilar could've just dropped this off at a drugstore? Nobody'd know?"

"The case and reel are like those you get at a big lab. I guess they have those labs over here." She knew so much only because Ron, who loved gadgets, was a home-movie buff.

"Do you think it's possible someone at these labs could pick films at random and watch them before they're sent out?"

"I guess."

"Okay." He downed the rest of his scotch and set the glass in the sink. "Do you mind if we wait a bit before we eat dinner? I want to make a few phone calls."

"Jim, I can't think about eating after watching that girl."

"Yes. Of course. Disgusting. You'll understand if we cancel our trip to Baguio this weekend."

"I'd forgotten all about it." She disliked this quick, terse manner, the man-of-action pose that did not quite fit Jim's thoughts.

"But matters should be settled in time for Samar."

"That isn't important! This film and that girl are what's important!" she snapped. "Don't play the host with me while *this* is going on."

He briefly bowed his head. "Okay. Right. You're right." He gave her a long, slow, measuring look. "I shouldn't pretend this is nothing. You know too much already. I'd prefer you didn't know." Deep lines radiated from the corners of his squint. "But it seemed only fair you see what you delivered and I had no idea it would be so raw. I can't wipe that out, Meg, but—as this unravels, do you want to be kept informed? Or would you rather I leave you out?"

"I want to know what's happening," she said automatically.

"All right." He closed his pink eyelids when he nodded. "Good. I don't *want* to exclude you. But I also feel bad about unloading everything on you. A ton of bricks. But good," he repeated, without much more conviction. "Be a new experience for me as well, having someone with whom I can talk things through while they're happening. My own personal historian." He tried out a half-smile. "How do you think people would respond if that were shown on TV?"

It took Meg a moment to catch up with his new thought. "They'd be horrified."

"Yes. I think so too. It would open a few eyes."

"You want to show the girl on television? Here or at home?"

"I could never show it here. I don't know if I can get it shown in the States. But it's worth looking into, don't you think?"

"Yes. I guess." Something in the idea made her uneasy, or maybe it was only the eagerness Jim couldn't hide when he gave lip service to uncertainty. He had a clear and vivid use for that girl.

"All right then. Let me begin my calls, find out what I can about the girl, see if I can start a few hares."

"Isn't your line tapped?"

"Oh, I never say anything important on the phone," he assured her. He hurried from the kitchen and Meg heard him quietly shutting his study door.

She was left alone with the movie still creeping through her.

She was impressed with Jim's cool sense of purpose, envious of his ability to keep his head and know what he wanted to do. Sickening knowledge and helpless doubt could be escaped in action. The film itself should be less obscene now that there was a chance it could lead to something else. The torture of this girl broadcast to the world was such a dramatic, disturbing prospect that Meg drew back from the idea, but her uncle believed in it, and this was his domain. She had never seen him in a public crisis. She was surprised he could be cool without becoming coldly self-important.

Meg wanted the urgency of the situation to take over her life, but it couldn't, not when she was only half-in, half-out. She couldn't imagine telling Jim to leave her out, yet this half-knowledge was an awful privilege, as frustrating as ignorance and far more painful. What could she do here except think of more questions to ask?

She could only steel herself for a limbo of watching and waiting, trust in Jim's competence and provide whatever he wanted, even if it were nothing. All doubts and uneasiness should be dismissed as the nervous thoughts of someone who was accustomed to watching events a hundred years after the fact.

17

"STRONG MEDICINE, JIM. Brutal stuff. If just a few seconds ever made the evening news, it'd wrench every gut in TV-land. Marcos would be Horror of the Month, if Iran doesn't hot up again. Uproar might last long enough to kick some sense into the peanut farmer. At least convince him to stop sending these people money and car batteries." Sokol snorted and shook his jowly, jar-shaped head. "A heap of subjunctives, Jim. But built on a big fat negative."

"It's an outrage," said Cooper, exasperated with the older man's cynical banter. "That film is an absolute outrage."

"I never said it wasn't, son."

"But you assume it'll never air on television."

"Like I said, it's *too* strong, *too* brutal." Sokol readjusted his portly weight into the corner of the sofa. "The networks won't touch it with a ten-foot pole."

The following day, late in the afternoon, Jim sat in his living room with Denny Sokol and John Cooper, listening to them argue about what they'd just seen. They were the two journalists in Manila whom Jim trusted most, or distrusted least, and he'd invited them to the house to get a professional opinion. Cooper was a stringy young reporter with UPI, on his first overseas assignment and very righteous, very irritable. He couldn't remain permanently indignant much longer, but Jim felt his anger made Cooper trustworthy while it lasted. Sokol, however, was beyond anger. A veteran TV journalist and old Asia hand of Jim's generation, he had no illusions about his trade, no further ambitions in his career; he was too overweight to be an anchor, too sharp-tongued to be a producer. He chose to work in this news backwater because he enjoyed the ease of Philippine life, especially the boys. Sokol was an unashamed pedophile who remained loyal to his lovers after they outgrew him, providing money and advice and frequently serving as best man at their weddings. Jim felt he could trust that kind of loyalty. Sokol was almost as contemptuous of the Human Rights program as he was of "TV-land" and the

Marcos government. Cynical resignation can be a disguise for self-serving opportunism, but Jim felt Sokol's was used to preserve his moral indignation. He wasn't encouraged when Sokol thought nothing could be accomplished with the film. ·

"I don't buy that," Cooper persisted. "If I were in television instead of print, I'd jump at the chance to send this to my producers."

"Then you're even more naive about the medium than our friend here." Sokol turned to Jim. "Sorry to disappoint you, old man. But what makes this item so devastating—actual torture, nudity, the fact it's a member of the fairer sex—are the very things that make it too hot for television. The networks have weak stomachs and no spine."

"You've given up, that's your problem," Cooper charged. "You're forgetting what TV did in Vietnam."

"Vietnam?" A smile warped Sokol's face. "Let me tell you about 'Nam. Living room war, my ass. You should've seen how they sanitized the footage my crew and I sent back. I'm not talking corpses with their heads blown off. We knew not to shoot that. But any kind of blood, edited out in the name of good taste. The curse of color film. And once the administration started blaming TV for people turning against the war, we couldn't even show *bandaged* wounds. And no dead G.I.'s, God forbid. Only dead gooks, facedown in medium-long shot. So don't give me that courageous television honesty crap, because it never existed. And what's happening to this young lady is much, much worse."

"Would it help if black strips were used to cover her parts?" Jim asked. "That wouldn't make it airable?"

"In their eyes, it'd only make it look more like a stag film. One of the things that'll scare producers off is the fear they'll be charged with titillation. Gratuitous sex with no value as news."

"Enéro's presence doesn't give it enough news value?"

Sokol remained patient over Jim's refusal to give up. "The American public doesn't know Ishmael Enéro from Adam's housecat. And we don't know for certain that's really Enéro. I mean, *I* assume it's Enéro. But when you clicked off the footage frame by frame, his face was as clear as mud."

"When I write this up," Cooper announced, "and I will, Goodall, I'm going to write that this reporter has come into possession of an amateur film that suggests Marcos's chief of security personally supervised the—"

"You can write that, John. But I'll bet you a month's salary your editors won't let it out on the wires. They'll ask to see the film and when they do they'll kill the story dead. Hearsay and speculation," Sokol grumbled. "Unsubstantiated."

His case against the film was so all-encompassing that Jim began to wonder if Sokol owed Marcos a favor. What if Enéro himself held something over Sokol's head?

"I don't know what to do with the damn thing," Jim groaned. "You sure there's nobody you could show it to, Denny? I'd consider letting you take it off my hands for a few days.''

"Thanks but no thanks. I don't know a soul who'd do you any good.''

No, Sokol had been speaking his own cynical truth, or else he would have jumped at the chance to pass the film on to interested parties. Another hope was smashed.

"Hang on to it, Jim, show it to a few more people you can trust, then get it off to Washington and out of your hair. You shown it to Chen yet?''—Lorenzo Chen was a local contact for Amnesty International.

"No, he's in Hong Kong on business until next week.''

"Show it to him when he gets back. At least it'll get into the record that an unknown woman was zapped on an unknown date by unknown members of the Presidential Security Unit at an unknown location.''

Sokol assumed the kitchen was in an abandoned army barracks, Jim that it was in the jail at Camp Crame where he'd heard cries a couple of months ago, but they were only guessing. As to the girl's identity, phone calls last night and today had given Jim no leads. He was hampered by not knowing how many weeks or months Aguilar had been holding this.

"Do you have a dupe I can send with my article?'' asked Cooper.

"Not yet.''

"Get your friend at this lab to strike a couple of copies,'' Sokol suggested —Jim told them a worker in a film lab had stumbled upon the film, then sold it to Jim; he wanted to protect Aguilar. "You should have at least one copy. Super–8 prints look like shit, but it's a bad idea to have only one of anything.''

Jim had discovered neither of the labs in Manila made prints of Super–8. He would have to send the reel to a commercial lab in Hong Kong or Japan, which would take at least two weeks. He didn't trust the lab at the embassy, of course, used chiefly by the CIA, and if he sent it on to Wheeler he might never see it again.

"Ah, this must be your houseguest,'' said Sokol, looking through the window at a cab pulling up out front.

Meg came up the walk, glancing at the extra cars parked in the driveway. Jim had dropped her off at the archives building that morning, telling Meg she should stick to her routine and that nothing would probably happen for a few days, if anything ever did. He'd left a note with the embassy's front desk, telling her to meet him at home and pay the cabbie no more than eighty pesos.

"A relative, I presume.''

Sokol knew about Jim. Cooper didn't. The young man was married, but he gave Jim a quick male-to-male look of appreciation when Meg came through the front door. With jeans and a heavy briefcase, she resembled a hippie businesswoman.

"Hi,'' she said, looking in on them from the front hall, feigning complete indifference at first, then shifting to mild curiosity as a more plausible reaction to Jim's visitors. "Hot today."

Jim called her in and introduced the men. Meg exchanged pleasantries about the heat and humidity and mice at the archives for a minute, then excused herself to wash off the archival dirt. Jim was impressed by her ability to keep all suspicions to herself.

When she was gone, Cooper whispered, "She hasn't seen it, right?"

"Of course not." Her involvement would be their secret.

"I know if my wife saw that, she'd blame the whole male race. You know how women get nowadays."

"Hmm."

Cooper left shortly afterwards, assuring Jim he'd show extreme caution in discussing this on the phone with his superiors in Japan, naming neither the source nor the exact contents of the film. "Let me find out what our chances are and I'll get back to you before I go public on this."

Sokol stayed behind to finish his bourbon and shake his head over Cooper's naivete. "Nice fellow. But a Watergate baby. He thinks Watergate was something the press did. When I was his age we pretended to be more jaded than we were, until reality beat out pretense." He leaned in and lowered his voice. "I don't need to tell you, Jim, you're playing with fire. But I'm serious when I say the only thing you might set ablaze is yourself."

"I'll take that under consideration, Denny."

Sokol smirked and shook his head. "You foreign servicers. If you didn't avoid us like the plague but dealt with us now and then, you'd realize our hands are as tied with red tape as yours. Well, good luck." He clamped Jim on the shoulder and stood up. "But my advice is send it to Cowgirl Derian. She probably won't be able to do squat with it either, but you're just going to break your heart trying."

Jim thanked Sokol for his advice and saw him out. He returned to the living room, gathered the glasses of melting ice from the coffee table and took them into the kitchen. He was not yet ready to face Meg. Jim was even more uncomfortable with his decision to discuss everything with her than he'd been last night, when he excitedly believed he had a powerful weapon in his hand.

Meg didn't come out of her room, though. Jim finally went to her and knocked on the half-open door. She sat cross-legged on her bed, back against the wall, forearms in her lap. She looked up at him with nervous anticipation.

"Who were they?"

"Journalists. I showed them the film." He leaned against the door.

"What did they say?"

And Jim told her, giving special weight to Sokol and denigrating Cooper, letting her know he had half-expected this but that he was disappointed, very disappointed.

"Did you find out anything about the girl?"

"No." He wanted her to know he'd tried. He explained his usual method, which was to call a competing security unit, the MSU in this case, and accuse *them* of arresting the person in question. Even killers resent being accused of a killing they didn't do. The MSU would then call around and get back to Jim, indignantly telling him the person in question was in the such-and-such jail, arrested by so-and-so, and the MSU was in no way responsible. The redundancies of a police state had their uses. "But I was able to get only so far with that, because we don't know the girl's name, don't know when this happened, don't know how long Aguilar has been sitting on this. The good captain didn't happen to pay you another visit?"

Meg mouthed a barely audible, "No."

"Well, if I'm wrong and he does, you might ask when this incident took place. If we could get the girl's name into the record, we'd not only strengthen our case, but give her some protection too."

"So there's nothing for you to do except send it to Washington?"

"No. Not yet anyway. It's too early. Maybe Cooper can come through with something after all. Maybe Amnesty will have some ideas, but their man won't be back in Manila until next Wednesday."

"And in the meantime all you can do is wait?"

Jim nodded. "There's far more hurry-up-and-wait in this work than suspense. We just have to be patient."

The knot of her body, the posture like a grimace, had untied itself a little; she set one foot on the floor. "How can you do this?"

"Do which?"

"Get so intimate with things you can do nothing to change?" Her tone was accusing, but she had a desperate, pleading look in her eyes. "Do you distance yourself, pretend they're not real? Do you numb out?"

"You get used to being helpless," he claimed.

"All day today, this kept creeping up on me, catching me off guard. I could go on with my work, amazingly enough, but then I'd see a girl, or a man, any Filipino, and suddenly realize what could happen to them. That nobody was safe. There's this horror under everyone."

"You get used to that too. You don't want to feel too much, but you can't feel nothing either."

Meg took a deep breath and shook her head. "I don't see how you do it. Without going a little crazy."

How did he do it? He had rolled all emotions and sympathy into a tight little ball. They were there, squeezed together, held in reserve. They seemed to have been held in reserve his entire life, but that was an advantage over here.

"Maybe I am a little crazy," he admitted. "Which is why I need to talk to someone I can trust."

"I'm not sure, Jim. Today I found myself envying all those wives who don't know."

She said it with a sour smile and Jim laughed, wanting it to be a joke, trusting Meg to understand it was too late for him to leave her ignorant.

But it was peculiar, sharing this slow-motion crisis with an outsider, a second conscience like self-consciousness, a sidekick of consciousness, a woman. Meg experienced this differently, which made Jim experience it differently. His own consciousness was not as watertight as it usually seemed, but leaked doubts and fears and hope. He knew he would have worked just as hard to do something with the film otherwise, but Meg's presence made him more willing to hope, more desperate to succeed.

Despite the food in the refrigerator, they ate out that night, in a restaurant in Makati. Neither of them wanted to spend the evening at home, alone with each other. Their shared knowledge was like a cramped room, and Meg said she needed to get out. Jim too wanted the spacious impersonality of other people around them. He wasn't sharing this with Meg in order to get closer to her, but he hadn't expected their bond to feel so confining, more a prison than a home. Failure was a difficult room to share with someone whose opinion mattered to you.

EVERYTHING CHANGED THE next morning.

It was Saturday. Having canceled their trip to Baguio, Jim proposed they drive to Cavite and the Emilio Aguinaldo Museum that morning. They were finishing breakfast when the phone rang. Jim answered it in the living room.

"Jim. John Cooper here. Can you talk?" He was breathless and excited.

Jim glanced at Meg, watching him from the kitchen table. "Yes. What's up?"

"They just left, Jim. They were here first thing this morning." He had to clear his throat to stop his voice from squeaking. "I didn't tell them a damn thing, but they sure as hell know something's up."

"Who, Cooper?"

"Major Valeriano and another man. From NISA." The national secret police, also commanded by Colonel Enéro. "They came to the house, said they wanted to talk and asked me to step out to the car. They wanted me to get in, but I refused. I told them to say their piece in the front yard, my wife watching from the window."

Jim heard a soft clicking underneath, like the tumblers of a combination lock falling into place. One could never be sure if it were the pops and shorts of a run-down telephone system or an inexperienced eavesdropper plugging into the conversation.

"They wanted to know what Sokol and I were doing at your house yesterday."

"How much did you tell them?"

"Nothing. Absolutely nothing. I told them we'd just dropped by for drinks and to shoot the breeze. But they didn't buy that. Valeriano got on to how easily my visa could be revoked and—damn it to hell, Goodall! I've only been here three lousy months! How would it look if I got expelled right off the bat from my first assignment!''

''They were bluffing. They can't lay a hand on you.'' The man was frightened. He worried himself into a panic just talking about it and, if they returned, Jim knew Cooper might tell them everything. Jim was thinking too quickly, weighing the consequences of that, to feel frightened or threatened himself.

''I think Sokol talked,'' Cooper declared.

''I seriously doubt that.''

''Then how did they know we were even there? I sure the hell didn't tell anyone!''

''The security guards at the gate must report all my visitors.'' He should have considered that possibility, just as he should have guessed that a passionate man like Cooper who could be easily outraged might be just as easily petrified. Jim did not dwell on his slip in judgment. He was too busy imagining a future in which Enéro knew what Jim possessed. ''It was just a routine visit, Cooper. A chance to intimidate the greenhorn with special attention.''

''I don't buy that. You've gotten me in deep shit, Goodall. I've got my wife to think about and you heard what Sokol said about your item. There's not a damn thing you can do with it.''

''What're you saying, Cooper? That you're going to tell them what you saw?''

''No! Of course not.'' His pride had finally kicked in. ''All I'm saying is I'm not going to be able to write about your item. The odds suck and the bet's off, that's all.''

Jim faked a disappointed sigh. ''Suit yourself. But can you do me at least one favor, Cooper? If they do get back in touch with you, and you tell them something, can you promise you'll call me and report what you told them?''

''I'm not going to tell them anything.''

''I appreciate that. But if they give you no choice and you do, can you promise to let me know?''

''Of course. But I won't.''

Cooper didn't seem to understand Jim was giving him permission to spill the beans. Jim decided it was futile to persist.

''This call isn't just for my sake,'' Cooper claimed. ''I thought you should know they feel something's up, so you could take the necessary precautions.''

''Thanks, John. Yes. I should get on the stick right away. If you'll excuse me—''

''Yeah. Gotcha. I can't tell you how sorry I am I won't be able to—''

''Goodbye, Cooper.''

Jim set the receiver in its cradle. He had sat against the arm of the sofa during the conversation and remained there, lightly patting his knees with both hands. ''Well,'' he said when he looked up and saw Meg watching him from the table.

She was alarmed by what she'd heard, and baffled by his calm. "They know you have the film?"

"No. But they will. Sooner or later."

"And that's not bad?" Disbelief tightened her voice.

"It might turn the film into a valuable property." Expressing the notion aloud enabled Jim to complete his thought: "If they think I've got something they want, it could put me in a good bargaining position." He smiled at her while he dug into his pocket for his address book.

"Who're you calling?"

"They're going to know sooner or later. I'm going to see if I can make it sooner."

He dialed Sokol's number. Sokol answered.

"Good morning, Denny. Have you had any little visitors dropping by for coffee yet?"

He hadn't. Jim told him about Cooper's call, Valeriano's routine visit and the young man's panic.

"Watergate baby," Sokol muttered. "Valeriano likes to stomp around and talk big, but you don't have to worry about me, Jim. I'm an old hand at playing the know-nothing gringo."

"That's why I'm calling, Denny. Cooper was in such a sweat they have to know I've got something up my sleeve. Go ahead and tell them what you saw. They're going to find out eventually. No use in getting them angry at you. Feel free to tell them what I've got."

Sokol was silent for several long seconds. "You sure, Jim?"

"Yes."

"No skin off my nose. That might even give me an in with Valeriano. I hope *you're* able to get something out of it."

"I hope so too."

Sokol knew not to ask for details. There was a good chance his phone was tapped as well as Jim's. Not wanting Sokol or the hypothetical eavesdroppers to miss the point, Jim added, "You can even tell them Colonel Enéro is perfectly recognizable at the scene of the crime."

"Hmmm." Sokol understood the danger of that. "Whatever you say. It's your funeral. Let me get my friend out of bed and dressed before company comes over. I don't want him to have a heart attack hearing cops in the living room. I'll give you a call afterwards."

"Thanks, Denny."

Jim returned to the kitchen and sat at the table to finish his coffee. Meg sat there with an elbow on the table, her hand clutched around her mouth, preventing herself from speaking until she'd thought this through.

"I don't know what'll come of this. Maybe nothing at all. But we shall see," Jim said. "We should wait for Sokol to call back and then go ahead to Cavite."

"You're serious? You're not kidding."

"Once the ball's in their court, they can wait for me. I'm not going to sit by the phone waiting for them."

"No, I meant you're serious you can actually gain something by letting them know you have this movie?"

"We've got nothing to lose. I spent all day yesterday running down blind alleys. But they don't know that. All they'll know when they finish talking to Sokol is I've got a damning piece of evidence. It'll be interesting to see what they might offer me in exchange for it."

"Money?"

"They should know by now I won't want money. But information. Names. The name and possibly the release of that girl, for starters. If anybody deserves to benefit from this, she certainly does. We'll have to see how badly they want it."

Meg looked both skeptical and intrigued, her gaze drifting off while the two responses chased each other inside her head. "You've bargained like this before?" she asked.

"Not really. But as I said, we've got nothing to lose."

Meg was silent. He watched her think, wanting to get a more objective measure of his own doubts and hopes for this scheme by seeing them expressed in her face. Meg bit down on one corner of her mouth, pulling it into a faint smile. "It would be great if you could get something out of it. Wouldn't it?" she said uncertainly.

"We'll have to wait and see."

Fifteen minutes after Jim spoke to him, Sokol called back.

"You were right, old man. Valeriano and a shavetail lieutenant just dropped by for a chat. Valeriano strutted around and acted like he knew everything, right down to the color of my stool. But when I let slip you had a movie, and what was in that movie, you could've driven a bus through his open mouth. He had no idea, Jim. Not the foggiest. I hope you know what you're doing, because he got nothing from Cooper."

"Did you tell him about Enéro?"

"Yup. And they were out the door like two bats from hell."

Good, thought Jim. Perfect. He could not afford to have doubts now. The machinery had been set in motion.

"You'll understand when I keep my distance on this one, Jim. Bullies can get very stupid and dangerous when nervous. You be careful. I don't relish doing a story on some freak accident involving a certain late American official," he said with a laugh.

Jim laughed with him, assured Sokol he'd be careful and thanked him.

He had to take a deep breath the instant he hung up. "All right. It's out of our hands. The ball's in their court."

"Good," said Meg. "It is good, isn't it?" Despite herself, she began to seem excited. She trusted his competence and calm, which made Jim more certain this was the right thing to do. It was clearly the only thing.

"I can't promise anything. We'll just have to wait and see how badly they want it."

"What're you going to do with the film while you're waiting?" Meg asked. "Or is that something to worry about?"

"Not yet, but yes. That's something I wanted to take care of. Thanks for reminding me." He left the kitchen and went down the hall to the study. He unlocked the drawer to his desk and took the reel from under the stack of folders there—it now looked like a thick blue and white poker chip with a hole in its center. He found a small padded envelope and returned to the kitchen. "We might have to get this out of the house. Just to be on the safe side. Orbit it in the Philippine postal system for a couple of days."

"You're mailing it to yourself?"

"Yes." It was a method Lorenzo Chen recommended. "They can't come here with a search warrant without violating diplomatic immunity. But there's always the chance of burglars and, well, I trust Tammy and Tommy implicitly, but it's not smart throwing temptation in front of them. There's far too many spooks at the embassy for me to consider keeping it there."

"What if you mailed it to me?"

Arms folded on the table, Meg looked serious and determined.

"Wouldn't that be better?" she asked. "In case people were checking your mail? You should send it to me care of the American Express office downtown."

The spirit of the game was contagious. "That's not a bad idea. But it won't be necessary. I've got a post office box here in Makati." He neatly printed his own box number and the address on the envelope, feeling Meg watching him. He wanted her involved, but not that involved, on the very slim chance a threat to personal safety arose.

She understood immediately. "Are you in any kind of danger? Or does your diplomatic immunity protect you from *that* too?" She nodded at the circle inside the envelope.

"To be sure. I'm safe. You're safe. You're completely safe." He looked up at her, understanding this was an important question that needed to be answered. "It's the one line they refuse to cross. Not just because of diplomatic immunity. They treat Americans with kid gloves here. Even the NPA has this enormous respect for the power of the U.S. They've never kidnapped an American. I'm not sure why. Except there seems to be a deeply ingrained habit of respect leftover from colonial days, and it carries over to the secret police."

"That must feel odd. To know you're invulnerable when everyone around you isn't."

"Yes. Well. It's something else you get used to," Jim claimed. The strangeness of the privilege sometimes deepened the distance between him and events he was powerlessness to stop—a spectator at the movies—although not today.

They drove out to Cavite, stopping by the post office to mail the packet.

Snooping around the musty hallways and stairs of the Aguinaldo Shrine and Museum, home of the man who'd led the Philippines in its fight against the United States, Jim told Meg how he'd met Aguinaldo himself back in 1957, when the embassy negotiated the return of the sword he had surrendered to the Americans in 1901. "He lived until he was in his nineties," Jim explained.

"Really," said Meg, not nearly as impressed as he thought she would be. Their thoughts were elsewhere this afternoon. "It's like hearing you saw the last of the dinosaurs."

"Well, the past isn't always as long ago as it seems," Jim admitted.

When they returned home that evening, there was no message on the answering machine, no evidence of anyone coming by the house. Jim told Meg this might take longer than he thought, but he wondered again if the film would have any effect at all.

THE CALL DIDN'T come until the following morning, Sunday, when they were both in the kitchen drinking coffee. Tony Wexler phoned.

"What the fuck's going on, Goodall? The ambassador just called from the golf course and he wants your ass down there pronto! Whatever it is you're dicking around in, Marcos is blaming *us*! Gough demands you settle this posthaste or your dick's in a meatgrinder."

"Good morning, Wexler." Jim hid his surprise that this had gone straight to the embassy. Flustered men with telephones had been very busy last night and this morning. "Did the ambassador give any indication what the president's problem appears to be?"

"Colonel Enéro has reason to believe you've obtained film that could create big misunderstandings, Goodall."

"Really? And does the ambassador know what's on this film?"

Wexler was surprised Jim immediately admitted its existence. "Yes. And it's fake, Goodall. Enéro is familiar with the film and says it's been making the rounds for months. You're the first bleeding heart who was sucker enough to swallow the thing."

Jim was impressed. It was an ingenious lie, and so plausible he might be tempted to believe it himself if he hadn't seen the footage. "If it's a fake, then what's the ambassador afraid of?"

"Don't play dumb. Marcos doesn't need us circulating fabrications that make him look bad. We've moved hell and high water to earn the man's trust, and you're screwing it up."

"I happen to think it's real," Jim said quietly. "For one thing, Colonel Enéro himself is clearly recognizable. He watched the proceedings."

Wexler said nothing; they hadn't told him that detail. "Look. I don't bloody care if it's real or not. This is their country. We let them run it as they please. You're meddling with internal affairs, Goodall, and that's inexcusable. You Human Rights people are as much a pain in the ass as the CIA. I'm not going to waste my breath arguing. Gough wants you at the Wack Wack clubhouse so you can fix this with the president.''

''Marcos is there?''

''Yes. They were having a very productive round of golf when Enéro called.''

Of course. Jim should have guessed. That was why Gough had been pulled into this so quickly. The interminable base negotiations had their dividends.

''Be there, Goodall. If you don't smooth this over with our man, you're on the next plane home. Derian won't be able to save your balls this time. You got that? Goodbye!'' There was a knock and clatter before the phone went dead.

Jim lowered his receiver, batting it like a club against his palm before he settled it in the cradle. He seemed to have struck gold; he had struck a nerve anyway. ''I don't believe it,'' he told Meg. ''I had no idea this'd go to the top so soon. Something might happen. I might actually be able to make something happen.''

''You didn't think you would?'' she asked.

He gave his doubts a giddy laugh. ''One never knows. Wish me luck. Wish *us* luck.''

THE SKY WAS bright and colorless, burned clean of blue. Cicadas chittered in the pine grove behind the clubhouse and the resin smelled like warm gin.

They were visible in the distance. A pair of canopied golf carts and a scattered platoon of figures drifted up the fairway of the ninth hole. Jim watched from the grove behind the green. Everything about the game was conducted in whispers, from the mosquito whir of the carts' electric motors to the completely visual, unheard sound of the bodyguards tromping beside the rough. Jim hadn't played golf in over six years; he was impressed with how sinister the game appeared to an outsider.

''Do you play, Colonel?''

''No!'' Enéro stood beside him in freshly pressed khakis, refusing to look at Jim, manfully straining to ignore the metaphorical fly that crawled on his face each time Jim looked at him.

With sunglasses, bald skull and the permanent little frown of a pit bull, Enéro did not look like a man who could take pleasure in anything, even the torture of a girl. The sip-sips called him the Scrotum, but maybe there was a Tagalog pun involved because Jim saw nothing baggy or testicular about the man. He had the stumpy body of a middle-aged wrestler and a head like a boxing glove with ears.

A loud snap sounded across the fairway; a black speck fell from the sky, and landed with a soft thud in the sandtrap to the left of the green. In the distance, the short blue and yellow figure that was Marcos jabbed the ground with his club, tossed the club aside and stomped toward the cart. A caddie immediately fetched the club.

On the other side of the fairway, the tall figure of Gough braced itself for his shot. He swung, and another speck hung over the green, only to drop neatly into the same trap with the president's ball. No wonder the man had succeeded in becoming an ambassador at such an early age.

Jim stepped from the piney shadows now that it was safe to approach, followed by Enéro. Bodyguards appeared on either side of the green, whispering on walkie-talkies, watching for assassins. The two golf carts pulled up, Marcos and Gough riding together in one, the other occupied by a PSU lieutenant who spoke on a telephone while he drove. Gough saw Jim standing with Enéro, pulled a face and looked away. Marcos pretended not to see anything except his ball in the sand. He snapped his fingers at his caddy, took a nine-iron and popped the ball up on the green with a clean chop. Gough followed, managing to get his ball a tactful ten yards further from the pin than the president's.

Hoping to catch a key to their states of mind, Jim watched them putt. Marcos gave away nothing, not even relief when he sank his ball in one stroke and the bodyguards respectfully applauded. Gough required two strokes, but they were sincere. A caddy ran over with the scorecard and gave it to Marcos, who held the card up to show his people he'd won. He was too busy to play more than nine holes nowadays, even when there wasn't a crisis at hand. Gough smiled at Marcos and bowed his head, then walked with him off the green. The two men in clashing pastel knits looked like Mutt-and-Jeff pimps.

"Goodall," Gough said curtly. "Pleased you could make it."

Marcos was coldly cordial. "Jim," he said, walking up with his hand and arm raised, the elbow lifted over his head to shake hands from above; here was a man who took the phrase "upper hand" literally. "You once played the game yourself, didn't you? I remember playing with you and Chip Adkins. On one occasion with President Nixon." He thought he was being friendly, but the charm Marcos used to turn on and off like a spigot no longer flowed.

"Yes, sir. Many years ago."

"A great man," Marcos sighed. "Unappreciated in his own country. Terribly unappreciated." He began to walk toward the pine grove and everyone walked with him.

Gough announced, "I've told the president you might be more comfortable chatting with him alone."

"You won't be joining our discussion, Ambassador?" said Jim.

"I'm treating this as a purely private matter between you and our host government. I've already made our own government's position clear to the president. I trust Wexler's made *your* position clear to you?"

"Quite clear." This was cagey; the less Gough knew, the easier it would be for him to deny any knowledge or responsibility.

"All right then. I want this matter settled with all deliberate speed. Mr. President, I trust you'll be able to settle this to your satisfaction. Goodall is a loose cannon, but *not* insensible to reason. I'll be in the clubhouse if you need me."

"We'll be fine, Donald. I'm sure Jim here is quite reasonable. Come, Jim. We'll chat in my hut."

Gough gave Jim a final admonishing look, then went with the others toward the clubhouse. Jim walked with Marcos and Enéro toward the river, and the little shack Marcos maintained on the grounds specifically for private meetings before and after games of golf, followed by a half-dozen silent bodyguards. Across the brown river, the baroque facade of the Malacanang Palace was visible among its bursts of palm fronds. The shack faced the water, a screened-in porch without a house, covered with the shade and needles of the pine trees overhead. Jim had never been here, but he knew this was where Ambassador Earp repeatedly met with Marcos in the months before martial law was declared. Entering the shack and seeing the wooden floor pierced and chewed by years of visitors in spiked golf shoes, Jim was impressed with the power of his movie, the mere rumor of it bringing him so close to the center of things.

The large wicker chair crackled when Marcos sat. He took off his sunglasses and mopped his face with a hand towel that had been left neatly folded on the table. Outside the screens, water lapped along the river bank, the clatter of cicadas rose and fell, and little radios hawked bursts of static while the bodyguards took their positions among the scaly treetrunks.

Marcos brushed his kewpie-doll forelock back into place. "Will you do the honors, Colonel? I want to finish this quickly."

Enéro gritted his teeth and stepped behind Jim. He frisked him, gingerly under the arms, then angrily up the insides of Jim's slacks. The torturer knew he was touching a homosexual, and it made him squeamish.

"You understand," said Marcos. "We can't speak man-to-man if you're wearing a bug. Please, make yourself comfortable." He gestured at a wicker chair slightly lower than his own. "I'd offer you a beer but all I drink is water." The president neither drank nor smoked.

"Water's fine."

While Enéro fussed in the refrigerator, Jim and Marcos gazed at each other. The man had put his sunglasses back on, but the lenses were photosensitive; the darkness cleared enough for Jim to see the tiny black eyes behind the smoked glass.

"July nineteen sixty-nine," said Marcos.

"I beg your pardon, Mr. President?"

"When you and I played golf with President Nixon. I never forget anything, Jim."

Enéro brought them their glasses of ice water and sat in the chair between them.

Marcos took a leisurely swallow. "Go ahead, Colonel. You know the situation better than I do."

Enéro noisily cleared his throat; he was not a man accustomed to explaining himself. "The movie you have is a fraud. It was manufactured by the Communists in an effort to discredit the president and cast shame on the Philippine people. We've known of its existence for months."

"You've seen it then?"

"I don't waste my time with movies. Members of my staff report its fakery is obvious. You'll look like a fool if you show it to the press."

Marcos continued to watch Jim and sip water, saying nothing.

"I don't know, Colonel. I found the film convincing. For one thing, I recognized people from the Presidential Security Unit."

"These filmmakers were clever. They found actors with vague likenesses to certain people."

"Extremely clever. They found someone who looks exactly like you."

Enéro exchanged a look with Marcos. They knew this already and it was Enéro's mistake. The president expected him to fix it. "Who else?"

"I don't know their names. Men I've seen around." Jim had decided not to mention Aguilar, for fear it would place the captain at the scene and make him suspect. Enéro would have to remember the time when a camera was seized, but Jim assumed there were other times, other women, when Enéro had been too absorbed in watching to know if he'd been filmed or not.

"We do not condone the torture of young women," Enéro announced.

"Only young men?"

"Torture is outlawed under the Constitution and tolerated neither by the president nor those directly responsible to him."

Marcos's chair creaked as he shifted around, bored with Enéro's stale phrases.

Enéro cleared his throat again. "We request you give us this film. We'll examine it and decide for ourselves if it's real. If that proves to be the case, the men responsible will be disciplined."

"Yourself included, Colonel?"

Enéro ignored that; he did not expect to be believed. "In appreciation for your time and any expense incurred in obtaining the film, we're prepared to pay you a reward. Fifty thousand dollars."

"You must want this film quite badly." Jim was uncertain how the amount translated into importance.

"We want to save both you and ourselves from embarrassment. In addition to the money, there's your own good name to consider. Your standing at the embassy."

"President Marcos should be able to tell you right off, after his talk with Ambassador Gough this morning, my standing is pretty low."

Enéro looked at Marcos.

Marcos shrugged.

Enéro said, "Not so low as it would get if your private life became public."

Marcos watched, waiting for Jim's reaction, treating him as little more than a game. The bribe and blackmail were the real purpose of this meeting. The preceding lies were only a courtesy to help Jim save face when he accepted.

"You know how our newspapers love gossip," said Enéro. "It could get very ugly. And once word reached your bureau in Washington that it was the First Lady's hairdresser who was your cocksucker"—he bared his gums on the word—"you'd be in big shit. They might even suspect you of spying for *us*."

"An interesting proposition," said Jim. "Very interesting." He smiled at Marcos, assuming this was his idea. Enéro's methods were more simple and direct. "I've already considered giving you the film."

Enéro lifted his chin in a Mussolini look of triumph.

"But not for money. And not for silence either," Jim said. "I live a plain life and I don't care who knows I'm a cocksucker—pardon my French. This is the proposition *I* suggest: First, the name and release of the girl in the film. Second, a list of people arrested and still in jail from the crackdown last April. I don't expect a complete list, but we can negotiate on the exact number. And third, permission to visit and interview those people. After my visits, *then* I'll give you the film. In the interim, you have my promise I won't leak it to the world press or television."

Enéro looked contemptuous, Marcos mildly surprised. He rocked one two-toned golf shoe against the floor, digging the spikes into the wood.

"It's not very much, Mr. President. I am a reasonable man. And it would be to your benefit as well, enabling you to rectify abuses nobody can blame on you." The list of names would help Jim keep people from disappearing. The interviews would give Derian more substantial evidence on the extent of political arrests and torture here. The claim of mutual benefit was an outright lie to help Marcos save face when *he* accepted.

Enéro swatted the air with the back of his hand. "Ridiculous horseshit. We have no political prisoners in our jails. Only criminals. This girl doesn't exist. Your film of the bitch doesn't exist."

Marcos, however, remained calm and interested. "Do we get to see this film, Jim? Or did you want to sell us a blind pig?"

"I'd arrange a screening on neutral ground—the Swedish embassy, for example. Colonel Enéro would be invited, to identify the girl. Also Tony Wexler from the embassy and maybe Denny Sokol, who's already seen the film."

"Mr. Sokol didn't want it for his network?"

"He's interested. But if I can do my job by dealing directly with you and Colonel Enéro, fine and good. Once the media gets its hands on something, there's no controlling what happens. Look at what they did to Nixon. I'd like to keep this under control."

Marcos drew his mouth together, the lips bunching together like a clumsily sutured wound. If Jim could overestimate the objective justice of television, it should be no surprise Marcos did too.

Enéro could stand it no longer. "Don't you know who you're talking to!" he snarled. "You don't make deals. *We* make deals. You're a nobody cocksucker. I make you a very good offer and you're too stupid to accept. You *bastos* pervert. Don't you know you put not just yourself in danger, but the people close to you?"

Jim kept control of himself, restraining his hatred of Enéro for threatening Meg. "You know as well as I do, Colonel, that if anyone lays a hand on my niece, not even the president's good friend Gough will stand by him."

"Jim's right," Marcos quietly told Enéro. "You should know better than to make idle threats against the man's scholarly guest." He smiled as if at a joke, gently shaking his head to himself.

It was inevitable they knew something about Meg; Jim was disturbed to think the secret police and even Marcos himself discussed her in small, private rooms.

"You surprise me, Jim," said Marcos.

"I would think nothing could surprise a man like yourself, sir."

He took the compliment with a minute nod. "My first reaction had been to let Colonel Enéro handle this alone. But I was curious. I had to see if the Jim Goodall who resigned in protest six years ago—should one be insulted or flattered?—was the same Jim Goodall now engaged in carnal relations with one of my wife's *catamites*."

"The one and the same," said Jim.

"Yes. I suppose you still are. Most real men can be bought too," Marcos explained. "But those of your persuasion generally come much cheaper. They have given up all honor to do what they do, which is why I let my wife surround herself with them. They amuse her and their loyalty is guaranteed. You on the other hand—I'd assumed money and the threat of disclosure would bring you around. But no. Curious. You engage in unmanly acts yet here you are, behaving like a *maharlika*."

It was the Filipino equivalent of *mensch,* yet with more blatant sexual connotations. The word could be translated as king or stud or phallus and carried a complicated cultural freight of prowess and power. Marcos, of course, considered himself the ultimate *maharlika*. He once proposed renaming the country Maharlika, after himself.

"Most interesting." He gripped the arms of his chair and forced himself up, requiring more effort than one might expect—perhaps the rumors about his health had a grain of truth.

Jim and Enéro stood with him.

"I'll tell Gough you and I had a friendly chat, without going into personal details," Marcos said. "Your proposition is something I need to discuss with Colonel Enéro before I make a decision. In the meantime, you won't show this little movie to anyone else, will you?"

"No, sir. I can keep it to myself for two or three days. Until Wednesday morning, let us say?" He did not want Marcos to think he could draw this out indefinitely, and the film wouldn't arrive in his post office box until Tuesday or Wednesday.

"You'll have my answer before then, I assure you."

They stepped outside and Marcos swooped one hand over his head again for a farewell handshake. He then marched briskly down the path toward the clubhouse, attracting his bodyguards the way a queen bee attracts drones. Enéro scowled at Jim and trotted after his president. He had lost and Jim had won, this round anyway. The dictator was willing to negotiate.

JIM WENT TO his office at the embassy before going home. It was after midnight on the other side of the world and Jim telephoned Dave Wheeler at his house. Embassy security monitored all calls, but Gough now knew everything Jim had to report to Wheeler.

Wheeler was still up. Classical music played in the distance until Wheeler turned it off while getting pencil and paper. "So. How's tricks?"

Jim told him about the Super–8 footage of Enéro, without telling him how he got it or that Enéro wasn't fully recognizable. He told about Enéro's people discovering its existence, without admitting his own involvement. And he told him he had just had a meeting with Marcos and the deals they offered each other, leaving out any mention of Gus: neither Wheeler nor Gough needed to hear he was using a spy for sexual relief.

"The monster himself talked? This film must be dynamite. I can't wait to see it. You got to get it to us right away. Is there a courier you can trust? No diplomatic pouch. If Gough doesn't snag it at your end, Holbrooke will at ours."

"I'm going to hold on to it, Dave. Until I see if Marcos gives me what I want."

"You're not actually going to give it to the bastards?"

"If they meet my terms, yes." Jim wanted Gough to know that Marcos could deal with him in good faith. "That way I'll know some good might come of it."

Wheeler understood what Jim was saying; they'd been arguing about this in cables and long-distance conversations for six months now. "Look Jim. You don't know what we're up against here. Iran's already got the Department scared shitless, and Nicaragua's ready to blow any day. It's not for lack of trying that Pat and I haven't been able to make capital out of the stuff you've sent us. But this film sounds different. We could jerk a few congressmen off the fence with it."

"Uh-uh. I don't want this girl collecting dust in the drawer with everything else I've sent you. No, if I can get some shortterm benefits with it, great, I'll give it to Marcos. If not, it goes to one of my television contacts."

"Lotsa luck with that," said Wheeler, already knowing how tricky it could be—his tone of voice wouldn't register in the transcript of their conversation

Gough would read. "All right. Can you promise me this? You'll call me before you make your deal with Marcos? If there's nothing special we can do with the film, yes, you should go for the short term. But if we can do more with it over here, you'll send it."

"I can't promise anything until I hear *your* case."

Wheeler was silent a moment. "Fair enough. I guess I can't blame you for not fully trusting us anymore."

"I trust your intentions, Dave. It's your ability to carry out half of what you think you can that I'm shaky about."

"No. None of it's turned out the way we hoped, has it? All right. I'll talk to Pat. You talk to the bastards. We'll see who comes out with the best deal. Good night, Jim."

"Good night, Dave."

He hung up and looked at the blaze of afternoon coming through his venetian blinds. For all their good intentions, they had no idea what life was really like over here; they didn't even know what time of day it was.

"I THINK IT's great. Isn't it? You'll actually be able to change something with that girl. She didn't suffer in vain. It's exciting. Frightening too, but exciting. You're excited. Aren't you?"

He was, but he didn't want it to show, wanted to seem calm and controlled instead. "It's too soon for me to feel anything," he claimed. "It wouldn't have happened without you, you know."

"No. I was only a go-between," said Meg. "But I'm glad to have been of use there at least."

They were in the kitchen, eating the dinner Meg had cooked. Tammy had weekends off and Meg fixed dinner chiefly to give herself something to do. "Don't look so shocked. I don't always eat in coffee shops and restaurants. Sometimes it feels good to chop onions." When Jim asked if she'd been nervous being alone in the house all afternoon, she said no, only restless, a feeling she put to work in transcribing her notes, then in making a pot of chili. "You were right. It's amazing how much someone can know, yet go on with the most trivial life."

Jim didn't mention Enéro's idle threat against "people close to you," but he told Meg everything else about the meeting: the hut, the golf shoes, Enéro's temper, Marcos's speech on homosexuality. He explained more about Marcos and *maharlika,* how the man was respected not only for his many mistresses and the medals he'd won leading guerrillas against the Japanese—although the rumor was the American medals had been given solely to buy his loyalty—but for murdering a political enemy of his father while still a young man in law school. Julio Nalundasan was shot one night when he stood on his porch brushing his teeth. Young Marcos was charged and convicted. He passed his law boards while in prison, defended himself in a higher court and overturned the conviction. Most people still believed he had done it, however, and many admired him for killing in the name of family honor.

"Ugh. These primal, so-called truths," said Meg. "A man's not a man until he kills somebody. A woman's not a woman until she's had a baby."

"Yes," said Jim. "Any fool can kill." He had never told Meg about his own murder, had he?

"But you can make a deal with a man like that? Trust him?"

"I trust in his intelligence. It's in his best interest for Marcos to make a deal. He's smart enough to understand that."

The doorbell rang.

Jim and Meg watched each other. Her mouth was full and she stopped chewing. She was not as nerveless as she pretended.

"Must be a neighbor," said Jim, getting up from his chair. "Otherwise they would've called from the gate." He went to the door, wondering if it were Enéro or somebody from the PSU. If the security guards were working for the PSU, they'd simply wave the car through without calling. Jim flipped the porch light on and looked through the peephole.

Standing on the porch, glancing over his shoulder at the street, was Gus.

Jim promptly opened the door. "What're you doing here?"

"Jim Goodall! Please. Let me in. I had to see you."

Jim let him in and closed the door. His jeans and knit shirt looked like they'd been quickly pulled on, without the usual care Gus took in getting dressed before he visited.

"Just Gus!" Jim called back to the kitchen, to put Meg at ease.

"Your niece is here?" Gus whispered. "We should go into the bedroom."

"Sure." Jim followed him down the hall. "You have something important to tell me? What's happened, Gus?"

"Yes. Just a minute. In here." Gus pushed the bedroom door shut behind them, leaned against the door and drew a deep breath. He was smiling as if he had good news to share—Jim had been expecting the worst. "Please, Jim Goodall. I have to tell you right away—" He gripped Jim's elbow and looked Jim in the face. "I am so damn horny."

Jim blinked. He jerked his arm from Gus's grip. "Damn you, Gus. I thought you had something important to tell me," Jim grumbled. "That the police had been to see you or I was in danger."

Gus laughed, his familiar hee-hah. "You *are* in danger," he purred. "Because I *am* horny. Please, I don't have much time. I tell Eleanor I am only going out to get beer and ice cream." To illustrate, or persuade, he peeled his knit shirt over his head.

"Gus, I'm not in the mood tonight. And I'm in the middle of dinner."

"Oh, but I'm in the mood, Jim Goodall." He stepped back, stepping out of his alligator loafers.

"Didn't we just do this two or three nights ago? I'm an old man, Gus. I've got too much else on my mind."

"You should let me take your mind away from that. Hmmm." He dialed his right nipple with a finger. He popped the button of his jeans and slowly drew down the zipper—the fellow had seen too many American porn films. "I have an idea," he suddenly said. "What if I take a shower? And you finish your dinner? I need to wash off. You need time to think about *sex,*" he smirkingly hissed.

"Take a cold shower," said Jim, more amused than annoyed. "Then you're welcome to join Meg and me for coffee."

"We shall see about that," he whispered. "You'll change your mind." He walked backward toward the bathroom, then turned and wagged his ass at Jim, shaking the loose jeans like a bell before he ducked behind the door.

"It's nothing," Jim told Meg when he sat down again at the table. "Our friend Gus is horny tonight."

Meg snorted and shook her head. "Well, don't mind me. I can stay out here and read or watch television."

"No. I told him to take a cold shower. I can't think about that in the middle of this." But the idea of sex with Gus did not seem as impossible now as it had a minute ago. Lust did not feel inappropriate at the end of this day; the chance of success was a kind of aphrodisiac.

"You don't think he's here to find out something in particular?" Meg asked.

"Possibly. Although I doubt Ferdinand's mentioned this to Imelda. And I don't know what he could learn that I haven't told them already. My state of mind?" Jim laughed to himself. "Would a man confident of success be interested, or not interested?"

Meg was listening to something in the distance.

Jim listened too. He thought he heard the steady sigh of the shower under the breath of the air-conditioning. Then there was a brief squeak, like a door being opened.

"Maybe I should check on our friend. See if he has everything he needs." Jim silently scooted his chair back.

"It's not in the house, right?" Meg whispered.

Jim nodded. He stepped quietly from the kitchen into the hall. The shower ran, uninterrupted by a body. The door to the bedroom gaped open, and the study door opposite was open too. Jim moved down the hall, keeping to the far wall so he could look into his study without blocking the light shining into the dark room.

Gus crouched at Jim's desk, his knees spread apart, the flattened W of his bare ass resting on his heels; he was jimmying the lock of a drawer with what looked like a bobby pin.

Naturally, thought Jim. Naturally. This was what he expected. But there was a stab of disappointment and anger when Jim saw what Gus was doing.

"Lose something?" he asked.

Gus tottered backward, then scrambled to his feet. "Oh. Jim Goodall." He drew a sharp breath. "You scared me," he laughed, pretending this was nothing. His hair was dry, his smooth skin grainy with goosebumps; he hadn't even stepped into the shower. His genitals were drawn tight by the shock of being caught.

"If you tell me what you're looking for, maybe I can help."

"Oh, uh, stuff." He stepped toward the door, looking across the hall into the bedroom where his clothes were, afraid Jim might grab or hit him before he could get to them. "You know. Greasy stuff. To fuck."

"You don't like that, remember?"

"Maybe I change my mind." He became bolder. "Maybe I wanted to fuck you," he said. "Oh, Jim Goodall, I am so horny."

Jim put his hands in his pockets. He didn't want to touch Gus, not even to slap him. "Get dressed and go home."

"You don't believe me?"

"Please, Gus. Before I lose my temper."

Gus produced a put-upon sigh. He quickly ducked past Jim into the bedroom. He entered the bathroom, turned off the shower and stepped out with the tangle of jeans in his hands. "You are so weird tonight, Jim Goodall. So sick in the head."

Jim stood just inside the door, keeping his distance. "Who sent you, Gus?"

"What're you talking about? *This* sent me." He pulled at his penis, stretching it like putty.

"Was it Enéro? Marcos himself? The least you can do is tell me which faction you're working for." He'd always assumed it was chiefly for Imelda that Gus gathered bits of information and news, gossip she could then proudly pass on to her husband. Jim decided it was discovering Gus worked directly for Enéro that made him feel hurt and angry despite what he'd known about Gus all along.

Gus flipped his underpants loose and stepped into them. "Why do you insult my attraction to you? I come here wanting you, and you accuse me of coming to steal something."

"Did they tell you what's on this roll of movie film?"

"Movie film? Who said anything about a movie film?" Gus looked down, tugging and adjusting his elastic longer than was necessary.

"It's film of a young woman being tortured. By members of the Presidential Security Unit, Gus. People you'd probably recognize from your visits to the palace. I know you'd recognize Colonel Enéro."

Gus pulled on his jeans and grabbed at his shirt on the floor, saying nothing.

"Enéro stood and watched his men take a young girl, undress her, hold her down on a bed and administer electrical shocks. They put the clamps on her breasts, Gus. The movie's silent but you can *see* her screaming." Jim wanted to keep his voice cold and dry, but his throat kept tightening in anger while he watched Gus hide his skin in clothes.

"I don't believe you. Or if it's true, she must have done something terrible," Gus declared. "She's a terrorist, a murderer. She was only getting what she deserved."

"No. Nobody deserves to be treated like that." Not even you, thought Jim. He was amazed to think such a thing, but he hated Gus right now, for his callousness, cynical lies and complicity.

"I have my own family to think about." Gus slipped his bare feet into the smooth scales of his alligator shoes. "I cannot feel for everyone in the world."

"I'm sorry I don't have the movie here or I'd show it to you."

"I don't want to see your movie. Where is it?"

"Someplace safe." Jim was no longer amused by his spy's brazen lack of subtlety. "Tell Enéro that. So he won't think your visit was a complete failure. Tell him the movie isn't in the house, but someplace where nobody can touch it. Not his people or mine either. I can't even get to it myself for a couple of days."

Gus listened carefully, then closed his eyes and sniffed. "You bark up the wrong tree. I came here to make love, Jim Goodall, and you have hurt my feelings."

"Fine, Gus. I was hoping you could be at least half-honest with me, but if you want to stick to that tale, fine. Let's go."

He walked Gus to the door, saying nothing more. He opened the door on a blizzard of white moths attracted by the porch light.

"I am very angry with you," said Gus. "I don't know if I'll ever forgive you enough to come visit again."

"In that case, let's say goodbye instead of goodnight."

"Goodbye, Mr. *Gágo*"—fool. "I expected more trust from a man who kisses me on the mouth." He marched out the door into the moths, his head held high, the seat of his jeans twitching poutily as he walked toward the sports car parked in the driveway.

Idiot, thought Jim, angry with himself for being so angry about Gus. He closed the door and hurried back to the study, turned on the light and inspected his desk. The obsessive neatness of his papers in the unlocked drawers seemed lightly ruffled, and on the rug in front of the locked bottom drawer was a bent bobby pin, the little droplet of plastic peeled from one tip. No, he had not misunderstood Gus.

"Then you were right about him after all."

Meg stood in the door, her arms folded, an uncertain look of sympathy on her face.

"Oh yeah." Jim showed her the twisted pin before he dropped it in the wastebasket. "He was here to get in my drawers, one way or the other."

She didn't smile. "I was able to hear only so much in the kitchen. At first it sounded like a lovers' quarrel."

"More like a whores' quarrel," said Jim with a laugh. "No, I had no

business getting angry with him. I hoped telling about the movie might wake
him up to what kind of people he's working for. But no. He has a convenient
gift for denial."

They returned to the kitchen. Their half-finished bowls of chili were cold
and congealed. Meg cleared them away while Jim made coffee.

"I won't pretend to understand your relationship," said Meg, sounding
more philosophical than sympathetic. "But I am sorry."

"Nothing to be sorry about," said Jim. "Actually it's a good sign they sent
Gus here on such a ridiculous errand. They've always used him very carefully.
But they're desperately looking for an alternative to my terms. They're cash-
ing in all the chips they have on me: my private life, my liaison with their
multi-purpose courtesan. They're very close to giving in." The idea had come
to Jim in the study, turning his feeling of betrayal into one of victory; it
became more convincing when said aloud.

Meg sat down again and lit a cigarette. "I don't know anything about
anything," she said. "But being desperate won't make them dangerous?"

"It could. Except there's no way they can touch you and me. What I've
asked for isn't so extraordinary that they should resort to violence. Marcos is a
tyrant, but he's a reasonable, practical tyrant. He risks too much going after an
American official or his niece."

Meg nodded, flicking her cigarette by brushing the filter with her thumb.
There was no trace of fear in her eyes, only a grim look around her mouth. A
shadow suddenly passed over Jim's thoughts. Her hair was up tonight and she
looked nothing like the girl in the film, yet Jim couldn't help being frightened
for Meg.

"Tomorrow morning," he said, "would you mind going in with me when I
go to the embassy? You can check out the Information Service's library,
which I understand is quite good. And, well, I'd feel a little better knowing
exactly where you were."

"Sure. I needed to visit the USIS library sometime." She hesitated, then
said, "So I do have good cause to feel nervous?"

"It's good to be a little nervous. It keeps one prudent. I'm a little nervous
myself," Jim admitted. "But rationally, you and I are in absolutely no danger.
If I thought we were, I'd put you on the next plane back to the States."

Meg smirked at the idea. "What if I refused?"

"Then you'd be an even worse masochist than I am."

"I would, wouldn't I? But it'd be like leaving a play at intermission. I'm
just an observer here, and I trust you know what you're doing. But I do feel a
little worried for myself. I just want to know if that's neurotic of me or
realistic." She looked pained asking.

"It's not neurotic. It's sane." But Jim realized he wasn't at all afraid for
himself, only for Meg; he could almost *want* something to happen to him.
"But there's nothing they can do to me except kick me out of the country,

which would be a relief. There's nothing they can do to you, Meg. Nothing at all.''

She inhaled her cigarette again, pulling the smoke in deeply while she nodded, seeming to believe him. After she exhaled she said, ''If I'm going to sit here with the spectators watching the Battle of Bull Run, I need to know if those are bullets zipping overhead or only mosquitos.''

''Mosquitos,'' said Jim. ''But you're more than just a spectator.''

She shook her head. ''No, that's exactly what I am. Thank God.''

Later that evening there was a telephone call from Zamboanga in Mindanao. Captain Aguilar didn't identify himself to Jim, but asked to speak to Dr. Frisch. Meg was startled to hear the call was for her, then unnerved when Jim whispered that Aguilar seemed to know the line was tapped and she should go along with whatever story he wanted to tell. She did, pretending she barely remembered him from their meeting at Oasis a few nights ago, feigning coy indifference when he said he had hoped to see her again but had volunteered that morning to fly down to Mindanao on government-related business. He would not return to Manila for another two or three weeks, and assumed she'd be gone by then. She managed a mild grunt of disapproval when he mentioned a few romantic might-have-beens, watching Jim's face to see how she was doing. Jim nodded to keep her going, surmising most of what Aguilar said from Meg's replies. He said something about Meg having a fruitful stay with her uncle and said goodbye.

''Good,'' said Jim. ''Very good. He knows something's going to happen. He's gotten himself as far from the scene of the crime as possible. We don't have to worry about him. And you handled that beautifully,'' he assured her. ''You were quite convincing.''

But Meg did not seem pleased with herself or excited by what Aguilar's call might mean, only relieved that she hadn't screwed up.

18

THE CITY STRETCHED NORTH in the dark along the bay. It was a half-sketched city, a picture map with a few luxury hotels, Rizal Park and the American Embassy clearly marked. A few known avenues cut through the maze of unknown streets, and a little river wormed its way inland from the crushed sprawl of Tondo to the rose gardens of the Malacanang Palace; the palace's front yard was a generic golf course where her uncle sat face to face with Napoleon in golf shoes.

Lying in bed that night, still floating on the surface of sleep, Meg strained to see the city whole, wanting to locate the different threats, needing to give this drama a geography. But what she'd seen for herself didn't help. There was no suggestion in her map of where the torture kitchen might be, the jails Jim had mentioned, the switchboard that listened in on every telephone conversation. Those places seemed to exist only in her head. You go halfway around the world to see the thing itself, and the only world you get is the claustrophobic cell of your own mind.

Meg imagined herself entering the Malacanang Palace, passing into it like a mosquito entering a man's ear. She expected to find there the torturers, eaves-droppers and solid banks of state computers. Instead she found Imelda Marcos, chatting on the telephone. She chatted with Meg's mother, assuring her Meg was a lovely guest and she liked her friend Doug, too, who did such nice things with her hair. Meg was alarmed, then relieved to realize she must be asleep and dreaming, then embarrassed the dream was so ridiculous and petty.

She awoke to a soft roar of water. She woke up every morning to the hissing shower on the other side of her bedroom wall, but this water was outdoors. The window was open—Jim turned off the air-conditioning and opened the windows every night when they went to bed—and a fresh smell of rain blew into the room. Rainy season was a couple of weeks away and this was just an early morning tropical shower, but it washed the air and drew Meg into her skin. She pulled on T-shirt and shorts and went through the silent house to the sliding glass doors of the dining room, pushed the glass aside and stood there. During so much weirdness, it felt good to watch something as normal as rain.

Fistfuls of water burst on the patio; the enormous green quills of the garden bounced in the downpour. The light itself looked green at this hour. Water raced down the trunk of a palm near the door, rippling over the bark wrapped around it like a bandage. The seething yard gave off a sweet breath of chewed cud.

It stopped, very abruptly, as if a knob were turned. Water continued to run in the gutters and pour from the spouts of long, heavy leaves, but it was over. Meg placed one bare foot on the wet bricks outside.

What am I afraid of?

Because she was afraid, even as she stepped over the patio to the spongy grass. Despite what she told Jim last night, she'd been uneasy yesterday afternoon while he was gone, mostly vague fears, sometimes fears for herself. She wanted to believe her fears for herself were out of sympathy for that girl, an attempt to close the distance between them. But Meg knew she was forgetting the girl, thinking of her in much the same way Jim had from the start, as evidence, a means to an end. When Meg undressed for bed the night she saw the film, she couldn't bear to look at herself. The next night she suffered a delayed pang when she saw her own hips and hair. Last night she remembered another use for the body and missed Ron, not just for sex but for the comfort of being with someone she could idly bump against and remind herself she was real.

There was only body and mind and world, and the things the world could do to the body. She was merely a mind looking on here. No wonder a backyard after a storm could feel so unreal and threatening.

Water ticktocking in the soil underneath, she strolled on the cool, sopping grass, glancing at the wet houses and other gardens outside her uncle's tall fence, then at the closed blinds of Jim's bedroom window. What tricks did he have for dealing with his own emotional weather? He clearly had emotions. He didn't suffocate them in Gary Cooper stoicism or kill them with smugly masculine competence. He could be excited. He acknowledged other emotions, yet spoke of them only as rumors, keeping them at arm's length, which might be the only way to stay sane during a crisis. This morning Meg respected and even envied such dissociation.

The thick stand of bamboo along one fence began to whistle, the water in its chambers audibly evaporating. There were further squeaks and cackles overhead as birds shook themselves dry. The sky lightened and cleared. The air felt clean and weightless for the first time since her arrival. Meg began to enjoy being out here, nerves and all, but a cigarette would make things better.

She was in the living room, looking for the pack she thought she'd left on the coffee table last night, when there was a squeak out front sharper and harder than the squeaks in the garden. Meg looked up at the windows. A jeep with a canvas top had pulled into the driveway; two men in white helmets sat in the fan-shaped eyes cleared by the windshield wipers during the rain.

"Jim?" she said.

In olive drab fatigues, trousers tucked inside their boots, the men were getting out.

"*Jim!*" she shouted, remembering his closed door, sealed blinds and the hour. She heard herself scream his name, but she wasn't frightened. She felt she should be, but she wasn't.

"What is it!" Jim shouted from his room, instantly shocked awake.

"Somebody's here! The police or something!"

The men stepped around to the back of the jeep.

"We're fine! Stay calm. We're safe!"

She stood back from the windows, her mind racing while her body remained paralyzed. She hoped they would arrest her too; she wanted to go inside the thing itself. And where would she go otherwise? What could she do to help him if he were arrested?

His unbuckled belt jingling, his feet thudding in the hall, he came into the living room. "What?" he demanded, seeing Meg staring at the windows behind him. He turned to look.

From the back of the jeep the men were lifting a body. They carried it under its arms, hauling the body up the driveway toward the window. Meg had never seen the man before, a Filipino whose heavy, nodding head was smeared with a brown mustache and chin beard: no, it was dried blood. Framed in a low-silled window with gold curtains tied in sashes, they dragged the man up the sidewalk toward the door.

"Moron!" said Jim. "Vicious, moronic bastard!" He ran to the front door and threw it open. "What the hell's *this*!" he shouted. "What the blazes is going on!"

"Mr. James Goodall?"

"You know damn well who I am! Who did this?"

Meg came up behind Jim in the door.

One man was thick and muscular. The other, who did the talking, was younger, an officer. They lifted the man like a rag dummy up on the porch stoop. His knit shirt was torn, his lower lip split and there was blood on his teeth.

"I don't know the details," the officer announced. "I don't care. All I know is our order to bring you your *friend*," he sneered.

And behind the dried blood and swollen nose, Meg suddenly saw Gus.

"Look like he cross somebody not nice," the thick man laughed. "Here. He all yours now." They hoisted the body and heaved it at Jim.

Jim lurched forward to catch him under the arms. "He's one of yours, damn it!" The body slid down in Jim's arms and Jim had to stoop to get a better hold. Gus's chin caught on Jim's shoulder, forcing his head back, displaying nostrils stuffed with caked blood.

"I know only what they tell me," said the officer, stepping back and ready to go.

"You can't just dump this man at my door without telling me what's going on!" A pair of brown scarecrow arms stuck out on either side of Jim.

The thick man was walking toward the jeep, but the officer lingered one moment longer. "He said you'll understand. He said he'll ring you up later to make sure you understand." He tapped the front of his helmet in a mocking half-salute. "Good day, Mr. Goodall." He turned and quick-stepped down the sidewalk.

"You morons!" Jim shouted after them. "He's your man, not mine!" He angrily jerked the body up by the seat of its pants. There was a faint moan, and a small bubble of blood in the bared teeth.

"He's alive," Meg whispered.

"Oh yeah. Damn them. *Damn* them." He backed toward the door, dragging Gus inside.

"You need help?"

"No. I got him." He hoisted Gus over his shoulder with as little tenderness as the police had shown. The dangling bare feet were spotted with dime-sized sores. Gus let out a higher moan as his chest went over Jim's shoulder.

Meg stepped out of their way. She saw the jeep race backwards into the street, reverse its gears and roar away. Then she saw a man in a bathrobe quickly open his door across the street and snatch the morning paper off his porch, pretending he'd seen nothing.

In his bedroom, Jim bent down to roll Gus off his shoulder and onto the bed. Meg came in to raise the blinds and give him light.

"Brainless, violent bastards. Pointless. Utterly pointless." He threw the pillows off the bed and laid Gus out on his back.

"Shouldn't we get him to a doctor?"

"In a minute. I'll get a doctor to come here." Looking down at Gus, Jim breathed loudly through his nose.

Gus's chest rose and fell. The bloody face bared teeth and gums like an angry dog each time he inhaled.

Jim fumbled at the collar of the torn shirt, as if to open it and help Gus breathe, but then he continued to yank, ripping it down the front and jerking apart the hem. He peeled the shirt back. "Damn. Bastards didn't do a half-assed job of it."

Standing by the window at the head of the bed, Meg could see two neatly symmetrical blood blisters stenciled over a nipple. The other nipple was puffed out, not erect but swollen in a burn blister.

"This is what their zaps can do when they don't care if they leave marks. They wanted to leave marks." His voice was dry and distant. He had sat on the bed to look at Gus's chest. He reached down to unsnap the jeans.

"No. *Paki.* Please," Gus murmured, a frightened whimper, one hand coming to life and grabbing Jim by the wrist. His eyes remained closed and his head rolled from side to side. "*Paki.* No. *Para.* Stop."

"You're okay," Jim whispered. He stroked Gus's head. "You're okay, Gus. You're with friends now. You're okay." He twisted his wrist free of the hand, undid the snap and opened the jeans. The zipper was already down or broken; he wore no underwear.

Meg instantly looked away.

Jim drew a long, dry breath through his nostrils. "They went all the way," he said, rubbing his hands against his legs. "No special treatment for the First Lady's hairdresser. Let me see if I can get the doctor. What time is it?"

It was fifteen minutes after six. Meg could look only at Gus's face. "Should I be washing off his face or something?"

"Go ahead. There's a basin under the bathroom sink." He stood and walked quickly across the hall to the study.

Meg went into the bathroom, found the basin and filled it with warm water. When she returned, she forced herself to look. There were pale brown blisters in the darker brown of his genitals, broken skin and dried blood. No, this couldn't mean to her what it meant to Jim. It could not go as deeply into her as it must go into Jim. And these wounds were only the aftermath, the residue of pain so intense she couldn't imagine what Gus had experienced, even when she pictured him twisting and straining like the girl in the movie. Kneeling beside the bed and wringing out the washcloth, she felt foolish for wanting to wash his face, but one had to do something. He had a sweaty smell of sickness and the metallic rainlike smell of blood.

"Very badly beaten," Jim was saying in the next room. "Burns and bruises. Electrical burns. No broken bones so far as I can tell. Yes, an acquaintance of mine. I don't know. He was unconscious when the cab brought him here."

His head twitched back when she touched his chin with the washcloth, then relaxed into her hand when he felt something warm and moist. She gently rubbed his chin and mouth, afraid of giving him more pain. His jeans were pushed down around his hips and she thought about pulling them back up, until she realized he'd be more comfortable and less obscene without them. She set the washcloth aside to wrestle the jeans under his ass, trying to keep the zipper and denim from touching the wounds. He seemed as weak and light as a child.

"Eleanor?" he murmured and said something in Tagalog.

Meg stood at the foot of the bed, pulling on the cuffs to ease the jeans past the sores on his feet. "No, it's Meg. Dr. Frisch," she told him. His wife must undress him like this when he came home drunk at night. Meg thought of women nursing sick husbands or, as their traditional duty in certain cultures, washing the dead.

Jim had finished his call, but was dialing the phone again. "Colonel Enéro, please. Yes, I damn well know what time it is. You tell the bastard when he gets in that Jim Goodall called.''

She had returned to his face to finish washing it when she felt Jim watching her from the door.

"Sorry, Meg. I didn't mean to stick you with that." He remained in the door, holding something in his hand. "The doctor's coming over. Filipino who works at the embassy clinic. But Ben's decent enough. I didn't give him the particulars of the case, but he won't be able to walk away once he sees this."

Gus looked more relaxed now, half-asleep, half-unconscious, his breathing steadier, the torn knit shirt an open vest.

"The police did this?" said Meg. *"Why?"*

"To get to me," said Jim. "They can't hurt me, but they can hurt one of their own. I never dreamed they could be so coldblooded and stupid." He lifted the rectangular box in his hand. "There's something I should do before Ben gets here. Only take a minute." He opened the hinged box: a Polaroid camera. "For the record," he explained. "While it's fresh." He looked at Gus through the viewfinder. "You might want to step back. I don't want you in this picture."

Meg left the bed, watching Jim, glancing at Gus. It made sense; it seemed necessary. Yet the sound of Jim's voice threw her, removed and mechanical, and the empty look on his face worried her. He could be angry with Enéro and the police, but he could feel nothing for Gus.

The electronic flash fired; a square of paper popped out beneath the lens. He stepped in closer and took another shot. Then another. And again. Gus stirred and grimaced as the flickers of light came closer. Each square card pushed out the one before, and the clearing pictures fell on the floor, then on the bed. When he finally finished, Jim wiped each eye with the heel of his hand, as though he'd been crying. Then he methodically picked the pictures off the bed and floor and stacked them together.

YOU WANT TO cry at such brute stupidity, Jim thought, setting the camera and pictures on the dresser. His eyes were already dry again. You only cry Polaroids, he thought.

"This was what he wore last night," he said as they lifted Gus to slip the torn shirt off his shoulders. The skin was warm, the perspiration cold. The cleaned face was swollen under its right eye. "He must have gone straight to Enéro when he left here."

"I can't believe people did this. People who knew him?"

"What happened to his shoes?" said Jim. "He had on alligator shoes. One of Enéro's men must have kept them for himself."

Jim decided Meg could feel more pity than he did; she hadn't known Gus.

All Jim knew, however, was his body, which had been transformed by bruises and burns into something else: a map of pain, a memo written in skin.

"Has he had a concussion? He keeps coming to and slipping out again."

"More likely shock," said Jim. "Trauma. The brain shuts down when the pain becomes too much. That's what they tell me anyway."

When Ben Corazon arrived, Gus was rolled over on his side, half-asleep, half-petrified by pain. Jim hadn't wanted to cover him for fear a sheet or blanket would rub against the cigarette burns on his feet and legs. Jim knew Dr. Corazon both from the embassy clinic and through Denny Sokol. A bald man with black-framed glasses and a little mustache, Ben was one of them, but he liked his young men tough and surly, which meant he was experienced in treating knife and even gunshot wounds outside of hospitals where they would be reported to the police. He understood what this was about as soon as he saw the burn blisters.

He asked Meg to go out to his car and bring in his other bag. He opened the bag he'd brought with him and examined Gus, fingering the skin, pulling the legs apart. "You didn't tell me this was government-related."

"I didn't want to scare you off."

"Nnh. Manila's full of young men who go to their doctors claiming they tried to fuck a light socket. They would rather people think they did it themselves than that somebody did it to them." He sat on the bed and prepared a needle.

"Will he have to be hospitalized?"

"You don't want him in a hospital?"

"I don't know yet." It would be much too easy for Enéro to pick him up again if Gus were in a hospital. Here at least there was the fiction of Jim's diplomatic immunity.

Ben stuck Gus with the needle, first in the groin, then near the blisters on his chest. "I can treat the burns and make it so he can piss without yelling. Your friend might have a broken nose, but that can wait."

"But I could keep him here for a few days?"

Ben shrugged and examined the mouth and swollen nose. "This a lover or just a playmate?"

"Occasional playmate."

He shook his head disapprovingly. "I can't see why you *or* the police might be interested in such a pathetic creature. None of my business though. None of my business."

Meg returned with Ben's bag, and the telephone rang.

"Excuse me," Jim said. "Meg, give the doctor a hand if he needs anything." He quickly stepped past her and crossed the hall to the telephone. "Yes?"

"Mr. Goodall?"

"Yes."

"I take it you received our answer. In response to what we discussed yester-day."

It was Enéro himself; one could hear the dull knife of his smile in the earpiece. Jim pushed the study door shut.

"I don't understand how this is an answer, Colonel. The president has one of his wife's friends tortured, the poor man is dumped on my doorstep, and I'm supposed to see that as an answer?" Jim's tone was sharp and firm, without panic or temper.

"The president had nothing to do with it. He's washed his hands of this affair and told me to do whatever was necessary. I think you understand my answer."

"All I understand is that you've inflicted enormous pain on an innocent, stupid man without any legal justification."

"We suspect him of working with the NPA."

"Bullshit. He was working for you."

Enéro was not distracted. "I might also point out that, as a suspected Communist, this man could be picked up again for questioning at any time."

"Why are you telling me this? I shouldn't have to remind you I am the Human Rights officer here."

"If you cooperate with us, Mr. Goodall, and hand over your movie, we'll regain our trust in you *and* your friends. We'll take your word that this Gus-Gus Luna couldn't possibly be a Communist, and won't ever touch him again."

It was everything Jim had feared since seeing Gus's bloody face, this blunt demand: Give up or we'll continue to hurt this man.

"Does Mrs. Marcos know what you've done to her friend?"

"The little sip-sip is hardly a friend. He was a servant, and servants are replaceable. A loyal wife knows when to bend to her husband's interests." The prospect of success made the bastard chatty, almost witty.

Pausing to think only gave Jim time to be disgusted. "Did you watch this session too, Colonel? Or did you let your subordinates handle it?"

"I watch such things only when duty requires it, Mr. Goodall. But in this instance, yes. I was curious. I had to see if a faggot screamed like a woman or struggled to maintain a little dignity. The former, it seems."

Jim saw the tight helix of the phone cord tremble slightly, but he could feel nothing, think nothing except that he'd been an idiot to expect any kind of sane behavior from this coldblooded imbecile.

"I'm speechless you could do this to your own man, Colonel. Agusto Luna is your man, your spy. He means nothing to me. You might just as well put a gun to your mistress's head and say you'll kill *her* if I don't hand over my film."

"This little cocksucker isn't *my* mistress."

"He was never mine either. I've known all along what he was."

"Hmm?" Enéro seemed to consider that. "You're more hardboiled than I thought you'd be."

"Useful cruelty is bad enough. But this cruelty is useless, insane. Because you can't accomplish a damn thing with it, Colonel."

"We shall see. It won't hurt me to call your bluff, Mr. Goodall. Only him," Enéro confidently declared. "I'll give you today and maybe tomorrow to think it over. In the meantime, I might add that the appearance of this film in any form, anywhere in the world, will ruin the trust you earn when you do give us the original. Our suspicions about Gus-Gus Luna will be reactivated and acted upon immediately. We'll be in touch, Mr. Goodall. Goodbye."

A gentle click was followed by a high-pitched hum, then the familiar tumblers clicking like dice before Jim hung up.

He sat very still, waiting for an emotion that showed he had already decided what he would do. His emotions seemed paralyzed, his thoughts paralyzed with them. All he seemed to know was that it would be wrong to bring more pain to the man in the next room. And that to surrender to Enéro would make Jim the prisoner of his spy for the rest of his days here: it would be wrong to give in to Enéro.

When he finally stood up and opened the door again, Jim saw Meg standing in his bedroom, a glum face watching Ben bandage Gus, her arms sternly folded over her chest. She looked at Jim as he came through the door, unspoken questions passing over her eyes and mouth: Is it over? *No?* Then what? She abruptly faced Gus again, biting her lower lip.

Ben had worked quickly. There was a gauze codpiece with a few inches of plastic tubing taped over the crotch. A white starburst of tape held a mound over the left nipple, and his legs and chest were splashed with brownish-orange disinfectant. Cotton was stuffed in his nostrils.

"I gave him a sedative. He'll sleep soundly for several hours. He'll be utterly exhausted when he wakes up, like a man who's been treading water for days. Worse than the burns is how these sessions keep muscles working long past the limit of normal endurance."

Jim nodded, barely listening to Ben. He'd hoped that seeing Gus would enable him to understand instantly what he had to do, but Gus was simply a body, and Jim had seen too many bodies. He'd told Enéro this man meant nothing to him in a futile attempt to protect Gus from further harm, but standing in the door, Jim did not seem to feel anything for Gus. He could almost feel pity. It stood off in the distance, a terrible sympathy that threatened to fill Jim with sorrow and guilt. The natural temptation to give in to pity and Enéro seemed petty, self-indulgent, a bone thrown to a sentimental conscience that would accomplish nothing of value for anyone.

MEG REMAINED BEHIND when Jim walked the doctor out to his car. Gus lay asleep with his arms outside the sheet, bandages on the thumb and ring finger of his right hand. The room was warm and humid, sick with disinfectant and sweat. Meg closed the window and lowered the blinds, then went to the other rooms to close all the windows so they could turn on the air-conditioning. The sun was very bright outside. Every trace of the early morning shower had been burned off the white sidewalks and green foliage.

She saw Jim standing out in the driveway, still in his sleeveless undershirt and bare feet. The doctor's car was gone and Jim talked to Tammy, who had just arrived in blue jeans and sneakers, her maid's outfit in one of the shopping bags she carried. He appeared to be suggesting, then insisting, they didn't need her today. He gave Tammy money. Meg was sorry to see her walk up the street toward the gate and bus stop. Of course she should be protected from this, but Meg wanted to have somebody else in the house today besides her uncle and the tortured sleeper. She assumed the last phone call explained and concluded everything. Even so, the world was no longer "out there"; it was in the bedroom and turned the house into a prison.

Meg was in the kitchen making coffee when Jim finally came back inside. "Good girl," he said, seeing the coffee maker spitting in its pot. "What a way to start a morning," he said. His face was grim, his posture slack and elderly. He stood beside her and laid a large, cool hand against her arm. "How you doing?" he mechanically asked.

"Okay. Overwhelmed. You?"

He shrugged and let go. He went to the sink and turned on the water. He watched the water run. There was no trace of the angry man who'd shouted at the police. She had never seen him angry, had never seen him show any strong emotion except remorse. He held his hands under the tap, rubbed his face and drove the hands over the snarled hair on his scalp. He turned off the water and gazed out the window.

"That was the police who called?"

"Uh huh. Colonel Enéro wanted me to understand that they'd pick up Gus again if I didn't turn over the film. That if the film were ever made public, they'd keep picking him up for questioning. For the rest of his life."

He spoke drily, reporting the threat as though it were a thing of the past and he'd had no choice except to give in to it. Just the idea of such endlessly repeated pain sickened Meg. "Could they really do that?"

"It's their country. They can do whatever they damn well please." He gripped the edge of the sink with both hands. He suddenly closed his eyes. "Idiot," he said. "What a sloppy, sentimental idiot I was. To think for an instant there was a line they wouldn't cross."

Meg didn't know what to say: I'm sorry? You must feel awful?

"What a tenderhearted ass. Of course they'd go after their own. And a faggot hairdresser? Hell, throw him out with the garbage. What the fuck have I been thinking?"

The face remained blank, but his voice grew tighter with anger and loathing. Her impulse to lay a hand on his shoulder was frozen by the sound of his voice.

"It's the same old fucking story. We talk and pat ourselves on the back, and they go right on killing each other," he muttered.

"But at least you'll know one man won't get killed."

He turned his head and stared at her. "*You* think I should give in to them?" He said it accusingly, contemptuously.

"I . . . I don't know." She was jolted to find the subject still open, to realize Jim hadn't given the police an answer. "I just assumed you had no other choice."

"Why? Because I'm such a sentimental idiot? Such a sweet bleeding heart?" The anger that had been muffled when turned against himself became sharp and cutting when he directed it at her. "A sentimental faggot who couldn't bear to hurt a fly? That's what *they* think. Is that what you think too?"

"I don't think any of that! All I meant was you have no other choice but to protect your friend!" She became angry to protect herself from his anger and her own disbelief. "You told them *no*?"

"But I've got until tomorrow to reconsider. Damn kind of them. Damn fucking kind. Film won't be back before then anyway." Gripping the counter, he slowly rocked himself back and forth. "Gus was never my friend. Just because I sucked the man's dick doesn't make him my friend."

"It's got nothing to do with *that*!" Yet it did, it must. Profanity made him sound crazy, this adult whom Meg had never heard say anything beyond "damn," and she needed to step around the craziness. "You know him. Isn't that enough? And there's nothing else you can do with the damn film. Right?"

"So I should give it up?"

"It's what makes sense. Doesn't it?"

He was looking at her, listening with his eyes. The blue-gray irises that could seem rational and human in their transparency had become two windows into blankness.

"Is it your pride?" she angrily asked. "You can't admit they've won? Is it the *principle*?"—she sneered the word. "Gus isn't the enemy. You said yourself he's just a dumb innocent they used as a spy."

"Yes, a poor dumb bastard who doesn't mean a thing to me." He looked out the window again. "No, it's not pride. They've won no matter what I do. But if I let them make Gus important to me, they've got us both by the throat. I won't be able to make a move without knowing that poor bastard could be dumped on my doorstep the next morning. We'd be married for life—his life anyway. So it's not like I'd be saving him for anything wonderful."

Suddenly his refusal stopped seeming irrational and wrong. No, the business wouldn't end with Jim surrendering the film. Her confidence wavered.

"Where's my cigarettes?" she said and went into the living room to get them and find the space to think.

But Jim followed her. "You think I'm as much of a bastard as they are, don't you?"

"*No!* I don't." She did. "I can't think anything yet." She found her pack and lit a cigarette, standing over the coffee table while Jim took up a position behind the sofa.

"You will," he accused her. "You're the historian. You know everything after the fact. I wonder how you'll call this five years from now."

"Damn it to hell, Jim, I'm not your judge!"

"Or maybe you need ten years, a century to understand. Right now you can only take it all in. Male violence and masculine pride. Men willing to be bastards for the sake of a cause. A woman would handle this better," he declared, staring at her. "A world run by women would be a happier place. But I'm impressed with how tough and cool you've been, Meg. You keep a cool, detached head."

It spilled out of him with his dry, cold anger, everything she suspected he believed about her, some of it true. "Am I supposed to be emotional for you too?" she charged. "Hysterical and sick to my stomach? Quit using me as your conscience! I am sick of playing your witness, your goddamn historian. You're going to do what you want to do anyway, no matter what I say. If I seem detached, you're the one who detached me and stuck me in the audience, Jim. I don't want to be here. But I am."

"What if I put you right in the center of things? You make the decision." The dry voice became sarcastically warm, the cold eyes continued to bear into hers. "I'll go along with whatever you say. Do I stand firm, wash my hands of Gus and, hope against hope, continue to try to do some good in this godforsaken country? Or do I give up to Enéro, making Gus his hostage and me their prisoner? Tell me. I'll do it."

For an instant, Meg was terrified he actually meant it. Then she was furious with him. "Fuck you. This was your screw-up, it's your decision. You're the one who'll have to live with himself afterwards. Don't ask me to play God, even as a joke."

He stopped, sobered by either Meg's anger or his understanding he'd gone too far. "Yes. You're right," he said. "I'm the one who'll have to live with it."

"And the man in your bed," said Meg. "He'll have to live with it too. Whatever you decide."

"Give me one of those." He snapped his fingers at her cigarettes, then came around the sofa while she shook one out.

She lit it for him. A cigarette looked so out of place in her uncle's face she waited for Jim to take it from his mouth and jab it in his arm: the sleeper down the hall gave cigarettes a new meaning. But Jim only looked at the thing in his fingers, sat down on the sofa and took another uncertain puff.

"I don't need to tell you it's remarkable what a man can do and still live with himself," he said.

"No." She sat in the chair on the other side of the table, wondering what he was talking about. The suspension of anger did not feel like peace, only exhaustion. Not until Meg had collapsed in the chair did she feel how exhausted she was, first by the adrenaline shock of handling a wounded body, then by this insanity of lost tempers. Jim was right: they kill each other and *we* talk.

"I've never told you this," he said. "I've never talked about it with anyone who wasn't there. But I once killed a man."

There was an involuntary shudder, but Meg lifted her chin and looked skeptical.

"This was ten years ago. But I've been able to live with myself. More or less."

"You feel somehow responsible for somebody's death?"

He smirked at the cigarette in his hand. "Oh no. I killed this fellow myself. At close range. A boy. Fifteen or sixteen years old. A Vietnamese boy in a village south of Saigon."

He was sitting back on the sofa, his legs crossed at the knees and the cigarette pointed upward, an Edward R. Murrow pose. His farsighted gaze hovered in the air above Meg's head while he told a story about a weekend in Saigon, some kind of all-night party and a helicopter ride the next morning over the Mekong delta.

Her skepticism stiffened before it gave way. Meg had heard her share of war stories; she recognized the smug note of "You can't imagine what the real world is like." She'd known several Vietnam veterans in school, even searched them out during her last year at William and Mary. She learned to listen for the bullshit in war stories. The vets who talked often wanted to shock you with horrors, silence you with their heartlessness, leering over gruesome tales about mamasans run over by jeeps for sport, or helicopter gunners firing at peasants in the paddies below for the thrill of watching bodies fly apart. Those stories were lies, Meg discovered, macho fantasies intended as a bleak joke on civilians who thought all soldiers were psychos. The true stories, the ones Meg heard when she'd earned a man's trust and was alone with him, either in bars or once in bed, had a different sound, one of confusion, quiet and embarrassment. They still shocked, but the teller was as stunned as you were, unable to understand what he'd seen or how he felt. Maybe that was a lie too, yet it was a more human lie.

That quiet uncertainty began to enter Jim's story, despite the cynical snorts and smirks he gave himself for getting caught in such a horrible situation, then for the way he "went bananas" when his host shot a man in the stomach.

"Next thing I knew, I had a gun in one hand. And this boy's face in the other. What else could I do but shoot? I pulled the trigger and shot." He said it calmly, but his eyes went blank; the fingers of his left hand closed and opened, remembering the face. "That's all it took. He was dead. Easy as that. The Arvins took the corpse. We got the living prisoner. We climbed into our chopper and hightailed it out of there. I was back in Manila that very night, no worse for wear than if I'd spent the weekend spearfishing in Puerto Galera."

Finished with the story, he folded his arms, frowned and looked off, as if he'd forgotten why he told it, what he'd expected it to prove.

Meg was silent too, not in sympathy or horror, but confusion. No, he didn't live with this as easily as he claimed, but who was he now? What kind of man did the experience make him? There was a feeling of sickness in her stomach and nerves, but she couldn't tell if that were because of Jim's story or simply her delayed response to seeing and handling Gus. No longer protected by urgency or anger, her own body began to respond. She nervously waited to hear how Jim's story would connect with the man down the hall, but he said nothing.

Finally, Meg spoke. "You didn't really murder him. You know that, don't you? You did the only thing possible under the circumstances."

"I know that. Yes. I've always known that." The distant look in his eyes suggested he didn't *feel* it, though.

"Do you think that might be why you came back?" she asked. "And for this kind of work?"

"Who knows why we do half of what we do?" But he wasn't surprised by the question, and he did not need Meg to explain what she meant. "Maybe," he said, addressing the ceiling. "Maybe I thought if I saved a few people I could square things between myself and the world. Or just one person. If I could save just one." He looked at Meg and sat up, shook his head at her and looked down. "But if that's the case, I was as ignorant as a swan. Ignorant and innocent and blind. To think for a minute this time might be different. History repeats itself. You think you'll handle it better the second time around. The first time it happened too fast for me to think clearly. This time it's happening so slowly I get to think about absolutely everything." He grimaced. "It was easier the first time."

"You couldn't tell yourself you were saving Gus?"

He raised his head and gave her a faint, condescending smile.

"If you gave them the film, you'd at least be saving Gus."

"Save him for what? So Enéro's people can continue to play zap-zap on him? So Mrs. Marcos can toss him back on the rubbish heap where Dominick found him? She won't be wanting to have her hair done by someone her husband threw to the wolves. It would be too painful, and Imelda has a very tender conscience. But out of sight, out of mind." He cast a cold eye toward the hall to the bedroom. "No, this is about more than what *I* feel. There is no easy way out. I better get dressed," he abruptly announced. "Maybe look in on Gus and see how he's doing."

She watched him leave the room, wondering at his polite concern for the man he would not save. But without her anger to sustain the belief, Meg was no longer certain she was right and he was wrong. Gus was his friend, his trick or whore, whatever. If Jim didn't love Gus, he seemed to feel something for him. And yet he was prepared to overcome his feeling for the sake of something larger.

Without Jim on hand to argue against, her automatic concern for what was here—the stranger under this roof—seemed narrow and easy, a compromise with evil. Meg lifted her feet into the chair, clutched her legs against her gut and thought: he's made me his judge, and I *am* his judge, but this is his choice and there's nothing more I can say that he doesn't know already.

19

SHE DOESN'T UNDERSTAND, thought Jim. But then he didn't understand either. This went beyond understanding.

He washed and dressed and glanced at the snarling face sound asleep on the pillow. It was the boy in the paddy field all over again, resurfacing in Jim's conscience, reappearing in his bed. He had told the story to explain *how* he could do this, then hoped against hope it would justify why he shouldn't. It didn't change anything. The decision remained.

The decision seemed to have made itself while he argued with Meg. He could not remember thinking: *This is what I will do.* But when he found himself taking that line with Meg, he knew it was the only stand he could take. He would not give in to their moronic cruelty, would not be blackmailed into being made responsible for what they intended to do. Gus was theirs, not his. Jim tried to believe something might still be accomplished with Aguilar's film, yet the film seemed like nothing now, just as his tender pity for Gus seemed like nothing. He hated Enéro for giving him these additional hours to live with this decision before it became final.

They ate breakfast, or rather, Jim ate, not heartily but merely to stop the slight burning in his stomach. Meg said little. She seemed to have given up on

Jim, only now she looked sick instead of angry. He apologized for losing his temper with her. "It's not you I'm angry with."

"Same here," she muttered. "But neither of us said anything we didn't already know, did we?" She asked what he intended to say to Gus when he regained consciousness.

"I don't know yet." He wondered how talking to Gus would affect his resolve.

It was after ten when the telephone rang again. Jim answered it in the study, thinking it was Enéro and that the bastard would hound him all day until he gave in. But the voice at the other end was very small and timid, a woman's voice.

"Jeem Goodall?"

"Speaking." For a moment he thought it might be Mrs. Marcos.

"You do not know me, and I am sorry to intrude on your home life. But my name is Eleanor Luna. I am the wife of your friend Gus-Gus?"

Straining to keep the nervousness from his tone, Jim was chillingly polite, saying no apology was necessary and asking what he could do for her. She continued to apologize while she said her husband hadn't come home last night and hadn't called either and she was a little worried. "Not to put my nose where it does not belong, but did Gus-Gus stay the night with you, Mr. Goodall?"

"No. I'm sorry, Mrs. Luna. He did come by last night, but left almost immediately." He cleared his throat. He wetted his lips. No, he couldn't do this. "I'm sorry, Mrs. Luna. I should tell you. Your husband's here right now." She would find out sooner or later, and it was cruel to think he could protect her. "They brought him here first thing this morning. I would've called you sooner, but the doctor left only a few minutes ago."

"*Ay dios ko!*" The small voice turned throaty and passionate. "He has been in an accident! He is hurt? Give him to me! Please!"

"He can't come to the phone. The doctor gave him a sedative and he's fast asleep at the moment. You should know that your husband—he was badly beaten last night."

She gasped and cried in a mix of Tagalog and English, too upset to ask by whom or why, immediately insisting she had to see him, needed to be with him and that she was coming over. Jim tried to dissuade her, explaining there was nothing she could do and he was fine for now; he promised he would try to bring Gus home sometime tomorrow.

The hysteria promptly dropped from her speech. "He is *my* husband," she said sternly. "I do not know you, Mr. Goodall. Gus-Gus says you are good. But I cannot trust you, cannot believe what you say until I see with mine own eyes the state of my husband."

There was no denying her claim on Gus. Jim couldn't understand why he'd been so softhearted in telling her as much as he had. He knew he had no choice but to give in to her. "All right, Mrs. Luna. You should come see him.

But I think he should stay here, for tonight at least." He did not want to make things easier for Enéro than they already were.

"Thank you," she declared. "A friend is very well and good, but a wife should be with her husband in his time of distress." She then discussed how to get there and what buses she should take—Gus had taken their car last night—and Jim offered to pay for a cab. He suggested she wait until that afternoon, when the sedation wore off and Gus might be awake. She said that was fine, a cousin would be back from work by then and could look after her two boys. Jim had forgotten Gus had children.

He finished with her and went back to Meg. "That was his wife. She's dropping by this afternoon. She insisted," he explained.

Meg looked at him, obviously wondering how the involvement of a wife and children would affect his decision, but all she said was, "You *want* her here?"

"Not at all. But I couldn't say no to her." It was as though something in him wanted to make this as painful as possible. If Meg weren't going to continue to prick and cut his conscience, the presence of an innocent wife would certainly do the job. If he were going to be a bastard, Jim wanted to be conscious every minute that that was exactly what he was.

THERE WERE NO further phone calls, no new thoughts or exchanges that morning. The air-conditioned house grew stagnant with the breathing of the man asleep in his temporary haven of drug-induced peace.

Eleanor Luna arrived shortly after one o'clock. She stepped briskly up the driveway, leading two small children by the hand. They were dressed up for the visit, the boys in new shorts and rugby shirts, their mother wearing a starchy ruffled blouse with her jeans, as though they were visiting Gus in a hospital. A solid, thick-jawed woman in her early thirties, Mrs. Luna looked much older than her husband.

"I am sorry, Mr. Goodall," she declared at the door, without apology. "But my cousin didn't come home and there was nobody to attend my children. They wanted to see their father besides."

Frowning at the small boys she eased through the door, Jim assured her no apology was necessary. They were four and five years old, all eyes and teeth, shy and giggly with the American towering over their mother. The youngest had a doll in his hand, a six-inch soldier in combat fatigues.

"Nonoy and Matt," said Mrs. Luna. "Say hello to Mr. Goodall."

They mumbled a greeting. The youngest stared into the enormous living room. His older brother looked up at Jim nervously, catching the distrust in his mother's voice.

Jim introduced Meg, who kept her distance, worriedly studying the two kids, then quickly said, "Let's see if Gus is awake. Last time I looked he was still dead to the world." He hoped Gus would remain unconscious and his family wouldn't stay long. Jim wasn't prepared to see his children. He forgot what he'd decided about how much to tell Mrs. Luna. She looked stronger than he'd pictured her, slightly masculine where her husband was slightly feminine.

He opened the bedroom door and stepped back.

She stood in the door and looked, gathering her sons in front of her, gently squeezing the shoulder of the eldest.

"Is Popo sick?"

"Yes. A little sick," she whispered. "Shhh. We must let him sleep." The boys stared, fascinated by the novelty of seeing their father confined to bed during the day. Mrs. Luna glared over her shoulder at Jim, as if this were something he had done. She already knew this was more than a street brawl or mugging. She sniffed and swallowed and jostled her sons. "You go play now. Go ask the lady out there if she knows any songs. I must see if Popo needs anything."

The boys ran off, Matt eagerly, Nonoy with his head lowered.

Mrs. Luna frowned at Jim and went into the room, slipping the strap of her bag off her shoulder and setting the bag on the floor.

Jim followed her, expecting her to ask for explanations.

"Pobrecito," she whispered and stroked her husband's hair. She gently lowered herself to the edge of the bed. She seemed to know what she would see when she drew back the sheet that covered his chest. She looked up at Jim, her wide eyes filled with two bright lenses of water.

Gus stirred. "Eleanor? Eleanor."

"Anó itó, baby?" What is this? Water spilled from her eyes when she angrily squinted at Jim. No, she wasn't innocent. "Why?" she demanded.

"You'll have to ask him," said Jim.

Gus continued to stir, slipping his arms around her waist and setting his head in her lap; they looked more like mother and child than man and wife.

"What did you do?" she said furiously, in Tagalog to Gus. "Why are they mad at you? You stupid fool, what did you do?"

"Sorry, Eleanor. I'm so sorry," he murmured, his eyes closed, his tongue sticking to his mouth. "So thirsty. Sorry. Please. Thirsty."

"Get me some water," Eleanor commanded.

Jim went to the bathroom, rinsed out the glass and filled it; she was tougher than her husband, and Jim didn't know if that would make this easier or more difficult.

"Here, drink some," she said, lifting his head and holding the glass to his lips.

His left eye, the unbruised eye, was half-open, but all he seemed to see was the glass and his wife's pink fingernails. He swallowed rapidly, then drew back, lightly coughing on the water. He blinked in surprise at the pains in his chest. He gestured the glass of water away with the back of his hand.

"Gago!" Fool. "What did you do to turn them against you?" Eleanor

cried, close to tears again. "You have ruined it! You have spoiled everything for your children!"

Mouth and eyes wide open, Gus was catching his breath like a man coming out of a nightmare. He frantically looked from side to side to see where he was, then closed his eyes and swallowed, relieved to know he was somewhere else. His eyes snapped open on Jim.

"Why?" he pleaded. "What did I do to *you*?"

Eleanor stared at Jim too, blaming him for this.

"It wasn't my doing," Jim said firmly. "You did it to yourself. You and Enéro and the Marcoses, Gus. The people you work for."

"It was that thing, no? That movie thing?"

"Of the girl you said must be getting only what she deserved," Jim reminded him.

Gus didn't hear. "I get back from seeing you, and tell them, and they grab me—" He stopped, frozen by a frightening thought. "My teeth," he said, putting his hand to his mouth. "Did they break my caps? Are they cracked?" He lifted his face to Eleanor but, before she could answer, he cut his eyes downward toward his middle, terrified by another thought. He gingerly pawed the sheet over his hip, afraid to touch what he couldn't feel.

"It's there," said Jim. "With a catheter so you can relieve yourself without removing the bandage. But it's blistered from electrical burns."

He was afraid mentioning the burns would bring back for Gus the horror of what happened last night. But no, Gus simply sighed, pleased to hear he was still intact. After intense and prolonged pain, the only thought he could give the experience was that it was over.

"They could burn it off for all I care," Eleanor snarled. "For all the good it's done us."

"Oh baby. Don't be mean to me," Gus moaned. "I ache all over." He rested his face again on the denim pillow of her lap.

She grimaced, then stroked his hair and frowned at the swollen bruise around his right eye. She saved her anger for Jim. "Can you leave us?" she said. "I must talk to my husband. And then I must talk to you, Mr. Goodall."

"Of course." Jim bowed his head and gently pulled the door shut behind him.

The television cackled in the living room. Nonoy sat on the floor very close to the screen. His little brother sat on the sofa with Meg, unable to decide whether to give his full attention to the army doll he undressed in his lap or the white lady sitting uncomfortably beside him. Meg looked straight at Jim, wanting to know what was up.

He shrugged and gave her a weary smile, acknowledging the children. He sat in the armchair and said, "You must be Matt."

"Uh huh." The boy was giving careful study to Meg's skin and hair.

Nonoy shifted closer to the TV, using it to block out everything strange and unfamiliar in this house. He seemed to know something was wrong, while his little brother treated the visit as a novelty, an adventure.

"You're U.S.A.," Matt told Meg. "You live in there." He pointed at the television and giggled.

"Don't be silly." She looked disgusted. "Can't you put some pants on your doll? He's getting cold."

Matt was clearly his father's son, happily innocent, which made Nonoy seem like his mother's child. Jim was sorry there were children involved, but even the Marcoses had children, and Enéro was a grandparent. Nevertheless, for a moment Jim imagined he could keep Gus and his family in his house, safe inside his shadow of diplomatic immunity, not just for a few days but for the rest of his tour in Manila. It was a foolish, sentimental idea, a scheme that would only postpone the inevitable. The legalities took time, but they could eventually get to Gus, and there were extralegal means, such as kidnapping Gus while Jim was out or arresting Eleanor while she was shopping. No, it wasn't practical and Jim did not want to make this family his prisoners.

He was shifting around in the thick, rubbery bag of his decision, groping for a way out. To save Gus for the sake of one's own conscience seemed like a failure of nerve. To save a man for the sake of his family might be justifiable. Jim thought he felt an opening, an escape.

Meg was looking at him oddly, sensing a change in his expression.

Matt was chatting nonsense while he dressed his doll. "U.S.A. Hey, hey, hey. A.S.U. Boo, hoo, hoo."

"Shut your trap, punk," Nonoy snapped at his brother. Their English sounded far more American than their parents', tuned by hours of television.

Their mother came out, slamming the bedroom door. She strode into the room, wiping her eyes with the flats of her hands. "Go play outside," she told the boys. "Nonoy, take your brother and go outdoors. There's a nice garden outside. Maybe this lady wants to show it to you."

"I'd like my niece to sit in on this." Jim wanted Meg to be here, simply because the presence of another woman might muffle the force of Eleanor's fear and anger.

Meg got up to open the sliding glass door and the children ran out, Matt squealing and going straight to a wiry acacia tree, which he climbed. She closed the door and returned to the sofa, sitting at the opposite end from Mrs. Luna. The woman seemed to frighten Meg, disturb her. Meg lit a cigarette, then scooted the pack toward Mrs. Luna in case she wanted one. She did.

Smoke poured from her nostrils. The filter was stained red by her lipstick. "He is not very smart, my husband. But he is not a bad man."

"Did he wake up enough to explain who did that to him?"

"Enough. He is back to sleep now. Poor *gago*. He knows nothing of pain." She sat back, her knees slightly apart; she frowned at Jim. "You have something they want. And they arrested my husband to make you hand it over. Am I right?"

Jim nodded.

"Will you give it to them?"

He hesitated. "I don't know. It depends on what they offer in return."

Meg lowered her eyes, assuming his uncertainty was a lie.

Eleanor Luna sighed. "Then you do not love my husband? You only use him for sexual pleasure?"

"One could say that." The wife understood the situation all too well. "I don't dislike Gus. But you know, don't you, that he was seeing me only because the secret police required it?"

"What else do you expect?" she snapped. "He has to stay in good with those people. You come and go, but we must stay and make what life we can. We made a good future for our children. But now?" Her face shriveled up, her cheeks and brow folding like an old woman's around the eyes that turned to water again. "We are ruined. Even if you give up this thing, you have ruined us."

Exasperated by her tears, Meg said, "Put blame where it belongs. It's the secret police and Marcos who did this, not my uncle."

She angrily shook her head. "One expects no better from them! They are vicious. They are sharks, and one knows what to expect from sharks. But you we thought would never hurt us," she told Jim. "And yes, Gus saw you because they wanted him to see you. But he likes you, Mr. Goodall. He always liked you. He cannot understand how his best friend could let this happen to him."

Even in her desperation, Eleanor Luna was a smart and careful woman. Jim understood she had to hold back most of her anger and hatred of him. She could not afford to be moral. A woman with less pride, however, might claim her husband loved Jim.

"What will he do when this is over?" Jim asked. "Can he go back to the Malacanang?"

"No! Of course not."

"You wouldn't want him to?" Meg suggested.

"They will not have him. They are finished with him, the president and his whore. Gus cannot understand that. He cannot believe the heartless bitch has washed her hands of him. But I understand all too well those are marks of Cain on his skin."

"Then you'll go back home?" said Meg. "To your families?"

"To the sticks?" Eleanor scoffed. "What can a hairdresser do for farmers? It would be too awful, the shame of returning to our jealous relatives."

It seemed a petty concern against the probability Gus would be picked up and tortured again. Eleanor had to know that, but couldn't think about it yet.

"What if you left the country?" said Jim.

"Where could we go?"

"I was thinking of the United States."

She looked surprised, then cocked her head. "But for that you need papers, visas and money."

This was the solution that had come to Jim, the way out of his rubber bag. "I can't promise you anything. But I might be able to arrange emigration papers." Gough and Wexler were so desperate to end this affair they should agree to that. "The snag is going to be in getting an exit visa for your husband. They might not let him leave the country."

Eleanor considered the proposal, her lower lip sticking out while she nodded, a farmer negotiating the sale of a cow. "Gus will not want to go," she said.

"I don't even know if it's possible, Mrs. Luna. All I'm asking is if you'd like me to pursue it."

"What will we do for money?"

"I could loan you some money."

Her nods became deeper, more deliberate. "Yes then. Pursue it. I see no other way." She did not look relieved or grateful, only practical. Jim didn't expect her to fall on her knees in gratitude, but he was stung when she looked him coldly in the eye and said, "What do you expect from us in exchange? The price?"

"Nothing," said Jim. "Not a goddamn thing."

Her faint eyebrows went up in mild surprise, but she believed him, took it as something owed her. "I will have to persuade Gus. Make him understand there is no other way. He loves his homeland, thinks it has been so good to him. I don't. How can any woman love a country where she must be her husband's pimp in order to succeed," she said without rancor, only sadness that it was so.

"All right then," Jim told her. "I'll have to make a few phone calls, then go out and meet with a couple of people. You're free to stay here while I'm gone. Make yourself at home. My niece will show you where everything is."

Meg was watching him, not surprised and pleased by his change of heart, but hesitant, her hand clamped over her mouth again.

Jim smiled weakly at her as he stood up to leave the room. He heard her knee knock the coffee table behind him when she got up to follow.

She caught up with him in the hallway. "What're you doing?" she whispered.

"I want to see if I can sell Enéro on a clean slate. I'll give him the film if he lets Gus and his family leave the country."

Her eyes were pinched with *Why,* but she restricted herself to practicalities. "Do you think he will?"

"I don't know. He might not want us back at square one. But this way he gains something. His way won't gain him a damn thing. You don't mind staying here and looking after Mrs. Luna, do you?"

Meg frowned in the direction of the living room. "She does a pretty good job of looking after herself."

"To be sure," said Jim. "Well, let's see if they'll bite."

He made his phone calls, scheduling a meeting at the embassy with Wexler for an hour from now, then trying to reach Enéro at Camp Crame. A major said the colonel was out, but when the man suddenly suggested Jim might come by around four, Jim knew Enéro was in the room, letting Jim turn in the wind, confident he'd won.

Getting his coat and tie in the bedroom, Jim took one more look at Gus. He appeared to be sleeping, but Jim felt he was faking, which was fine with him. He didn't want to talk either, and he wasn't doing this for Gus.

TIME PASSED IN fits and starts for Meg while Jim was gone, now racing like a deathwatch in a hospital waiting room, now suspended like the obligatory visit after a funeral. Mrs. Luna and her children immediately made the house theirs, and Meg felt as though she were the unwanted visitor. The woman occupied herself in making a big pot of soup with what she found in the refrigerator and cabinets. "For my husband," she explained. "And anyone who's hungry."

She continued to smoke Meg's cigarettes, and Meg sat at the kitchen table so they both had access to the pack. The situation felt disquietingly familiar, and Meg realized she was reminded of sitting in the kitchen while her mother fixed dinner. She did not want to think this black-haired, slightly butch, Buddha-faced woman had anything in common with her mother.

Meg didn't know what to make of a woman who seemed so at home in crisis and compromise. She'd been startled when Mrs. Luna described herself without apology as her husband's pimp. Meg wanted to feel sympathy with her, but that was difficult when Mrs. Luna seemed so certain *she* was the injured party here. Meg was relieved that her arrival had loosened Jim from his decision, her wild shifts of emotion succeeding where Meg's indignant reasoning had failed, and yet there was a cunning strength in Eleanor Luna that suggested she didn't need Jim, she might not even need Gus.

"Have you always wanted to emigrate, Mrs. Luna? Or is today the first time you've considered it?" Meg had been surprised at how promptly open the woman had been to the idea.

"Always I consider it. For the pursuit of opportunity. Now that all opportunity here is died—" She shrugged and continued peeling the green shrimp she dropped into the pot; alone with Meg she was very patient and unemotional.

"If my uncle can't get an exit visa for Gus, would you take the children and leave the country without him?"

"I would rather not. But if I must cut my loss and there is no other way, I could." She calmly looked at Meg. "You think your uncle wants Gus-Gus all to himself?"

"No. I'm sure he doesn't."

Mrs. Luna accepted that as just another fact. Meg had mentioned emigration just to find out how important Gus might be to her.

"You are a career woman, Dr. Frisch? You have not a husband and family?"

"No. Although the one has nothing to do with the other."

"You are lesbian?"

"No. Are you?" Meg asked as matter-of-factly as Mrs. Luna had, but the question had been on Meg's mind since Eleanor Luna arrived.

Eleanor held out one hand and indifferently waffled with it. "I have loved women," she said. "Now I am loving my children and have no love to spare."

"I was involved with a woman, but—I don't know. I guess it's not in my biology." Meg only wanted Eleanor to know she wasn't shocked or contemptuous, but it sounded so completely beside the point that Meg wasn't sure why she said so much. She didn't know if she liked Eleanor, yet she wanted Eleanor to like her. "I hate being called Dr. Frisch. Please call me Meg."

Eleanor nodded. "You want to know how much I love Gus, don't you?"

"No, that's none of my business," Meg said guiltily.

"I love him. As the father of my children and my partner in living. Without me being practical, he would not have built on his friendship with Dominick. He would be maybe a too-old hustler in the Ermita or a village street barber. And without him, I would be a mean, mannish *dalága,* a witch insulted by men and feared by the girls, working at a factory sewing machine for a dollar a day. We have a good marriage. I hope to continue it in the United States."

"And if you can't? If they won't let Gus leave?"

"My children come first. I myself come second. And then, if there is room in the boat, comes Agusto."

Her lack of sentimentality was brutally honest, the clear-eyed realism of the underdog. What else could she believe in her situation? Eleanor Luna was outside morality and judgment. It was wrong to judge her by a different set of standards than those Meg used for her uncle and herself, but she did. Her own doubts and values were luxuries, a privileged language that couldn't be translated into anything she could give Eleanor. All she could do was sit and smoke and hope very hard that Jim was convincing the secret police they gained more from a clean slate than a bloody one.

Frowning at the garish, suffering Virgin on the refrigerator, Meg felt she finally understood why good women were constantly shown praying in novels and movies from Catholic countries. What else could they do while waiting for the men to decide things?

Six o'clock came and Jim was still not back. Eleanor called her sons in from the backyard and served the soup. Meg sat with them while their mother took a bowl to their father. Nonoy had lost the angry shyness he'd used to hide his fear, as if sensing from the change in his mother that things were no longer hopeless, that something good might come from their visit to this peculiar house. He asked Meg if there was snow where she lived and what kind of car she drove. Matt wanted to know if she had boyfriends or girlfriends or lived with her mother.

It was nearly seven when Jim came through the front door. He looked surprised, then shaken, to find all these people sitting in his kitchen. He stood over them with his jacket bunched in one hand, his shirt soaked gray at the armpits. The women gazed up at him; the children continued to scrape the last of the ice cream from their bowls.

"Well?" said Meg.

"He has to think about it." Jim attempted a smile. "Wexler said yes. There were no problems at that end." He watched the kids, knowing not to say too much in front of them. "But Enéro says he has to think it over. He'll come around. I'm sure he will. But he has to think it over."

His smile grew wider. And Meg suddenly felt that Enéro had said no. Absolutely no.

"I have an idea," Jim announced. "It's awfully late, Mrs. Luna. Would you and the boys like to spend the night? The boys can sleep in the guest room and Meg can sleep in the study, if she doesn't mind. I'll sleep in the living room. You can sleep with your husband, of course. It's a big bed. You shouldn't have to worry about knocking his injuries in your sleep."

Eleanor seized the invitation, as if she too sensed Enéro had refused Jim's deal; spending the night might be the only way she could make sure Jim did right by Gus. Meg watched her uncle while he and Eleanor discussed pajamas and breakfast, hoping to catch his eye so he could give her a look or nod to signal that what she suspected was true. His face told her nothing. He asked Eleanor for some of her soup, then pulled out a chair and joined them at the table. Even when the children raced out of the kitchen to watch television, Jim continued to chat about such nothings as sleep and soup. When Eleanor wondered aloud how American schools compared to schools in the Philippines, Jim delicately smiled and said she shouldn't worry about that.

HE COULDN'T TELL them yet. He wanted everyone to enjoy the comfort of hoping; he wanted his house to be a sanctuary to this family for at least one night.

He could feel Meg seeing through his smiles. She already seemed to know, but Jim carefully avoided being alone with her. When he finished the soup, he joined the kids in the living room. When Mrs. Luna put her children to bed, he told Meg to move her things to the study so she wouldn't disturb the children later. When the women returned, they sat silently in front of the television, Mrs. Luna smoking Meg's cigarettes and accepting Jim's invitation to help herself to his liquor cabinet.

"I've zombied out," Meg announced at the end of the next TV show. "I'm going to try reading myself to sleep." She stood up and stared at Jim, wanting him to understand this would be their chance to talk. When he simply said goodnight, however, she accepted and left the room with a quick, light step, as if relieved.

But without Meg there to disperse his attention, Jim felt very alone and uncomfortable with Eleanor Luna. She didn't say a word; she didn't have to. She sat like a stone facing the television, utterly solemn despite the American laughter imported with the show they were watching. A match sizzled when she lit another cigarette.

"Mrs. Luna?"

Her head turned, her full lips and heavy eyelids equally immobile and inexpressive.

"Do you mind if I look in on Gus before you go to bed?"

"Do as you please," she mumbled. "This is your house."

No, she found no comfort here; she already knew that Enéro said no and hope was inappropriate. Jim apologetically thanked her and went to see if Gus were awake.

He didn't stir when Jim stepped inside and softly closed the door. He was genuinely asleep this time, his bare chest rising and falling in the white light from the bathroom. He looked like the survivor of a shipwreck cast upon a beach, each breath a sigh of relief to be on solid ground again. He never dreamed he'd be pitched back into the ocean.

I got you by the balls. I got you by your boyfriend's balls.

Enéro had growled the phrases over and over while he strutted up and down in his office against the slashes of sunlight coming through the blinds, his saw-toothed shadow cutting across the carpet. He seized the new offer as a sign of weakness, proof positive Jim would do anything to save his *catamite* from harm. He couldn't comprehend how someone might do this not from selfish affection but for reasons of common decency. "I got you by *his* balls. I'd be a horse's ass to let him leave the country."

Not even an appeal to self-interest could get through the man's vindictive stupidity. Jim told him this was the only way Enéro would be able to protect his name. "I don't want to protect you, Colonel, but I want to spare this fellow and his family further suffering. Your terms gain nothing for anyone, yourself included. Because if I can't use the film to buy Agusto Luna's free-dom, I have no choice but to use it to discredit you and the Marcos govern-ment."

But Enéro was too confident of success to see that. His only fear was that Jim might try smuggling Gus out of the country, with or without the em-bassy's complicity. He warned Jim against it, telling him the house was being watched and that Gus would be arrested the instant he left private property. "We will keep him here until you see the light. A guest of honor at Camp Crame. You see? I got you by the balls, Mr. Goodall." He clutched a handful of air and laughed.

They would not let Jim lose humanely. They forced him to win viciously, although the only thing he was certain to win was the freedom to lose again.

The choice had been easier to accept in Enéro's office than it was now while Jim watched Gus sleep, but Jim firmly accepted it.

"Lovey? Sweetness? *Ay.*" Gus was awake. He looked about in a panic when he saw Jim standing at the foot of the bed. "My wife is gone?" he asked, terrified to be alone with Jim.

"No, she's here. She'll be spending the night. In here with you," Jim assured him. "I'll be out on the sofa."

Gus sank back again, and sighed.

"How do you feel?"

"Tired. So dead tired. And very sore. Like I am sick." He made a face and angrily shook his head. "I have to pee again."

Jim looked around the bed, thinking there must be a bowl or jar they were using as a chamber pot. When he didn't see one, he said, "I'll help you over to the toilet."

Gus let Jim give him a hand sitting up. "No, no, I am no baby," he grumbled when Jim moved to lift him in his arms. "I just need you to lean against."

They hobbled into the bathroom together, Jim supporting Gus with one hand on his hip and the other clutching the wrist of the hand with bandaged fingers over his right shoulder; it was difficult finding places to touch that weren't discolored by bruises or disguised with gauze. They stood over the toilet bowl, both of them looking down at the clear plastic tube that had replaced his penis.

"That thing makes me always feel I need to pee," Gus snarled.

"Take your time. We've got all the time in the world."

Did he love Gus? People assumed he did—Meg and Enéro and Gus's own wife—when Jim didn't. He hadn't, until tonight. It was like love, his feeling of tenderness and pity for this fellow he couldn't help. It was similar to the final rush of affection one might feel for an unlovable animal once you've decided to have the beast put to sleep. Jim wished it were as easy as that, and he could put Gus to sleep. He did not know how to save anyone except by killing them.

He flushed the toilet when Gus was done and helped him back to bed.

"Now leave me," said Gus. "I have nothing to say to you."

"No?" Jim had so much to say to Gus, but nothing that wouldn't give the man new pain.

Gus curled his upper lip above his gums. "You are stupid. You are so stupid. If you had let me take the movie to them this would never have happened."

"No. Probably not," Jim quietly admitted.

"I don't want to go to the United States! I don't want to start over. I was top of the heap here. Until you ruined everything. Why? Why? We were such good friends, Jim. Weren't we?"

Not "Jim Goodall," but simply Jim now. Jim crouched beside the bed, but he didn't have the heart to tell Gus the door to the United States had been closed and locked. "I'm sorry, Gus. I never dreamed they'd hurt one of their own. I don't know what I would've done if I knew, but the possibility never crossed my mind."

"We had it so good. We had everything," Gus cried, his anger giving way to grief. "We had money and importance and a nice place to live." His face twisted up in a scowl and tears, the mask of Greek tragedy that became inhuman when a person wore it. "Oh God," he moaned. "Why has she forsaken me?"

"She hasn't forsaken you. Your wife's still here."

"No!" Gus cried. "Imelda! Mrs. Marcos. I was her friend. She liked me. I had my hands on her neck and in her hair. How could she let them hurt a good friend like this?"

"I'm sure she has nothing to do with it." Jim was so surprised by Gus's passion over Imelda, he said, "And you were just an employee, a servant, Gus. She barely knows you exist."

"What do you know? You're as stupid as Eleanor about Mrs. Marcos. I was her good friend. I laughed at her jokes and she laughed at mine. I would still be her friend if you hadn't turned them against me." He was regaining control of his voice and tears. "I must talk to her. When I tell her it was your fault, she will understand and forgive me. She will fix things with the police."

"Maybe," said Jim. He knew she wouldn't. As Enéro had made clear on the phone and in his office, the First Lady had washed her hands of Gus. Enéro wouldn't have dared to touch him if the Marcoses hadn't given him their full permission. But Jim had to leave Gus with some kind of hope. "We could try that. We'll call her tomorrow and see if she'll talk to you."

"She will. I know she will," he stubbornly insisted. "You got me into this, but I must get myself out. I always have to do everything myself. Eleanor thinks I'm a fool, but I'm not. I know what I'm doing."

Jim nodded. "All right then. We'll try Mrs. Marcos in the morning." He stood up, resisting the impulse to stroke or even kiss Gus goodnight. He couldn't be angry with Gus for absolving his employer of all blame, or for continuing to put the full responsibility on Jim. His arrogantly naive, self-healing ignorance was one of the qualities Jim loved in Gus right now. Maybe it was only the trauma that blocked out so much, but if Gus were going to suffer the physical pain, it seemed right he be spared the mental pain of too much understanding.

"Who needs the U.S.?" he scoffed as Jim stepped toward the door. "I love my homeland."

"Goodnight, Gus. I'll let you sleep. You'll need your rest."

Jim hadn't wanted to make Gus understand. He had needed this odd encounter solely for himself, a chance to measure his decision against his feeling for the fellow. You always hurt the one you love, he thought as he pulled the door shut. Except Jim realized he got it backwards, loving those he hurt.

He gently knocked on the door to the study before opening it.

Meg sat at the far end of the leather couch, still dressed, her bare feet up, a notebook propped on her knees.

"Sorry. I have to use this phone. Mrs. Luna's in the living room."

"You want me to leave?"

"No. You might want to hear this."

He took out his address book and found Dave Wheeler's number. It would be Sunday morning there. He wished it were still Sunday here and that the past twenty-four hours hadn't happened. He sat on his end of the sofa and dialed the number.

"They said no," Meg whispered.

Jim nodded.

The telephone was ringing. The tumblers were clicking into place. Jim wanted both Dave and the electronic shadows, whoever they were, to know what his final decision was.

Meg sat very still, watching. She settled back against the leather arm to sit more motionlessly.

The phone was picked up. "Wheeler."

"Dave?"

"Jim." He immediately knew who it was. "How are you? Hoped you'd call this morning. I spoke with Pat at length last night." His official cheerfulness sounded foreign and inappropriate.

"And?"

"She's terrifically excited by your item. Unless you've hit paydirt at your end, there's beaucoup good we can do with it at ours."

"More definite maybes?" Jim hadn't intended to be skeptical with Wheeler. He faced forward on the couch to avoid seeing Meg's overcast face.

"No, something very definite. Our congressman from Brooklyn, Solarz, has a few friends in the House ready to throw in with him on Marcos, *if* we can prove how out-of-hand things are."

"My reports and photos should be proof enough."

"But they wouldn't have half the effect this movie would. These people have short attention spans. You've got to hit them quick and hard. We get three or four more Congressmen in our camp, and we can sock Marcos where he'll hurt, in his upcoming World Bank loan as well as the next foreign aid package."

This would be so much easier if they could accomplish something real, topple a government or save a life. Instead the film was just another counter in the civilized game of temptation they played with large sums of money.

"What've you got on your burner, Jim? They give you any indication they'll give you something of value if you play ball?"

"Nothing," he said. "Not a damn thing."

"Then send it over. Because we can do plenty with it. And if it's media coverage you want, we got a better chance of getting it through Congress than you do playing Deep Throat with a couple of stringers over there. What do you say, Jim?''

"I say yes. Sure.'' He took a breath, wondering if he'd breathe relief or grievous error with his oxygen. "Yeah, I'd already come to the conclusion there was nothing for me to do but send it on. All right then. You'll get it.''

"Good, Jim. I knew you'd see this was the best solution all around. You might want to use other channels, even regular mail. Is your niece still visiting? What if you sent it out with her when she flies home?''

"That won't be for another week or two.'' He glanced at Meg. Her posture and expression hadn't changed; there was no surprise or disgust, only quietly sustained scrutiny.

"Plenty of time. We could arrange to have someone pick it up from her at the airport or her home.''

"I don't know, Dave. I'll have to ask her.''

She blinked when she heard herself mentioned, then frowned.

"Whatever. I'll leave that to your discretion. But I can't wait to see the film, Jim. It sounds like absolute dynamite.''

Jim shifted forward again, away from Meg; he did not want to use her as his courier. "There's something else you should know about the circumstance surrounding my decision, Dave. I don't know how it'll affect your attitude toward this film.'' He had to clear his throat. "But in the course of negotiating with the secret police, I exposed a man to arrest and interrogation. Colonel Enéro has told me point-blank that the man will be rearrested and subjected to further interrogation if I don't surrender the film.''

Wheeler did not need to be told *interrogation* was a euphemism; *torture* had a shrill, meaningless sound, even in Human Rights. "Jesus,'' he muttered. "Ruthless bastard, ain't he? Who's the man? Not the person who gave you the item in the first place, I hope.''

"No. An innocent bystander. Or not so innocent, but without direct involvement in this. A police spy who's also an acquaintance.''

"What sort of acquaintance, Jim?'' He was silent a moment. "Sexual?''

Jim was surprised he understood so quickly. "Uh huh.''

"Shit,'' he grumbled. "Shit and damnation. You've been taking your jollies with a police spy? Couldn't you have saved it for weekends in Bangkok? Damn it Jim, you sat on it for forty-some years.'' He scolded Jim for what he saw as simply a minor complication, not for ruining everything. "Bad judgment. Very bad judgment. I don't understand how you could've done something so stupid.''

"Yes, well, I never imagined they'd resort to this kind of moral blackmail. They've made me responsible for the welfare of their spy. They're not bluffing when they say they'll subject him to the worst. I saw him myself this morning. Bruises and electrical burns.''

"But he's one of theirs? He works for them?''

"Oh yeah. He's a Marcos man. Even now.''

"Then you can't feel responsible for him, Jim. I understand your qualms. But we can't let their ruthlessness stand between us and our mission. In the long run, we might be able to save hundreds, maybe thousands with this film. We can't be deterred by what the bastards'll do to one man, and their own man at that."

"You're not telling me anything I haven't told myself already." Jim had hoped the arguments would be more convincing coming from someone else, but they had a tinny, routine sound.

"What if I take full responsibility for what happens?" said Wheeler. "I'm *ordering* you to send us the film. Anything that happens to this spy is all on my head."

Jim wanted to laugh. "That's easy for you. You don't know the man. You've never had his tongue down your throat."

Wheeler hesitated. "It *is* easy for me. Which is why you should let me take the blame and responsibility."

"Uh-uh, Dave. We don't have to play Eichmann with each other. You'll get the damn thing. But it's on my head, not yours. I just wanted you to be cognizant of the price tag attached." Yes, that was the only reason why Jim mentioned these facts.

"You're in a tough spot, Jim. I don't know what else to say."

"I'm sending the film," Jim declared, wanting to end his sympathy. "One way or the other, you'll get it in the next couple of weeks. And I'll send you pictures of what they do to their spy. In their rush to put the screws on, they've given me some first-rate evidence."

"It's the best decision all around, Jim. The only decision."

"It is," Jim said firmly. "Goodnight, Dave."

"Goodbye, Jim. I'll tell Pat the full situation. You'll have her sympathy and gratitude. Good luck."

They hung up together and Jim took a deep breath. He was sad, terribly sad and mournful. It wasn't guilt, which Jim experienced as an angrily knotted numbness, but grief, expressed in a soft, palpable warmth beneath his muscles, and a moistness under the eyelids. He had been afraid he'd feel nothing when it was done, only cold and right. If he were going to be a bastard, he wanted to be a feeling bastard.

"You didn't tell him Gus and his family are here."

Meg watched him, an elbow on one knee, the hand pushed up beneath her hair. Her voice was low. There was a look of toothache to her mouth.

"It wouldn't have changed anything. He didn't want to hear the details about Gus."

She closed her eyes and sighed.

"You think I'm wrong, don't you?"

"I don't know, Jim. I couldn't do what you're doing, but—" The look of pain narrowed her eyes. "They won't let Gus go even if you give them the film?"

"No. Enéro's vindictiveness is stronger than his common sense."

"And that's what you were telling Gus before you came in?"

Jim shook his head. "I'll tell him tomorrow. And Mrs. Luna too, although she seems to know something's wrong."

Meg drew a deep breath through her nose. "But until then, you'll suffer for both of them."

"I'm not proud of what I'm doing."

"No, you feel like shit. I'm sure you feel like shit."

There was anger in her words, and his words too, but they had to keep their voices low and anger was turned inward. They spoke like two people angry with themselves rather than with each other.

Meg drew her bare legs more tightly against her chest. "I've been thinking about that story you told me this morning. You don't live half as easily with that as you claim."

"I do and I don't," he told her.

"But this one will be even worse. Won't it? You're throwing another man on top of the first, and you're not coldblooded enough to live with both of them, Jim."

"What I might feel is irrelevant," he declared.

She bit her lower lip, plucking at it with her teeth before she said, "What if you quit? What if you just give them the film and resign from the State Department?"

"What would that accomplish?"

"It would get you out of this no-win trap. And it'd free Gus from you, Jim. What difference does it make if he and his family are out on the street? They can take care of themselves. Talking with Eleanor this afternoon made that much clear to me."

It was an option Jim hadn't considered; he couldn't seriously consider it now. "Wash my hands of this and walk away? Save my own soul and say the hell with Marcos and the rest?"

Meg winced at hearing the idea expressed in those terms. "It's a solution that makes *some* sense," she insisted. "To me anyway."

"No," said Jim. "I can't. And it has nothing to do with pride or ego. I was willing to bend. I offered to compromise. But to completely give in to them and walk away from this, scot-free, would be wrong. Cowardly and wrong. Not for the sake of my conscience. Not even for the sake of that poor son of a bitch in my bedroom." Jim was frustrated to find his reasons for staying less easy to articulate than the ones for not surrendering, but such words as *principle* and *moral duty* were dry and empty right now. "I can't give in to cruelty. You're the historian. You of all people should understand that."

"I understand that. Perfectly. But I also understand what this might do to you as well as Gus. That first boy is what put you here, Jim. God knows where you'll end up with this on your conscience too. It could fuck you up for good."

"My mental health has nothing to do with this." She'd been harder to fight when she argued out of concern for Gus instead of concern for him. "And awful as it is, I'd rather have this on my conscience than knowing I caved in to brute cruelty. Maybe that sounds masochistic to a woman, but it's what I believe and what I have to do. I can't appease their brute cruelty by sacrificing the larger issue for the sake of personal feeling."

Meg was silent for a moment. She lowered her head and said, "Part of me knows you're right. It does," she admitted. "It even recognizes that there's something admirable in your knowing what you know, and still be able to do what you're doing." She narrowed her eyes at Jim again. "But I just can't admire it."

"Nothing to admire. I screwed up. I overestimated their intelligence and decency. But I can't walk away from this."

She nodded and took another deep breath. "I don't know why I want to argue you out of this. Maybe it *is* because I'm female, and emotionally— narrower? closer to the ground?" She shook her head. "I'm just not ready to believe there's no other way out."

"Believe it. Accept it," said Jim. "I have. There's no way out."

Her gaze turned inward and she lightly rocked against her knees, nodding with her whole body, seeming to accept, apparently giving in.

Her retreat forced Jim to wonder if she might be right after all; no, his resignation would only assure Enéro that cruelty was power and torture an effective means for controlling anyone.

"Frustrating to study history," Meg suddenly said. "But an awful privilege too. I sometimes get frustrated reconstructing old errors I can do nothing to change. But here I am in the present, and there's not a damn thing I can do here either. And it's a relief." Her eyes focused on Jim's. "I actually feel relieved I can't change your mind. Because if I could, I'd be terrified it was the absolutely wrong decision, and partly my fault if you quit."

"You don't need to be afraid, because I can't quit."

"No. You can't. You won't," she added. She settled back to sit very still and grow accustomed to the fact. "What happens next?"

"We wait. I get the film back tomorrow or the next day and send it to Washington. Wheeler suggested I send it with you, but I won't."

"Why not? You don't trust me with it?"

He was surprised she didn't flatly refuse. "I want it off my hands as soon as possible. And I don't want you feeling in any way responsible for what might happen."

She frowned, but didn't object or thank him. "And Gus?"

"I'll keep him here for as long as I can. A few more days. Maybe a few weeks. Maybe when Enéro hears his film is making the rounds in Washington he'll see he has nothing to gain by taking Gus back into custody."

"Do you think that's likely?"

"No," Jim admitted. "A vengeful man like Enéro? Not bloody likely at all."

There seemed to be nothing further to say in the matter. Her acquiescence —no, it was more like resignation—seemed to declare the business settled, the decision final, yet they continued to sit at their opposite ends of the sofa, unable to look at each other, Jim testing his decision one last time by picturing the body across the hall and what would be done to it.

20

THE TELEPHONE RANG.

Meg saw Jim calmly turn and take it. The world entered this prison of nerves and words only in beaten bodies and disembodied phone calls.

"Speaking."

Meg had tried to use their silence to get a better grip on her decision to disengage, but all she could seriously consider was Jim's statement that this waiting could go on for days before the police came for Gus. It would be like a long illness and Meg wished she could escape this hellish house and country. But to fly home now would be cowardly and wrong.

"Yes, it's been a few weeks, Dominick. How are you tonight?"

Jim faced her without seeming to see her, his eyes blinking in erratic bursts.

"She does? Uh huh. When? May I ask what the occasion is?" His eyes darted to one side; he faked a sociable laugh. "Hen party or no, I'd like to come too. If you qualify, so do I. No, I trust you, Dominick. The First Lady too. I understand. Woman to woman. My niece would be honored. It's almost eleven now. How does midnight sound?"

Her mouth went dry and her heart was in her throat. No, this couldn't mean what she thought it meant. Wouldn't Jim put down the phone to ask if she would go?

He was seeing her now, his eyes wide and serious while his mouth curled in sociable chatter. "That's very kind, but if it's all the same to you I'd rather bring her myself. Fine. One last question, Dominick. Would this have any connection with a mutual acquaintance? I think you know exactly who I mean. Uh *huh*. I see. No, I understand, I understand perfectly. Very good then. I'll have her there at twelve sharp. No, no, the honor is ours, I assure you."

He set the receiver in its cradle, very gently, as though starting another story on a house of cards. "I'll be damned," he said.

"What?" Meg demanded.

"Imelda wants to meet the Human Rights officer's niece. You've been invited to the palace tonight."

"Tonight?" That was her first fear. *"Why?"*

His mouth was on the edge of a smile. "She wants to talk about Gus. There's no other explanation," he told himself. "Why else would she—? Damn." He glanced at the phone. "Our eavesdroppers are in *her* camp. She knows what I've decided about Gus. Well!"

"Shouldn't she want to talk to *you* then? What can *I* do?"

"She must think she'll be more comfortable talking to you. Woman to woman. Maybe she thinks she can sweet-talk you into sweet-talking me out of this. I don't know. But the important thing is she's curious enough about Gus to want to talk to somebody. Maybe he's not so deluded about his patron after all."

Meg was overwhelmed; he had to be kidding. Her next thought was that Jim did this to her as a mind-fuck, in revenge for all her criticisms and charges. "I don't know, Jim," she pleaded. "What am I supposed to say to her?"

"I wouldn't worry about that. She'll do all the talking." He stood up. "Come on. You have to get ready if we're to be there by midnight."

"This is real? You really expect me to go?"

"You won't?" He looked at her with disbelief and fear.

"No, it's just—" She covered her confusion with a nasty laugh. "It's not a joke? She wants to meet *me*. No, of course I'll go. It's our only chance, right? Oh shit."

"Dominick was noncommittal, but yes, maybe. Who knows? But it's worth trying. Okay?" His tone was stern, his face pleading.

Meg swallowed and nodded. Even if there was unconscious vengence in the quickness with which Jim accepted the invitation without consulting her, that didn't change the fact that Imelda Marcos wanted to meet Meg, and this was their one chance to get the ear of somebody at the top.

When Jim knocked on the door to his bedroom, Eleanor opened it, wearing one of Jim's undershirts. He told her what was up and said they needed Gus's advice. She quickly woke him. Gus was overjoyed to hear Meg would be meeting his employer—"She hasn't, she wouldn't abandon me!"—while Eleanor maintained her doubts—"She must only want to hear the gruesome dish." Jim became cool and careful in their presence, insisting nothing might come of this but any channel of communication was worth exploring; he spoke with an impatient quickness that hadn't been there when he thought the situation was hopeless. Meg's fears swung wildly from the prospect of meeting a monster to the trivia of which blouse to wear.

"No, no, those sleeves do not show proper respect," Gus scolded.

He sat propped on his pillow, imperious despite the bandages, telling Meg what she could and couldn't wear. She changed several times, going back and forth between the bedroom where his sons slept soundly and the bedroom where Gus held court. He ordered Meg to wear her hair down. "You look younger then, and she is more forgiving of cheap clothes on young women."

He hated the only lipstick Meg had and went through his wife's purse until he found a becoming shade. He applied it himself, firmly holding her chin while Meg bent over the bed. The swelling beside his right eye was a deep shade of purple turning yellow along the edges, like a bruise on a peach. "Tell Mrs. Marcos her loyal friend thinks of nothing but her tonight. And that I must talk to her real soon." He released the chin and gestured Meg back. "You look okay. She will think you're a careerwoman, but a young one, so she'll be amused."

Eleanor remained off to the side, a woman afraid to hope. She might be willing to cut her losses and go on without Gus, but she had to empty herself of emotion in order to accept the idea. When Jim and Meg left, however, she followed them to the door.

"Please," she whispered, clutching Meg's arms. "Remind her how funny Gus can be. He does not deserve to suffer." She embraced Meg, her soft breasts trembling in the undershirt, and planted a ticklishly frightened kiss on Meg's neck.

She made it worse. They all made it worse, even Jim with his repeated claim in the car that nothing might come of this but that it should be an interesting experience for a historian. No, he did not want to sacrifice Gus. Another possibility, another door had opened just a crack, and Jim expected Meg to get her foot in and force the door open.

Not until they were out of the compound and on the highway did Meg have the concentration to focus her nervousness on the important question. "What exactly am I supposed to tell the woman?"

"The truth. Just tell her the truth. What I intend to do with the film. What Colonel Enéro intends to do to Gus. You should let her know that at this stage, she's the only one who can save him."

"Do you think she will?"

"I honestly don't know. I have no idea how much say Imelda has with her husband or the secret police. But use tact and discretion when you tell her what's happened. There'll be other people present, so you might look for an opportunity to speak to her alone. Mentioning this in front of her friends might embarrass her."

Her stomach knotted at the thought of protecting this woman, then at the very idea of talking to a monster "woman to woman."

"Oh God, Jim. I don't know if I can go through with this. I'm sure I'll say the wrong thing or lose my temper and tell her what I think about the *shit* she and her husband do to this country and Gus and everything else.''

"You can't do that," said Jim, frowning. "You won't," he claimed. "She's very charming. Just let yourself be charmed. If you want to lose your temper, save it for me when you get home.''

It was absurd. She'd been furious with her uncle all day, but here she was on her way to meet someone who actually deserved her fury and blame, and Meg would have to keep it to herself. What frightened Meg about meeting Imelda Marcos was not so much the woman and what she might do or say, but the violent anger the idea of her awakened in Meg. She had spent much of her career studying the violence of men, but her own violence, rare though it was, frightened and debilitated her. She had thought she'd outgrown that phase, left it behind when she decided to write about teachers instead of soldiers. Strummed nerves shook Meg loose from her chronology, jumbling past and present selves. Sitting beside her uncle in a fancy blouse and faintly adhesive lipstick confused Meg with the memory of being chauffeured by her father to the junior prom.

Jim attempted to put her at ease by talking about details: how to address a dictator's wife, who might be there, how late this might last, speaking briskly even when he joked. "No telling when she'll say goodnight. She suffers insomnia, like Lady Macbeth, only she'd rather entertain than wash her hands.''

"Can I smoke?" Meg asked. She was relieved to hear she could; the subtle violence of lighting a cigarette should save her from larger, more aggressive gestures.

They came down from the elevated highway to a factory district. They crossed a bridge into a dark park, a cluster of lights winking in the trees ahead. Jim turned off the street and stopped at a white stucco gatehouse. A guard in a chrome helmet telephoned a superior while the car idled at the closed iron gate.

"What's the best we can hope from her?" Meg whispered.

"That she'll take Gus back. If not, I'm still willing to make the deal I offered Enéro this afternoon. Yes. I could live with that," he muttered to himself. "A clean slate.''

The guard came out, unlocked the gate and walked it open.

Jim shifted gears and casually saluted the man. When he lowered his hand, he felt around for Meg's hand. "But you'll do fine," he whispered, clutching her palm. "We have nothing to lose. You can't make things worse, only better." His fingers were thick and cool, his palm very large and damp. Meg tightly gripped it, not knowing if she were expected to take assurance or give it.

The palace floated out from behind a ragged grove of trees, a large white mansion with three layers of arched loggias at this end, balconies that were brightly lit although the tall windows in each arch were black, as if the owners were away for the evening. The fronds of the royal palms overhead were folded downward, like sleeping bats. The long drive curved toward the front of the building—or maybe it was the back—and under the fume-stained archway of a carriage entrance that jutted from the facade. Jim slowed the car and stopped under the vaulted roof. A fat, grinning man in a barong and slippers bounced down the wide carpeted steps to open the door on Meg's side.

"Dr. Frisch, I presume." He greeted her with a plump, boneless hand knotted with jewelry. "Good evening, Jim. Good to see you."

"Hello, Dominick. My niece, Meg. Dominick is a close friend of Mrs. Marcos and, at one time anyway, Gus."

Dominick lightly laughed. "I am still his friend, when it's convenient." He pulled on Meg's hand to draw her from the car. "I promise to look after your niece, Jim. I'll bring her home myself when we finish here." Meg resisted the tug and remained seated.

"I don't mind waiting," said Jim. "I can even park out here and sit in the car if you don't want me inside." He nodded at the limos parked in the little lot outside the covered entrance, their drivers standing in a bunch and looking at Jim's Toyota.

"Not necessary, Jim. I don't know how long this will take. And if we wanted to kidnap this lovely young lady"—he squeezed her hand to let Meg know he was teasing—"we could do it if you were out here or sitting comfortably at home. Go home."

"You're right. Yes, I trust you, Dominick." He gave Meg a concerned, slightly sheepish smile.

"I'll be okay," she told him.

"It should be very interesting for you. Whatever happens." He put his hand on her shoulder, bent in and kissed her cheek, pressing slightly to get past the dried skin of his lips to something softer inside. "I'll wait up for you. Listen to Dominick. Good luck," he said and gently pushed her toward the door.

Meg climbed out. Dominick swung the door shut. The car gritted sand and slowly rolled away. The red eyes of the taillights receded into the darkness with insects clacking and squeaking like a hundred unoiled wheels.

She had burned to see the inside of things. She had wanted, and not wanted, to have a say in what happened. Here was her chance, for better or worse, and there was nothing to do now except try.

"A good man, your uncle." Dominick took her hand again and twined his arm with hers. He sweated cologne and had a thick crown of ageless black hair that might be a wig. "Good men can be mysterious and unpredictable, but admirable now and then."

He led her up the steps and past a pair of guards in more chrome helmets. The sullen men didn't snap to attention for the old queen and his American guest, but impatiently waited for them to pass so they could resume chatting or daydreaming or whatever guards did at this hour when nobody was watching.

"You don't consider yourself a good man?" asked Meg.

"Me, my dear? Oh no."

The long hallway inside suggested a museum after hours, public antiques and potted plants, with an unidentifiable sickly sweet smell like perfumed dry-rot. Here she was at the center of all ills in this country, and the place seemed deserted, lifeless, dead. No, the real center was that kitchen where the girl and maybe Gus himself had been tortured. It was dangerous to picture torture before meeting the torturer's wife, but Meg couldn't stop herself. She wondered if she should be worried about her own safety. She wasn't. There was something about the large, effeminate man who held her hand and arm—a wise old fish in a wig—that put Meg at ease.

"Gus speaks highly of you," she fibbed, seeking an opening to the subject of why she was here.

Dominick sighed skeptically. "How is the foolish boy tonight?"

"Not in great pain. But sore. Exhausted." She expected Dominick to play dumb and ask why; he listened with his thick, fishlike lips pursed in a glum pout, his heavy eyelids sadly lowered. "He doesn't seem traumatized," said Meg. "Yet. Or understand that it can happen again. But then nobody's had the heart to tell him."

"Silly boy," Dominick grumbled. "I told him not to allow himself to be loaned out for government services. But he thought I simply wanted to protect my position on the ladder of my First Lady's heart. He thought this would enable him to leapfrog over me. Also, I think, he wanted to get into your uncle's pants." He gave Meg an amused, sidelong glance.

He steered them past a marble staircase as smooth as soap into an enormous twilit room full of heavy Spanish furniture and heavier shadows.

"We'll be in her private chambers tonight," he explained. "*En famille.* Just my First Lady, a half-dozen of her closest friends and her special guest for the month, a famous Hollywood actor and star you will recognize immediately."

"Does she know why I'm here?" Dominick seemed capable of arranging this meeting completely on his own.

"Oh yes. I put the bee in her bonnet," Dominick admitted. "We had just learned your uncle wasn't going to deal with Colonel Enéro. Little birds, y'know. 'Wouldn't it be amusing to meet this man's niece?' I suggested, and she agreed."

"Then she wants to talk to me?"

"She didn't say exactly. And I couldn't ask." He lowered his voice as they entered a mahogany-paneled corridor. "She is surprised by your uncle. That is all. She is a woman of enormous life and spontaneity, a creature of many moments. One cannot press her too hard. I promise nothing, my dear. Much will depend on how she takes to you."

Being polite wouldn't be enough; Meg would have to woo Imelda Marcos. "I'm not famous for my charm," she whispered.

"When in doubt, look at me and I'll let you know if you're treading too close to her train."

Meg had done her share of departmental schmoozing and politicking, but these stakes were much higher. "*You* want to help Gus, don't you?"

Dominick used his heavy lips and eyelids for a blasé look. "Oh, one wants to at least try, my dear. If it's not too inconvenient. Here we are." He set one jeweled hand on a shiny brass door knob in a mahogany door at the end of the corridor. "Shall we?"

"How do I look?"

"Lovely. Very natural and American." He curled his fingers at her face, a coaxing gesture. "Smile," he said. "A big smile. She wants her guests to be happy."

Meg drew a deep breath and smiled. "Okay."

He opened the door on a deep, bright room and loud laughter. A broken carillon of giggles poured from a woman who sat with her back to the door. The hilarity around her was more careful and measured.

Imelda Marcos lounged on a yellow silk sofa as long as a whaleboat, facing a matching sofa where three guests smiled and bobbed their heads: Blue Ladies, although none of them wore blue tonight. A herd of other sofas, armchairs and love seats filled the vast living room like a hotel lobby, brass light fixtures glowing against the polished oak walls. Above the cold fireplace were two panels of folk art, paintings of Adam and Eve in the jungle of Eden. Adam stood behind a bush; Eve wore a sarong and had her hair piled tightly on her head: they were actually Ferdinand and Imelda.

"And then Colonel Qaddafi said to me, 'You are such a good woman, you must study the Koran and become a Muslim.'" More hysterics followed, Mrs. Marcos rocking back and forth. When she caught her breath, a petite hand with crimson nails abruptly reached up to pat the black hair woven snugly against the back of her head, as if feeling somebody's eyes there. Whatever regret she might feel for Gus, she'd already found someone else to do her hair.

Dominick brought Meg forward. The head turned, and the famous, slightly puffy china-doll face covered Meg with dark, soulful eyes. The center of gravity shifted; Meg's stomach dropped. It was like seeing a photo of Adolf Hitler and having human eyes stare back at you.

"Ah!" she exclaimed, with a schoolgirl smile and blink of delight. Then, "Ah," again, smile softening for a sweeter, simpering look, an actress experimenting with responses. Her crinkly gold lamé blouse suggested the gold foil on expensive candy. "You must be Dr. Margaret Frisch, Jim's niece. Thank you, Nicky," she said, dismissing him. "I am so tickled you could drop by on such short notice."

"The pleasure is mine, Madame President."

Imelda burst into giggles again, covering her mouth. Was she insane or merely drunk? The highball glass on the end table had been barely touched.

"If Ferdinand heard you say that, he'd have a heart attack! And then I *would be* Madame President, wouldn't I?" she told the others. "No no no, I am simply the First Lady, Mrs. Marcos. But you must call me Imelda."

"I'm honored. Thank you."

"And I will call you Margaret? Or no, I hear you're called Meg."

"Yes. That would be nice."

Meg thought the habit of good manners would get her through this fraudulence, until Mrs. Marcos held out both hands and Meg had to touch her, then bend down for the kisses the woman stuck on each cheek. Automatically, despite herself, Meg kissed back. Perfume caught in her throat and her lipstick picked up the pollen of face powder. When she straightened up, Meg resisted her impulse to wipe her mouth off.

Mrs. Marcos patted the shiny yellow fabric beside her. "Sit with me," she said, and Meg sat, pointing her knees toward her host in an effort to get some distance. She smiled at the others and Mrs. Marcos introduced them: Mrs. Cocojuanca, Mrs. Benedicto and a sullen young beauty named Miss Torres. The willowy young man lighting Mrs. Cocojuanca's cigarette was introduced simply as Barney. Finally, Mrs. Marcos came to the very tanned American dressed in casual whites at the other end of their sofa. "And you know who *he* is," she proudly whispered.

The movie star whose name Meg could never remember sat with his perfect nose and chiseled chin tilted backward, fast asleep despite the noise around him.

"Poor dear. We have worn him out with our festive Philippine vitality. But this way we can still look upon his beauty and sigh."

The others looked at him enviously, wishing they too could go to sleep. They didn't dare say goodnight or doze off before the First Lady was finished with them for the evening.

Mrs. Marcos told Meg to tell Dominick what she'd like to drink. Dominick had remained standing off to the side, smiling at Meg to encourage her.

"Is there, uh, coffee?" Meg asked. It had been a very long day and she didn't know if fear and adrenaline would keep her alert much longer.

Mrs. Marcos laughed. "The night is young. You can't want coffee. We want you to relax and let down your hair."

Meg laughed with her. "You're right. A white wine spritzer?"

Dominick pinched the air with his thumb and finger to assure her he'd go light on the wine.

"You must not go telling Dr. Frisch your aches and pains," Mrs. Marcos teased the others. "She is not a medical doctor, but a history doctor. She teaches history at a major American university. Isn't that marvelous? We women are everywhere. We can do anything men can do, and still keep our femininity."

Could a woman supervise the torture of another human being? Meg looked for a way to bring up Gus, but this wasn't it, and she was thrown hearing such beliefs mentioned in this place.

"I was telling tales of my travels when you arrived," Mrs. Marcos explained. "I am the Henry Kissinger of Asia, always on the go, spreading my woman's touch throughout the world. This year I have traveled to London, Libya, the Soviet Union and the Big Apple. I am a good-will ambassador, not just for my own country but the entire world." And she sang: "I'd like to teach the world to sing . . .", warbling a whole stanza of the song before she dissolved into giggles.

Everyone laughed with her, including Meg. Meg felt her mind and body split apart each time she laughed, disgusted with herself for playing this game, then worried she played it badly and Mrs. Marcos would see straight through to Meg's contempt. But the others' laughter sounded no more sincere than Meg's, courtier hilarity that was a mechanical matter of big grins and rapid breaths. They laughed when Mrs. Marcos told a long anecdote about the futility of shopping for boots in Moscow, although they must have heard the story a dozen times. Meg wondered if the woman had forgotten about Gus altogether, but Dominick gave her a hopeful look when he brought Meg her drink, indicating it was a good sign his First Lady of many moments was in a good mood.

"When you were in London," Miss Torres blithely asked, "did you see this new show called *Evita*?"

Eyes shifted nervously on either side of the young woman; Mrs. Cocojuanco looked ready to jab the girl with her elbow.

Miss Torres noticed nothing. "My cousin saw it last month when she was in London and said it was fabulous. I am surprised you haven't heard of it. 'Don't Cry for Me, Argentina'? Eva Péron?"

Mrs. Marcos's gaze grew colder, her pout more petulant. She lowered her head and the slight pad of flesh beneath her jaw became a double chin.

"It sounds wonderful," Miss Torres persisted. "We must try to bring it to Manila."

"No," said Mrs. Marcos flatly. "I know this show. I cannot understand why anyone would write a musical about *her*. She was a nobody. A whore who married far above her station. I will not let my people pay good money to see such nonsense."

Miss Torres finally understood she was on thin ice. "I didn't know," she apologized. "All I know is what my cousin told me, and she's not very bright. Yes, it's silly to glamorize a woman like that."

Dominick frowned, worried his patron's mood might be ruined. "What's most irritating is that there's another woman who genuinely deserves to be celebrated for her accomplishments, noble nature and singing abilities. I think I'll write this composer a letter and tell him he should seriously consider writing his next musical about a particular lady in this very room."

Meg was certain he'd gone too far, but he knew his First Lady quite well.

She brushed the flattery aside with a sweep of her hand, then wryly observed, "These theater people are more interested in shams than in the real thing. Not since *Camelot* has there been a good show about politics."

With Dominick leading the way, they got Mrs. Marcos to talk about her favorite musicals, attempting to coax her into a better mood. Meg wondered if the others knew about Gus or why she was here, then decided they only wanted Mrs. Marcos happy so she would go to bed and they could go home. Meg knew better than to look at her own watch; she turned to look at the sleeping movie star and the Rolex on his brown wrist: it was after one o'clock. Timing was everything: Meg could not bring up Gus until Mrs. Marcos was in a good mood, and if she were in too good a mood she might go to bed without Meg getting a chance to talk to her.

"And what about you, Meg?" Mrs. Marcos asked. "What is your favorite musical? I bet I can guess. *Hair.* Am I right? You are of that age."

"Uh, yes. I like *Hair.*" Meg slipped into telling the truth. "Actually, I'm not very big on musicals."

"You think they're silly?"

"No no. Not at all. I just—I'm not very big on music, period. I don't know why. I guess I don't have an ear for it." She feared she only dug herself in deeper, although what did any of this have to do with Gus? "It's my failing, I admit. Something missing in my nature."

She gave Meg a deeply pitying pout. "You poor thing. I know I couldn't live without music. Maybe you are like your uncle that way. Music is the language of the heart, and your uncle is a heartless man."

"I have a heart. I just don't have an ear," said Meg, wondering how she could use this to talk about Gus. Not here though, not with Imelda's retinue watching.

"Your uncle pretends to enjoy music, but I can tell he doesn't. So serious, so solemn. He does not know how to enjoy himself," chuckled Mrs. Marcos, going off in a different direction. Maybe she wasn't referring to Gus after all. "Do you know what we used to call your uncle?" She shared the joke with the others. "The Vicar! We called him the Vicar!" And she broke into new peals of giggles.

Meg laughed with her, pretending never to have heard the epithet.

"Oh but that was before we knew," Mrs. Marcos declared when she caught her breath. "Like all men, even the Vicar has his naughty side. And naughty in a way one would never guess to look at him." She arched her precise black eyebrows at the man's niece. "You can't judge a book by its cover."

"There're all kinds of gay men," said Meg. "I know about my uncle."

"I do not condemn. Certainly not. I'm a very modern woman." She smiled lasciviously. "He is the scandal of your family?"

"Nobody knows except me. I assume my mother knows without knowing she knows. Or maybe she does. He is her brother. But I've never discussed it with her or anyone else." Meg tattled away simply because Mrs. Marcos was curious and Meg needed to please her. There was unease over sharing family secrets with a dictator's wife, but Meg heard herself declare, "I found out the hard way."

"Yes?" Mrs. Marcos's eyes lit up. "Do tell."

"It's too embarrassing," said Meg, surprised by her interest, then wondering if she could use that interest.

"We adore juicy *tsismis*. Gossip, you know."

"I'm sorry. I couldn't tell a roomful of strangers."

"You and I are friends," Mrs. Marcos sweetly pleaded. "Can't you tell me?"

"I don't know. Maybe if we were alone?"

"I understand. Yes. Some pains are too private to be shared with the masses." She gave a dismissive glance to her little court. "I need to go freshen up. Come with me and we can talk in private."

"I'd be flattered," said Meg. "Sure."

They stood up together and Mrs. Marcos took Meg's hand in hers. "Don't leave yet," she told the others. "I thought we might watch the videos of the party I gave President Nixon in New York last year." She led Meg toward the bedroom, past Dominick who bowed his head and raised his eyebrows, congratulating Meg on her cleverness.

Meg might have been pleased herself if she thought she could invent a good story. There was something unseemly about reducing an important personal matter to gossip for the entertainment of Imelda Marcos, even in a good cause. Meg didn't know if she could get from gossip to Gus, or exactly what she might win from this cluster of whims and poses.

In heels and puffed hair, Mrs. Marcos was taller than Meg, which was a surprise in a country where most of the men were Meg's height. She amiably patted the back of Meg's hand: it was a very touchy-feely regime. "You must tell me what your uncle did. I am all ears."

They had entered a bedroom as large as the living room, an enormous canopied bed on a dais to one side. A young maid snapped awake in her chair beside the bed when her lady's shoes clicked across the parquet. She jumped up and ran ahead of them, turning on lights in a dressing room, bathroom and clothes closet, each of which appeared to be the size of Meg's apartment in Madison.

Meg waited until the maid returned to the bedroom to say, "In a nutshell, he went to bed with my boyfriend in college."

"Oh? Ohhh." Mrs. Marcos looked delighted. "You poor child. Make yourself comfortable. I will be right out." She gestured at the armchairs grouped around a high-tech vanity table, then stepped into the bathroom, closing the door just enough to shield herself from view. "I'm listening," she called out.

Meg told the story quickly, too thrown by the situation to make up a new one. The mirror over the vanity table was framed in a white tube of light that placed the dressing room somewhere in outer space. The closet had an unearthly glow from the rows of illuminated shelves that covered one wall, where a couple of hundred pairs of shoes were displayed as if for sale. And Imelda Marcos herself sat on a toilet a few feet away. Meg gave the dry, circumstantial version of what happened: the invitation to visit, the bad timing of her ride, the proudly guilty faces of two cats with identical mouthfuls of canary the next morning at a rally.

Mrs. Marcos was disappointed Meg hadn't scratched anyone's eyes out. "But the Inauguration?" she said. "I was in Washington that very weekend."

"You met them, ironically enough. Jim introduced Doug to you at a party or reception somewhere. Doug was very impressed."

"You don't say. That weekend is a blur to me. Parties, parties, parties. But if I had known what your uncle intended, I would have stopped him, I assure you."

Meg was amazed by the coincidences here, and the thought that Imelda Marcos was a kind of evil fairy godmother to her uncle's sex life.

"You must have been heartbroken."

"Not at all. But angry. Very angry." She wanted to dismiss the affair as ancient history, but Mrs. Marcos's prurient pity might prove useful. "There was no future between me and this boy. But I felt my uncle betrayed his loyalty to me. I was far more hurt by what he did than what Doug did."

The voice inside the bathroom said nothing for a moment. Then, "I know exactly how you feel. I am betrayed by your uncle myself, and very angry with him."

"Because of Gus?"

"One moment." The toilet flushed and there was a clink of porcelain when the sitter stood up. Water ran in a sink.

When Mrs. Marcos came out of the bathroom she looked as solemn as a nun. "Sit. Please. I'm not finished yet." She sat down at her vanity table and examined her face and throat in the mirror, smoothing skin with her fingers.

Perched on the edge of an armchair, Meg saw herself in the half-light behind Imelda's evenly illuminated head.

"You know what your uncle's doing to my good friend Gus-Gus?"

Meg nodded. "Except Jim's not doing it. The secret police are." She had to stop herself from saying, *your* secret police.

Mrs. Marcos relaxed her face to look over the elaborate arsenal of lipstick cartridges and muddy rainbow of backlit perfume bottles that covered her table. Then her lower lip bulged, her dark eyes glittered with water. She snatched a tissue from a gold-plated box and quickly dabbed them.

"No!" she declared. "It is your uncle who does this. The police do only what they always do. If your heartless uncle gave Ishmael this item he needs, nothing would happen to Gus-Gus. You must talk to him and make your uncle change his mind."

Meg gazed into a mirror world where everything was reversed: it was always the other person's fault, even here at the Malacanang Palace. "You can't talk to this colonel and get him to change *his* mind?"

"He says it is a question of national security and he has no choice in the matter. No, it is Jim Goodall's decision now, nobody else's."

"But he feels *he* has no choice in the matter."

"Nonsense. All he has to do is give them this thing. Not go sending it to our enemies in Washington."

Meg resisted the urge to tell Mrs. Marcos what "this thing" was. "But the police will still go after Gus the next time Jim does anything wrong. That's what he thinks anyway."

Mrs. Marcos closed her eyes and sank back in her chair. "Why does Jim not trust us?" she demanded. "What makes him think we are such monsters? Yes, our police sometimes do harsh things, but only to prevent our enemies from doing worse things to us. Why is your uncle out to get us?"

It was like talking with the mentally ill: you had to take on some of their madness just to communicate with them. "There's nothing personal involved," Meg assured her. "It's his job, and my uncle is very devoted and proud about his work. I've already tried reasoning with him. I don't want to see Gus hurt. But Jim is a very stubborn, principled man." Meg slipped in that last adjective for the sake of pride; she disliked finding traces of her own response to Jim's decision mirrored in Mrs. Marcos's blinkered blaming. "He's determined to be just as tough and stubborn as your police chief."

"But my little Gus-Gus is the one who'll be hurt."

"Were you going to let him work for you if this ended well?"

Her eyes briefly glittered again and her breasts rose when she shifted her shoulders against a chill under her skin. "Ferdinand won't allow it. He will say it is a security risk and make our police look bad, or something." She firmly shook her head. "Is Gus-Gus angry at me?"

"No. He told me to tell you he's still your loyal friend and is thinking of you tonight." Meg noted she didn't ask how Gus was or the extent of his injuries, only what he thought of her. "He doesn't understand what he did wrong that made you abandon him."

"I'm not the one who abandoned him," she said indignantly. "It is your uncle who's abandoned him. Gus-Gus means little to me," she insisted. "He did my hair, that's all, and not very well either. But he seems to mean far more to me than to your uncle, who made love to him!"

"But Jim doesn't want to see Gus hurt. He's willing to bend."

"Yes? How?"

Meg played the only real card Jim had given her. "He says he'll give up the film if you let Gus leave the country."

"Oh." Mrs. Marcos pouted again. "An exit visa, yes. Ishmael told me about that. He says it's a trick."

Meg was surprised she already knew. "It's not a trick. My uncle's absolutely sincere. Because he does not want Gus hurt again."

Mrs. Marcos irritably shifted. "What's to prevent your uncle from circulating copies of this thing after he gives us the original and we let Gus-Gus leave?"

"His promise?" said Meg. "The fact I know he hasn't made any copies yet? And I think he's proven he's willing to circulate the movie whether Gus is in danger or not. The only definite thing it changes is that Gus won't be hurt again." Meg tossed different reasons at her, hoping one might stick.

"But it means Gus-Gus leaves the country he loves!"

"Uh, yes. It does." Meg searched for a tactful response to that. "But it's the one decent alternative my uncle has given us."

Mrs. Marcos said nothing for a moment, which was startling. She drew several quick, deep breaths to help herself think. "I don't understand. I hoped this would be a beautiful love story. Where a man sacrifices everything he believes for the sake of love."

"I don't think my uncle ever loved Gus. Romantically."

"No? I think he did. But a man like that will sacrifice love for the sake of *principles*." She scornfully enunciated each syllable. "Women are less principled, hence more human."

Meg stared, blinked twice and used the statement. "Which is why it's up to us to save Gus from the men. Or up to you. Imelda." The name did not come naturally. "There's nothing more I can do. But you can. Can't you?"

Lifting her chin slightly, Mrs. Marcos watched herself in the mirror. "I must. Jim and Ishmael have given me no other choice. Yes. An exit visa for Gus-Gus."

Meg held her breath. She couldn't believe Mrs. Marcos was coming around.

"I must intervene," she told herself. "It's silly for Gus-Gus to suffer when the solution is so simple. I will make Ferdinand see. He is *my* hairdresser. I should be able to do with him as I please."

"You mean, I can tell my uncle you agree?"

She didn't hear Meg's disbelief. "Ferdinand has gone to bed, but I will speak to him in the morning. You must speak to your uncle and hold him to this promise. Gus-Gus will get a visa, Ishmael his thing, and your uncle can keep his principles. Everybody wins. I don't understand why the men didn't see that." She rolled her eyes upward and snickered. "They were too busy proving who had the biggest gonads."

"What's the next step?" asked Meg.

"I feel so much better. And tired. Whew." She sank back against her chair again. "A good tired. People think power is all fun and games. But the responsibility is *exhausting*."

"Did you want my uncle to call you? Will you speak to Gus?"

"Oh no. It would break my heart to talk to Gus, knowing he's saying goodbye. Just tell Jim to ring up Colonel Enéro tomorrow and they can arrange how they want to swap their toys. I am sure they will want to play James

Bond with this. But Ferdinand and I will hold Ishmael to his side of the bargain, if you can do the same with Jim."

"It's what my uncle wants too," Meg pointed out.

But Mrs. Marcos was already off on yet another tangent. "I feel right now like a mother whose child is leaving the nest. So many people leaving our country for foreign lands. We think of our people as our children, Ferdinand and I, but we'll always be in their hearts no matter where they are." She blinked a few more glimmers from her eyes, and raised the back of her hand to cover a yawn. "Excuse me. I am suddenly so sleepy. I don't know why. I really must get to bed."

She rose and Meg promptly stood with her.

"Say goodnight to my friends on your way out. They'll understand. And thank you for your help in solving this predicament." She gathered Meg's hands between her own, a sincere sandwich. "I could not have done it without you."

"My pleasure, Mrs. Marcos."

"No!" she laughed. "Imelda! You must call me Imelda! After what we've accomplished tonight, we will be the best of friends." She leaned in and kissed Meg on the mouth, a sticky, rubbery kiss that didn't register until it was over. "Now off with you. We angels of mercy need our beauty sleep."

Meg backed toward the door, stunned it was over, relieved she could say goodnight and go. Not until she was crossing the bedroom did she think: *What happened? What did I do?*

The guests in the living room were happy to hear the First Lady had gone to bed. Mrs. Cocojuanca teasingly asked if Meg had a secret massage she could teach the rest of them. Everyone stood up and moved toward the door, except Dominick, who was grinning at Meg. She assumed she looked blank, absolutely stunned, but Dominick recognized she was stunned by success.

"What about *him*?" asked Miss Torres, pointing at the comatose movie star.

"Let him be," said Dominick. "I'll take care of him later." He walked with Meg, letting the others get further ahead in the corridor before he whispered, "She said yes?"

"I think. She'll make the secret police accept my uncle's deal."

"Oh thank God," Dominick murmured. "And thank you, Dr. Frisch. You performed handsomely."

"Then we should believe her?"

"If my First Lady said it, she meant it." He squeezed Meg's hand happily, his rings pinching her fingers.

"But will she remember tomorrow what she said?" The scholar wondered if she should have gotten something in writing.

"Of course. And if it slips her mind, I'll be there to remind her."

"It's just she changed so quickly and she seems kind of, well . . ."

"Mad? Oh no." He shook his head. "Perfectly sane. She seems a bit scattered when she hasn't had enough sleep, that's all. And people in her position in life don't worry about form or making sense. They feel free to let their thoughts fly as they occur.''

Out in the parking lot beside the carriage entrance, the early-morning quiet was broken by women scolding their drivers awake and the solid slam of limousine doors. Dominick opened a door for Meg and said his chauffeur would take her home. "I should go back and take care of our Hollywood guest. But again, I can't thank you enough for helping Gus. Not only for him but for her. She is very fond of Gus, in her fashion. Good night, Dr. Frisch.''

The plush backseat was wide and soft; Meg wanted to stretch out on it and sleep. She didn't. She drew the tinted glass panel aside so she could see the driver and road ahead of them—she couldn't bear being enclosed right now. She lit a cigarette. She'd been too nervous in the palace to remember that she smoked. More adrenaline buzzed and chimed through her now than when she'd been with Imelda Marcos.

What had happened? What did I do? Her conversation with Imelda felt like a helpless ride on somebody else's stream of consciousness, Meg able to do little except try to nudge the stream this way or that. They seemed to have won. Dominick said they had. What had they won? The "history doctor" had intervened and, instead of recording suffering, she'd prevented it. There was relief that it was over, but no feeling of triumph. Meg began to fear she'd been too complicitious, too kissy-face, humoring and indulging the woman when she should have confronted her with the horror of what had been done to Gus. Meg hadn't even told her what was in the "thing" that Imelda seemed to know was a movie yet treated as a complete mystery. Where was the girl in the movie tonight? What would happen to the girl? Who could save *her*?

Such second thoughts were an absurd self-punishment. Meg knew she'd obtained the one concession that Mrs. Marcos was willing to grant and that it was ludicrous to feel guilty for not winning more. Nevertheless, to come away from this full of joy and self-congratulation would have been more ludicrous, pathetic and deluded. You do what you can and, even when you succeed— especially when you succeed—it never feels like enough.

JIM AND ELEANOR were both up and sitting in the kitchen when Meg came in. They faced her with identical anxious stares when Meg stood in the kitchen door. Jim wore his reading glasses; Eleanor had pulled on her jeans under the T-shirt. The clock above the sink said it was three in the morning.

"She said yes. She'll help Gus get out of the country.''

Eleanor let out a great sigh like a moan as she jumped up to embrace Meg. *"Salámat, salámat,"* she chanted—thank you, thank you—squeezing Meg tight and kissing her on the neck and cheek.

All doubts lifted for a moment.

"You saved Gus. You have saved *us*. Oh you are great, Meg. You are so great." She passionately shook Meg against her chest. "I must tell Gus." She released her and raced out to wake her husband.

Never a hero in her own life—is anybody?—Meg was startled to be taken for one in Eleanor's.

Jim stood by his chair, gazing at her over the tops of his glasses. "What did Mrs. Marcos say?"

"That she'll make sure Gus gets an exit visa if you give Enéro the film."

He received the news with a slow nod, bowing his high forehead at her. He looked very old tonight, tired and pink-eyed.

"That *is* what you wanted?" she asked.

"Yes. It is. Definitely." His heart wasn't in his words. He attempted to smile and his heart wasn't there either. "If I don't seem more relieved, it's only because, well, I can't quite believe it."

"I can't believe it either," Meg admitted. "But that's what she told me."

"Here. Sit." Jim pulled out his chair for her. "You look exhausted. As well you should be. You must feel like you've been to the moon and back tonight."

And here I am in the kitchen again, thought Meg, remembering her skewed metaphors as she collapsed in the chair. "Then you'll do it?"

"How can I not do it?" He sat in the chair next to hers, peeling off his reading glasses and laying an arm across the back of her chair when he looked into her face. Meg remembered her old joke about him: my uncle is too farsighted to see anything closer than Southeast Asia.

They heard Eleanor down the hall shouting the good news to Gus.

"Thank you," said Jim. "You succeeded where I failed. I didn't want to sacrifice Gus, but you saved him from my principles."

Meg felt uncomfortable with the praise, the responsibility. "Not me. Imelda Marcos saved him. With your compliance." She shook her head and snorted. "We're all in this together, Jim. You and me and Imelda."

"Strange bedfellows," he admitted. His arm came forward and the hand gingerly gripped her shoulder.

She leaned into his chest with her other shoulder, surprised by the comfort of his weight, the sudden bond of complicity and regret.

"But it *is* the right thing to do?" she asked, looking at the reading glasses on the table. "Giving up the film to save Gus?"

"For now. A bird in the hand," he claimed. "Although in the longterm scheme of things . . ." His voice trailed off, unwilling to finish.

"History will judge otherwise?" she said skeptically.

"No. This is too private for history." His arm held her more firmly and he took a deep breath. "We've made it private anyway. But time will tell if I blew it in choosing Gus. Only time will tell."

They sat at the table in their awkward, exhausted half-embrace, listening to Eleanor in the distance celebrate the survival of her family with a husband who was disappointed they hadn't done better.

21

TIME DOES TELL, but not always what's expected.

Imelda Marcos kept her promise and forced Colonel Enéro to accept Jim's terms. Five days later, when Gus was well enough to travel and Wexler had expedited the emigration papers, the exchange took place at the gate for the daily flight to San Francisco. Major Valeriano was there as Enéro's representative. Wexler was there to mediate and assure Valeriano that the film was whole and Jim hadn't cut out any pieces to keep; Wexler refused to let Jim show him the movie that morning but ran it between his fingers as it went from one reel to another, feeling for splices. Meg came to watch the conclusion, and Eleanor brought the boys to see their father off. The family would follow later when Eleanor finished tying up their personal affairs and selling what they couldn't take. They looked like just another Filipino family sharing tearful goodbyes at Manila International. Sad to be leaving but excited to be going somewhere new, Gus hugged and wept on everyone, even Major Valeriano. He hesitated only for a second before he embraced Jim and said, "I forgive you. You did what you thought you were supposed to do, that is all." When he was aboard the plane and the ramp pulled away, Wexler handed the film to Valeriano. The plane lifted off, became a speck in the distance and was gone.

The house in Makati was eerily quiet that evening without the Lunas. Jim and Meg left for Samar the next day and spent a desultory week bouncing in a jeep on hilly trails from one nondescript village to the next. When they returned, Eleanor and her sons had already left for the States. Meg flew home two days later.

Dave Wheeler was more exasperated than outraged by what Jim had done. Attempting to make use of the Polaroids that Jim sent as an explanation, Wheeler flew out to California to interview the subject, thinking detailed testimony might give the photos more clout when he showed them to congressmen. Wheeler came to the motel where the Lunas were staying. Gus denied ever being tortured. When Wheeler showed him pictures of himself—naked and covered with fresh bruises and burns that were now just patches of bad skin—Gus stared at them in disbelief. His face turned pale and he blacked out. He fell out of his chair to the floor, his right arm rigid and trembling beneath him. The horror that Gus had suppressed was now far enough in the past for his body to remember the pain. The seizure lasted less than a minute. When it was over, Gus felt no worse than if he'd simply fainted. Eleanor screamed at Wheeler; Wheeler apologized and left. A doctor told them these attacks could continue for years whenever Gus was caught offguard by anything that reminded him of what had happened. Physicians were familiar with the phenomenon in people who'd been in traffic accidents and, more recently, refugees from Central America and Asia.

Jim was furious when Wheeler told him over the phone what had happened. He sent the Lunas more money with a brief note saying he understood Gus might need "special medical attention." Meg received a shorthand version of the incident in a card from Eleanor. "We now living with my Cousin in Daly City until Gus find good work. He has apolapsi once but better in time. Nonoy and Matthew fine. I am in shock at the prices."

Jim's work seemed more futile than ever, a charade of effort, yet he stuck with it, hoping against hope he could win something besides a clear conscience with his clean slate. Wheeler and Derian in Washington were unable to gain more support for their cause, not for the Philippines, not for anywhere else in the world. When the embassy in Tehran was seized and all national attention focused on the Americans held hostage there, even Wheeler admitted it was time they packed it in. Human rights was a luxury a panicky superpower would not pursue. Jim was ordered home to finish the term of his contract in D.C. He regretted their failure, mourned their defeat, but found satisfaction in feeling he might have done right by Gus after all. Even if the film had earned them more support in Congress, there was no way in hell the government would have moved against Marcos, not this year at least.

Jim stopped over in San Francisco on his flight home. Daly City was near the airport and the Lunas were still staying with Eleanor's cousin in a crowded shingle box apartment, depending on relatives just as relatives had once depended on them. Gus seemed overjoyed to see Jim again. "I want to come see you at your motel tonight. Like the old days," he whispered, an offer Jim nervously declined. Everything had changed, especially Gus. There was a cynical coldness beneath his friendly noise, bitterness and resentment. He didn't talk about it but Eleanor did while her husband was out getting beer. Ashamed of his fall in status, hating himself for failing to earn enough to support his family properly, Gus was coming apart. San Francisco was full of hairdressers and nobody believed Gus had done Imelda Marcos's hair. He worked as a washer in one salon after another, getting fired because of his arrogance and temper. When Jim offered to loan them more money, Eleanor shook her head. "We owe you too much already. And this is about pride, not money." Desperately needing to prove he was somebody, Gus spent more nights in the Castro, which Eleanor said she wouldn't mind if he didn't come home drunk and depressed. Sharp-tongued Filipinos with slight builds were not the sex object of choice in San Francisco. When Jim attempted to defend Gus by suggesting his odd behavior should be expected after what he'd been through, Eleanor said that that was the very excuse Gus used whenever she confronted him. "I am sorry you are *not* boyfriends or maybe you could talk sense to him. I am close to giving up."

Meg heard about the next change from Eleanor, in one of her brief cards that meant more than they said coming from a woman who found writing in English difficult: the Lunas were moving to Washington. Meg's first thought was that Imelda Marcos had been right and Jim actually was in love with Gus. Then she got a full letter from Jim announcing that he and the Lunas were to be business partners, "in a beauty parlor or whatever they're called nowadays." He would put up the money; they provided the labor. "I know what you're thinking, but it's strictly business, without hanky-panky."

Here was his chance to have his cake and eat it too, yet Jim refused to eat. Meg wondered what kind of self-denying scruples were at work, or if maybe her uncle believed that saving Gus would cancel out the Vietnam episode only if he weren't saving Gus for himself. She even wondered if Jim had outgrown sex, until she came to a line at the end of the letter mentioning a Peace Corps administrator he'd been seeing.

Life in Madison reabsorbed Meg with surprising quickness. She taught her classes, met with students and resumed work on her book. She moved in with Ron shortly after she came back. If the experience had shaken or changed her, the changes had nothing to do with Meg's feelings for Ron. But she found coming home to him such a sane, well-deserved peace after Manila that she wanted to see what might happen if they made their pairing less provisional. Nothing happened. They remained the same people they'd been before, just as committed to their work, just as skeptical about life in general. The aggravations of routine intimacy were more visible than its slower, subtler comforts, yet their occasional fights assured Meg she hadn't gone to sleep. Despite her fears, living with Ron did not finish her off or mire her in the idiocy of private life, fears Meg had suspected all along were false although she hadn't been able to let go of them until she'd been to Manila and back. It was as if she'd been afraid domestic love could keep her from making contact with the world at large. Well, she'd made contact, briefly, and come away with a deep awareness that that world could break into any life, but that she was capable of confronting it if the need arose.

Meg told Ron everything that had happened, in different versions as her understanding of it changed over the next months. She feared it would become just a story, an elaborate anecdote, but Ron listened each time with a changing mix of pity, confusion, disgust and admiration. The medical doctor had no doubts that the history doctor and her uncle had made the right choice. "It's like an obstetric emergency where the doctor has to decide whether to save the mother or the child. All things being equal, you go for the mother."

Meg saw Jim roughly once a year, usually over Christmas when she visited her family in Virginia. He visited her once in Wisconsin, but Jim was terribly self-conscious around Ron, either too stiff or too noisily masculine. Jim remained in Washington, first to teach at the Foreign Service School, then in an administrative position with the Asia-America Trade Council. He was offered a post with Americas Watch, one of several private organizations that now filled the gap left by the collapse of the Human Rights program, but he told Meg he needed to put that work completely behind him. She knew his real reason for staying in the area was the Lunas. They had an apartment in Reston, Virginia, just outside the Beltway and not too far from their salon. Jim took Meg over for dinner each time she visited. They received her like family, or rather, like a dear family friend. She was amused to hear Matt and Nonoy—who insisted he be called Ben—refer to their parents' business partner as Uncle Jim.

Her book on the Thomasites, much revised and expanded, was finally published in 1983 under the new title, *Good Works: American Teachers in the Philippines After Conquest.* Meg intended the title as both ironical and an acknowledgment of the Thomasites' admirable intentions. She dedicated the book *To my parents.*

Benigno Aquino was assassinated that summer, gunned down at Manila International as he stepped from the plane that brought him home after living in the United States since his release from prison three years ago. Suddenly, the Philippines was newsworthy in a way it hadn't been during Jim's time there, and *Good Works* was widely reviewed. Meg felt peculiar benefiting from a fickle media climate that had failed her uncle and so many others. Her book was hardly a bestseller, but it received enough attention to get an untenured professor attractive job offers from several good schools. After discussing it with Ron, she accepted the offer from Harvard. Ron had no trouble getting a position as a liver specialist with one of the Harvard hospitals and they moved to Cambridge together.

The Philippines remained in the news. Revelations of Marcos's greed, his overseas bank accounts and U.S. real estate holdings became common items in the press, although what fascinated the general public were Mrs. Marcos's omnivorous shopping sprees. Her notoriety helped the Lunas' salon, Manila— For Hair. Gus already had a framed photo of her over the cash register and his customers now wanted to hear more of the stories many assumed he was making up. Would Imelda Marcos's hairdresser *really* be doing hair in a shopping center in Reston, Virginia? Eleanor handled appointments, bookkeeping and the hiring of additional cutters. Jim remained a silent partner, except when Eleanor wanted to pay a Malaysian without a green card less than scale and he had to argue her into a more sympathetic position. The shop began to show a profit and they all made money. The Lunas put a down payment on a townhouse in a nearby development. Jim had bought an old two-bedroom house when he returned to D.C., in a neighborhood of grandparents and one middle-aged gay couple tucked away in Maryland across the district's southeast line. Jim considered the house more an investment than a purchase, but he'd never felt comfortable spending money on himself. The house was a good forty-five-minute drive from Reston.

On Saturdays, when both parents were at the shop, Jim sometimes came across the river to take Ben and Matt to the movies, shopping mall or into Washington to visit museums. He liked how the boys tolerated and even humored "Uncle Jim" when they weren't exploiting his generosity. Ben grew more deliberately American, tough and scowly, while Matt enjoyed being the spontaneous, defenseless baby of the family. When Jim brought them home, Eleanor frequently invited him to stay for dinner, particularly on nights when her husband went into town alone to do the bars with his new friends. Jim and Eleanor would sit in the kitchen after dinner, have another drink and discuss business, the boys' schooling, the cost of living and life in general. Jim had grown very close to Eleanor, very fond and respectful of her.

One evening after the boys went to bed, Eleanor asked, "You're not sorry nothing ever came of you and Gus?"

Jim laughed, amazed she could ask that after five years. "Gus and I are a thing of the past. I'm not here because I still expect anything from Gus."

"I know that. And we both know my husband well enough to know he can be fun in small doses, but no prize. No sirree." Gus clung to his accent but Eleanor's had become slightly southern. "But it is strange," she said. "When I stop to remember how you became our benefactor."

Jim had to deflect the word with another laugh. "I'm nobody's benefactor but my own, Eleanor. Honest. I've benefited all around from this arrangement."

It was true. His life now had the density of family life, with none of the pressures and constriction. Only with Gus did he sometimes have fights, such as the week-long argument they had before Gus gave in and went with Jim to the Whitman-Walker Clinic where they were both tested for antibodies. And Jim had a full life outside this family, a leisurely series of friendly romances with men in their thirties and forties, usually with the government and as emotionally settled and self-sufficient as Jim was. A few hours each month on an AIDS hotline—begun solely to meet new faces—led to involvement in fundraising and gave Jim a fresh use for his Hong Kong-tailored evening clothes. His only real regret was that while he had other lives, and Gus had his too (white boys in their twenties, a reversal of roles that meant more heartache than sexual hijinks), Eleanor had only the shop and her family.

"But this is what I want," she told Jim. "I'm happy. When I get bored with peace and want some fun though, watch out. I will be hell on wheels."

Jim didn't miss his old life, for the most part. He experienced occasional flickers of old ambition and regret over his failure to make any mark on the world, but they passed quickly. He suffered a peculiarly virulent attack one Sunday when a brunch date canceled and he spent the day at home. Overcome by a desire to justify what he had become, Jim suddenly wanted to write his memoirs. He made a strong pot of coffee, unplugged the phone, sat down with pencil and paper and—all that came out was an old anecdote about his recently rediscovered Richard Nixon golf ball. He added a few remarks and sent the pages to Meg as a letter. That seemed to cure him, exorcising regret and suggesting this must be the life he had wanted all along.

"There is this thing called history, of course, but history is something unpleasant that happens to other people," Arnold Toynbee wrote in a satirical vein. Which makes Marx's description of what's now known as the Third World as "people without history" sound like an enviable condition. Most people want only to stand clear of the machinery, others want to watch the spectacle from a distance, but some of us ache to affect the machine. I still believe that we need to connect self and world, private life and public action, the kitchen and the moon—whatever we call the two extremes—if we want to make history livable. But they're already linked, whether we like it or not, and there are occasions where the best one can hope to do is to disconnect one from the other. You disconnected a family from history at its worse, Jim, and that's nothing to be ashamed of. You've earned the right to disconnect yourself as well, although you seem to have connected nicely with a smaller, more human community.

Looking back over your letter, I see you weren't really fishing for answers with your claim to have been "a tourist in the empire, a houseguest of history," and suspect that I've regressed to my old role of playing your conscience, your mirror. So be it. We continue to speak past each other to larger issues, Jim, using each other to argue with ourselves. What a curious pair we make. For the longest time, you used me as your mirror while I used you as a window. It was a situation I resented so long as I feared you affected me far more than I affected you. But now that I know I can affect others, I see our extended dance as a privilege, a gift, an education. We need to affect other people—preferably for the better—if we're to assure ourselves we're not just tourists in this life, and individuals must suffice if nations won't cooperate. (One can get sloppily philosophical on a rainy afternoon in Cambridge.)

That was the heart of the letter Meg wrote back to Jim. The exchange took place in the fall of 1985. A few months later, on the weekend of February 23, 1986, Meg was in Baltimore for a conference at Johns Hopkins when it became clear that the disturbances in Manila could become a revolution and overthrow a dictator.

Newspapers and TV news had filled slowly over the past month with the acceleration of events in the Philippines: the "snap election" Marcos announced to prove he had his country's support, the public protest when he claimed victory over Cory Aquino, the walk-out of the women manning the

election-return computer terminals when they saw how votes were being jug-
gled, then the mutiny of soldiers at Camps Crame and Aguinaldo led by
Marcos's former allies, Juan Enrile and General Ramos. Even the Church
became involved, Cardinal Sin calling over the radio for the people of Manila
to pack the streets around the camps and prevent Marcos's tanks from getting
to the rebel soldiers. Meg was frustrated to be sitting out a revolution in an
auditorium full of academics picking apart the dead horse of the Progressive
era. She telephoned Jim Saturday night, then rented a car Sunday afternoon
and drove down to watch the spectacle with people whose life it was, past,
present and future.

Jim met her at the door. "Keep your coat on. We're going straight to Gus
and Eleanor's. They're expecting us."

They went in Jim's car, Jim punching channels on the radio in search of
news while Meg asked what he knew about Cory Aquino. He'd met her,
several times in fact, first when she was a devoted spouse pouring coffee for
guests while Benigno talked nonstop, later as the patient, melancholy wife of
a political prisoner whom Jim encountered in prison reception halls. Not until
after Aquino's assassination had she emerged from her husband's shadow.

"So what do you think will happen? Will she succeed?"

"She or Enrile or the army." But Jim was too excited to remain a hardnosed realist. "Maybe even the people. Whatever happens, the Marcoses are
finished. There's no way they can continue after this."

Gus and Eleanor were overjoyed to see Meg again. Taking her parka and
scarves, they asked about Boston and Ron and said nothing about the news.
Jim hung up his own coat himself, as though he lived here.

"Big doings, huh?" said Gus, sitting Meg in front of their color television.
"Special report coming up," he explained. "I am wearing yellow for Cory,"
he added, gesturing at his crewneck sweater. He and Eleanor brought out
potato chips and beer and they all settled in to watch the news.

"Crisis in Manila: A CBS Report" began with talking heads speculating on
whether Marcos would abdicate, compromise with the rebels or use violence
against the crowds jamming the streets. A helicopter shot of Edsa Boulevard
from the day before suggested a street festival, a mile-long rally, a Mardi Gras
celebration.

"Look, look," said Gus. "That's the palace where Popo once worked." He
pointed at the top of the screen as the camera panned over the city. Gus was
disappointed with how little his sons recognized. Matt sat cross-legged at his
father's feet, fascinated with it all, but Ben kept getting up and leaving,
returning to watch from the door, then leaving again. Twelve years old and
layered in a sweatshirt and long underwear, Ben was a fastidious adolescent
who made faces and finally said, "Everything looks so gross."

"Does this mean we'll be going home?" asked Matt.

"*This* is your home," Eleanor declared. She frowned at her husband, then worriedly lifted her eyebrows at Jim. "But maybe we can visit relatives now. When the time comes."

Gus didn't catch any of that, but continued to watch for familiar places. A homesick look came over him during a shot of Roxas Boulevard, the hotels and bay and royal palms, the wide boulevard completely deserted except for a solitary tank creeping down the wrong lane.

There was a quick summary of the Marcos regime that downplayed American complicity—a State Department spokesman explained it was against U.S. policy to interfere in other country's affairs—and highlighted Imelda's excesses.

"Poor Imelda," Gus sighed. "She must be heartbroken tonight."

When the commentator mentioned "allegations of torture," there was a blurry color photo of a bruised body. Jim stared at it: no, it wasn't one of his Polaroids. Stealing a glance at Gus, though, Jim saw the pinheads of perspiration on his friend's upper lip. Jim reached over to touch his shoulder, only to have Gus brush away his concern with a flick of his hand and roll of his eyes. Gus settled back in his leather recliner, the man of the house, the lord of his castle. Eleanor came over and sat on the arm of her husband's chair.

"Well, I don't know about the rest of you," said Meg. "But I wish I were there."

"Me too," Gus said eagerly. "It looks like one big party in the streets. Noisy and festive and *warm*." He hated cold weather.

"I'm perfectly happy to watch it from here," said Eleanor. "It won't be a party if bullets start flying or the crowd stampedes like a herd of cattle."

Matt twisted around, surprised to hear the adults talking as if they could actually be there and this was not just a television show.

Jim said nothing. He folded his arms across his chest and watched, frowning against moistness he could feel gathering in his eyes.

There was live footage of Edsa Boulevard now, beamed by satellite from the other side of the world where it was five in the morning. The sky was pink, the land still dark. A crowd of grinning faces thrust themselves into the light from a television camera, men and women in brightly colored shirts and yellow neckerchiefs making *L*'s with their thumbs and index fingers, the sign for *Lakas ng Bayan:* People Power.

"You wish you were there. Don't you?"

"No. I don't. Not at all," said Jim. "I'm overjoyed it's happening, and happier still it has nothing to do with me." But he couldn't look at Meg, knowing she would see in his eyes that he was lying.

It was miraculous, like watching the hatching of an egg that Jim had once feared might only be a stone. Miraculous and heartening and chastening too. It was painful yet fitting that it happened without him there to think he could help it along. Only time would tell what kind of animal was being hatched, but for now, for the next few days, history could be something miraculous that other people *do*.

ACKNOWLEDGMENTS

MANY CONVERSATIONS, interviews and works of nonfiction went into the imagining of this novel. The Foreign Service officers who spoke to me know who they are: I can't thank them enough for their time and willingness to talk. I owe special appreciation to my friends, Dick Wall, Bart McDowell and Ed Sikov, who not only put me in touch with people from the State Department but shared their own travel experiences. Chris Westburg, Dr. Neil These, Mary Jacobsen and Al Weisel provided important details. I have a strong debt of gratitude to my new friend in Manila, Dominique James, for his knowledge, openness and generosity.

Waltzing with a Dictator by Raymond Bonner was indispensible for its detailed picture of the State Department during the Marcos years. *In Our Image* by Stanley Karnow and *Sitting in Darkness* by David Haward Bain provided valuable information about the Philippines. Also useful were *Rebolusyon!* by Benjamin Pimentel, *Priests on Trial* by Alfred McCoy and *All the Wrong Places* by James Fenton. Real organizations, events and names have been used fictionally throughout the book and imaginary characters should not be confused with actual people who held the same posts or titles during the time described.

My partner, family, friends and colleagues sustained me during the long work involved, but I particularly want to thank my editor, Lisa Healy, for her support and judgment. And Mary Gentile gave so much in the way of eye and ardor and involvement that I know this would be a poorer book without her friendship.